**A**

AGE OF THE ALMEK



**SHORT STORIES**

IT'S IN THE PUDDING
LOCK LANGAVUT

# AGE OF THE ALMEK

TARA A. LAKE

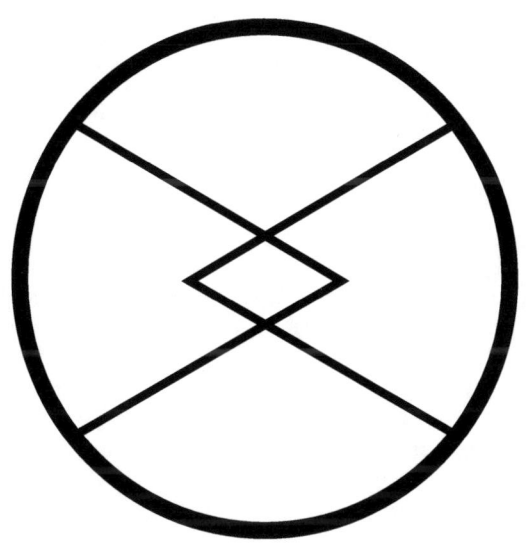

BOOK ONE OF THE ALMEK SERIES

LAKE PUBLISHING

First paperback edition published by Tara A. Lake/Lake Publishing in Canada in 2020



ISBN: 978-1-7771194-1-6
Ebook ISBN: 978-1-7771194-0-9



Cover illustrated by Lauren Kyte
Cover designed by Lauren Kyte & Tara A. Lake
Map illustrated by Lauren Kyte
Map designed by Lauren Kyte and Tara A. Lake

Book Layout Tara A. Lake & Vicki Cloutier

www.taraalake.com

LAKE PUBLISHING 2020

LAKE
PUBLISHING

For Alex, Averi and Owen. My biggest supporters.

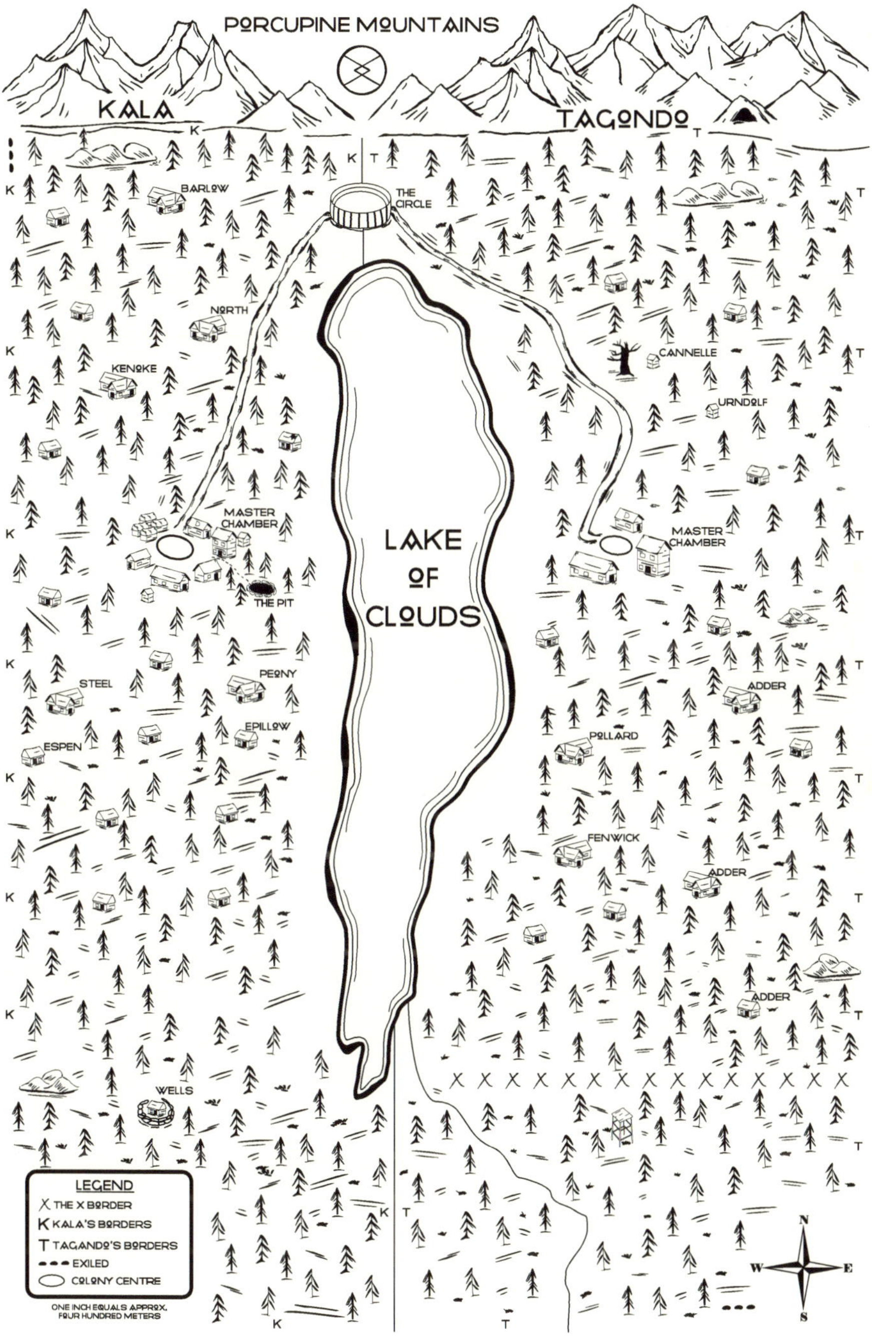
PORCUPINE MOUNTAINS
KALA
TAGONDO
THE CIRCLE
BARLOW
NORTH
KENOKE
CANNELLE
URNDOLF
MASTER CHAMBER
THE PIT
LAKE OF CLOUDS
MASTER CHAMBER
STEEL
PEONY
ADDER
EPILLOW
POLLARD
ESPEN
FENWICK
ADDER
ADDER
WELLS
LEGEND
X THE X BORDER
K KALA'S BORDERS
T TAGANDO'S BORDERS
EXILED
COLONY CENTRE
ONE INCH EQUALS APPROX. FOUR HUNDRED METERS
N
W
E
S

# Prologue

Hendrix North's eyes sweep across his surroundings, the scents of dirt and iron waft in the breeze. Mountains, a lake and forests all sit welcomingly in his view. So does a crowd of four thousand, sitting amidst the sunrise, famished, scared and worst of all – unpredictable. He glances around at these people – the ones who have survived the Water Crisis and now surround him. They are all here because of him.

He moves his sights to the children play-fighting beyond the thick gathering of people; they are naïve to the permanent damage the Water Crisis has inflicted on humankind, while the adults, who can better comprehend the severity of what has happened, are terrified for their lives – they can't stop thinking about what has happened, neither can Hendrix.

It was five days ago that the water became too toxic for human consumption and when the city of Oregon, The North family's home, began to fall. Hendrix knew it wasn't partial to Oregon though – it's a global event.

The water that poured from their taps suddenly came with a yellowed hue that only darkened and a putrid scent that only grew stronger. Some risked drinking it, and those that did died. It wasn't long before people began looting for bottled water - water that was stored and bottled before it became too dangerous to consume - smashing store windows, home windows as well, just to get their hands on the one thing no one can live without. The looting turned to rioting, threats were posed against government officials and when the killings started, the President presumably fled the country – no one knows for certain of course. It was only a matter of days until the country was no more – all form of regulation gone, vanished.

Before long, bodies were strewn across the sidewalks, while abandoned vehicles blocked most of the roads. Many had fallen from the toxic water, others murdered. Once there was no controlling the masses, there was no choice but to move, to get his family out of Oregon and to safety. Safety, he decided, was the Porcupine Mountains in Michigan. Hendrix, from his profession in hydrology, knew this place to be their best chance of survival for the Porcupine Mountains houses the only source of safe drinking water left on the planet.

He gathered as many people as he could and fled with several buses to Michigan. On the way they picked up many stranded survivors – the fear in their eyes have yet to subside, for that he is sorry. He shudders in knowing that fear will never leave his eyes too. He squeezes them tightly shut as the image of bright red rivers flow down the streets of Oregon in his memory. *It was just paint – deep, red paint.* In fact, paint is what Hendrix tries to focus on – red paint like Ida's car, or the shade they painted the office walls in their first house. Surely it was not the same colour as the insides of another human being.

Hendrix stands near a man who steps upon a large boulder, he speaks out loud to the people: "Calm down everyone, there is nothing to be fearful of here in this New World. We have made it, here we can survive." The voices quiet down to less than a whisper as they turn to face him, then they begin moving closer to listen to the man that addresses their thousands.

"It's not a New World, it's a Broken World," a voice drifts from somewhere in the crowd, correcting the man.

The man smiles, and somehow, his smile helps to release some of the weight that recent days have imposed upon the people, “You’re right. This isn’t a New World at all, it is a Broken World, but you know what? We’re going to fix it.”

Merek, Hendrix’s older brother, stands at his side now – he leans over and asks: “What now?” Merek looks to him for guidance, presumably because Hendrix is the one who brought them all here.

“I’m not sure, just listen… wait,” Hendrix replies. His eyes shift to his wife, Ida, who stands at his other side. Ida holds their infant, Atticus, in one arm while also gripping their six-year-old daughter Vera’s wrist with the other.

“But what are we waiting for? Why are we just standing around doing nothing? These people have been through enough,” Merek begins to grow more heated. Hendrix knows this isn’t the time or place for his brother’s temper.

“Don’t you think I know that? We need to decide on a leader – the entire group does, before we can move forward,” Hendrix retorts, though his voice stays steady. He knows his brother is anxious to establish living quarters.

The calm man that continues to pull the crowd’s attention speaks again: “It wasn’t easy leaving our homes, it wasn’t easy seeing all those terrible things…but that was all in the Old World. Here we stand, in this Broken World. We got here together. And here we will stay, together,” he nods as his dark eyes paint over the crowd.

The people move in a little closer toward him in sync, as if they are one moving unit. Hendrix stands near the boulder and glances up at the man who speaks; his olive skin glistens in the morning light and shows a face more indifferent than the rest. It’s clear to Hendrix that this man has a way about him as he somehow pulls the people’s focus and holds it.

“Zev, right?” a dark-skinned man says as he approaches the calm speaker. The speaker steps down from his place upon the boulder.

“Zev Astor, curator,” he nods. It has become the new norm to introduce one’s self along with their Old World profession. Such information comes in handy.

Hendrix seems to be involuntarily a part of this conversation as the two men stand openly in front of him.

“You have a talent, they listen to you – why?” the newcomer asks.

“Thank you. It’s like you said – a talent.”

“My name is Oberon Kenoak, federal judge,” the dark-skinned man says, as he extends his hand out to shake Zev’s. He turns to Hendrix and extends his hand towards him as well – a gesture that now almost feels out of place. Perhaps it’s far too normal a thing to do after they just witnessed civilization crumble.

Still, the social etiquettes of the Old World haven’t yet been lost on Hendrix, and so he reaches out to reciprocate Oberon’s handshake, “Hendrix North, hydrologist,” he replies.

“I know who you are,” Oberon says. “That was something. The way you gathered all these people, and got us here.”

“Anyone could’ve done it.”

Oberon smiles, “Well now, we must elicit a positive mindset amongst these people, especially after what they all just saw.”

“Would you say a few words?” Zev asks Oberon, he nods and Hendrix releases a sigh of relief.

Oberon now stands upon the boulder and his low voice booms across the whole sum of people: “People of this Broken World, I know it may not seem it, but it is a good time to be grateful. The Earth has given mankind a grave awakening. Treat her as though she doesn't matter, and she will treat us as though we don't matter. It is time to treat her differently – it is time to treat her as though she matters.

"It is time to focus on cleansing the water by clearing out the toxins and cleansing ourselves so that we can learn from our mistakes. The very fact that we stand here alive is all the proof we need that we have been given a second chance. We must make it count." The crowd claps in agreement with Oberon – the crowd's voices overtake the space once again.

Zev begins to whisper up toward Oberon as Hendrix peers over to check on his wife and two children once again. He notices that they have drifted from him through the sea of people, and in his effort to stay in tune with Zev and Oberon he didn't notice. Their infant, Atticus, now rests on the ground several feet from Hendrix, his cries fill what is left of the quiet space beyond the inaudible chatter of people. But Ida and Vera are nowhere to be seen. *Why has she left him lying there?* Hendrix wonders uncomfortably, though his thoughts are still muddled with shock and uncertainty from the events that have recently unfolded from the Water Crisis, but whose aren't?

He sees a boy then, a toddler, who hangs his head over baby Atticus, eyeing him curiously, though mischievously. Hendrix begins moving toward Atticus, closing in on the twenty-something feet and countless bodies that separate them, until he catches a glimpse of what he thinks to be Vera's auburn hair. He releases a sigh – at least Vera is there with him.

Hendrix sees that Oberon is now off of the boulder, conversing more intimately with Zev. Hendrix stills his stance and his attention is pulled away from his family once more as he attempts to overhear their conversation:

"We must decide on a leader, someone who is level headed and respectable," Zev says. Oberon nods in agreement.

Hendrix wants to focus on the conversation between the men, he feels some sort of responsibility, but his eyes refocus on Atticus – his other responsibility. Hendrix watches as the toddler that hangs his head above Atticus pulls what looks like a tiny knife out of his pocket and moves it toward Atticus. Hendrix can only assume that the young boy is mimicking something he's witnessed in the Old World – because they all saw that sort of brutality. Hendrix has lost the shine of Vera's auburn strands, there is no hint of her watchful presence over Atticus and his search for her comes up empty.

"Ida!" he shouts above the crowd in urgency to alert his wife to retrieve their infant, as the bodies between he and Atticus are still plentiful – and who knows how many more there are between him and Ida.

Ida suddenly appears, dipping down and scooping Atticus up in an instant, fleeing from the blade-bearing toddler.

She grabs Vera's shoulder then with her one free hand and begins shaking her daughter, "I told you to watch him. I asked you to watch him," Ida shrieks as tears pour down her face.

"I'm sorry Mama," Vera says looking down to the ground in shame.

Ida brings the two children to Hendrix's side, "Did you see that?" she asks him, breathless. What is left of her voice is raspy and her face betrays her creeping insanity.

Hendrix simply nods, remaining collected while attempting to ignore the feeling of his heart pounding against his insides, "What is that boy's name?"

Ida glances back towards the toddler, "Digby Espen."

“We need to keep a close eye on him,” Hendrix tenses then glances at the lake - Lake of Clouds - as its yellowed waters sit still. It is his first time seeing the lake, or ever being in Michigan and witnessing the beauty of the Porcupine Mountains. Though, the lake is not the water they came for - the spring is - buried somewhere in the southwest beyond the lake. The details of the coordinates are all in his briefcase, one of the few belongings he was able to bring from the Old World. He will need to get started on locating the spring and preparing a lab as soon as possible.

Zev stands upon the boulder once again, “We must elect a leader, someone who can guide us during these trying times, someone with experience in guiding others, someone who is fair.” Zev stands silent for a moment, but still holds the crowd’s attention, “Seeing as he was a federal judge in the Old World, I would like to nominate Oberon Kenoak as leader.” The crowd applauds.

A different man, one much smaller in stature and hair so black that his skin looks pale in contrast, approaches them. He pulls Zev down off of the boulder and stands upon it himself. Zev stumbles to catch his footing.

“We need an army, soldiers. Don’t you want to be prepared? Don’t you want to survive? I will lead this place, we will become the strongest civilization to ever grace this planet,” the man announces. Hendrix notices a peculiar look about this man’s eyes – they look almost white in colour, but upon looking closer he sees the slight hue of blue.

“What do you have to offer us?” a voice calls from somewhere amidst the swarm of bodies.

“What’s your name?” Zev questions upward, “What are your qualifications?”

“My name is Regan Adder,” he answers, then resumes his response to the crowd, “Who wants to be transformed? Choose me as your leader and together we will make mankind strong again.” The crowd erupts in cheers.

A man appears behind Regan, as if out of nowhere, and grabs a hold of his shirt in an attempt to pull him down off of the boulder. Regan doesn’t take kindly to the intrusion and instantly grabs the knife that rests in the side of his boot. He lifts it towards the man.

“You want to see qualifications?” Regan bellows to all who watch. The man held tighly within his grasp raises his trembling hands in submission. His eyes spread wide in plea. The thousands erupt in acknowledgment. They want proof of his qualifications.

“Very well. If this is what it’s going to take!” Regan calls as he plunges the knife into the man’s stomach.

The man’s body falls to the sand in a series of convulsions. Many in the crowd release gasps of horror, Hendrix included. Perhaps that was not the kind of qualifications they had had in mind. Still, Regan stands tall, proud. His blood-covered hand drips while still holding onto the knife.

“Was that enough proof of my qualifications?” Regan inquires. Not a single breath is heard for what feels like an eternity.

Oberon says under his breath, “This is the sort of behaviour we just left behind.”

Zev stands beside the boulder; fear riddled across his face, still his voice is able to carry across the crowd, “You heard the man – we need to choose. Let’s vote. Those for purifying the water and respecting Mother Earth – raise your hand for Oberon.” A couple thousand raise their hands. “Those for developing an army and becoming a strong civilization raise your hand for Regan.” The other half, evidently, raises their hands.

"It appears they want different rulers," Zev says to the men near him.

Regan plants his feet upon the dirt next to the three men with a scowl, "Two rulers? What are we – about four thousand people? You think two thousand soldiers is enough of an army to survive this Broken World?"

"Without fresh water no one will survive," Hendrix says.

Regan jerks his face toward Hendrix, "What's stopping me from gutting you too? And *him*?" he points to Oberon.

"We need them," Zev urges.

Regan sneers, "We have the spring, right scientist?"

"For now. It won't last forever."

Zev whispers to the men, "We can simply give the people what they want – two leaders with two separate colonies."

"But why divide us? We are stronger together," Hendrix counters.

Zev shakes his head while glancing at Regan, "Staying together won't be possible. These people are on-edge, they'll riot, or worse. They have spoken."

Oberon nods, "We will make laws that all must abide by, while ruling two separate colonies. As time goes on our population will only grow, which means more people for your army," Oberon nods to Regan, "and more people to work on the water."

"I think this is the only way to ensure our civilization will prosper," Zev agrees.

Regan stands still in thought – his eyes crinkle into slits. Hendrix's chest rattles as he awaits his decision. Regan is right – nothing is stopping him from gutting Hendrix or from killing anyone who crosses him.

"Very well," Regan finally says with a grin.

Hendrix releases a sigh of relief, although splitting up doesn't sound like the best course of action, given the circumstances with Regan it may be the safest.

"It is settled then," Zev says, "You two must discuss details," and with that Regan and Oberon step off to the side.

Some time later Regan and Oberon address Zev with the details of their plans for the colonies, including the name of the civilization, colony names and the significance of the soil they stand upon.

"What shall we call you both then?" Zev inquires.

"Masters," Regan sternly states.

Hendrix looks to Zev thoughtfully, whose smile is warmer and more calming than any man's smile ought to be after everything they've been through to get to this moment. He looks to his family with hopeful eyes, as he wonders what their future with these people will look like.

Zev nods at the two newly elected Masters and says to them: "I'm going to introduce you both," The Masters nod to Zev - their endorsement for him to speak on their behalf - to be their Orator. He stands upon the boulder once again and places his finger on his lips in a request for silence, the people oblige.

"May I officially introduce you to your Masters: Master Oberon Kenoak of Kala and Master Regan Adder of Tagondo. Please congratulate your Masters!" Zev pauses for the people to cheer in satisfaction. He stands down then and allows The Masters to claim the people's attention.

Master Oberon's voice fills the quiet, "Thank you. Thank you for your vote. The laws and details of the two colonies are to come, but for now, know that the Earth is ready for change and we are going to give her change – because you are The Almek.

We are The Almek. Named as such to mark us as the only civilization to survive the Water Crisis.

"Together, we will account for all of our needs. Together we will build our civilization; we will rebuild humankind. But let us not forget how we've been granted this opportunity, how The Almek began. It was here, upon this sand that we stand, that myself and Regan - your Masters - have been elected to guide you – here within The Circle."

Hendrix, like many within the crowd, glances down at the sand below his feet. It sits just north of the Lake of Clouds. His gaze rises, sweeping over the circumference of land that the sand occupies. *It is a circle,* he thinks. *How interesting.* Naturally, he wonders how the sand came to be, and why it's in the shape of a circle, though the people in the Old World formed it as such.

A voice in the crowd calls out: "What is The Circle?"

Hendrix is curious too: what *is* The Circle?

"It is the place in which we will all unite, in which we will all be cleansed." Oberon states.

# Laws of the Motherland

We gather to unite as one and we gather to pay respect to Mother Earth.

May we be cleansed.

## Duties

1. All shall pray to and respect Mother Earth
2. All shall fulfill their working duty by meeting share requirements and working full eight-hour days
3. Insignificants must yield allotted seasonal provisions set by their respective Master every week
4. Favoured of Kala and Tagondo are entitled to half the share requirements as supplementary time must be put towards their professions
5. Those that do not fulfill share requirements shall face tribulation as an Offender
6. Positions are born into and passed on to offspring and assumed offspring
7. None shall receive a Favoured position unless by blood or by merge
8. All colony members shall wear their family crests at all times
9. All shall abide by the curfew siren at sundown
10. Ceremonies and celebrations held by one's respective Master are mandatory
11. All minors must attend school during the January to December calendar year: Insignificants attend school from the age of five to thirteen-years-old; Favoured must attend school from five to eighteen-years-old and apprentice in their family's profession during this time. Upon the completion of school in December, Favoured and Insignificant graduates will be placed into their family's respective fields

## Deaths

12. The dead shall be respected and given a proper burial ceremony attended by all colony members
13. Any acts of violence or murder against a fellow Almek will result in tribulation
14. Upon death, if there shall be any living family members that do not hold a Favoured position themselves, – they are to be demoted to Insignificant
15. In the event of the death of a spouse, the respective Master will determine when re-merge agreements are to be set
16. Homes of undetermined deaths must be demolished or burned

## Births

17. Pregnancy and childbirth are forbidden outside of merging
18. All pregnancies and births must be immediately reported to one's respective Master and a birthing ceremony for the infant will follow upon said Master's date of choosing
19. One's respective Master can decide when a re-birthing ceremony can take place for those over the age of twenty and not bound by merge

## MERGES

20. Merge agreements shall be between a male and female and decided upon by their respective Master
21. Merge agreements will be made on or thereafter members' twentieth year of birth with merge date decided upon by the colony Master
22. All colony members are to practice abstinence prior to merging
23. The colony Master will arrange for housing for new mergers
24. Following the verbal merge agreement, presented by the colony Master, the woman is to maintain the patriarchal home until the merge date, decided upon by the colony Master
25. Homes of failed merges must be demolished or burned

## DEFENDERS

26. All shall respect the colony Defenders
27. Defenders shall not rule over any members of the opposing colony
28. Defenders shall follow his mandate provided to him by his Master

## ILLEGAL ACTS

29. None shall leave their respective colony unless exiled by his/her Master
30. None shall speak of or step beyond the colony borders
31. None shall speak of the Old World
32. None shall communicate with the opposing colony members
33. None shall consume the poisonous waters
34. None shall commit treason, assault, theft or abuse
35. None shall commit suicide
36. None shall possess weapons within the Kala colony
37. Violation of any illegal act will result in tribulation, including possible death

## THE MASTERS

38. All shall respect The Masters
39. The colony Master shall plan tribulation for any Offender as they see fit
40. The Masters are each entitled to one rest day of rest every seventh day

# 1

# VERA OF FAVOURED NORTH KALA

Vera takes to her seat, allowing her bottom to quickly press into the wooden bleacher below her. She doesn't want to be here, but she is an Almek, which means she has no choice. She squeezes her hands into fists - white knuckled and bordering on numb - and glances to her father. Hendrix sits on her right followed by her mother and younger brother. The last of The Almek arrive and take their seats within The Circle. Almost without pause complete silence washes over the colonies. It is about to begin. Hendrix gazes down upon Vera, a reminder to sit still, to stay quiet – to do as they expect. Though the reminder is unnecessary, it is every time. He offers her hand a brief squeeze and she returns the reassuring gesture. Every time she graces The Circle she recalls, but only vaguely, when it all begin – when The Masters were chosen eighteen years earlier.

Her eyes trace to the stage where the infant - the guest of honour - is contently embraced in Brene's arms. Light from the morning sun beams down upon their faces as she admires the white-hooded cloak that rests atop the baby's delicate head; shielding its eyes from the sun's yellowed warmth. *There is something serene about that embrace*, she thinks. To Vera, that embrace is the only true act of what it means to be human, at least here within The Circle.

After one last caress of the child's rosy cheek, Brene - a dark-skinned Tagondian woman - holds the Kalian baby above the ceremonial pedestal. Ida, her mother, mentioned that the baby's given name is Lilith; though there is no guarantee that will endure. Vera admittedly could've done without Ida telling her the name, even though she would find out today along with the rest of The Almek. For the past two days, since Lilith was born, the infant belonged to her birth mother, Lidia of Favoured

Peony. However, every person present, including Lidia, knows there is no certainty that Lilith will remain hers beyond this ceremony. For there is a purpose for this ceremony, it is meant to ensure bloodlines mix between colonies to prevent the sort of genetic defects that a lack of diversity in bloodlines would offer. Vera watches Lilith lay atop the pedestal asleep with a grey fur pelt wrapped around her small body, as if it were a blanket. Lilith would one day wear that fur pelt as the rest do - all but Vera - up around her shoulders. Vera can't pull her eyes away from the baby, observing Lilith from some four hundred feet. Although her visual of Lilith isn't clear from this distance, she knows the bottom edges of Lilith's petite white dress barely extends out past the fur blanket– the needle workers always make an infant's first outfit a little too big. Her fur slippers shield her precious feet from the cool March air.

The ceremony begins, there is no signal to initiate it, at least not one that Vera is aware of, but The Masters have everyone's undivided attention. Brene, the aide of The Masters, carries Lilith down the steps of the stage and traces through the sand down in front of the stage toward the pedestal. The Almek watch as she lovingly sets Lilith upon the pedestal and cups one hand over Lilith's head and the other over her heart, but only for a moment. She begins to perform a dance, one spiritually brimming in nature and yet distasteful in all aspects with the jerking motion of her arms and a pivot of her head. Vera writes off the awkward dance as one of the lesser qualities of the Tagondians. Granted, she doesn't know exactly what their admirable qualities are, if any. As the musical ones drum a quiet steady hum, Vera, tempted by irritation, thanks Mother Earth internally at the dance's finale. To this day she is still unaware of the purpose of the arbitrary dance. She finds it grandstanding of The Masters to allow it to continue, ceremony after ceremony. But she reminds herself that is the way, regardless of their claims that it eases the baby's senses during the ceremony. In reality, it likely soothes the people, offering them hope before the unfolding of a bloodbath, because here in The Circle it is a life for a life. It pains Vera how Lilith is entirely innocent and wholly unaware of what is to come. Vera knows what is coming and that it is brought on by The Masters.

Vera glances to the westerly stage where The Masters sit; she watches their eager stares anticipate the events to come – her head begins to spin slightly in a dizzying fashion. As a means to ground herself, she attempts to focus on The Masters and their Barons. Master Regan sits on the right side with his Barons Jarot, Orsen and Burke who rule alongside him. Meanwhile, Master Oberon sits on the left side with his Barons Quim, Hogard and Martil. The sights of them alone heat the colour in her cheeks. She moves her gaze upward to the sky as a means to distract herself. The Almek symbol catches her focus for a brief instant as her eyes sweep over the roof of the stage; two mountains turned on their side and carved into the wooden arch, the horizontal peaks uniting inside a sphere – one peak representing the colony of Kala, the other Tagondo.

The glint of the circular crests that rest over the hearts of every citizen captures Vera's attention as the sun rises above the treeline. Her thoughts are distracted then by the Kalian whispers, something Kalians are particularly good at. The whispers surround Vera and like a school of piranhas the Kalians attack and lacerate the Tagondians with their painfully quiet words. Her eyes then shift to the Tagondians and she notes how they sit upon their bleachers a little less neatly and a little less quietly; they appear more rugged in stature with messier hair and dirtier clothes.

"They are filthy, vile looking human beings," she overhears someone say.

"Much like their ruler," a second speaker agrees.

Her Kalian counterparts are not wrong. Though she doesn't partake in the gossip, it doesn't mean she disagrees. Still, she reminds herself they are the pursuers, the hunters of the land. Maybe in some animalistic way that warrants them some extremely petty defense. Their hair falls wild much like animals - men and women alike - whereas Kalian men trim their hair short, while women must tie their hair up. There is no reason really, other than the fact that it allows Kalians to look uniform according to Master Oberon.

The Kalians are the foragers, botanists and scientists of The Motherland and that, she reasons along with the rest, does make Kalians superior. Even through these sharp mutters the Kalians sit prim and proper. Vera ponders briefly how they must appear to the Tagondians, for she has never spoken to a Tagondian, nor stepped on their soil. The Kalian Orator, Zev, interrupts her thoughts.

"Welcome my friends, here we gather at The Circle," he begins reciting the ceremonial scripture, "We gather to unite as one and we gather to pay respect to Mother Earth. May we be cleansed." The entire crowd perks up across The Circle at his presence upon the podium, gentle snaps proceed during his brief pause, "Please, welcome our Masters: Master Oberon, his Barons of Kala and Master Regan and his Barons of Tagondo."

Colony members welcome the two men by snapping their fingers. Vera snaps her fingers in harmony, she must if she is to stay under the radar. The Masters sit beside one another with their respective Barons lined to their sides, as if to signal an alliance of the colonies; however, Vera knows the history of the colonies to be anything but aligned. She briefly wonders who could fall for such a ruse.

All members face The Circle as they watch Zev adjust the podium's microphone and continue to address the audience: "The Masters would like to thank you all for gathering here today."

*Though it is hardly optional*, Vera thinks to herself. The podium sits just in front of the stage, The Masters look down upon Zev's back as he speaks.

"We would like to begin the ceremony. The infant currently known as Lilith, at just two days old, comes from blood of Kalian brains and strength. Her Father, Kobe of Favoured Peony, has blood of strength and forages like no other. Her mother, Lidia of Favoured Peony, has blood of brains with impressive intellect and a position as a botanist in Kala's greenhouses. This infant has several interested families. Pip of Insignificant Cleary from Tagondo is first in line. As per usual, it will be a fight-to-the-death between the willing participants. If Insignificant Cleary fails, the next family in line has the opportunity to fight for complete rights of the baby against the successor. Same goes for Favoured Peony. The last man or woman standing will be the winner. Weapons of choice are located along either side of The Circle. Will the two opponents please step forward?"

Vera glances at Lidia, the mother of baby Lilith and wife to Kobe Peony. It surprises her to find Lidia, subdued on the stage in her seat. The Masters hold a special seat on the stage for the lucky Almek whose family is forced to participate in the ceremonies. Kobe steps into The Circle. He stands tall and proud, the girth of his muscular arms flex and glisten in the sunlight. Pip Cleary, a Tagondian man whom Vera doesn't recognize, enters The Circle. Pip will be at a great disadvantage due to his size, she thinks, in both height and muscle mass. The top of Pip's head barely reaches the sturdy curve of Kobe's shoulders.

Zev continues, “A welcome to our opponents – Kobe of Favoured Peony and Pip of Insignificant Cleary,” the colonies’ repetition of friction on their fingers once again cause Vera to stir in her seat, “We will initiate the standard countdown: ten, nine, eight…” Zev continues. Vera scans the crowd and watches the Defenders as they examine the seats; an exaggerated tapping of their clubs pound against their palms in search of any conflicting members.

Brene sounds the horn and the opponents retrieve their weapons. Kobe chooses the ceremonial sword and Pip follows his opponent’s lead in also selecting a sword – the men circle one another as the fight begins. Kobe charges at Pip and although Pip initially hesitates by back-stepping, seconds later he comes forward with his sword swinging. Vera closes her eyes, squeezing them tight, for she can’t bear to look. Her heart races, pulsing in the background of her conscious. It is her stomach that diverts her attention; there is a sour feeling that stirs, a nausea that begins assaulting her insides. The sounds that engulf her ears make it so: the clang of the swords, the groans from the opponents, the occasional scream when one wounds the other echoes off The Circle’s wooden fence and the nagging worsens. The Kalians sit calmly, detached even, and Vera isn’t quite sure if the alternative is worse because when she glances at the Tagondians they are scowling and waiving their fists in the air ever so indecently. That is the kind of involvement The Masters want – the people are beguiled in their ceremonies.

Vera wishes nothing more than for the fight to stop, for there to never be another ceremony. She holds her head and cradles it in her lap – it is the same thing every time. *Get it together.* She fights her higher moral ground and slowly raises her head. Not only is she worried about letting her parents down, she knows the repercussions of not watching. There is a danger in disobeying, should someone - a Defender - spot her uncommitted. Just as likely, a fellow Kalian with an urge to report her misconduct could disclose her actions. So, she opens her emerald orbs and lowers her sight towards The Circle once again.

Suddenly something catches her attention – a boy directly across The Circle on the Tagondian side is standing.

“STOP!” he shouts.

*Who is this boy?* He looks as though he couldn’t be a day over fifteen-years-old and is as skinny as a praying mantis, though hardly as intimidating. However, unlike a praying mantis, that young boy stands out amongst the crowd. From a distance it is hard to get a clear visual of him, though she can make out that his hair is cut, almost as if his mother quite literally placed a deep-set bowl atop his head and cut around it. Most male citizens have long hair in Tagondo – whether they do not have the luxury of a hair tender or they simply don’t care, she does not know. Either way, their lack of grooming magnifies their boorish nature.

The young boy stands scared, yet resolute. Within this instant of the boy yelling out the blood and sweat-covered opponents freeze. Bewildered heads turn to look in the direction of the voice that disrupts the ceremonies of The Masters. In fact, every single person has his or her eyes on the boy. Shock upon the faces of the people; surely a bloodbath would be more heinous. Vera looks to the stage where The Masters sit. Master Regan, whom Vera has not met, holds an angered look in his eyes and yet, a devilish grin on his face that suggests otherwise.

Zev remains calm and glances to the stage for guidance from his superiors, Master Oberon hastily swings his hand in motion to Zev to signal a request of his presence on stage. Zev walks up the stairs and approaches The Masters, his hands held together in a clasp and his body bending at the waist in a bow it is necessity for all to bow when approaching a Master. The three men exchange whispers. The Barons sit with heads tilted inwardly, a part of the conversation, and yet not entirely. After a few moments Zev nods his head and returns to his place at the podium in front of the stage set to deliver his oration. The boy's life is in the hands of his Master now, it matters not what he does next.

Zev begins, claiming the attention of the people once again, "People of the colonies-"

The boy interjects, only this time louder: "-STOP! No more people may die. Except Master Regan!" The boy holds up a bow and arrow in his maturing hands and aims it with conviction and heart, though with naivety in its most innocent form. The boy lets loose the first arrow. It shoots forward like a bullet, zooming through the air. In a moment of panic Master Regan lowers his head to avoid the arrow. It flies above his skull and lands somewhere irrelevant behind him on the platform. Zev still stands indifferent, his composure unwavering even though he is presumably unequipped to deal with this kind of outburst one that has never occurred before. Still, he is the Orator of The Masters and so he looks for guidance to fulfill their orders once again. It is almost unsettling to see Zev appear just as unaffected as the day they came to this place. Or perhaps it is the very opposite. Perhaps that is the point.

Master Regan, with a flushed face, confidently holds his hand in the air toward Zev, a request to stop. Now a Defender, who is a rather tall brute, engages with Master Regan then swiftly marches toward the seats where the boy stands. The Defenders are the guards of the colonies; men of titan strength that keep the people in their colony aligned and orderly. This particular guard is the Tagondian Defender in charge of all Defenders and Master Regan's Lead. He clearly didn't expect the boy to release another arrow, but release another arrow he did. It seems a mark of bravery, or perhaps stupidity as his arrow pierces the Defender in his thigh. A moan of sorts expel out of the man's mouth – though it doesn't sound human, rather the deep growl of a giant. This Defender has to be beyond six feet tall and apparently has a rather unimaginable pain tolerance. There is only a slight pause, followed by a flex of his thick neck - which briefly exposes more protruding veins - then onward he continues.

Though it is rare for a Master to address the colonies at The Circle, Master Regan stands to do so: "Remember this – this is what happens when you act out of line. When you are an Offender you must face Tribulation – no one is exempt of it. Rimmy, please do the honours."

Vera glances at the large stone perched in front of the stage beside the podium; on it is carved The Laws of The Motherland. These laws make one an Offender when broken.

Rimmy, the Tagondian Lead Defender in pursuit, effortlessly picks up the boy and walks toward the Tagondo exit. The boy screams and kicks, though the Defender is unyielding; the boy's efforts are wasted.

Vera's heart pounds, she places her hand over her chest. The powerful thuds radiate down her arm. *That poor boy.* A man and a woman loudly stir in their seats, Tagondians on either side of them hold the two down, as if to keep them quiet. *His parents*, Vera thinks painfully. How she wishes she could help. Master Regan offers Zev a nod of affirmation to continue.

"Well then, let's get back to why we are here," Zev announces, his smile painted on his face once again as the very sound of his voice soothes the crowd into a lull.

Brene sounds the horn a second time and the fight immediately continues as if the boy's outburst was entirely imagined. It seems so surreal, no one interrupts The Masters' ceremonies. The grunts and moans of the opponents continue and are heard by all. Vera squeezes her shaking hands into fists as if to cope with the dissent that grows inside of her. Though she tries so desperately to blend-in, to sit still, tall and proud as her people do, as her family does – she can't pretend to tolerate this. The struggle between opponents continues, how confused she is to want it all to end as soon as possible and yet for it to continue in order to postpone a death sentence.

Kobe's legs are long, allowing him to jump up and land behind Pip. A stealthy move of his sword sends Pip to his knees.

*How could he?* Though she knows the answer: in The Circle it is kill or be killed.

Pip moans in agony and in defeat as the blood pours from his back and marks the sand. Suddenly the Kalians begin to cheer; it is timely, their involvement. It only happens when one of their own has won. A man has died. He will become one with the earth. Several Tagondian Defenders enter The Circle and form around Pip's body, which lies in the sand. There they stand in silence, Vera knows why they are waiting.

Zev steps back up to the podium and opens his palms to the sky, a gesture for all to join in the ritual chant: "One with the Earth," the entire Circle recites once.

The unsettling mantra, though brief, comes to an end. The Defenders pick up Pip and drag away his lifeless body. There will be a burial ceremony that night in Tagondo, Vera assumes – the laws will it.

"Congratulations Kobe, a fair win. Everyone, congratulate Kobe of Favoured Peony," Zev announces as the crowd's fingers snap. "Now, Baby Lilith isn't Kobe's just yet – who is next in line to fight for the rights to this baby?"

With that, Kobe raises his fists painted with crimson red in the air and shouts: "Who's next?" If Kobe is fortunate enough that there is no one else in line, he will win the rights to his daughter.

However, Keaton of Favoured White, another Tagondian man and the next opponent, approaches to stand in the confines of The Circle. Vera wonders briefly what it must feel like to step onto its bloodlust granules – to confront the choice to kill or be killed, to join the list of murderers or victims. She will never be that person. How could she when even a glance towards The Circle haunts her so? Besides, she will never bear a child, not if it means bringing it into this Broken World.

The Circle, and Zev, wastes no time, "A welcome to our opponents: Kobe of Favoured Peony of Kala and Keaton of Favoured White of Tagondo," Zev pauses, it is an intentional pause meant to build suspense, the crowd snaps their fingers eagerly. "We will initiate the standard count down: ten, nine, eight…" Zev chants; his voice is the only sound to fill The Circle and each Almek hangs on his every word, "one."

Following the countdown Brene once again sounds the horn. In that instance the opponents retrieve their weapons – Kobe chooses the ceremonial sword once again, while Keaton chooses the chain. The chain is a thick, eight-foot-long weapon of braided steel with spikes along the tip of its frame – only the fiercest of fighters choose such a weapon. One will need great strength to manipulate its weight.

Vera does not doubt Keaton's ability to manoeuvre his weapon of choice and as he charges at Kobe she receives her proof. Keaton thrashes the chain, this way and that, as if it is as light as a coil of rope. The chain smacks down onto the ground; bringing up with it granules of sand into the air. With each rise of the chain, Kobe winces and turns his face away; his eyes squinting in discomfort.

*How can he fight with sand in his eyes?* Surely Zev will call for a respite. *Come on Zev, call it. Call a respite,* she hopes.

Kobe's steel sword clashes with Keaton's metal chain and the gut-twisting sound echoes off the bleachers. Each interaction is followed immediately by a second clatter from the movement of the chain. The chain has a way of wrapping its long and mouldable frame around whatever object it comes into contact with. Kobe swings his sword to defend every wrangle until a blow of the chain hits his forearm, Kobe jerks his arm away quickly before it takes hold of him. Then it comes for his leg as Keaton whips his weapon toward Kobe effortlessly like a snake. As if it has a mind of its own the chain reaches for Kobe's remaining limbs. For a split second Vera can't take her eyes off of the chain, she forgets that a man is controlling it. It seems so ruthless as it violently entwines Kobe's body. Swing upon swing, thrash upon thrash, the spikes cut into Kobe's flesh and rip him apart, exposing his mauled muscles. Kobe screams in agony at each blow; regardless, his sword continues to swing, desperately attempting to fend off the steel snake, but the sword does him no good. It can neither cut the chain nor reach his opponent.

Kobe backs away from Keaton, "I'm done, I can't…" he shouts as he faces The Masters in their cushioned seats. The crowd's ears perk – they love a good show. It is then that Keaton thrashes the chain across his opponent's back, a splatter of blood sprays Keaton's face as the spikes slide into Kobe's muscles, tearing raw flesh from white bones.

On his knees, Kobe screams once more, "Please!" The clatter of the chain fills the air, along with his pleas for mercy.

Vera hopes The Masters will oblige such a plea. Though she has seen similar commotions in the past and such compassion isn't the precedence of The Masters.

Lidia's face appears to be soaked in tears and sweat. Vera can only image how hard it must be to watch one's husband in this moment: a defending father against a hungry ogre. Vera argues with herself about the lack of fairness. Though, fairness doesn't matter in the world they live in – she wishes that it did. Keaton's chain swings once more and wraps itself around Kobe's thigh; a tug is all it takes to knock him down. No, fairness is not implemented here. Keaton continues his ruthless takedown by then wrapping the chain around Kobe's neck, a series of twitching limbs and gasps for air follow – it is obvious when life leaves Kobe Peony's body.

The Tagondians thump their boots in unison as screams and cheers erupt upon the victory. Keaton has won; he has murdered Kobe. Kobe's lifeless, mutilated body lies in the sand, sand that is once again tainted with the blood of another. Keaton has been tainted much the same, covered in speckles of Kobe of Favoured Peony's blood. A malicious grin possesses his face as he licks the blood off of his hands. Lidia flies across the stage then.

*What is she doing? She's gone mad.* Several of Master Oberon's Defenders grab Lidia, their grasps firm on both of her arms. She waves her arms and kicks her feet in a fit, but her eyes remain fixated on Lilith. *She's not trying to get to the baby*? Vera asks herself in shock as she glances down at her own hands, which are shaking uncontrollably. The sounds that surround her now filter in, muddled, as she debates for a second on running to the baby herself, for Lidia, though she knows the thought in itself is ludicrous. She doesn't really know Lidia. Besides, the chances of her even getting to the baby before a Defender gets to her are extremely unlikely and she would then face tribulation on the spot. The muddled sounds continue as her mind becomes a cloudy haze while she contemplates her next move in a conflict between obedience versus morality. For Vera, obedience always comes first. Or is it survival? One can say there is a fine line between the two. She wishes she could be braver, more daring.

A group of Defenders enter The Circle and surround Kobe's body with intentions to procure the same brooding chant as before.

Zev raises his arms toward the sky once again to signal The Almek to join in: "One with the earth," the sadistic chorus booms in Vera's ears as the words roll off the lips of every Almek. She speaks them too of course; she has too. Though she shifts in her seat, restless and resisting the urge to scream. She hopes it is over.

"Who's next in line to fight for baby Lilith?" Zev speaks to the crowd. It is known that The Circle is open to man or woman; however, his question is answered with silence, "Very well then. Brene, would you please do the honours?"

"Halt," Master Regan orders, "the mother, Lidia of Favoured Peony, has stepped out of line."

"She has-" Master Oberon begins, possibly coming to her defence.

"Bup bup bup," Master Regan holds his hand out to silence Master Oberon, "Tribulation for offending," his tone a barter. It is heinous to speak of another's life in such a way, but it has become the norm of The Masters and therefore of The Almek.

"Very well," Master Oberon agrees, "bring her to The Circle centre." Huron, Master Oberon's Lead Defender in Kala, escorts Lidia to the centre of the sandy circle – this is his duty since Defenders can never touch opposing colony members, only those of their own colony. Her footsteps graze over the blood of her deceased husband. Upon reaching the centre, Huron forces Lidia to her knees and instantly rips her shirt off.

"Ten whippings," Zev announces, a verdict of The Masters.

Huron holds a leather whip, much smaller in girth from the ceremonial chain. It isn't as life defying and so Vera hopes it will not abuse Lidia's body the same way Keaton's weapon has done to Kobe. The Circle sits in silence as the whip bounds against Lidia's bare back. She screams and wails in distress. When the whip opens her flesh, lines of crimson red contrast against the peach coloured backdrop of her skin.

Acid quickly rises in Vera's throat. *Keep your head,* she recites in her mind. By whip number eight Lidia's body falls forward; passed out from the pain. Huron marks the last two whips on her body as she lay unaware in the sand.

"That will do Huron," Master Oberon states. Huron picks up Lidia's unconscious body and takes her away.

Upon the removal of Lidia from The Circle centre, Brene removes Lilith from the pedestal and carries her over to Keaton whom she hands her to. There he stands in front of the stage: a proud, blood-brushed man beside his wife.

Poised and indifferent to the residual affects that The Circle seems to have on its audience, Zev addresses the crowd once more: "A grand congratulations is in order to Favoured White, they have won themselves a beautiful baby girl. On behalf of The Masters and myself we would like to thank you for joining The Circle for this birthing ceremony. May I remind you, this is one of the many ways that we unite as one and pay respect to Mother Earth. May we be cleansed. You may be excused."

On Zev's cue, the colony members stand and soon a swarm of people move about. Slowly The Circle empties, including Favoured White who depart with their brand-new baby girl in hand, probably to rename her, bathe her and call her their own.

^

Vera begins her walk back toward the colony centre through the footpaths with a dreariness that follows her after every birthing ceremony like an unwanted shadow; beckoning her toward the darkness that it encompasses. Though she tries earnestly to hide her growing misery for the ceremonies she always despises them. However, if she is honest with her herself, it isn't just the birthing ceremonies that make her question their ways, it is so much more beyond that. But, The Almek aren't raised in their new life to question things – not like in the Old World where people seemed to question everything. Maybe they just weren't asking the right questions back then to have humanity end up where they are now.

As Vera walks the paths, the clamour of chatter, laughter and boots scuffing the dirt fills her ears. She darts off the main path to veer away from the noises that signify people forgetting. It is almost as if once they leave The Circle, their memory of the events are erased. But, it isn't some supernatural force that's responsible, it is their own doing – they choose to forget. It is evident in the way they carry on about trivial matters. She never forgets.

*"It's all for naught,"* the whisperer says.

Vera hears the whispers tickling the trees as a breeze blows past. The whispers are only heard when the paths are quiet. Vera pictures some odd Kalian hiding in the forest amongst the brush, sending whispers through the paths. She wonders why on earth this person doesn't have better things to do with their time, never mind how they manage to reach their weekly shares for Master Oberon runs a tightly wound society.

Master Oberon has heard about the whispers and ruled that no Kalian may speak of the whisperer. His Defenders have been searching for the culprit for years with no luck. But that pitiful rule is mild in comparison to some of the laws they are forced to live by.

School, work, supplying one's required shares and humouring The Masters are the ways of The Almek. Though Vera isn't exactly sure how things are run in Tagondo, it is merely assumed. Still, she ponders the soughs of the heckling Whisperer.

Through the footpaths in the forest each Kalian, including Vera, travels their separate ways back to work or school, there is no rest for The Almek. After daily duties the colony will gather tonight at The Pit for One. The Pit contains a circle of wooden seats, enough for all Kalians, and in the middle rests a circle of stones that functions as a fire pit. It is used for many purposes, such as Coakai, which is a spirit celebration requested and led by Master Oberon. During Coakai he is able to influence rainfall from Mother Earth by communicating with her. The form of communication is bizarre, and yet, it is simply ordinary at the same time, seeing as it has been a tradition for the Kalians since their settlement. No one questions it because rainfall has been lacking since the Water Crisis. The musical ones play drums and many will drink whiskey, all while a fire blazes and smoke bellows above the treetops like a cloud. Master Oberon will display a dance which is said to ask Mother Earth to give The Almek rain. Somehow, it rains every time. Vera isn't sure she is convinced of Master Oberon's 'powers.' Though it doesn't bother her all that much, Coakai is certainly not the worst thing The Masters conduct.

Another function of The Pit is for burial ceremonies, which are referred to as: One. They are a celebration of life for the dearly departed. An informal good-bye of sorts that appears to make the living feel better. It is always a merry and lively celebration, which is what Vera struggles with. People think they are celebrating the life of someone who has passed, they aren't wrong. But they are also celebrating a life that died in The Circle as a result of the The Masters' ceremonies. The dead are as so because they died at the hands of a fellow Almek, but also by the tongue of their Masters. But that doesn't change the fact that in Vera's opinion, when it comes to the ceremonies, all colony members are witnesses, aiding and abetting these barbarous acts.

^

Following her afternoon spent working in the lab Vera tends to her hair, ensuring pins hold it back snuggly, to be presentable just as The Master likes it. She gives one final glance in the mirror as she tugs at her black clothing, bound tightly against her curved frame. She would like her clothing to be fitted more loosely. She then makes her way to The Pit for One.

Ceremonies at The Pit are the only time in which the Kalians are granted allowance to be out past the sundown curfew. As her legs drag her across the colony centre the sun sets in front of her in the west. Vera can hear the celebration beginning – the drums are upbeat on this night, always upbeat for One. She makes her way across the spacious tree-lined dirt circle of the colony centre. To her right are the three Kala greenhouses and the lab. Straight ahead sits the Kalian hospital, run by Doctor Theodus of Favoured Harrow. To her left is a tiny cabin called Division, this is where a single Kalian works per shift, accepting the shares collected by the colony throughout the day. Beside Division is the tiny Kalian jail, beyond that rests the largest building in all of Kala: The Master's chamber, which is where Master Oberon and his Barons meet and discuss matters of the colony in private. Directly on the other side of The Master's chamber is a pathway, which leads to The Pit, and beyond that sits the school, that she once attended. She soon turns down the tree-lined path lit with solar lights, solar lights are located outside of most cabins and throughout the colony centre. These lights aid the Night Defender, the Defender scheduled to roam and keep watch at night, and assist citizens in navigating their way home during the occasional evening celebrations.

As Vera enters The Pit, children play and dance while most adults mingle whilst holding a drink in their hand, most likely fermented grapes or corn. Vera will have neither, regardless that she is of age for the drink. The smell of burning bones and flesh waft in her direction. It is a weird smell, the smell of a body on fire. It reminds her of deer on a frying pan; she hates the scent. It always clings in her nostrils, thick and heavy like a gas. But she has to remind herself that they do it for what Master Oberon calls, "good reason." The body of the deceased is cremated in fire to purify them from their previous life and ready their spirit for its next life. Once cool, the bones will be passed around the fire as a good luck omen.

Vera takes a seat in the designated area for Favoured, which are located closest to The Master. A couple Defenders begin pulling Kobe's bones out of the fire pit using large clamps and place them on the ground in a pile beside Master Oberon's seat at the head of the circle. The others continue to dance to the musical one's enchanting drumming, Master Oberon dances as well. There are few who sit and avoid the dancing, though Vera doesn't know their reasoning. She only knows her own. It isn't simply that she doesn't enjoy dancing - though she doesn't - it's the principle of it all. Vera listens to the party that surrounds her, as if she is invisible. However, she is pretty certain to most that she is. She gazes into the fire as the flames reflect in her emerald eyes. *Even though he is dead, did Kobe feel any pain while lying in that pit? While his flesh dripped off of the very bones that had at one time anchored his body together?* Her breathing catches slightly at the thought.

Master Oberon begins addressing the crowd, which means all of the bones have been retrieved and cooled. The others take to their seats, smiles of satisfaction across everyone's naïve faces.

"It is time, my friends. The time has come for 'The Passing.' We pass Kobe around the fire with love and in unity. With a vision that if we work together, one day our water will be cleansed and we can expand beyond The Motherland."

"One," the crowd hums.

"Now we must pray," a slight pause in Master Oberon's speech, likely for effect, "Oh Mother Earth, we pray for you to carry this man's spirit to his afterlife and to bless us with abundance on this Earth for the rest of our days," Master Oberon says as he faces the circle of gleaming eyes around the fire. Their awe-struck stares seem to satisfy him in a way Vera doesn't quite understand.

Master Oberon begins The Passing and Kobe's bones move amongst hands around the fire. The Passing is done in silence; even the drums halt. Each Kalian caresses each of Kobe's bones, one at a time in a brief embrace of their choosing and then passes them along to the person to their right. Some stare longingly, others merely wrap their arms around them. To Vera The Passing seems senseless. *How could it in any way right the wrongs of one's life?* Maybe she is just being smug. Vera has no wrongdoings in her history. Actually, her life is fairly stale, even as a child before coming to The Motherland.

Vera glances up into the trees as she awaits the first of Kobe to come, trying not to think about it all. She notes that the eastern phoebes are in for the night, they are her favourite birds to watch. She decides that when it is her time to become one with the earth the birds will suit her just fine. That way she will never have to be caged in one place ever again. A bone finally comes around to her, she doesn't caress it in the same way the others do. Really, it takes everything in her to co-operate and hold onto it – but co-operate she must. *I'm sorry Kobe,* she thinks. He was a healthy, strong, good-looking man, one that any woman would've been lucky to merge with. It was a life wasted. Vera hates waste. Even though the very idea of her own merging surfaces frustrating thoughts, still, that doesn't mean she can't feel for what Kobe is missing out on, and for whom is missing out on him. *Poor Lidia.*

As Kobe's bones continue past her, she holds her breath - something she always does - and passes them on as quickly as she receives them. There is a pinprick of a thought that prods at her, sometimes it's more invasive, more mauling than others: she is a fraud. She doesn't believe wholeheartedly in The Almek ways. Surely someone will catch on soon enough and report her. If it isn't this it'll be something else. Moreover, she is surprised that her lack of fur scarf isn't the thing that gives her true thoughts away and in turn has her reported to The Master. Kalians like things to look clean, well-kempt and matching. Different is frowned upon. In fact, the needle workers make the same clothing for everyone – black and simple. Each Kalian fashions long sweaters and coats, fitted pants - to make foraging easier - and a fur scarf cozied around their necks to keep the chill in the air from nipping at their throats during the cooler months. Thankfully it isn't a law, which means she has done no wrong. Vera does not wear a scarf for she can't stand the thought of an animal being skinned for her own comfort. Yet, somehow, it seems incredible to herself that she is not reprimanded for that very act.

Although Master Oberon has his hand in making unjust laws and creating inhumane ceremonies, she holds a form of respect for him. He is a stern ruler, but patient in nature. He is strong and kind and seems to truly love his people and Mother Earth. Which is why the Kalians carry on in a spiritually scientific way of life. Though, in Vera's progressive mind, they speak of nothing truly impactful. The very fact that merge laws were made and enforced is proof of that. *Why hasn't Master Oberon merged as the rest of Kala is mandated to?* As an answer to her own question, she supposes that all rulers are exempt of laws and can make exceptional ones for themselves. Wasn't that what most rulers seemed to do in the history of mankind? Whether it is out in the open or behind closed doors?

Upon completion of the passing, all bow their heads at Master Oberon's signal and recite the closing script: "One with the earth."

Lidia, Kobe's widow, is handed his crest, one last good-bye. She holds it snug in her hands, appearing uncomfortable with all eyes on her – *who can blame her?* Her hands cup the crest for a brief moment, and then she releases it and offers it back to a Defender. At that time, two more Defenders come and gather up Kobe's bones in a wheelbarrow, while the third holds his crest. Kobe's bones will be buried in the bone hut, a place behind The Master's chamber that holds all of the bones of the deceased in Kala. The bones are kept locked in the bone hut as a means to prevent the mammoth wolves - enormous grey wolves who have mutated from the toxins in the Water - from disrupting them.

With that, the ceremony is over and Vera is itching to rid herself of the dusty remains littered across her hands. She holds her hands out awkwardly and wipes them across the cool grass below her. The celebratory drums begin and with them the dancing. Fortunately, removing one's self is allowed following the closing script. She feels as though she has paid her dues and as a result of feeling singular in her own community, she decides it is time to turn in for the night.

Vera spots her mother, Ida of Favoured North, and approaches her. Ida is always distracted and fully absorbed in the mood, whatever the celebration.

"I'm going back," Vera says into her mother's ear as Ida continues dancing gleefully with drink.

"What's that dear?" Ida shouts in a drunken slur.

"I'm going home."

"Father can walk you home. Or… where's James?"

"That's not necessary, thank you. I'll be fine."

"Be careful," Ida says in warning, lifting the drink to her mouth.

Before leaving Vera goes to check on Atticus, her younger brother, as she always does. She finds him with his friends deeply immersed in a game incorporating sticks and rocks, flipping and throwing; the game is of no significance to Vera, and so she doesn't ask about it.

"Atticus, I'm going home. Do you want to walk with me?"

"No, I'm going to stay," he replies, barely removing his focus from the game.

"Make sure you walk home with Mother and Father then, okay?" she warns, "And steer clear of Digger."

"Yep," he waves her off.

"Good night," she says as her watchful gaze lingers on him just a little longer. He pays no mind to it.

Atticus is a scrawny teenager and lacks in both muscle and common sense – attributes that always seem to find him trouble. Trouble: such as his long-standing feud with Digger. Atticus has been at odds with Digger, or perhaps more fitting, it is Digger that has been at odds with Atticus since their arrival in the Porcupine Mountains. Digger is a fellow Kalian, brawny and with enough brains to isolate Atticus before meeting his fist to his face. Vera thinks back to years ago when Digger had Atticus cornered at Lake Cloud, attempting to push Atticus in - and would have - if it wasn't for her being there. Digger threw his fist at Atticus as he always does when he thinks no one is around to see. Luckily, Vera was picking leaves off an abetzi plant nearby and heard the commotion happening down towards the water. She saw Digger and instantly flew out of the bushes and grabbed Atticus' shirt just before he fell into the poisonous waters – waters that if touched, would have killed him. Digger laughed, as though it was a joke and ran off, naturally, as betrayal is true to his character – desertion too.

When this instance was brought to Ida and Hendrix's attention, they hushed Vera's concerns of approaching Master Oberon to discuss the dangers of Digger. Though they've known for years that Digger has been a source of agony, it seems they are determined to hide the trouble, to keep their family agreeable in The Master's eyes. Vera can only assume this is to do with her and Atticus' Uncle Merek who had once been a member of The Almek. Back in the early days of the society forming, bravely or stupidly, Merek spoke out against the laws that The Masters were creating. He stated that they were dehumanizing – he was exiled on the spot. As Vera recalled, Uncle Merek was the first to be exiled. It was then when the North family knew silence was safer. Thereby, Vera takes it upon herself to look out for Atticus.

The walk back from The Pit is quiet, except for the shouts that travel from those gathered around the fire. The calls eventually fade the closer Vera gets to home. She doesn't drag her feet as she wants to as she knows someone is always watching, Defenders often sit among the shadows patrolling, and on a celebration night it is important for the security of the people to have more than one. This only means that it is a guarantee that someone is watching her as she walks. At least her thoughts are private, even if her words and movements can't be. The evening air is cool and seems damp now that she is out of the fire's warm reach. She wraps her sweater around herself a bit tighter to keep the breeze off her bare skin.

*"They're watching,"* something whispers amidst the breeze. *I know.*

A creak in a nearby bush startles Vera, causing her to jump and release a small squeal from her throat. Though she is used to the whispers, the darkness is different; it always makes her uneasy.

^

Vera spends the next day working at the lab while Atticus works at the greenhouses and attends his law class at the school. Following their workday, the two meet to forage by the lake. As Vera walks through the forest just before sundown, she surveys the water's edge of Lake Cloud, for when one forages they are required to scout edibles for their family's portion of shares for the week. Atticus dawdles not too far up stream – it's typical, his dawdling. He is lucky to be cute, with sea green eyes and light freckles. The two resemble one another, though Vera is less fair skinned and she doesn't bear freckles as he does.

On this day, and with little time, the pair manages to gather four baskets full of spring berries and dandelion. *Mother will be happy,* Vera thinks. It is often a challenge to fulfill their weekly shares, especially during the winter months. However, it is appreciated that The Masters lessen the share requirements per household by half during those months. And she is grateful that Favoured are granted a lighter share load two pounds per week during the summer months. It is important Favoured are allowed to gather less shares as their profession is expected to require a lot of their time, knowledge and attention to detail. The Insignificants however, have higher expectations when it comes to foraging shares. Those that are strictly foragers must reach four pounds per week, while society workers need three pounds per week. Still, prayers to Mother Earth have been essential to their share fulfillment – it was Mother Earth, after all, who rebooted herself. It is she who allows the colonies of now six thousand people to occupy the lands of Michigan – The Motherland.

A leaf from a dandelion stem lightly tingles against Vera's thumb as it hangs over the edge of the basket. At the beginning of their settlement following the Water Crisis, the Almek learned that the plants vibrate against human flesh. The scientists admittedly have no clue why, for all of their efforts since forming The Motherland have been focused on the fresh water supply and attempting to cleanse the toxic water in Lake Cloud. Regardless, it is a vibrating they have all come to know.

"We best head back," Vera says as she notes the sun beginning to set in the west. She pauses to admire the beauty of the vibrant sunset; it is so rare that she allows herself a moment's glance upon one. But a moment is all that she allows herself, for it is ill advised to be out during dark – the curfew siren will wail upon nightfall.

"Okay, see you at home," Atticus hollers as he rushes off, sprinting within an instant in the direction of their home.

*Now he wants to be mindful of time management,* she thinks. However, when Vera glances down she notes that he has run off and forgotten his basket. If it isn't picked up by another Forager and claimed as their own at division, animals will eat it – his hard work all but forgotten. She ponders if she should teach him a lesson again and let him figure out that his basket is missing on his own – it isn't the first time he's forgotten it and it won't be the last. But she has done that once before, and she saw the repercussions of what happens when she doesn't look out for him. Their family almost missed their shares that week and she had to search the forest in a hurry to gather another basket before the week's end to meet their shares. It didn't appear that Atticus had learned anything from that experience – but she certainly did.

"Wait, your basket!" Vera decides to shout after him, scooping it up and now carries a total of four baskets in her hands. Her shoulders begin to slump forward – not from the weight of the baskets, but from the exertion settling into her muscles from the long day.

Atticus returns promptly, scooping his single basket out of Vera's full hands. His tall body already towers over her average frame, she wonders when that happened. She sighs as the short strands of his light brown hair, barely touched by the breeze, disappear into the green of the forest. Some days she finds it hard to believe he is seventeen nearing eighteen, she doesn't remember being so careless at that age, so irresponsible. Then again, it has been six years since she was his age.

The sky grows dark as sundown approaches, and with it takes the petty warmth in the air. Vera's skin shivers, she quickens her pace; a vigorous walk seems appropriate for timing. Her heart rate accelerates as she moves her limbs in an exaggerated motion through the trees, careful to not bump the baskets. Deciduous trees envelop her, tall and proud, while the Porcupine Mountains - and both colonies - surround her, all of which was once merely camp ground in the Old World.

The curfew siren sounds as it always does at sundown. The hand-wound siren, sounded by one of the musical ones, was presumably made beyond one hundred years earlier. *It may have been a fire siren,* Vera thinks, but then again, she isn't an historian. The noise starts low and the pitch rises as it winds faster. She hates that sound, it causes her stomach to cringe. It's a nagging reminder that they aren't alone, mammoth wolves are always lurking at night. They have come to call them mammoths, the word itself merely references to their enormous size for they are said to stand as tall as the fence at The Circle and weigh some fifteen hundred pounds.

Her breathing quickens and the cold air makes her throat feel dry, she swallows to moisten it once again. Though she is grateful the planet can still muster the temperature drop of minus six degrees Celsius, she longs for warm summer days and they aren't too far off now, around the corner really. She isn't much of a fan of the cold months; however, there are two things she admittedly loves about the winter. First, a snow-filled landscape, she has a certain appreciation for beautiful scenery, never mind that she often doesn't have the time to admire it. Second, it is remarkably, sometimes eerily, quiet in the winter. It is a good kind of eerie though, if there can be a good kind. She often finds herself wanting more of that kind of quiet, it is peaceful, serene. During these moments, only occasionally she worries that maybe they aren't as safe as they think. After all, the colonies have only been established for eighteen years post the Water Crisis. *That is the eerie part,* she thinks, as though something bad is in the midst. *Does Mother Earth intend to clear the planet of all human beings? Or are there other civilizations out there, other than The Almek?* She buries those thoughts, pushes them deep inside her core. If she were to share them aloud, she would be considered an Offender and face tribulation. For it is The Masters who claim The Almek to be the only surviving civilization - the civilization that is to solve the global Water Crisis - they pride themselves in this fact.

As a means to veer her thoughts away from looming angst, Vera tries to listen for the chatter of the noisy and rambunctious forest creatures that are soon to come with warmer weather. They are often in a dizzy and quite entertaining to watch as they begin to make their way out of hibernation mode. Her personal favourites are the birds; she envies their freedom. To come and go as they please, to soar through the sky - no real obligations - aside from feeding their families and building nests, of course. *But isn't that all that I do?* She relates, *More or less... Throw in a disobedient brother and a merge agreement with a future husband that I never wanted, sure.*

As the siren continues wailing Vera's eyes wander upward. Above the trees a thin orange slice of what looks like a row of orange pansies rest in the sky. She reminds herself that she mustn't pause to admire them, for she needs to focus. A rumbling sound comes from the distance - the wolves - a rumble that she doesn't want to get too close to. They only roam the paths when the sky grows dark. She moves her legs as fast as they can march without breaking into a sprint. Her heart rate increases and her body begins to sweat. She doesn't bother taking any layers off as her temperature rises. She doesn't have the time to spare, she knows better than to be out this late. *Mother will be disappointed.*

Suddenly a Defender appears out of the trees, "You're to be indoors," he says sternly. Though he startled her, she isn't surprised; the Defenders are a nagging presence during all hours of the day or night. The crest resting on the left side of his chest is silver like hers. However, his has the squinting face of a fox carved into it,

Vera curiously tilts her head as she recalls never having seen this crest before. Regardless, all Defenders' crests are silver, because they are of the Favoured.

"With the earth," she pauses momentarily so he may recite the understood greeting, when he doesn't, she continues, "I do apologize, I'm minutes from home," she says calmly, hiding her nerves. The Defender wraps his large hand around her arm, just above her elbow, and escorts her home. This is the first time that she has been accompanied by a Defender, for she always makes it home on time. An instant worry for what Ida will think overcomes her. *At least Atticus will make it home on time*, she presumes.

The solar lights that surround her family's log home are in sight: House of Favoured North.

"Don't let this happen a second time, or I shall notify The Master. This is a warning," The Defender turns and leaves without another word as Vera walks up the front steps.

"With the earth," Vera says as she enters, speaking the accepted Almek greeting while setting the baskets on the counter – careful not to knock Atticus' over as he left his basket sitting right at the counter's edge. The slightest bump would send the shares soaring to the floor. She moves the basket away from the edge without a second thought.

"May we be cleansed," Ida replies with the reciprocated greeting, "You're late. Was that a Defender walking you home?" Her voice is stern as her eyes are fixed on the vegetables she's cutting.

"Yes... it was a long day... longer than planned. But, we pulled some great shares."

"Thank you, I'll take them to division tomorrow – but don't cut it so close next time," Ida warns, "In before curfew – I don't want to see that a Defender has to bring you home again."

"Yes, Mother," Vera pauses a moment at a twinge in her stomach for having disappointed Ida.

"You know we're lucky we don't have as many share requirements as the Insignificants."

"I know."

"You would've been foraging full time after you turned thirteen, or working full time as a society worker cleaning the colony centre, or making clothing with the needle workers." Ida lectures, "It makes me wonder how late you'd be if that were the case."

"Yes, Mother."

Hendrix comes down the stairs and interjects with a smile, "The Almek share requirement is a delicate system calculated with great care. Whereby one's profession determines the amount of shares they are subject to. The Insignificants are just as important as us Favoured are. The servant ones ensure ceremonies at The Pit run smoothly, the musical ones play songs dear to our ears. This colony wouldn't function the same without them. We need to respect our roles."

"Yes, Father." Vera clears her throat and continues. "The meadowsweet are almost in bloom – another couple weeks," she exclaims lightly with a hope that it will distract Ida from her tardiness.

"Oh yes, I just love those flowers, so many creditable reasons they are great," Ida notes. Vera has heard her mother say that before, Ida loves their smell and their petals – a great tool for cleaning wounds.

Ida moves about the kitchen with slouched shoulders and a pain in her eyes that Vera can't place. She wonders if she is having an off day. However, Ida is fleeting like the wind and what is one minute isn't the next. *Like Atticus,* Vera thinks.

"Any progress today with the water?" Vera asks Hendrix, hopeful.

"Well, Miss, the levels were looking good today. Not quite there, but getting a bit closer." Vera releases a sigh. "Closer is progress," he firms and she simply nods her head. She supposes it depends on how close 'closer' is.

"Can I give you a hand?" Vera offers Ida.

"Yes, that would be great," Ida steps aside, allowing space for Vera to take over. Ida turns towards the cast iron pan to stir the white-tailed deer. The steam from the deer cooking wafts by Vera, causing her nose to twitch. She detests the smell – memories from the recent birthing and One ceremony unwantedly resurface briefly in her mind of raw flesh burning, the thought is repulsive in its own right. It is this very scent that makes her struggle to eat meat. In fact, it surprises her that humans are able to even consume the animals at all, what with the animals still drinking the poisonous waters. But the animals themselves seem to be entirely fine – except the mutated wolves. They are ravenous creatures of the night, and seemingly the only animals affected by the toxins. *Perhaps the other animals can drink the water because of something in the breakdown of their digestive system an acid of some sort that allows most animals to be immune to lethalyn,* Vera think as she continues slicing the blade through the vegetables.

Soon the four Norths sit on old, teetering wooden chairs with the table itself also equipped with a wobble. It isn't terrible, and only a slight inconvenience when a small amount of pressure from one's forearm is placed on the tabletop's edge.

"We should wait for James," Ida points out. Hendrix nods as he sips his glass of water.

Water is never consumed unless one knows its source. The only source from which one will drink is the lab, which houses the spring water – the safe drinking water. Once a week, on Sundays, Kalians line up by the lab entrance with their jugs and Master Oberon fills them with water from the spring. One jug per family member is the allotment. However, Kalians also collect rainwater, or let snow melt into liquid in large rain barrels, this is typically the water used for washing.

"Yes, Mother," opposing only in her thoughts with regards to waiting for James. She would rather have her bones dragged to The Pit with its fire lighting the darkening sky like the sun. Then she decides, maybe she doesn't truly want that alternative.

Ida clears her throat, most likely because she's irritated,"So Atticus, how was your day, love?"

"It was okay, I had to help move some soil at the greenhouse in the morning with Lidia, had law with Educator Barlow and then helped Vera forage," he shrugs.

"Great, and Vera?"

"Good, I spent my day doing some things in the lab for Master Oberon before foraging-" The front door swings open then and in walks James of Favoured Barlow, or Educator Barlow as most refer to him as.

"With the earth. Hello everyone. Mrs. North, Vera," he approaches Vera with a kiss ready on his lips to plant on her cheek. She shudders inside.

"May we be cleansed!" Hendrix welcomes.

"Hi, James," Vera forces a smile, "You know, there's no need to call my mother that anymore, right?"

"Yes, James. Please do call me Ida. Soon enough it'll be Mother," Ida nods. It's obvious to Vera that Ida's trying too hard. This knowledge only makes her feel more uncomfortable.

"Okay," he smiles, a plain smile, as he sits on an unsteady chair at the table. *There's nothing extraordinary about that smile.* An awkward silence fills the room for some time. The man that sits beside Vera is more or less a stranger to her; yet somehow, in a few short weeks they will merge. Ida stares at Vera expectantly.

Vera inhales sharply, "So, you had a good day?" The question is meant for James.

"Yes, the students were great today. There was a written test on the foraging rules. It's straightforward stuff such as: What is the share division? Though it baffles me that some of them still aren't aware," he says glancing at Atticus. Atticus' eyes dart away and face the table.

"Our house gets 25%, our colony gets 25% and then Tagondo colony gets 50%." Ida chimes in, desperate to continue the flow of conversation.

"Yes. Some of them got it correct," James adds.

Ida smiles, "They must have a good teacher." The table sits in silence once again, until Ida adds: "So you two must be eager for the merge day? Pretty soon your new cabin will be built, and you'll get to move in together." Her own mother couldn't know her any less. Vera already dreads just visiting James' home, for until their new cabin is ready Vera has been in and out of James' current home keeping house, as the laws so require - another law she despises and she can argue many reasons why, the top reason being she has better things to do.

"I'm really looking forward to it," James says in between mouthfuls of food.

"Great," Vera adds. *I can't stand you,* she thinks as she scoops another mouthful of vegetables. At least her thoughts will always be her own, but then again Vera isn't great at being optimistic.

# 2

# COLE OF FAVOURED POLLARD
# TAGONDO

It's sundown after baby Lilith's birthing ceremony. Cole walks down the footpaths that lead from his house to The X, an area of pursuing grounds where the trees are carved with X's and the pursuers regularly hunt. He still has on his grey coat, fur scarf and black pants. Tags wear dark colours – it is said the dark colours are less noticeable to the mammoths.

*"She's coming,"* the Whisperer speaks. Cole has been hearing their whispers since he was a boy of eight-years-old, when he first settled in Tagondo. He never really paid much mind to the whispers, until of course they suddenly coincided with what Murdina told him. He wonders how the Whisperer would know what Murdina knows, as she is such a mysterious old woman, one who appears to know much more beyond human reasoning.

His ankle aches as he walks, the slight nag pulls his focus from the whispers. He twisted his ankle when pursuing a rabbit a couple days earlier and tried to ignore its bite, but his attempts are proving useless. However, on the plus side, he was successful in his pursuit of the rabbit and deems his sore ankle a sacrifice, a trade of sorts: the rabbit's life for his sprained ankle.

When he took the rabbit to division, Arn - the Division Keeper and sprightly old man - said: "Another one for the ol' Mammoth Slayer," his chipper tonality rare amongst the Tagondians. Cole likes Arn; he always pictures him as a man that one would want on his side, a man that does the right thing, even in the face of adversity.

"It'll do for today," Cole responded.

"You've got the blood of a winner," Arn complimented, referring to his reputation.

Cole is known for his face-to-face combat with mammoths. He never pursues them, quite the contrary, they almost seem to come looking for him. He has managed a couple successful escapes, but two encounters resulted in him winning the battle. There is no one else in Tagondo who has faced a mammoth and survived. Still, he hates the way everyone gawks at him upon his jaunt. No matter where he is awestruck eyes gaze at him with a sort of praiseworthy glimmer. Cole could do without their admiration. He forgot what it was like before his first mammoth kill, some four years previous to this day, when no one paid any mind to him whatsoever.

He walks through the trees, still remembering the day they carved The X's into the trees. He was eleven and cut his hand during the job. He still has the scar that runs along the length of his index finger.

The sun sets in the west and the forest grows darker, orange shadows casting amongst the foliage, an owl coos above. His ears listen to the rustling of the evening critters coming to life for another night. Another sound arises: Kala's curfew siren, he hears it, but only faintly. Even though the law states all Almek are to be inside at curfew, Tagondo seems to be the exception to the law. Their Master, Master Regan of Favoured Adder, doesn't seem to enforce that law upon his people. Granted he is a merciless ruler – one his people fear, and so they do not protest. Regardless of the ruler, protest is not the way of The Almek. Still, Regan has been infamous for breaking the laws or making up his own upon a change of heart, upon the moon rising, upon a drop of rain – any unforeseen reasoning of his choice really. Cole reasons that they mustn't need the curfew in Tagondo because all are trained in combat and also make and carry their own weapons.

Later that evening the Tagondians will be having a celebration for their win. The family Favoured White won at The Masters' ceremonies. Which is cause for celebration – drinking and dancing always follow such an occasion. The Master likes winning. Cole will go, as the celebrations are mandatory, and he will indulge in drink and dance. Admittedly, he enjoys a good celebration – though he'll try not to think too hard about its origins. Master Regan requests a dress code at his celebrations, which Cole finds a waste of time, but in the end he doesn't mind all that much. As a result of the dress code though, Cole is on his way to his lookout that he built it in the forest past The X. The lookout is a platform built up in a tree and the last time that he was there he was intoxicated with drink, following one of Master Regan's gatherings, and left his black blazer there – an item Murdina had sewn for him. Cole makes his way through the forest, carrying in his hand a jug of corn whiskey. He isn't often intoxicated, just on the nights Master Regan holds celebrations, something that seems to happen a handful of times during each month. As he sips on his drink he finds the altering psychoactive effects to lighten the nag of his ankle upon each step. A cluster of dandelions sit to his left, the leaves brush against his pant leg. Even through the fabric of his pants he can feel the light vibrations from its petals, as though it's searching for his skin, the tingling will grow stronger once its green surface comes into contact with human skin. Though Cole doesn't know why the plant does this, he knows the tingling has nothing to do with him being intoxicated – *that* he is certain of. Plants are different in the Broken World; something during the Water Crisis triggered a change. He hopes to goodness the scientists in Kala know what that change is. Regardless, Tagondians never hear news from Kala regarding this.

Upon reaching his lookout, Cole glances around before climbing up the ladder to his platform, one hundred feet up and built on the widest and tallest tree that he could find. He prefers to keep its location private, which means no one else knows about it. He spots, crumpled in the corner atop his lookout, his blazer. He takes off his coat and pulls the black blazer on. Next, he reaches for the knife that he keeps tucked away in a wooden box in his lookout and carves one line on the side of the tree for the exiled, for he isn't sure what will become of the young boy who acted out of line that day. Sixty-four lines total now. Cole doesn't enjoy the ceremonies of The Masters and he certainly doesn't like to see a life wasted. But, there is a need inside of him, a need to know how many. Which is why, when he was eight-years-old and witnessed the first man to ever be exiled, he began keeping track. When he looks at the tree marked with lines and it reminds him that life is short. It's possible that's why he doesn't possess fear, as most do; maybe that is why he is able to defeat a mammoth wolf when no one else can.

Cole climbs down the lookout ladder, having barely taken a moment to glance at the movement in the night sky from the treetops, and begins his trek back towards the colony centre. As he approaches the centre, the footpaths are lit up with solar lights around The Master's chamber. Tagondians, dressed to impress Master Regan, walk the stone steps and enter the front doors. Cole glances up at the wooden pillars flanked on either side of the door, each carved with a serpent - Master Regan's family crest - wrapped around a mammoth. Without an explanation Cole understands the symbolic nature of the pillars. He finds it ironic considering Master Regan has never faced a mammoth himself, never telling a tale of fighting such a beast nor sharing the sobering thoughts that possess one's mind when they think they may die at the hands of such a creature. Perhaps that is why Master Regan speaks so tough, so vile; he lives in fear for his life, but he cannot truly protect himself, he needs the protection of the Defenders. To stay in power, he must ensure that his people live in even greater fear than he.

The servant ones play music and the dance floor fills with tipsy Tagondians, all in their finer-wear, men in high collars and women in dresses. Cole takes note that most even take time to manicure their hair, it is a strange sight and always surprises Cole how nicely the Tagondians actually can clean up.

"Cole!" Treena says as she runs to his side, slipping her arm inside of his; it's the norm for her hawkeyes to quickly spot him.

"Hi Treena," he says with a faint smile.

"You're not gonna believe it, Daddy finally wants to have the Agreement Party for us. It's been forever, I've been asking and asking…"

"Oh… Wow. The party eh?"

Treena releases her feet off the floor in tiny pulsing jumps of excitement, "Yes! Finally, our merge agreement will be set in stone. And then after the Agreement Party we can plan the merge!"

"Yeah," the slight fluctuation in his tone is the only tell that he's hesitant.

"I know, it's been what, like three years?" she asks.

"Since our Dads made an agreement for us to merge? Something like that," He wasn't keeping track.

She steps closer to him then, "I can't believe I'm going to merge with the Mammoth Slayer," and leans in to whisper into his ear, her moist words irritating, "I want to do all kinds of filthy things to you on our merge night."

It's exciting, a female saying such things to him. He wonders what kind of filthy things she would do, suddenly the blood rushes to his groin. He has bed a woman once before, though it was a mistake and it will not be one he will make again. For he agrees with Law #22 - of practicing abstinence before merging - it makes sense to avoid unwanted pregnancies and the spread of disease. However, it doesn't come easy, a man can only masturbate so much… He imagines his cock being tugged and squeezed fiercely by a woman's soft warm hands, then he imagines that woman to be Treena and he shudders slightly.

"Hey now," another fluctuation in his voice as he steps back from her, the swelling in his pants subsiding.

Treena is Master Regan's only child – a spoiled monster of a child, even at twenty-four-years-old. Treena is pretty with thin black hair that falls to her shoulders, light aqua blue eyes and a pointed nose that is in perfect proportion with her facial features. She always smells nice, like coconuts, better than most Tagondians. But she is also bossy, impatient and selfish – her father sees to it that things are done for her. Cole struggles with finding things to like about Treena, he figures that in bed things would be no different. Nevertheless, he will go through with the merge agreement and merge with her, mainly because he has no way out of it – no way but death. Besides, there are no women in Tagondo that he is even remotely interested in – not that they are given the freedom to choose. He is nearing thirty and has no family of his own yet. With that in mind, he can accept his fate.

"Bud! I heard the news," Lincoln says as he approaches Cole with a high five.

Cole reciprocates the high five, "You did?"

"I'm gonna go chat with Nin," Treena whispers in Cole's ear.

Mostly indifferent, though slightly relieved, Cole replies, "Okay."

"So, when are you gonna consummate this thing with Treena?" Lincoln presses.

"On the night of the merge, no sooner," Cole affirms, "Though knowing Master Regan, he could suddenly schedule the merge for tomorrow." If that were to happen Cole would follow his fate. Even if it meant complete unhappiness for the rest of his life he'd at least be alive and have a family of his own, which was more than the rest of the world was granted.

"Pffft. I bet she'd let you hit it sooner. She is dying for some Favoured Pollard cock."

"Not interested, although I am interested in your hair – what the hell did you do to it?" Cole's hand gestures with a fiddling of his fingers at Lincoln's pouf and laughs.

"I cut it, left the bangs a little long."

Cole can tell Lincoln is amping up to defend his choices, this reason is only the beginning. Still, Cole pays no mind and chuckles once again. "Man, I've been telling you for years – don't cut your own hair."

"We can't all grow a nice thick mane like yours," Lincoln teases, but it comes out more so as a pout. There's argument number two.

"Leave my mane out of this," he says with a smirk. Cole's dark waves sit at his chin and are often tucked behind his ears. He doesn't mind its wild appearance and prefers that he can just leave it without fussing over it. Most Tagondians have long, untamed hair; it is the brand of the Tagondians. However, Lincoln is one of the few that obsesses over his own head of hair, and sometimes over Cole's as well, it drives Cole mad. But, he has been that way ever since Cole can remember.

"You need a drink FP?" Lincoln asks. FP stands for Favoured Pollard, a nickname Lincoln came up with years earlier.

"Sure, thanks," Cole stands solo a moment, the music tickling his ears. The light and shadows are mesmerizing on the dance floor. Suddenly a strong hand urgently grabs his wrist and pulls him towards the door.

"Come quick, quick lad," the woman urges.

"What is it Murdina?" he asks. Her short, sturdy figure pulls him outside and down the steps – as if he isn't a grown man, strong and capable of following her steps on his own accord. Murdina has always been a mother figure to him, which means this sort of thing happens naturally between them.

"This way," her Scottish voice articulates in a tempered whisper. The two run deep into the forest, Murdina's murky blue eyes searching the trees. Cole follows Murdina's example and glances about, catching an eyeful of their surroundings. Although he is uncertain of what she has called upon him for, he perceives that she wants complete privacy.

When she is satisfied that they are alone she speaks: "It's happenin'," she warns.

Cole falters a moment all the while Murdina looks to him with impatience, "Sooner than planned? Are you sure?" he asks.

"Sure as shite."

"Okay. What do we do?" There is something to his voice, hidden amongst his laboured breaths and his purposeful articulation. It isn't obvious at first, the way his nerves lick at his words. Still, he notes its subtle presence, knowing how Murdina regards him, she likely heard it too.

"Tell nea a body, but get ready lad. She's comin'."

# 3

# VERA OF FAVOURED NORTH
# KALA

The next morning, the eastern phoebe wakes Vera once again. They are known to migrate back to Michigan at the onset of spring – from where? Who knows... but, she knows that tune anywhere; their distinctly repetitive, yet light and cheery two-syllable whistles are ones that she has grown to love. It is still dark outside; the sun has not risen yet. Although, it will in a matter of minutes so Vera quickly gathers her things and gets dressed. She will make her way to James' to tend to his home before he wakes. She decided that she prefers him asleep and unaware of her presence.

As the light is seen peeking through the trees she scurries to Favoured Barlow down the path, across the colony centre and into the trees. The colony is quiet, no one is out at this hour even though it is allowed as the sun is shining light on The Motherland, meaning there will be no mammoths out, because for whatever reason lights deter them.

Vera enters Favoured Barlow without a knock, for there is a mutual understanding that Vera has a right to access it at all times for tending. As she enters the narrow hallway she smells eggs cooking from the kitchen. *Damnit, he's awake after all.* She takes off her shoes and rounds the corner, entering the tiny kitchen. There he stands, her future merger and father of her unborn children. The very thought sends a disturbed jolt across her body that almost causes her step to falter. If she has to have children in this world, James of Favoured Barlow has to be the least probable man she would ever want to do it with.

“With the earth,” he says as his empty eyes meet hers. She has grown sick of his stare, along with his British accent.

Vera nods uncomfortably, eagerly attempting to be agreeable, “May we be cleansed.”

“Have you come to join me for breakfast?” His voice is cold as he speaks, nothing ever seems to change that.

“No, thank you. I’ve come to tidy for you.”

“I see,” he fills his steel plate with eggs and walks to the square table that is pushed up against the wall at the far end of the kitchen, though it is anything but ‘far,’ it is merely the only open space in the room. Seeing as the table is against the wall, there are two chairs on either end of its build. As James takes his seat her eyes are pulled to the empty chair. That seat is for her, physically and figuratively. She hurries to the sink and begins washing the dishes. Scrub, rinse, repeat. *Just finish and get out.* James will be happy that his house is clean, which means he won’t report her for failing to keep house and she can get on with her day which is to be spent at the lab with her father.

James is a much older, quiet man who she once had as an Educator for many years. Although she heard stories, it wasn’t until they entered a merge agreement that Vera saw the inside of his house. There is an eerie feeling inside it. It isn’t only James that brings unnerving sensations, of course he is about the half of it, but it is also the feeling that they aren’t alone. It is said that his previous merge partner committed suicide in this very house because she couldn’t conceive. Which is why, just as soon as James and her new build is complete, this very house will be burned to the ground. Suicide is seen as a contagious ailment; therefore all precautions are taken to rid the colony of its disease. Vera often wonders if it was truly a suicide, or if it was James himself who claimed the life of Elle Barlow for not being able to conceive. Regardless, her body was never found. She could have possibly jumped in the lake and finished herself off that way. A cool set of goose bumps prickle Vera’s skin, even with the hot soapy water encasing her hands.

Once the kitchen is tidy Vera moves to the bedroom. As she tugs and tucks the disheveled sheets from James’ sleep he comes to the doorway, leaning on the wooden edge of the doorframe. Vera turns to glance at him – a force of habit when one sees movement in their peripheral. It is unnerving, the way he stands there in silence, fixating on her. She moves slowly, keeping her breaths shallow, wanting to hold the least amount of his attention as possible. Her leg itches down by her ankle and she ignores it, even when it sends a jolt down her body. It takes a certain kind of will power to ignore such a feeling. He continues to stare at her, the force of his gaze piercing into her minimally exposed skin, making her feel as though her off-white flesh is transparent. She pulls the blankets up as far as they go and tucks them in an urgent manner. More movement in her peripheral, the floor creaks as he approaches her. She’s bent over the bed when he pushes his hips into her behind, holding his force there. She freezes at his touch, unable to move away even though she desperately wants to. *What is he doing?* He has never laid so much as a finger on her at Favoured North in front of her parents, except for the odd dry kiss that makes her cringe with a wanting to scrub her cheeks with bleach.

“This is your place,” he says. She swallows and recites a brief prayer to Mother Earth in her mind. However, when she doesn’t respond to him, he thrusts his hips into her, she almost chokes on her own saliva in response.

"Yes," she manages. Her body tightens in alarm, a knowing of what he wants from her – what he expects. Her hands tremble on the edge of the blanket. When he finally backs away from her, she breathes once again. She finishes tidying then quickly gathers her things and heads for the door.

James appears lurking again, this time in the hallway by the front door, "This is going to be a good arrangement," he says while the tiniest glimpse of a smile tugs at his lips.

^

"With the earth. Good Morning," Vera says to Hendrix as she flies through the front door of Favoured North.

"Good morning, Miss. May we be cleansed. Listen… I forgot to mention, my P tester broke yesterday. It's urgent that we fix it this morning once we get to the lab."

*Terrible early-morning news,* Vera tenses, "How will we fix it?" She knows what he is going to say, it's something he's said many times before.

"It's not impossible, Miss, we will find a way. You know, sometimes the greatest lessons are in the set-backs," Hendrix says humbly. The words themselves she understands, though in her mind she disagrees. The setbacks are setbacks, because they inconveniently, and quite literally, set one back in their ambitions. No, Vera will not be grateful for the setbacks, if it isn't a step forward, it's a step backwards and that is unacceptable.

"It can be hard to see the positives that you speak of," she looks down at her coffee.

Hendrix reasons, "Ah that, my dear, is half of the battle. It is never easy, but it is good practise."

"This may be off topic, but… how do you cope with… the ceremonies? I mean… the challenges that come with witnessing the ceremonies?" It is true that Vera finds many things about life in the colonies difficult, but her question is inspired by the events of the recent birthing ceremony. However, the way Hendrix lifts his head quickly to catch her expression tells her that he is surprised by her question.

Ida approaches the table and takes her seat, "Everyone has to endure them, it doesn't mean we need to like them." Vera purses her lips out of frustration, the ceremonies are purely barbaric and have no real purpose other than tearing families apart. She glances down at the steel crest that rests over her heart a symbol of her family, a compass made out of silver steel. Each family has one: same in size, different in symbol. Favoured have silver while Insignificants have bronze.

"I for one am all for the ceremonies. It controls the population; it keeps people lawful, it's honest. Consider too, the fact that it's better than what our government was doing before the Water Crisis evoked great change in the world," Hendrix offers.

Vera assumed that his opinion on the matter must largely be based on the fact that the North's presumably think they are safe – their family name will never be pulled because they are needed. It is evident to Vera as well that Hendrix likely has some influential information on precisely what the government had been working on in those days. Hendrix is a scientist, even before the Water Crisis as he worked closely with several members of congress in the Old World. She was a mere child of six-years-old when they moved to Michigan as the rest of the world fell, which means she lacks perspective on how one should rule. Still, it hasn't stopped her from speculating on that front, nor from despising the laws.

Vera leaves the kitchen to wake Atticus. If she doesn't, everyone will leave to begin their days and he would still be in bed fast asleep, none the wiser. Atticus moans as Vera pulls the blankets off of his long, slender frame.

"Wake up sleepyhead," she opens the blinds to his window. It doesn't matter that his window faces south; the light from the sky still shines through his room. "I'm about to make breakfast." All but a moan escapes his mouth. That is signal enough to know he is awake so Vera heads downstairs and starts breakfast. She fries eggs and toasts some bread over the stove. Just as breakfast is ready, James walks in through the front door and plants a routinely dry kiss on Vera's cheek then everyone sits around the table to feast together.

"Good day, everyone. With the earth," James announces in greeting.

"May we be cleansed," Ida tugs at her toasted bread, "Are you hungry James?"

"No thank you, I'll just have coffee."

"James, do you enjoy the strategic ruling of The Masters?" Hendrix asks, he always loves a good debate on perspective. Though in this world it isn't so much a debate as a retelling of The Master's beliefs.

"I do quite enjoy The Master's unions, very much so," James notes with an indescribable passion to his voice. Vera almost spits out her water. *He must be deranged,* she thinks.

"What exactly, do you find so intriguing?" an elated Hendrix inquires further.

"As you know, I study the laws, it is remarkably fascinating how The Masters develop and ceremoniously enforce the laws," James proclaims in response.

Atticus looks to Vera and through his slumberous expression a question rests on his lips. She can tell by the way he opens and then closes his mouth, barely waiting his turn to speak. She lowers her brow in a glare briefly, just long enough for Atticus to notice. No matter his question, James Barlow is not to be trusted.

^

It is a hard realization for Vera to accept – that there are people in the colonies that look forward to the shows of The Masters. That is what Vera thinks of them as, shows: barbaric displays of power that she desires nothing more than to end. She shouldn't be surprised though, the laws are burned in the brains of all The Almek. Even Hendrix is in support of the ceremonies, and Ida doesn't seem to object. James, well, they excite him to a level of fervour she has never seen in him before. Goosebumps cover her arms at the recollection of his enthusiasm over breakfast that morning.

Vera moves her gaze towards the sun; it has risen into an orange-blue sky, bringing out with it the morning wildlife. Her walk to the lab with Hendrix is quiet, which isn't usually the case. He glowers towards the ground as they walk. She wonders what is bothering him, his moods have been a tad unsteady lately, likely stress from trying to find a cure for the water – it is a responsibility that seemingly rests upon the shoulders of the Norths. Once they get to the lab, the two manoeuvre around the space effortlessly. It is as if they are two pieces in a moving puzzle, gliding elegantly from one place to the next. Always thinking ahead, determining the next move. Vera, in many ways, is a lot like Hendrix beyond just their Favoured title, in which they hold great pride.

In reality, there is a certain level of preferentialism to the Favoured that is unspoken. She assumes that is why they are given such a name as 'the Favoured.' This actual favouritism is evident in most things, beyond just a title, specifically in the school system. The schooling is more sophisticated for the Favoured. They are granted an apprenticeship in their appointed field and a longer, more thorough education as a result, which means they have the opportunity to learn in the classrooms as well as practise their knowledge on-site. Their school days run according to each individual Educator's planning. Thereby a student gets their schedule at the beginning of each new year in January, at which point they move up in grade level and a new school year commences. School for Favoured is mandatory all year long, from age five to eighteen. In December of the year they turn eighteen, they are placed into their family's respective fields. And finally, sometime after their twentieth birthday members are placed into a merge agreement – that too, is mandatory. This is the story of Vera's life in Kala so far, like it is for all.

Though Vera has graduated some years earlier, Favoured are always given the opportunity for additional learning. Since her family consists of botanists and scientists, she and Atticus are born into their positions and they are fortunate to have the choice between the two Favoured fields for their chosen profession – something few Favoured have. A Favoured's education is seen as essential to The Almek way of life, which means more education is always available, should a Favoured so desire. Vera has always taken to more classes, while Atticus plans to be done just as soon as he can.

The Insignificants, on the other hand, aren't granted such opportunities with their schooling nor their professions. As stated in the laws, they are schooled from five-years-old until the age of thirteen. Like the Favoured they are given a schedule from their teachers at the beginning of the year including courses such as law, the Water Crisis, foraging, reading and writing, but these classes are specific to Insignificants. Classes beyond that are seen as too sophisticated and unnecessary for an Insignificant's role in the colony. The Insignificant classrooms are far more tightly packed, as there is less of a need for them to obtain quality learning. Sharing a classroom between the two social groups is prohibited, which is why Favoured are set apart for a more thorough learning experience. Regardless, it is essential that all Almek know and understand the laws, the unfolding of the Water Crisis and foraging to establish proper collection of plants, and above all uphold their responsibilities within the colony.

Vera does not take her responsibilities lightly – those that know the ways of the lab are few. The two students that work in the lab intermittently for their apprenticeships were also born into science. Isla, who is thirteen and as innocent as a flower, was granted a position in the lab through her mother who passed away just three years prior; she had a blood condition they couldn't seem to get a hold of. Then there is Ellis, seventeen and ill tempered – often upset over incredulous things like his pencil breaking or his hair windswept into disarray. Atticus has mentioned to her that the entire science class hears about it, including Wymen Ferris, also known as Educator Ferris, who happens to be Ellis' uncle. Ellis' parents died in a tragic car accident when he was young, back before the Water Crisis and as a result Uncle Wymen took on the noble duty of raising Ellis. Perhaps Ellis' unfortunate past was sufficient enough an explanation for his rotten nature and unpredictable outbursts. Either way, neither Isla nor Ellis are fit to be left in the lab alone. Educator Ferris helps a couple days a week, when he isn't fulfilling his teacherly duty of enlightening his students with the ways of science. Although Atticus could pursue a job in the lab, he didn't take to the science realm. He is a botanist through and through, if he could just remember all that he learns in class lectures.

Vera ponders why Atticus appears to detest science so, or more specifically why he dislikes being in the lab. He's always stared at the cylinders in apprehension, ever since he was a young boy. They are likely intimidating to Atticus and with good reason; perhaps that is why he diverted from science. Vera glances at the cylinders herself and examines the tall vats full of water. These giant cylinders were built back in the early days of settlement made with a thick shatter-proof glass. Their size takes up half of the lab, which means desk space is limited but sufficient enough. A long steel table runs along the east wall starting near the entrance, and another along the west wall, the cylinders take up the south end of the building. These cylinders sit about seven feet off of the ground, which means a ladder is necessary when accessing water samples. But falling off of a ladder in the lab isn't the greatest danger, a leak in the Lake Cloud vat would be.

The Lake Cloud water is housed on the far right in cylinder #3. In the middle, cylinder #2, holds much less in quantity, this is the ground water. Meanwhile, cylinder #1, on the left, houses the natural spring water. The spring water is found hidden and protected underneath Michigan's soil and is the fresh water that the colonies drink - the reason they have survived - and as far as we know, it is the only safe drinking water on the planet besides the rare occurrence of rainfall. Thankfully, the rain water continues to test negative for lethalyn, however the lack of its presence is undetermined.

Back in the Old World, scientist Hendrix North, among others, discovered the spring water – an underground aquifer that isn't contaminated with chemicals due to several lucky and coincidental circumstances. The first being that it is completely confined underground; which means its location makes it impossible for humans to contaminate it. Second, it is surrounded by clay and other non-porous rocks below ground level, which are impermeable and create an ideal site for a healthy aquifer. Lastly, they believe that only parasites and bacteria are able to live in such an environment – both of which they can rid the water of easily. Installing the filters and testing the water several times on a daily basis is pertinent to the safety of the spring water.

"Can you get out the TXE tester please? It's time to conduct the test on cylinder number three," Hendrix asks Vera.

"Do you want the lethalyn tubes as well?"

"Yes, please. I'll have you test for lethalyn this time," Hendrix states casually, but Vera looks at Hendrix with surprise. It will be her first time testing the lethalyn levels. It is something Hendrix has always been authentically obsessed over. Without hesitation though, Vera gathers the necessary items and places them on one of the smaller metal lab tables, which is on wheels for mobility. The work surface is covered in papers of Hendrix's scribbles, which means no test tubes are to be put on there. With a pair of gloves pulled up beyond the cuffs of her lab coat, nearly reaching her elbows, she puts a pair of safety goggles on and proceeds with the test. On the large steel table, at the edge of all the papers, there is a single element used for boiling. Vera crushes and then boils the bark off of a birch tree, the white substance that collects on the surface of the water is a chalk-like powder called betulin. Betulin is used in pain relief, but it is also thought to be a natural cleanser. Vera scoops the betulin out and mixes it in a dish with chlorine dioxide and ozone. Chlorine dioxide will disinfect the water and ozone will immediately breakdown any bacteria or viruses that are present in the water. Ozone is a valuable chemical because its molecules will break down naturally – allowing oxygen to be all that remains. The one problem with chlorine dioxide is that it leaves residual molecules; however, the hope is that with the right ratio of betulin, ozone and chlorine dioxide together they will rid the water entirely of all chemicals – lethalyn included. Vera adds the mixture - betzonide they call it - to a 0.5mL test tube filled with Lake Cloud water. The TXE tester will reveal the ratios of chemicals in the water while mixed with betzonide.

"Lethalyn 0.25mL, Arsenic 1.5mL, Coliform 3mL, Cryptosporidium 0, Turbidity 0," Vera reads the results aloud to Hendrix with a sigh of disappointment.

"Slowly but surely. Next time add more betulin to the betzonide," he says with his back turned to her as he works on something of his own invention at the west-end table. Vera then uses the HP Vac to suck the lingering chemicals out of the water. It's not probable that the vacuum will work, but she tries. The TXE tester reveals the result, which makes no difference. Her heart sinks just a little every time she reads the results. *Lethalyn is impossible.*

"Vera, what's the evacuation plan?" Hendrix asks, with an inquisitive tone to his voice that she finds rather suspicious. Regardless, the very thought sends a brief feeling of worry through her core. She can't stand the idea of the lab being compromised. Her life's work is in here – her life, rather, has been spent inside these walls. But she knows Hendrix and that he likes to keep her prepared and on her toes, she knows that she must answer, so she briefly explains that she would pull the alarm and leave.

Hendrix presses further though, "What do we do if cylinder #1 has a leak and it begins pouring out onto the floor?" Vera looks at him with humouring eyes, he nods eagerly, "Five steps."

"One: pull the alarm," she gestures to the lever that hangs on the wall beside the exterior door, "Two: grab as many toxin suits as I can and evacuate everyone." She pauses a moment, not because she doesn't remember what comes next, but because it irritates her.

"My lab coat," he urges.

A sigh releases from her chest, "Yes, step three: grab your lab coat," though she nods her head in agreement she says it rather off-the-cuff. Vera holds a deep lack of understanding for his persistence with his coat. If the lab goes down it wouldn't bother her if her lab coat should go with it – so long as lives are saved, people protected.

"You cannot forget that should myself or the lab ever be compromised. Understand?"

She nods her head yes as she focuses her eyes on him more attentively.

"And what about cylinder #2?" Hendrix questions.

"Four: push the air-tight button on the side of the spring cylinder to close the lid, preventing contamination."

"Very good. Is there anything else that you need to remember?" he asks.

"I'd like to be able to take all the years of paperwork and tests…"

"That's impossible," he affirms.

"I know."

He persists, "Five?"

She turns to look at her father whose face forms a smirk, though she assumes his smirk a means to be playful, "Evac-"

He interjects, "Run like hell."

# 4

# LIDIA OF FAVOURED PEONY
# KALA

The next morning Lidia receives word from Atticus that Vera will be working in the greenhouses with her as Ida had some business to tend to with Hendrix in the lab. It isn't uncommon for approved Favoured to cover for one another upon a sick day, or needing–reinforcements, but she has never worked alongside Vera - a scientist - before. Seeing as Vera has covered in the greenhouses on a handful of occasions in the past with Ida, she will somewhat know her way around at least. Lidia is quite close with Ida, Vera's mother, they've worked together as botanists in the Kala greenhouses for years now. If Lidia is honest, the idea of working with Vera unsettles her, though it also intrigues her – the way Ida speaks of Vera offers Lidia a very different impression than what she herself has of her. For one, it's odd that Vera doesn't wear a fur scarf as everyone else. She wonders if that means the rumours of her not eating meat are true. There also seems to be a constant scowl upon Vera's face and Lidia wonders what on earth the poor girl has been through that could make one so sorrowful all the time. Lidia knows what sorrow is, and is struggling with it herself, at least since Lilith's birthing ceremony. The greenhouse door opens and in walks Vera.

"With the earth. It's nice to finally meet you," Lidia attempts to hide her timid feelings, "Your mother has said so much about you."

"May we be cleansed," Vera responds coolly while readying herself with a pair of scissors for trimming the dead leaves. Silence follows. Lidia watches as Vera presses the pin that holds her dark brown hair together, and runs her hands along the sides of her head, willing her hair to stay flat, to stay perfectly tidy against her scalp. Vera eyes move to Lidia's, and as they do so they glow an emerald green, and are framed in an oval face that rests unhappily in this moment. Perhaps in most moments.

However, Lidia isn't easily discouraged and attempts further conversation, "So, do you know much about the greenhouses?"

"I know some, just tips my mother has shared with me." There is a sort of stale atmosphere in the air with Vera there, like the way one feels when cooped up indoors during the evening. Lidia detests the feeling of being restricted and she doesn't much like unexciting things, but mostly, she is curious about the sadness that Vera seems to carry.

"Okay good. Well, Ida has some helpful tips, though she does often repeat herself - like a cicada insect - sometimes a ringing is all I hear," Lidia laughs as her straight blond hair loosens in its tie behind her head. She quickly reaches her hands up to adjust it.

Vera releases an instance of laughter and Lidia smiles deeply with her dark eyes that almost appear indigo-blue in the right light, they crinkle at their corners. Lidia feels pride for making Vera of Favoured North laugh. If anyone in the colony had seen it, they'd be speaking of it for days.

As the morning progresses it comes as a pleasant surprise that the two seem to get along. It is nice for Lidia, she doesn't have many friends, though she isn't sure who does, Kala is a fairly isolated place to live.

"So what's with your fur scarf?" Lidia asks. It isn't just a question, it's a test.

"What fur scarf?"

"Exactly."

Vera's eyes flicker upon Lidia, then her eyes wander away upon her response, "I am free to choose how I feel about fur scarves."

It isn't a direct answer to Lidia's question, and yet it is precisely enough to suggest that perhaps there is something within Vera that she can trust, and something beyond the reserved, somber persona.

"Very well," she clears her throat, "I know we're not supposed to talk about it, but I have to ask… how are things with James?" Lidia questions Vera in a whisper, aiming to pinpoint her source of presumed unhappiness. Her voice is faint so no one can hear her sows of offence. Although they are alone in the greenhouse, the walls of glass aren't all that thick.

"Oh," Vera pauses a moment, appearing taken aback by the question. Lidia knows that it is against the law to speak of merge agreements – she doesn't mean to make an Offender out of Vera.

However, Lidia watches as Vera's hands being to quiver at her side, "It's fine, it is simply part of my duty," Vera says as she turns the fans on for the lavender plants. Words of intimate details are never to be spoken.

"I get that. That's what I'm trying to tell myself now, all this pain – it's just part of my duty," Lidia says, looking towards the ground in sadness, while also digging for details from Vera.

"I'm sorry…" Vera adds, seemingly with hesitation.

"Well, I wasn't overly happy with Kobe – I didn't love him. And I didn't want children. I'm not sure those things make this any easier though," Lidia confesses.

"I don't believe in love. The laws are above all things," Vera urges. Lidia wonders if Vera truly believes they should be, or if she's just worried that someone could be listening.

"Yes, yes of course they are," Lidia agrees. *Maybe freedom over a fur scarf is much different than freedom over the laws*, a sudden worry for her possible misjudgement envelops her if Vera wanted to, she could report her for her words of offence.

"Even though I may not agree with all the laws," Vera whispers. Lidia, surprised by Vera's statement, notes her feelings and is now put to ease.

"Me neither," Lidia adds, glancing around them. A thought crosses her mind that she would normally never dare tell anyone, but for some reason has a desire to tell Vera, "But I still have hope for love. Even in this crazy world. And Lilith? I pray to see her again one day."

"Why? It's not even considered in our way of life."

"I don't know, I just do."

"Suit yourself, but we better stop talking about this," Vera states, "I hear footsteps outside."

Regardless, Lidia continues, "I just… I can't stop thinking about her. I wish there was a way to get her back, you know?" she sulks, wishing there is light amongst all of the darkness that encases her.

Vera pauses her trimming and looks at Lidia, "I'm sorry, I truly am. I can't imagine what you must be going through. But we need to get back to work."

Just then Huron, Master Oberon's Lead Defender, opens the door to the greenhouse; his legs carry him in like two stone pillars, unwavering. He walks about the greenhouse inspecting the plants, while slipping a suspicious eye toward the two women. Lidia jitters her foot against the ground in a nervous manner, while the rest of her body freezes. She half expects Huron to arrest them, to say that he heard their words of offence. But when a door slams and she realizes that he has left, she exhales in utter relief. Her eyes glance at Vera, whose lips are pursed in what Lidia thinks to be fear.

# 5

# VERA OF FAVOURED NORTH KALA

Despite Lidia's push to speak such private words of offence, Vera feels a sense of ease in her presence. The very fact that Lidia speaks of true feelings inspires Vera – no one, not even her parents speak of real matters, aside from the water. Even she herself would never normally speak of such things for the simple fact that it can mean the difference between survival and death. It is reckless to make such thoughtless decisions, but Lidia seems different compared to the others, she seems honest. To her own surprise, Vera agrees to have Lidia join her for a pull day - a common term Kalians use when they must forage - surely Lidia will be bright enough to keep her thoughts to herself while rummaging among the paths.

The next morning, the two meet in the colony centre and head for Lake Cloud where they are hopeful to gather a good portion of their shares for the week. It is a lively spring day and the March sun is growing warmer and shines bright as Lake Cloud reflects its light like a mirror; so much so that one almost can't see the tinge of yellow poison in its waters. The forest is alive and sprightly and the commotion from its creatures fills the morning air with a sense of rejuvenation.

"We will split our pulls that we gather from today," Vera states while on route to the lake.

"It's not my day to pull though, you don't have to do that."

Vera swiftly shakes her head, "Nonsense."

It would be an understatement to say Lake Cloud is one of Vera's favourite places to be, aside from the lab, it is her home away from home. She relies on this place for its serene landscape. It is a dependable place, once she can go when she needs clarity and time alone. She values her alone time graciously and yet, she is completely content spending her day with Lidia. A cracking noise echoes from the forest across the lake, loud laughter follows. Vera and Lidia freeze to watch two figures appear from the trees across the lake, and walk towards the lake only a few hundred metres away from the water's edge.

"Tagondians," Vera whispers.

"What are they doing over here?"

Vera contemplates, "I suppose it is their lake too. They pursue there."

"Should we leave?" Lidia asks.

"If they get too close, we will. We are here to do our job. Though, I'm not exactly sure how they think they will accomplish theirs with how noisy they're being," even Vera knows this – pursuing needs to be done as quietly as possible.

Moments later the two Tagondians spot the women, "Hey ladies," the tall, fair-haired one calls across the lake.

Vera and Lidia quietly stand side-by-side looking off into the forest as if something particularly interesting is holding their attention in the opposite direction, a façade of sorts, all while keeping in mind Law #32: None shall communicate with the opposing colony members. Vera has the laws memorized, and for good reason.

"What's the matter? Too good to chat to a couple hard workin' Tag boys?"

*More or less,* Vera thinks. It is a silly question to pose, of course Kalians are superior to Tagondians – it is basically written in stone. Besides, she has no interest in breaking the laws and becoming an Offender – that desire overrules her mild curiosity.

"Leave them alone Lincoln, I don't think they're interested in your shenanigans," the somewhat shorter, brown-haired one laughs.

"No, they're being stuck up. I said hey," the tall guy shouts again.

"With the earth," Lidia nods her head, pleasant as the day is young.

"Don't talk to them," Vera barks in a whisper.

"That's better," says the tall one.

"Lidia," Vera tugs on Lidia's arm begging for her attention, "We have to go, we can't talk to them, it's the law," clear contempt in her voice. She won't let her parents down. Should someone find out she's speaking to Tagondians, it would reflect poorly upon their family name, or worse.

"What are ya ladies doin' out here today?"

"Foraging," Lidia replies, "What are you guys doing?" Vera still tugs on Lidia's arm in opposition.

"Well, we were pursuin', takin' a break now. Just got ourselves a *nice big buck*," the tall guy explains, exaggerating his words slightly.

Vera tugs harder on Lidia's arm once again, as if to guide her away from the Tagondian men. Even at this great distance across the lake they appear vile and unkempt.

"That's a good pull for you guys," Lidia continues to engage.

Vera ponders Lidia's mental stability as her own stomach begins to twist with worry. They will get caught and have to face Master Oberon in tribulation. Who knows what kind of backlash this will mean for her family – higher share obligations or worse, they could lose their positions as Favoured. There has only been one Favoured Offender to face tribulation in the history of Kala – Uncle Merek.

"Wait, why don't you come on over here? We can hang out for a bit," the tall guy questions.

“No Lidia, we need to get out of here,” Vera begs, raising her voice slightly in urgency.

“Let’s just go over and talk. This is a once in a lifetime opportunity. Have you ever seen a Tagondian up close and personal before?” Lidia tempts with wonder and curiosity in her eyes.

“No. And I don’t want to.”

“Okay, but isn’t there at least a tiny, tiny part of you that’s curious?”

“Curious, maybe… stupid, no.”

“This doesn’t make us stupid. This makes us adventurous. Besides, what if we end up liking these guys?” There is something in Lidia’s eyes as she looks fixedly at Vera.

Whatever it is, Vera has to get rid of it, “Liking them?” The thought in itself is outlandish. “There is no room in this world for Kalians and Tagondians to interact. We cannot be friends with them.”

“But, what ever happened to adventure? To breaking free of chains… or fur scarves?”

“There is no breaking free of this place and its laws,” she reminds Lidia.

“Don’t you ever just want to soar above the trees? To feel as though you’re a free person, even if it’s just for a moment?”

*Yes*, Vera thinks. If she could grow wings and be an eastern phoebe, she would most certainly soar above the treetops and leave this place. Warmness fills her heart at the thought. If only they could fly, right across the lake and to meet these Tagondian men.

“Please!” There is an excitement in Lidia’s eyes, a sparkle; it’s likely more of a shine but Vera refers to it as a sparkle. The joy that spreads across Lidia’s lips forms a smile and Vera feels hopeful in a way that she possibly never has. The idea of a brief escape also seems to offer Lidia relief. That thought begins to sway Vera. She can’t see a way to convince Lidia otherwise and so begins reasoning that talking with a couple Tagondian men isn’t as bad as missing shares or committing treason… It will be, after all, just a conversation. Perhaps she can do that for her friend, only if she can ensure it’s quick.

“Okay fine, but just for a minute,” Vera agrees, “Any longer and I’m leaving. You know how the Defenders do their rounds.”

Lidia beams, “Okay, thanks!” and they begin walking north along the water’s edge towards The Circle, located only a few hundred metres away.

“I’m doing this for you. Just know that I don’t like it,” Vera clarifies, and it’s true. In doing this she’s fighting against her conscience. However, this promise of a brief taste of freedom urges her legs to keep moving in the direction toward The Circle.

“I know and I appreciate it. I will return the favour one day.”

“Return the favour?” Vera asks quizzically.

“Yes, I’ll do a favour for you one day – even if I really don’t want to do it.”

“Okay,” Vera agrees hesitantly, but she can’t see herself asking her friend to do a favour that involves offending.

As both pairs approach The Circle, the brown-haired Tagondian calls, “We’ll come to you.” The men climb the gates of The Circle and run across its tainted sands.

The two women stand by The Circle’s edge as the medallion of sand that signifies death and abduction stares back at them between the slats of the gates. Vera glances over to Lidia who suddenly looks pained and doesn’t once glance towards the pedestal.

The men make it across seemingly so effortlessly; though they have already offended by climbing the gates of The Circle, which is an offence in and of itself. It is the norm upon an introduction to inspect one's family crest and so they get close enough to do just that. The tall guy's crest is a bronze dagger, while the others is a silver eastern phoebe. Vera intakes a sharp breath of air. She knows an eastern phoebe anywhere; it's her spirit animal, if she were ever to have one.

"Ladies," says the tall guy with a smile.

"Hi," Lidia says as Vera stands silent.

"What, does she not talk?" the tall guy asks, gesturing to Vera.

"She just-" Lidia begins.

But Vera can't stand someone else speaking for her, and so, she interjects: "I'm just trying to figure out: is it now socially and morally acceptable for our people to *hang*?" Through her defensiveness Vera attempts a level of casual conversation that she isn't sure that she is achieving. It likely doesn't matter, they are just pursuers, lowlifes of The Motherland, she tells herself. Still, she wonders why the one man has a crest of the Favoured.

"Um, sure?" the tall guy answers questioningly while laughing, "I'm Lincoln, this is FP… well, Cole," he continues as he gestures to his friend who has a head of thick brown hair tied at the back of his neck in a stubby ponytail.

"Vera," she says, then gestures over to her friend, "This is Lidia." Lincoln stares at the two women with a mischievous look to his eyes, while the other guy, Cole, spends most of his time staring off into the trees and watching around them. *Not something a Kalian would do*, Vera thinks. She glances around the field and forest that encases them. *What is he looking at?* She thinks, irritatingly. Then she begins to inspect the bushes. When she isn't distracted with Lidia, she always worries about prying spectators; maybe he does as well. But when she looks back at him, his stare is intently upon her, until her eyes catch his and they flutter away once again.

"So, why do you guys think they won't let us talk?" Lincoln asks.

"It's definitely strange," Lidia replies.

*We shouldn't be speaking about this. Nor speaking at all,* Vera thinks to herself.

"It's easier to control two smaller groups of people than one large group," Cole notes, "But, I'm just a mindless Tag barbarian, so what do I know?" he chuckles.

*Maybe not so mindless,* Vera perks. There is something peculiar about him, she admits to herself, even with his thrown-together Tagondian look. Maybe he isn't mindless, though he is stupid to speak so honestly – especially when one's words can be used against one's self – the rumours of the lack of common sense in Tagondians are at least now proven to be true.

Everyone is quiet for a moment, until Vera breaks the silence, her words chosen carefully, "Control is merely done by the hands of those whom are lacking." It is entirely safe she reasons, an innocent statement, free of offence.

Cole looks at her with a curious expression on his face, as if he wants to hear more. *Not a chance Tagondian.* Or perhaps he didn't understand the words she said for his lack of schooling so the rumours go, the Tagondians don't actually attend school, a chuckle leaves her throat.

Lidia laughs and adds nervously, "My friend is feeling sour at the moment, she has been arranged to merge…"

"Oh," Cole says.

"Don't worry. Vera won't be sour to you guys, though."

"V," Cole simply says.

“Hmm?” Vera hums in question.

“Short for Vera,” Cole says with a sort of pride for coining the nickname.

“Yes, Vera starts with a V,” Vera speaks slowly, intentionally, as if she is speaking to a deaf person.

“Oh good, as long as it doesn’t stand for villain,” he chuckles at his own joke, while ignoring her sarcasm.

To both her surprise and irritation she laughs, though she wonders who laughs at their own jokes as Cole does. “Do you suppose you would know a villain if you saw one?” she humours him, while her eyes squint in judgement.

“Well,” he thinks about it, “They’re not usually attractive, and I bet they have bad breath.” Is he complimenting her? No one offers compliments in Kala.

Desperate to change the focus she reaches for a plant out of her basket, “Well, not if they have this they wouldn’t,” Vera passes Cole a green stemmed plant with yellow leaves from her basket, “Abetzi: a natural breath freshener,” she states. The leaves are soft and fuzzy like a peach, though its taste is strong like mint, but a bolder flavour. Vera puts a leaf in her mouth, she ignores the tingling and begins chewing.

“It’s safe to eat?” Cole asks.

“I’m not about to risk poisoning myself for your entertainment. Yes, it’s safe,” Vera replies.

Cole pulls off a leaf and examines its surface, as if questioning the strange plant from the Kalian woman, but in the end he puts it in his mouth and nods satisfyingly.

“Here,” Vera passes Lincoln and Lidia each a leaf.

“Wow, that is strong,” Lincoln shouts. Suddenly, a high-pitch whistle, one long blow followed by three short blows comes from the Tagondian woods.

“I’ve heard that before, what is it?” Lidia asks.

“That’s our boss man callin’ us in,” Lincoln says, “Hey, you Kals aren’t all that bad.”

“Kals?” Lidia questions.

“Yeah, you’re the Kals and we’re the Tags,” he says while pointing his thumbs back at his own chest.

Vera speaks then, “It was almost pleasant… Now let’s all pray to Mother Earth that we don’t get caught for offending.”

“I’m also pretty certain that villains don’t pray, nevermind use the word ‘pleasant,’” Cole smirks, “and they aren’t worried about breaking laws either,” his brown eyes playfully await a remark from Vera.

She fights a smile, “Things are not always what they seem, Cole. But I think you already know that.” With that Vera turns, readying herself for the walk back to the colony.

“Wait,” Cole calls while gently reaching through the gate and just grasping Vera’s wrist – willing her not to rush off. Her skin immediately tingles at the presence of his touch, though it is unlike the tingling from the plants. Still, she pulls her wrist away, “Should we all meet here again?” he asks, holding her gaze.

“Yes,” Lidia says without hesitation.

“I don’t know about that,” Vera has now broken the law once, she can’t do it a second time, she has been irresponsible, flying up in the clouds long enough. It is time to return back down to earth and focus on things at the lab.

“Come on V,” Lincoln says.

“I’ll bring the snacks next time,” Cole tempts.

Vera contemplates a return visit, can she really commit to a second offence? Though in the end, she didn't mind meeting these Tags, and the thrill of doing something she wanted with total disregard to the laws was exciting – still, her stomach twists at what it can mean if they get caught. The other three hold smiles spanning across their faces. Surely they fear The Masters – everyone does. However, there is something to be said for the taste of excitement, Vera can now testify to that.

She smiles, "No meat," she says, wondering if this means that Lidia now owes her two favours. Lincoln holds a quizzical stare in disbelief at Vera's comment.

"That's right, I figured because no fur scarf - I practically had you pegged - no problem," Cole says without flinching at the idea.

"Pegged as a weirdo," Lincoln interjects. Cole immediately backhands him in the stomach.

"How's tomorrow? Before lunch?" Cole suggests.

"Eleven. That should be fine," Vera agrees as she and Lidia begin walking away. However, Vera knows they can't return, it is far too risky. She entirely plans to avoid the lake at all costs the following day – she isn't going to see the Tags again. She will break the news to Lidia during their walk back.

The Tags are just out of view and nothing can be more obvious – Lidia can barely hold it together. She squirms in excitement as they walk side-by-side.

"Oh my goodness," Lidia yelps, "They were nice. What harm did it do?" she babbles on.

"We mustn't tell anyone about it," Vera warns, interrupting Lidia's chatter.

"I won't, you don't need to worry about that. But that was insanely liberating, I felt so free. Didn't you?"

"I…" Vera doesn't really know what she felt. She was worried they'd get caught. She was irked by Lincoln. Distracted by Cole.

"Okay. Do you think they'll come tomorrow?" Lidia asks.

"I really don't think we should-"

"Vera, come on! You saw how great they were," Lidia pleads.

"You and I clearly have different descriptions of what 'great' means," Vera teases, "Let me think about it."

The two women spend a few more hours collecting and gathering along the lakeside with intermittent chatter – eventually calling it a day's work and dropping their shares off at Division together before heading home.

^

While venturing home, now alone, Vera's mind is distracted; a problem she rarely faces, perhaps never. But like a cardinal whose tune is arguably over-done, so too are her thoughts as they rhyme off the events of the day. She is distracted then, her eyes looking in every which direction but forward and as a result she unexpectedly crashes into a young girl. Vera thinks she recognizes the girl. *Is she in one of Atticus' classes?* She isn't entirely sure, regardless, she feels foolish for the collision. Neither were looking where they were going. Almay, Vera is sure that is her name, had fallen to the ground, Vera reaches out her hand to help her up.

"I'm terribly sorry, are you alright?" Vera asks. It comes as a shock when the young girl's cloak falls down just as she stands, for there, hiding underneath is the bump of an expectant mother. A secret. Vera knew secrets are to be held at a cost –

if it isn't tribulation, it would be guilt or pain. Vera looks up at Almay, who couldn't be more than eighteen-years-old.

Almay fumbles with her cloak, frantically attempting to cover her stomach, "Please, I beg you. Don't tell them."

"I…I…" Vera stutters as an uncontrollable reel of thoughts sift through her head.

"Please. I can pay you in shares, anything!"

Vera's hand finds her way to her chest, there it rests in shock. She glances at Almay's bronze crest – the poor girl has enough shares to worry about. With the bump of Almay's stomach still barely exposed from her cloak, Vera becomes curious – she's never touched a stomach with a growing child inside.

"May I?" she asks, gesturing to the girl's bump.

"Sure," the girl nods nervously.

Vera's hand touches Almay's stomach, just in time to feel a slight nudge. She jumps back, startled at first. Then she places her hand on Almay's stomach once more, "It's incredible, truly…" she says in awe.

"I can't be out long," Almay explains, "They'll find me."

"How old are you?"

"Eighteen."

"How did this happen?" For if it's true that Almay is indeed eighteen, she has broken more than one law, Law #21: Merge Agreements will be made on or thereafter members' twentieth year of birth, and Law #22: All colony members are to practice abstinence prior to merging.

"I'm in love, not merged." Almay replies, her face turning downward in shame. Vera steps back a couple paces, appearing detached, though she is quite the opposite. She didn't think there was room for love in a place like this. For just a moment, it is as if her vision shrinks inward and all that is left is a tiny tunnel in which to see out of. It is all she can do to stare at the young girl and her bump that protrudes well past the rest of her body. She looks as though she will be due to have the baby in a few months time.

"Then, you must go," Vera says, "Protect your child and… your love," as the word *love* leaves her lips she feels foolish for its utterance. Though she can't very well report Almay, the birthing ceremonies are barbaric enough, never mind what could be done to Almay – she has to think of the unborn child and how it needs its birth mother.

"Thank you," Almay begins running as fast as her body will allow it down the footpaths home.

Vera stands stunned, as she offers a brief thought to what Almay said with regards to love. She doesn't think Almay is right, though she doesn't think she is wrong either.

^

Vera walks through the front door of Favoured North, something she has done thousands of times before, like breathing. However, this time is different. She is an Offender, not only once, but twice, and can be punished as such. She walks right up to her room, her hands in trembling fists – she can't face Ida and Hendrix, not tonight. She lies on her bed face down with Almay on her mind. She has many questions and evidently wishes she wasn't so bewildered and had asked them.

She decides to pray to Mother Earth, "Dear Mother, there are secrets. Secrets surround the colony and whip through the footpaths; they reside within me. Help me," she says out loud, though a private whisper.

Her stomach aches as her insides twist and with it her thoughts entangle like the dandelion stems she used to make into bracelets as a child. She would wind the stems so tightly that one couldn't tell which end belonged to which stem. That's how her stomach feels, a mangled mass of confusion. The only difference being, the bracelets were beautiful and came at no cost. *I am an Offender*. The thought irks her to her very core, she will hold these secrets, and she will take them to her grave. She is Vera of Favoured North, daughter to Ida and Hendrix, scientist of Kala – not some reckless girl who runs about toying with Tags.

But that's when she thinks about him. Memories of Cole swirl through her mind and instantly her cheeks warm. The thing that stands out to her most is the memory of his voice, she wasn't aware of it at the time, but it is multifaceted, if ever a voice can be such a thing. Yes, it is deep and masculine, but there was a gentle sincerity in its tone. She had never heard such a voice nor seen such a pair of eyes in all of Kala, granted Kala isn't very big. But he is a Tagondian, a wild animal of a human, one that is neither graceful nor as well-kempt as she. Favoured or not, he is quite the opposite of her: boorish and scruffy while she is far more intelligent. But as a smile creeps across her face, she realizes then that she is completely curious to learn more about Cole the Favoured Tagondian. Which means, Lidia doesn't owe her a second favour – this time, she is going to offend on her own accord.

# 6

# COLE OF FAVOURED POLLARD TAGONDO

Later that day, the Tagondo pursuers reconvene at the combat call of Master Regan they are required to train. The call comes without warning and every Tagondian flocks immediately to the colony centre. Lined beside The Master's chamber sits an alarming abundance of weapons, though it is merely normality for the Tagondians. The Defenders, who are physically the most intimidating men and known to be the fiercest in combat, teach all Tagondians in such affairs, though they certainly don't share all of their secrets. Master Regan wants the Tagondian citizens to know just enough to win at The Circle. The way he sees it: the more power in Tagondo, the better. Besides, the Kalians are bookworms, they know not how to wield a sword or cast a chain like a Tagondian, which means winning against them comes easily enough.

During training in Tagondo, men and women will combat one-on-one. Several fights take place at the same time: Bruisers they call their opponents. This all takes place while Master Regan sits upon his perch, watching with his Barons. The Defenders call upon fighters at random, the two in combat choose a weapon and immediately charge at one another. The fight commences and lasts for five minutes. There is no reward for winning, it is just practise after all.

Cole stands in the warped circle that encompasses the colony centre, rows of people are piled in. Rimmy brings forth the Bruisers - the ones that will fight - though it isn't done amicably. Cole watches as Rimmy clasps his paws onto the coats of two citizens, children no less, and heaves their bodies into the centre. The two children straighten their jackets as if to brush off Rimmy's rough handling of them and eagerly take to combat stance earlier than necessary. Rimmy carries on down the circle, tossing in more Bruisers to form numerous sparring partners. Master Regan doesn't seem to object; in fact, the action casts a grin across his pale face.

Rimmy approaches Cole, his intentions obvious. He grabs Cole's coat and thrusts him into the centre with Issac following him in with a whimper at the shove Rimmy inflicts on him.

"Favoured Pollard and Insignificant Urndolf," Rimmy booms.

"Me and him?" Cole asks bewildered. It hardly seems fair. *The Mammoth Slayer versus the weakest link in all of Tagondo?* Cole sighs. There are children that can put up a better fight than Issac. Thankfully, Master Regan ensures children face-off in their rightful age groups.

After dozens of pairs are assigned, Rimmy's glass stare sweeps over the Bruisers, "Weapons," he orders.

Cole heads straight for the arsenal, his hands wrap around the cool handle of a club, choosing it specifically so that he can bang Issac around a little bit, but without inflicting too much pain on him. Cole watches as Issac steps uncertainly towards the weapons, his fair complexion looks to Cole with an uneasy stare. Issac juts his hands out - palms up - as if posing a question to Cole on which weapon he should take. As a means to draw attention to his choice, Cole swings his club casually, letting the handle leave the grasp of his fingers as it spins up into the air. He holds his hand out, slightly cupped in anticipation of the wide head of the club's landing, and a second later the wooden frame lands upon his capable hand, precisely as he knew it would. If Issac is bright enough, though Cole seriously doubts it, he will acknowledge Cole's tossing of his club as his answer to Issac's question. Issac blinks absentmindedly and reaches for the sword. Cole sighs and runs his free hand through his hair… he knows how Issac handles a sword and that he'll have to try to predict each mindless swing, wherever the tip of the sword ends up will not be where Issac intends it.

Rimmy blows the first whistle to warn the Bruisers to take combat stance. Everyone's feet are parted shoulder-width apart, one foot planted out front and their legs slightly bent at the knees. Weapons are held up and outwardly, defending their fronts. The immediate ringing of two whistle blows indicates the beginning of the fight. Several pairs of Bruisers begin circling one another. Cole stays slow, barely moving, merely watching. His eyes hold firm on Issac's. Issac begins moving his legs and speeding up his footwork, displaying typical movements of a nervous bruiser, but that's not what gives him away. Cole waits for the sure sign. A couple more paces and Issac runs his hand up to his brow wiping away the sweat – there it is. Cole stops a chuckle from escaping his throat.

"What do I do?" Issac whispers to Cole. Cole begins moving in a circle, though his pace increases only slightly, Issac follows suit. Grunts and growls from the other Bruisers sound through the colony centre, while Issac and Cole merely stare at one another.

"Pollard – those who waste time waste blood," Rimmy warns over the crowd. This means that if Cole makes a joke of the combat calls and doesn't use the allotted five minutes adequately, Rimmy will take him for lashings. He'll have to hit Issac a couple of times, maybe knock him on the ground, that will possibly satisfy Rimmy and Master Regan. Cole jumps forward suddenly, slamming his club toward Issac and just in time Issac hesitantly raises his sword and its flat surface somehow meets with Cole's club. Issac begins swinging his sword this way and that, the swings and jabs are anything but methodical they are quite the opposite. Cole rolls his eyes. *If I get sliced from this breach…*

There is no way to predict Issac's sporadic jabs, but Cole will surely find a way to wrangle him or at least make it look like they are in legitimate combat. So, Cole comes at Issac again, forcing his club forward and this time slamming it into Issac's chest. His movements are more exaggerated than the hit actually calls for, but he knows Rimmy holds a close eye. The sword dangles at his side as Issac's body crashes backward causing him to land on his bottom.

"Shit, Cole," Issac moans. As Issac's body is unmoving, Cole's eyes dart to Rimmy, it is obvious that Rimmy's stare is lingering on Issac. At least Rimmy saw the hit, that is good, but it won't be enough. Cole motions with his hands to instruct Issac to his feet. It takes longer than he likes, but Issac finally makes it to combat stance once again, or at least his version of it.

"Hit me," Cole whispers under his breath.

"What? I can't," Issac replies, still panting.

"Just do it. With the flat end, not the tip or the edge," Cole whispers, knowing that Rimmy's gaze is still upon them. Issac eyes his sword, as if he has never seen one before, as though he needs to see where the flat surface is. Cole exhales. Issac raises the sword, winds up and swings it at chest height toward Cole. There is a slight angle to Issac's wrist, which means the smallest of tweaks and the sword's edge will fiercely meet Cole's chest. In an instant Cole brings up his club while simultaneously moving his footing backward. The sword's edge slams into Cole's club and just as he thinks it will, it etches a slice into the club. As Issac's sword lowers to his side Cole pounces once again, slamming his club into Issac's arm. Issac's feet fumble, but he regains his footing without fall. The pair manages to drag out their combat long enough that Rimmy finally moves his gaze elsewhere, soon thereafter Rimmy blows the whistle to signify combat completion. The first round of combat comes to an end and chatter fills the colony centre.

"You didn't have to go so hard on me," Issac says as he holds his arm, it will likely bruise by the night's end.

"Hey, we're not called Bruisers for nothin'," Cole quips. If only Issac knew how soft he had gone on him. Though that doesn't really matter, so long as Rimmy doesn't know.

"Pollard," Rimmy calls Cole over. *Shit.* Cole approaches Rimmy and glances up toward his brow, which is lowered and wrinkled at the moment.

"Yes, sir?"

"What did I tell you about waste?" Rimmy states, his eyes staring into Cole's, it's a warning.

"Yes, sir," Cole says. Rimmy turns away and begins calling out the next set of Bruisers.

^

That night, Cole and Lincoln head to The X and set up targets in The X using wooden stands with circles painted on them. They practise regularly, seeing as pursuing is their sole job and their livelihood. However, in the springtime they amp up their evening skill perfecting in preparation for Master Regan's Pursuing Challenge, which happens annually in the spring and there is always at least one who doesn't make the bounty – that poor sucker gets exiled. Cole knows that he'll never be the unlucky bastard in Master Regan's games. He is intelligent and skilled, yet he prides himself in never letting those qualities go to his head, instead he only practises harder.

"Those Kal girls were hot," Lincoln breaks Cole's silent focus.

"You have got to be the horniest bugger I know," Cole laughs, though the mention of Kal girls gets Cole thinking. The very fact that he laid eyes on Vera means more to him than he can even comprehend. It all comes back to that *feeling* that Murdina had. "Someone is coming with the green eyes of an emerald," is what she had said.

"Are you tellin' me you didn't think they were hot?" Lincoln heckles. Cole subtly shakes his head as Lincoln pulls him out of his thoughts, "I'd like to bend the brunette over… V was it? And give her a taste of this cock," Lincoln says while grabbing his groin.

Cole reaches out and smacks Lincoln across the chest, "Easy there." Lincoln releases a moan from the smack.

"You. I bet you could have them. Both at the same time," Lincoln goes on, but Cole stays quiet, "Come on man, your mouth always runs a mile-a-minute. Why so quiet now?" Lincoln pushes – and he is right, Cole normally has a lot to say, some would wager too much, though he isn't one to speak of indecencies with regards to women. Cole sighs and waves his hand to dismiss Lincoln's comment.

"All the ladies want you, all the ladies want the 'Mammoth Slayer'," Lincoln continues.

"No they don't. They just want to feel safe, protected," Cole reasons.

"I'll protect them with my cock, it's as good as a sword," Lincoln laughs. Cole begins to laugh too, though primarily at Lincoln's stupidity, just a couple of men howling into the night air like a couple of wolves.

Lincoln is a boorish man and at the ripe age of twenty-four has the mouth of a seasoned Defender – so Cole thinks. The Defenders are the guards of The Masters and the colonies, generally chosen for such a position because of their size and strength. Only the strongest men can be among the Defenders and only the strongest stay, which results in a form of arrogance that gives the Defenders a bad reputation amongst citizens. Though Lincoln is tall in stature, he's scrawny, and so when he speaks, curt like a Defender, Cole can't take him seriously.

Cole refocuses and shoots his arrow, rarely a miss. He has been a perfectionist at making his own weapons; perhaps aiding him in his pursuing ability – it is important to have reliable weapons as a Tagondian.

Twenty yards, thirty yards, forty yards they compete against each other, a game of sorts. Lincoln hits twenty yards and thirty yards, but he can't quite get to forty yards, his arrow always falls short.

"Fuck," Lincoln shouts, easily angered – another reason he mirrors a Defender.

"Just keep trying man, you'll get it," Cole encourages, "Try aiming higher, pull back farther."

"Yeah, yeah," Lincoln says as he tosses his bow to the ground, "I'm done for the night. You?"

"Sure," Cole agrees. For a guy who puts a lot of stock in himself, Lincoln has always been a quitter. In some ways Cole feels a responsibility to his friend to keep him afloat. Cole has had Lincoln's back since they met eighteen years prior, even when Lincoln falters – including when he got Cole in trouble for shooting an arrow into The Master's chamber window when they were teenagers. Rimmy gave Cole twenty whips to his back. The tribulations were harsh enough to make a person want to behave. And although it was a mistake, and Lincoln didn't mean to rat Cole out, Cole forgave him nonetheless.

"So tell me, what do you really think about this merging with Favoured Adder?" Lincoln asks.

"I'm fulfilling my Tagondian duty man, that's what I think about it." The two begin collecting their arrows and stacking the targets against a tree to use the following night.

"That's it? It's a big deal and you're not even showing excitement. You're going to basically be royalty. Almek royalty."

"I know… The Masters put a lot of stake into merging – when we were kids it was all we'd talk about," Cole reflects, paying no mind to the royalty comment that Lincoln made. Cole has enough unwanted attention being the Mammoth Slayer, he doesn't need anymore, and so he doesn't want to think about being royalty too.

"Yeah, that and bedding women."

"No, that was all you talked about," Cole points out.

"I can't help it," Lincoln admits with his hands raised in the air accepting the guilty verdict, "This whole abstinence thing is killing me! I beat my dick raw."

Cole chuckles, "I don't know. I guess it seemed exciting back then, back before I knew my sentence. But for the past three years I've known the day will come when I merge with Treena. Just like I know tomorrow morning I will wake up and go pursuing. In the end, I guess it doesn't really matter."

"Yes, but soon you'll wake up, get laid and then go pursuing," Lincoln adds with a smirk.

Cole rubs his hands down across his face, "Yea, I guess so."

"I know so – Treena's a horny little kitten."

"Quit talking about her like that," Cole warns Lincoln into silence, which wipes the smirk off of his face. Cole has no desire to speak ill of Treena, nor imagine bedding her. Even if he does desire to speak in such a way, if he was caught, Master Regan would turn psychotic right before ordering Rimmy to whip Cole's back into fleshy shreds.

Lincoln moves on, unaffected by Cole's warning, "So, we're gonna meet up with the Kal girls tomorrow, right?"

"Yeah."

"Good," Lincoln moans a pleasurable sigh.

"Please, just go home and jerk off," Cole replies exhaustedly, though a tease etches his voice.

^

Later that evening, Lincoln and Cole reunite, and walk to The Master's chamber to join in on the celebration. The Claiming they call it, for Favoured White.

The husband and wife caress the baby in their arms and pass her to one of the Defenders. As the tradition goes, an appointed Defender holds the baby over a cask of water, when Master Regan signals the Defender drops the baby all the while the parents have to catch her before she reaches the water – a symbol of their capable hands in raising a child together. As if the poor infant hadn't been through enough, though a baby has not once fallen in. Cole watches because he knows he has to. He saw what Master Regan did to the poor woman who didn't watch the last time; after he was through with her she only had one eye with which to watch the next ceremony.

The commotion carries on in the background of Cole's conscious until his thoughts drift to Vera and Lidia once again. He looks forward to seeing them the following day and like a child, for the first time in a long time, he feels a sense of eagerness. It's new and exciting speaking to Kalian women, even in their brief encounter, he found a likeness in Vera.

His visual memory wanders to her pink lips and down her neck - thankful she wasn't wearing a scarf - to her chest. An admiration for her curvy figure overcomes him. *Those hips. Those hips and childbearing.* His pants tighten at the thought of her silhouette against the sunlight. *Stop thinking of her like that*, he tells himself. She is the woman Murdina spoke of, Murdina said she was coming: *A brunette with the green eyes of an emerald,* Cole reflects. He hasn't seen any other set of eyes quite like hers. At first he wasn't entirely sure it was her, and when Lidia had mentioned that Vera is in a merge agreement, it caught him off guard for a moment – Murdina didn't mention that part. But the description of her eyes and the lack of fur scarf – he is sure that is her. However, the one element still confusing Cole is that Murdina said she saw Vera in Tagondo. *A Kalian scientist in Tagondo?* Cole didn't understand it, but he knows that he believes her. He doesn't know how or why, but she is coming. Murdina is in preparation for her welcome, she advised Cole to do the same. *How to prepare?* He isn't quite sure what exactly he's preparing for, but after meeting Vera he can't wait to find out.

# 7

# Vera of Favoured North Kala

The next morning Vera manages to completely avoid Ida and Hendrix. They aren't home when she wakes, which is odd; however, her desire to be invisible trumps her curiosity over their whereabouts. Chances are they are cooped up at the lab, they've seemed distracted in recent days. Hopefully they will be occupied for the day so that she can inconspicuously meet with the Tags. She will say that she was foraging all day with Lidia – that will be simple and believable.

After breakfast Lidia and Vera meet in the colony centre and begin their walk down the footpaths to meet with the Tag boys later that morning. Surprisingly, Vera is feeling grateful for her new friend - her only friend - if one is concerned enough to count their friends. They share stories and speak as if they have known each other for a lifetime. Vera knows about the dreadful scar on Lidia's leg and Lidia knows of Vera's horrendous middle name – one so embarrassing that only her family, along with Lidia now, knows it. She has even threatened certain death to her brother if he is to ever utter its existence.

"So, seeing as you're a scientist, I have to ask you, what's your theory on the weird sensations that the plants cause?" Lidia whispers.

In an attempt to shut this particular conversation down, Vera replies abruptly: "I'm not supposed to be talking about that stuff."

"I know, but I'm Favoured and a botanist. Besides, if anything, me working with the plants suggest that I ought to know."

Vera's eyes squint ever so slightly, as they always do when she is curious or set in her mind about something, "I don't know," Vera simply states.

"Or you're just going to pretend like you don't know?" Lidia continues with the insistent questions.

Vera tenses under her breath, "No one really knows."

"It's been eighteen years since the Water Crisis and plants have never been the same since… How do you guys not know yet?"

An irritated sigh escapes her, "The plants aren't exactly the priority in the lab, the water is." Vera is certain she can't possibly get in trouble for saying that – as it is true on multiple levels. Regardless, a quick glance over her shoulder offers her some peace of mind that no one is around to overhear her.

Though she feels quite excited about reuniting with Cole and Lincoln, Vera's nerves heckle her like a mosquito; rapacious and devouring in nature. Today her stomach is swooshing, like the small waves in the lake. Vera and Lidia approach the tree line and pass the tiny wooden cabin that sits empty off to the side, it has been broken-down ever since she can remember it having been there. The two women walk along the dirt footpaths that zig-zag this way and that, twisting through the foliage of the forest, they are narrow and often connect with other pathways. Years of a couple thousand people trudging across the ground will do that by way of wearing down the grass until it no longer grows. They pass the north edge of the lake and approach The Circle.. They are slightly early and so they sit down in the grass at the lakeside, after all it isn't unreasonable to sit and wait for a short period of time. Although, it could be said that being idle for almost an hour is unreasonable.

"I can't believe they aren't coming," Lidia finally whines in disappointment. Vera rises to her feet and wipes the damp grass away from her bottom. March is coming to a close and so the ground is beginning to dry. Spring weather is never as wet as it once was, it is sad how the earth seems to be drying up.

"They're Tagondians, Lidia. They're practically wild animals," she responds, coming to terms with a certain level of disappointment. She decides that she can bury her feelings away and eventually never think of this again. In some ways she is relieved that they did not show.

"I don't know… that sounds a bit harsh. Wait – what are you doing?" Lidia asks.

"Well, I'm not very well going to sit here and throw away any more of my time," Vera begins walking back, "Are you coming?"

Lidia looks to the ground with a pout, "Okay. But, can we try again tomorrow?" Lidia asks.

Coming back is just about the last thing Vera wants to do, but when she sees the sadness in her friend's eyes, she somehow understands, and decides that she can't very well say no. *Those animals better show.* She can't stand the thought of Lidia being let down again – not now, not when she needs something happy in her life so desperately. If she comes with Lidia one more time in search of the Tags at least it will give Lidia something to look forward to, as opposed to living in the pains of her past.

^

Vera walks in the door of Favoured North to find her family sitting at the kitchen table and the room notably quiet, eerily quiet, at least compared to normalcy within the North household. *Oh no, they know,* she internally panics. *They know about the Tags. They know I'm an Offender.* She walks into the kitchen and can practically feel the toxins of offence seeping from her skin.

"What's going on?" she finds the courage to ask.

"Vera, would you have a seat?" Hendrix gestures to a chair. He never calls her Vera, always *Miss*. And no one said the Almek greeting this time – a first.

"What is it?" she asks, sounding more impatient than she'd like. *Get to the point,* she thinks. *Get the punishment over with.*

"I'm just going to get straight to the point, because I know that's what you prefer," Hendrix takes a deep breath, "There's a re-birthing at The Circle tomorrow, in your name."

"My name was drawn?" she asks disbelieving.

"I'm afraid so darling. You're over the age of twenty, and out of a merge. Their timeline holds true – it's already been 6 months since the last re-birthing," Hendrix pauses to wipe the water from his eyes and continues, "I will be fighting. There is one Tagondian family so far - there may be more - that are willing to fight for the rights to you." Vera stares at Hendrix in silence, he leans forward and squeezes her hand. *I did this. How could I have done this?* Her words internally and silently nag her.

After some time Ida speaks softly, "Honey, say something," she gently insists. But Vera can't, it's as if her mouth is clamped shut, a force of unknown origins sits there holding the clamps. Even if she could open it, what would come out? There are no words.

"Miss, listen, it's going to be okay. You're going to be okay, I promise," Hendrix explains.

"We have no choice, no options here," Ida begins crying, Vera can barely understand her words through her sobs and the fog in her own head.

"I'm going to be there for you, I'm going to fight for you Miss," Hendrix looks at Vera's eyes warmly and squeezes her hand once more.

"No," Vera manages to sputter, "I did this. I'm the coward. I'm the one who screwed up."

"Vera, sweetheart, what are you talking about?" Hendrix asks as his eyes widen briefly. He seems shocked at the words that echo in her own mind after she says them: *I screwed up.*

"You did nothing, this is not your fault," Ida tenses with bloodshot eyes. Neither of them sit comfortably while hearing Vera speak with such indecency as she never has before, even Atticus sits silently with a wet face, shock present in his eyes.

Vera hesitates a moment and then lets the words she'll forever regret saying slip from the hollow crack between her lips: "I broke this family."

Flashes of what's to come haunt her thoughts: Hendrix's figure standing amongst the tainted sand at The Circle. She fears for his life – he's neither a warrior, nor the kind of man that can ever hurt another. He is gentle and kind, a most compassionate man and if he is forced to fight he will be crushed like an ant, helplessly and silently. She can't live with herself if that happens, but what if it does? Her family will not survive. She gives into the pulsating ache in her throat and begins to sob.

"Miss, what? What is it?" Hendrix asks.

Suddenly her tears of regret turn into droplets that seem to sizzle against her flesh. She can't bear to tell her family what she's done.

"You've done nothing wrong dear. It is the luck of the draw," Ida explains.

Vera snorts, "Luck."

Ida eyes Hendrix nervously, "You will have to witness your father fight, we all will."

"No, I won't let that happen. I will be the one to fight."

"You can't, they won't allow it," Hendrix states calmly. He is always the voice of reason. But Vera is sick of his reasons; her fists shake at her sides.

"I have to try," she says.

"No. Miss, listen to me. You have to accept it."

"No," she shakes her head. "You never went to a single strength training session, you know nothing about combat."

"Nor do you," he affirms. "To be honest, I never thought they'd even enter our family name into the draw… to risk losing one… two of their scientists…" Hendrix's words fade.

The strength training sessions are optional in Kala. Only those who are motivated to partake in the ceremonies, or worry they could be forced to participate, actually go to the training.

Hendrix's eyes wander in thought and after a moment they find and focus on Vera once again, holding her gaze while grasping her hands, "We need to talk about what is going to happen if I die."

Atticus interjects, it is obvious he is on the verge of shouting, his entire frame trembles, "Why didn't you go to strength training? Why haven't any of us?" His lips quiver with a sadness and an anger that Vera wishes she could take away.

"It was stupid of us," she agrees.

"I see that now," Hendrix nods solemnly. "But, we mustn't dwell. We must prepare. Now listen… first off, you have to follow the rules and sit quietly during the fight. If I lose - that clearly means that I have been killed," Hendrix looks to Vera, "which means that you will be going to a new home as a Tagondian. You must go with that new family, that is where you will live your coming days."

"But I don't know them," *You know two of them.*

"I do, I know a couple of them from meeting during our settlement days. Ask them what D is for trust, if they answer correctly, you'll know you can trust them."

"What's the answer?" She asks in a panic.

"You'll know," he simply says and continues, "Do the absolute best you can, lay low, live as they live. You will find it's a bit different than how we do things on this side of the lake. But you must learn how to pursue. If you fail… they exile the ones who can't keep up."

Vera's mind begins spiralling. *What will become of our family? How will Atticus function without me watching over him, guiding him? And the lab: does Father honestly think the others can run it? What if Hendrix does win?* There is a chance he could, she hopes. If he wins and no one else stands in line to fight for the rights to her, Hendrix will live.

"What will happen with the lab?" Vera asks through tears as she rises to her feet in dispute.

"The lab will go on, Educator Ferris, Ellis and Isla will take over, Atticus too," Hendrix explains.

"How will Mother and Atticus get enough shares each week?"

"We'll manage," Ida adds.

Hendrix stands and puts his arms around Vera in a warm embrace, she hides her face in his chest and lets her hands wander to her stomach, caressing the aches that begin to throb and nag on her insides. The realization slowly begins sinking in, Hendrix will be forced to battle for her position in the North family. *How can I live with myself if he loses?* Vera's thoughts wander to Lidia, she needs to tell her.

"What time is the ceremony?" Vera asks Hendrix urgently.

"10:00 tomorrow morning."

"Oh no, I need to see Lidia. I was supposed to meet her tomorrow. I need to tell her… I need to…"

"Honey, it's almost curfew," Ida warns.

"I have to, I'll run. I can make it back before the sun goes down."

Vera stands in a hurry and in her urgency she barrels out of the front door, forgetting to close it. She sprints down the footpaths past the neighbours, past the greenhouses and beyond the lab. She flies past The Master's chamber, thoughts of anguish and betrayal are immediately directed toward the sight of the building – but they are meant for The Masters themselves. Favoured Peony is just beyond the colony centre. The sun has almost set, but only a flash of orange shoots across her peripheral view. The cool evening air encases her skin, giving her goosebumps, though perhaps the evening air isn't the cause of the goosebumps at all.

Soon enough she reaches Favoured Peony, out of breath she instantly thumps her fist against the wooden door. Under normal circumstances Vera would feel apologetically out of line – but not tonight.

"Hi, with the earth…" Lidia's mother answers the door, clearly concerned to see Vera on their doorstep at this time, "Can I help you Vera?"

"I need to talk to Lidia," she says, barely able to choke the words out.

"She's not home right now," her mother says with distress, "She went out with her father, but the sun is setting – she should be back any minute." Vera looks to the sky and sees only a tiny sliver of light, she can't afford to wait, mammoths hunt in the dark.

"I need to hurry. Tell her I came by – tell her I have a re-birthing tomorrow and that I will not be able to meet her tomorrow."

"Oh Vera…" Lidia's mother pauses and her eyes soften, "Okay, I will."

"Tell her…" Vera hesitates, her mind scans over all of the things she would want to say if she were able to say good-bye to her friend. She'd tell her how much she appreciated the recent days of her friendship. Vera knows her mouth won't be able to articulate those thoughts, nor pass them along to Lidia's mother. Instead, all she can muster is: "Tell her I said good-bye."

Vera turns and runs down the path, tears running down her face. She can't breathe, not even to let the slightest of sobs out. The sun tucks behind the mountains and she can hear the mammoths begin to cry out. She runs harder, faster. She prays to Mother Earth that she won't catch sight of a mammoth, or that one won't catch sight of her. Before she knows it she reaches home and flies through the front door of Favoured North and just as the siren rings the door slams closed behind her. Leaning her back up against the door, letting her legs collapse beneath her, she crumbles to the floor.

8

# Cole of Favoured Pollard Tagondo

On the morning Cole and Lincoln are supposed to meet Vera and Lidia a second time at the lake, Lead Defender Rimmy arrives with a blow to Cole's front door – surely he wants to knock it down. Cole opens the door and bids Rimmy a good morning.

"Your presence is requested with The Master," Rimmy instructs.

"Okay."

"Now," Rimmy states more impatiently.

"Let me just tell my sister that she's going to have to take over looking after my dad."

Rimmy nods his head. The sole reason Rimmy accepts this brief pause is for the simple fact that Burke is Baron to The Master. Cole calls for Nin, who is upstairs, still Rimmy huffs in the doorway with agitation. He is used to getting what he wants, an entitlement that brews amongst the Favoured, but especially the Defenders. When Nin comes down to take over, Cole leaves, following Rimmy down the footpaths.

After a silent march towards the colony centre, they walk up the stairs to The Master's chamber and go inside. There sits Master Regan, in his cushioned chair with a drink of wine in his hand and two Barons at his side.

Cole takes a bow in the presence of The Master "You called for me, Master."

"Yes. I wanted to get your insight on the upcoming Pursuing Challenge," Master Regan states.

"Oh, okay. What can I help with?" Cole asks, surprised. Though it isn't the first time Master Regan has asked for his assistance.

"Well, seeing as you're quite savvy with pursuing and you will one day, after you merge with my daughter, be of Favoured Adder I thought you would have a valuable opinion to offer. You see, I want to up the ante so to speak – to make the Pursuing Challenge more difficult."

*Shit.* Offering advice to Master Regan is never the place one wants to be. He doesn't want to have an influence over his dealings.

"Change the weapons… Bows only?" Cole offers a meagre suggestion.

"I like it… but it's not enough."

"No solar lights?" Cole says, hopeful.

"No, not enough."

"Increase the bounty?"

"Yes!" Master Regan exclaims, "From two, to four!" His eyes light up as Cole nods his head in both agreement and regret.

"That's final then, four bounty per-person. This will make it more interesting – thanks to you," he smiles a menacing smile.

"It will," Cole agrees. *Not for the better though.* He begins to bow and leave, but Master Regan continues.

"One more thing, Treena told you about the Agreement Party did she not?" Master Regan asks as he rubs the tips of his fingers together in an unsettling motion, his glass held still in the other hand.

"Yes," Cole responds.

"Good. I will let her choose the day and how she would like it done."

"No one has ever planned a party at The Master's chamber but you," Cole points out.

"You're right, it is unnerving. However, she has waited a long while to merge with you – I am rewarding her for her patience."

"That is kind of you, your grace."

"Indeed. That's all, you may leave," Master Regan waves his hand as if to shoo Cole on his way and with a final bow Cole exits the chamber, escorted by Rimmy. Cole runs back toward home to meet Lincoln, jogging along the footpaths with hope that he will still be on time. As Cole closes in on his home he spots Lincoln on the path.

"FP – Where were you?" Lincoln shouts.

"Oh hey, I was just coming to meet you…" Cole begins.

"I've been waiting at Favoured Pollard for over an hour. It's too late, it's after 12:00 now," Lincoln whines.

"Shit," Cole hollers and throws his weight out to punch the side of a nearby tree. He has no way of knowing if that day at the lake was going to be the first and last time he'd ever see her. He immediately hopes that Murdina is right.

"You fucked us both, ya shithead!" Lincoln shouts, throwing his arms in the air.

"You weren't getting laid Lincoln, pull your head out of your own ass."

"Yeah, you're probably right," Lincoln admits, "So then why are you so pissed?"

Cole can't be entirely honest, he will get himself into trouble, "It was a good time yesterday, surprisingly," he simply states.

Lincoln nods his head in agreement, "Oh well, time to focus my efforts back on the unmerged women here, I guess."

Cole shakes his head at Lincoln in disgust and goes on to wish for a way to contact Vera, to let her know that he wanted to be there – that he tried to be there. He imagines her showing up at the lake to find out he didn't come. For some reason, he can't stand that thought. Cole breaks out into a sprint in the direction of the lake; down the footpaths and across the field to the lakeside. *Asshole,* he thinks to himself as he glances across the lake, seeing only the green and brown shades of an empty field and an endless forest beyond it.

# 9

# VERA OF FAVOURED NORTH KALA

Vera wakes after having a terrible sleep – if she even slept at all. She lays there favouring her left side as a kink throbs in her neck. Still, she rises from her bed and walks down the hall, glancing into Ida and Hendrix's room to see only Hendrix there, still asleep. *Where's Mother?* She wonders as she walks downstairs.

"Mother?"

"In here, Honey," Ida quietly calls from the kitchen table.

"What are you doing?" Vera asks.

"I was just looking at this… dress. I was saving it for you – for your merging day. But, I think you're going to have to wear it today. We didn't have enough time to have something made up for you. And well… white is requested by The Masters for the guest of honour," Ida stands, holding up an exquisite white dress.

Vera reaches out to touch its silky-smooth contours. Her hand moves up to the ridges along the sweetheart neckline, then down to its cinched-in waist. It flows out into an A-line beyond the waist, the bottom resting on the floor, waves of milky white fabric contrast against the dark wood floor.

"I have never seen a more beautiful dress. Where did you get this?"

"It's from Oregon, I packed it back in the Old World, when I knew we had to come here. We were told to grab whatever we could fit into a single suitcase the day we evacuated. It was my mother's, she wore it on her wedding day," Ida sniffles.

"It's incredible."

Ida then chuckles, though it is pained and her face glistens with tears as if a memory passes through her mind, "Your grandmother wanted me to wear it at my wedding, but it just wasn't me. I kept it, with the hope that it would one day work for a daughter of my own."

Tears tickle Vera's eyes, "Thank you. Do you think it will fit though?"

"Why don't you try it on? Today will be the only opportunity I will ever get to see you in it."

Vera rests her hand on her mother's, "I would be honoured." With the house quiet and still, Vera quickly slips into the gown on the spot – it clings to her sides, almost as if it's painted on her. It accentuates her hips, she doesn't much like that, hips are seen as a symbol for child-bearing and can even be enough of a reason for a man to fight for rights to her in The Circle. "I think it may be too tight," she says regretfully.

"Sweetie, it's perfect," Ida says while wiping her eyes, she then simply heads toward the stove to start breakfast.

It's all Vera can do to not think of the upcoming ceremony. The worries of what this day will bring brews inside of her – like a terminal illness, simmering below her surface, tugging and altering her insides. And much like a terminal illness, there's no cure, no chance of redemption, not even Mother Earth can help her now. Her throat forms a hard lump, making it difficult to swallow. Her hands tremble with the urgency of solace. She raises her quivering hands and stares at them. Pondering then, but only for a moment, what she can do with her two hands that can put a stop to this dreadful ceremony, to stop Hendrix from dying. She could end her own life with those two hands – a life for a life, as it were. Only this way of taking one life would be to save a particular one. There would be no need to carry on with the ceremony because there would be no guest of honour. But suicide, it is forbidden and those that commit it are sure to have spirits trapped in the unknown – the place that is black and the epitome of nothingness. Favoured North would be burned to the ground. *I can't*, she decides, knowing it would be absurd and wouldn't help her parents in any form. Besides, Atticus needs her; even if she is out of reach she'll be alive for him, in case. After she ensures her hair is tied back tightly, Vera joins her family for their last breakfast together.

"Miss," Hendrix says while holding out his arms to her, she approaches him for a hug.

"Vera, I don't want you to go. I wish we had more time," Atticus says as he looks toward her with red, swollen eyes.

"Time," she says aloud, pondering the luxury. "What if there was a way to get more time?" She thinks of Almay and how she is getting away with hiding an entire pregnancy from The Masters and Defenders alike.

"You mean, like stall the ceremony?" Atticus asks, bewildered. His nose is congested with each breath in.

"It's a thought," she says.

"There's no way to stall. Besides, Miss, why postpone the inevitable?" Hendrix asks.

"You couldn't cheat The Masters if you wanted to. You would be killed for such treachery," Ida states as though she is irritated by such a proposition.

James, who is also present at this final family meal, sits quietly and simply stares across the table at Vera with what she considers to be untrustworthy eyes, eyes filled with darkness and deceit. Despite her knowledge of treason within Kala, Vera knows she can't share the news about Almay; secrets are not only held at a cost, but they are also shared at a cost.

She sits down at the table to eat, "You're right. I don't know what I was thinking," she says monotonously – a façade for James. She doesn't say another word about stalling the ceremony. Instead, breakfast is shared in silence, with the exception of shallow breaths and obstructed nasal cavities – it is torturous. *Why can't they just treat today like any old day*? She canters in her head. *It's not any old day*. She wishes so deeply that she could pretend it is. *Why can't they help me do that?*

When it is time to walk to The Circle no one wants to leave. The family stands at the front door not wanting their bodies to cross its frame, as if it is some sort of bad omen. Vera doesn't believe in such things. She deems the superstitions and myths that circulate the colony by way of shared beliefs and also by the Whisperer, to be implausible. With the exception of the afterlife beliefs. But who actually believes in the whispers? *Only a fool.* Vera opens the door and steps through it, after deciding that things can't possibly get any worse. The footpaths are crowded with the entire colony heading to The Circle. People walk single file or two-by-two down the narrow paths. In wider pathways they form groups to carry conversations, some whisper, others speak louder than they ought to – especially the ones who speak ill of Vera, spreading rumours as to what led to her re-birthing. No matter what they whisper or shout, nothing will change her circumstances for the better.

Even still, their clamour is accusatory and the onslaught fills her ears: "I heard she took Master Oberon to bed," one colony member shares with another, "It's why he takes his rest days."

"She probably bedded Educator Barlow and couldn't satisfy," another tunes in.

"It's surprising she didn't disappear like Elle," rants another. She shudders at that one.

"Maybe the Tagondians will find some normalcy in her."

It is impossible to tell whose mouths spit these putrid lies, though she reminds herself that it doesn't matter anyway. Still, she wonders: *Am I that strange?* Granted, she isn't very social, surely she has at least one admirable quality. She is rather proud of her work at the lab, but it is also classified work, and so, the general public isn't aware of the doings behind those walls. It seems invaluable to keep the happenings in the lab private from the people, but that is strict orders from Master Oberon. None of it matters now, their stings, the lab it is all going to be but a fragment of her past. Not to mention the ceremony, enduring it will be far worse than any rumour they conjure up. But, to Vera, transferring to Tagondo would be the worst life sentence any one person could ever receive.

As they continue their walk, several Kalians approach her parents with their façade of apologies for their unfortunate circumstances, noting that they will pray to Mother Earth that Vera will get to stay in Kala, but at the chance Hendrix doesn't win, that she'll have a smooth transition into her new life in Tagondo. In reality, these condolences will not stop all this from happening, so these words don't make a difference to Vera. Though, she can tell by her parents' weary smiles that these condolences and prayers are nice for them, and Atticus, to feel supported through this. And who knows, maybe Mother Earth really is a force that can ignite positive change amongst the world; if she is, she better step in.

Suddenly, a cold hand tugs on her arm, pulling her off the path and into a nearby bush. Shocked, and having no knowledge of self-defence, she stumbles and falls backwards, the man's grip loosens and she lands on the ground. Vera glances up at her assailant in shock.

"It's really too bad," the man begins, his fine black hair cut in a bob to align with his chin – the sides swept around the back in a nub of hair. She instantly pulls herself up and stands amongst the foliage. He reaches for her arm to assist her.

"Excuse me?" Vera says, pulling her arm out of his hold this time. She glances at the footpaths, but they are shielded from the others by a wall of green leaves and branches, no one can see them.

"This situation that you're in. Make a deal with me and it will all go away," he sneers. His small, intense eyes are fixed on hers.

"What are you talking about?" she asks, appalled.

"I can secure your place here. Your father won't have to die, you won't have to leave."

"How?" she questions skeptically.

"Have my child," his sky-blue eyes continue to pierce into her own, making her feel queasy. His face is riddled with pain, though she wants nothing of it, "What I mean is – merge with me, and then have my child."

"How dare you," she says and then storms off.

"It's the only way you'll be able to stay," he shouts after her, but when she looks back he is gone. Running to catch up with her family, she fixes her dress and pushes back her shoulders.

"Where were you?" Atticus studies her face briefly, as though he is suspicious. Vera decides it's not worth anything to speak of the strange man.

"I tripped," she simply states. Atticus nods then, seeming satisfied by her response. After all, Vera reasons with herself, she is having a hard time ignoring her thudding heart and buzzing head, it does feel as though it is all she can do to not trip over her own feet.

As she once again trails closely behind her oblivious family she rubs over the spot the man had touched her, as if to clean off the perversion. They pass the old abandoned shed that sits near Lake Cloud and it reminds Vera of Lidia and their walks together. The last time she walked by that shed was for a much different reason – to see the Tags. Ironically, this time, it is to fight against them so she doesn't become one.

^

The North family enter The Circle and instantly two Defenders grab Vera's arms and guide her toward the stage. Hendrix runs to her, puts his hands on her shoulders and whispers something in her ear. She can't make sense of the words over the commotion four muffled syllables, she hears though.

Within moments the Defenders guide Hendrix to the edge of The Circle and away from Vera. Just then, she's directed up the stairs and motioned to sit in the chair that Lidia had last sat in, Vera sits down as directed. How surreal it feels to be an extension of that chair. *No, no, no, no, I shouldn't be here*, she thinks. *It must be a dream. It has to be a dream.* She feels a tingling sensation in her feet, an urgency to run. Though how can she run in this dress? She could tear it off for all she cares, if it means saving Hendrix. She needs to get away, if she can flee to safety and find somewhere to hide, Hendrix will stay safe. However, nowhere outside of these colonies is deemed safe - the mammoths are everywhere - and fresh drinking water, what of that? She'd be dead in three days, if not sooner.

The Tags show up in flocks and are guided to their seats. Vera quickly notices Cole and Lincoln sitting down beside one another. Cole takes his seat and instantly his eyes find Vera on stage. There his gaze stays. She doesn't quite feel anger, not like she thought she would in seeing them again. However, her mind is in too much disarray to establish any one real thought or feeling. She glances over at the Kals, who sit quietly and calmly, that makes her want to scream. They could lose two of their own today - scientists at that - and still, they follow The Masters blindly. There are no other scientists in the world to help solve the Water Crisis – but they already know that. Zev approaches the podium to speak, breaking her scattered thoughts. The Masters are already seated next to their Barons.

"Welcome my friends, here we gather at The Circle, we gather to unite as one and we gather to pay respect to Mother Earth. May we be cleansed." Following a brief pause, he continues: "It is with great pleasure that I stand here today, to introduce the 36$^{th}$ biannual re-birthing ceremony, put in place by our Masters as a means to ensure bloodlines are fresh amongst the colonies. Please welcome our wonderful Masters: Master Oberon of the Kalians and Master Regan of the Tagondians."

The crowd forces their fingers together in unison. However, Vera barely notices the snaps over the intense pounding of her heart, it reverberates in her ears. She turns her head from side to side, not able to focus on anything in particular. One person blends into the next – like the way she imagines the drink influences one's vision. She realizes then, if Hendrix loses, she will never drink and dance with Ida at one of those ridiculous ceremonies. Why does tragedy make one feel for things they've never once cared for?

"The Masters would like to thank you all for gathering here today. And with that, we will begin our ceremony," Zev pauses for snapping fingers – The Masters relish in it. "As per usual, this young lady has been drawn at random for re-birthing. She is twenty-four-years-of-age and comes from blood of brains. She is of Favoured North: science and botany intelligence run through her veins. In terms of reproduction, she is a very promising candidate; any family would be fortunate to have her. There are several interested Tagondian families at this point, up first: Hendrix of Favoured North and Opi of Insignificant Cannelle. As per usual, it will be a fight-to-the-death between the two willing opponents. Following the battle, the next family in line will have the opportunity to fight for complete rights for Vera of Favoured North. As always, the last man or woman standing will be the winner. Weapons of choice are on either side of The Circle. Will the two opponents please step forward?" Hendrix and Opi both enter The Circle.

Zev speaks to the audience once again, "A warm welcome to our opponents, Hendrix of Favoured North and Opi of Insignificant Cannelle," the audience snaps. "We will begin our countdown: ten, night, eight…" It is the same thing every time, only this time it is Hendrix's life at stake. "One!" and with that Brene sounds the ceremonial horn in one long blow.

The fight begins: both choose a sword as their weapon of choice, a typical choice and a safe choice. The opponents circle one another, possibly to defer the clashing of their blades. A few gentle whacks back and forth and the Tagondian crowd pounds their fists into their hands like a pack of hungry wolves, they want blood. Vera can't bear to watch, she bends her head down into her lap, squeezing her eyes tight and covering her ears with her hands.

"You do not wish to watch?" Master Oberon's booming voice speaks to Vera. *Surely he isn't surprised at that?*

Out of respect for Master Oberon, she sits up straight to address him, "No your grace, I can't. I hope you will understand."

"You are here, you are listening – that is enough," he nods.

"It is insulting that you do not watch," Master Regan sneers from the other side of Master Oberon.

"It shouldn't be," Vera says the words aloud, though she didn't entirely mean to speak back to a Master. Her thoughts are not aligned as they should be.

"Oh?" Master Regan replies, "It shouldn't be insulting that you do not follow a simple request? A Master's request?"

"It is not my intent to insult you, your grace," Vera states. Master Regan's eyes stare at her with intent, until he suddenly looks away. Zev is called to Master Regan's side and whispers take place between the two men. Zev nods his head as he backs away from Master Regan. Zev returns to his place at the podium, clearly set to give an unprecedented oration – the opponents stop at his interruption.

"Dear people, there has been a slight interference – Vera of Favoured North has spoken out of turn and so, we need to make amends. Do not be in fear as we render a tribulation accordingly."

Vera looks to Hendrix, she isn't exactly sure what she did. Nor is she certain about Master Regan and the shrewd look that is meant for her on his face. A commotion begins on the other side of the stage, whispers break out amongst the crowd. Zev waves his hands to request silence. The tall Defender, who resembles a giant, walks toward the battlegrounds and stops just before his shoes reach the sand. As soon as he knows he is visible to everyone, he raises a bow. He looks like a giant in black, who likely knows not of the word mercy, who is a killing machine. Vera feels her pulse quicken and whatever form of calmness may have resided within her is slipping away. She squeezes her hands into tight fists to fend off the trembling. A current of some kind soars through her body, sending jolts like electric shocks to this limb and that, making her shift about in her seat, unable to sit still – adrenaline, perhaps. She stands up and leans against the railing that keeps her captive. Her eyes are fixated on Hendrix.

Oberon straightens in his, "Absolutely not!" he shouts.

But the Defender aims his bow toward the opponents and in one swift release, without a thought or mere hesitation, almost as if he didn't hear Oberon at all, the metal arrow soars across The Circle and burrows itself into Hendrix's right shoulder like a giant bullet. He stumbles and falls down onto his knees.

Vera feels a sharp pain in her chest as she drops to the floor. The hard lump in her throat that sat there since she left the confines of her home engorged with pain grows, until there is a pressure from deep within her stomach. Suddenly acid rises up her throat and vomit spews out of her, attempting to take all those disobedient words with it. The lady who handled baby Lilith in her birthing ceremony, Brene, approaches Vera with a cloth. Her dark skin glistens in the late March sunlight. Vera looks up at her, their eyes meet for an instant. Vera is surprised by their delicacy, their sadness. It doesn't exactly correlate with what they are told about the Tags. Brene gives Vera's hand a short, sympathetic squeeze and backs up just as quickly as she appeared. She must be scared of what The Masters may do if they see the interaction, or Vera looks like a pathetic damsel and Brene feels pity for her. Vera's instincts force her head to turn, she locks eyes with Master Regan who sits in his elegant chair with a sideways, devious smile upon his pale face. Vera is pretty sure he didn't see her interacting with Brene – at least she hopes. She dabs her face with the napkin.

"That was unwise," Master Oberon says to Master Regan. Oberon glances about, his professional demeanour resolute. Tension fills the space between the two Masters, somehow in Vera's debilitated state, she notices.

"What? Not entertaining enough for you, Oberon?" Master Regan says with a sly smile.

"Quite the opposite, actually," Master Oberon responds, his deep voice smooth and steady like the lake on a windless day. Master Regan laughs, a snicker that only adds to Vera's unsettling nerves. Her gaze moves back to The Circle. She must watch, so that Master Regan does not have another excuse to cause more harm.

Vera is well aware that the arrow in Hendrix's arm will be a grave setback for him, and what is that thing that she hates about setbacks? *They prevent one from getting ahead. But what about Father? He would view this as a lesson. I see no lesson for him here.* She annuls her thoughts, stubbornly resisting the urge to find anything positive in this darkness.

Bringing herself to her feet, she leans on the railing for support. With her hands clasped around the railing and the cloth from Brene in one hand, she grips the railing harder, digging her nails into the wood. The sensation, somehow, lightens the trembling in her hands. Vera watches as Hendrix holds his sword with his left hand while keeping his right arm still by his side, the arrow is still protruding out of his flesh, red pouring from the wound and dripping down his bicep. Vera has to look away, she can't watch him struggle, she knows it will tear her apart, disembowelment, like the mammoths are known for If the pain of watching him fight alone can harm her this much, what will become of her if he is killed? *You have to watch*, she reminds herself as she feels Master Regan's eyes upon her.

The two men swing their swords, Hendrix much slower than previously. Opi stops several times to catch his breath. The clang of their swords sends goosebumps pricking at her flesh. The grunts of the men grow louder as their efforts become more trying. The arrow still sits in Hendrix's arm, willing blood from his body. The Circle is laced with the blood of the best scientist that Kala will ever see. The one who lead them here, to the spring - saving them all - and yet, no one does a thing.

Her eyes sting at the visual in The Circle, she needs a distraction. She scans the audience instead, but when she does she comes across the constant stare and unrelenting brown eyes of Cole. Cole who doesn't deserve to wear the mark of the eastern phoebe over his chest. She wants to scream, though she knows right well she won't. *Why must he stare? I'm not the show, you buffoon.* She knows Tagondians are supposedly known for their love of the ceremonies. They are, after all, combat savvy. So that must mean Cole is quite entertained. It takes her a moment to realize that vomit covers the front of her grandmother's beautiful gown. *How could I be so careless?* She wipes her face more desperately then, and moves the cloth down to the dress with the intent to remove as much of the mess as she possibly can. But she begins to feel drowsy, she examines the stains on her gown that cling to the fabric like grass stains on trousers – only grass stains are bright green and smell like the earth. These stains are brown and muddled with the faint scent of stomach acid. Still, they will be just as stubborn to remove – she is stubborn. Does that mean then, that she and these stains have a likeness? Her vision begins to fade.

A strange whine erupts from her throat as one loud thud interrupts her thoughts, like a tree branch falling from the top of an evergreen and crashing down on top of her. *No, stay! You're supposed to be resolute.* A shrill scream sounds. Vera turns toward The Circle – heaviness takes over her body, her head sways. She sees Hendrix lying face down on the ground. His lifeless body imprinted in the sand as if the earth has already claimed him, willed him, to be a part of its own matter. Nothing, she feels nothing, just weight pressing down on her, forewarning unconsciousness. In her haze, she gazes back up at Cole who is no longer in his seat. No, he is running toward the stage, towards her. *But why?*

An unpleasant feeling beyond heaviness washes over her and the sound of a falling tree branch echoes in her ears, over and over again until the thud begins to sound like her name, but it is such a low boom that it can't possibly be the voice of a human being. She feels pressure in her back, as if a tree persists in crashing down and thudding against her body with an appetite to assault her so destructively, as if to thrust her into the earth as well.

"Just take me, take me and leave him," she mumbles. The echoes slowly grow quiet, distancing themselves from her. She takes one wobbly step toward the stairs, but her legs give way. Her vision closes in and she falls toward an endless black pit.

# 10

# Lidia of Favoured Peony
# Kala

The dirt fills the cracks under her fingernails and stains her fingerprints, it is the life of a botanist and Lidia has never thought anything more of it. She sits, motionless, in the greenhouses. Working by herself on this day, now a solitary mission to keep the plants alive. The greenhouses are solely her responsibility now that Atticus and Ida are forced to work in the lab since Hendrix and Vera left Kala.

Hendrix left Kala in Lidia's eyes, Kobe just the same, and darling Lilith... That's how she views all the people that have come and gone from her life in Kala. No matter where they end up, they simply *leave* Kala. Her world seems so small, so insignificant when she thinks this way. Lidia picks at the dirt that lingers on her hands with desperation to remove it. Why she suddenly worries now, it's not a thought that crosses her mind. Though she is unaware of a desperation building inside of her to rid herself of the life she is living and to clean the filth that marks her; however, that filth is merely a symbol for the tragedies that are bestowed upon her.

Her body constantly reminds her of her pain, being only one month since giving birth; her cervix still bleeds rather profusely from having baby Lilith. Aches and pains still sting at her perineum, but the stitches Doctor Navede left in between her legs will dissolve in the coming weeks. Lidia looks forward to that time when she can feel, at least in some minor way, a reflection of her old self.

She uses the edge of a prong off a small hand rake to push the dirt out from under her fingernails. *Plynth,* she thinks. It is one of the best plants used for cleaning. She'll soak her hands in it later that evening. She puts the rake down when she realizes there is no point. Hours of work lay ahead of her, the dirt will soon find its way back in between her skin and the underside of her nails – it always does. Whether it's the same dirt, or different dirt, it doesn't matter.

As she cares for the tomato plants she uses her scissors to cut the leaves along the bottoms. The plants are getting tall and so it is important to prevent the bottom leaves from getting too humid causing disease amongst the plants. It is also pertinent to the plants' health to consider where the light will fall, bottom leaves need to get enough light to continue to prosper. She remembers when she taught Atticus that. He argued that he didn't believe it was necessary to cut the leaves, though in the end, he regarded her suggestion as valid and clipped them accordingly. As far as teenagers go, he is pleasant to be around.

Her thoughts drift back to Lilith and she wonders if she'll ever see her daughter in her teenage years. The wonderment in dreaming up what she will look like is both heartfelt and heart wrenching. Lilith should be here, in Kala, to grow as a botanist like her mother, with her mother. She wonders: *Why did The Almek have to be life takers?* They didn't literally take Lidia's life and yet, they did. She begins to sob at the thought, sorrowful moans escape her mouth, she tucks her head into her chest and knees on the floor of the greenhouse. Her body stays frozen, and yet vibrating ever so subtly from her distressing wails of mourning.

"What is the meaning of this?" Huron's voice fills the humid air. Lidia fumbles to wipe the tears off her salty face and to bring her legs to stand.

"I-I..." she fumbles again, over her words.

"Get on with it," he requests.

She takes a deep breath in submission, "I'm sorry. It's hard to work right now."

"There are no excuses in Kala."

She pauses a moment, how should she talk to the Kalian Lead Defender? She never knows, but decides to simply speak the truth: "I'm hurting," she finally says, "Not just on the inside, the outside too – everywhere," her voice choppy in between bouts of sniffles.

"It's unruly to speak of such things," he wades in the doorway, his face wrinkling with dislike.

"It's the ceremonies..." she begins sobbing heavily once again.

"The ceremonies are The Masters' gift to us all."

"I know, and I am grateful for their gift. I'm just not sure how to make the hurting stop," she says.

"Pray to Mother Earth and speak to no one about it," he orders.

"Okay." Prayer to Mother Earth is Master Oberon's favourite course of action when faced with opposition.

"I came to see how the peppers were growing and when they will be ready to send shipment to Tagondo," he continues on with business.

"Oh, of course. They will be ready next week," she sniffles.

"Good. Get to work. I won't report you this time – for your father. But if I catch you brooding again, I will have no choice but to report your idleness to The Master," Huron states then simply turns to leave, closing the greenhouse door behind him.

Lidia presses the palms of her hands over her eyes, as if by some gentle force she could prevent the flow of expelling tears. Even if she can never see Lilith again, at least for the time being Lilith will get her nourishing breast milk as they ask Lidia to express her supply several times a day to ship off to Tagondo. Everyone knows that's what they force the mothers to do, except no one speaks of it. There is the odd mother that doesn't agree to it. Their days don't end as well as they begin. The ones who agree, must express in The Master's chamber, as a witness is pertinent to ensure the supply isn't intentionally tainted with toxic water. No matter, it still hurts – the knowing that she's feeding a child she can never hold.

Perhaps it is all a nagging reminder. No one – she has no one. Her parents don't listen to her cries for help and her Master certainly won't. Vera was the only one who listened to her. Huron was gracious in offering her a warning, she knows that. He knows her father, Wade of Favoured Peony, well. Regardless, she knows he won't be able to offer such a pass again. Lidia of Favoured Peony is falling and if she isn't careful, she'll crash and break into a million pieces.

# 11

# VERA OF INSIGNIFICANT CANNELLE TAGONDO

An intense noise - a thud of some sort - torments her rest and brings her from sleep to wakefulness after sleeping for what feels like weeks. Her body jolts up to a seated position as she realizes that she is no longer in her home, but on a stranger's bed. Last she remembers walking through the threshold of Favoured North on her way to her re-birthing. Whispers… she remembers the stings from colony members. She remembers the strange man who assaulted her, however mildly, in his stupor to convince her to have his child. She shudders. *But what happened following that?* She can't recall. She can merely assume it didn't end the way she wanted it to. But without a concrete memory to lean upon she wonders where Hendrix and the rest of her family are. Lidia too. In her foggy mind she suddenly grows fearful that the strange man has abducted her since she can't remember being at The Circle.

With her heart pounding and her vision slightly blurred, she tirelessly attempts to gauge her surroundings. Forest green: the colour that encases the walls of the bedroom, a glass of water sits upon the bedside table – it is always peculiar to see a misplaced glass of water no matter where you are in the colonies. It isn't enough that she is in a strange room, but she most certainly won't be drinking that water even though her mouth is dry like the peeling white bark on a birch tree, her tongue feels like paper. She can't recall when she had a drink of water last. Her head spins; however, dehydration is not her primary concern. She slowly moves her legs and scoots her bottom to the edge of the bed, letting her feet slide over the edge to rest her soles on the cold, wooden floor. She comes to a standing position, but her knees buckle beneath her and she collapses to the floor with a thud. She has been detained here longer than she imagines. Though the timeline in which she has been here is entirely unmarked. Even the weakness in her muscles can't be a reliable indication.

A light series of footsteps thread their way toward the bedroom. She freezes, her breathing comes to a halt as a means to listen in uninterrupted silence. It's the strange man, she is sure of it. Her pulse quickens. The door swings open and a mysterious face peers through the open door. It's a short, stocky woman with white flyaway hair that walks into the room. It isn't who she is expecting and Vera finds herself relieved. *She looks rather ghostly*. If it wasn't for hues of orange in her eyebrows and eyelashes Vera would assume that the woman before her is an apparition. Vera rubs her eyes and they open to find that the woman has moved further into the room, she now stands at her bedside.

"Alright, princess?" the woman says rather stoically, though Vera is startled by her closeness with a sudden jolt. She notes that the woman's *R's* roll in an accent that she is unfamiliar with.

"I… I think so," Vera hesitates, her voice hoarse. She struggles once again to get to her feet. The woman holds out a sturdy hand to offer support. Reluctantly, Vera accepts. Gently holding Vera's hand and elbow, the woman helps pull her to her feet. Her legs are still quite shaky, which tells her that backing up and sitting on the bed is necessary to avoid another fall.

"Did ye fall out of bed lass?" The woman asks.

"No, I tried to get up and my legs couldn't seem to carry my weight."

"Aye, ye should be drinkin' that water."

"It's um… stale," she blurts.

The woman holds her inquisitive stare upon Vera with a single raised eyebrow, "We canna be havin' that, now can we? Ye stay put, I'll be right back." The woman scoops up the glass and wanders out of the room. To sit upon the soft bed in silence, with the light blue quilt that warms her, seems like the thing to do for there is a severe feeling of exhaustion throughout her body, none like she has ever felt before. Resting back upon the headboard, her eyes begin to close, a beckoning for more sleep.

"Princess, ye canna sleep anymore."

Startled, Vera opens her eyes and sits up, "I can't help it," she musters.

"Aye, yer body needs the food and drink," she says, forcing a glass into Vera's hand.

Vera's quivering hand accepts the glass and brings it up to her mouth, uncertain if she can even stomach the liquid. She decides that if this woman wants her dead, she'd already be dead. Therefore, the glass meets her bottom lip and she tilts back, drinking forcefully initially, and is pleasantly surprised that emptying the cup is not a trial.

"That's good, will ye have more then?"

"Not right now, thank you."

"Well then, tis time for ye to get up. Come to the kitchen, I made apple muffins." If one couldn't smell the apples and cinnamon wafting down the hallway from the kitchen surely they'd be mad. The rich aroma fills the house with the warmth of fresh baked goods; something that isn't often had in Favoured North for Ida isn't much of a baker. The sweet waft coming from down the hall is pleasing to Vera and she inhales deeply. Vera notices that the woman walks with a slightly bow-legged saunter, she leads Vera to the kitchen table; it isn't without effort to get herself there, but for her age this old woman is seemingly quite sturdy and capable.

"What's your name?" Vera asks, only now realizing her caregiver - if that's what she is - hasn't mentioned it.

"Why, have I forgotten to mention it?" she looks puzzled, until Vera nods. "Murdina," the lady says. Vera nods once more as she observes the crest resting on Murdina's chest: a bronze tree. "Tis a Rowan tree," Murdina says when she notices Vera's gaze.

Vera nods and moves her examination to the kitchen walls, which are the same green as the room she was resting in. *Evergreen,* she thinks, *like the forest.* There are paintings on the walls made from pieces of wood. The paintings are exquisite, none like Vera has ever seen, Rowan trees with red leaves and white heather flowers.

"Ye fond of the paintins, Princess?" Murdina says, noting Vera gaping at them.

"They are lovely."

"I do suppose. My wrist is not what it once was." As Vera admires the paintings in silence Murdina continues, "Good luck omens." She gestures with her hands towards the paintings.

"The Rowan trees?"

"Aye, indeed."

Curious, Vera questions: "What would you need good luck for?" *Good luck is for the superstitious – any true scientist knows that.*

"For the things in this world that need changin'," Murdina answers simply, as if it should be obvious. Vera offers Murdina an unhinged glance as she wonders just what exactly she is referring to that needs changing. Though she herself knows there is far too much, especially for luck to hold any weight. Then again, she supposes Murdina's beliefs don't matter much, nor do they affect her. She won't be staying long, as she will need to get back to her family. Though food and drink will be necessary to get Vera back to health before she can travel back home. Besides, she needs to figure out where she is and why.

"Tea?" Murdina offers.

"Sure, thank you."

Murdina's step is peculiar at best, her hands wave about in a jerking motion, though her jaunt is solid and confident while simultaneously light-footed. Vera watches her with weary eyes as Murdina brings steaming muffins to the kitchen table on a wooden plate. She has light brown-orange freckles splattered across her skin and is of considerable weight, which is a possible cause for her pace, but it doesn't explain her light-footedness. The tea is soon ready and quite hot; Murdina brings it to the kitchen table as well, placing it in front of Vera. Lemon and bergamot scents escape the teacups and find their way to Vera's nose. The scent is familiar, somehow, but it doesn't make sense as to why, for she's never tasted Lemon tea before. The sweet and spicy notes are intoxicating. Taking a sip she notices the tang in the lemon, its zest making her tongue feel sprightly. It isn't long before the teacup is empty and she is asking for more. It fills her belly with warmth, warmth that she has unknowingly missed.

It isn't common to have tea in Favoured North too. The rare occasion happens when one is ill, which isn't often. They used to drink tea all the time back in Oregon – white raspberry – back before the Water Crisis. Vera still remembers the day the Water Crisis swept the globe killing billions of people. Her thoughts drift back to how the chemical levels reached a maximum and the attempts of the various organizations fighting to clean the water had been futile. Overall, the number of individuals who cared was severely lacking and unfortunately, the oppositional force - those that didn't care - was of mass numbers. Vera now knows what a mass number of people with lax values can be capable of.

"How's the tea?" Murdina interrupts her thoughts.

"It's good, though the zesty tang of the lemon zips the edges of my tongue ever so slightly, it has a nice balance of flavours overall," the words fall out of her mouth before she even had time to think of them as she sits there wide-eyed. She glances in the teacup, examining its contents. She didn't mean to speak her thoughts aloud.

"Yes," Murdina smiles knowingly. "Eat."

"Oh yes, how could I forget. These muffins smell delicious. I sure hope you didn't add any Lake Cloud water to the recipe," she laughs nervously at the words which are meant to contest only in her thoughts. Vera picks at a muffin and places pieces into her mouth. It is still warm and seems to practically melt on her tongue.

Murdina seemingly amused, simply nods, "Ye must be wonderin' where ye are? What do ye recall?"

"I don't remember anything. Where's the strange man? He had assaulted me, told me to have his child and then disappeared into the trees – is he here? He's here isn't he?" She stops to take a breath, though her eyes continue to sit wide in discomfort. Confusion rattles her, she is babbling – she never babbles. It's as if Vera's mouth is a river and the floodgates open. Words bound out of her mouth, out of the safety of the walls that reside inside of her head, tickling off her tongue mindlessly, carelessly.

"The strange man isn't here," Murdina says.

"Are you sure? Because I distinctly remember what he looks like. If I were to ever see him again, there's no-"

"Shhh, lass, yer fine. He won't be botherin' ye while yer in Tagondo."

Silence encases the room for a brief instant before Vera's mouth begins motoring once again, out of her control, "Tagondo? What on earth am I doing in Tagondo? Did he bring me here?"

"No, yer at Insignificant Cannelle. This is my home and Opi's. Ye slept for a long while."

She wants to sit quietly, to reflect upon her options. To find a way out of the situation she is in, but it's as though she no longer carries any agency over her own tongue.

Her thoughts continue to spill: "I need to leave... to get back home before someone finds out I'm in Tagondo… I'll be tried as an Offender. Can you tell me which way my home is?"

"I think's it's almost time for ye to go have a soak."

"That would be a good idea, my personal hygiene is severely lacking," Vera slaps her hand to her mouth.

Murdina chuckles, "Aye."

"There's something wrong with me," Vera admits uncomfortably.

"Hmm?"

"I think I need to go lay down…"

"Alright, give it here," Murdina's fingers reach for and tug on the teacup in Vera's hand.

"I'm not finished-"

"Ye've had enough," Murdina states. Vera nods, pursing her lips to keep them from moving and pulls the mug toward her mouth, out of Murdina's reach. She tilts her head back and empties the contents into her mouth. Murdina's eyes grow wider for a brief instant, surprised by Vera's audacity. Vera sets the mug on the table and wipes her sleeve across her mouth.

Shaking her head, Murdina quickly scoops up Vera's mug and brings it up close to her face and inspects the contents. Vera watches, feeling slightly loopy, as she lowers her brow in curiosity at what the odd woman is doing. The cup is empty except for a few tea leaves in the bottom.

"Ah, just as I thought," Murdina says with a nod of her head.

"What is just as you thought?" Vera inquires as she rubs her hands across the tops of her legs. "This sensation feels weird," maybe her legs are slightly numb from lying for days or weeks. Or perhaps the dehydration is making her experience what she imagines intoxication to feel like. *Could it be the tea?* One thing is for certain, she's not thinking quite clearly.

Before she can answer the front door opens and a short, balding man with a round stomach waltzes inside.

"Oh, hello there!" a chipper voice projects from the man with the black makeshift glasses that sit crooked on his nose.

"Yer sooner than expected. Princess, tis a pleasure to introduce ye to my husband, Opi."

"How do you do?" He asks Vera. That face: she recognizes that face the second it comes into view and yet she can't recall where or how. Something inside her tells her she should not like this man, but when she glances upon his face all she can do is observe its apparent innocence. Still, she has a bad feeling.

"How do I recognize you? I mean… I've never seen someone with such a round stomach in all of Kala, but somehow, somewhere… I've seen you before," Vera exhales, this babbling thing is sickening the longer it carries on. "I'm sorry if I'm being rude. I can't seem to-" His eyes simply shift towards his wife questionably.

"Er, I think she means 'what did ye get' – did ye pursue anythin'?" Murdina intervenes.

He sits back in his chair, pushing his glasses up his face with one chubby finger, "Oh, no sadly, I did not."

Vera inches forward toward Opi, the urge to correct Mrudina stews inside of her – she wants to know why she recognizes his face. But upon her sudden movement, Murdina darts her eyes to Vera and gives a sudden jerk of her head, as if to signal Vera to be quiet. Vera purses her lips.

"Next time. Here ye go, lovekin," Murdina says while handing Opi his tea, his tea is different, Vera can tell by its floral sent.

"Thank you, bumpkin," Opi replies as he rubs his palms together in anticipation.

"So, I guess we need to have the talk," Murdina announces.

"Yes, I suppose we do," Opi agrees.

"What talk? Is it about who brought me here?"

"In a round-about-way we brought ye here. We chose ye so ye can pursue for us."

Vera releases a belt of laughter, though its presence feels out of place even to her, "Are you insane? I don't pursue, I'm Kalian."

"You can learn," Opi suggests. Vera shakes her head in response.

"Yer not as daft as a chair. Surely ye can learn a thing er two." Murdina speaks, forwardly. She is right: Vera isn't a *daft* young lady. Though pursuing isn't one of the things she has studied – she shakes her head *no* once again. However, the shaking act accentuates the distorted sensation in her head.

“We have a friend who will help teach you,” Opi says, as if satisfied with his addition to the debate.

“I can’t stay here...”

“You are where you are supposed to be.” Opi says. “Besides, Cole is a great teacher.” “Cole?” Vera pauses. *Could it be the same Cole?* “I’d rather swim in Lake Cloud and drink its poisonous waters than speak to the likes of him,” she spits.

“We best talk about it later,” Murdina nods sternly to Vera. Opi’s face wrinkles in confusion then follows with a shrug. “Tis time for that soak. Down the hall an’ to the right.”

Vera’s legs wobble, threatening to collapse below her once again. Murdina quickly appears at her side and helps her get down the hall and to the bathroom. It is there that she stays for some time, soaking her sore muscles. No thoughts circulate her mind in relation to the recent past that has led her to this place. No memories float about succeeding her walk down the footpaths to her re-birthing. She can feel something missing, memories misplaced. It’s as if some things have been wiped clean from the workings of her brain. A fog has been present since she awoke earlier and there it lingers. Though somewhere in the depths of her conscious, she assumes she is in Tagondo for the one reason she fears the most. If it is true that means Hendrix is dead. *It can’t be true,* for she has no proof. She pushes the thought away as quickly as it surfaces. The loopy feeling won’t let her focus on any one thing for very long anyway. After some time, Vera begins to doze off when the bathroom door opens and in her dreamlike state it sounds like the echoes of the booming tree branch once again – she sits up in a panicked haze. When she sees Murdina in the doorway she lets out a scream and makes a sad attempt to cover her bosom and cross her legs.

“Calm down lass, are ye forgettin’ I have a bosom and a duilef too. I just came to check on ye.”

Vera sits speechless, frozen in place until Murdina leaves.

“Listen, ye canna mope about all day. Get dried off, get dressed and we practise.”

“Practise what?” Vera questions.

“Yer pursuin’ skills. Mother Earth canna help wi’ that,” Murdina leaves the bathroom and slams the door – startling Vera and causing her to jump and let a few splashes of water wallow out of the tub.

The glimmer of an urge overcomes her, like a light shining through a wall of fog, her hands form into fists briefly. *I will never be a Pursuer.* And she won’t, not if her life depends on it. She clasps her hands together and prays to the Mother. She prays for her memory to fully return, she prays that she’s wrong about why she’s in Tagondo… that Hendrix is still alive. But the wave of intoxication pulls her back into the fog, it makes her disregard her thoughts of worry and muddles all reason once again.

# 12

# ATTICUS OF FAVOURED NORTH KALA

Atticus walks to school sopping wet from the rain, but pleased that there is rain. Coakai must be to thank, that or the prayers to Mother Earth. It is after all April and The Almek need the rain. Since spending more time in the lab Atticus has learned that somehow the rain doesn't seem to contain lethalyn, which makes him believe there is possibly something that rids the water of chemicals within the evaporation process. The scientists are still trying to figure that out, but it is seemingly thrown to the wayside – apparently cleansing the lake is more important than studying rainwater. Even though Atticus doesn't consider himself a scientist, he is required to take on more responsibilities in the lab, which is tiresome, as it will take the team longer without Hendrix and Vera to make progress on solving the Water Crisis. Thankfully, Ida is often there to offer help, however senseless it is, but her presence is appreciated. At least she is familiar with the lab, having gone in to work with Hendrix on several occasions. On the other hand, Atticus was essentially thrown into the lab – a most undesirable place for him to be. He is forgetful and clumsy and if he is honest, he prefers playing in the dirt to handling glass test tubes and running strange machines that always beep at him. Machines are complicated, he thinks, whereas plants aren't; plants are the least complicated things on the planet.

The footpaths are mud puddles and Atticus is covered up to his ankles. The sky is a dreary grey, but even when the sun shines it still feels much the same. No matter the weather, he doesn't like the way things feel in Kala without Hendrix and Vera. He misses Vera's guidance and, to his surprise, he misses her heckling. She was always there for him, like a steady beating drum, predictable and consistent. Somehow, he feels weaker without her there. He always pushed her away, often even ignoring her, which saddens him. He could use her insight now though, as Ida wallows in her grief, unable to find herself. However, the colony can't know that – especially not The Master. Which means Ida must continue to appear to manage her workload, however Atticus carries the weight of it now. He doesn't blame her any, quite the contrary, he understands. He misses Hendrix and the calming presence he offered Favoured North, too. He was a patient and gentle man intelligent beyond Atticus' comprehension; the house seems cold now. He worries now too, he never used to, for Ida's safety and his own – they are vulnerable. Perhaps feeling alone creates a sense of vulnerability and he is learning that he doesn't like being alone. When he prays to Mother Earth for guidance, he catches himself asking for the impossible: to bring Hendrix and Vera back. Neither of which he knows can ever be done though.

Soon Atticus enters the school just as he does every other day. No time off, even for the poor souls who lose a part of their hearts in the ceremonies. Though Atticus doesn't want time off, not really. He prefers to keep busy. If he is busy, he doesn't feel alone. The teenagers pile in the classroom as Educator Barlow sits at the front to teach them more nonsensical Kala laws. Atticus despises rules, he believes they are meant for bending – and on a good day, breaking.

"With the earth," Educator Barlow clearly states, as he awaits the follow-up greeting.

"May we be cleansed," the class responds in synchronization. A subtle smile rests on his face, this greeting always pleases him, Atticus wonders why.

"Alright then, where we left off…" Educator Barlow states to the room.

*What an arse,* Atticus thinks as he opens his notebook to the lengthy list of laws he needs to memorize before graduation. He wonders then, what he hates more: the laws or James Barlow himself. To think that Vera was almost forced to merge with the man. Atticus' mouth forms into a frown in disgust. He wonders how the likes of this man had the nerve to eat breakfast and dinner amongst Favoured North, and with a pitiful look to his face most days. James still lives temporarily in his old house where his wife died. Their plans to burn the house were briefly put on hold when his merge agreement with Vera was revoked. Now a new living arrangement is in order for James. Atticus hopes The Masters are right – that suicide is contagious.

Atticus scans the list, forty. Forty laws he needs to memorize and understand their origins by December. He has a poor memory, probably the worst of anyone he knows. His best friend, Ulyd, on the other hand is a law master-genius, or so Atticus calls him as a tease. Ulyd is at the top of the class, the top of every class actually, and Atticus both praises him and heckles him for it. He is proud of his friend, but there are times Ulyd takes things too far. Like spending an excessive amount of time with Educator Barlow after class, Atticus finds that much dedication to be odd.

"Why were the laws put in place eighteen years ago when we came to The Motherland?" Educator Barlow questions in his Brit accent.

"To cleanse, to unite us as one and to pay respect to Mother Earth," the class chants in unison, as per every other day – it is the morning routine that replaces standing to one's National Anthem. There are no nations to hold pride in, just The Motherland. Atticus mouths the words.

Atticus speaks out to the class, "Do you really believe that?" his question is aimed for Educator Barlow to answer. After the ceremonies tore his family apart, he has been second-guessing the ways of The Masters.

"Atticus, if you don't believe that then we are in trouble. Or more specifically, you are."

Atticus glances over to Illandra who sits a couple of rows to his left; he wonders what she believes. She smiles at him, a small pleasant smile, though the very movement of her lips send tightness to his pants that he doesn't expect. It's unpredictable lately – always creeping up on him whether he wants it to or not. Illandra is always a source of inspiration, in more than one way.

"I'm still trying to grasp an understanding for all the laws, and what they actually do for us," Atticus reasons. He likes to send Educator Barlow reeling with annoyance at any chance he can get, and it is easy.

Giving Atticus a blank look James asks the class, "Is anyone wondering if the laws really do cleanse us, unite us and assist in our respect to Mother Earth?" A couple head nods are initiated throughout the room. "It is true, the laws do help us achieve this greatness. By way of helping us work together and survive in ways that we didn't in the Old World. They encourage us to be the best people we can be to each other and to the planet. Which in turn, makes Mother Earth proud. The repercussions we face if we do not follow the laws is essential to the success of them," Educator Barlow explains.

Barlow's chatter fades into the distance; the current laws and their history are really of no interest to Atticus. His thoughts drift to how the way they separate Favoured classes from Insignificants, he deems that it is as pointless as the scripture itself. There is no legitimate proof that Insignificants are any less intelligent or capable to be among Favoured classes – or to learn the ways of a higher, more respectable profession. Illandra shuffles in her seat, Atticus can only assume that she is intrigued in the law lecture; however, he is intrigued in how to go about changing the laws.

He has reason enough to wonder on the legitimacy of the laws because of the one girl that he is always drawn to – Illandra. The fact that he can't ask her out on a date, or courtship - or whatever they used to call it in the Old World - frustrates him. Dating has been on his mind a lot, and he's been reading about it in books. Sure, the pages are yellowed and ripped, arguably falling apart, but that doesn't stop him from reading stories of courtship and adventure. As the class comes to an end, Atticus leaves immediately and heads for the lab. His afternoon will be spent there deciphering Hendrix's old notes. However, he can't read Hendrix's writing to save his own life, "mammoth scribbles" are what Atticus always called them. Hendrix would laugh his light, airy chuckle and then he'd always say: "I'd rather it be a mammoth than a Master," whatever that means.

On his way to the lab to see Ida, Atticus passes the greenhouses and pops in to see Lidia. He often checks in on her, even on the days he isn't working in the greenhouses. In some ways she has suffered even more than he has, in the last month she has lost her baby, her husband and her best friend.

"Hey Lid," he says as he leans over her shoulder, she is sifting soil around the basil plants.

"Oh, hi Atticus," she replies indifferently and without a smile. Lidia doesn't smile anymore, no matter how hard Atticus tries.

"How are you feeling today?" he asks her.

"Same as yesterday – tired," she simply states. She looks tired, her hair is a knotted mess on the top of her head. Is it the same knot from the day before? Her eyes red and swollen, even the way she moves her limbs is tiresome to watch.

"I can help today, if you need it. I have to go to the lab for a bit, but I can come back," he offers.

"Thanks Atticus, you're always so kind. I'll be fine though."

He persists, "You sure? Even if I said I was *dying* for someone to talk to?" She looks at him without a change in her expression - her face sits dull, lifeless - as though she's looking through him. Her eyes barely blink. In an effort to humour her, he jumps and then releases a squeal from his throat that sends her startled and spooked within an instant. She inhales a loud frightened moan and then laughs the first laugh he's heard escape her in weeks.

"Ah, so you're not just a bag of bones!" he exclaims. A troublesome smile is strewn across her face then. It doesn't reach her eyes, nowhere near, granted it is better than a frown.

"No, not just a bag of bones. Though some days I think that's all I am. Just waiting for the day that Master Oberon sends this bag of bones around the fire."

"Ooooh, come on!" he exclaims, "You're not just a bag of bones. You're a cool person and fairly smart. Not crazy smart or anything, just fairly smart," he teases. She jabs him in the side with her elbow.

"Ow! But really, things will get better from here. I keep telling myself that too."

"You think so? Somehow it seems it's only getting worse," she says.

"You can talk to me. I know it's weird: I'm your friend's little brother… But, I miss her too."

"I know, thanks," Lidia pauses a moment, "It was easier with her here, she listened so well and always had the most logical advice."

Atticus chuckles then, "Painfully logical."

"She helped keep the darkness away after I lost Kobe and Lilith. Now that she's gone, I worry the darkness might swallow me whole."

"You have reason to be here, more than most of us. You're one of the best, most capable botanists," he offers.

"Being capable doesn't make me feel any better. Neither does being here."

Atticus wonders then, what will help her to feel better? It is difficult to imagine being in her shoes: to have a dead spouse and an infant living across the lake – an infant who probably cries for her unknown mother's arms. Atticus feels her pain in an understanding sort of way and realizes then that she has said something of significance. Something that can possibly be the answer to helping her, "You said Vera was a good listener and always gave the best advice?"

"Yeah?"

"Maybe that's what you need to help you feel better – someone to listen to you, so you can get out what you're feeling."

"It's actually against the law to talk about. All of this is. We could be tried as Offenders for even speaking about our feelings of the ceremonies."

"Fuck the laws!" he shouts.

"Shh, Atticus, you're being too loud."

"Sorry," he pauses and thinks for a moment, "But if you're waiting for the day Master Oberon sends your bones around the fire – why are you so worried about being caught talking, if that's what's going to help you?"

"That's actually… pretty logical," she says, surprised.

"My sister and I do both share North blood… my logic just tends to be slightly minuscule by comparison," he chuckles.

"I'll think about that. Thanks Atticus."

"Hey, anytime. I better run though, the lab awaits. I'll talk you later, okay?"

"Okay," and she turns to focus her attention back on the weeds in the soil.

Atticus leaves the greenhouse feeling slightly less empty than he had upon entering. A part of him thinks that he helped Lidia feel better today, even just a little. Perhaps he 'cracked the code,' if Lidia's a code that needs to be cracked.

From a distance Atticus can see Digger walking up ahead on the footpaths, his arm is around Illandra, as it always is when he thinks no one is looking. He is a gutsy one Favoured and arrogant as all hell about it. His father, Imeldo Espen, built the greenhouses and the solar panels – a task that not just any builder could do, which means that he is a necessity. Digger is in training and will one day be just as much a necessity as his father, if he can figure out how to do anything other than break things with his fists. Atticus walks a fair distance behind them as he doesn't want to be noticed. Whenever he's alone with Digger he ends up with a goose egg the size of a walnut, at minimum. However, Atticus finds himself distracted, his eyes preoccupied by the views of Illandra's backside, he steps on a branch – the crack echoes down the footpaths.

*"Hide,"* the whispers howl in the wind. He jumps, immediately throwing his body into a bush so they will not see him. Hopefully Digger will think it's an animal and be none-the-wiser. There Atticus will lay until he is sure that Digger is long gone. Until he hears no more rustling along the path and is certain the coast is clear, only then will he get up and run for the lab.

# 13

# VERA OF INSIGNIIFICANT CANNELLE TAGONDO

There is quite a variety of weaponry in Tagondo, the only form of weapon not allowed are guns. Apparently firearms are forbidden and were not brought over from the Old World. Vera remembers to keep these thoughts to herself, since speaking of such a time can very well make one an Offender, regardless of which colony one is in. Nevertheless, Tagondians are pursuers and therefore they make their own weapons. Some are known to be skilled craftsmen, others more or less useless in such happenings – like Murdina and Opi. Having the know-how seems to be the difference between life and death in Tagondo.

That afternoon Murdina and Opi try their best, a worrisome best, to show Vera their hunting tools and how to use them. Though Vera has no inclination as to what proper weapons should look like, it is evident that their tools are lacking as their sad bows and arrows are falling apart and their axes entirely crooked, along with the Canelles' sense of aim. The three fiddle all afternoon with zero progress, aside from Vera's arm getting sore, if it can get any sorer from her recent immobility.

She glances up at the tiny piece of land that surrounds the Cannelle house. Beautiful, tall pine trees encase the back of the property, providing a generous amount of privacy from the footpaths; a single Rowan tree sits out front of the house. It is the largest Rowan tree that Vera has ever seen, with the girth of its trunk as wide as her outstretched arms. A few tiny gardens rest randomly about the yard, clearly this woman likes to garden. The shed where the tools are kept is ready to fall apart and is derelict, though somehow the inside looks as if it has barely been touched. The house itself is plain, with dishevelled wooden steps leading up to the single front door entrance. Another glimmer, an urge to flee right now and escape this place, overcomes her. But an intoxicated feeling still encases her and it makes her ignore the urge. At least her thoughts aren't spilling out of her mouth like they were. She picks up the axe, readying herself to throw it at a makeshift target that Opi set out, when suddenly someone approaches her from behind.

"Hey, fancy seeing you here," a deep voice speaks over her shoulder. Vera jumps and releases a squeal of shock, dropping the axe, which almost land on the newcomer's foot. She turns to confirm who the guest is, though the sudden weight in her stomach tells her she already knows. Her cheeks warm.

"Cole," Murdina welcomes from across the lawn. "I wondered when ye were comin'."

"Whoa, you almost took my foot clean off," Cole teases.

Vera rolls her eyes and turns her back to Cole. "A shame," she mumbles. Though she says it so only he can hear. Although her mind is filled with fog, she remembers without a shadow of doubt the anger she has towards him. After their first meeting they had planned to reconvene at the lake a second time, but Cole stood them up. Although it seems a tad juvenile of a thing to be angry over, she is likely more upset at herself for having wasted time on a mindless Tagondian.

"Hey there, *Sport*!" Opi shouts as he walks over from the shed at the onset of conversation.

Vera quickly picks up the axe that she dropped with a slight flush of pink remaining on her cheeks from her scare.

"What are you doing here?" Vera asks Cole, attempting to hide her irritation and immediately wishing she did a better job. The fog that presses in on her vision isn't helping. Still, she doesn't want him to know that he's causing any sort of reaction within her. Her eyes squint in the sunlight as she peers over her shoulder at Cole; her visual drifts up and down taking in his stance, while shifting the axe's weight in her hands.

"I came to help you," he offers.

"I don't need your help."

"You two know each other?" Opi asks, bewildered.

"No-" Vera quickly spits out, perhaps a little too eager.

"No," Cole adds while eyeing her. She is glad he's at least quick enough to catch on to her façade in front of Murdina and Opi. "And to be honest, I'm kind of glad that we don't," he beams. She rolls her eyes when she knows no one will see her.

"Come Opi, let us get drinks," Murdina suddenly says as she saunters off. "Good luck to ye both."

"Coming, my love," Opi calls as he follows behind Murdina; they soon turn around the front corner of the house and are no longer in Vera's sight.

The two stand in silence for a moment, the axe dangles at Vera's side. The heavy weighted weapon in her hand feels so foreign, but it doesn't take her mind completely off of her frustrations toward Cole. Still angry about the lake and him disappointing Lidia, she wants to offer him a piece of her mind, but it isn't like her to speak without filter – this morning's episode aside.

Murdina appears again, a glass in her hand, "Here, drink this. You must be thirsty after all that practicin'." She hands the glass to Vera. Murdina's not wrong Vera is parched, so she downs the glass of mint flavoured water.

"Thanks," Vera hands the glass back and Murdina turns and retreats back inside.

After a moment of Cole and Vera standing in silence, Vera looks at Cole once again, with a critical stare, "You may as well go," she says aloofly while turning away from Cole and back towards her target. She throws the axe and walks to the target to retrieve it, and repeats this endeavour. Her attempts are pitiful and sadly unsuccessful, but she notices the fog slowly begins to fade.

Cole stands quietly for a moment with his arms crossed in a relaxed stance and finally says, as if ignoring her last comment: "You know, if you begin with a smaller axe, it'll be easier."

An exacerbated exhale leaves Vera's mouth, she throws the axe a few more times without acknowledging him or his suggestion, assuming he will leave if she ignores him long enough. Eventually, his footsteps fade away, in which direction, she's unsure. She does note, however, a sigh of relief that escapes her. She stops throwing the axe toward the target and instead tosses it on the ground. She's wasn't getting anywhere with it anyway.

"Try this one," his voice re-emerges over her shoulder once again as an unwanted startle.

Vera's shoulders shoot up slightly from the scare, but it is frustration that keeps her back turned toward Cole.

"Are you handling things okay?" Cole asks gently and out of nowhere. His concern for her is entirely unwelcome – along with his presence.

"I'm not sure what you're referring to," her words shoot through gritted teeth. "Or why you're speaking to me like we're old friends." She picks up the axe that she tossed on the ground, entirely neglecting the other axe that Cole holds in his offering hand. She continues to throw the same axe, purposely avoiding eye contact. "But I've never been better."

Cole stands there, unmoving, merely observing in silence, "Okay," is all he says. She throws the axe a couple more times toward the target. The silence is numbing to her ears, normally all she wants is silence. A glance over her shoulder at him and it is obvious he is waiting for her to do or say something. Meanwhile, all she wants him to do is leave. He stares at her, almost apologetically, though she doesn't understand why.

"Wait… you don't remember, do you?" he asks, breaking the piercing silence. But his voice is equally as piercing right now; she can't decide which is more bothersome.

"Remember what?" she questions sternly, admitting only to herself that she couldn't stand it if he knew more than she. Especially since she is well aware that there is a missing link in her brain, but what could he possibly know about that? *Likely not a thing.*

Cole sighs, a moan that expresses that he's come to a conclusion of sorts, "I think you were drugged," he finally states.

Shocked by his presumption, she fires back: "Drugged? I wasn't drugged," still she searches what little short-term memories she has for a link as to why Cole would say such a thing. She knows that she is missing information from the time she walked to The Circle for her re-birthing ceremony and waking up in the Cannelle household. *But drugged... how? And when? The strange man?* It was a far-fetched assumption. There are no drugs in the Motherland in which to incapacitate people with, or to make them lose their memory.

"Brene, the aide, she gave you a cloth and then you started acting funny at the ceremony. You're still acting funny, even today."

"I don't…" Vera pauses and tries to think back.

"It happened, trust me. I saw the whole thing," Cole reflects. Vera stumbles backward a few paces and shakes her head, she can't recall what he speaks of and so she disagrees. Though through her dumbfounded exposition she can't seem to collect herself either.

"It all makes sense... it's the reason you're not even acting like you lost your father," the words blurt out of his mouth. A look of pity immediately strewn across his face, "Shit." He moves toward her then. Mechanically and instinctively she backs away. The words surge into her ears, but don't register – they are meaningless syllables.

Vera looks directly into Cole's eyes. She stills herself as he steps closer. Now face to face with him, she notes his unrelenting, brown-eyed stare. It stirs a feeling in her that she recognizes, a flash of an image shoots through her memory of Cole running to her through a crowd. Her grandmother's dress smeared with what looks like vomit. A Defender shoots an arrow. *But what does it all mean?* Still photographs flash through her mind without reasoning, snippets that feel as though they are from someone else's past. She turns away from him, squeezing her eyes tight. Her hands remain down by her sides in fists, but still grasping onto the axe in her right hand. Cole's fingers brush her left wrist just as they had that day at the lake – she jolts back from him.

"Your Father, he's dead V. That's why you're here," he says softly. An image of Hendrix lying in the sand, lifeless, flashes before her eyes a dark red pooled around his body. She suddenly feels other memories shoot through her mind, memories that can't possibly be someone else's that begin to fill the gaps of the temporary void inside her head. She realizes that she can't deny that they are real, especially when she sees the pained look on Cole's face. These memories are hers. *He is dead.* She falls to the ground, tears well up in her eyes. Still, stubborn as an ox, she prays to Mother Earth for Cole to be wrong, but she knows it's true. She doesn't bother praying for her father's return. Death is permanent. It has to be.

"It's okay, V," Cole says gently, squatting down beside her.

"Don't call me that," she wails as she sits up on her knees to meet his level, "Nothing's okay," her voice cracking, "You wanted a show – you got one," she sobs so loudly that she disrupts the birds in some nearby trees and causes them to scatter from their nests. Her body gives way and her bottom slides onto the grass. She covers her face with her hands; maybe it will all go away if she hides. Maybe *he* will go away.

She sits in a mound of flesh slumped on the ground, a carcass, dead within and without. A loud thud echoes through the trees in the distance. Terrified of the falling branch, she jumps forward. Cole catches her and holds her tightly for a moment, his embrace is warm against the goosebumps on her skin. In her mind, the tree branch crashes, over and over. It scares her down to her very core, like a nightmare, only in the daylight when one is wide-awake and can't escape with wakefulness.

"Shh, you're fine," Cole whispers as he presses his arms across her trembling body.

As if his words snap her out of her trance, she stands up, pushing herself away from him, "I think you're forgetting that I don't need your help." She begins walking toward the house and oddly feeling the most clear-headed she's felt since she woke up that day.

"Ah, but I think you're forgetting that you're the one who jumped into my arms."

"Must you have an argument for every insignificant incident in your life?" Vera coolly shouts back.

"Yes. If I know my argument is right."

"Well then, argue away…" she mumbles under her breath, "Buffoon…"

"I'm not a buffoon, many a fellow Tag enjoys the light-heartedness of my sense of humour," he is smiling, she can tell without looking. A wide grin, meant to tear her very heart out.

"You're forgetting that I'm Kalian," she states, and without a falter to her step she continues walking, up the stairs and inside.

^

That night Vera lies in her new bed, the one in Insignificant Cannelle, as scattered thoughts of the ceremony seep into her awareness. He heart aches for Hendrix, she misses him deeply, but she's relieved that the fog has left her conscious and that the memories that have returned to her are crisp. A worry for how Ida and Atticus are doing surrounds her like a swarm of bees. Every single concern pricks into her skin. *Are they okay? Is Atticus making it to class? Will Ida manage the shares every week?* She can't recall a time in which her heart has felt such agony. She cries, and when she thinks she has no more tears left, she cries some more. Amidst her emotional realizations, she hears the floor creak outside of her bedroom door.

"Murdina?" she calls in a whimper.

"Aye, Princess?" Murdina opens the door, as if coincidentally walking by at the precise time that Vera called for her.

"How many days?" Vera asks.

"How many days what, my dear?"

"Since the re-birthing."

Murdina's eyes slant the tiniest bit with the upward movement of her brow – she realizes what Vera is truly asking, "Five," she answers.

Five days ago Hendrix of Favoured North had been walking and breathing. Five days ago, he had been a tangible presence that Vera could touch. A brain she could pick for hours on end over their shared interests. She was beyond lucky to have been a part of his life. But she wished she was better, perhaps she could have humoured him a little more with his wacky antics and obscene theories. A different unease fills her heart – guilt in disguise. The tears begin to fall relentlessly.

"What is it Princess?" Murdina asks softly.

"It hurts."

"Aye, it does."

"What will happen to him?"

"Sith upon him." Vera looks at Murdina, bemused at her ability to speak words and yet absolute gibberish at the same time.

"Hm?" Vera replies.

"Peace, my dear. Yer faither's in peace. Sith."

"How do you know?" Vera inquires.

"Ye musna worry lass."

"What is it that tells you he's okay?" Vera urges.

Murdina simply replies, "Mother Earth."

When Vera scans back through her hazy memories on the day of her re-birthing, something sticks out: highlighted amidst the morning sun, a round face, pudgy in frame with glasses and squinting eyes. Though it looks innocent enough, it belongs to the entity of a murderer. For Hendrix was in The Circle that day – he died there, murdered. There was only one man who stood inside that very circle with him, that man owes her the life of her father. In that instant, her own face grows red at the image of this man, it burns her thoughts and causes her hands to form fists. Opi of Insignificant Cannelle is his name and she will see to it that he faces the repercussions of his actions.

# 14

# COLE OF FAVOURED POLLARD TAGONDO

After he leaves Insignificant Cannelle, Cole walks the paths toward Favoured Pollard to help with some chores. It isn't typical that men have their hands in house tending, but without their mother Cole has always aided his sister Nin. Upon returning home he sees Nin out back washing the laundry. Cole collects the rest of his father's laundry and brings it out for her. He places the basket at her side and sits down on a log beside the nearby fire pit. He keeps a stone here, one meant for sharpening his pursuing weapons. Cole picks it up and assumes sharpening his dagger.

"Where have you been?" Nin heckles upon noting his presence.

"I was helping Murdina and Opi."

"You were not – you were helping the *Leech*. Admit it," she demands.

"What's wrong with that?" he asks.

"Leeches are useless. You've seen Hilard and Jacob, what about Liev? They're all painted with the markings of death – you know they are."

"I don't know anything and don't call her that." Leeches are a term used to describe the Kalians that transfer to Tagondo. They are said to be useless: unable to pursue and tend to latch onto the backs of the Tagondians, freeloading, relying on them to supply them with bounty – to Tags they are the blood-suckers of The Motherland.

"It's only a matter of time before they're exiled. Cole, please just focus on things here, help Murdina and Opi - fine - but not *her*," Nin orders, "She's not one of us."

"Nin, has anyone ever told you to take that stick out of your ass?"

Nin releases a huff and storms toward Cole, scooping the basket of laundry off the ground in a jerking motion, "You need to shift your focus to your future wife," she spits. A jab meant to insult him as she knows he isn't over-the-moon about merging with Master Regan's family.

"On one condition," he says.

"What?"

"Go find yourself a merge agreement and please get some relief for all that pent-up anger," he laughs as he walks back inside.

Master Regan has yet to arrange a merge agreement for Cole's older sister, Nin, who's twenty-nine and not getting any younger. He knows it causes insecurity within her, as if she's a waste - unwanted and undesirable mating material - which is why he sometimes is able to take a dagger to that particular wound. In reality Nin is beautiful and kind, to most people. Nin even befriended Treena, likely to learn why Master Regan hasn't granted her a merge agreement just yet. Though Cole doesn't believe that Treena knows, nor has any part in such operations of the colony. In fact, she seems entirely useless.

Cole wanders inside to flee from Nin's perpetual nagging while Burke, Cole and Nin's father, lies asleep on the couch in the living room. He has been sleeping more and more these days. Burke holds the elite position as one of three Barons to Master Regan; however, his acting role as Baron has lessened greatly over recent months as his health has been declining significantly. Cole begins cleaning the kitchen and his thoughts wander to his conversation with Vera. He chuckles at the memory of her jumping in fear and then at her incessant need to be horrible to him he laughs at that too. She is stubborn and surprisingly curt, but she is hurting and confused – who wouldn't be in such a predicament? She needs his help. Especially if she is going to survive Tagondo. Besides, Murdina said *she* will come and *she* came. Which means Murdina was right. That is reason enough. When he had asked Murdina why he needed to be involved, she just said: "Help *her*." There is a reason Vera is in Tagondo, a reason that Murdina knows about – he just doesn't know what it is yet. But if there is anything he has learned about Murdina, it's that she divulges when the time is right.

Regrettably still, Murdina's instructions seem to have only worsened Vera's hostility toward Cole. Possibly even beyond the standard Tagondian-Kalian animosity – he admittedly never dreamt it would be this bad. But Cole knows he must continue to move forward if he's going to hold up his end of the agreement with Murdina, even if it sends Vera reeling in blood-red anger towards him.

Now, there is something else that is potentially working against them and his ease in helping her: her memory loss. He didn't know that her memory would collapse on itself and that he would have to be the one to rebuild that bridge. A genuine concern for whatever the drug was that Brene placed upon that cloth for Vera circulates his conscious. It is another thing he should look into, but another thing that could find him trouble. Still, even through her bitterness toward him and the comical relief it has provided him, Cole hates what Vera has been through. Amidst it all, he remembers Murdina's words: "Be patient when *she* comes lad." And so, patient he will try to be.

^

As Cole wanders through Tagondo, he walks along the border where the forest grows thicker. He notices someone, a young girl, and stops to admire her drawing in her notebook. She sits leaning against the girth of an oak tree, sketching the landscape of the Porcupine Mountains. He has never noticed this girl before, nor does he know her by name, but her drawing is impressive and an urge to comment on it overtakes him.

"That is some drawing," he says to the girl.

The young girl, who couldn't have been older than seven-years-old, drops her pencil and fumbles to snap the notebook closed. Her untamed hair rests in blond swirls down her shoulders framing her doll-like face smudged with dirt. She says no words, she merely stares at Cole in a wide-eyed gape.

"Sorry, I didn't mean to scare you. You are good at that – at drawing," he nods toward her pencil that now rests in her fingers once again. She simply continues to stare, as if dumbfounded by his presence, or his words, he wasn't quite sure. "Do you have others? Can I see?" he approaches the tree trunk to sit next to her. But before his legs bend him into a seated position the girl is gone – off with her notebook and pencil, vanishing into the forest as if she'd never even been there. "Oh. Maybe next time then," he says to the space beyond the tree where she disappeared. He stands up and carries on, locating the path that will lead him to the colony centre.

Before long he sees and approaches Lincoln from behind, "Aren't you a sight for sore eyes."

Startled, Lincoln jumps and turns, "Oh, FP, I didn't hear you there."

"Most don't. It's kind of like the staple of being the Mammoth Slayer. No one hears me coming, not even a mammoth."

"Yeah well, you should warn a person."

Cole chuckles, "Sorry. It's habit." After a slight pause and moment of silence Cole continues, "So, do you want to go hit some targets?"

"No man, I'm busy," Lincoln says as he speeds his jaunt, Cole slows his.

"Busy doing what?"

"Stuff," Lincoln simply states while continuing to march down the path.

"Okay… later then?"

Lincoln stops abruptly in his tracks and turns to face Cole, "If you don't remember, we were supposed to pursue earlier today."

"Oh shoot, I forgot, sorry man. Murdina asked me to help with something." Cole could neither say exactly what that thing was, nor that it was specifically in reference to a person.

"Well, I was counting on you to help me with my bounty. I still haven't reached my shares for the week."

"Oh shit, you should've told me," Cole reasoned.

"What did she ask for help with?" Lincoln inquires, but there is an accusatory tone to his inquiry.

Cole runs his fingers through his hair, "Just something odd, I can't really talk about it. You know Murdina," he chuckles.

"Yeah, I know Murdina. But she's never made us keep stuff from one another before."

"I guess not."

"And that makes me wonder what's changed. And you know the only thing I can come up with?"

"What's that?" Cole humours.

Lincoln eyes Cole with an angered stare, "The Leech," he accuses, then turns and walks down the path.

# 15

# VERA OF INSIGNIFICANT CANNELLE TAGONDO

She isn't a murderer, not by a long shot, but now her circumstances and thoughts are clear – she's stuck in Tagondo with no lab or ability to work on cleansing the water, and no little brother to incessantly watch over, so she has all the time in the world to seek revenge on Opi. The next morning Vera lies awake in her room – a room she is destined to change in. She is already changing; she could feel it since the moment the intoxicated fog began lifting. Maybe Cole was right, maybe she was drugged. The anger that she feels toward Opi she has never felt for anyone before. She can't help but feel angry towards Cole as well – only that anger is different and not even remotely comparable. Her chest aches with resentment towards these men and in mourning for her old life. Suddenly Murdina barges into her room without knocking.

"Out of bed wi' ye," she pulls the blankets right off her. "Ye canna lay in bed all day. Breakfast, then off to practise." Vera lays silent, another memory floats amongst the waves of her conscious.

"What is D?" she asks Murdina, she remembers her father telling her to ask this in order to find out whom to trust. Though she herself has no clue what 'D' even is.

Murdina eyes Vera intensely, unblinking. Then suddenly a wide smile spreads across her wrinkling face, "Deneen," she whispers.

Vera gasps. It's her middle name.

"Now, practise," Murdina repeats, "Ye will not pursue a thing if ye dinna practise."

"Why? How?" Vera asks.

Murdina squeezes her hand, "Not so many questions. Practise"

Vera simply nods, stilled in shock and wonderment. Though she isn't sure why or how Hendrix could've passed on this information to a Tagondian, especially on to Murdina, she realizes that it was a wise strategy on his part – he knew Vera's struggle in trusting people. He knew that only those she trusts know her middle name. *Who would have thought such significance could come from such a terrible name.*

Now feeling more confident in Murdina, she focuses on Murdina's instructions – if she doesn't practise, she won't get better. If she is going to force justice upon Opi for Hendrix's death, she needs to practise.

Vera dresses and when she enters the kitchen and sees Opi she freezes. Her eyes fixate on him, a twinge of adrenaline courses through her veins. A twitch shoots through her neck. She glances about the room; the pan on the stovetop looks promising. She envisions herself grabbing the pan and colliding it with the shine on his bald skull. She scoffs at the vision, pulling herself free from it. It is the first violent daydream she's ever had. Shivers creep up her spine and across her neck.

"What is it lass?" Murdina asks. It is then when Vera realizes her scoff sounded itself outwardly, for all to hear.

"Oh nothing, I… it's my neck, it's bothering me." Sure, she could ask Opi what D is, but in the end his answer won't change her desire to seek justice upon him. In the end, he still killed her father.

"Botherin' ye?"

"Yeah, it's fine though."

"Then get food in yer belly and off wi' ye," Murdina scolds.

"Yes," Vera agrees, she needs to get outside – to get away from Opi and collect her thoughts.

^

It isn't long before Vera grows tired of the repetition of aiming, throwing and retrieving the axes, evidently ending up with blisters on her hands. *Is completely missing the target considered failing?* She is pretty certain the answer is *yes* – and that isn't an option. Even still, she persists, all-the-while the sadness in her heart remains; though as time passes it's size and shape will shift and morph into different complexities. In this moment in time it is substantially large with frustration towards the axe, which then grows into anger. She feels defeated and throws the axe to the ground, turns around and runs right into a mass – Cole. Their bodies collide, nearly causing the both of them to fall to the ground if not for Cole's sturdy reaction in quickly catching her. A thudding heart from a scare like that is standard she reminds herself.

"Whoa, someone scares easy," he laughs with a deep but breezy chuckle.

"Yes, well," she jerks her arms out of his gentle grasp and clears her throat, "perhaps your persistence scares me. The nerve one must have to continue showing up unannounced, unwanted." Cole puts his hands up in a sort of 'caught-red-handed' manner, but ultimately it comes across more so as an innocent 'because I'm so goddamn handsome' sort of way. He is and Vera knows it, this only angers her more.

"I had no idea," a smirk rests upon his face.

"It is a real pleasure to clear that up for you," she says. He bites his lip as a crease forms across his forehead. He takes a breath and his eyes shift to sincerity. She watches his sudden change and looks away.

"Vera," he pleads. "This isn't the you I remember meeting that day at the lake."

*That's what this is? A 'you're not who I thought you were' conversation?* She wants no part of it.

"One day you'll understand the significance of not placing expectations on people," she responds coolly and shifts her body with clear intentions to walk away. His hand grazes her wrist as it has many times during their short correlations, willing her to stay – she freezes.

"Listen, I know the other day was a bad start. Give me another chance," he says. She listens to the softness in his voice – it is patient and kind. She can't decide what she hates more, the fact that he won't get as angry as she, or that there is a longing that dances among the edges of his voice, as if that longing can somehow hold her accountable for who she was then versus who she feels like now. Maybe she just wants revenge on him for standing her and Lidia up, but that is childish and she is better than that – she decides that she doesn't care enough to consider doing that.

"Cole, you don't need chances. You need to mind your own damn business," she retorts, all the while she can't believe the words that continue to sound off her lips – she can't believe how good they feel to express too. Like metal arrows that shoot through flesh like bullets. *Does it hurt, Cole?* She meant it as an insult, but to her dismay he laughs so hard it comes from deep within his gut. Her father once said: "One cannot resist to laugh at the sight of another laughing." Vera had never experienced that revelation – until now. Come to think of it, even in the limited time she has been in his presence, she hasn't seen someone as humoured as Cole so often is. She resists with all of her willpower, but to her disdain a measly smile slips across her lips. She hopes he doesn't notice. He doesn't comment on it.

Instead, he says: "You know what I think? You're a funny one, Vera of Insignificant Cannelle."

"It amazes me that your brain has the capacity to register anything beyond killing and eating. However, sadly, it can't tell the difference between a joke and an insult," evidence of the smile long gone, pursed lips replace its curve. She catches sight of his eyes and something tightens in her chest. She ignores it. She reminds herself why she despises him, otherwise she might accidentally let slip a choke of laughter at how maddening he makes her feel. But she does despise him as well as all of his ill-humoured jokes. How can she get rid of him this time? Telling him to leave, insulting him and not accepting his help all prove useless so far. Perhaps it's time for Vera to find a different, quieter place to practise. She turns to disengage, heading for the house.

"Okay, well, I'll see you tomorrow," he says casually and presumptuously.

"You probably shouldn't count on it," she notes, walking away while looking down to inspect her blisters.

"That wasn't a question, I'll definitely be seeing you tomorrow," he chuckles, as if in pleasure of her torment. Vera, still with lips pursed, neither looks back nor responds.

^

The next morning Master Regan sounds the combat call – Vera only knows its cry because Murdina told her that it would one day demand her. She makes her way down the footpaths, Murdina saunters closely behind her and they head for the colony centre. The Tags engulf her with their putrid scent and she wiggles her nose uncomfortably. Their hair long, and wild. Hers still sits, tied back in a bun behind her head; in her mind she is still a Kalian. The Tags gather around the colony centre, looking to their Master for guidance.

Rimmy begins pushing pairs into the centre, his hand immediately reaches for Vera and he flings her body in. *Great.* It is her first ever combat call and she hasn't had an opportunity to watch one beforehand to know what to expect. Vera stands face-to-face with her opponent as Rimmy fills the circle with several duos. She doesn't know her opposer by name, but the girl's slender frame isn't all that intimidating.

"Get your weapons, Bruisers," Rimmy shouts. Vera glances around, a dizzying feeling overcomes her, as if she's in a dream. She attempts to solidify her balance and then makes her way over to the weapons. She retrieves a club because she doesn't intend on truly hurting anyone on this day, especially not the likes of this friendly-looking Tagondian girl.

The pairs take to their spots once again, weapons in hand. A slight unease rushes through her body as she glances at the glint of the sword that her combat partner has chosen. Rimmy blows the first whistle. Vera, having no clue what it means, looks about for any indication on what to do.

As her opponent bends slightly in an awkward looking position, the girl calls to her: "Psst," to get Vera's attention. Vera looks to her and says nothing, still confused. "Combat stance, like this," the girl instructs, demonstrating with her elbows up, weapon out from her body, bent legs and feet apart. Vera is instantly so very grateful for the instruction and attempts to mimic her opponent, however awkwardly.

Without another thought, two more blows of the whistle sound and movement breaks out around her. She is stunned and looks about the colony centre, watching as Tag after Tag begins battling their opponents. She is lucky, at least her opponent doesn't seem to be like that. Vera shifts her gaze to her opponent who is charging toward her and swings her sword with great purpose. Vera gapes at her partner, but it doesn't bring her movements to a halt. Vera dodges her partner's swing by bending her legs and crouching down in a hurry – the blade soars overtop her head.

"What the hell!" she calls out. The girl's eyes look different than they did just moments ago, before the two whistles sounded – her hazel eyes squint slightly and are filled with fire now. Her mouth forms into a grimace as she moves toward Vera, swinging her sword once again. Vera doesn't know how to fight – she's never been given a lesson. However, instinctively, she brings her club up and holds it out in front of her as if it's a shield, though she knows there is no way it will prevent that sword from reaching her. Still, she has to try. She must ignore the way her stomach has dropped and threatens its acid, or the way her club trembles in her hands.

The girl lunges at Vera again, this time pressing the blade against Vera's arm, Vera is lucky that the flat edge of the sword is what makes contact. Still, Vera stumbles in her step, but her arms swing the club back up in front of her torso and she bends her legs.

"I don't want to hurt you," she whispers to the girl.

"You won't," the girl says as she swings at Vera, marking the tiniest slice across the back of her hand. A line of red appears instantly. Vera gasps then returns to combat stance and begins jerking her club back and forth. Surely if she is fast enough the girl's sword won't get past her club. In the flash of a second the girl charges at Vera and knocks her backwards, Vera crashes onto her bottom. The girl holds her sword up to the edge of Vera's throat, there she freezes. Just then, Rimmy blows the whistle to signify that this round of combat is over. At the flick of a switch the girl's face begins to smooth out; there is no more grimace, no more life-threatening stares. Instead, she smiles at Vera a most pleasant smile - almost as though she is an entirely different person - and reaches out to help Vera stand up.

"You definitely have got some work to do, Kalian," the girl says as she pulls Vera up, and then walks off. Vera stands speechless, her gaze shifts to Rimmy. An evil stare possesses his face, one that is enough in and of itself to knock her back on her ass.

# 16

# ATTICUS OF FAVOURED NORTH
# KALA

Three short whistles sound in Kala upon sunrise; the citizens dress themselves and make their way to The Pit. The fire is burning hot, tickling the immediate Favoured seats with its warmth. Smoke bellows up into the air creating a thick mass of grey fog. Atticus sees Master Oberon standing beyond the fire as he always does, awaiting the arrival of his people. He is dressed in a makeshift cloth, a triangle that hides his groin and bottom and hangs down to his knees. The cloth is embroidered and beaded in an intricate design. The shape of an animal is stitched in the centre, an eagle, to represent freedom and courage – to represent Oberon of Favoured Kenoak. He is shirtless, with the exception of his fur scarf, which rests across his shoulders with his Favoured Kenoak crest placed contentedly upon it. The silver metal with an eagle carved into it stares back at Atticus as he takes his seat.

Musical ones sit off to the side of Master Oberon as they bang makeshift drumsticks – sticks wrapped in a cloth at their ends with some type of animal skin stretched across the hand-carved wooden base. Their thumps create a steady beat that fills The Pit with echoes, almost like a metronome, adding in an extra beat every fourth boom. Atticus, still exhausted from his slumber - one that was not nearly long enough - begins closing his eyes, begging for more sleep. It is still dark out and he worked late the previous night tirelessly aiming to catch up on household chores at Favoured North.

"You're not sleeping, are you?" Illandra asks as she sits down beside Atticus.

He opens his eyes wide in surprise, "Oh, hi. No, I'm not. Well, not anymore," he says groggily. He raises his hands straight above his head in a stretch.

"Sorry to wake you. I saw you over here, so I thought I'd sit with you. Not to mention, you're close by the fire."

"Have a seat," he sleepily beams. Illandra gazes into the flames of the fire in silence. He watches her, staring at the dainty curves of her profile – the way the bridge of her nose barely protrudes outwardly and how it smoothly turns downward ending in a tiny, round bend, like a button. He sighs, *She's beautiful in this light – in any light really.* If only he could tell her. She shuffles in her seat, a reminder that he needs to look away now. He turns his head in a hurry, then worries that it was too sudden, too drastic of a movement that she's noticed.

He clears his throat, "So uh… what do you think about these gatherings?" he asks her, breaking the silence.

"What, Coakai?"

"Yeah…"

"It helps bring the rain… So… I like them I suppose. The rain is a good thing, remember?" she responds playfully.

"You think it works though?" he asks her, disbelieving himself, but still intrigued by her opinion.

"It has not failed us yet. Prayer to Mother Earth helps all things. Why, what do you think about it?"

"I think it's good if you like to see The Master in nothing but a skirt," Atticus admits. Though he is serious, he presents his thought as a joke.

Illandra giggles and leans over giving him a gentle slug to his arm with her shoulder, "Stop it. Come on, what do you really think?" she pleads.

Atticus bites his lip in thought, "To be honest, I don't know what I think." The drums increase in sound and speed, they always amp up right before The Master begins. They slow and quiet to a light hum as soon as everyone is sitting.

"With the earth," Master Oberon announces to the people. The people nod in the wake of his words, though not one soul speaks. Normally, the people are the ones that bow to The Master, but not for Coakai. Coakai is different – it's Master Oberon's turn to demonstrate his respect to his people, and to his Earth. The air is so quiet that it feels thick, as if in order to speak and be heard one would need the loud sound waves of the drums to break through its density. And yet, somehow, an owl coos nearby, his song heard perfectly from up amongst the trees where he must be sitting. The fire crackles and pops of amber fly out from the center of the pit and onto the ground beside it.

Master Oberon continues: "It is the dawn of a new morning, and with this day we shall be cleansed. Let us pray to the Mother." All of the people lower their heads in a bow, as does Master Oberon. He brings his hands up, palms touching one another in a prayer stance, and he recites his prayer for all to hear: "Dear Mother Earth, we pray to thee. We pray in love and gratitude, but also in fear and longing. We pray for a shift in your atmosphere, for a change in your tides. We pray for your temperatures to regulate, for your rainfall to grace us. We pray for the health of your creatures and all other living things. We pray to be cleansed," he pauses a moment and ends the prayer in a routine closing, "With the Earth."

"With the Earth," the people recite in unison. The drums pick up once again, louder than before, as Master Oberon takes to his dance. His feet pound into the dirt, his arms flutter in soft, elegant lines and then he suddenly jerks in a series of quick movements. He reaches for two branches that lean up against a large rock to his right and lights them using the fire. He spins and tosses the flaming branches – catching them before they collide with the ground and snuff out.

Everyone watches in awe, anxiously awaiting the rainfall. Somehow, it has come every time he holds Coakai; Atticus still can't figure out how he does it. As Master Oberon throws the branches higher and farther up, they threaten to extinguish, but upon their descent the flames grow larger once again. He tosses the lit branches behind his back, under his legs and around his arms – catching them without fail every time. Every time, the people are fascinated.

"It works every time, Atticus. How can you be so skeptical?" Illandra whispers to him.

"I'm waiting for the time it doesn't," he simply replies. And there it came, almost as if to prove Atticus wrong – to shove his foot in his own mouth. The rain pours down in buckets, soaking each and every person. But no one minds that it bathes them – they are ecstatic. The second rainfall within a one-month window, such a thing hasn't happened in the past two years, so this is reason to be particularly happy. Master Oberon stands with his face pointing up to the sky, his mouth wide in a gleeful grin and his arms agape in a welcoming embrace. He chuckles, his deep soulful song. In the background, the drums still quietly hum. The people rise to their feet and look to the sky, their hair flattens to their faces and their clothes are sopping wet.

Master Oberon shouts over the rain in a cry of joy, "You see? This is why we are here. This is why we survive. We are the ones to cleanse this Earth. She has chosen us."

# 17

# Vera of Insignificant Canelle Tagondo

The eastern phoebe begins its familiar two-syllable song at 6:15 the following morning. A satisfying feeling encases Vera's body, like a blanket, *home*. She is home – it has been all but a bad dream. She lifts the blankets and peers out the window; it is dark though she can see, without a doubt, the silhouette of a Rowan tree in front of her window. Satisfaction quickly turns into ache in her chest – she isn't home at all. Her green eyes well up with tears, a forest of anguish.

Already having seen things that no one person should have to see, how does one continue on? She isn't sure, but she knows it's pertinent that she fights her desire to flee back into her blankets; it's pertinent that she gets out of this bedroom. She decides that she will leave early this morning to target practise in quiet, before the sun comes out and before Cole shows up. She reminds herself that practising will help her with whatever she plans for Opi. Moreover, between Murdina invading her privacy and Cole sneaking up on her, she has no alone time. She desperately needs it – it's time to get her training moving and she thinks that practising on moving targets is the best way to do that – she chooses to ignore the warning that sparks in her stomach, the one that won't allow her to kill an animal. In a hurry, she gathers her things and gets dressed quickly in the dark, which proves to be difficult, but not impossible. The black pants and sweater should allow her to sneak down the footpaths unnoticed; it is important she isn't seen, for she doesn't want anyone to alarm Cole and have him come find her.

It has just finished raining after a long night and her boots make a sloshing sound against the sopping ground. She steps a little lighter so as to not stir any attention, it's too early to deal with Cole and she has no desire to meet anymore Tags.

Vera makes her way down the unfamiliar paths realizing in hindsight that it probably isn't a grand idea to wander them alone in the dark for the first time. Still, with the crooked axe in her blistered hands, she walks. It's peaceful here at this hour; only the odd bird is heard for miles. Vera isn't out in the dark for long before the sun slowly peeks up from the east, bringing with it the orange of a thousand fires. Vera wanders off the paths and into the forest.

*"Watch out for The X,"* the wind sows. *So, the whispers are here too. What is The X?* Vera thinks to herself and continues on, paying limited mind to the whispers.

Finally, she finds a spot that she deems appropriate to sit and watch the wild come to life. A robin circles the oak tree above her, landing on the ground and back up into the air in a hurry. She watches on knowing that it's in search of worms for its babies, she's willing to bet the nest is in the nearby oak tree. She sits, slumped against a tree, and though the ground is wet that isn't what bothers her, it's the weight of the realization that she is in unfamiliar territory. Though admittedly, being in this forest is the most she's felt like her old self, still, it isn't home.

Curiosity for how far away the Kala forest is and where the two forests connect crosses her mind. The forest would be the only way to get back home, but why would she escape the place where Hendrix's murderer resides before dealing with him? She can't go back home anyway. As the sun continues to rise, along with it comes its warmth. April is significantly warmer than the March mornings had been. Vera decides to move deeper into the forest. She soon approaches a row of trees with X's carved into them at eye level. She wonders if this could be what the whispers were referring to, so she decides to continue forward and walks toward The X's on high alert.

She hears a scuffing across the ground before someone speaks, "Hey, V," a high voice comes from behind her. She turns to see who it is.

"Oh, Lincoln. With the earth," she says.

"Hmm? Where are you off to?" he asks. Something about him seems different. His hair, she notes, is evidently shorter, though just as ridiculous looking as it was at their first meet. She decides it must be his hair.

"I'm just practising," she says, though she feels slightly leery being alone with him out here, his mischievous gaze still lingers upon her the way it had at the lake.

"Well, the best place to practise is there," he says as he points toward the trees marked with the 'X's.' The wall of trees that are marked sit a few feet to her right, she looks beyond them and can see neither poisonous plants nor signs of mammoth wolves. There is, however, a tiny stream with a tree that has been knocked down resting over the water like a bridge – she decides that it seems safe enough to head in that direction.

"Great, thanks," she responds.

"Anytime," he smirks. "I'll be seeing you around," he calls as he turns and walks in the opposite direction.

Vera suddenly blurts: "Don't tell Cole."

Lincoln turns back around, "Tell Cole what?"

"That you saw me out here," she explains.

A smile stretches across his mouth into a thin curve, "You don't have to worry about that." She nods and turns toward her destination, thankful for her seclusion once again as she decides to sit by the stream.

Vera listens to the pleasant gurgle of the moving water, which is low for this time of year; a rising concern over the past century. Less snow, less water and warmer global temperatures: if only her ancestors had seen it decades beforehand. Meadowsweet sits just down the stream, which is a pleasant surprise. Vera wanders over to the plant to gather a bouquet of the bright pink flowers and as she bends down something flies past her head – it makes an odd airy sound. *What on earth?* She ponders. There is no sign as to what made the funny noise. So, Vera continues picking the meadowsweet. She hears another swoosh – only this time the something grazes her hair. *Pesky bugs,* she thinks, with warmer temperatures they come out earlier now. While she moves her hand in a swat-like motion to shoo away any possible insects, another swoosh sounds and this time Vera has no opportunity to react before a sharp edge grazes her hand, making her drop the bouquet. A metal arrow burrows itself into the ground beside her foot. She freezes.

A twinge gurgles in her stomach, is it a bad thing that she is camouflaged with the shadows of the forest? It's still dusk and easy for her to blend in with the dark tree trunks. Worry fills her, if she is to stay put she may very well face an arrow burrowing itself somewhere other than the ground. In a flash she drops her body down to the ground and begins crawling toward a wide tree. Another arrow zooms past her, cutting through her shirt and braising the skin on her left arm. A cry of pain leaves her mouth, for her arm instantly burns.

"*Move,*" she hears a voice whisper – a warning for her to escape before she becomes a puddle of blood. She moves her limbs in sync and as fast as she possibly can. It seems as though she is a part of a race, a kind that she has never encountered before, an unfair kind of race – for she is being pursued.

Vera reaches the wide tree with heavy breaths expelling from her chest – it feels as though she can't get enough air into her lungs. She ponders if she could be losing too much blood, while also realizing that she knows next to nothing about the body and its extremities. She pushes herself up against the tree and prays to Mother Earth that the metal arrows can't get through a tree as thick as the one she is leaning on. She places her hand over the slice in her arm, wincing in pain. Touching it only makes it sting more, and now her hand is covered in blood from her wounds; however, the slice on her hand is minor in comparison to her arm. Her eyes widen at the red liquid, the very sight of blood sends her into a spiral of panic. Her body begins to vibrate uncontrollably: *Maybe this is it*, she thinks. *Maybe this is where I die.*

# 18

# Cole of Favoured Pollard
# Tagondo

The air feels slightly damp following a rainfall in early spring – but the rising temperature of the Earth's crust only allows that dampness to linger until the sun appears over the horizon. It is a happy time when the rain comes; it fills the empty buckets that sit alongside the exterior of houses with water and with hope. Tagondo holds Defenders responsible for dispersing the water – just because one collects it, doesn't mean the water is rightfully theirs - after all, water is more valuable than Old World gold - Cole has seen Tagondians get killed over the smuggling of the resource. It's expected that Master Regan will plan another surprise probe. Though the probes operate weekly, they will take place twice this week seeing as the rain came for them.

The probes are intrusive inspections whereby Rimmy ventures door-to-door with a handful of other Defenders. They enter homes unannounced and tear the insides apart until all is a heaping mass upon the floor. It's inconvenient, but it's the norm for the Tagondians. Although Cole doesn't see the reason for the mess, he understands how vital it is to share the water resources. However, that doesn't change his worry on Master Regan being responsible for governing those resources, though, he cannot act on these concerns.

He walks the paths in the early morning, heading for Insignificant Cannelle to meet with Vera for practise. He thinks about how he'll wrangle her today – to make her cooperate with him. It isn't as though he is expecting her to be a pushover, he just wants her to listen to his instructions – to make his job a little easier, or at least give him a fighting chance at succeeding. But how can he say that, without telling her that it's his assigned job from Murdina? *It's already enough of a challenge to train a Kalian how to pursue, let alone one with the attitude of a lioness*. At least he has experience with haughty women – Nin is the queen-of-haughty, Treena too. If he can handle them, surely he can handle Vera. Maybe he needs to simply view her as an animal, stubborn and fearful. However, animals are meant to be hunted or kept as pets. He reconsiders that comparison.

His knuckles press upon the front door of Insignificant Cannelle in brief taps, Murdina answers immediately.

"Cole, what are ye doin'?" she asks with a concerning look upon her aging face.

"I came for Vera."

"The lass is not here. I thought she was wi' ye."

"She's not with me. I haven't seen her since yesterday – after she stormed off heated," he recalls briefly humoured. "She must be sleeping still. I'll go wake her – she'll love that."

"She's not here, I've already checked," Murdina says, her eyes slowly widening in concern.

"Oh shit," Cole says as his body simultaneously turns and darts down the stairs towards the footpaths.

"Ye must find her, or she'll be Tagondian meat," Murdina shouts, her raspy voice following him down the path. "Remember, she's a scientist – one of the few who can cleanse the water!"

Cole's legs launch his frame through the trees as fast as they can muster. He doesn't know where exactly Vera is, but the first place anyone would go for pursuing training would be The X. Therefore, he needs to rule it out first and foremost. She doesn't know her way around Tagondo yet, and if she enters The X unprepared, unaware of the possible dangers she'll end up hunted – she'll end up dead. His concerns aren't fleeting ideas that blow in from the seeds of the wind, after seeing Vera's combat call with Finara the other morning, his concerns are sound as the very earth he stands upon.

His chest huffs as he runs, though in the grand scheme it is effortlessly done. Cole is in immaculate shape, which isn't a surprise for a typical pursuing Tagondian; perhaps it's his physical capability that encourages his lack of fear. And yet, fear seems to prick at his chest as he runs. He knows why though, *What if I'm too late?* He does not want to fail at the only thing Murdina has ever really asked of him – the only thing that seems to place some form significance and also excitement upon his time in Tagondo. To him, being the Mammoth Slayer is trivial, hardly worth anything at all. But, Vera is a scientist and who knows what good she can be for the water – for The Almek.

19

# Oberon of Favoured Kenoak
## Kala

"The all merciful Mother Earth has answered our prayers again!" Oberon exclaims later that day, following Coakai.

"It is baffling, each time it happens… I do not understand your grace," Quim adds.

"It is not a thing that needs understanding. It is merely a thing in which needs celebrating," Oberon suggests.

"And celebrate we did," Hogard responds.

Quim clasps his hands together in satisfaction, "Yes, I think they rather liked this Coakai. The rain plundered down in large deposits… It's incredible one person can encourage Mother Earth to create such things."

"Isn't it though?" Oberon beams his genuine ear-to-ear smile, "It feels good to be just exactly what this colony needs, what Mother Earth needs."

"That has always been the case your grace," Hogard compliments.

Oberon and his three Barons sit upon their chairs in The Master's chamber, it's the place in which their daily meetings are held and laws are enforced among other meanderings of the colony. Master Oberon chooses to sit upon the same plastic chairs as the rest of the colony – after all there really is no grave distinction between him and his people in terms of behaviour and appearance. Oberon has a contagious energy about him, it draws people to him and he knows it. Any leader would use that to their advantage.

"Must we count the barrels of water?" Martil asks.

"Yes, as usual, we will have Huron run a count," Master Oberon states, "but as always, we will allow the people to keep what they have so collected – that doesn't change."

"Are you sure your grace?" Martil urges.

"Martil, we may be nearing the end of our fresh water supply from the aquifer… that knowledge hasn't phased me. However, I am quite confident in our scientists… they will pull through for us. Besides, taking from the people in a time like this is… not just," Master Oberon calmly explains.

"They don't yet know about the aquifer coming to a shortage," Quim reminds him.

Master Oberon nods in agreement, "You're right, and we must keep it that way a little while longer. Taking their rainwater supplies will only cause panic. We don't want that."

"I urge you to take control while you still can," Hogard warns.

"We are not takers. When have I ever tried to produce such a mindset within this colony? Not once. The moment we insist on taking is the moment we lose all control. We have their love, their admiration and most importantly their trust," Oberon reminds the room.

"How will we keep those things if we can't supply them with enough safe drinking water?" Martil asks.

"You know that all must trust in me, the vessel which communicates with Mother Earth to supply us with rain. And I know that we must trust in our scientists to cleanse the spring water. There is nothing more that needs considering," Oberon states.

"Very well your grace," Martil nods her head in acceptance.

"But what will we do in order to keep the people on that wavelength?" Hogard asks.

"Hmm, yes. We must do something…" Master Oberon pauses, "Something to keep them hopeful and distracted."

"A gathering maybe? A communal dinner?" Martil offers.

"Precisely. Let us meet for a group prayer to Mother Earth. A prayer and a dinner – unity always brings about desirable feelings and behaviours."

# 20

# VERA OF INSIGNIFICANT CANNELLE TAGONDO

Footsteps - fast footsteps - are getting closer and coming for her.

"Just please, make it quick," she pleads quietly to Mother Earth. It won't be all that bad, dying right now. They say in death there is no pain – she can get on board with that idea.

"Make it quick? Vera, what the hell are you doing out here?" Cole shouts at her while catching his breath. *Cole?* He instantly notices the blood and a look of terror sweeps across his face. He swiftly bends down to get a closer look at her, his eyes pierce into hers and then begin scanning over her body intently. Suddenly, a falling tree branch lands nearby with a heavy thud; she throws her arms over her head to protect herself.

"Hey, it's alright," he says calmly, then quickly rips a piece of cloth off of his shirt and wraps it around her arm in an attempt to lessen the bleeding.

After some time, she pokes her head up and out of the enclosure of her arms – she can see no more falling branches from where she sits. Was it a hallucination? She glances around and up at the tree that she's leaning against, for confirmation, which makes her realize that no branches have fallen after all. She turns to Cole and his handsome face looks genuinely concerned. But if she imagined the tree branch falling, is she imagining him too? She reaches out a trembling, blood-covered hand and touches his face – he is most definitely not a hallucination.

"Umm, are you alright?" Cole asks with curiosity, his eyes gleaming over her reddened hand.

"Yes, but your face isn't…" she says as she pinches her lips together as a means to hold back a sudden sense to laugh.

He brings his hand up to his face and wipes the red smudges off of his cheek, "It's alright, I'm used to blood," he replies through a raised eyebrow.

"Well that's not concerning."

"Animal blood I mean – not human blood," he clarifies with a chuckle, "But let's leave the finger painting to the children. Okay?" A goofy grin possesses his face. She laughs, letting her head roll back, her laughter echoes off of the trees.

Without notice, Cole scoops her up in one stealthy movement and begins walking. She feels loose, lightheaded even, perhaps from blood loss, though she doesn't think she's lost that much. She glances at Cole and notes the light on his face; his eyes are amongst the shadows and appear darker than usual, but his lips and jaw are touched by the light of the morning. It is a pleasant sight.

He looks at her, his expression tense, "What were you doing out here anyway?"

"I came to pursue," she says shakily.

"I told you I was going to teach you. There are rules out here that can either save your life or get you killed if you don't follow them. This place isn't about picking flowers and berries – you could've been killed."

"I didn't know."

"You would've known if you listened."

"You should have told me. Perhaps even one of the first things you should have mentioned upon seeing me," she mimics his deep voice: "You know Vera, the forest is a death trap so whatever you do – don't go there."

He smirks slightly and then shrugs his shoulders, "Yeah, maybe. But somehow I don't think you would've listened anyway."

"Perhaps not."

"How about a *thank you*?" he says after a moment.

"What?"

"A thank you for rescuing you," he adds while nimbly carrying her across his forearms.

"Thank you. But to clarify: you didn't rescue me – you inadvertently came to share prudent information with me that you neglected to tell me upon my arrival. That is hardly a rescue. Some mentor…"

"You are the most difficult woman I have ever met. You know that?" he laughs and shakes his head. She breathes in what she identifies as a citrus scent.

"Why, because you can't boss me around? Can't force me to kill an innocent animal?" she asks.

Playfully shocked by her tempered response he replies: "Uh, no. Because you're a stubborn Kalian."

"We are not stubborn."

"Maybe the rest of them aren't, but you…"

Vera cuts him off and her voice raises above a chatter, "I what?"

"Well, maybe in Kala you're the genius that gets to treat people like shit, but here you're fresh meat baby. You best learn to listen if you don't want to be devoured."

Anger rises inside of her, "Put me down." She squirms in his grasp.

"Why? Don't like being told how it is?" he states. She sits in silence, unsure of what bothers her more: his obnoxious nature or his nerve to assume he has her all figured out.

Finally she speaks again: "Put me down I said!"

"Relax, you need to go to the hospital to get fixed up."

"I'm fine, let me go," she wiggles and tosses, but his strong arms are unyielding in their hold of her.

"It's not that much further – you'll get your stitches and then you can go on your merry little way," he explains. So, there she dangles: four feet above ground and against her own will.

Anger tempts her while feeling unsure of what her next move should be – this is an unprecedented situation. In all of her years she has neither been spoken to in such a manner, not even by a Favoured, not directly at least, nor has she been picked up and thrown around by the likes of an ill-mannered man. Surely Hendrix would be shaken to his core if he knew the kind of defective man she's interacting with.

Vera's eyes dart to his face with an intention to scorn him with her glare, but his eyes are still set in the shadows, his lips still highlighted by the yellowed rays of the sun sending both confusion and intrigue through her head. Aside from his handsome appearance, every other possible quality this man has drives her nuts. The noise that comes out of those lips is maddening. Her ears begin ringing. She decides then that she wants nothing more to do with him. The rest of the walk to the hospital is quiet; several people pass by them on the footpaths, all seeming to be less unkempt than Cole. She feels a sense of disgust at each of their appearances – they all greet Cole with envious, welcoming eyes while not a single one acknowledges her, the newcomer.

Still, she wonders, *What it is about Cole that has everyone so enamoured? It barely even phases him.* Furthermore, the lack of greetings to her burns her behind, mainly because the Kalians always welcome newcomers from Tagondo. Granted, with caution, but always with a smile – no matter how phoney of a smile it is. It's always interesting to see a Tagondian move to Kala, it's a rare occurrence since most birthing ceremonies are won by the Tagondians as their training is far-superior.

It's surreal for her to be in Tagondo, to be within arms reach of the citizens whom she was taught from a young age to dislike. To some degree the Kals have always been right on their presumptions of the Tags. Vera can remember her curiosity as a child: wondering what it would be like on the other side of the lake. She imagined groups of kids playing together, running free – their classes were outside all the time. The kids in her mind were friendlier than the Kal children – who were snobbish brats when their parents weren't around. What young Vera would have given to see the other side… But the curiosity and imagination of a child will only run wild for so long, it didn't take much time before she recognized it for what it was. She was about eight when she stopped daydreaming and concerning herself with Tagondian life.

Finally, they make it to the hospital: a small log building ran by the head Doctor, Dr. Yani. Cole carries Vera in and the young nurse on shift greets them with a smile.

"With the earth," Vera begins while still in Cole's arms. The two glance at Vera quizzically.

The nurse shifts her focus to Cole then, "Cole, everything alright?"

"Well Mae, you're not gonna believe this but newb here went out into the forest and lets just say they thought she was a deer," he explains. Vera initially scowls at Cole for having shared the details of her embarrassing venture; Cole humorously ignores her sideways glare.

She can't let it go and so before she knows it her mouth is moving again, "It's silly, I know, seems I had no one to properly inform me and show me around."

Possibly sensing the tension, or entirely clueless to it, Mae chimes in: "Oh dear, here. Come this way," Mae leads them to a room with a small bed in it. There is a table with alcohol and clean cloths, among other things set out. Cole places Vera on the bed.

"You can go now, I'm fine," Vera says. Mae pulls Cole out of the room to speak with him. Vera watches as they stand just outside of the door, though she is straining to hear them. Mae, with her lovely stark blond hair and sweet demeanour, rests her hand on Cole's arm. Cole doesn't brush it off, if anything it appears as though he moves in closer to Mae. Vera sighs to herself and looks away. She decides instead to examine the room: the lighting is dim and there are no windows for natural light. The walls are bare, making the room feel even smaller than it is, though the dim light of a lamp casts a yellow glow in the corner, offering some warmth to the barren interior.

Vera hears Mae let out a carefree giggle, which sounds like an eastern phoebe serenading them with her sweet song. Well, not them – Cole. Vera's cheeks grow hot, but why? She deems there to be no rational reason to be jealous, Cole is not of interest to her. Through the log walls Vera hears playful screams carry on outside – the kids do run wild here, that is one thing she did foresee. Mae enters the room and it appears that Cole has left.

"Hi, Vera. So, what do we have here?" Mae's golden eyes contrast with her blond ringlets. Her features are round and beautiful. Vera explains to Mae what happened, leaving out a few of the more embarrassing details. Mae gives Vera a swig of corn whiskey - her first taste of alcohol - she gags in disgust at the bitterness of the drink. She wonders how on earth her mother has a liking to it.

After a series of cautioned movements, and sharp intakes of breath from Vera, Mae finishes stitching up Vera's arm. Vera glances down at Mae's crest: a silver daffodil, which signifies to Vera that their nurses are considered Favoured in Tagondo as well, just as in Kala.

"You need to keep it clean Vera. Does Murdina have whiskey at home?" Mae asks.

Realizing Mae already knows where she lives, Vera wonders then what else she knows about her.

"I'm not sure-" Vera begins.

"Yes," Cole pops his head inside the doorway, "She's Scottish, she definitely has whiskey." Vera lets out a sigh of frustration for she thought she was free of Cole's nagging presence. "How'd it go? She going to live to see another day?" Cole chortles. Mae giggles while Vera rolls her eyes.

"Yes, she's going to be just fine. She's a tough cookie," Mae smiles at Vera, "But no more going into the pursuing grounds by yourself – it's not safe there." Vera purses her lips and tries to force a smile, though she is pretty sure she can smile more genuinely than she is. Actually, she knows she can.

"Alright then, thank you Mae for your help," Vera says as she stands and walks toward the door.

"Oh, Vera," Mae calls after her.

"Yes?"

"Welcome to Tagondo," Mae says with what sounds like sincerity.

Vera continues walking, "Thank you," she says over her shoulder as she scurries as fast as she can to exit the hospital. Mae's welcome stays in her mind, which she thinks was actually quite nice. Cole comes running out of the building and catches up to her in what feels like a single heartbeat.

"You could've been nicer to Mae, you know. She helped you out a lot. And she's right – you can't go to The X on your own, ever again."

"I was perfectly nice to Mae. If it wasn't her stitching me up, it would've been someone else."

"Not necessarily. Going back to the rules here – Master Regan has to approve every single hospital visit. The unnecessary use of hospital supplies is considered an offence. I've seen guys with their arms practically falling off and he didn't approve hospital access."

"What is the point in having the hospital then, if you guys don't use it?"

"We do use it. It's just, he makes the calls." Cole explains. *So that's what Cole and Mae spoke about in the doorway*, she reflects.

"So, how did you get Mae to agree to give me access?" Upon asking her question, Cole hesitates while looking off into the trees, away from her.

"Well, she doesn't mind doing me favours…" he replies, lowering his voice.

"Why? Are you and her close?" she mimics his quiet tone. Cole halts his speech as a Defender walks by, the man's tall, wide frame marches purposefully, as if he's on his way to something of significance. Cole nods his head to the Defender. Once he's out of sight Cole resumes the hushed discussion.

"Sort of, we used to be," he continues.

"What does that mean?

"We liked each other at one time…"

"I thought so," she proclaims.

"What?"

"Nothing, it was obvious. You two appeared to be quite cozy in there."

"Me? No. I don't do cozy – don't want to face tribulation," he establishes.

"She sure seems to do cozy," Vera remembers the way Mae's hand rested on Cole's arm. It was too sensual of a gesture to be considered simply friendly. Though what does she know about amorous relations? "I think it's for the best you know – that The Masters ruled out sexual relations until merging," she continues.

"Why?" he asks, his fiery gaze provoking her, she turns away.

"Though I don't agree with all of the laws… this law controls the population. Think of how many poor women have ended up pregnant in the history of humankind: pregnant without a home, without a partner to help care for the baby, perhaps even pregnant without wanting to be. This law… it controls the population. And another bonus is that it helps to ensure babies are loved," Vera says as she feels like a mere shadow of Hendrix.

"I know all of that – I have a sister. It's a good point though – babies being loved. But women are still forced to reproduce in this world, even if they don't want to."

"And it makes me sick to my stomach," she admits, speaking louder than she means too.

"Shh," he reminds her, "Why? You don't want a family?"

"No. I don't."

"How could you not? We need family… what will you leave behind?"

"I have my younger brother to care for – that's enough for me," she answers his question coolly.

"According to The Masters, he is no longer your brother."

"He will always be my brother. That will never change."

"I guess you're happy to be out of your merge agreement then?" Cole inquires.

"Thank Mother Earth I got out of it. It was cancelled due to my re-birthing. Which is the one good thing to come from that dreadful experience."

"Would you have gone through with the merge agreement?"

"What sort of question is that? I had to – it was my duty. No matter how repulsed I was…" she admits. He nods his head as if somehow he understands exactly what she means. "So, how will I hide my stitches from The Masters?" she asks.

A woman walks by them with her infant in her arms; the baby boy must be no more than four months old. His head is rather full of hair for an infant his age, little tufts of strawberry blond blow in the breeze. She's distracted a moment, realizing she knows that baby – he came from Kala. His name was Fergus and he had belonged to Ingrid of Insignificant Tommel. Vera wonders where Lilith is then.

"Wear long sleeve shirts," Cole says reclaiming her attention, "A few weeks and you'll get the stitches taken out, it's not a big deal. I've done it – but only because I had to."

^

When they reach Insignificant Cannelle they are met with a tunnel of Defenders lined in front of the house. The door is wide open – Murdina and Opi are standing silently outside.

"What's going on?" Vera asks Cole as they approach the tiny house.

"Probes," Cole pauses a moment, he must assume Vera knows what this means. She looks at him with her eyes narrowed in asking and he seems to take that as a cue to explain further: "Master Regan probes the cabins once a week, especially after a rainfall - well Rimmy does - someone's got to do his dirty work, right?"

"He searches the houses? What on earth is he looking for?" she asks.

"The illegal holding of water… he's a slob about it though." Vera can see Murdina and Opi are still standing on the deck, waiting for the men to finish. The search doesn't appear to bother them.

"Is there anything I can do?" she finally asks Cole.

"Just wait here, they don't take long. We'll clean up afterwards." Cole is right, after a minute or so two Defenders walk out behind Lead Defender Rimmy.

As Rimmy tramples down the stairs he shouts, "Probe complete on Insignificant Cannelle." The redheaded Defender that follows closely behind Rimmy checks his list. Rimmy stomps down the footpaths toward the next cabin and the other Defenders follow behind him two by two. With the 'all-clear,' Vera enters in through the front door behind Murdina and Opi. The place is turned upside down: drawers and cupboards open and emptied onto the kitchen floor, mattresses flipped in the bedrooms, dressers and their contents thrown about.

"What have they done? This is a mess," Vera asks, shocked at the lack of care.

"Just another day in Tagondo," Opi reasons with a sigh.

"Tis not all that bad, get to work," Murdina mumbles as she begins putting the kitchen items back in their places.

"Once a week," Cole says as he walks in, "and never the same day twice in a row. The only exception to the law is when it rains."

"It's done at random?" Vera questions further.

"Aye," Murdina nods while slamming the forks and knives back into their drawer.

"That is awful. Murdina, what are they looking for, it can't just be water?" Vera asks with desperation to understand.

"Yer guess tis good as mine," Murdina responds.

"It's nothing. It's the way it's always been," Cole says.

Vera adds in thought, "There must be something aside from just the surplus water. Why flip the mattresses to look for water? It doesn't make sense. What can possibly fit below a mattress?"

Vera wonders what kind of colony ruler Master Regan is after all – as far as she can tell he is entirely different than Master Oberon. He is ruthless and inconsiderate – two characteristics a Master should never possess. But what does she know? Master Oberon has his flaws. Maybe that's all this is, just one of Master Regan's flaws. Still, something about the probes and Master Regan's logic doesn't sit right with her. In everything there is cause and effect. If the probes are an effect, what is the true cause for them?

# 21

## REGAN OF FAVOURED ADDER
## TAGONDO

Regan of Favoured Adder sits in his velvet armchair upon the platform in his chamber. Here he spends most of his days answering to Tagondian matters, no matter how grand or insignificant. His leading officials report to him daily and on this day the top concerning issue at hand is the massive amounts of rainfall that the colony barrels have collected. No one, in his mind, has more right to that water than he, and he has a strategy - the threat of exile - to keep the people honest.

He has put the probes in place to snuff out any deceit amongst the colony, whether it be by means of smuggling the depleting precious resource or otherwise. At his request, the barrels are made by the colony's welding ones out of iron or steel, whatever metals they can get their hands on, and these hold the rain water. Each household is given an allowance of one barrel to keep for themselves, beyond that one barrel the Defenders retrieve the surplus. Those who hide their own reserves, and keep more than allotted, are punished by exile. It is pertinent to Master Regan's dealings that regular citizens do not know the whereabouts of the additional barrels, and they have to accept that. Master Regan holds the water – which means he holds the power, and he plans to keep it that way. Although, there is something else that he'd like to get his hands on – something so valuable that it will change the ways of The Almek forever.

"Your grace," Rimmy enters with a bow.

"My Lead – has it been completed already?" Master Regan questions.

"Yes, with great success."

"How many barrels?"

"Three thousand two hundred full, and another one hundred thirty partial barrels."

"Excellent," Regan states. Rimmy stands still, his mouth forms a straight line – perhaps he has more to say. "Well? Get on with it," Regan impatiently instructs.

"There's one problem,"

Regan sighs, "What is it?"

"We have a smuggler."

"Is that so?"

"Yes."

"Who then? What pitiful soul could be so stupid as to-"

"Your daughter… sir," Rimmy clears his throat. Master Regan is silent for a moment, his fingers press against his lips in thought, while his other hand swirls his wine that sits thick in his glass.

"Does anyone else know?" he finally inquires.

"No one, your grace."

"Very well then. Bring her to me."

"What shall I do with her surplus?"

"Is it hiding? Where is it?"

"Yes, in her basement."

"How the hell did she get it down there?" Regan wonders out loud.

"Sir, the Defenders are at her beck and call – you know this."

Regan spits as his temper grows angry at her foul behaviour, "She's out of control!"

"What will you have me to do, your grace?" Rimmy asks.

"Just see to it that no one finds the surplus, I'll deal with her. Send her over right away."

"Yes, sir," Rimmy says as he bows and then takes leave. Amidst silence once again and left to his thoughts, Regan considers his options with Treena. She is growing increasingly rebellious in recent months – he doesn't know what has come over her. She is spoiled and he knows it: she begged for him to have a new cabin built for her and so she has her very own Favoured Adder cabin before she's even merged. But isn't it all too pleasing to offer one's child the things they did not have? Just then, the chamber door swings open and slams shut.

"Daddy. You called?" Treena waltzes in as if she owns the place.

"Treena, my dear. We must talk," he begins gently. She rolls her eyes, though she is twenty-four she still somehow acts like her actions don't have consequences. "The surplus you have been smuggling."

She moans, "What about it?"

"It is unacceptable. Use up the surplus that you have collected and ensure no one finds out about it."

"But, I don't want to run out of water. You don't even tell me where you keep the colony surplus."

"You mustn't know, because it is dangerous. The less you know the better."

"You tell the Defenders your secrets. You tell them more than you tell me!"

"You will one day know all there is to know about ruling Tagondo. Until that day comes you must stay in the dark," he explains, though he has told this to her many times. Treena turns toward the exit in a huff and pulls the door shut behind her with a blow. Regan downs his glass of wine and pours a fourth.

# 22

# TREENA OF FAVOURED ADDER TAGONDO

Treena leaves The Master's chamber in a heated rage. *How dare he try to tell me what to do.* As she charges through the colony centre she spots Cole – just the man she wants to see. Her eyes shrink into angry slits when she notices that he is walking with the Leech. *That bitch.* She heads straight for them, ready to slap that pretty face right off of her skull. But, to her dismay, and her joy, Vera turns down a different path, likely heading toward Insignificant Cannelle. Cole is all hers now; she lurches toward him.

"Hey Treen – whoa!" Cole is seemingly caught off guard as she grabs a fistful of his shirt and pushes him off the path, "W-What… what's up?" he stutters. Her jaw clenches as she slams his back up against a tree on the path's edge, out of sight but still visible if one looks from a certain angle. He releases a gasp of wind that's forced out of his lungs from the impact.

"Is everything-" he begins, but she stops him and forces her lips on his, hard and firm, pushing her tongue at him.

This is it, after all these years of her asking he's finally going to give himself to her; frankly, she is sick and tired of asking – she isn't asking anymore. She wants him so badly she'll just about devour him, like the way she often devours a pint of wine – thirsty and eager. But oh, it is satisfying; the way it causes her stomach to burn, her lips to tingle from the effects of the drink. As she kisses him she realizes that he too makes her lips tingle with heat. He is like a drug to her, a drug she's never been able to try. She kisses him harder, more desperately. Her fingers slither in such a way that they grasp onto his shirt, determined. She pulls then, tearing his shirt right off.

"Whoa, what the-" but she stops him from continuing by biting his tongue, "Ow!" he cries.

"You're mine," she warns him. He has stopped her before from kissing him – he won't get away with it this time, "I'm taking you."

An unknown voice speaks from behind them: "Treena, at least do this indoors." It's a Defender walking by, shaking his head as he leaves them. She can get away with anything she wants – she can get away with murder. But for now, she just wants sex.

Cole pushes her off of him then, "Treena, stop it."

"What?" she questions, panting.

"We can't do this. We have to wait until we merge – I don't want to be made an Offender."

"But you want me, you want this," she tells him.

"Just wait, it'll happen soon enough," he presses. Cole: always so noble, so level-headed.

Right now she doesn't need any of that, she's angry and wants someone to fill her and shake her until she isn't angry any longer. But fine, she can find someone else to satisfy her for now. She storms off without another word down the paths, her face flush in both anger and arousal – the two seem to go hand-in-hand for her. She can't believe Cole shot her down, as if she's just some Insignificant. He never treats her as though she is a Favoured - Favoured Adder at that - the family which rules the colony. Three long years in a merge agreement and he refuses to put his hands on her. *Why is it so hard to convince him?* It is easy to sway others – and she has, countless men. But Cole doesn't need to know about the others. She storms down the path, a lightning bolt of fury, ready to zap the first man in her path that will have her. There is something thrilling about breaking the laws her father has laid out for her. Each time is more thrilling than the last.

As if she planned it, she spots a familiar face, "Lincoln," she states indifferently.

"Treena, what's happenin'?" he asks as they approach one another.

In her tunnel vision she doesn't respond, not to offer a single word or explanation. She simply grabs him by his shirt and drags him down the path toward Favoured Adder – her house. They are not far and when they arrive she opens the front door and in one swift movement pulls Lincoln inside then slams the door.

"What are we doin'?" he questions, dumbfounded. Still in the front entryway, Treena raises her hands to the bottom edge of her shirt and pulls up, lifting it over her head and tossing it onto the floor. She unzips her pants and tears them off without a word. "Oh," Lincoln says as his voice rises in surprise.

"Take your clothes off," she orders as she leads him around a corner.

"Yes, ma'am," he says and he pulls his shirt and pants off in a hurried fashion. Treena smirks in knowing that he will be hers too. Lincoln slowly moves toward her, she places her hands on his bare chest and pushes him, forcefully, into the place that she wants him. Lincoln glances around nervously for a moment as he lands on her bed, and then brings his eyes back to focus on her, "Treena… you are smokin'," he says.

"Stop talking," she states, then rips his undergarments off. His face holds a satisfied grin that lets loose a moan when she settles, but this isn't for him. She moves as fast as she can, though she still feels the anger stewing inside of her – anger towards her father for keeping things from her and treating her like a child, anger towards Cole for turning her down and not giving into her desires. But she likes it, the knowing that she is doing exactly what she shouldn't be. Somehow it all seems to anchor her closer. Lincoln makes more noise which disturbs her focus, "Shut your fucking mouth," she breathlessly demands. He tries to move too, but she doesn't let him; instead, she pins him back down. His face looks ridiculous as he ogles over her, "You fucking idiot," she calls. Once she finishes, she gets up and begins gathering her clothes and putting them back on.

"Umm…" Lincoln begins.

"What?" she says, irritated.

"I didn't…"

"That's a shame."

"You're joking right?"

She crouches down in front of him, placing her face an arms-length away from his, "Does this face say I'm joking?"

"Well no, but-"

"Get the fuck out of my house before I tell The Master you fucked his daughter."

# 23

# Vera of Insignificant Cannelle Tagondo

Later that day, following the Probes, Murdina and Vera sit at the kitchen table having tea. It's odd how Vera has melded into the workings of Insignificant Cannelle fairly easily, but she tries not to think too much about that. She reminds herself that her father wanted her to trust Murdina, though, if he were here she would question him on it. There is something about Murdina, something mystifying. So, naturally, when Murdina chooses to discuss matters of Favoured Pollard, Vera listens – even if Cole is the last person she wants to reminisce over.

"Cole's maither, Dion, died back in the early days of The Motherland, she was a wonderful lass. His faither Burke has been ill for some time, goin' on three years now," Murdina explains.

"That's horrible. What's wrong with Burke?" Vera asks.

"They dinna ken. The man can barely walk. So Cole, the poor lad, meets shares for his family so they dinna face exile. Even though they are Favoured – Master Regan willna hesitate to get rid of those who dinna reach their shares."

"And yet he spends any extra time he may have, caring for you guys too?"

"Aye. The lad has got a heart of gold," Murdina says with a smile. A twinge pricks within Vera's chest. She has been horrible to Cole, and for what? He missed coming to the lake that one day? Vera didn't know that Cole has faced such struggles in his lifetime – he hides it well. She wonders then, *How does one appear so untainted by death, illness and pain and still care for others?* Vera sits in a trance with her thoughts.

"Tis a sad story, Princess," Murdina continues, tugging Vera from her thoughts, "all the more reason to be decent to him. Besides, us Cannelles are connected wi' the Pollards. Opi and Burke are close – Cole's always been a good lad to us, like a son."

"It's complicated. He's a… handful." Vera replies with caution.

"Aye, but so are ye," Murdina chortles, an open book when she wants to be. Vera shifts in her seat, moving in such a way that it makes her wince from the gash on her arm.

"What's the matter?" Murdina asks.

"Oh, nothing. I bumped into a tree this morning in the forest," Vera says. The more people she can avoid knowing that embarrassing story, the better. She wonders more about the story with Opi though – she still needs to figure out what she's going to do about that, but Vera is never one to make rash decisions, especially in the instance of life and death.

Murdina scoffs: "In the forest? Not The X?"

*Busted.* "Yes, The X."

"That boy is supposed to be watchin' ye."

"What do you mean?" Vera questions. The blue in Murdina's eyes shift back and forth nervously.

She hesitates as she speaks: "I wasna supposed to say that…He an' I… we have an agreement," Murdina states.

"What sort of agreement?"

"I've already said too much."

"Murdina? What agreement?"

Murdina inhales sharply and continues, "He is to protect ye, to keep ya alive, unharmed."

"I don't understand… I can take care of myself."

A scoff as loud as the hum of the kettle escapes Murdina's mouth, "Ye think that. All the more reason ye need him."

"I don't need him. Or anyone."

Murdina raises her eyebrows, "Tis a fool who believes such things." Vera shifts her arms, crossing them over her chest as she glances down upon the wooden grains of the table. Who is Murdina to tell her what she needs and should believe in? Vera has always taken care of herself.

^

One long, high-pitch call reverberates throughout the colony – the nag whistle sounds. Murdina, instantly in a dither, drops her teacup, which crashes to the floor creating a wreckage of tiny navy blue shards. She speaks to herself in angry Scottish jibber-jabber that Vera can't understand.

"Eejit," Murdina moans to herself and walks for the front door in a panic, leaving behind the pile of jagged china pieces spread across the floor. Murdina steps outside and swiftly closes the door behind her. Knowing that a single whistle blow isn't for combat calls, Vera rises to her feet and heads for the doorway too, with a wonder on what it does mean. Just then, Murdina opens the door and pokes her head back in, "Are ye comin', lass?"

"Yes, I'm coming," Vera answers as she rushes to catch up to Murdina.

"Move quickly," Murdina calls back.

"Why, what does this particular whistle mean?" she asks with an uneasy feeling that it isn't going to be good.

"If ye dinna get there fast, he'll mean to have yer head on a stake."

"Pardon me?"

"Dinna be testin', lass. Master Regan tis a dark force not to be reckoned with," Murdina looks to Vera with light blue orbs wide like walnuts and possessed with suspicion. *She must be scared of Master Regan,* Vera thinks. Though after her re-birthing, and seeing the evil in his eyes, she wonders who isn't.

A vast amount of Tags, scruffy and rough-around-the-edges, flock to the footpaths. Vera feels out of place and seeing so many of them is a teeth-clenching reminder of just that. She glances around, some have patches of dirt smudged across their cheeks or a rat's nest for hair a top their heads. *Surely they have mirrors in their houses? Or perhaps they have quite seriously taken to a prehistoric way of life.* On the other hand, others dress a bit finer and attempt a minimal level of grooming.

Nevertheless, the swarm of Tags smell like salty sweat and raw meat, *or is it raw sweat and salty meat?* Regardless, a well-educated Kalian doesn't belong here amongst such filth. Vera supposes they know it too, for she can feel their eyes on her. In no time they approach The Master's chamber where the nag whistle is being called from and it seems to be comparable to The Master's chamber in Kala, at least in Vera's mind. She looks up and there stands Master Regan on the stairs, holding a knife to the stomach of a pregnant woman. Vera's brain rattles in confusion, all she truly wants is to get away from the stench of damp bodies that surround her. The colony members gather within minutes of the nag whistle sounding, bodies press up against hers – she can practically feel their dirt rubbing off on her clothing.

"Bastard," Murdina mumbles under her breath.

"What is it? What's going on?" Vera asks in a hush tone, while squeezing her arms tightly to her sides in an effort not to touch the Tags at her front, side and now back.

"Tis Jeanne, a lovely young lass – quite good wi' needlework that one."

"What did she do?"

"What did she do? I dinna ken. Nothin' I'm sure. Nothin' but love a man an' carry his bairrn," Murdina whispers; clearly concealing her words from nearby ears.

"Oh, is she pregnant illegally?"

"Aye, an Offender."

"You knew?"

"I ken."

"Why didn't you report her?"

"Didna have the heart. Someone did though," Murdina says with sadness evident in her voice. Master Regan gives one last blow to the nag whistle. The crowd falls quiet as Jeanne squirms under his grasp.

"This is what I like to call: dual Offenders. Here, I have one of the two-part offending unit. But you see, I need the other part," the crowd stomps their feet - one, two, three times - in an expression of approval, while Master Regan's eyes scan the crowd hungrily. Vera glances around, a pulsating thudding in her ear; excitable, dirt-covered faces stare back at Master Regan. "She didn't do this on her own," Master Regan urges through gritted teeth. The crowd stomps three more times. All are frozen in place, as if their lives are on the line should they move an inch. Or maybe they're just enthralled with the show. "You always make me do this the hard way," Master Regan shouts as he shoves Jeanne to Rimmy and takes to his seat. Rimmy grabs her in his giant-like hands and she squeals in fear. Regan offers a nod to Rimmy and, as if in an unspoken agreement, he knows just what his Master so desires. Rimmy tears the woman's shirt and undergarments down the middle until they descend and lay in a dark heap on the stone steps below. Jeanne winces. Her bosom now exposed to the entire colony with a swollen, pregnant bump protruding from her.

Vera has never seen such a sadistic display – it's evil. In all of her days as a Kalian she's never seen a woman's dignity taken from her. The uncomfortable realization of being in such close proximity of the unkempt Tagondians leaves her mind as heat begins to spread through her body like wildfire. *Where the hell is the father?* Master Regan offers another tilt of his head and Rimmy takes his knife and runs it deliberately in between Jeanne's breasts, thinly slicing her skin and leaving a fine red line down her torso; Jeanne begins to cry in a piercing scream as Rimmy holds her by her hair in a fistful of rage. Vera's hands shake in fists, she wants to speak up so badly, but she knows it's not wise. *Keep your head*, she tells herself. After all, she has managed to keep her head all those times at The Circle.

"Where is he?" Master Regan questions the crowd once again. She feels the words at the tip of her tongue, ready to spill out of her mouth at the drop of a hat. *Don't do it,* she tries to convince herself. She feels sick at the thought of making an outburst, but she can't very well do nothing. Jeanne is shaking, from head to toe in fear as Rimmy holds her. Vera can't bear it – the very look of Jeanne is enough to sway her – someone has to do something. Without another thought she pushes her way to the front of the crowd, heads turn in glances of concern as she makes her way forward.

When she arrives at the bottom of the steps she speaks, "Enough!" As the words come out she doesn't recognize her own voice; her courteous tonality turns stern and hoarse, cracking slightly under the pressure. "Let that girl go at once," she stares Master Regan in the eyes, her lips pursed.

"Well, if it isn't the scientist," Master Regan sneers.

"This is inhumane what you're doing," Vera's voice echoes off the crowd; only silence follows. She can't sit back and watch another person be treated so poorly, even if it means tribulation for herself. In her mind, it's a fair claim that Jeanne is in a more delicate state than she.

"It appears that the newcomer is not clear on our laws. She has spoken out of turn – now an Offender. And what do we do with Offenders?" Master Regan yells to the crowd, the crowd stomps their feet into the ground. Surely the strength of their stomps will trigger an earthquake that'll swallow her whole. A jolt of surprise shoots through her as someone grabs her hand unexpectedly – it's a warm, gentle touch. She glances to see Cole squeezing in beside her. Of course it's him, he has an agreement to fulfill.

"You need to stop this, now," he whispers out the side of his mouth, keeping his eyes steady on Master Regan.

"Cole, we can't just let this continue!" she says to him, infuriated, as if he's suggesting that the safety of her life is more important than the safety of Jeanne's.

"We can, if we want to live," he whispers again to her. He then speaks out to Master Regan and the crowd, "She is new here, yes, and isn't that all the more reason to give her a chance to learn our ways? Besides, she comes from Kala – the weaker colony." Vera looks at Cole, *The weaker colony? Ah.*

"I don't need you to speak for me," she spits. But the crowd seems to like his point, as they stomp their feet briefly in agreement, then they watch their ruler give the idea some thought.

Rimmy still holds poor Jeanne by her hair, a line of blood drips down her chest and protruding stomach. A stunning young woman approaches Master Regan's side then, Vera doesn't know her by name, but she possesses the same black hair as Regan, the same blue eyes. The young woman bends down filling his ear with whispers. He nods and then she walks off the steps and returns to standing amongst the rest of the Tags.

"To offer an Offender grace is to be weak. She must learn our ways quicker to avoid retribution," Master Regan pauses a moment, "Rimmy, take her." Within a split second Rimmy passes Jeanne to a Defender to his left and makes his way down the chamber stairs. He reaches out his grasping hands to Vera – she freezes in fear. He holds her in his grip, restraining her by her arms. Master Regan locks eyes with her, "Bring the newcomer up," he adds as he gives his wrist a flick, a request for Vera's presence. How easy it is for him to get what he so desires.

Vera's hands begin to tremble – Cole inconspicuously squeezes her hand tightly for a brief instant, he must've been sure Rimmy wouldn't notice. Though, as her hand slips out of Cole's she doesn't know exactly what the squeeze means. *Is it pity? Worry?* Whatever it is, it doesn't make a difference, she is about to face some form of tribulation. The last tribulation she witnessed was Lidia's lashings that day at The Circle. She remembers how the Defenders ripped off Lidia's shirt then remembers her own lashing - the aching gash on her right arm - that she is to keep hidden under her long sleeve shirt at all costs.

Rimmy forces her up the stairs in a push; all the while her hands shake in fists at her sides. She hopes no one in the crowd can see her trembling hands, especially the likes of Master Regan. As she approaches him, she realizes that he isn't all that tall. Though he's sitting upon his chair he's quite tiny for a man, let alone a ruler of an entire colony, though size shouldn't be a direct statement to one's capabilities. No, it isn't in his size at all that frightens her – it's in his eyes. They are small and just as she remembers them, but this time the intensity in them makes her worry for her life. His pale blue - almost translucent - eyes make him look as though he may not be human at all. She swallows hard, certain that everyone can hear the loud gulp that echoes through her ears.

Rimmy squeezes her wrists harder. The pressure nags at the base of her hands; she bets that he could tear her hands clean off if he wanted to. A brief panic encases her in that moment and she uses a small amount of force to fight him off, but she remembers Cole's words. Cole still stands there, serious – angry even. He must be angry with Vera for speaking out, as everyone else appears to be. Disgruntled stares from unfamiliar faces heckle her as she peers out to the crowd. That's when the realization hits her that she is completely alone. No one is here for her, not anymore, Cole is merely here because of an agreement. The people who would be here for her are either dead or forbidden to see her again.

Rimmy, takes her by surprise by locking her wrists together within one hand's grasp, he then grabs her shirt and tears it off of her with the other hand – her peach skin is now exposed. Tears immediately fill her eyes though she refuses to sob. Thankfully, her undergarments have stayed in place, covering her breasts; however, her recent scars are no longer hidden, she doesn't know which exposure is worse.

"Well, well, well, it appears we do indeed have an Offender on our hands. Look: Tag stitches. This means we have another set of dual Offenders," Regan smiles, an evil smile. His eyes wander to Cole suspiciously then back to Vera. Rimmy continues to hold her wrists firmly in place. "Whom, may I ask did these stitches for you, Vera of Insignificant Cannelle?"

She shakes her head *no*, she won't say who, but decides to correct him: "It's North. Vera of Favoured North," she says through gritting teeth.

Master Regan snickers then, "Did you hear that? She thinks she is still a Favoured," he chuckles and nods once again to Rimmy, who grabs her shoulder and presses his fingers into her wound, she winces in pain. "Tell me, won't you," Regan persists.

"Me, I did them myself," she spits.

He laughs, "Do they teach such things in Kala?"

"Yes," she lies as she continues to moan in pain, Rimmy presses harder.

"Well then, the only way to settle this is to have you show us. Does everyone agree?" he addresses the colony and the crowd answers by stomping three times in unison once again. *So, they also get whatever they desire – at least when it comes to savagery.*

A sudden worry encases her: she can't do stitches. Rimmy adjusts his hold on her; he releases her shoulder and then grabs her by her hair with one hand. He pulls forcefully and she knows she is at his mercy. Rimmy reaches down to the side of his belt and when his hand returns within Vera's field of vision his fingers wrap around the handle of a knife. Without hesitation he digs the knife into her wound, opening the stitches. Vera yelps in pain, blood pours down her arm. She glances about the crowd, noticing the watchful eyes of many children – a sudden worry fills her heart for them. But this life is all they have ever known and so their tentative eyes gaze upon her, appearing just as hungry as the men and women, if not more so.

"Someone, get the necessary supplies," Master Regan demands to no particular person. However, within moments, a redheaded Defender brings the supplies as requested. Vera glances over the items and thinks that they should be everything she needs to clean and stitch herself: towels, alcohol, a needle and thread. Rimmy releases his hold on her and she stumbles to the top stair and sits down. *Just do it,* she thinks to herself then begins mentally running through the steps that she saw Mae do just the other day.

Mae first used a towel to wipe the blood and then applied alcohol to clean the cut. Vera knows that she needs to closely mimic Mae's work in order to save both of their lives – Cole's too. Vera traces her memory to follow the exact procedure while taking a swig of the booze for herself. *Thread through the needle then pierce the needle into the skin. Move back and forth in a zig-zag motion.* She's used to doing fine work with her fingers at the lab, and over the years she has stitched up holes in garments as needed – she hopes that will be on her side. After sanitizing the wound, she finally pokes the needle into her arm and pulls a sharp intake of air, right before she begins stitching. *Back and forth, Vera.* The pain is sharp and intense. *Keep going.* She holds her breath, exhaling when she takes a break from moving the needle. The pain is almost unbearable, she pauses a moment, grabs the bottle of alcohol, whiskey she assumes, and takes another swig – anything to help with the pain. Tears run down her cheeks, though she still refuses to sob. The droplets that stream from her eyes blur her vision slightly, she wipes the tears away so she can finish. *Keep your head.* After what feels like hours, but only minutes have actually passed, she finishes and ties the knot using her one free hand and her teeth. Finally she cuts the excess tail off the thread and exhales in relief.

"Well, I'm almost impressed," Master Regan says as he gestures to the audience, raising his hands up in the air. The crowd snaps this time. "I only hope you can show as much enthusiasm with your tribulation as you do your first-aid."

Vera stands up, her face flush. Master Regan's words flow in through her ear canals, but they don't register for she feels dazed from the adrenaline of the procedure. She holds her wounded arm carefully by her side, thinking that she is free from the torment, ready to make her way down the stairs. She leans down, before making her way back to Cole, grabs the bottle of whiskey and takes a final swig.

"Three lashings," Master Regan suddenly spits.

"Wait what?" she inquires, she can't help but think that she has misheard. For she did what he wanted her to – she completed the stitches. *It can't be.* She eyes Regan, blood-covered and confused. Rimmy grabs her once again and ties her hands up with a coarse rope, which scratches at her already tender wrists as he tightens it. He then ties the rope to one of the chamber's mammoth pillars. She turns her weary face toward Cole as she stands shirtless in restraint. He nods his head a couple times in encouragement. Rimmy pushes her and without her hands to grasp at anything for support she slams down onto her knees. *No. No. This isn't happening.*

"You should probably try to keep your shirt on the next time we meet," Rimmy whispers the words in a haunting threat. She begins to sob, she doesn't care anymore who sees as tears leave her eyes and moans of sadness leave her mouth. She hears the whip ready before it collides into her back. She screams at its sting, already hoping for it to be over. The second lashing hits her back with more force than the first and she coughs as she fights to catch her panicked breath. It hurts like nothing she has ever felt before. Even the stitches hold nothing on these lashes. She doesn't think she can make it through one more lashing. But it comes before she even has time to consider it and it slams into her flesh.

Suddenly she realizes she now knows some of what Lidia felt that day in The Circle at Lilith's birthing ceremony – her back stings as though it has been licked by flames. Lidia survived ten lashings, Vera can barely handle the three she was so graciously gifted. She is dazed when Rimmy grabs the rope that binds her wrists together, he pulls her to her feet with force. The rope unravels in an instant; Rimmy's perverted eyes remain on her chest. There's a twinge of something unsettling within her, but in that moment she feels nothing. The tears have stopped spilling out of her eyes, the remaining ones simply slide down the sides of her red cheeks.

"Go," Master Regan says as he shoos her down the stairs, "But, Vera…" she turns to glance back at him, her shredded shirt still strewn on the steps a few feet from her, "Don't forget where you are. You're in Tagondo now, and here – I am Mother Earth," a sly grin spreads across his pale face. She turns and rushes to Cole in a light-headed daze, stumbling into his arms.

"Are you okay?" Cole asks as he embraces her. Vera doesn't say a word; she just stays there, in Cole's arms, staring up at Master Regan. Master Regan's eyes flicker, then a frown instantly spreads over his face. As Cole's arms carefully and slowly descend, releasing their hold on her, the sly grin returns. Regan continues with an order to Rimmy for Jeanne, though he uses no words, a simple nod of his head, and Rimmy knows. Rimmy violently grabs Jeanne by her hair once more.

"Last chance, who fucked this girl?" Regan yells across the crowd, his anger growing.

When no one comes forward Rimmy holds his knife up in the air, turns to Jeanne and ferociously shouts, "Death to the Offender!" Without pause Rimmy's blade slams downward and digs deep into Jeanne's stomach, after a slight pause he rips his blade across her abdomen and slices from left to right. Her insides spill across the stairs: a bloody fetus amongst the guts. Jeanne falls to the ground, her body twitches in a mound of burgundy and honey-coloured convulsions. There is no longer hope in saving Jeanne. The baby on the other hand, its cries pierce the air like a wailing siren.

The crowd erupts in applause by way of stomps and low reverberating chants of: "He, he, he." It pulls Vera out of her subdued trance, startling her. Her eyes gaze over the blood-covered stairs, where she realizes – there is no telling her blood from Jeanne's.

# 24

## COLE OF FAVOURED POLLARD TAGONDO

It wasn't help, at least not good help, that Cole offered Vera the previous day. He feels pain for her, having to go through what she did. *Why can't I seem to do for her just exactly what Murdina has asked of me?* He's to help and protect her and is failing miserably. He doesn't like failing – which is why it never happens. He tells himself that Vera is just an issue he needs to sort out *but damnit she's a big issue.* And nothing is going as smoothly as Murdina seemed to imply it would. He wonders how he can possibly protect and help Vera without having the ability to talk any sense into her? It almost seems like a sick joke – as though even attempting it is impossible because she refuses to oblige. *Speaking out of line at a Tag meet – what the hell was she thinking?* Of course it would wind up with her being beaten – there is no other way that could have gone. Still, his stomach feels slightly ill knowing the degrading feelings that goes along with an event like that – the discomfort and pain that she'll be feeling today will be unbearable. If only he somehow could've prevented it all from happening. It was her first Tag meet and though most are along such lines of brutality and barbarity, this one was extreme.

Cole's eyes water slightly at the image of Jeanne, dead upon the stairs. He cared for her – she was a most kind woman. And now there's a child… one that needs claiming. Seeing the child, alone and vulnerable - lucky to be alive - makes him feel guilty. He bites his lip in thought, *No, he can't come forward, it would change everything.* He'll have to move on, pretend as though the past never happened – now that Vera is here, he has reason to do that.

Cole makes his way through the colony centre that morning, walking past the chamber's stairs with his hands in his pockets. The stairs are still discoloured, but it'll be only a matter of time before the Defenders scrub clean the markings of death. All go about their day, as though nothing has happened, Cole tries his best to do the same. But if he is honest, his life sort of turned into shambles when Vera arrived, and continuing to behave complacent toward Master Regan is proving to be trying – she's making it harder on him to do that. How in the hell can he be complacent with Master Regan when he's whipping and mangling the very woman Cole is to protect?

He thinks more about Vera and how she pushed him the previous day. She didn't appear to want his help at the meet – he wasn't all that much help after all. They could've both been killed had things gone anymore out of hand. The problem isn't his uninvolved demeanour toward Master Regan - that's how one stays alive in Tagondo - anything beyond being complacent in this world and one is just asking to be killed. *Is that it? Does she have a death wish?* She is the problem, and every little outburst or stubborn whim she entertains of speaking out will ruin them. It will not be possible to help her if this continues, he'll have to tell her that. Admittedly, he doesn't know how, and so, as he approaches Insignificant Cannelle that morning he racks his brain.

# 25

# Oberon of Favoured Kenoak
## Kala

Master Oberon stands with Zev upon The Master's chamber stairs. Zev signals with the whistle - two short blows on repetition - which informs the colony that there is to be a communal dinner at The Pit. There is no need to give notice, as Master Oberon never instructs a change in Kalians' attire for any gathering, except a merge. Kalians are always well dressed, and so when a last-minute gathering is called they hurry to the colony centre.

"Should we head to The Pit your grace?" Zev asks as Master Oberon and his Barons stand upon the stairs of the chamber awaiting the colony to gather before them. Zev stands wearing his tall collared black coat, which hangs so low it goes down past his knees. His fur scarf rests on his shoulders, but still purposefully shows the tall collar. His short, brown hair is swiped slightly over to his left side in a swoop of short strands. Being the Orator for Master Oberon, it is pertinent that Zev is both pleasant and presentable.

"A couple more minutes and we shall." Oberon loves watching his people gather before him, he finds such pride in their entrancing stares of affection. The way they stand so willing before him, he knows they're content in doing just about anything for him.

Several Kalians flock to The Pit, after a few minutes Master Oberon makes his way down the aisle of trees and solar lights himself. The musical ones play music and a Defender already has a fire popping in the stone hearth. The servant ones line tables with an array of foods while another servant one stands post at the drink table, pouring whiskey or wine for those of age. A communal dinner is always a grand occasion.

Master Oberon sits in his seat and tells stories of Mother Earth and how she is making change for The Almek. Change and movement that are a direct result of their efforts and it's all happening right below their very feet: the sort of thing that one can't possibly see with their eyes or feel with their hands. On this night he decides to tell one of his stories about Mother Earth, he poetically describes how the earth's crust is cooling down day by day from the way The Almek are caring for her and once the water is cleansed, she will be back to her normal temperature. His stories often pull from The Almek ways, however they often include fictional characters with fictitious circumstances. The story he tells on this night is about an Almek woman whom believed she couldn't bear a child. Upon prayer to Mother Earth, day after day, she was finally gifted the presence of a fetus in her womb – another child to offer Mother Earth the love and respect she needs, to till her lands and care for her waters. The people love his stories – he can see it in the way they look at him as he tells them. The way their mouths fall open in silent gasps, the way their eyes sparkle with love and warmth. However, his favourite part of a communal dinner is always the prayer.

"Let us pray," he lowers his head, "Mother Earth, we speak to you on this night and we ask of you three things: we ask that you provide us with as much rain as you can possibly muster, we ask that you love us, for it is in your love that we unite, and we ask that you bless us with the ability to cleanse your waters. In return, we promise to care for you and treat you with the respect that you so deserve. With the earth," he then raises his head and with a wide stretching smile he says, "Now let's eat."

# 26

# VERA OF INSIGNIFICANT CANNELLE TAGONDO

Vera finally gets out of bed after hours of restless sleep. Her arm aches with a burning pain, her back too, though her knotting stomach is causing her the most agony. To no help, she's been thinking about Cole through the night. She replays in her mind the way he asked her to keep quiet at the nag whistle meet and the look on his face following her tribulation after she hadn't listened. But how could she? The ceremonies at The Circle were one thing, but that nag whistle meet was something entirely different. She could never be okay with such barbaric happenings.

Cole will be coming by this morning, as usual, to pick her up so she decides this time she will listen, she will join him for a pursuing day. She sits outside on the front stairs awaiting his arrival. Soon enough Cole appears from the footpaths, greeting Vera with a loose smirk.

"Good morning," Vera greets him, it's unlike her Kalian greeting and she can't help but feel weird without it, but weird isn't necessarily bad.

"You look tired," he says and they begin walking down the footpaths.

"Do you tell that to all the girls?"

He smirks, "Only the tired looking ones."

"I suppose that's why you still don't have a merge agreement then?" she smiles, though it is half-hearted.

Vera notices that he hesitates for a moment, "Could be…" he says, shrugging, "most of them are just intimidated by my charm."

"Oh? It's not your sense of humour they're scared of?"

"You're smiling today, and telling jokes – what's going on?" he asks.

"Nothing," she simply states. She was good at pretending in her old life, at burying her truth. However, it has been a dire challenge for her this past week - between Cole and Master Regan - she is beginning to feel like a ball of gas on the verge of exploding. She needs her white lies to stay sane, to stay safe.

"I don't believe you," Cole says suspiciously. *Shit*, she thinks. She just wants to be left to her facade, so she can hide within the walls of their safety – like a lizard in camouflage skin. Her cheeks blush.

Cole turns towards her, "So?" Her mind wanders to her conversation she had with Murdina the previous day and the pain that Cole has faced in his lifetime. She feels torn on how to deal with him, as though she should be more pleasant to him and yet, she can't stand being near him. It is an awkward position for one to be in.

She releases a sigh and decides to partially fess up, "Murdina told me about your father... and your mother... I'm sorry."

"Oh. My mom... That was a long time ago. And my dad – it's not a big deal. Just a bit of a set-back for him, he'll come around."

She pauses a moment, looking up at him in bewilderment, "Just a setback?" she asks, cautiously.

"Yeah, Dr. Yani will figure out what's wrong with him and treat it. One day, that's all this will be – a setback. I know he'll get better." The very words send shivers down Vera's spine. *Just a setback* – a series of words that always irked her when Hendrix said them, and hearing them on Cole's lips is unnerving. She doesn't know what to say.

"It's good that you see it that way," she finally adds. They walk in silence for some time. *Silence,* she thinks, *is an underrated thing.* It's also a rare occurrence when she's with Cole, so she relishes in it and takes to an admiration for the shades of the forest.

Several Tags rush by, no one really greets one another, which is still strange for Vera. But she realizes, she really doesn't want to say, "With the earth" on repeat anymore. It's sort of refreshing that no one here seems to say it. Her eyes thoughtfully wander to the greens and browns of the wildlife that surrounds her; they are in their own league of beauty. Soon they pass the trees with the giant X's carved in them, she reflects on recent memories that shine a light on her stupidity and stubbornness. She's surprised that Cole doesn't say anything as they pass into The X, neither a snicker nor the slightest of teases, as she expects. A part of her feels let down by the lack of instigation, which she deems odd. They walk further into the forest as the morning sun rises into the blue sky, a blue that bears with it the possibilities of a new day. Vera walks in an oddly harmonious state – she survived her first brutal run-in with Master Regan. Somehow, she wonders if that makes her braver. There is no question though that it makes her a more capable Tagondian.

Cole breaks her wondering thoughts, "The trees marked with X's are the pursuing grounds. We call it The X. This is where we train and pursue. It's not the safest for a newb to be here, but Master Regan has made no changes – even after a young boy was shot through the heart with an arrow last month."

"Last month?" Vera proclaims with unease.

"Yeah, it's rough in this neck of the woods – not like Kala I'm sure."

"No, not even in the slightest resemblance."

"We usually try to wear bright colours when we're in The X, so no one accidentally gets shot – that happens all the time. But a boy dying – that was a first."

"That's so sad. There has to be a better way to manage The X."

“There is always a better way,” Cole exhales, “but no one challenges The Masters.”

“I suppose not.”

“Just up ahead is my lookout, it’s a secret,” Cole says as he reveals his loose smirk once again, she wonders if he’s looking for a reaction.

“Why is that necessary?” Vera asks coolly, though secretly envious, dreaming how nice it would be to have a secret spot of her own.

“It’s nice to get away from it all, I guess,” he shrugs. She nods then, in understanding.

After zigzagging through the forest for some time, they approach a wide tree with a ladder built on the far side of it. When Vera looks up she notices a platform that sits at what looks to be about eighty feet or so above ground.

Cole grabs the ladder with one hand and holds his other hand out to Vera, “Here, you go up first. I’ll go up after you to make sure you don’t fall,” he offers. She steps toward the ladder, admittedly heights are not her forte, but she figures in the afterlife, as an eastern phoebe, that won’t be a problem.

“Is it strong enough to hold both of us?”

“Yeah, you don’t need to worry,” he assures her.

Vera rests a shaking foot on the first step while both of her hands grip, white knuckled, on either side of the ladder. She lifts herself off the ground while Cole places a single hand carefully on her waist to help steady her. His touch briefly distracts her from her bearings, but the burning of her back from the lashings pulls her focus. Her arm is merely a dull ache initially, though as she begins the climb it stings from the constant stretching motion. Nevertheless, she continues to climb until she reaches the square entry at the base of the platform. Manoeuvring herself up on top of the platform is the most challenging for her wounded arm, but she’s determined and makes do. Cautious to avoid bumping either of her wounds against the tree, she settles to standing upon the soles of her feet. It is small atop the platform, but there’s more than enough room for a few people to fit on it. Cole swiftly stands and moves to the edge, his hands resting on the railing that encases it, he looks out in pleasure.

“Want to see the view?” he asks eagerly.

“Yes.”

“Here,” he reaches out his hand to help guide her toward the railing. As he touches her hand he notices the trembling, “You alright?”

“It’s my nerves,” she says ashamed and pulls her hand out of his grasp, “It’s not going to collapse under our feet, right?” she asks with worry clear in her voice.

“No, but if it does I have a backup plan.”

“You don’t,” she says with a nervous wide-eyed smile.

“I do,” he says as he walks to the corner of the platform and grabs a thick rope that appears to be secured to the tree trunk. A portion of it dangles down from the railing, the rest of the rope sits in a pile in the corner of the platform.

“You’re going to do what exactly with that?” she asks, unbelieving.

“If I have to, I’ll grab the rope, go over the railing and climb down – it’s long enough to reach the ground.”

“This thing better not collapse with me on it,” she says with raised eyebrows and a growing fear of ever having to use Cole’s ‘backup plan.’

“Listen,” he says, placing his hand on her shoulder while carefully avoiding her wounds, “It’s not going to break, okay?” Vera nods her head, though she isn’t entirely convinced.

She reminds herself that he's been trying to keep her alive so far, because of the agreement, so why would he stop now? She reasons that his backup plan must be sufficient enough to save lives. The two stand side-by-side, looking out at the grand landscape of the forest with greenery as far as the eye can see. This platform must be built on one of the tallest trees, for they can look down upon the surrounding trees and relish in the expansive panoramic beauty. The white, feathery clouds sit motionless against the pale-blue backdrop – they are fortunate, it's a calm day, no wind. Vera gazes out, speechless at the tranquil view. She decides this is her favourite spot in all of Tagondo colony – she doesn't need to see the rest of it to know that for certain. After a few moments she settles in a little more comfortably, even gaining the courage to lean forward, placing her hands on the wooden railing.

"So, what do you think?" he asks after a few minutes of quiet. She doesn't respond at first, she isn't quite ready to fill the silence. Instead, she turns to look at him, his eyes pinch at the corners in a smile.

"It's incredible," she admits in a whisper.

"You like it then?" he's clearly pushing for more, but doesn't he always push for more?

"Yes, very much so," she gives him.

"You can come here anytime," he offers, sincerity in his voice. She doesn't respond, *If no one else has been here, why now, why me?* She must be overthinking it all – it is, after all, just a platform attached to a tree.

"It's difficult to see the ground. How do you manage to pursue an animal from all the way up here?" she asks, not fully addressing his offer.

"I have gotten a couple deer, but I don't pursue much from up here," he replies as he gazes out. She didn't take Cole as the sentimental, reflective type; she assumed the purpose of the lookout was to have a place to pursue, but clearly this is more of a personal sanctuary. She won't be so invasive as to probe further. She turns and notices lines etched into the tree, a tally of sorts carved into its bark. She quickly counts the markings – sixty-four. *What is he keeping track of?*

"Do you pray to the Mother?" he asks, once again distracting her thoughts.

"I do. Do you not?"

"I'm surprised," he says, "I didn't have you pegged as someone who leans into the laws of The Masters so gracefully."

"Oh? And why is that?" she asks, knowing right well he is wrong and has no clue who she is.

"I don't know… you seem like someone that wouldn't take a notion and run with it blindly."

"I suppose," she responds. *But it is all that I have known,* she thinks. "Do you pray to her?"

"Pray… I guess it depends on what the word means to you. I ask the earth for forgiveness for our centuries of disrespect and mistreatment, I ask the earth for abundance in meat to keep us alive, but I don't pray to an imaginary Mother of the Earth," he explains.

"I suppose that is fair, though the first law states-"

"I know: *All shall pray to and respect Mother Earth,*" he states, "It's a stupid law. They can't control my thoughts and who I do and do not pray to. Besides, Master Regan seems to think he is Mother Earth." He glances at her then, waiting for her to react. Humour plays across his expression.

She considers his statement for a while, she does pray to Mother Earth as if she's a mother figure – she spent countless hours trying to cleanse the water, she watches and participates in the ceremonies – all because she's told to. But yes, perhaps forcing someone into prayer is not the way to go about it. No one has ever admitted such an opinion to her before. She glances at Cole and holds his gaze for an instant. *Maybe he is worth trusting.* After all, he did save her the other day in The X, even if she won't refer to it as a rescue – and if he is sworn to protect her, maybe keeping her secrets and extending help when she asks is included in that promise.

Without another thought she speaks out of desperation: "I want to get revenge on Opi for killing my father. Help me."

"You what? Are you nuts?"

"I am not," she eyes him defensively.

"No way. If Opi dies, guess where the first place Master Regan will look?"

"The X?"

"No. To you! You are the only one here with motive to hurt him."

"I can tell him I didn't do it. I'll make sure I do it when Opi's in The X," she reasons, "It can look like an accident – like that boy."

"It won't work. Master Regan has his ways, including torture: physical and mental. He will get the answers that he wants, he always does. Rimmy sees to it." Cole's reaction is an honest answer – even if it opposes her wishes. "Besides, you really think you're the killing type?" it appears as though he is holding a smile back, but she can't tell for sure.

"Obviously, I'm not. But it doesn't seem that impossible to pull off, I got through my tribulation fine. And it's not as though he would be able to do anything without proof."

"You got through it just barely. Don't be stupid, V," he urges, "He has his eye on you now, if he didn't already from the commotion you caused at your own re-birthing ceremony. Besides, killings at the ceremonies aren't anyone's fault but The Masters'. They are the ones who organize it and enforce it."

"That's true, but how would you feel if you were forced to befriend, never mind live under, the same roof as the man that killed your own father?" she asks.

"I don't think I could hold that strain against someone, if they were forced into such a situation as yours. Like a puppet on strings," Cole explains, "If it wasn't Hendrix, it would've been Opi. He was forced to defend himself. He was forced to please his Master."

"I'm stuck Cole. I've been forced into a situation that I can't help but feel unhinged about."

"I get it, I've been forced by Master Regan into doing things that I don't want to do," he says earnestly.

"Like what?" she questions, curious as to how he can relate to her.

"... Just things that you wouldn't understand," he pauses a moment, clearly choosing his words carefully, "Listen, I can't help you. I'm sorry. Opi has been my friend for many years, my dad's too."

"Fine. I'll take care of it myself," she says coolly. Turns out his agreement with Murdina to help her isn't without its exemptions. *That must mean that there are exemptions in his protection as well*, she thinks.

He shakes his head, "Listen, I've been wanting to talk with you and since you've brought this all up..." She glances at him expectantly, waiting. He takes a breath and continues, "You're new here right? And you don't know your way around, how to act… If you want to survive here you're going to need help. But if you're on a mission to stir shit up in the colony and get yourself into trouble all the time, I won't be able to help you."

"What are you saying? I've already told you that I don't need your help," she reminds him, saying it all the while unaware of her own hypocritical behaviour. She notes that he has yet to tell her about his agreement with Murdina though.

"After yesterday, you and I both know that you do. Listen, the only way I have survived here in this place is by being indifferent and getting good at what I need to, to survive." She knows exactly what he means, for she too is guilty of living a life of intentional ignorance

"I can't pursue," she spits.

"I'm not asking you to, at least not yet."

"Then what are you asking of me?"

"For now, just try to fit in – stop standing out so much," he reaches around to the back of her head and pulls the tie out that holds her hair up. Her thick waves fall down her back.

"What was that for?" she asks irked, her hands instantly jolt to her long strands, as if a part of her has been unwillingly exposed as she's never had her hair down in public.

"This is the start of you blending in," he tucks the tie in his pant pocket.

She scoffs, "You can't just take things from people."

"Well neither can you." She knows he's referring to Opi, and her desire to take his life, or something close to it.

"I don't know if I can just pretend as though Opi didn't kill my father," she says, looking away from his stare.

"That's the thing – I think you're going to have to," he concludes, she shakes her head in disagreement as she remembers a disturbing vision she had of colliding the pan into Opi's head the other day. *Death changes a person. Tagondo changes a person,* she decides. She touches her hand onto her aching stitches. *No, I can't pretend anymore.*

"It might seem strange, but talk to Murdina about it – she is a force, if anyone can help you through this it's her," Cole suggests.

"The person I'd really like to talk to is my father. He would know what to do."

"I can tell you he wouldn't agree with you on killing a man for revenge. Especially when he isn't prepared and can't defend himself."

"You don't know my father."

"I know that you don't want to be like Regan."

Vera pauses, "What about the probes? Will you help me with that?"

"What about the probes?" he asks quizzically.

"I want to know what Master Regan is looking for."

"I told you – surplus water," he chuckles in irritation, "You're bothered by the probes? You're forgetting that things have been this way since the beginning."

"And you seem content with these ways…" she tenses.

"I have been, I've convinced myself to be. We all have to be if we want to stay alive," he admits.

"Well I won't stand idle. I refuse."

"I can't seem to crack you, no matter how hard I try to figure you out… Or convince you not to be stupid."

"Maybe I don't need to be convinced or cracked," she reasons.

"Maybe neither does Master Regan."

"Maybe not, but I have to try."

"I know that feeling," he smiles now, but it's half-assed. She doesn't know that he's referring to her. A silence lingers amongst them for some time as they take in the sweeping view. Maybe Cole is thinking about ways to find out more about the probes, perhaps he isn't. He's a difficult creature to read, but she thinks all humans are. Then she thinks about Cole's advice, she should talk to Murdina. Murdina is, after all, the closest thing to a mother that she has.

^

Vera waits for Cole to lead their departure from the lookout. Cole notes that it's time to teach her to pursue. So, once grounded, he leads her to a nearby open field where they sit at the tree line, quietly waiting, for what, Vera isn't sure. After some time a wild turkey hobbles by, it doesn't appear to notice them.

"Watch this," Cole whispers and slowly sits up. He winds his arm and ejects an axe through the air – it pierces the turkey square in the chest. The creature flaps its wings obnoxiously, fluttering up in the air and then drops down to the ground. Vera's stomach instantly twists, she closes her eyes in disgust. "Are you alright?" Cole asks, dumbfounded.

"I'm… I'm okay," she responds, unsure herself, and slowly opens her eyes.

"You're pale, Vera."

"I actually… I need a minute, excuse me," she jumps up and runs quickly into the forest. Hiding behind a bush she releases the building acid from her stomach. She turns and looks to see Cole behind her with a pile of leaves in his hand.

"Here," he offers. She accepts the leaves, attempting to ignore how her cheeks are burning with embarrassment, and wipes her face.

"So… are you like, a nervous-vomiter. Is that a thing?"

She is mortified, "I... I don't know."

"It's not everyday someone vomits when a turkey is pursued… In fact I've never seen it," he dramatizes.

"It's called having a conscience. You should try it."

"It's all about survival."

"Survival for you. Death for something else," she says. He looks at her in a peculiar way – his one eye squints as if he is trying to figure something out.

"You're different, Vera. Different than anyone else here," he simply adds. She doesn't know how to respond, but she knows he is right.

She has always felt different. Blending in with one's colony has always meant unity. Perhaps that is why she is a loner. No matter how hard she tries, the fire in her stomach burns her with its flames at every turn. As she reflects on his statement, it doesn't insult her as he isn't wrong, but in any uncomfortable situation, silence, she thinks, is often the best course. And so, she says nothing to it.

Cole walks back toward the field, picks up the turkey and begins tending to its dressing. She doesn't much like the term, nor does she know specifically what it means, and though she can take a guess she prefers not to give it another thought. Vera stays clear of the dressing process and specifically tells Cole not to tell her what he is up to. After the tragic story of the turkey ends, they travel back into The X. Cole brings his weapons and sets up targets for them to practise with. Vera silently admires his homemade knives – he seems to be quite the craftsman. Though they are sleek and straight, they make no difference for her throwing or aiming skills. He gives tips for every weapon, including how to hold them as a means to avoid blisters. He also says that over time her hands will build a callus. She listens to his teachings attentively.

^

The days begin to blend into each other as Cole and Vera try to develop her pursuing skills and knowledge. It doesn't take too long - merely a few weeks into May - before her aim improves and she is consistently hitting targets. She practices through brief instances of rain, through the damp evenings – pushing through the pain of her arm and her back. And even when her arm gets infected, still, she practices. She practices until her muscles ache and her eyes can no longer focus. She doesn't know how or why, but she knows in her gut that these pursuing skills can only help her in her ultimate goal.

When Cole suddenly places his two hands on her shoulders and speaks into her ear: "Let's take a break," a memory shoots through her mind: she's in The Circle, Hendrix is being pulled from her, but before they part he places his hands on her shoulders and whispers something into her ear - four syllables - as if hearing him through a speaker from the Old World, muffled and distant, she remembers his words: *Step number three.*

# 27

# TREENA OF FAVOURED ADDER TAGONDO

Treena sends another one of her male suitors on his way, just as quickly as he showed, from Favoured Adder. It wasn't satisfying, but come to think of it there are many things on the go that she isn't feeling satisfied about: Cole is giving her all kinds of grief denying her his bed, not to mention getting too close for comfort with the Leech, while Regan is being difficult about providing her with more power in the colony. No one is giving her what she wants. But she wonders: *Who is truly satisfied anyway?* Anyone that claims they are being given just exactly what they want are either delusional or liars.

Besides, there is more excitement in the game of taking and it's in the *how* that she finds thrilling. Coincidentally, Cain, one of the top Tagondian pursuers, is someone who knows how to go beyond to impress. He's the son of Orsen of Favoured Fenwick, whom is Baron to Master Regan. Regan has never been fond of Cain and that suits Treena just fine. In fact, it's better than fine as she likes to cause a stir and as of late she's angry with her father.

Treena reflects back to the promise that he made to her when she was younger: he said that he would always give her everything because when he was a child he had nothing. He said that when she turns twenty-five he'll place more responsibility on her shoulders, he'll give her a part of the colony to rule. She's worked hard to ensure he follows through with his promise and she lives obsessively through each day of her life dreaming of that day with only one thing in mind: taking power.

She wants more water, she wants more sex, she wants to rule the colony - one day she will - she wants Cole too, and she will have him, she will take him. Her twenty-fifth birthday is approaching, it's in only a few months time and she is quite ecstatic to finally get more power in the colony. She's been waiting a long while, though her patience is growing thin. Regan promised – her time is coming.

She gathers her things from her bedroom and makes herself look presentable by way of fixing her hair and straightening her shirt in the bathroom mirror. She retrieves her fur scarf from the hooks by the doorway, pulls on her boots and walks out the front door of her house; she's on her way to The Circle.

The footpaths are overflowing with Tagondians who are also on their way to The Circle: it is baby Jed's birthing ceremony. He was Jeanne of Insignificant Toley's baby, though no one knows who the father is. Not a single man came forward in claim for the baby. It doesn't matter anyway, even if the father wants to keep baby Jed he'll have to fight and survive The Circle. *She was a waste anyway*, Treena thinks, having no compassion for the murdered woman or her bastard child. Besides, Jeanne had always looked at Cole in a way that irked Treena. She didn't much like Cole's glazed-over eyes every time she was near either. *Where is Cole?* She hasn't seen him since yesterday, since he pushed her off him. It isn't as though Treena is happy about him shoving her off, she's furious. But there's this obsessive desire to have Cole that she is willing to ignore his disdain and focus on finding her release elsewhere until he finally caves.

The thing is, Cole's the only guy who has ever turned her down. She's had many men, both younger and older, but they aren't Cole. Though she relishes in the power she holds over those men, the best part is how it's like a game – each one thinks he's the lucky bugger to sleep with a Favoured Adder, none of them know there are actually tens of them. She knows that they will never find out too, because if they tell a soul that they have bedded her, Regan would have their heads on the spot and her skin would go unmarked. So really, it's a win-win for her.

Cain, on the other hand, is the exception to a lot of her rules. He sees the dark side of Treena for what it is – he has a dark side too. They've collaborated together on more things than she likes to admit, as she's been screwing him for years all the while he's been entirely aware of the countless others. Cain could be defined as the closest thing Treena has to an ally, although Nin is becoming a close second. Cain bumps into her then, intentionally, making her aware of his presence.

"What," she says, though her voice doesn't fluctuate as it does for most upon the end of a question.

"Have you seen *lover boy* hanging around the Leech?"

Treena scoffs, "Yes. It's driving me fucking nuts."

"How predictable," he chuckles as he pats her back. She doesn't like being called predictable.

"Won't you do something about it?" she pouts as she adjusts her Favoured Adder crest over her shirt, pulling his attention to it - or rather to her breast - either way the focus will remind him who she is and what she could potentially do for him one day. Well, what she wants him to think she would do for him. If he plays his cards right, if he does exactly as she asks, she could ensure Cain a position of Baron. Though she isn't stupid, he wants more than just Baron. He eyes her crest, licking his lips, though unaware of the hunger strewn across his own face.

"I'll take care of it," he says. She knows he will. *Who's really the predictable one?* She smiles internally.

"What are you gonna do?" an excitable curiosity arouses her. She remembers the last time Cain said he'd take care of something for her – she ended up in that same room having a threesome with two men and a severed hand. He truly could do anything to Vera and she would squeal with delight from her depths. "I just want his focus back on me," she says with determination.

"You got it, your highness." Cain says.

She isn't the ruler of The Motherland – not yet. Still, hearing it articulated on his lips arouses her, though she won't show it.

"Just take care of it okay? Don't touch Cole."

"Gladly," he grins as though possessed. She wonders then what terrible things he'll do to Vera. Then she realizes that she doesn't care.

^

As the Tagondians arrive at The Circle they find the Kalians already seated: proper postures and poised as ever. *Ass kissers,* Treena thinks to herself. She takes to her seat, her mind fades away from the ceremony as Orator Zev rambles and follows the motions of a typical birthing ceremony. She isn't interested in the talking part, all she wants to see is the raw reactions of human beings fighting for their lives.

"Welcome my friends, here we gather at The Circle," Zev begins reciting the scripture as always, "We gather to unite as one and we gather to pay respect to Mother Earth. May we be cleansed," a brief ritual pause and Zev continues: "Please, welcome our Masters: Master Oberon and his Barons of Kala and Master Regan and his Barons of Tagondo." The Almek all welcome The Masters by snapping their fingers. As Treena snaps her fingers she glances about, boredom setting in.

Brene brings the baby out dressed in head to toe white clothing with fur slippers and a blanket scarf. She places him on the pedestal and proceeds to do her dance. Treena glances away, it's the same damn thing every time. She looks for Cole, whom she finds sitting with Vera. Oddly, she feels at peace, Vera has no idea what's coming for her, but Treena does. An evil smirk plays across her lips.

Once Brene's dance ends Zev adjusts the podium's microphone and addresses the audience, eyes admirably shift to him as he over takes their focus: "The Masters would like to thank you all for gathering here today. We would like to begin the ceremony. Baby Jed, at just one day old, comes from blood of strength. His mother Jeanne of Insignificant Toley was both Pursuer and society worker. His father is unknown. Nevertheless, this boy is a Tagondian and it is without a shadow of a doubt that he will grow up to be strong, with capable hands in either Foraging or Pursuing. This infant has had no interested families report to their Masters prior to the ceremony. Is there anyone interested in the claiming of this child?" Not a single sound stirs in The Circle, "Who is first in line to fight for the rights to this beautiful baby boy?" Silence.

Treena ponders if she can hear Zev's heartbeat through the microphone, though his stature stays calm in welcoming. This is a first - no one in line to fight for an infant - though she can't help but feel slightly let down, she was looking forward to a good show. She's certain it would be a good one, what with the dramatics of how his mother died.

Zev looks to The Masters for guidance in this unprecedented situation. Master Oberon signals for Zev's presence, he immediately walks in an elegant sway to The Masters' place on the stage. He bows upon greeting The Masters and bends down to meet them at eye and ear level. Several minutes carry on as The Circle sits in utter silence, Treena contemplates grabbing someone's arm, reaching it up in the air and volunteering them herself. *That would be interesting.* Suddenly, that gives her an idea, a rather thrilling idea. She stands up in the bleachers and runs around The Circle, flies up the steps and whispers in Regan's ear. When she rises a devilish grin is cast upon her pale face, then she simply returns to her seat. Many weary eyes offer glances in Treena's direction, she hopes they are worried – scared is even better.

The Masters continue their whispers back and forth, including Zev and their respective Barons in the conversation. It's obvious that they are completely unprepared for something like this, they are lucky they have her. Finally Zev rises up, back to his abnormally straight posture and returns to the podium. *Oh this is going to be good.*

"I would like to apologize on The Masters' behalf for the pause. We are facing an unprecedented situation here; however, we have come up with a resolution. We are going to need one crest from each household of people who are either merged or in a merge agreement." The two colonies' Lead Defenders each hold up a large steel bowl and walk toward the bleachers of their rightful colony. Rimmy approaches the Tagondian stands as Huron approaches the Kalians. Though Treena can't hear what Huron is saying to his people, she watches as their faces do indeed turn from concerned, pinched brows to fear-filled, wide-eyed panic.

"You heard him, one crest per household – in the bowl, now," Rimmy barks. The Tagondians do as he asks in a hurrying manner. The clang of steel meeting steel echoes circle-wide. Once the bowls are full and the Defenders receive all requested crests, they each carry their bowl to Zev. The citizens stare, unmoving.

"I'm going to draw one crest from the Kala bowl and one from the Tagondo bowl. Whichever crests I pull, someone from that family must volunteer to fight in The Circle for the rights to baby Jed," Zev explains.

Treena thinks then, *What if my crest is pulled?* She'll have to fight – her father doesn't fight. She'll be fine up against a Kalian though, they fight like little helpless children, it's pathetic. Then she ponders on what would happen if Cole's crest is drawn. *He'd win too*, she confidently thinks. *But then we'd end up with a stupid baby to care for, one that isn't ours.* She decides that it won't be that difficult to fake an accident: leave the baby in the woods for the mammoths to get. *It'll be easy.*

Zev places his hand in the Kala bowl and stirs the crests, the sound - or the anticipation - causes the people to stir in their seats and pull Treena from her thoughts. His hand stops and he pulls a crest out of the bowl. There it sits, in his hand hovering over the steel bowl filled with the lives of others.

"Insignificant Bohymn," Zev announces and with it the Kalians release a sigh, "Please establish your volunteer and make your way to The Circle."

A woman stands instantly in the bleachers. She glances down at the man she sits beside; he appears to be glaring up at her, Treena wonders why. The woman makes her way to The Circle.

Zev greets the woman, "Melda of Insignificant Bohymn, thank you for volunteering," Zev states. He then puts his hand in the Tagondo bowl and stirs the crests with seemingly more enthusiasm. The same clatter of a noise is all that is heard, soon his hand stops and it lifts out of the bowl. Everyone in their seats are at way too far of a distance from the podium to see what crest has been pulled.

"Favoured Wilder, please establish your volunteer and make your way to The Circle."

Treena sits back relieved and then glances around her in the bleachers, realizing she doesn't know the name 'Wilder.' *Which family is it?* Suddenly a dark-skinned woman flies around the edges of the sand and approaches the bleachers, it's Brene.

She bends down slightly at her hips, her face is both stern and calm and as she speaks to someone her feet shuffle slightly, it appears as though she is in a disagreement with someone. *But who is it?* Treena shifts her body to see – it's a man who sits with crutches in the front row. He isn't wearing his crest, which means that it is likely resting in Zev's hand. Treena decides that the man must be Brene's merger.

"I'm fighting. I won't take no for an answer," Treena hears the man say as he raises his voice in anger.

"Arkish, you can't fight. You're in no condition. I'm the one who must fight. It's me," Brene says as she backs away from the man, her decision looks final, that much is obvious. Brene stops in her tracks and runs back at the man then, embracing him in one last hug; one that could very well be their last. *How touching*, Treena thinks as she rolls her eyes. Brene makes her way to The Circle and for the first time she places her feet on its sands to fight.

"Brene of Favoured Wilder, thank you for volunteering. My people, we now have our volunteers. Let the ceremony commence!" Zev raises his arms up into the air in a joyous expression. The crowd, affected by his contagious energy, snaps their fingers. "As per usual, it will be a fight-to-the-death between the willing participants. The winning opponent will have the rights to the baby. Should we end up with a volunteer next in line, the ceremony will continue. The last man or woman standing will be the winner. Weapons of choice are along either side of The Circle. Will the two opponents please step forward?" The women hesitantly step a few feet further into The Circle.

"A welcome to our opponents: Melda of Insignificant Bohymn and Brene of Favoured Wilder!" the crowd snaps their fingers once again. "We will initiate the standard count-down: ten, night, eight, seven, six, five, four, three, two, one," and in a moment of panic realizing that Brene is not available to blow the ceremonial horn, Zev reaches for the horn and quickly blows it.

The opponents retrieve their weapons: Melda chooses a sword, the most likely choice for an inexperienced fighter, while Brene chooses a spear. Melda charges toward Brene and in one swift movement Brene brings her throwing arm back and with great strength thrusts the spear forward. It soars through the air across the entire circle and swiftly pierces through Melda's body – through her heart, killing her instantly. In its wake, the blow brings Melda to the ground, pinning her to the sands of death.

# 28

# VERA OF INSIGNIFICANT CANNELLE TAGONDO

A loud hissing sound surrounds Vera, fear for what it represents sends a wave of chills through her body. Then she sees the snake: its upper body rises to waist-height while its bottom half coils. The tips of its sharp fangs move closer towards her in a vicious wanting. Suddenly, the eyes on the snake begin to change – they morph from their yellow-green amphibian-like shape, to a more human-like form. Their colour takes on a light blue, so pale that it contrasts with its earthy green skin. A panic rises inside her chest, she freezes and listens a little closer; the sound melds into a high-pitch ringing.

She abruptly wakes to the nag whistle – a reminder of Master Regan's power over everyone, perhaps that is the entire point of it. She opens her eyes and sits up in her bed, still shaking from the realness of the dream. She shudders at the thought of the human-like eyes that suddenly occupied the snake. The nag whistle still sounds, Vera places her hands over her face feeling overwhelmed. She can't go to another of his meetings, she can't sit back and watch an innocent be harmed. She glances to the window and is confused to see that it's still quite dark outside. She looks at the clock and it's still technically nighttime: 1:00 in the morning. She's tired from the commotion of the Favoured Wilder claiming celebration only hours earlier, but Master Regan doesn't bear any patience or compassion. Which means, she knows that it's time to go, so she reluctantly jumps up and quickly gets dressed before locating Murdina. As she gets ready she thinks back to yesterday's birthing ceremony and how it all played out. It's unfathomable, the things The Masters do to continue their rituals, and the people – they sit and let it happen, to themselves and their families no less.

Vera reflects on how she was able to see Atticus and Ida from a distance in their seats at baby Jed's birthing ceremony. Their weary faces only stoked the fire in her belly. The Masters had no right to take her from them. But she is at The Masters' mercy – they all are. She remembers Melda and the thud her body made when it collided into the sands of death – she sees then her father, and his body meeting with the same sand at her re-birthing. It's the same sound of the imagined tree branch slamming into her. Her breath catches slightly as she realizes what what truly haunting her all this time. It doesn't make her feel sorrowful as she expected though. Now, more than ever, Vera feels angry – it isn't despair, it's fury at The Masters' ceremonies. The one plus to come from the recent death of Melda is that sweet baby Jed now has a loving home. Vera hears the distracting sounds of Murdina moving about in the kitchen – once she's dressed she makes her way there.

"Take this," Murdina says, handing Vera a brown satchel.

"What is this?" Vera asks.

"Use wi' a keen mind an' open eyes," Murdina says and then darts toward the front door, without further explanation. Before she flies out the door Vera watches as Murdina reaches for some other unknown object. Vera carries on knowing that she does not have time to investigate the contents of the bag right now, instead she puts the strap of the satchel over her shoulder, resting it diagonally across her torso.

"And this," Murdina turns back and as they stand upon the deck out front of the house, she pulls a piece of fabric over Vera's neck, resting it atop her shoulders – a pine green scarf made of warm fleece.

"Did you make this?" Vera fluffs and adjusts the scarf around her neck.

"Aye, I did, tis fabric from Scotland. I havena much fabric left from the Old World, but I had to use it for ye – it matches yer eyes."

"Matches my eyes?" Vera questions. She glances down at the green fabric, noting that it does indeed match her eyes, but also the forest. The soft fuzz brushes across the skin on her neck, it makes her feel warm. As the nag whistle sounds again, she notes its ability to instantly make her skin crawl with goosebumps, even with her new scarf. Regardless, she's grateful for the gift, she's never had a scarf before.

"Thank you, Murdina."

A thoughtful smile rests on Murdina, "We should go now," she quickly states. Vera follows Murdina through the footpaths, noticing that Opi only now joins them in their travels to The Master's chamber. She wonders where he was before he showed up as she moves behind him, not allowing herself to be vulnerable to him. The sudden movement makes her dangling hair sway subtly from the slight breeze. As she walks behind Opi she silently wonders if she could use whatever is in the satchel against him – likely not.

As they travel the footpaths Murdina and Opi speak quietly to each other while Vera's focus finds the empty feeling of uncertainty in her gut. Now that she knows what the Tag meets are like, she prepares herself for the worst.

As they approach the chamber, Master Regan stands on the stairs, his Defenders are circling the crowd while his Barons sit in chairs beyond the top stair.

"Tagondians, tonight our young will partake in the annual Pursuing Challenge. Many of you have done this before and many of you will do it again. This challenge never fails us in weeding out the weak and allowing the strong to prosper. If you do not come back with four kills in bounty – you will be exiled." The crowd gasps - at what - Vera isn't quite sure. Perhaps it is in their fear of potential exile.

Murdina leans over and whispers to Vera, "He increased the bounty, the bastard."

Master Regan enthusiastically continues, "Thank you to Cole of Favoured Pollard, Mammoth Slayer and our top Pursuer, for the suggestion of increasing the bounty!" the crowd stomps their feet three times. Vera eyes Murdina suspiciously as a disappointed expression overtakes Murdina's face. "The individual with the largest bounty will be awarded a grand prize. Do not be complacent, this has happened several times over the years. You know the drill, people ages 13-30: you are our future and our future is reserved for the strong. Every man and woman for themselves… Go – now!"

"What the hell?" Vera snaps at Murdina.

"Ye best go lass," Murdina waves Vera off.

"What is this? Why the hell didn't you tell me?"

"Wouldna made a difference. Ye still have to do it."

"I have no weapons with me."

"Good luck," Opi and Murdina say in sync, though she can hear Murdina's confidence stand apart from Opi's voice.

The crowd begins to separate into distinct segregations: the older pursuers disperse and head down the footpaths, likely returning to bed as they don't have to partake in the challenge. Meanwhile, the younger division heads toward the east side of the colony, a section of the forest that Cole has never taken Vera to before. *Where is Cole?* She can't believe, after everything, that he helped Master Regan plan this challenge.

As the swarm of colony members clear away from The Master's chamber steps, a different worry now seeps into Vera's thoughts. She has never been successful at pursuing moving objects and has no weapons to speak of. She can't pursue an animal, she won't. Not to mention the mammoths are out there. She stands, frozen, in the darkness as people fade into the black abyss and with them their chatter.

She shivers as a chill traces along her extremities, though she isn't sure if it's the night air or the grave awareness of her solitary mission. After forcing several deep breaths, her chest begins to heave, but it doesn't seem to lighten the pressure. In fact, it feels as though the weight grows heavier, pushing her down. Tears pour over the delicate skin of her lower eyelids and run down her cheeks. It seems hopeless, but a spark travels across her skin and tickles her gut, telling her that she can't give up – she always manages, she always takes care of things herself.

A stirring in the bushes breaks the silence, along with her opposing thoughts. Suddenly, two strong hands grab her from behind: one wrapping across her ribcage under her breast and the other covering her mouth. She is forcefully pulled deep into the bush, further into the darkness. She wants to scream but she can't, still, she fights against its restraint.

"Shhh, it's me," a warm, moist breath tickles her ear, Vera sighs in relief. If only she took a moment to relax and pay attention to the scent on his hands she would have known it to be him. The musky odour of cedar mixed with the aroma of orange peels pleases her nose once she notices it – his lookout is built of cedar and oranges are his favourite. Of course it's Cole, he couldn't leave her behind because of his standing agreement with Murdina. She turns to look at him in silence, "Say, did you get a new hair tender? The twigs in your hair are really screaming 'wild Tag' to me."

"You are outrageous!" she says as she shoves him, unable not to smile in relief.

"I will settle for outrageous," he smirks.

Her voice turns harsh, "What's this about you helping Master Regan?"

"It was a trap. He forced me into it," Cole admits innocently.

"How?"

"Remember we talked about Regan forcing us all to do things we don't want to do. Things that we have to live with?"

"Yes."

"He made me tell him to up the bounty, he wanted to do it all along. He just waited for me to say it so he could put the added pressure on me."

"I don't understand why someone would do that? Why wouldn't he just add the rule himself if he wanted to," Vera inquires.

"I don't understand a lot of the shit he does. But I wondered if it was his way of priming me."

"Priming you for what?" she asks. His eyes dart then.

"Maybe… to become… a Baron one day… or something? I don't know… He loves the whole *Mammoth Slayer* bit," he fumbles over his words. She suspects that he's hiding something from her.

She examines his face in the low light: he is a beautiful creature with his deep-set eyes that appear so genuine, his curved-into-a-smile lips that are silent in this moment – for that she is surprised. In many ways Cole is built for this life as a Tagondian: his wide shoulders frame the weight of his muscular arms. She imagines the strength within those arms and her breathing falters slightly.

As usual, Cole breaks the silence, "Listen, we need to move. Here, I made you these," he says while passing her a knife, an axe wrapped in suede as well as a bow and arrows. In the glow of the nearby solar lights she can see "V" carved into the metal of each of the weapons. Her heart both aches and fills with warmth, but she shows neither.

"Thanks," she breathes, "Where do we go?"

"Follow me, stay close and stay quiet," he says before darting northbound. The two scurry through the forest, climbing up the mountain's ridge. It seems as though they are going in a different direction than the large group of pursuers who appear to be heading east. "A North always sees north," her father would say. Even though it's now evening and Vera isn't very well versed in navigating in the dark, she knows they are heading north at a slightly westerly angle – she can feel North pulling her.

The faint shouts of the other pursuers echo in the distance. It seems as though Cole is trying to put as much distance as possible between them and the others. She isn't sure why, but she wants to trust him. Suddenly, a scream sounds in the near distance. The struggles of an altercation cloud the air like a fog.

"Fuck, this way. Hurry," Cole says as he pulls Vera by her left wrist, forward, away from the screams.

"What?" she asks with worry, but Cole doesn't respond. Some yards ahead and through the brush she sees a solar light sitting on the ground. It illuminates the trees around it, but that isn't all. There are people there – three of them standing around one lying on the ground. As Cole guides Vera hastily away from the group she can't help but gaze at the unfolding brawl that seems to be filling the silence of the night. "What's happening over there?" she asks as she looks to Cole for reason.

"Just don't look. Keep moving," he tenses, as they circle wide around the group, through the forest, seemingly careful not to involve themselves, or to be seen at all. But she can't not look, her stare darts back to the group of people. She sees fists and feet meeting the frame of the person that lies in the grass, a dark liquid covers the person's face. The night is too black to make out its true colour from such a distance, but she can guess what it is. She's seen enough of it in Tagondo to know.

"Finish him off!" exclaims one of the low voices.

"But dragging it out is so much more fun," a second voice explains.

"Cole, are you hearing this? W-We have to do something," Vera begs as she notes one of the assaulters walking slightly away from the rest of the group. The moving assaulter stops, he then stands with his arms raised, he's holding an object that she can't quite pinpoint through the trees.

"He's being too loud," a female voice speaks.

"We'll cut off his tongue then," the second voice declares before bending over the victim. A series of muffled screams follow.

"Just do it already," the female says.

"Cole, please!" Vera tugs at her arm in an effort to escape his hold. But there is one last sound that tells Vera that it's over: a metal arrow soaring through the air, only briefly, the surge that pushes through the wind upon its release is unmistakable. The finalizing sound is one that the arrow makes as it meets with the flesh and skull, digging into the ground in its last movement.

"Vera, Run!"

^

After what had to be an hour of sprinting, they finally stop. Vera tries to catch her breath.

"This way," Cole says as he reaches for Vera's hand and begins leading her to the dark opening of a cave. Standing at the cusp of the cave's entrance Cole pauses to fumble with his backpack. Vera stands motionless, constantly looking behind her for fear that the mammoths, or more likely the group of muggers, will surprise them.

Once the item of Cole's focus is removed and glowing over his face, she realizes it to be a solar light. He grabs her hand once again and leads her into the vast unknown of the cave. It's dark and damp inside the cave, but the solar light offers enough light that Vera can comfortably see her immediate surroundings; beyond that of which the light touches, she can see nothing but blackness. Rock walls are formed around and above them, the stone ground below their feet is wet, they step diligently so not to slip. The musty scent of the cave fills her nostrils like a thick gas; she grimaces in displeasure.

"Don't touch the puddles," Cole warns.

"Why? Is there a river running through here?"

"No..."

"Then it's likely collected rainfall. The rocks are full of calcite so the only thing likely abundant in this water is calcium carbonate, which is only harmful in large amounts."

"Say what now?"

"It's not technically ground water and it's not attached to another body of water, which means it should be fine," Vera summarizes.

"All this time I've avoided it like the plague."

She chuckles then, but in an instant a frown rests on her expression once again, "What is that foul smell?" she asks Cole, sounding a touch prudish.

"Have you never been in a cave before?"

"No."

"Oh, well, it's not gonna kill you. It's better than being out there. Out there will kill you," he notes as he sets the light on the ground and takes his backpack off.

“What happened back there?”

“These competitions are crazy – they go to everyone’s head. Everyone wants to win the grand prize…” he pauses, “It’s basically a free-for-all.”

“So they actually kill one another?” she asks. “For what? This prize you speak of?”

“It’s not just about the prize. If you don’t make the required bounty, you’re exiled. But not before Master Regan gives you tribulation. They think they’re fighting for their place in the colony, when really no one needs to be harmed – there’s enough bounty out there for everyone.”

“Why didn’t anyone tell me?”

“I didn’t want to scare you, besides – you’re staying in here until it’s over.”

“So you mean to keep me locked up?” she says in bewilderment.

“It’s not safe out there… you saw for yourself.”

“I won’t just sit here and do nothing.”

“I should go out for a bit, see what I can get for us,” he says, standing and ignoring her comment.

“What about the dangers out there?” she asks.

“You’ll be safe in here. And out there – those dangers should be scared of me,” he winks.

“But, what if –”

“-Shh,” Cole waves his hand nonchalantly through the air, “I’ve been doing this for half of my life, V. Don’t worry about me, I won’t be long.”

“I’m not worried,” she says, almost as if she’s insulted by his suggestion that she could care enough to be worried for his well-being.

“Well good then, that makes two of us,” he smirks and continues with a warning, “Don’t leave this cave. It is literally the only thing keeping you alive while I’m gone. Also turn the light off, you don’t want to draw attention to yourself.”

“But-”

He interjects, more casually now, “Don’t wait up – catch some Z’s.” He turns then and disappears from her sights.

She scoffs in disbelief and bends her legs to sit down on the rocks. *The nerve he has. The self-assurance. To try and tell me what to do*? It’s maddening, especially coming from a Tagondian. She wonders what it is that makes him so sure of himself. Is it the fact that he has slayed a mammoth before? Because killing an animal is certainly not impressive in her books. Or is it the fact that he isn’t scared of being mugged in the darkened forest? Anyone can be fearless – it doesn’t take a genius to be that. It takes a genius to solve the Water Crisis, even though she hasn’t thought about it in a while for she has been so preoccupied with Tagondian matters. She should be working on cleansing the water right now, not being held prisoner in some cave by Cole – who could never be a scientist, he doesn’t have the brains for it. She finds herself questioning his age, knowing it has to be somewhere near her own. If he has in fact been doing this competition for half of his life and started when he was 13, that’ll make him twenty-six-years-old – only two years older than her.

As she sits in the cave alone, all that is heard is the steady drip of water falling from the rock ceiling. The odd sprinkle drops on the back of Vera’s head, slowly cascading down to her neck. She wouldn’t mind it if it wasn’t for the smell. She imagines the musty water soaking into her thick brown hair and causing it to match the cave’s unappealing scent. For all she knows she already smells like one of them – like a Tagondian. Their differences from the Kalians boggle her mind, especially considering she never dreamt that she’d live to see the differences up close.

Thinking of Kala and the Water Crisis reminds her once again of the message Hendrix whispered in her ear: "Step number three." She knows exactly what it means – retrieve his labcoat. His silly coat must be more important to him than she understands, since he whispered it to her at her re-birthing, minutes before he died. Which means she needs to escape Tagondo and get back to Kala to get it, but she'll need help if she's going to be able to pull it off. There has to be a way to convince Cole to help her.

After some time she finds herself wondering about the depths of the cave that she sits in. The thought alone sends shivers down her spine, causing her shoulders to squirm. She, for the desire to remain naive, doesn't risk shining the light behind her. This cave certainly isn't an ideal place to be stuck – it's far too dark, even more so than outside. At least there's light from the moon to gaze upon, it creeps tranquilly into the cave's entrance.

A couple hours pass by before a tapping noise alarms her, claiming her attention. The subtle rhythm mixes with the beat of the water droplets, then a slight scuffing across the rock floor begins. It's rhythmic too, like moving feet, and sounds like it's coming from deep within the cave. Sitting upright and still, she wonders what it is – her mind races. *Oh no! A mammoth!*

She jumps to her feet and grabs her axe, holding it out in front of her like a complete amateur. The sound grows louder – it's coming closer. An eerie feeling washes over her, as if there are eyes upon her – she can't see them, but she doesn't have to. She wants to scream, but instead she closes her lips tightly together, they quiver with a desire to cry for help. Realizing that there is no one here to help her, her limbs begin to tremble – she's on a solitary mission after all, she reminds herself. Maybe she can dash for the cave's entrance and flee the cave and whatever creature dwells within its rock walls. Instead she remains frozen in place, her feet planted in what feels like cement blocks. She may be an amateur, but she is entirely ready to fight for her life.

# 29

## COLE OF FAVOURED POLLARD
## TAGONDO

Cole wanders across the slope of the mountain heading northeast, he figures that it's better than whatever lies south, on the flat ground of the forest. He worries about Vera being around the other pursuers who can be unpredictable on this night. But more specifically he's worried about Cain. Cain of Favoured Fenwick, or as Cole likes to refer to him: *Fenprick*, is a sneaky, slithering snake-in-the-grass. Cole doesn't trust him, never has. Admittedly, Cain is, next to Cole, one of Tagondo's top pursuers, which only makes the tension between them greater.

Cain's father is Orsen Fenwick, one of Master Regan's Barons as well, and being a Favoured means more than offering fewer shares, it means you are treated differently. Master Regan is more willing to turn his back on the indecencies of the Favoured, of which Cain often takes full advantage. Perhaps that curates an entitlement. They have known each other since they were young boys and just joining The Motherland. Back then they were friends, until Cole caught onto pursuing much faster than Cain. Upon reflection, Cole thinks that sometimes it's the big things that turn a person mad and sometimes it's the little things that keep them there. By the time they were teenagers Cain became quite competitive in a destructive and disturbing way, often trying to get a reaction out of people. Once he even left the bloody fetus of a baby fawn decapitated on Cole's doorstep. Over time Cain only became increasingly aggressive; taking his competitive nature to physical levels, often attacking Cole as well as other pursuers during hunts to get the bounty, especially at the annual Pursuing Challenge. However, three years ago things got worse when Master Regan decided to place a merge agreement between Cole and Treena – Cain went mad. Cain wants to be the one to take over Favoured Adder. Cole assumes that he wants to rule Tagondo with Treena and for some reason he feels it's owed to him since he has won every Pursuing Challenge – no one even wants to try to beat him out of fear for what he will do to them. He wants to be the best and the best he'll be, even if it's purely from inflicting pain or fear on others.

Cole's mind veers easily toward Vera, *If Cain ever got his hands on Vera…* he shudders at the thought. He doesn't know what Cain is fully capable of. He would harm Vera just out of spite, to harm something dear to Cole. As a result, Cole's ultimate goal is to keep Vera as far away from Cain as he can, to help Vera is to keep her safe, besides that's what Murdina asked of him. But if he is honest, he's beginning to grow a liking for Vera. Being near her, beyond just his call of duty, is becoming more enjoyable. At any rate, Cole's reminds himself that he can be at ease because Vera is safe in the cave while Cain is soaring through the forest, fighting for his number one spot; nothing is more important to him than that. And Vera? She isn't a threat for that seat.

A flock of wild turkeys wander by and pull Cole from his wandering thoughts. With ease he picks four of them off while the rest get away, but he's content, and as usual he guts the turkeys in the field to make it easier to carry their weight on his hike back. After he retrieves and cleans his arrows, he returns them to their case on his back. His bow is his favourite weapon when pursuing – the string running so closely across the side of his face is familiar, comforting even. Still, the feeling of sending an arrow reeling through the air is even better: a high that at one time sent his head buzzing and his nerves jittering. Now, it sends him into a state of tranquility. *What is it that Cain feels every time he draws his bow?*

Cole continues to hike through the night, both at peace and also on edge, if one can be both things at once. He enjoys the black of the night, the rhythmic songs of the crickets and the smell of the April air, and yet, he readies himself for the unknown. He easily pursues and obtains his last four bounties and though he has several opportunities to take more – he doesn't. He is satisfied that he's obtained enough kills to secure both his and Vera's safety in the colony. On his way back to the cave he picks up speed, his heart races from the hike and with an anxiousness to get back to Vera. He hopes that she's able to find sleep and if not, at the very least, finds the cave to be a good place for peace and reflection.

# 30

## Lidia of Favoured Peony
## Kala

Eight weeks have passed since Lilith's birthing ceremony. Though her superficial wounds have healed, there is much that remains sore within her. No one seemingly struggles the way Lidia is, at least that's how it appears. Her body aches with a pain that possesses her muscles and joints – nothing can remedy her hurt. No herb, nor drink. Each movement takes an unbearable amount of effort and her mind is a foggy mass of troubled thoughts. She wonders how she has even made it through the last few weeks. It's as though her body has been operating on autopilot, for she can't even remember yesterday.

The days blend into one another and form into a series of time and experiences within her life, she feels as though she's an onlooker over her own existence – watchful eyes from afar. She constantly questions what's happening to her and whatever it is, she is alone in it – no one else can possibly feel this way, not with the smiles they all carry. She pushes aside her views of her life, she can't bear to watch any longer. It's ironic to her really, that The Motherland is supposed to be this joyful place of unity. This place where the survivors of the Water Crisis can coincide with a community for support; and yet, all they wear are depressive shades of black and grey. Not to mention the support is only physical. It isn't a joyful place at all – no one is united, are they? Then again, maybe they are united and it's just her that's incongruous, the black sheep.

Lidia walks her fatigued body to the greenhouses, another day alone with the plants. She talks to the plants, perhaps out of desperation, or perhaps she is just losing her mind – it's a possibility.

"There, there little ones. You'll be healthy yet," she says as she waters the onions; however, she worries they aren't getting enough sunlight. There is something to be said for sunlight and water – not to mention words of affirmation. Maybe she isn't all that different from her plants, her plants that continue to tingle against her skin, as she brushes by them day by day.

A commotion in the colony centre interrupts Lidia's dazed routine, she runs outside. Defenders encircle a young woman, one whom Lidia recognizes as Ingrid – if she's remembering right. Ingrid is the mother of a baby boy and wife to a deceased husband – both have left Kala. There are only three ways in which one leaves Kala: in death, exile or by transfer won in a re-birthing ceremony. Her baby boy's ceremony took place this past winter, only months prior to this day. Ingrid's screams of agony both echo and haunt the colony centre as the Defenders struggle to keep her contained in their grasp. She resists with jabs of her fists and whirls of her legs.

"Let me go!" Ingrid wails.

Lidia can just barely hear the muffled words of the Defenders; their voices grow louder with their lack of patience. Her neck tingles with nerves at the sight – she has never seen quite an outburst such as this in Kala.

"I want to see Fergus," Ingrid screams in high pitch squeals of distress.

*Fergus, that's right,* Lidia thinks. She recalls the cries of baby Fergus when he had been placed on the pedestal, it was cold outside and white flecks of snow fell from the sky. She remembers her feelings well, for she was pregnant with Lilith, the dread that filled her heart knowing Lilith would be next was unbearable. Out of worry and love she talked to baby Lilith while in her womb, "Stay in there, don't come out little one – not for a long while," she begged of her baby that day.

Colony members stop at the commotion and gather to witness the revolt, as they too are shocked to see such a scene occur in Kala. Defenders are holding Ingrid by her arms and legs, dangling her body over the surface of the ground. There are too many of them, she'll never get away. Then Lidia sees the words painted in black across The Master's chamber: "Salvage our humanity" with a strange symbol marked beside it. A labyrinth of some sort – it starts small and rounds out in size until it suddenly stops. *What is she thinking? Revolting? And in the daylight...* She must be crazed, for no one would dare do such a thing. In fact, no one in the history of Kala has.

A lady stops and stands beside Lidia, "I've never seen an Offender before. Have you?" she asks.

"Yeah," Lidia replies, for she's looked in a mirror.

Appalled the woman says, "When?"

Lidia doesn't respond, instead she considers that she possibly recognizes this lady, but doesn't know her by name.

The woman continues, but not without a crinkled nose for Lidia's lack of response, "I think her baby is better off without her, after seeing this display."

Lidia wishes she could stop the woman from speaking words of gossip that fall thick off her tongue, "But, she's hurting," is all Lidia can muster. She wishes she could do more than that though.

"No one hurts here."

"How can you say that?"

"Mother Earth absolves our pain – The Masters see to it," the woman says with stern certainty.

Master Oberon appears from his chamber with his Barons at his side, "A tribulation of stones for Ingrid of Insignificant Tommel," he orders with a pained expression.

The Defenders then form a circle around Ingrid while another dumps several piles of rocks around the exterior of their circle. Before Lidia can comprehend what is happening, it begins – Ingrid is released and each Defender throws rock upon rock, harshly marking the white flesh on her body.

"Fergus!" she wails as she circles the border that surrounds her – she is looking for an escape, though there is no escape, not from The Motherland, at least not alive. "No, no, no, no!" her calls fill the colony centre along with the hammering of the stones against her body.

Lidia can't help but watch, for that is all there is to do. Besides, she imagines that the Defenders won't let her leave now; they'll force her to watch should she try to leave, as it would be a sign of contesting. The Defenders will be on high alert now because of Ingrid's outburst, Lidia wishes that she had just stayed inside the greenhouse.

Blood begins to ooze out of Ingrid's body, wounds on her head and face wet and glistening in shades of red. Still, Ingrid calls for Fergus. Not her deceased husband, not Mother Earth – Fergus. The Defenders work tirelessly, determined to end her agony. That's what they'll say when they are done – that they helped her find peace. That they cleansed her. The Kalians watch – attentive and without emotion. She wonders what everyone else feels about the stoning, what they think about it. Lidia will never know. When the last rocks are thrown, the silence of Ingrid's rasps signify that it is done. Lidia glances at Master Oberon, his brow wrinkles in displeasure. As far as Lidia can recall, this is a first for him – having to deal with an Offender in this way. But what else could he have done? Ingrid marks the first act of defiance against Master Oberon – the first revolt in Kala.

"One with the earth," the Defenders say to Ingrid's corpse. Oberon and his Barons then turn and walk back to The Master's chamber – leaving the mess for the Defenders and society workers to tend to, the ones who regularly clean the colony centre. Slowly thereafter the colony members begin moving again, dispersing in whispers amongst the footpaths, back to their daily routine; however, Lidia remains unable to move. As fellow Kalians pass by, Lidia can't bear listening to their whispers, she knows them all too well.

"She deserved that, she wasn't a true Kalian," one man says.

"All Offenders deserve death," notes another. Lidia's heart aches for Ingrid, maybe all of her body does – there is no way to tell where one ache stops and another begins.

She watches as the cleaning ones pour buckets of water on the ground to rid the colony centre of Ingrid's blood, while Defenders carry her corpse toward The Pit. A burial ceremony will take place tonight. Lidia doesn't want to go, but she has to. She is tired of the exhaustion, the worrying and the putrid acts that everyone accepts as normal. All the while, the vision of Ingrid's drawing on The Master's chamber haunts her mind. *What does it all mean?* She wishes that she could have asked her. Maybe Ingrid just wanted to leave Kala. Lidia doesn't want to be here anymore either, it seems like things in Kala are changing for the worse. She wonders then, if she could leave Kala too, as Ingrid has.

# 31

## Vera of Insignificant Cannelle Tagondo

With no time to react, a dark figure hurls toward her, unexpectedly springing at her from the depths of the shadows. She barely catches sight of the attacker, who is a moving blur in the dim light of the solar lantern. They swiftly knock the axe out of her grasp and land on top of her on the cold, hard ground. Then they pin her down, their hand presses the side of her head into the rock floor. The jagged edges of stones pierce into the fleshy part of her temple while her hair lingers in a puddle of murky cave water, the tip of her nose just barely hovers over top of it, forcing her to inhale the putrid scent at a more concentrated level. All she can hope for is that her estimation on the state of the water is correct – that it's just rainwater. She's restrained though, immobilized due to the force pressing against her and she isn't be able to get away from the water source. Her eyes ache as she desperately pushes to see as far as her sockets will allow her to view, but it isn't far enough for her to identify her attacker. They straddle her and she struggles under their grasp, all they require to detain her is but a single hand: strong and merciless.

"I've heard about you," he finally says though a raspy voice.

"Funny, I haven't heard of you," she quips, though she realizes it's merely her nerves talking back, for she has no clue who this man is. He presses on her skull – she winces as her head is forced further into the ground. She thinks back to Cole's advice then: *The only way to survive in this place is by being indifferent.*

"I've heard that you're all kinds of trouble," her attacker taunts.

"I don't want any trouble."

"Good. Then tell me, what is the cure?" he demands.

“The cure?” Vera is dumbfounded. *What does the cure have to do with the Pursuing Challenge?*

“Don’t play dumb with me scientist – I know you know,” he pushes her head into the ground harder. *What does this Tagondian want with the cure for the water?*

“I don’t know what the cure is,” she states truthfully. The man then swiftly grasps her head and forces her face into a nearby murky puddle. It sends her into a state of panic when water fills her mouth and nose, her arms flail out uselessly. After an unbearable amount of time he eventually pulls her face out, pushing her head back against the stone ground, still not revealing his identity. But she’s still alive, so she is right about the water. She realizes though that her attacker would most likely not have that knowledge – not unless he’s been in here the entire time and overheard her conversation with Cole.

“The cure – now!” he warns. A stream of water spills from her throat as she coughs.

Through panting and trying to retain her breathing she speaks: “I don’t have it. They took me from Kala before I could figure it out-”

The force of his hands shift once again, she knows this time around to hold her breath – the water is coming. It fills her nostrils, but she keeps her mouth closed for as long as she can. When her face finally feels the air, she begins gasping and coughing in an attempt to catch her breath again.

“Last chance, Leech. You give me the cure and I’ll let you go. Don’t, and you’re pretty little face won’t see outside this cave again.”

“I can’t…” she wishes she could, she feels utterly powerless.

“Fine… then we’ll have to do things the hard way. Give me the cure… or I go hunt down ol’ Coley-boy and finish him off. He’s a pain in my ass as it is – so I’ve got plenty of motivation beyond threatening you to go through with it.”

“Don’t… don’t hurt him,” she tenses.

“Oh, she cares about him,” he speculates amused.

“Just, leave him out of this.”

“Then…?” he says as he lifts his hand off of her head and spreads his arms out in a welcome reveal of his face. She slowly turns her head to sneak a glance. The man is wearing a black hooded sweater, thereby preventing her from seeing his hair. But she sees the front of his flesh that inhabits that hood – his face is fair skinned, plain looking and houses a pudgy nose at its centre. Although she can’t make out the colour of his eyes in the low light, the very sight of his face offers her nothing but unease. She wishes that she could be stronger in that moment, that her arms had the ability to force him off of her, that her hands could hit him swiftly in the temple and cause him to falter, or her knuckles could knock his front teeth out and maybe even his consciousness. But she isn’t strong like that and she doesn’t hold the self-assurance that Cole does.

Her mind soars through her choices, granted they are scattered because of her nerves. Her hands find fists amidst trembling, *I have to save Cole.* Although he drives her to anger more times than she can count – she can’t stand the thought of him being killed or even hurt for that matter. She has begun feeling a feeble ease around him though she doesn’t want to admit it. But maybe that means he is her friend – if friends get heated, easily pissed off at one another and can barely stand each other’s presence. It doesn’t matter though – realistically she has no idea how to help him or even herself. She isn’t strong and she doesn’t actually have the cure. *Unless… I could lie about the cure*, she thinks. It would be a horrible thing to do and Hendrix would roll over in his grave, but she can pretend that she knows what the cure is - hell - she can even pretend that she has it with her. Hendrix would understand, especially if it means that she saves a life. She sighs in disbelief of what she is about to do and for fear that she may not be able to pull it off.

"I'll go right now, it won't be hard to find him. I know all of his favourite places," the man threatens.

"Please…" Vera tries one last time. His face distorts in anger then. It's too quick, the way his hand comes colliding with the side of her face. The smack holds her in a daze of shock for just a moment. However, when she sees his hand raise once again, she throws up her arms instinctively to defend her head, his fist meets her forearms in a blow.

Pulling together all of the strength she can muster, she uses her forearms to push against his chest and manages to move him off of her. He must not have been expecting it because he stumbles backwards. This gives her a moment to sit up, she struggles to a seated position. Her heart races, moving the blood faster through her veins, she is weak in comparison to Tagondians – she can never beat this man and she knows it. His hands then grasp at the fabric of her shirt, bunching it up in his fingers. He effortlessly picks her up and tosses her against the cave floor; her tailbone slams into the rocks, a moan of pain escapes her mouth. He comes at her again as she lies vulnerable on the floor, his hand grasps her shirt once more and he drags her back toward the puddle. A terrifying assumption crosses her mind: *He's going to try to drown me.* Then he will likely go for Cole, she can't let that happen. She raises her foot, pulls in her leg and kicks his ankle as hard as she can. The man stumbles and falls landing on his knees.

"You fucking bitch," he spits. As he stands to his feet her eyes catch a glimpse of her satchel over by the puddle. She realizes the only probable way she can survive this is if she gives him what he wants: the cure.

"Wait," she says urgently, trying to stall him before he comes at her again. She holds out her right hand, shaking in front of her in plea.

"Are we scared yet?" he teases.

"I'll do it," she says rising to stand on her feet.

"Do what?" he taunts as he moves to stand directly in front of her.

"I'll give you the cure," she grits, though she speaks through clenched teeth merely to stop them from clattering.

"That's my girl," he lowers his head to hers, imposing his profuse sour odour as his sweaty skull pushes against her face. She closes her eyes, for she can't bear to look into his.

He then backs up and begins adjusting his clothing, she walks over to her satchel and sits down in a hurried fashion. She fumbles for her satchel, pulling it out of the puddle of water, while feeling an urge to clench her fists she wishes that she could have saved Cole in a different way, an honest way. She opens the satchel and quickly glances at the first red-lidded vial her eyes catch sight of, the inscription reads: "Thone: its poisons will seep into the skin, time will reveal burns." *Burns?* She has known the oil of certain plants to cause a reaction when in contact with skin – that has always been the case though, even before the Water Crisis. *It's worth a try,* she decides, hopeful.

"Hurry up," he shifts his stance impatiently. She hesitates for a moment while the tiny tube of thone sits sprightly in her fingers.

"I just want to ensure Cole's safety," she reiterates the basis for their agreement. A half chuckle that sounds more like a growl escapes his throat.

"Sure, whatever, Kalian." As he adjusts his fur scarf she glances in the satchel a second time. She quickly picks up a vial and reads it: "Ivani: a wet leaf on your wrist will offer you strength." *Strength?* Murdina said that whatever was in this satchel would help her, though she isn't exactly sure how. She brushes her wet hair away from her face and moves her hands back inside her satchel. Through the fumbling she's able to place the tingling ivani leaf on her wrist – a backup plan, should he try to attack her again. Though the thought of relying on a leaf sounds ridiculous, but she doesn't have the time to hypothesize on why and how a leaf could offer her *strength.* Instantly her skin begins buzzing lightly where the leaf rests. With the thone vial in hand, Vera stands up and faces her attacker.

She holds the vial out to show him, "Here it is," her voice shakes slightly. The buzzing on her wrist sends sparks shooting up her arm unlike anything she has ever felt before.

"What is that?" he demands.

"This… This is the cure," she says with an agonizing tightness in her throat.

"That's it? That's the fucking cure?" he says almost disbelieving. Vera pulls the only stem out of the vial, it has a couple leaves attached to it. She intentionally holds the contents carefully.

"Yes," she mumbles, aiming to sound defeated. In some ways she is, just not entirely in the way he thinks.

"If you're fucking with me…"

"I'm not – that's it," she offers – a sad attempt to reassure him. She needs to do better.

"What does it do?" he asks.

This is it. Her chance to do better. She clears her throat, "It takes the poison out of the water so that you can drink it," however, her voice shakes as she speaks. She'll be lucky if he believes her, at least it's a decent explanation.

"Show me."

"I can't… I have no Lake Cloud water in which to test it."

"Fine," seemingly satisfied he grabs the tiny stem from her hand and tucks in behind his right ear. She swallows loudly, but it feels as though the tightness that tugs at the walls of her throat slowly begins to ease off. He turns his back to her, it appears as though he is preparing to leave. "Cain."

"What?" she questions.

"Cain of Favoured Fenwick."

"Who is-"

"That's me. So you know when you hear about the guy that discovered the cure for the water," he says as he turns to face her a mere few feet away.

She is about to sigh in relief, he believes her after all and he's going to flee the cave – all will be fine. She'll deal with the repercussions of her lie later, she decides, as she begins to turn away from Cain. But as her mouth opens to exhale he slowly creeps forward.

"But there's something else I need," he goes on, his voice husky. Vera sees that his hand fiddles with something at his side, but the cave is dim so she struggles to pinpoint the object – within a millisecond he motions his arm upward while simultaneously closing the petty distance between them. He springs toward her. A surge of adrenaline spikes through her as she darts out of his grasp, but she reacts a little too late, the object in his hand meets her face, covering her nose and mouth entirely. He holds the soft fibres firmly against her, her vision begins to blur as she breathes in a woodsy and sharp scent that she is only vaguely familiar with, but it begins to fade. The pungent odour dissipates until it's a mere prick to her nose every time she inhales. She quickly melts into the recesses of what her conscious mind knows – but it isn't long before her entire conscious begins to fade until there is nothing.

# 32

# COLE OF FAVOURED POLLARD
# TAGONDO

As Cole backtracks southwest toward the cave where Vera waits, he hears oncoming footsteps, loud footsteps that thump into the ground, likely stirring the grass in their wake. One thing he's certain of, they are footsteps that aren't afraid to be heard. He slinks his body behind the trunk of a wideset tree and waits as the sound approaches him. The footsteps grow louder, he can vividly hear the grass crunching and rustling. Still, he stays stiff against the tree. There is no need for him to be fearful, but during a Pursuing Challenge he knows it's wise to go about unnoticed, always ready.

He motions his body slightly around the right side of the tree, his movements calculated and in direct opposition to the sounds of the oncoming visitor. A slight breeze sways the tall grass surrounding him and his shield - the tree - and then it's gone. As the breeze passes, so too, do the footsteps. Instinctively Cole readies his bow in his hands. He pokes his head out from behind the tree as a means to peer out, to see who else is venturing this far outside of Tagondo's borders. The steady beats that sound off the earth's floor fade, but he's certain he sees the back of Cain of Favoured Fenwick – he knows by his sandy-coloured hair and the faded black jacket that he wears, which has a sword blade tear in the back put there by Cole himself, during a combat call.

"What the hell is Cain doing over here?" he mumbles under his breath suspiciously.

Once he knows the coast is clear, and Cain is long gone, he picks up into a light jog and continues toward the cave. He listens to the sound of his own feet as they bound into the dirt and grass: a thump followed by a rustle, followed by another thump and a rustle. There is a slight unsettling in his chest, which he tries to ignore.

*It's silly to worry,* he tells himself. No one knows about that cave and the least likely person to know about it is Cain. Cain is a headstrong Tagondian, focused on his bounty, he isn't the type to wander – at least not in the forest and without purpose. *But Vera is fresh meat, and doesn't Cain have a sort of obsession with fresh meat – animal or human?* Cain also obsesses over being the best and his calculations upon how to become the best have proven to be skewed and unnatural. He wasn't carrying any bounty as he passed by, which is unusual, however, Cole reminds himself that the challenge is quite literally the most important thing to Cain – it's the thing he trains for most. He likely has some poor Tagondians carrying around his ridiculously large pile of bounty around for him, which is cheating, as one is supposed to carry the weight of their own offerings.

The emerald, sage and olive greens of the forest rush by Cole in a blur – shades of green are his favourite colours ever since he was a young boy in The Motherland. He couldn't possibly be one of The Almek and not have an attraction to such an earthy colour; it's practically written in his DNA now. Then again, a lot of things are.

Soon, the grey-black entrance of the cave is within sight and he slows his pace as he wanders inside, dropping his bounty off of his belt just inside. The cave is dark, the only light coming from the low glimmer that the moon casts just inside the entrance. It does nothing for his visuals, but he seems to see well in the dark compared to most.

"Vera?" he calls into the darkness. He can't see her, nor her solar light. "Are you in here?" he asks.

A sound which he thinks to be a moan hums from somewhere in the cave. His fingers grab at his pocket, instantly retrieving the box that encases a few matches for emergencies. He holds the box and a single match out in front of him and slides the match across the gritty side of the box. A slight spark sounds and the match bears a tiny flame and with that tiny flame he sees Vera and her frail-looking body strewn across the rocks.

"Vera?" he says under his breath. He moves his feet towards her, careful not to slip on the wet cave floor, while holding the match tentatively in between his thumb and index finger for guidance. He spots her solar light, though it's unlit, the faint match flickers orange across its surface. He bends down and retrieves the light, giving it a quick tap across his thigh in case the connection merely loosened – he's pleased when the light comes on once again, though dimmer than it was before.

Cole blows out the match and tosses it into the puddle behind him. He sits down beside Vera, placing the solar light in front of her face, she has a cut on her temple, bruises on her face and her clothes are ragged.

"No, no, what happened?" he shouts, his voice echoing in the cave as he examines her body. He places his hand gently, but urgently, under her chin and on her throat, checking for a heartbeat. He feels the subtle thudding of blood pumping through her veins. *Thank you,* he desperately thinks. She's alive. He then places his hands in the cool puddle and quickly presses them across her forehead and cheeks as a means to gently wake her. His eyes graze over her face, then to the torn clothing upon her body and back to her face once again. "What happened to you?" he questions. He then sees her satchel lying beside her – he grabs it and pulls out a tube of abetzi. He knows two things in this moment: one, he knows Murdina fiddles with plants and gave Vera some to fiddle with – and two, he knows abetzi, Vera introduced it to him that first day they met. He can recall its strong scent and flavour, although he doesn't know if it will help her now. He pulls a fuzz-covered leaf out of the tube and holds it under her nose. As she breathes in the features on her face turn to wakefulness. Her eyes open, revealing emerald green orbs that suddenly remind him of the forest. "Hey," he says cautiously.

"Hi. What happened?" her voice scratches as she slowly sits upright. "Ow," she reaches to caress her tailbone.

"I don't know. I was going to ask you the same," he replies casually, attempting to hide his concern, "I just got back and found you lying here," he glances away to offer her some time to gather herself. She coughs then and his eyes quickly, yet tentatively, wander back to her once again. He wants to help, but truth be told he doesn't know how to. She seems so delicate, even more so than when he first met her.

"I…I was attacked," she finally says as she rubs at her right temple.

"By who?"

"I don't know… I didn't get to see his face," she says, coarsely. He can't ignore the hoarseness of her voice – she must be thirsty.

"Here, drink this," he says offering her his water bottle. Vera takes it without hesitation and thirstily drinks most of its contents; he notes her lack of hesitation. *She must've hit her head, no one in The Motherland drinks a glass of water without knowing its source – unless she's beginning to trust me.* Cole can feel creases in his forehead forming - they are always faintly there, at least in his more recent years - however, it's as if he feels them in that very moment creating new permanent lines of worry, ones that didn't exist upon the surface of his skin before Vera.

Cole holds his arms out, now resting his elbows on his knees as if bracing himself, "Just tell me, was it Cain?" he asks, immediately regretting even suggesting the idea that it was Cain, but also needing to know. He instantly thinks, following his question, that if it was Cain she likely would be in far worse condition – if not dead.

"Cain?" she repeats his name, testing her memory as it passes over her lips. "The name isn't familiar."

"Fuck," he spits as his head turns sharply in anger. A nervous exhale escapes his lips, as he tries to remind himself even though he saw Cain wandering the forest several hundred yards from the cave, it doesn't mean it was him. For if it had been Cain, he wouldn't have just attacked her and left. This sort of thing isn't typical for him, he would still be here because Cain is the kind of man for whom proving a strong point is always necessary and letting his presence be known is priority. With that being said, Cole decides that he can rest in assurance that it probably wasn't Cain, but he now needs to find out who it was. *I'll crush them with my bare hands,* Cole zones out briefly as he gazes at the jagged rocks set into the cave floor.

Vera's voice pulls him from his reverie, "I'm sorry."

"It's not your fault," he returns, matching her inflection.

"I've never been attacked like that before…" her frame shudders then, Cole assumes likely at the brief memory she holds of it. Seeing her like this brings anger to his chest once again.

"I'm going to-" Cole rises, resting one knee on the ground and the other bending in front of him – feeling utterly exacerbated with fury. He failed to protect her. He will hurt the man who did this - hell - he'll tie him on a rope and hang him from a tree as mammoth bait.

Shh, sit down. My head hurts and you're being too loud," she begs as she wraps her fingers softly around his forearm, willing him to sit.

"Sorry. It's just, I don't know what this man did to you – he obviously put his hands on you. I'm going to tear him apart when I find out who he is," he says intensely.

Her voice, however, is calm, still wrapped in a haze, "I'm sure we'll figure out who he is. By the unkempt looks that I remember of him, he's definitely a Tagondian though."

"And you didn't catch even a glimpse of his face? Do you know what he wanted?" he asks skeptically and in a begging for her to remember even just the slightest clue. The condition of her clothing suggests the man may have had his way with her and she doesn't seem to have any inclination.

"I don't remember," she says inertly. Cole tries to relax, she's right, they'll figure out who it was because he won't stop until they do. This thought, however, neither settles his mind nor stops it from running through the possible scenarios of what this man may have done to Vera before or after she was unconscious – things that she seems entirely not worried about. Perhaps she was drugged again though – her snippets of recall in memory remind him of her state following her re-birthing.

"He could've…" Cole abruptly stops speaking, acid rises in his throat, something that never happens to him.

"Could've what?" she pulls for more. Though, Cole doesn't want to say it, he'd rather mention death than the word that actually jabs at the tip of his tongue – at least death in this world is natural.

"He could've killed you," he finally says, hiding his original thought.

"And what, this stranger would've become an Offender? I doubt it."

"You don't know what Tagondians are capable of, especially during a Pursuing Challenge. Even after seeing that fight break out in the forest, you really don't even know the half of it. So, let this be a lesson, V, don't ever turn your back to a Tagondian. Not any of us."

"Okay," she says. It appears as though, for once, Vera might actually listen. Although her voice still articulates in a haze when she speaks, she doesn't sound confused about where she is or who she is – not to mention she is still breathing. Cole warmly decides that is, in the end, the most important thing.

"Tagondians are the worst people in The Motherland," she finally speaks again, as if the realization just came to her.

Cole releases a howl of unexpected laughter as the light gleams across her face and with it igniting a warmth in his chest. *And you*, he thinks, *You're the emerald amongst the trees.*

# 33

# OBERON OF FAVOURED KENOAK
# KALA

In the days following Ingrid's stoning, the month of May releases an increase in warmth over the people of The Motherland. However, that warmth doesn't offer any solace to Master Oberon, who feels such shame, such regret. He allowed his Barons to convince him that striking back against Ingrid's threat of revolt was the best course of action.

"They will get over it, they will move on," Martil says.

"We have had nothing like this happen before – the people are scared your grae," Quim adds.

Oberon knows this to be true – they are scared. He sees it in the way they look at him now, in the way they side step to avoid conversation with him in the colony centre on his walks. He feels his power slipping. He thinks in silence for a moment, he is not a person that makes rash decisions.

"I need to regain their confidence in me. But how?"

"Consistency is key, we should shy away from drastic dealings for awhile," Quim encourages.

"Maybe we need to start lining up merge agreements for those of age without one. Perhaps that excitement will take their minds off of Ingrid," Hogard offers, "It will keep them hopeful."

"It's not a bad idea," Martil agrees.

"How many are there?" Oberon inquires.

"There are several your grace, I'll gather their names and get back to you," Hogard states.

"Excellent. Thank you, Hogard."

"My pleasure."

"In the meantime, have you heard word from the scientists on the condition of the water?" Martil asks.

"The levels of the water have not yet changed," Oberon simply says, though he has something in the works of his own; but he isn't about to tell all of his secrets, not even to his Barons.

This has been in the works for quite some time, something that will change lives forever. However, he likes to keep his conversations with his scientists separate from that of his Barons – keeping his allies segregated and within a close eye. There is good reason too – if one person knows everything there is to know about Oberon of Favoured Kenoak, they may not think of him as the wonderful leader that his image depicts him to be.

"Okay, we'll stay posted on that. What about the mammoths? Any sightings there?" Martil asks.

"A few Kalians have reported sightings by the lake and on the southeast side of the forest near the Kalian border at sundown," Hogard reports.

"A couple spotted on our footpaths by Defenders," Quim adds, "Still only during the night hours."

"There has been no mammoth killings in eight months," Hogard states.

Oberon is pleased, "Excellent," he says.

"I hate to say it your grace, but another option we have, is to use the fear..." Hogard's words drift in hesitation.

"What exactly do you mean?" Oberon, already having decided he doesn't like the sounds of it, humours Hogard with his question.

"Well, we need the people to look to you most in moments of fear. Is there something that we could use to increase their fear? It would make them look to you for guidance... resulting in their unyielding trust," Hogard explains.

Oberon looks at Hogard with intent, "I despise the use of fear."

Still, Hogard continues with his idea, "We could use the mammoths... Set up bait stations that will attract them and in turn cause more of a scare."

"Absolutely not," Oberon states.

"What about the colony members that know too much?" Martil asks.

"Whom exactly are you referring to?" Oberon questions.

"The Norths..." Martil mentions.

"I've got things under control. The North's don't know any more than all of the other Favoured, or beyond their professional duty to the colony. It's just the tender feelings following Ingrid's stoning that I need to tend to," Master Oberon responds coolly.

"Are you certain your grace?" Martil asks.

"Why yes, Hendrix - however capable - left us when we needed him most, and Vera, I wasn't entirely confident in her abilities to cleanse the water at such a young age anyways. Anything that Vera knows about Kala will do her no good in Tagondo. Ida and Atticus are merely trying to get through their days following their tragic circumstances. Now please, let's leave that family be," Oberon demands.

"If you're certain. Although I should mention that we have noticed that Atticus has been acting out of character, which is cause for concern. He speaks out in class, doubts the laws, doubts Coakai. We've been keeping a watchful eye, but pretty soon things could get out of hand," Martil explains.

Oberon begins to feel his throat tighten, as though someone is holding a rope around it, pulling it tightly, willing the air out of his lungs.

He clears his throat, "We can't have Kalians doubting our ways," Oberon finally agrees.

"If one is in doubt, one seeks answers," Martil tenses.

"Yes," Oberon agrees once more. Although he can't have anyone questioning their ways, a single teenager isn't his sole concern – assuming that teenager doesn't pass their doubts to others like an infectious disease. The trust of the thousands is his sole concern, if he can convince the thousands first, he will succeed. He thinks then, that knowledge breeds understanding, which in turn breeds trust. Surely there's a way to fix everything – a painless and respectable way.

"What's more…" Martil begins.

"What is it?" Oberon asks, almost in a wince.

Martil continues: "They're beginning to speak about your rest days. Whispers fill the paths – we're not sure who is responsible… But they're speculating on where you go during your rest days."

"My rest days are my days, no one needs to know about my own personal business," Oberon defends.

Martil nods, "You are right, your grace. I'm simply letting you know of the whisperings."

"Isn't today your rest day, your grace?" Quim asks.

Oberon glances at Quim, "Yes, it is. I'm going to leave once we settle up here."

"That was all I had for today," Martil notes.

"Myself included," Hogard adds. Quim nods in agreement.

Oberon sums up the result of the meeting before his exit: "Very well then, we will begin to line up merge agreements in the coming weeks to offer a sense of hope and ease among the Kalians. And we must increase our Kalian meetings. The more we gather and unite, the more it will encourage their trust within us."

"With the earth, your grace," the three Barons speak in unison.

^

It's still dark out, the sun has barely begun to rise – this is when Oberon prefers to meet with his Barons. It's also when he likes to journey out on his rest day; watchful eyes are less likely to see him and where he is heading in the dark.

He carries with him a bag, it's always pre-packed the night before his rest day, but within it there are no weapons. Oberon ruled a law of no weapons in Kala - aside from their weekly strength training meetings - and he did so to keep the peace amongst his people. Which means he has no weapon to take with him on his journey, that fact always makes him feel a sense of unease, he should have something to protect himself. But he believes that no one is above the law, at least not without a startling good reason.

Oberon ventures through the paths quietly and with a confidence that he will not be spotted. In the forest, the trees shuffle at the mild breeze, which is warm and seems to calm his jittering nerves. He makes sure to carefully pass Favoured Wells - a peculiar house in his mind - he always wonders what goes on within those walls, he'll never be so arrogant as to enter uninvited though. His eyes lock upon the rock wall that surrounds Favoured Wells, there is something so mystifying about it. He knows the rock wall has been there upon their settling in The Motherland, he can't help that it beguiles him with its charm. He reaches a hand toward the rocky surface, with an urge to let his dark skin rest upon its rough exterior.

Oberon jumps then at the sound of a sudden crack in the forest, which startles and distracts him from his thoughts on the rocks. He picks up his jaunt then and hurries to pass the Kalian border – the line of trees that are engraved with K's to signify the edge of Kala. Oberon swiftly moves into the vast darkness of the forest beyond the colonies.

# 34

# VERA OF INSIGNIFICANT CANNELLE TAGONDO

Vera wakes to a tapping noise coming from the back of the cave. She instantly shoots up onto her knees and freezes. *Footsteps. Someone's here.* The tapping sounds again, but it can't be footsteps she decides, it's too delicate of a noise and too erratic. It reminds her of a tiny pebble cascading down a rock wall. Still, in silence, she waits for footsteps for a part of her is not entirely convinced that it isn't an unwelcome guest. After some time and when no footsteps follow, she exhales. Though, still, she has a great sense of unease. *My attacker could come back.* She scoffs at herself then – there would be nothing she could do if he did. Cole is right – she is fresh meat. Just then she feels a rumble of vibrations from the ivani leaf still on her wrist, she forgot all about it, likely because it no longer buzzes against her skin.

Cole speaks in a sleepy but urgent haze located only a few feet from her, "Vera?"

"Yeah, I'm here," she says, holding up the solar light.

His voice is softer, calmer, following her response, "Did you sleep?"

"For a bit," she says as she rubs her face, noting the slight lump that protrudes at her temple from her altercation. Her ribs and tailbone ache, her head also throbs something fierce, but mostly her entire body aches.

"I was thinking, at least we have our bounty and can head back at first light," he says.

"Yes," she nods in agreement.

Suddenly, a voice calls in hesitation from outside of the cave, "Cole?"

*He's back!* Vera quivers. Cole rises to his feet and wanders toward the entrance as Vera instantly feels a shot of worry soar through her chest, but Cole doesn't appear to be miffed in any way at the visitor.

"Issac," Cole greets the voice. Some indistinct mumbles sound and he responds: "Oh shit, yeah come in." A man walks in with his arm wrapped around an injured woman. A slice of flesh is exposed on her calf and a kink to her hobble suggests that her ankle is broken, though Vera certainly isn't a doctor.

"She's here? The Leech," Issac notes, eyeing Vera.

"Put me down here," the woman moans in annoyance. It's obvious that the man Cole refers to as Issac is struggling in assisting the woman. Cole walks over to help her to a seated position.

"What the hell happened to you?" Cole queries.

The woman speaks through sharp breaths: "I was attacked. It's fine, it's not the first time I've been injured during one of Regan's Pursuing Challenges." She settles her hands by her sides and lets her injured leg lie flat against the rock floor.

"Who was it?" Cole asks.

"We didn't see faces," Issac claims.

"It was Cain," the woman raises her voice as her eyes dart to Issac in irritation.

"You said that already, but we don't know for certain," Issac counters.

"It was him – I saw his blade. I know the handle of his blade anywhere."

"They wore hoods this time, we couldn't get a good look," Issac continues.

"I know an asshole when I see one," the woman retorts.

Vera releases a low giggle – she would never dare call a man an asshole out loud, or to anyone, it's too easy for words to get thrown around and to end up meeting with the wrong set of ears. Suddenly she feels unsure again, she admits to herself that she felt a little less worried when it was just her and Cole.

The woman's face turns to Vera, "What? You think this is funny?" she asks forwardly.

Vera, taken back by her boldness, shakes her head apologetically, "No."

"It's not a joke. Cain and his troop are dangerous," she says.

"I understand…" Vera says quietly.

"What's up with her?" the woman motions her head to Vera.

"She uh, she had a run in with an unknown visitor…" Cole hesitantly explains.

"Oh shit! Is that why you're all banged up?" the woman asks. Vera simply nods her head.

"Well, you faced your first encounter with a Tagondian during a Pursuing Challenge… and survived. I'd say that means you're hard."

"What does hard mean?" Vera asks.

"You mean aside from being the description of an object?" the woman teases, "It's like… when you step on an old tree stump and you think it's rotten and falling apart, but then it surprises you and it's actually solid… *Hard.*"

"You thought I was a rotten tree stump?" Vera questions, slightly amused.

"Yes," the woman notes with a smirk.

"Well, glad we cleared that all up," Cole adds.

"I think you need stitches," Vera gazes at the woman's leg.

"And you are the one to do them!" the woman says. Vera assumes that she is likely referencing the day that she did her own stitches in front of the entire Tagondo colony. Her arm is a mere scar now – she glances down at it and winces at the memory. She has new painful injuries now though, her tailbone feeling the most sore.

"Thanks for reminding me…" Vera's voice trails off.

"I don't mean anything bad by it. You were hard. I've never seen a Kalian do anything like that before."

"I suppose we all do what we must to survive," Vera simply says even though she has no clue how she managed to survive her attacker. She's constantly tugging at her memory for a hint. Vera turns to the backpack that Cole packed for her and searches for supplies that can help the woman. She gathers cloth, thread, a needle and alcohol – it'll be enough to make due. She turns to the woman to tend to her wounds – her right eye is swollen, her nose is crooked, her ankle looks deformed and her left calf has a deep slice through the muscle, about the length of Vera's index finger. The cut looks like a clean slice – she isn't sure if that's good or bad. Vera doesn't know what to do with the possible broken ankle, so she decides it's best she leave that alone.

"What's your name?" Vera asks.

"Ezla."

"Well, Ezla, this may hurt a little," she warns.

First, Vera pours some alcohol on a cloth and wipes at the gouge to remove excess blood in an effort to clean the wound, while also getting a better look at it; Ezla releases a sigh of pain.

"It's okay," Vera reminds her. She'll have to ignore the fact that she hates the sight of blood, something she blames The Masters for – it doesn't necessarily make her queasy or ill, it simply reminds her of The Circle, of every life that's been taken in their ceremonies.

She shakes her head at the thought – she can't let it affect how she helps Ezla. She continues gently cleaning Ezla's wound and internally hopes that whatever form of stitches she can do, will be sufficient, if not at least something temporary to make do until they can get her to the hospital.

"Is Mae working tomorrow?" Vera asks Cole, though her focus stays on her fingers and the needle that's about to pierce Ezla's skin. *She may be our only hope in Ezla's admittance into the hospital*, Vera thinks.

"Yeah, she'll help us if Master Regan doesn't admit Ezla," Cole says with certainty.

Vera recalls Cole saying that Mae sometimes helps him. *Maybe Mae's desire to help is solely based on an interest in Cole,* but she pushes the thought away. She has to focus on Ezla.

"I'm going to begin stitching," Vera states.

"Bite down on this," Cole passes Ezla a piece of torn cloth from his backpack. Ezla accepts the cloth into her mouth and bites down as he suggests.

"You sure you can do this V?" Cole asks. Vera nods, though she isn't entirely convinced herself.

Issac scoffs, "*V?* I guess the rumours are true that Cole is getting in close with the Leech."

Cole shakes his head in warning at Issac, "Don't call her that."

Meanwhile, Vera is distracted from their brief clash as she holds the whiskey out toward Ezla to offer her a drink, but Ezla shakes her head – her refusal to indulge in the whiskey somehow surprises Vera. Why she wants to feel more pain than she ought to seems odd. Regardless, Vera brings the bottle up to her own mouth and takes a swig.

"This is going to hurt, okay?" Vera repeats, as if reminding her of what happened and what is to come. Maybe she'll take the whiskey after all, it would make Vera feel better if she did.

"Just get it over with," Ezla demands, muffled by the cloth in her mouth. She bites down harder on it once she finishes speaking. Vera rips Ezla's pants where the wound is on her calf to get a better look, realizing she should have done that step initially. She cleans the area once more and pours some whiskey on the wound, then on the needle and thread.

"Hold the light over here," Vera directs Issac.

"Fine," he brings the light closer, appearing to be bothered by his forced closeness to Vera.

"Deep breath Ezla," Vera instructs her, remembering the way she guided herself in her mind the day she completed her own stitches.

Vera grasps the needle precisely, yet firmly, and with only mild hesitation. She takes a deep breath and then pierces the needle into Ezla's skin, pulling the thread back and forth across the wound, consciously ignoring Ezla's painful moans. It's different, stitching someone else's skin, but with each prick she recalls the sharp ache it ignited within her own nerve endings. Her hand begins to jitter slightly at the memory. *Steady*, she thinks. But Vera reminds herself that the goal is not to be 'pretty' - no - the goal is to keep Ezla alive and free from infction.

"How many carcasses did you yield, Cole?" Issac asks, his British accent only now evident to Vera.

"Why?" Cole's voice lowers, knowingly.

"Ezla got two and they took both of them," Issac explains. Cole looks to Issac, as if calling upon him to speak up with regards to his own bounty. "I hadn't gotten any," Issac admits as his hands rise up in a shrug.

Cole sighs, "What's eight more?" and at that he stands, readying himself to go back out.

As Vera continues suturing Ezla's wound, she notes a small black bag buckled to Ezla's belt, "What is that for?" she nods in its direction.

"It's my knives," Ezla speaks around the cloth in muffled breaths, "I've been using them since I was a kid."

"For pursuing?"

"Yes," she removes the cloth from her mouth so she can speak to Vera more clearly, "And target practice and fending off attackers during these stupid challenges."

"I guess your knives didn't fail you tonight," Cole teases sarcastically.

"This still isn't as bad as when your bow failed you with the mammoth in The X," Ezla chuckles at a memory then pulls the knives out of her bag, silver steel gleams in the solar light as she holds them up to show Vera.

"Hey, the bugger caught me off guard," Cole defends himself.

"Yeah? A fifteen hundred pound mutated wolf caught you off guard?" Ezla heckles.

"You're talking to the Mammoth Slayer here – only one there is, remember?" he beams, though it's obviously all in fun.

"Oh forgive me all mighty *Mammoth Whisperer*," Ezla praises in sarcasm at Cole then places the knives on the rock floor near a beam of light for Vera to view them.

"Those look as though they have been made by one who bends steel," Vera says, glancing at Ezla's knives. She knows that the one who bends steel makes the family crests – in Kala Curshman of Favoured Steel makes them, but she doesn't know who makes them for Tagondo. Ezla's knives, she thinks, look just as intricately made though.

"Maybe. I don't know who made them," Ezla states.

"Who bends steel in Tagondo?" Vera curiously asks.

"Eardin of Favoured Jenisk-" Cole begins.

Ezla interjects, "He was an ironworker back in the Old World – practically a job-match made in heaven."

"Do you think he could've made your knives?" Vera inquires.

"It's possible. Why don't you go ask the guy if you want to know so badly?" Ezla quips.

Vera shakes her head, she isn't about to approach some gruff Tagondian man and start asking him nonsensical questions – especially not now after her experience in this very cave. She glances at the wooden handle of one of the knives, it's carved with a symbol she thinks she recognizes: a circle with a raven inside. She can't recall where she has seen that symbol before.

Still curious on the origins of the knives, she asks: "Where did you get them?"

"A man, a long time ago. I traded my mom's locket for them."

"Why would a man want your mother's locket?" Vera questions.

"It was gold… I figured that was a good enough reason. Besides, I'm not exactly one to wear jewellery," she says, waving her hand up and down to showcase her lack of pristine presentation.

"It just seems odd, a strange man wanting a necklace from the Old World," Vera thinks out loud.

"I'll leave you guys to your banter of lockets and old men," Cole offers, uninterested.

"Wait, let me finish stitching Ezla. I'll come with you," Vera pleads – *Anything but being stuck in this cave.*

"Not a chance. There are more dangers for you out there than there is in here."

Vera argues, "But, you have double the bounty to get."

"Are you eager to hunt rabbits already scientist?" Ezla teases, "Most Kalians don't make it in these parts on their own."

"Damn Leeches," Issac interjects.

"No… I suppose not," Vera admits, eyeing Issac with uncertainty at his comment.

"What did I tell you?" Cole warns with a glare at Issac. Issac flattens the curve of his lips.

Not sure what to do or think of the sudden strain between Cole and Issac, Vera supposes she can stay, moreover, if Ezla and Issac stay with her it'll mean she's not alone and if her attacker comes back at least he'll be less likely to strike all three of them. Besides, Ezla is right, she can't hunt an animal, not even if she wanted to – but it's her decision to stay, not Cole's.

"Fine," Vera concludes.

"Whoa… Now that is the first time you've ever agreed with me. I don't even know what to say," Cole jokes.

"He has no words? Is it really true?" Ezla mocks. Cole tosses a tiny pebble in her direction.

"I'm staying because I want to. Now go before I change my mind," Vera states. Cole, probably knowing that she might change her mind, turns and leaves through the only exit.

"He's a good guy," Ezla states seemingly out of nowhere. Vera knows she's referring to Cole.

"Is he?" Vera asks as a means to humour Ezla.

"I've known him forever, he's different around you. I can't figure out what it is though."

Vera forces a laugh, “Different? You mean bossier?”

“Softer, actually. I think…” Ezla adds thoughtfully.

Vera doesn’t know what to think of that and instead of giving it further thought she quickly straightens her shoulders and refocuses on Ezla’s stitches.

“Ouch! You know, you’re pretty shitty at this, right?” Ezla calls out.

“I know, I’m sorry. If it’s any consolation, I’m almost done.”

“Any news about this wrapping up is good news as far as I’m concerned,” Ezla quips and Vera finishes her work by tying a knot and cutting the tail with a knife.

“There! All done. Now do not let Master Regan see this one, there is no way you’ll be able to stitch that one up on your own.”

Ezla smirks, “Yeah, I’m not as *hard* as you.”

“I’ve never seen a hard Leech before,” Issac notes in what seems a thoughtful manner and not quite a personal jab.

“It’ll do you good to pay no mind to it,” Vera interjects before this conversation prolongs – she doesn’t feel that way about herself. In fact, the very instance of her being attacked earlier that night in the cave is a good indication that she is not *hard.*

Suddenly images of her attacker’s corrupt face flashes through her mind and her thoughts worry about what may have happened while she was unconscious – did he lay his hands on her?

She looks at Issac and Ezla with a forced smile, “Well then, does anyone need something to eat?” She fumbles through her backpack and pushes the memory from her thoughts.

# 35

# Lidia of Favoured Peony
# Kala

It's decided – she will take control of her life in the only way that she can, by jumping in Lake Cloud. She wants to leave Kala, to no longer bear its torture. There is no part of her that wants to go exactly as Ingrid did – death by stones is so prehistoric, so barbaric. She, Lidia of Favoured Peony, won't give The Master, or Huron and his Defenders, the joy of holding a burial ceremony for her, the joy of ripping apart her flesh to burn her bones – she'd rather taste the poisonous waters of Lake Cloud, she'll relish in it. No one will get to watch in pleasure as Lidia leaves Kala, no one will share whispers of her and no one will be the wiser.

Lidia has thought it all through: there will likely be a search for her for a period of time after she goes missing. However, the search will be short and the effort minimal, because it won't take them long to realize she's not in Kala and no one survives outside of the colonies – they don't search out there. She also knows that they won't be able to search the lake - that's something she has on her side - they'll never know what happened to her. All that needs deciding is her timeline, when she will do it and what she wants to achieve before meeting with the lake. This creates a sense of purposeful pressure for Lidia, for upon reflection she finds there is a lot she wants to accomplish before her departure. She promised herself that she won't leave before seeing to it that her list is complete, and Lidia has a thing about promises. Atticus suddenly enters the greenhouse, disrupting her thoughts.

"Hey," he smiles.

"Oh, I wasn't expecting you," she says nervously, while returning a small forced smile with hope that her face hasn't betrayed her.

He closes the door tightly behind him, "What's going on? I've been worried," he whispers. The two pause to glance around, looking through the glass walls of the greenhouse as a means to ensure no one is eavesdropping outside – she clears her throat.

"You've been worried?" she asks quizzically, aiming for casual.

"Yeah, you've been distant."

"We're all distant in this colony."

"More so than normal, I mean."

"Sorry if I've been distracted."

"Distracted with what?" he pushes. *Shoot,* she thinks. *But I trust Atticus – don't I?* He knows her and she him; they've worked together in the greenhouses for years next to Ida. Not to mention, he's been the only one that continues to check on her following Vera's ceremony. She trusts him. Who is she kidding? She needs someone to trust.

"I've been thinking about Ingrid's stoning," she whispers.

"That was... barbarity at its finest," he says cautiously, "What's troubling you about it?"

"She was calling for Fergus," Lidia says, trying to sound indifferent even though heat buzzes at the edge of her voice.

"Yeah, a mother always wants her offspring," he says softly in agreement. He reaches for her hand. She accepts his touch as warm and genuine, momentarily forgetting that he's not yet eighteen. Although she is thirty this year, the years between them don't seem to make a difference to her. She hugs him.

"Oh!" Atticus says, seemingly surprised as she wraps her arms around him.

"What? Never had a hug before?" she asks, pulling away just slightly.

"I can't remember the last time," he recalls as his arms dangle at his sides.

"Me neither," she adds sadly. Atticus places his arms around Lidia and a few reflective seconds pass as they embrace.

Atticus breaks the silence, "Vera's ceremony," he answers, continuing to hug Lidia, his head towering over hers; his slender body allows her to wrap her arms all the way around him. She feels a strength in his maturing muscles that offers her comfort.

"I want to leave Kala," she finally says.

"What? How? Why?" he asks, holding her now at arms length.

"I'm not happy here anymore."

"But, where would you go?" he asks. She can't tell him the details of her plan just yet, not before she has everything in order.

Instead, she simply responds, "I don't know."

"It would be a stupid move – do you know how to survive outside of the colonies?" he asks while backing away from her, perhaps he wants to look her in her eyes. It doesn't bother her either way, though she did enjoy the touch of another's skin against her own.

"That's a trick question. No one does," she meekly replies.

"Well? You'd be sentencing yourself to death."

"Yeah. Well, what if that was the point?"

His eyes widen, "Lidia! What are you saying?"

"I don't know. I need some time," she responds, confused.

"Time for what? Don't leave, you belong here."

"I just want it all to stop," her voice drifts.

"Then be here. Do something to make it all stop. Don't wither away," he pleads. *Wither away,* it sounds so appealing, like she's already halfway there.

# 36

## VERA OF INSIGNIIFICANT CANNELLE TAGONDO

Issac and Ezla have dozed off, but Vera couldn't dare sleep, not at the chance of Cole needing her help. She feels restless without him being there with her, but truthfully there is something more that's keeping her awake – she wants to know what exactly happened to her. There's no way to know what truly happened, unless her memory returns. Even still, there is that absolute unmarked timeline in which she was unconscious.

She decides that she has to push those thoughts aside in an effort to distract herself, she feels slightly envious of Issac and Ezla. It appears as though they don't have concern or worry in regards to helping Cole, or anything beyond their most basic human needs – they sleep quite peacefully. Even though Ezla was also attacked she doesn't seem worried. Vera has always been one to worry about things beyond her control though. She glances at the two: Ezla is sprawled out across the rocky terrain and Issac is sitting upright and snoring abnormally loud, his reverberations remind Vera of one of the machines at the lab. *The lab.* The thought instantly carries memories into the forefront of her mind and brings with it the urgency to get back to Kala – to tend to the message that Hendrix whispered in her ear. However, she knows there's nothing she can do right now, while in the thick of Master Regan's troughs. Instead she reflects on working with Hendrix and how much joy she got out of the work they did, the pride that coincided with trying to save the water. She misses it – she misses him.

Vera finds herself fighting noiseless tears, withholding the sobs that want to escape. Between coping with Hendrix's death and trying to survive Tagondo, it seems she hasn't had a moment's reflection on her work at the lab until now. It was important to her at one time. In fact it was everything. But here, in Tagondo, what's important now? Feeling safe, she decides. She misses the privilege of wandering the forests alone and foraging at the lake, even though Kala came with its dangers as well. Ultimately, the only way to truly ensure safety is to cleanse the water so that she can leave The Motherland altogether. Tears stream down her face as a pitied feeling engulfs her. She thought she was meant for great things, that she would find the cure to the water eventually, but she can see now that is likely never going to happen. She fights the tears that tempt to fall. *What good does crying do anyway?*

^

Several hours pass before Cole returns and admittedly Vera almost nods off a handful of times. She looks up at him as he enters the cave, his face drawn with what she assumes to be exhaustion, the sun is beginning to rise and he's been up most of the night.

"Well," he says as he flops his body down beside Vera, "That was interesting." His eyes are heavy, his hair an actual mess – more so than normal.

"Did it go okay?"

"It did up until I ran into a mammoth."

"No!" Vera shrieks, and though her reaction lags from her own need for sleep, she sits up as though she's ready to jump swiftly out of her own boots in concern.

He laughs, "I'm kidding."

She lifts her hand and gently pushes his arm. As her fingers graze the curve of his muscle under his cotton shirt she suddenly hesitates and pulls her hand back. A flashback shoots though her mind of her placing her arms up attempting to fend off her attacker while he hovers over top her, a quick flash of his face appears and then nothing.

"You okay?" Cole asks. *I don't know,* she thinks. And she wonders what determines someone being 'okay' or not after an attack.

Still, she forces words out of her mouth that Cole will think to be a normal reaction: "Yes… I just… I should've known that you were joking… about the mammoth," she accuses him, hoping he doesn't notice her hesitation.

"So, did these two lazy dogs sleep the whole time?"

"Practically." Vera rubs her hands across her face in an effort to keep herself awake.

"You're tired," he says.

"Yes, well. So are you."

"We still have a few hours, get some shut-eye," he insists.

"What about you?"

"I'm fine for now. Here, take this," he tosses her his bearskin scarf.

"Ak-" Vera sounds with hesitation at his offer.

"-No arguing. Get some rest," he simply states.

She rolls her eyes and tosses the scarf back at him - no way will she use a fur scarf - not to mention, it still irks her when he tells her what to do. But this time, she won't fight it further, she needs sleep if she is going to function and be capable of getting back to the colony in a few short hours. She takes her fleece scarf off that Murdina made for her and places it on a rock to act as a pillow. When she lies down she realizes that although he's bossy and insists on knowing her every move, there's an ease that sweeps across her in his presence. Soon she closes her eyes and finds sleep.

^

Waking to Ezla's laughter isn't the most pleasant wake-up call as it's a sort of obnoxious cackle that urges one's ears to want to close, if only ears could do such a thing.

"Wakey wakey, Vera!" Ezla chortles.

"Is it time?" she sits up with squinting, drowsy eyes. Her brown waves stick in a sleepy disarray of strands, she uses her fingers to mimic a brush and quickly combs though her locks.

"It is," Cole apologetically looks to Vera in understanding.

Ezla fumbles with locating her boots, "Let's roll. I'm starting to get sick of you guys."

Issac gathers the group's belongings while Cole divides up the bounty so each have their rightful number; Vera notices that he has ensured not to go over the required lot, and she knows why – it's safer. Ezla retrieves her boots and begins the struggle of putting them back on. Vera walks over to Ezla and helps her to her feet.

Cole brings a long stick in, one that Ezla can use to help steady her footing upon the uneven ground as she walks, "Here."

"Thanks."

Vera lifts Ezla's arm over her shoulder for additional help, knowing Cole will be guiding them back. The group exit the cave as the sun slowly rises; wherever the light of the day touches there will be no mammoths. At the cave's entrance, Cole and Ezla pause to chat about the path that they should take to get back to Tagondo. There seems to be a trust between them that Vera can't quite understand why or how it came to be. Issac on the other hand, she still isn't sure about him.

After the two men walk ahead, Ezla states: "Moment of truth."

Vera looks at her quizzically, "What is?"

"If you're gonna be able to help carry my weight down the mountain side or not."

"Oh, it should be fine."

"You're alright," Ezla chuckles, "for a scientist."

"What, do you have something against scientists?"

"No, not really. It's just that they all seem like asshole know-it-alls."

"That sure sounds like something to me," Vera notes.

"I guess we'll find out."

Cole guides the group up the mountains, even farther off track from the path that he thinks others may occupy. The view from where they travel is immaculate – Vera can see some of the buildings in Tagondo, deep-set in and amongst the lush trees. She even spots some fellow pursuers also making their way back to The Master's chamber, bounty in hand, though they appear to be quite tiny in size and such a distance away that they can't hear but a sound from them.

Throughout their journey, Ezla and Cole tease and poke fun at one another, primarily at Issac - he appears to be the laughing stock of most jokes - he seems like easy prey with his high-buttoned shirt fastened all the way up to his neck, right below his chin and his dirty blonde puff of hair that sits atop his head. There's also an unusual nasal tone to his voice that irks her slightly, but she tries to remind herself that isn't fair – one cannot control the way their voice sounds. Maybe she will get used to it over time. Cole and Ezla must have, after all, those three have known one another since they were children. It amazes her that their friendship has carried on beyond that childhood phase of naiveté and innocence. She was eight when she stopped 'playing' and searching for her friends down the footpaths, no longer responding to their pleas of shenanigans and imagined fantasies. Eventually, they stopped calling for her altogether. But she had a responsibility to fulfill, countless responsibilities actually.

"Shhh, be very quiet," Cole interrupts her thoughts and the chatter between Issac and Ezla. He stretches his arms out in front of the group as if they're a force that could stretch for miles.

"What is it?" Issac asks, paying no mind to the volume of his voice.

Meanwhile, Vera stops promptly; an aching concern rises in her chest, all she can think is that her attacker has come back. Her eyes dart behind them in desperation to see what Cole sees. When she finds no sign of concern, she turns to him and examines his face. It's difficult for her to pin his expression, because there's something in his eyes she hasn't seen before. Then she gazes down the path and sees what he is focused on so intently. His eyes are locked on the large, grey creature that is weaving through the trees. Its body looks just like that of a wolf, only twice the size, easily. Its face has mutated into something out of this world, though from this distance she struggles to see its mangled details. It moves some 200 yards away from them.

Vera places a shaking hand on Cole's arm, "What do we do?" she asks. Perhaps this is the one time she'll easily let him tell her what to do.

"Stay quiet, stay calm," he responds while readying his bow and arrow.

"He's killed one before," Ezla nonchalantly whispers to Vera while still using her as a means for balance.

"Two, actually," Cole corrects, banter in his voice and a half smirk on his face. Though his eyes remain steady on the mammoth.

"I-I can't," Issac stutters as his eyes widen in terror, he begins to back away from the group.

"Issac, stay still," Cole urges as Issac continues to separate himself from the group.

The mammoth catches sight of the movement and in an instant breaks out into a sprint toward the group. While Vera stands paralyzed, Cole lets loose several arrows, they shoot about 150 yards, two of which pierce the mammoth in its side – as if it doesn't even phase the giant creature, onward it charges. The mammoth's steps pound the dirt, each thud sending a jolt through Vera's chest.

"Ezla, you go east, get your knives ready," Cole instructs, "Vera stay with me."

Ezla manages to hobble off to the side in an attempt to escape the path of the mammoth; she hides behind a tree. While leaning on its frame to still her stance she steadies knives in both of her hands. Vera can see Ezla's pained expression from putting pressure on her injured leg. It's then that Cole pulls Vera with force across the path to the opposite side of Ezla. Her feet fumble over the rocks at his urgency. She jerks her arm out of his grasp, irritated by his need to drag her about like some helpless child.

"What are you doing?" he barks.

"I asked for instruction. Not to be dragged about."

"I'm just trying to keep you alive."

"I'm not completely helpless," she retorts.

Cole snorts as he releases another arrow, "You got lucky back at the cave with the Tag so you think you're strong now?"

Vera's body trembles, even through her pride she's still fearful. Cole positions his body so that he now stands in front of her acting as a shield, like he's some impenetrable force, brimming with power and strength. Vera's breath catches at his nobility, but she reminds herself it is all because of his agreement with Murdina. Still, she rolls her eyes.

"You think you can take one of these guys?" Cole questions her as he holds another arrow pointing at the creature, awaiting the most ideal opportunity to strike.

The mammoth is heading directly for Issac – Issac, who turns and begins running as he notices that the mammoth's demonic eyes are fixated on him. The beast runs up the path passing the armed three: Ezla throws knives, Cole lets loose several arrows and Vera stands helpless, but she doesn't want to be helpless, she's sick of being seen as weak.

In a moment of conviction, she makes a decision and reaches into her satchel and quickly grabs the tiny stem that holds several ivani leaves. Vera swiftly places a leaf upon her wrist, grabs her bow and arrow and runs for Issac. She notices the leaf tingles against her flesh, and after a moment it buzzes even stronger. A sudden surge shoots through her veins, her pupils dilate, her heart rate accelerates and as she moves her body she increases in speed. The trees beside her now blur – fear, she realizes, does not freeze her thoughts and cause her to tremble. Instead her mind focuses in on one objective and it is crystal clear: save Issac from the mammoth. She moves her legs faster, weaving in and out of the trees at a speed that seems like a surge of adrenaline, but there is no time to think about why.

The mammoth is quickly approaching Issac, luckily, she's quite savvy in mobility from her days foraging and running after Atticus, she'll have to thank her little brother one day for that. Vera cuts westwardly off the path and takes a shortcut to get to Issac before the mammoth. When she reaches Issac she immediately pushes him off the path with a strength that seems to come out of nowhere, he flies a few feet and lands in a bush with a crash, moaning from fear or injury, she isn't sure which follows. All she knows is that he is no longer visible to the mammoth.

Swiftly, Vera turns to face the approaching monster with her bow aiming directly at its heart and ready to soar an arrow right into it, ready to take the creature's life – but she can't. She can't put aside all of her inner feelings of killing an animal. She isn't a Tagondian. Even though she still feels the surge in her veins, she drops her bow and arrow and freezes. Her eyes squeeze tightly shut as she waits for the mammoth to take her. Maybe it won't be all that bad - dying - for in this world only the fittest survive anyways. But somehow the creature begins to slow down its pace, standing now, but a few feet from Vera, and then it falters. The beast falls to the ground in a thump that almost seems as though it shakes the earth's crust, she stands frozen, staring down in shock and confusion. She glances up and just beyond the creature is Cole. Cole lowers his bow as his gaze moves down upon the mammoth. Vera's eyes follow his line of sight to where she notes several arrows, Cole's arrows, sticking out of the back of the mammoth and one that protrudes out the back of its skull.

"Vera?" Cole shouts, a sort of pain etched in the cracking of his voice. His shoulders slump forward as he catches sight of her.

Ezla limps in Vera's direction, "Holy shit! That was something scientist!"

Issac appears, crawling out of the bush by Vera's side, "I think I broke my elbow," he whines.

"Honestly? If it's not broken, which it better be after all of your whining, I'm going to break it just so you know the difference," Ezla warns as Issac frowns in response.

"Sorry Issac," Vera says, worrying that she did indeed break his elbow with the sudden force that she collided into him with. Her trembling hands return as the buzzing from the leaf slowly begins to subside.

"What the hell was that anyway? I feel like I ran into a rock wall," he moans. Vera looks down at the leaf that barely tingles on her wrist anymore. Issac's question makes her aware that what just happened seems entirely unnatural. She ponders her symptoms briefly and it's as if the oil from the plant entered her bloodstream and offered her a shot of adrenaline. It seems like a long shot, she'd love to run some tests in the lab to learn more… She quickly tears the leaf off of her wrist.

Cole throws his weapon to the ground in what seems like both relief and exhaustion. His brow tenses as he runs his hand through his hair, just as he always does. He stands there curiously, as if contemplating something, *But what is he contemplating?* He's angry with her – that much is now obvious. She resisted his help and then tried to interfere. Vera adjusts her posture, uncertain of what to expect from him and yet preparing herself. She put her life in danger and potentially the lives of everyone else here – it was entirely reckless and irresponsible. Sure, she tried to save Issac, but perhaps she put him in more danger by acting on her foolish convictions, which resulted in her succumbing to the mammoth in the end anyway. *A Kalian can't defeat a mammoth.* It was stupid, but at least the mammoth is dead and everyone else is alive. *Can't that be all that really matters?* She exhales at the realization that Cole saved her – which is both relieving and bothersome.

Cole begins walking toward Vera, his chest huffing up and down, but she notices that his eyes start to soften as he approaches, which confuses her. She doesn't let her eyes soften. Then, there he stops and the two stand inches apart.

"You can't tell me what to do. I only tried to help-" she begins her case.

But he cuts her off, "-That was the stupidest thing I think you've done yet. I'm not even sure exactly how you pulled it off or how you weren't mauled!" his tone is firm, but his expression heartfelt. *Mauled?* She repeats the word in her head.

As she slowly comes to terms with the severity of what could've happened, her emotions begin soaring through her bloodstream as the effects of the leaf completely wear off. He's right, she could have been mauled, or worse, she could also still be reeling from the altercation in the cave.

Cole's stare lingers on her face, she looks down to the ground unequipped to cope with his gaze. Tiny droplets of water brim her eyes, though she refuses to let them overflow. Nor will she look back up, she can't. He drives her mad. To appease him or to anger him – she doesn't know which she prefers. He's like a wild card, one she doesn't know how to play. Like that stupid card game – five-card draw is it called? Hendrix tried to teach her as a kid back in the Old World, she never got it.

"It was also, the bravest thing I've ever seen," he continues, "I mean, for a Kalian," he smirks.

She looks up into Cole's eyes, only because she feels the pressure to do so now, "I had to try to help Issac."

"You saved him," he says, stepping closer until his torso is parallel with her face. She can feel the warmth radiating off the contours of his chest. It would be nice to use that heat to warm her rosy cheeks and cool-tipped nose. But she won't.

"And you… saved me," she admits.

As she looks away, suddenly and uncomfortably aware of Ezla and Issac's gaze on them, he reaches down and places his hand gently on her chin.

She subtly winces as he raises her eyes back to his, "And I'll do it again and again." She swallows hard, the gulp sounds in her ears. "You piss me off Vera North," he breathes, "but what you did was incredible."

Incredible? She wasn't expecting that. She inhales – cedar and orange ignite her sense of smell. This scent has become familiar to her, like the way spring brings forth its routinely earthy fragrance. It's predictable, welcoming. She also realizes that something else warms her cool demeanour, he called her by her true name – for she will always be a North.

Cole leans in then, his eyes heated and fixed on hers. When his gaze moves down to her lips it's as if her feet are standing on shards of glass and within an instant she shoots back, stepping away from him. Perhaps nothing can truly warm the coldness within her. There she stands, at a distance, with her heart beating slightly faster than normal. She worries that she has embarrassed him; however, not much seems to spark embarrassment in Cole Pollard. Still, there's a chance he'll be angry with her for turning his presumed kiss down.

"Sorry. I wasn't thinking, I shouldn't have," Cole starts. Then she realizes that he's too good of a man to be angry with her for that, and that very fact pains her. Cole turns around and heads to collect his weapons from the mammoth's cavity. Vera feels a brush of cool air as he turns his body away from hers, maybe she imagined the whole thing.

"It's alright," Vera whispers back to him, slightly delayed, but it's a lie. Lying always seems to be the way to navigate life among The Almek. No one really wants the truth here. However, there is one immediate truth that she notes: something unfamiliar grows inside of her, a spark of some sort that tugs at her limbs and nestles in her core. It digs into her flesh, like spikes on a rose bush.

# 37

# COLE OF FAVOURED POLLARD TAGONDO

They dragged the mammoth deep into the bush so that no one will find its carcass and ask questions - of course, if they were to bring it as bounty Cole would win the Pursuing Challenge - but more attention, and pissing Cain off, is the last thing he wants. And so, after much debate, the other three agreed upon his terms. His terms were simple: no one finds out about the mammoth attack.

The rest of the walk back was quiet and as they enter the footpaths outside of the colony centre, Tags flock in and fill the empty spaces amongst the trees. Each of the foursome carries their bounty of four carcasses. Vera carries her offerings in her hands as she doesn't have a belt like the others have: a common Tag accessory meant for gripping any one limb of a dead creature as it dangles, flopping lifelessly at one's side. A chuckle rises in Cole's throat as he watches the way Vera adjusts her hold on the creatures' tails within her grasp – her arms spread out, away from her body as if to keep them from touching her and a grimace spread across her mouth as though she hates every minute of this.

As they approach the colony centre Cole sees Master Regan sitting in his chair next to his Barons upon the platform in front of The Master's chamber, a glass of wine is in his hand as per usual. The men and women that partook in the Pursuing Challenge gather around the circle of the colony centre, they must take up over half of Tagondian population. The younger and older citizens - the ones that weren't required to participate - stagger in behind them, less in numbers. Defenders make their way about the warped circle, several carrying lists and marking the bounty number beside each participant's name. Cole notes Lincoln standing among the line, alongside a few other Tags closer to The Master's chamber stairs. Lincoln holds a glare on his face meant for Cole – he is sure of that. Cole stands amid the same line of salty smelling Tags, but with Issac, Ezla and Vera at his side. Issac's frame trembles as the Defenders approach them.

"Stop it – you've done this before," Cole reminds him, but there's no teaching Issac new tricks, he's like an old dog that can't see past the fog in his eyes.

"I'm nervous…" Issac admits.

"No kidding," Cole says with irritation, "Just play it cool." He glances to Vera and although she still holds the carcasses out abnormally far from her torso, she isn't shaking, nor does she look nervous. This slightly surprises him.

"It's easy for you to say, everyone will easily believe you got four," Issac grumbles.

"Yeah, well, you could at least try to look believable," Cole whispers.

Rimmy approaches them and grabs the four carcasses from Issac first and, as if it's possible, Issac's body seems to tremble even more in Cole's peripheral. Cole runs his hand through his hair, without directly looking at Issac – if Issac doesn't calm down, he'll give them all away. His pulse begins to quicken slightly, but he has to remind himself that it's the same thing repeatedly with Issac, if it wasn't for Cole secretly helping him, he'd be long gone. Cole knows that he's a sucker – the only one who continuously has Issac's back and knows that, yes, he has a soft spot for the weak and timid. He has a soft spot for those that are not capable of meeting the hefty requirements of Master Regan. He realizes then that he technically plays for both sides as with Master Regan seeking his input, he was forced to play on the dark side. Again, he had to be indifferent to simply survive. Rimmy stares Issac down, his dagger-stare remaining on him, he watches him squirm under his gaze.

Finally he speaks: "Four for Issac of Insignificant Urndolf," he says then tosses the carcasses to the Defender that follows closely behind him. Another Defender puts his pencil to paper, marking his list. Cole exhales in relief.

Rimmy reaches for Cole's bounty and simply shouts without another glance at him, "Four for Cole of Favoured Pollard." Then he moves onto Ezla, who has propped her wobbly stance against Vera for support of her wounded leg. "Broken leg?" Rimmy asks, though a slight smile plays at his lips. Cole knows he's an evil man, he doesn't need this moment to prove it.

Before Ezla can respond Rimmy grabs her bounty and knocks into her injured leg as he continues onto Vera, Ezla wails in pain and leans on Cole for support.

"Four for Ezla of Insignificant Adder," Rimmy pauses a moment as he stares at Vera now. Though there is emptiness to his eyes, he moves them across her body as if she's a meal, one that he can help himself to.

Cole shuffles his feet in discomfort. *Fuck you Rimmy, just keep walkin'.* But Rimmy notices Cole's uneasy movements and his eyes dart back to him. Rimmy smirks. Cole's tensing must make it obvious that he is protective over Vera; Cole stills his feet and aims to hold his indifferent posture.

"What happened here?" Rimmy asks as his rough hands grab Vera's chin. He pulls her face closer to his, tugging more roughly than he ought to, inching her closer toward him.

Cole's eyes shift to Vera, though he tries earnestly to not turn his head. Vera stands, steadying herself with her arms tightly stacked at her sides, but frozen, as if to allow him to finish what he has set out to do. Her expression is unreadable, maybe that's intentional. Rimmy's hand forces her head to slightly turn as he eyes up the scuff on her temple. Cole knows exactly what he's doing, he's showing his power, his control. Of course Rimmy knows that Vera didn't get the bounty herself - he isn't stupid - but he has no proof, which means he won't report it to The Master. In an attempt to pretend as though this doesn't bother him, Cole stares straight ahead while he waits for Rimmy to move on, that's all he can do.

"Four for Vera of Insignificant Cannelle," Rimmy spits though his eyes stay on her as he says it. He releases his hold on her chin and though Cole remains still, in his irritation he clenches his jaw. Rimmy's eyes shoot back to Cole and his evil smile spreads, showing his yellowed teeth. After a few uncertain seconds, Rimmy thankfully turns his body and continues on down the line of Tagondians. Cole exhales again in relief. It appears as though Vera does too as her posture seems to slouch ever so slightly upon Rimmy's exit.

Following Rimmy's check of the Pursuing Challenge bounty he leads three men to the Tagondo jail, several Defenders follow in watch. Cole knows they'll face something horrific, he also knows it'll be at the Aftermath Party – Regan has one following every Pursuing Challenge. He only hopes their tribulation will be less gruesome than the last one. An image of two men having their ears removed by Rimmy scars his memory; Rimmy staring intensely with blood-covered hands.

"Wow. That was… something," Cole says as the line of pursuers disperse.

"Another Pursuing Challenge in the books," Ezla smirks.

"Yeah!" Issac says, followed by a wince for his elbow.

"Pfft, you barely did shit Urndolf," Ezla heckles.

Vera takes a few steps backward, "I need to get back to Murdina's."

There is something off about her and he knows it. He shouldn't have tried to kiss her. "Yeah… I need to get these two wackos to Master Regan to report their injuries."

"Good luck," Vera says, as she turns to walk down the path.

"I'll see you at the Aftermath Party?" Cole asks.

"There's no way around that, now is there?" she says.

"No," he smiles. Cole then goes with Issac and Ezla to report their injuries to The Master while Vera heads back to Insignificant Cannelle.

By this time, Regan has settled back inside the chamber while a large line with several Tagondians from the Pursuing Challenge seeking admission into the hospital forms outside. Seeing as Cole is unable to go in with Issac and Ezla, since he isn't injured, he stands outside of the building and waits as each member goes in individually. Issac goes in first and when he comes out his face is sullen in frustration.

"He wouldn't give it to me," he grumbles.

"Well, your arm looks fine," Cole suggests.

Next, Ezla stumbles her way out, smirking through her pain, "I got it."

"Good… You need it," Cole says.

Issac exhales sharply, "It's because you're his niece."

"It is not. Have you looked at my leg?" Ezla retorts.

"Come on, let's go," Cole says as he wraps his arm around Ezla's waist to help her to the hospital.

"What, not going to carry me like you did Vera?" Ezla teases. Cole is used to her teasing and he normally dishes it right back, but not tonight. He reflects on how Ezla is more like a sister than his own who shares his blood.

"How'd you hear about that?" Cole asks.

"Nothing stays secret here, Coley boy, you know that don't ya?

"Well in that case, hell no I'm not carrying you," he replies with a chuckle.

"You like her," Ezla teases through pained breaths as they walk.

“Yeah,” he admits.
She pauses, then notes: “It’s weird…”
“Yeah,” he agrees.
“Be careful. You liking her is only going to taunt Rimmy more,” Ezla warns.
“I know. That’s what I’m worried about.”

# 38

# VERA OF INSIGNIFICANT CANNELLE TAGONDO

Vera flies into the shower as soon as she gets back to Insignificant Cannelle that afternoon with an earnest desire to rid her body of the filth that her attacker imposed upon her. Her body aches from head to toe from the altercation, which means there is no telling what sort of abuse has been done to her. She lets the scalding water run over her body and scrubs her skin until it's red. A different kind of red streams down her legs and turns pink with the water - her monthly cycle. She reflects again on how little she knows of the incident and hatred fills her. She imagines his face inside his hooded sweatshirt, the visual of his grimace encourages a memory to the forefront of her mind - it's distorted and foggy, but she suddenly recalls the man asking her for the cure and in turn she gives him the thone plant as trade for Cole's safety. *Thone? Why did I give him thone?* She questions herself, a reckless decision. Though she can't remember much after that instant, she feels a suffocating feeling, one that suggests that she had no other option. She immediately gets out of the shower, quickly wraps a towel around herself and searches through her satchel, she finds the thone vial and reads the inscription.

"Burns!" she says out loud in shock. *How could I?* This man was already angry enough, had enough reason to harm her and she lied to him – but not just any lie, not like the white lies she tells to keep herself from being vulnerable. No, she lied about the cure to the worldwide Water Crisis. She flops herself onto the floor, still wet from her shower, she sits in disbelief and regret of her terrible decision.

After some time, she rises and sits atop her bed immersed in thought, *Cole is alive though.* If it weren't for her lie he'd possibly be dead. The truth is, no, she isn't a terrible person, she's a weak person. Her track record in Tagondo of making poor choices only continues to grow.

^

It's a daunting obligation that they must dress up for the Pursuing Aftermath Party. Master Regan sent specific, mandatory instructions by means of Rimmy who delivers the message door-to-door. Rimmy stands like a dark shadow in the doorway, hovering over the Cannelle's like a giant. His eyes dark under his hood are two black orbs that mean to torment whatever crosses their path.

"Master Regan says dress in your finest," his voice booms. Vera wagers that his frame is much too large, his voice much too deep for any normal human being. Murdina and Opi accept the instructions and immediately wander to their wardrobes to find something appropriate. Vera is left to bid goodbye to Rimmy.

"Thank you," she says and begins closing the door.

"My pleasure," his jaw clenches as he speaks and she thinks he wants to say something else. His evil stare lingers as she closes the door with an urge to flee from his peering eyes, her heart erupts in spasms of unease.

Vera walks to her room, unsure of what to wear. It's hard for her to see the purpose in dressing in elegant clothing and, like many of Master Regan's commands and meanderings, they have no true purpose towards the greater good of the colonies.

"Quick, quick lass!" Murdina hurries Vera along to her room.

"I'm hurrying," Vera mumbles, unenthusiastically tugging at her hair – it's thick and so it isn't easy to persuade it into any specific style.

"This frock, put it on Princess," Murdina shoves a dress at Vera.

"This is far too-"

"-Pish," she speaks over Vera, which is typical of Murdina, "Didna want ye to go lookin' like…"

"Looking like a Kalian?"

"Like… Ye dinna belong," she simply says.

Vera glances down at the bronze crest on her chest that's etched into the shape of a Rowan tree: the Cannelle family crest, an Insignificant Tagondian. She bears the crest, but she definitely doesn't belong.

Vera slips into the gown that Murdina mentioned she made earlier that day. Blue teal clings to her chest and down to her waist, there it meets a gold coloured crinoline that widens at her hips and falls to the floor graciously. The straps set off to the sides of her shoulders rest just at the edge, in beautiful ruffles. It's quite lavish, far beyond the extravagancies of Vera's taste. When Murdina comes over to fuss with the dress, Vera can see such intensity in her expression. This is important to Murdina: this senseless, trivial evening. It touches Vera as it reminds her of the day her mother readied her for her re-birthing ceremony, her chest aches at the memory. *What is it about mothers and dressing their daughters?* It's as if a sense of pride is innate in females when it comes to dressing their young – another argument for why Vera thinks she is not fit to be a mother.

As Murdina continues to tug and adjust Vera's dress, she can hear the fireplace crackling in the living room in its stone hearth, it always creates shadows amongst the room.

Vera doesn't enjoy the fussing, though she doesn't mind it all that much either, and she finds Murdina to be growing on her, even though she's a tad pushy. Vera breathes in cinnamon – a typical spice that Murdina simmers over the stove claiming that cinnamon cleans the stale air indoors, while also offering goodluck to those who breathe it. Vera could believe the former.

"There," Murdina exclaims as she looks Vera over in the dress as though it's a grandiose piece of artwork. Perhaps it is. Still, the inspecting stare makes her feel uncomfortable – Vera looks away. Murdina places her hand atop Vera's, "Are ye alright lass? Ye can talk wi' me… about anythin'…"

A twinge of embarrassment settles in. Maybe Vera's weakness is etched all over her face, defying her attempts to stay hidden. Inside her head she contemplates if she should tell Murdina about what worries her. Her thoughts quickly dart away and ponder on what she'll do if she sees her attacker again, he'll likely be at the party tonight, but she really doesn't want to talk or think about it anymore. So, out of necessity, Vera wanders to the tall mirror that hangs on the wall near the bedroom door. She needs space; she needs to rid her mind of the thoughts that only make her feel terrible and scared. She focuses on the dress instead. It isn't exactly what she would desire in a dress, though it admittedly looks nicer than she presumed it would.

"A Princess, indeed," Murdina smiles a serious smile that doesn't quite go as far as her eyes. "I must get myself dressed," she notes as though she forgot that fact, before turning and scurrying down the narrow hall toward her own bedroom.

Having given up on her hair, and deciding to just leave it down, she wanders to the living room. The fire creates the shadows across the walls and floor just as she pictured, even though the sun has not yet set. Opi waltzes into the living room wearing a grey collared shirt that houses his double chin within its tall neckline. His pants are plain, just black, but the blazer he wears surely has the eccentric flare of Murdina's touch for it has beads sewn onto its chest and a tall, plaid collar that stands against the sides of the collared shirt.

*Have his pants been made too short? Or does he just prefer them hiked up past his belly button?* It isn't for Vera to decide. A different, more impactful question raises in her mind then: *Is he a murderer?* As she gazes at him, she ponders that it isn't for her to decide either, but it is for her to find out. She knows no other way than to simply ask him. Though, how far will she go if he doesn't willingly answer, she isn't certain just yet.

"You look nice," Opi says while adjusting his belt.

"Yes, well, you can thank Murdina for that."

"Isn't she lovely? I've never seen a woman with such taste for flavour!" he exclaims.

The two are alone, they are never alone – now is her chance to confront him, if only she can muster the courage. Her mouth opens and then closes again. The tips of her fingers pulsate, and she feels a spark that taunts her insides. She steps toward Opi with an intention, a sudden urgency that reminds her she needs to know the truth. Hendrix had been brave enough to fight for her in The Circle so she needs to find the strength to at least talk about it, even if it's uncomfortable, even if it means speaking with her father's murderer.

"What happened that day in The Circle?" she finally blurts.

"W-What ever do you mean?" Opi stutters as if her question appears as a surprise, beads of sweat suddenly glisten on his forehead.

"How did the downfall of my father unfold?" she questions, knowing she missed some of the fight, it was too hard to watch – as well as the possible matter that she was drugged.

"I-I don't know what you mean," he stammers again.

She huffs in frustration, "Did you or did you not kill my father?" she demands.

"I-I did, I mean, I didn't. I mean," he takes a breath – his face worry stricken.

"Tell me!" she yells, then retrieves from under her dress one of the knives that Cole made her, "Tell me or I will use this," she threatens, holding the blade up while shaking. She points it toward Opi.

"I don't know what happened, okay?" Opi's stubby finger moves his glasses up his nose, as he always does – nervous or not.

"What do you mean, you don't know what happened?"

"If… I shouldn't be speaking of this," Opi runs to a nearby window and glances out, then travels to look out another. He runs about, looking and closing the windows tightly before he continues. "I didn't kill Hendrix," he whispers.

"Who did?"

"I don't know. One minute he was holding his sword and I mine – we were in battle. And the next I looked and he was lying on the ground."

"So you didn't kill him?"

"No. But Master Regan thinks I did, please Vera, you mustn't say a word. If he knows I wasn't the one responsible for Hendrix's death he'll have my head, or worse." Vera looks at Opi confused, her eyes form suspicious green slits.

"All I know is, he died," he affirms.

She purses her lips. There is a sadness to Opi's face, a quiver in his lip that makes Vera somehow believe him. Just then, Murdina walks out of her room with a bright purple gown on. It's decked in frills along the edges and filled with plaid on the bell skirt. Shiny beads are spread randomly about the dress; it appears as though they were placed with as much intent as the stars in the night sky. Her hair is knotted in a large mass at the side of her head and two pink circles sit upon her cheeks, almost as if they are tattooed on.

"What is it?" Murdina demands at the sight of the two, standing in opposition with sullen faces.

Vera turns to Murdina, "Do you know how my father died?"

Murdina's eyes hold firmly on Vera, her brow slightly wrinkles, "Whatever do ye mean? Yer faither died in The Circle, we all saw him."

"Opi says he didn't kill him. So?" she shrugs, all the while her lips remain pursed in order to control the sobs that threaten to erupt in her throat. Murdina's harshly wrinkled brow softens and her eyes return to their natural, slightly downturned shape. She breathes in heavily, but she says nothing for some time, Vera waits.

When Murdina finally speaks, she appears flustered: "Well then, if nae a body knows, it's settled."

"Settled how?" Vera asks.

"That Hendrix is dead."

"We're trying to figure out how he died Murdina."

"He died in The Circle. Leave the poor man be, at peace in his grave."

"But I-"

"We have to go, we canna be late for the party," Murdina says, "Dry yer tears."

^

Vera, Murdina and Opi walk through the footpaths; wooden cabins and trees fill the spaces between the pathways. Vera pulls her scarf tightly up around her neck as the sun sets and the air of this late May evening grows unusually cool. The paths flood with Tags scrambling toward The Master's chamber, each in his or her own elegant attire – even little children and babies garnish their finest. Vera learned from Murdina that some Tags make their own formal wear while others hire someone well versed in needlework to ensure they have something fitting for such occasions. One that does not possess such needlework skills have to trade something of value to have an outfit made and to most that something is usually their shares.

Soon Ezla appears along the path with Issac by her side, his weak arm is held tight to his side while his good arm stretches out to assist Ezla in her step. Ezla has a tensor bandage around her ankle and a cane to help take the weight off.

"Vera, you are looking wonderful," Issac calls as they catch sight of one another. She wonders why the sudden compliment.

"V, pullin' out all the stops," Ezla says, throwing her arm around Vera's shoulders.

"You two look quite nice yourselves," Vera nods as she joins their pace.

The three continue walking the path together as Opi and Murdina toddle ahead of them. Vera instantly thinks that it's odd to not have Cole apart of the group after their camaraderie the previous night. Vera soon takes over for Issac and lifts some of Ezla's weight as she helps her hobble toward the chamber. Issac slows to walk closely behind them; Vera glances back at his simple brown suit that buttons all the way up to his neck and he smiles at her – opening his lips baring his crooked, yellow teeth. His pouf of dirty blond hair sits atop his head, sort of brushed over to one side. Meanwhile, Ezla is wearing a dress simple in style and dark blue in colour, like the night sky. It almost looks like a t-shirt and skirt set, with a belt separating the two. It complements Ezla's orange hair and pale skin-tone – even covered in bruises and fashioning an injured leg, she's pretty.

"Your dress is nice. Did you make it?" Vera asks her.

"Yeah, is it that obvious?"

"It looks great."

"Hersh said he thought it looked like garbage. But he probably won't make it out tonight anyway, so I won't have to listen to it."

"Hersh?" Vera asks.

"That's my Dad. The father figure," Ezla rolls her eyes. Vera isn't one to pry so she doesn't ask what the sarcastic 'father figure' reference means, although she is curious. However, Ezla continues on to answer her curiosity: "He's drunk everyday, and kind of an asshole."

"Oh." Vera doesn't know what to say to something like that.

"It's okay though, it's just how it's been."

"How is your leg anyway?" Vera asks.

"It's fine. Master Regan approved my access to the hospital, so Dr. Yani looked at it. She said it's actually just a torn ligament, should be healed in a few weeks."

"That's not so bad. Did she say anything about the stitches?" Vera asks.

"No, at least not to me."

"Well, I'm glad you're okay. Can you report your attack?"

"Pfft, no. Master Regan doesn't accept reports like that," Ezla states. Vera presses her lips together.

"It's not fair, The Masters only seek to hold people accountable when it suits them," Vera speaks heatedly.

"The pricks!" Ezla agrees.

As they approach the stone steps to The Master's chamber, Defenders line the wall beside the wooden doorway. Tags flank in through the doors; a constant flow of traffic. Shouts of annoyance and moans of ignorance filter into the room ahead of her. The lack of respect for one another strings through the air as noticeable as dirty laundry clinging to a clothesline. She braces herself upon entering The Master's chamber for the first time. It's a large building that houses a kitchen in the back and enough space to accommodate everyone in the colony to sit at tables and chairs. It might have been used as a mess hall for a camp back in the Old World. On the far back wall a wooden stage sits with stairs off to the left leading up to it. The same wooden carvings, only much smaller in size, rest on either side of the head table atop the stage. There, Master Regan sits with his three Barons: Orsen, Jaret and Burke; a feast lies out on the table in front of them. As Vera's eyes scan the front of the chamber, she sees that there's a tiny, circular table below the stage, just in front. Vera wonders what that table is for. She imagines, just like the pedestal in The Circle, it too has its purpose.

Murdina explained to Vera earlier that it's customary to sit with one's progeny, so she follows Opi and Murdina to one of the tables, designated for Insignificants, along the wall. The tables are quite large and so there is room for others. Ezla waves down Hersh, while Issac goes to search for his parents to guide them over.

As everyone takes to his or her seat, Vera notes Ezla's father, Hersh, did come after all, reeking of drink, it's quite obvious that he's intoxicated – which is what Ezla must have been talking about earlier. His dress shirt is only halfway buttoned, exposing his gut down below. Issac sits on the other side of Hersh – beside his own father, Hugh, who looks and dresses much like Issac. They hold the same pointed nose rather high and their mouths house the same crooked, yellow teeth – evidently those particular genes are quite strong in that family. However, Issac's mother, Innis, seems rather poised in comparison. Although Vera struggles to hear what Innis says to Murdina, there is a smooth, featherlike flow to the way Innis sways her fingers as she speaks.

Vera turns, searching the room for Cole, but her search comes unanswered. Ezla clears her throat and gestures with her head and eyes to a table across the room – the tiny, circular table up front closest to The Master's table.

"That who you're lookin' for?" she questions Vera. Vera turns her head to follow Ezla's action.

"Oh, I suppose it is," she responds casually.

"He has to sit there, that table is reserved for The Master's immediate family and Barons," Ezla explains. Vera remembers that Cole's Father, Burke, is a Baron. She looks to the table where Master Regan sits and sees a frail looking man whom she assumes to be Burke. She glances back to Cole's table and wonders who the woman is that Cole's sitting with.

"Treena," Ezla says, as if Vera asked the question aloud.

"Who is Treena?"

"She's Master Regan's daughter… And my cousin." Vera nods then, as she clearly recognizes her as the woman that often runs to whisper into Master Regan's ear during ceremonies.

"Cousin? So that means Master Regan is your uncle?"

"A dear uncle indeed," Ezla says sarcastically. "My Dad wasn't always stuck on the drink… Let's just say that," Ezla whispers. Vera ponders that for a moment, she looks over at Hersh. Yes, she can see now that Hersh could be related to Master Regan

– similar black hair and pointed cheekbones, though their eyes are different, Hersh's dark eyes hold a sadness that pains Vera.

"You must look like your mother," Vera presumes, as clearly Ezla didn't get her burnt orange hair from the black of Hersh's.

"Yeah, a lot actually," Ezla reverts the subject then, "So, Treena, she is to be the next Master when Regan is gone."

"I notice she looks awfully comfortable with Cole," Vera says. Treena has her arm around Cole's shoulder, leaning into him as she speaks into his ear.

"Yeah she would, with their merge agreement and all," Ezla notes.

"Their what?"

"You didn't know?"

"No."

"I thought Cole told you..."

"It's fine, I'm glad you did," she says, aiming to sound indifferent. She sits in thought a moment. All this time Cole has been lying to her, even when he's had countless opportunities to tell her about his merge agreement. But why?

"You alright?" Ezla asks, concerned.

"Yes," Vera says, her distant eyes return from their daze.

"Their fathers have been best friends since after the Water Crisis, them merging was kind of written in stone," Ezla explains. *Written in stone? Could it be love?* Vera ponders the word. *Is it like Almay said? Or Lidia? True love?*

Vera glances back at Cole and scoffs at the sight. She doesn't think so, but she decides she doesn't want to know any more about his merge agreement with Treena, so she doesn't respond to Ezla out of necessity. It's second nature for Vera to bury her thoughts and feelings – like bodies in a grave, gone but not forgotten. She straightens her posture, clasps her hands together and sets her brow accordingly. In response, Ezla raises her right eyebrow at Vera.

Ezla goes on: "So, beside Treena is Nin, that's Cole's older sister, then Delaney, Cain's mother and Baron Orsen's merger. Then beside her sits my nemesis - everyone's nemesis - Cain of Favoured Fenwick." Vera coughs suddenly, choking on her own saliva.

"Cain who?" her eyes move up toward the table as they absorb the man that Ezla speaks of.

"Fenwick," the name articulates off Ezla's lips in harsh syllables that reverberate in Vera's ears. For just a moment it's as if she is in a dream where she is the size of an ant and everyone else that sits around her at the table towers over her.

"Wait a minute…" Vera stares at his face. *That's the face.* She knows it is. *Cain of Favoured Fenwick, that's him.*

She suddenly recalls then how he told her his name, how he wanted to be the one to get the cure so that he'll hold more power. His eyes suddenly find hers in a possessive, evil glare and as he turns his head she sees burns of red across the side of his face. *Thone.* His stare pierces her, she can practically see the anger radiating from him. *He's going to come for me.* It's an illogical, paranoid thing to think and yet, she knows it with all certainty. She's going to have to figure out how stop him this time. Master Regan stands then, interrupting her thoughts as he addresses the crowd.

"Welcome Tagondians, it is an exciting evening indeed to bear witness to another Pursuing Challenge – to see how successful you all were, most of you," his neon-blue eyes scan the crowd, there's an intensity to them that Vera finds unsettling – it seems to be a trend in Tagondo.

In this moment the servant ones, the ones who cook and wait on Master Regan, bring out dinner plates filled with food and place them upon all of the tables.

Master Regan continues: "Some of this meat has been supplied because of the Pursuing Challenge. Let us eat in that honour," the crowd of Tags snap in celebration.

Master Regan takes his seat and begins eating the steaming meal that lies in front of him. The people sit in silence and watch him eat while two servant ones stand on either side of his table, hands clasped with diligent eyes on his graciousness. Regan gestures to his glass and the servant woman closest to him quickly retrieves his drink off the table and takes a sip. She sets the glass back down and stands upright, straight like a soldier. Not a full minute passes and Master Regan collects his glass and takes a drink for himself. He then resumes eating and the room echoes with the chomping and smacking of an animal; it irks Vera, though she sits still as everyone else does. A servant one dabs Master Regan's face with a cloth, signifying that he's finished.

He then sits back with drink in hand and raises his glass, he shouts to the room: "Dig in, my broken ones," and everyone does as he says – they shovel fork upon fork full of food in their mouths, like pigs in a pen, gluttonous in nature.

Veal, potatoes, green beans and freshly baked biscuits all sit in front of each colony member. It's important to Vera not to waste the veal, though she knows there's no possible way her stomach will allow her to eat it. When she was younger, Hendrix asked her to try meat again – he suggested that perhaps her taste buds had changed, as they seem to do as the human body ages. She knew he was wrong, her taste buds hadn't changed – she knew it by the way her stomach nagged and twisted at the smell and the way her mouth unpleasantly watered. In her experience, there are two different reasons in which the mouth salivates and the option that applies to her isn't the pleasant one. But she didn't have the heart to tell him. She agreed to try it again with hopes it would appease him; unfortunately, the moment she placed that piece of meat in her mouth, out came the vomit – spewing like a fountain. It is for this reason she offers her meat to the rest of the table. Hugh happily accepts it, he holds out his plate and she gently places the veal on top. Potatoes, beans and a biscuit will be plenty for her.

Soon it is time for Master Regan to announce the Offenders: the ones who didn't quite make the required bounty, which as far as Regan's ruling is concerned, is a sure-fire way to get exiled.

Master Regan stands to address the crowd: "It is not an easy duty that we possess – to supply this Broken World with enough meat to sustain the life of thousands. As the two colonies grow, it is evident we must increase our bounty year by year. I am not oblivious to the fact that we house many weak Tagondians.

"Far too many of you are not pulling your weight, while others work double time. And as far as I'm concerned, one weak member is one too many. Tonight, we bear three. Three Offenders lack the urgency and skill to complete a simple task, a task that will keep us alive. Do we not want to stay alive?" he asks the room.

Snapping fingers fill the quiet in response like pellets of hail hitting the ground. "Is it not important then, that we rid ourselves of the poison that lingers beneath our skin?" the Tags boast an encore with their ice pellets, "Because that's what they are: poison. And what does poison do?" he pauses then, his next words are deliberately spoken slowly yet articulated with such exaggeration, "It slowly kills you from the inside out!" he states as the room cheers in shouts and howls for Master Regan.

In that moment Vera begins to cough rather profusely, she puts her water-filled glass down on the table and covers her mouth as she coughs into her hand, trying to muffle the sound. The cough worsens until she feels her throat swelling – she can neither breathe nor speak. She moves her hands up to her neck in desperation for air.

"Vera, what's wrong lass?" Murdina speaks with urgency.

When Vera can't respond, Murdina appears standing by her side to quickly assess her vital signs.

"Yer eyes, they're turnin' black."

There isn't much time, Vera can feel the light fading from her eyes; her vision begins closing in.

Murdina picks up Vera's drink and smells it, "Stein!" she scoffs, "Aye smell yer bevvy lass, have ye got brains?" Murdina rummages through her bright purple satchel that hangs across her shoulder, though Vera is in far too much of a panic to pay mind to what Murdina is in search of. She tries to force a cough but nothing comes. The pain in her throat burns and nags as if someone has set fire to it.

The members at her table stay in their seats, frantic eyes search Vera and Murdina. Ezla begins screaming for help, her deep voice scratching the air, but no one can hear it above the room's cheers for Master Regan. Suddenly Cole appears by Vera's side, somehow he must have heard the screams of desperation.

"Murdina, what's wrong with her?" he demands.

"Stein,"

"What's stein?" he asks urgently.

"Poison," Murdina says while still rummaging through her satchel and mumbling Scottish curse words under her breath that no one can quite understand.

"Can you help her?" he pleads.

"Pish. Here it is," Murdina pulls a tiny glass vial out of her satchel with what appears to be crushed leaves of some sort inside of it, "Get me a glass of fresh water and a spoon," she demands to no one in particular, "And smell it first."

Cole grabs a glass of water nearby and sniffs it, "Here," he offers instantly then passes her a spoon. Murdina pours a spoonful of crushed leaves into the glass of water and stirs it rapidly, the water begins to turn a light, misty green.

"Drink this now lass. Ye havena much time," Murdina demands as she tips the glass towards Vera's quivering lips.

Vera reaches for the glass with her shaking hands and attempts to hold onto it, Murdina continues to steady it with her wide-set hands. Without a notion as to how she'll manage to swallow the mixture, she accepts it. Once Murdina's concoction touches her lips and enters her mouth, the liquid shoots down her throat, opening the pathway to her lungs and oxygen begins to flow through her body once again – a subtle buzzing and tingling flows through her insides. She breathes heavily, coughing, her throat burns from the poison.

"Is she okay?" Cole asks with tense eyes.

"I'm fine," Vera clears her throat and then turns to Murdina with a sweat-covered face, "Thank you."

"Ye dinna have to thank me Princess. But boy, ye've got some trouble on yer hands."

"What do you mean?"

"I'll explain later," Murdina says, turning her head with a questioning eye as she looks around them, "For now, dinna drink or eat anythin' while yer here. Cole, stay with Vera. Dinna let her out of yer sight," she says with certainty and a strictness that one wouldn't want to test. However, Murdina's expression most days looks this way: a raised brow and a straight-lipped mouth. It's a face Vera sees often and finds it difficult to judge the necessity of its dramatics. Though she knows it's fair on this night – someone poisoned her drink.

A glance to her glass indicates a black tint to the water that she didn't notice earlier, but she hadn't really looked. She slowly stands, grabs her glass and dumps it into the plant that sits in the centre of the table, while cursing the person who attempted to poison her.

As she glances around the room a few seconds later, she realizes, she was poisoned, almost killed, and it happened entirely unnoticed by the colony members who continue to cheer for their Master. Though their shouts don't prevent her entirely from hearing a few whispers from skeptical Tagondians. In this moment, following her brush with death, she looks even more unkempt than them.

"She is Kalian, maybe she's come to harm us with her science," a voice at a nearby table whispers, a storm of emotions swarm in her head.

By some uncontrollable force Vera scoffs rather loudly, it seems accusatory whispers are unavoidable; however, she can hear no whispers that point to the responsible Tagondian, the one who poisoned her. It could very well be anyone – anyone who doesn't want a Kalian around. But she hasn't been the only Kalian sent to Tagondo. Over the years there have been several. She is, however, the only scientist.

Then she thinks, maybe it wasn't meant for her. Though that's an incredibly awful mistake to make, to poison the wrong person. She hopes it to be true. Her eyes scan the room and they quickly meet the same possessed stare, and such a stare it is – the kind that sends prickles across one's flesh. She can see him clearer from where she's standing now – the blisters clearly evident on the side of his face, she supposes that he isn't all that fond of the thone plant. And even less fond of her.

# 39

## ATTICUS OF FAVOURED NORTH KALA

Atticus walks the paths as the celebratory drums for One hum in a buoyant tune. When he reaches The Pit he catches sight of Lidia as she takes her seat, he walks over to her.

"With the earth, Lidia," he says.

She responds in a rasp: "May we be cleansed."

"How are you holding up?"

"Holding up? I'm not. A woman just died," she whispers under her breath.

"I know," he wraps his arm around her shoulders then, tightly yet gently, and pulls her into him. "I know."

The bones are pulled from the fire and placed to cool before Master Oberon's seat. Many still dance and drink, though slowly they flock to their seats. Atticus doesn't know what it is that suddenly sends people to their seats, there is no signal, no siren that goes off. He wonders if it's the way the smell of the fire changes, one minute it smells like burning flesh and eventually the scent of burning hair consumes the air.

Master Oberon sits in his seat and addresses his people: "With the earth. It is time, my friends. The time has come for 'The Passing.' We will pass Ingrid around the fire with love and in unity. With a vision that if we work together, one day our water will be cleansed and we can expand beyond The Motherland."

"One," the crowd hums.

"First, we must pray," Master Oberon pauses, an intentional pause, and then continues, "Oh Mother Earth, we pray for you to carry this woman's spirit to her afterlife, to cleanse her and love her. And we ask that you bless us with abundance on this Earth for the rest of our days."

He smiles at his people, their adoring faces smile back. He begins The Passing of One: one bone, one embrace, and then continues passing them on to his right.

When the first bone comes to Atticus he always feels strange and thoughts circulate in his mind: *Who was Ingrid? I never even knew her and yet I'm caressing her bones.* It's the norm, but it's strange. He holds it gently in his hands, he stares down at the dust covered bone then passes it to Lidia while trying not to stare at her reaction. The Passing is intimate and meant as a means of reflection for the self and for the group as a whole; however, it's hard not to look.

Lidia holds Ingrid's bone, caressing it in her small, delicate hands. Her index finger almost appears to tap on the surface for a second, but it's merely the beginning of her hands moving. She grazes the bone with her right hand, as if moving away the dust to inspect it, like there's some sort of secret inscription written just for her. Her bottom lip trembles as a single tear falls from her eye and lands in the dust on the bone. As if Lidia is then pulled from a trance, she passes it on to the person next to her. Atticus feels a wave of curiosity flow through him, he wonders what it all means to Lidia. An hour or so goes by before The Passing is finally complete.

All bow their heads at Master Oberon as he recites the closing script: "One with the earth." Seeing as Ingrid's husband is already one with the earth, Master Oberon is handed her crest. He holds onto it, his hands lie flat as he stares intently at it. He then sets it against his heart and places both of his hands, one over top of the other, on the crest. He presses it there, embracing the crest for a brief moment while his eyes close. It is a peaceful ritual. He is a peaceful-looking man. Just as soon as Master Oberon opens his eyes, he holds the crest out and passes it to one of the Defenders. Two Defenders gather her bones in a wheelbarrow and the three of them head to the bone hut.

"Are you okay?" Atticus asks Lidia.

"Sort of. I'm not really sure."

"Do you want to go dance, take your mind off of it?"

"Sure," Lidia says with a faint smile.

The musical ones play their instruments livelier now, as most of Kala stay at The Pit to drink, dance and rid themselves of the weight that bears down on them from another death in the colony. Atticus won't forget the display earlier that day, but he admits to the freeing sensation of dancing. Is it so bad if he wants to pretend as though none of this happened? If only for a moment?

# 40

# VERA OF INSIGNIFICANT CANNELLE TAGONDO

Cole immediately sits down at the table beside Vera, she feels safer with him at her side, she is safer with him at her side – though she won't admit it aloud, especially not to him. The crowd's applause for their Master slows and the room finally grows quiet once again.

Master Regan continues the night's agenda: "The three Offenders are as follows: Trey of Insignificant Wisen, Karim of Insignificant Schol and Liev of Insignificant Wick. Please proceed to the stage," he states.

The three young men make their way to the stage, led by Master Regan's Lead Defender, Rimmy. They walk in a single line formation like a depressed flock of sheep on their way to slaughter. It pains Vera - Tagondians or not - to see this, they are human beings and are hardly being treated as such. She worries at the thought of what Master Regan's plans are for the three young men. If it's to be anything comparable to his previous displays of ruling, she knows these men are in trouble.

"It is customary that when we send off an Offender who has not been able to fulfill our needs that we take something from him before he leaves. A payment, or apology, if you will. Seeing as this was a pursuing competition, we all need our hands for pursuing do we not?"

The room chants, "He, he, he," in response. It seems to be the chant they do when they want blood, Vera notes.

"I want one finger from each of you. It doesn't make a difference to me which one," he nods to Rimmy who then grabs Trey first and holds his left hand down on a tiny square wooden table – the one she noted earlier. *So that's what it's for: a torture table*, she realizes.

Rimmy holds a large, rusted pair of scissors in one hand while gripping Trey's wrist with the other; Vera inhales sharply at the sight. The room grows quiet, the slightest creak of a chair is all that is heard. Vera, still reeling from her recent brush with death and awareness of her attacker, looks about the room in disbelief. The Tags lean forward in what appears to be interest, elation even. *They want to see this!* Then, a crippling crunch: the sound of bones breaking and a single, lonely scream of agony signals that it's done. Rimmy tosses a towel at Trey as he desperately wraps it around his limb to control the spray of deep red fluid coming from his hand. Trey stands in front, on display, just as Master Regan so desires. Tears run down Trey's cheeks, his face red with pain or anger – or both. Master Regan's stare lasers through Trey while he smirks at the onset of torment – Rimmy's face stays inexpressive, emotionless.

Karim is called upon next and his feet move slowly forward toward the table. As he passes Trey, they nod at one another. Trey means to encourage Karim that he'll be okay; if misery is a brotherhood, they would both be members. Rimmy removes Karim's left pinky; careless about it in a way one roughly takes off a dirty glove. Vera worries what kind of infections these young men will be subject to – that'll likely be the culprit of their deaths, maybe not today but in the coming weeks. The remaining part of Karim's finger, the stub that's still attached to his hand, emits a spray of red liquid about five feet in front of him. He barely flinches though, his expression is lifeless – he's in shock. Though it takes him a few seconds to react, when he does he moves quickly to care for his wound. He rips part of his shirt off and wraps it across his hand then raises his blood-soaked limb above his head before taking his place beside Trey.

Liev Wick is next. Vera has never met him but it's obvious he's not intending to cooperate. With one robust push, using what looks like the force of his entire body, he knocks Rimmy down. The Lead Defender falls backward and in an instant jumps back to his feet and wrangles Liev in a headlock— Liev's face quickly reddens with lack of oxygen and it looks as though Rimmy's sure to kill him. Vera's eyes dart back and forth from Master Regan to Rimmy. *Stop!* she thinks, *Someone needs to do something!*

"Enough," Master Regan finally says.

Rimmy stands up right and holds Liev tightly in his grasp by the back of his neck. Master Regan's gaze is suddenly upon Vera's table.

"Stop!" his palm raises to the room, "What do we have here? Cole of Favoured Pollard. You have switched seats without my consent? And to an Insignificant table no less?" Master Regan states. They have been caught. Vera's heart races up into her throat. Only Master Regan would stop a deadly fight to concern himself with seating arrangements. Perhaps it is more than that though.

Cole stands up, "Yes, I was worried about my friend," he says calmly, without a flinch.

"So I see. Well the only thing that concerns me now is your lack of respect. Move back to your table with the Favoured, unless you don't want to stay a Favoured?"

"If it means that I can ensure Vera's safety, I think I'll stay right here," he states, sitting back down. Master Regan's eyes grow wide, for the first time Vera sees what she thinks to be surprise on his face. She worries what that means.

Vera leans into Cole and whispers: "Cole, go back to your seat," she brushes her hand gently across his forearm, "I'll be fine. Don't lose your position as Favoured over this. What happened to being indifferent?" She fears he could lose much more than just his position in the colony.

“No way, you’re fresh meat – anyone could’ve done this,” he argues.

She rolls her eyes then. She couldn’t live with herself if Cole lost his Favoured status - or worse - because of her. This, she thinks, must be his first time ever disobeying his Master.

“Cole, come to the front,” Master Regan says as he gestures a slight nod toward Rimmy and his scissors. Cole stands to his feet and without a second thought walks toward the torture table. Rimmy shoves Liev toward one of the other Defenders to confine.

“You’ve surprised me Cole, it isn’t like you to be so… disobedient. Perhaps that has something to do with a certain someone,” Master Regan’s eyes fixate on Vera for a moment before he refocuses on Cole, “But to be honest, it adds a sort of exciting twist to tonight’s events. Rimmy – a finger from Cole as well, if you will.” Master Regan moves his hand forward in a sort of bowing motion.

Rimmy holds Cole firmly in place, Cole doesn’t fight. Instead, his eyes fiercely focus on what’s to come while his lips push tightly together in a line.

“No, stop!” Vera shouts, rising to her feet.

“Oh, my, my… another outburst! That’s more than I can count from you my dear,” Master Regan bellows toward Vera.

“Master Regan, please. He didn’t do anything. Let him go back to his seat and you won’t hear another word from either of us,” Vera pleads.

“I won’t hear another word from you? My... that is a tempting offer. Does that mean I get to sew your mouth shut?” he pauses a moment, “Hmm, on the other hand, a finger… or two from Cole would be more effective. And in the end, a small peace offering from one of our best pursuers...”

Cole’s father and Baron to Master Regan stands up, it’s clear that rising to his feet takes effort.

Burke then speaks in a slow, tiresome tone, “Master Regan, this is my son you’re talking about. Put a stop to this nonsense at once.” Burke breaks out into a fit of coughs and returns to sitting.

Master Regan’s eyes thin into two malicious slits. He waves his hand to Rimmy. Rimmy steadies Cole’s hand on the table.

“Daddy no!” Treena shouts.

“Bunny… You must stay out of daddy’s dealings.” Master Regan is clearly getting annoyed at the constant stream of interruptions.

Still, Treena runs up the steps and to her father’s side. She whispers a series of words into his ear while he nods agreeably then she steps back with a smirk on her smug face.

Master Regan holds his hand up, as a means for Rimmy to stop, then raises his index finger and lets it rest across his lips as he ponders, “Okay, I have made up my mind. We won’t remove a finger, but I have another idea, which has gotten me excited. Instead, it is clear that I need to set a merging date for Cole and Treena, say… Next month? Thirty days from now. Reproduction to start immediately following.”

Treena merely walks to her seat while holding a lingering stare on Vera. Vera slumps her bottom down onto her chair, Cole’s eyes meet hers, his eyebrows lift apologetically in defeat; if this is how he plans to tell her about his merge agreement with Treena, she’s not impressed. For a moment, it was almost as if she forgot all about it. But, she decides, she won’t say a thing, she won’t even be mad at Cole for him not telling her about the merge agreement if it means he keeps his limbs.

Cole walks back to his seat next to Treena, and as he approaches his designated table Treena throws her arms around him and extends her lips out to kiss his cheek – all the while Cole's eyes remain locked on Vera.

"This feels so wrong Ezla," Vera says, looking away.

"It is wrong. So wrong. Treena is a huge breach."

"You think so?"

"Yeah, she's a piece of mammoth shit – even worse than that."

"Well, this isn't all her fault. At least she saved Cole. I tried and it only made things worse."

"There's not much you could've done," Ezla tries to convince her.

The celebration continues and yet somehow through all of the commotion of Liev and Rimmy throwing chairs and shouting obscenities to one another, it's all a blur to Vera. However, Master Regan looks pleased – her pain appears to offer him exuberance, it's sickening.

In the distance of her consciousness she overhears Rimmy's triumph as he takes one of Liev's fingers after all. Liev screams and falls to the floor, the room roars in excitement. *For goodness sake I can't take these dramatics right now.* For now the three men are restrained, surrounded by Defenders off to the side beyond the table of torment. Vera wonders what Tagondo does with their exiled, and if it's the same as Kala.

After the brutality ends Master Regan makes another announcement: "It has come to that time, where we announce our reigning champion of this year's Pursuing Challenge!" The room snaps their fingers.

Master Regan rises to his feet as he holds a shiny object in his fingers. He stands and walks to the very centre of the stage to address the room.

"Cain of Favoured Fenwick, would you please come forward." Vera tenses at his name, the very utterance of it is enough to send her head in an unsettling whirl. What did he do to her? She can't stop thinking about it.

Cain rises from his seat and walks forward until he stands in front of The Master's stage and in front of The Master himself. As Cain stands a few steps below, he glances up at Master Regan with eager anticipation.

"Cain, you have procured a bounty of ten – far more than required. You are a true Tagondian, a true Pursuer. Strength runs deep in your veins, fear does not. Your prize…" Regan holds his hand down as Cain reaches his up to grasp the shiny object from his Master.

Cain fiddles with the tiny prize, pulling the length of it over his head and around his neck. When he turns to face the stare-filled room, curious eyes gawk at his reward that now rests, dangling on his chest. It appears to be a small coin of sorts, possibly made from gold judging by its yellow hue, it sits attached to a leather necklace. Cain stands with his shoulders back and a grin on his face that one can't quite explain. It's a proud grin, but it also shows something else - a hunger - as though his desire to win isn't quite fulfilled. Vera shudders at the thought. The entire room breaks out in stomps of glory for Cain of Favoured Fenwick.

After Cain takes his seat, Master Regan encourages everyone to dance. The musical ones, bring out several instruments including a drum, chimes and a guitar. Instantly, many in the colony stand and begin dancing in the centre of the room like a psychotic, brainwashed cult. It reminds Vera of the One celebrations back in Kala and she wants no part in it.

She approaches Murdina who still sits at their table, "I'm going to go home."

"Lass, ye canna go, ye canna be wanderin' alone anymore."

"Are you kidding me? I can't be a hostage, I need to be alone right now," Vera then turns and moves to the door, hoping no one will notice her sneaking out.

A thought crosses her mind then: *I have to be quick.* The last person she wants to notice her alone is Cain, but hopefully he'll be distracted with his recent victory. She walks through the doors and just barely makes it to the first stone step when a warm hand gently tugs at her wrist. She sighs knowingly.

"Hey," he says.

"Hey," she replies.

"Well shit, that was some night. You almost died and I almost lost a finger," Cole chuckles, "We both got lucky."

"You didn't get lucky – you had Treena."

"I didn't have Treena," he says while turning her body around gently with his hands so she's facing him, "What's up with you?"

She ignores his question but can't ignore the thought of Treena, "No? It does seem that way, especially now with the merging date set."

"I'm sorry that I didn't tell you… I was going along with it because there was no better option for me. But I know now that I can't let it happen, that I need to get out of it. The last thing I want is to be with her."

"It doesn't matter. It's what *they* want. And they get whatever they want Cole - they're Adders - royalty." And they clearly don't want her and Cole being friendly with one another.

"So, what do you care?" he asks.

"I don't care," she crosses her arms.

"You don't care? You don't want anything to do with me, but the second there's another woman in the picture you're pissed off?"

"I'm not pissed off."

"What are you? Tell me."

"I-I need to go. Excuse me," she says turning and walking down the steps.

"Damnit Vera, you're impossible!" he calls to her, but she keeps walking and doesn't look back.

He's the one that won't stop pushing her for more – while he's in a merge agreement with another, no less. *I'm not impossible – it's him.*

With things seeming to worsen in Tagondo, at least in Vera's mind, what she needs to do is figure out a way to get back to Kala and complete step three.

# 41

## Atticus of Favoured North
## Kala

It's been a few days since Atticus spoke with Lidia about her leaving Kala. Nevertheless, he keeps a close eye on her – he wants to know what she's up to, which is probably unfair to her, he isn't sure, but he is concerned. *Why would someone want to leave at the risk of death?* He also didn't like the way she acted at Ingrid's One.

Atticus goes to class, but he can't focus due to his worry for Lidia. He notices that she has been trying to avoid him lately, or so it seems, and he thinks that there's no reason for her to avoid him, unless she has plans. Plans that she doesn't want Atticus to get in the way of. But Atticus is good at sneaking about, he always has been. He's snuck away from Digger before being spotted more times than he can count, and he begins doing the same with Lidia.

Atticus often follows Lidia in the evening, on her way home at sundown like a hawk or a lost puppy – or something in between. Mostly she just cries when she thinks no one is looking or she'll pray out loud to Mother Earth, whispers that beg for solace. *Doesn't she know that someone is always watching?* That was a lesson his parents taught him in his younger years, when he was reckless and caused trouble – someone was always listening, whether it be the Whisperer or a Defender. The more he thinks about it, perhaps he's still young and reckless, but he just knows to keep an eye out now.

Atticus witnesses Lidia travelling back and forth from the greenhouses, but more interestingly he's spotted her visiting Torant of Insignificant Wells' house. Torant's an odd and mysterious man, one that the colony people generally steer clear of. Atticus hears the odd whisper, possible reasons as to why, but he doesn't know Torant and so he doesn't technically know if the whispers check out.

On this day Atticus follows Lidia once again to Torant's house, keeping a fair distance back and weaving in and out of the brush along the path. In all honesty, he's never seen Insignificant Wells before following Lidia, though many talk about the old rock wall that comes before the house. Insignificant Wells is one of the farthest homes from the colony centre and sits just at the edge of Kala. Southward, beyond his house, has never been ventured – the reason being mammoths are of greater threat out there, though Atticus doesn't think that is sufficient enough a reason.

Today, Atticus gets a closer look and can see that the rock wall actually encases Insignificant Wells – a circled wall of stones surrounding the cabin. Atticus watches as Lidia, in her black pants and fur scarf that sits atop her charcoal long sleeve shirt, walks in the front door of Insignificant Wells without a knock. *What are you up to?* He has never been inside the walls of Torant's house, nor will he ever. So, there he stays for some time, watching and waiting. He hopes that she is safe. He hopes she isn't being touched or fondled or hypnotized. He doesn't really know what kind of rituals go on inside those walls. Voodoo dolls have been mentioned in the whispers by the colony people that he's heard surrounding Torant's name, he prays to Mother Earth that Lidia comes out unharmed.

When Lidia finally emerges - alive - Torant sees her down the front stairs. His slick-black hair is greased to his head, almost appearing as though it's painted on, and his eyes are so dark that it looks as though, from where Atticus is hiding, there are no irises to speak of.

"You know you and her both made a terrible decision speaking to those Tagondians that day," Torant says, seemingly continuing a conversation from inside the house.

"You don't think that was what initiated her re-birthing, do you?" Lidia asks.

"What are the names of the Tagondians you spoke with?"

"Cole and Lincoln. They called us over, asked us to talk with them."

"Cole of Favoured Pollard?"

"I didn't get his full name."

"Oh well, it's done now," Torant responds. "You must go."

"Well, thank you for the peace of mind with Lilith," Lidia calls back as her feet hit the ground and she begins walking down the footpaths.

"Speak of this to no one," he says to her as she nods her head and ventures into the forest. "And don't forget payment," he calls.

Atticus plans to stay crouched in the bushes until Torant goes back inside. However, Torant turns then and scans the surrounding forest, as if knowing. His eyes form suspicious slits as he studies the greenery. He scans over the bush that Atticus hides in. *Shit! He knows.* An urgency to run soars through Atticus' limbs, but if he moves even the slightest of muscles Torant will definitely see him – and who knows what Torant will do if he catches someone spying outside of his house. So, there he stays and he'll stay as long as he needs to, he can push the feelings that want him to run to the back of his mind, he can forget them. For it isn't the first time he's had to hide in a bush, and it won't be the last.

When Torant finally turns and retreats inside, Atticus stands to his feet and flies up the path. He's fast and stealthy as he dashes through the footpaths knowing that Lidia will be long gone by now. He's relieved that he was able to see her leave Torant's, relieved to know she's still alive and not strung on his wall like a puppet.

Atticus replays Lidia and Torant's conversation in his mind over and over and he wonders, who is Cole of Favoured Pollard? He decides that if he ever lays eyes on this guy who has even the slightest part in making his sister an Offender - and taking her away from him - he'll kill him.

Atticus runs through sundown as the curfew siren rings in his ears, all the while he has an ill feeling in his stomach that stretches beyond his worry for Vera. *What is it then?* His mind keeps wandering back to Lidia – no one ventures out to Insignificant Wells. And if Lidia is, she's in greater trouble than he thinks.

# 42

## Vera of Insignificant Cannelle Tagondo

"Where do the exiled go anyway?" Vera asks Murdina the next morning during breakfast. Since she left the party early the previous night she missed seeing off the exiled, though it isn't exactly missed in the way some would suggest. She wonders what one would do once being exiled, for there is no where to go.

"They will never be seen again," Murdina's eyes suddenly widen in intensity. She glances away from Vera and her tone drastically softens, "Ye need not worry about that."

"But, I do. Those men won't survive out there on their own." As quickly as the topic of conversation had begun, it ends.

"How are ye feelin' today anyhow?"

"I'm fine," she says with irritation for being ignored. She focuses then on a different matter at hand, one closer to home, "What was that substance that you put in the water that you gave me?"

"Oh," Murdina shudders, "Last night twas a close one. I ken someone gave ye stein, just like the black poison. Not many people ken about the plant's properties. I'd be keen to watch yer back."

"The plants properties?"

"Tis time ye ken, that the plants are different now, after the Water Crisis."

"I know that, but different how? Why do they buzz on our skin? What caused…" she can't bring herself to say out loud what happened the day of the Pursuing Challenging, that a plant had caused such a reaction in her body. She feels foolish at best.

"Ye used one, didna ye?" Murdina asks knowingly. Vera simply nods. "The oil of the ivani plant seeps into the blood, an' releases a hormone… I canna recall the name though."

"Epinephrine and norepinephrine," Vera says, recollecting a brief study done in science class years earlier. It's the only thing that can explain the reaction. "Adrenaline," she affirms after a quizzical look washes over Murdina's face.

Murdina nods, "That sounds right."

"Why does it happen though?"

"If ye figure it out..."

"What about stein and the black poison, what are those?"

Following a deep breath, Murdina explains, "I gave ye plynth: its cells counteract wi' stein. I dinna leave the house without it."

"Is there plynth in my satchel?"

"Of course. That satchel can save yer very life more times than ye can count. Give it to nae a body."

Vera recalls how it has already saved her life twice. That she decides, is good enough reason to listen to Murdina about the plants.

"Can you tell me... what is black poison?" Vera inquires.

"Some call it stein, some call it the black poison – some believe it is what's in the water."

"But stein made the water in my glass black, the water in Lake Cloud is yellow…"

"I dinna ken if they are the same."

Vera contemplates telling Murdina that the poison in the lake is called lethalyn. It is highly sensitive information - information that only a handful of people know - but she feels that she can trust Murdina. Besides, she isn't in Kala anymore, which means Master Oberon can't hold her responsible for her choices now, only Master Regan can. However, there is one reason wagering against entrusting this information in Murdina: Opi. Vera knows that Opi proclaims to be innocent of killing Hendrix; still, Vera could never trust the man who fought her father in The Circle.

Vera intakes a sharp breath of air and decides to fully trust the significance behind "Deneen," and speaks, "It's called lethalyn. Seeing as one tints water black and the other yellow, they appear different to the naked eye, which makes one assume that they are entirely different substances. However, I'd like to test them in Kala's lab to know for sure," Vera explains. "I'll have to escape Tagondo and break into the lab of course…"

"Tis a good idea… not right now."

"I have to go soon. I need to know."

"When it's safe."

"I'll have to go soon, I don't want to waste any time. Besides, there's something else I need to tend to in the lab…" she subtly mentions as she recalls the whispered message from Hendrix.

"No! Now is not the time to go to Kala. Now is the time to focus on yer pursuing," Murdina pleads.

"Don't worry, I'll get Cole's help. I figure if anyone is going to keep me alive and get me to Kala, it'll be him – the man bound by your agreement." Vera rises to her feet and heads for the front door.

"Lass! Wait-" Murdina shouts to no avail as Vera runs out the door.

She runs down the footpaths, past the log homes on either side, carrying a hope inside of her chest that she hasn't felt in a long time. She must fulfill the task her father asked of her, it means more to her now than pursuing, understanding the probes or anything else – those endeavours can be put on hold for now.

Vera runs to Cole's house, a small log home that sits on a slightly elevated plot of land, and walks up the small hill to reach the front door. She knocks and Cole answers the door, his face sunken in despair.

"What's the matter?" she asks in a slight panic.

"It's my Dad."

"What?" she demands.

"He's dead."

"What? What happened?"

"I-I don't know. He foamed at the mouth, his eyes went black – like yours started to last night."

"Where is he?"

"Come in," he says.

She treads inside the house, "Where?"

"The kitchen," he states in a haze. She runs to Burke and kneels down beside his body in a hurry.

"Where's Nin?" she asks.

"Out pursuing," he says as Vera examines Burke, she notes the complete blackness to his eyes: lifeless ovals. She barely notices the mess surrounding them as she focuses on Burke – black foam fills his mouth and moves down the side of his face, settling itself on the wooden floor. Vera feels for a pulse but there is no sign of a heartbeat.

"Grab me a glass of water, now," she instructs Cole. He holds the glass out for her and she quickly grabs it from his hand, pours in crushed plynth and stirs it – the water turns the same familiar green from the night before. She fills the spoon with the green concoction and dumps it gently in Burkes open mouth. After a moment she desperately pours more.

"What's happening?" Cole asks.

"Nothing. I think it's too late," she replies under her breath.

Cole drops down to his knees, to be near her and his father.

"I'm so sorry," is all she can muster.

After a moment, Cole stands suddenly, and without saying a word walks out the front door, it closes behind him with a bang. Vera collects herself and rushes to follow him, thinking he shouldn't be left alone. She stands out front of the house, but he wandered off too quickly. She calls for him only to hear no response. When she hears rustling from the back of the house, she wanders in the direction of the sounds and finally catches sight of him staring into the vast forest.

"There you are," she says relieved, "Are you okay?"

He stands with his arms limp at his side, his back turned to her, and for the first time she sees Cole of Favoured Pollard truly speechless.

"I'm so sorry Cole," and she is sorry, but the tone in her voice doesn't express warmth as she knows it should. She catches sight of his profile as he looks to the side and she sees that his eyes are watered down. "Are you okay?" she asks again. Though even if he wasn't, she wouldn't have the slightest clue how to help.

Cole doesn't respond for some time, maybe it's only a few moments, but it feels like a lifetime to Vera.

"You care? Why?" he blurts, it catches her off guard.

"Cole, of course I care. I'm not some heartless breach."

"Breach?" He turns to look at her, the pain still brimming in his eyes.

"I'm catching on," she affirms. His stare pierces her; she looks away.

"If you're not heartless, then tell me why you care." He's forever trying to push her, force her to say things that she'd rather keep hidden beneath the depths of her smile, or in this instance, her frown.

He steps a few paces closer to her, his expression unchanging. Their closeness makes her uncomfortable, but it also provides her with an urge to let a series of words fall from her lips that she wants to say. She wants to confide in him too, and tell him about her worries of Cain, but she decides against it. Maybe speaking those words out loud will only make them seem truer.

"Because… you're a good person," she stumbles over her words. It isn't like her to mumble; still, she kicks herself for saying it.

"I'm glad you think so," his voice remains flat, but there's an impression of sarcasm and she knows its purpose – it's to make her talk, to say more. She huffs, wishing that she wasn't there in that moment, but also happy that she is because he needs her, or at least someone.

"I… I like you," she finally manages. She clears her throat following her uncomfortable response.

"You like me? Well that's the most life altering sentence a girl has ever said to a guy," he says monotonously, though she knows that sarcasm still lingers from the essence of his words. He isn't getting any more from her than that, she decides firmly.

"You're in a merge agreement," she says in almost a whine, begging for silence.

Somehow, Tagondo has done a fine job of exploiting her weaknesses, while leaving nothing to be said for her strengths – her involvement with Cole has been no different.

He walks over to her then and places his hands on either side of her waist; he leans in without hesitation and presses his lips firmly against hers. She freezes. She can't pull away – he just lost his father. Though she doesn't know how to move forward, how to be what he pushes her to be, she isn't a woman whose sole purpose is to have a family and grow old with a man next to her – to bear his children, to care for them until they no longer need her, or until they are won in the ceremonies. She can't even grasp that as an option, it isn't for her, at least not in this Broken World.

She decides to stay, unmoving. She doesn't pull away from his lips, though she doesn't quite engage. His arms squeeze tighter around her waist, as if begging for there to be something inside of her, something that he can squeeze out of her. *I'm sorry Cole*, she thinks.

# 43

# Lidia of Favoured Peony
# Kala

There comes a point when one feels so much pain that they can't continue on the same path – a path that only amplifies that pain or prolongs it in some way, like friction on a blister. Lidia's burning, longing, to get off that path. *But not yet,* she reminds herself. *Not yet.* She still has things she needs to tend to before she leaves Kala.

For one, Lidia cannot leave this earth without knowing that Lillith is okay. She decided to seek information from Torant of Insignificant Wells for this. It's also important to Lidia that upon her leaving the greenhouses for the last time that she leaves them in pristine condition; her mother, Bethin, will never live it down otherwise. She also wants to leave a note for Atticus – he's been there for her when no one else was. He deserves to know she's forever grateful – even for his childlike attempts to make her laugh regardless if they worked or not. She also wants to leave a mark: something for the others to see, something like what Ingrid left. She thinks her mark should be a message on The Master's chamber, like Ingrid did. *But what?* Lidia hasn't decided yet. *What could possibly be significant enough to leave behind in the form of a mark?* She'll defer this until it comes to her.

First on her list: Lillith. She's aware that Torant has been scrutinized amongst the Kalian whispers for years. However, alongside those whispers are assumptions that there's a man who knows the future before it happens and so she wonders if that man is Torant. In fact, the whispers in the paths told her to go see Torant of Insignificant Wells. When she first reached out to him he pretended as though he had no clue what she spoke of. But, she insisted and continuously appeared at his doorway in desperation. Today is the day she'll get answers though.

Following her work in the greenhouses, Lidia walks the paths through the colony that lead to Insignificant Wells. A slight flutter hits her heart as her nerves jitter. Though she's been to Insignificant Wells a handful of times now, no matter how brief those instances were, she still feels a worry that she's doing something wrong, that she shouldn't be meeting with Torant, but she ignores those thoughts. She reaches the edge of Kala and nears the rock wall. There's a rustling in the bushes, but she doesn't have much time so she focuses on her task. She walks up his steps and raises her hand to knock but the door opens before her knuckles graze its surface.

"What now?" he barks in annoyance.

Lidia notes that Torant never offers the Kalian greeting, though her nerves are too jittery to push for it. She reminds herself that no one else is out this far anyway.

"Please, I need to know. I won't bother you ever again. Just tell me," she pleads. He stands there, his eyes appear light up close, they stare into hers making her feel unsettled, she rubs at the sides of her arms in a subconscious means to comfort herself.

Torant releases a sigh, "Fine, come in." She follows him inside and sits immediately at the kitchen table. The last couple times she's been here, that's where they sat as they spoke. He refused to give her answers, up until today. Today she will get her peace of mind. "So, what is it this time…?" he questions her.

"I told you…" Lidia shakes her head, "Please, tell me about Lilith. Is she okay in Tagondo?"

"You truly think I know the answer to that question?"

"Yes. I… I hope you do."

"Will it stop you from doing what you're thinking about doing?" he asks.

Her mouth drops open, "So you do know."

He raises his hands as a means to silence her.

"But you do. You know about my plans to meet with the lake. How do you know that?"

"If it won't change the outcome, then what's the point in you knowing anything more beyond what you know right now?" he asks.

"I just want peace of mind."

"It's tragic. A mother who longs for the touch of her child is willing to seek death to rid herself of the pain that distance has caused," he rises to his feet then and paces about the kitchen.

"Please."

"If I tell you what you want to know, you must do something for me in return as payment."

"Anything."

"It may not be today, or tomorrow… But you must remember…"

"I will, I'll remember," she insists.

"I am going to ask you for help."

"Me help you? I don't understand…" she shakes her head in confusion.

"That is all you need to know right now."

"Okay – I will do anything you ask. Now please, tell me about Lillith."

"Lillith is…" he pauses a moment, possibly for effect, though it's working as Lidia leans forward in eagerness to hear more, "Happy and healthy." Lidia releases an exhale that fills the room with her breath.

"Are they nice to her? Do they read to her? Give her hugs and kisses?"

"I can't explain any further – you got what you came here for," he states then walks over to the door, reaches for the knob, and opens it, motioning for her to make her way through. She does as he suggests.

Torant sees her down the steps, "You know you and her both made a terrible decision speaking to those Tagondians that day," he says.

Taken aback by his knowledge of their meeting, she pauses a moment. She reminds herself that of course Torant would know, he knows all. But what if The Master knows too? Would that be enough to cause a re-birthing for Vera?

"You don't think that was what initiated her re-birthing, do you?" Lidia asks.

"What are the names of the Tagondians you spoke with?"

"Cole and Lincoln. They called us over, asked us to talk with them."

"Cole of Favoured Pollard?"

"I didn't get his full name."

"Oh well, it's done now." Torant responds. "You must go."

As she steps onto the pathway, she can't help but turn and say: "Thank you for the peace of mind."

"Speak of this to no one," he says to her. "And don't forget payment," he calls. She nods and turns down the path.

She did it: she got answers from the man who knows all. Baby Lillith is in a happy home, loved and cared for – that is all Lidia can ask for. At least she has a chance at a good life, even if it isn't with her. She breathes in a sharp inhale as she glances at the trees on her walk back. Somehow, they seem more vibrant, more appealing. The sky is bluer even though her body still aches with every step in a strong desire for rest – not the kind one gets from sleep though. She reminds herself that the trees appearing more vibrant is likely just the effects of relief soaring through her bloodstream – the first item can be scratched off her list.

^

The next day Lidia puts her head down and begins a deep organization of the greenhouse. Even though her body still drags with the same exhaustion, she pushes through it. She tills the soil in all the greenhouses; pulls off all the dead leaves of every plant; trims the bottom leaves off the plants that need it and sprays them at their roots with Ida's homemade fertilizer – pureéd compost. The green peppers are ready for picking. *To hell with Huron, he can come pick the peppers.*

Lidia has now completed two things off of her list, meaning she's closer to her rendezvous with the lake. She sits in the greenhouse with a blank piece of paper in front of her. Now, what to say to Atticus? They have known each other for many years, she watched him grow from a little bean to a tall, handsome man. Technically he's almost a man as his eighteenth birthday soon approaches; she isn't that much older, eleven years and it barely crosses her mind. But they have been through a lot, seen a lot, laughed a lot, learnt a lot. She begins writing, tears fall from her cheeks and land on the yellow piece of paper.

After some time she folds it up and writes: 'Atticus' on the back. Knowing where Ida keeps her spare lab key secretly hidden in one of the greenhouses, she slinks to retrieve it and then sneaks into the lab and places the letter on the counter. He'll find it tomorrow, after she meets with the lake tonight.

Lidia reflects upon how there will only be three things left behind after she is gone: baby Lilith, the letter for Atticus and her mark. Now, for the final thing on her list, she'll do it at sundown, after the curfew siren rings. That way, everyone will be inside and no one will catch her. Only one Defender roams the paths at night, surely she can avoid him too. Her eyes light up then, for the first time in a long time, for it has just come to her: the mark that she will leave for all of Kala to see.

44

# Regan of Favoured Adder
# Tagongo

Early in the morning Master Regan announces his plans to have a celebration of life for Burke of Favoured Pollard. Truth be told he's somewhat miffed that Burke passed away. What's more, Cole is now an Insignificant – without a family member in a Favoured profession, the Pollard household can no longer be Favoured. Which also means his merge agreement with Treena is null and void. However, he likes Cole, and he doesn't like many people. Cole always puts his head down, he always gets the job done. Perhaps he should make Cole a Baron – perhaps one day he will, seeing as such a position isn't passed on by one's parent, one must be appointed to Baron by their Master. It would be good for keeping up appearances to have the Mammoth Slayer as a Baron – a man following in his father's footsteps. Yes, Regan likes the visual. The citizens would eat it up.

There is however a problem, and it's a big one – Vera. She's distracting Cole from his duties, distracting him from Treena. He'll need to do something to remedy that. Under normal circumstances he'd find a reason to exile her or make her disappear as he has done with annoyances in the past. This is different, she's in her origins a North and there is no way to explain a reason for exiling her, at least not one that would be easily justified yet. Nonetheless, it is now evident that Cole would not look the other way if she up and disappeared. She's a scientist from Kala – everyone knows it and no one would forget it. No one has forgotten when Merek of Favoured North was exiled, even the Tagondians remember. He would need Vera to act out, he could push her to do something of an Offending nature and thereby qualify her for exile. However, an easier idea crosses his mind: *I could hire someone to kill her.* That is a viable option. Her dead body would need to be out in the open so many Tagondians could see it for themselves. Just then his two remaining Barons enter the chamber.

"Have you handled the body?" Regan asks Orsen as they join him, taking to their seats.

"All is taken care of," Orsen assures.

"Excellent. Now we just need to ensure the celebration of life goes smoothly. Jaret, have you readied the servant ones?"

"Yes your grace – they are busy at work prepping in the kitchen."

"And the black poison?" Regan inquires.

"Heaps of it coming in from the forest tonight – all will be stored where you want it," Orsen confirms.

"Excellent. The citizens mustn't know about it, which means we must keep everyone inside at the celebration, that will ensure no one sees us transporting it," Regan states.

"I will collect a group of Defenders to tend to it," Orsen says.

Jaret then inquires: "Have you decided on appointing a third Baron?"

"Not yet," Regan responds distractedly, "I'm still thinking about that." "Is that all then your grace?" Orsen asks.

"Yes, you may go," Regan confirms.

The two Barons rise from their seats, bow to their Master and leave. Master Regan remains sitting in contemplation. All seems to be aligning, except his plans for Cole and Treena. He wants to ensure that their merge takes place. There will be nothing better for Treena than to merge with Cole. He now faces the predicament of having to get Cole's permission, since Burke is dead.

There must be something that will convince Cole – some sort of deal that will tempt him into it. Regan decides that he doesn't know him well enough and doesn't want to risk a chance that he'll turn the offer down. Then, it hits him: instead of having a private Tagondian Merge Agreement Party that they normally have, he'll plan a gathering at The Circle for all The Almek to attend. It is, after all, his daughter. Still, he needs more than just making Cole the centre of attention. He will speak with Cole one-on-one before the ceremony, to guarantee his cooperation, so that Cole won't be able to turn it down, nor be able to avoid it.

^

Master Regan sits on the deck of the Master's chamber as Rimmy blows the whistle. Just one blow is all that's needed to get Bruisers into combat stance. The colony centre is lined with Tags, twenty pairs ready to fight. Regan watches as Vera takes her stance. Sure, her combat stance is looking more refined, she has been in Tagondo long enough, and so one would hope for a decent amount of improvement. However, what little improvement she's made is no match for his daughter.

Vera and Treena stand facing one another, Treena with her daggers held out in front of her, Vera with her sword. When Rimmy sounds the two-whistle blow, the fights begin. Treena and Vera encircle one another, Regan watches with pure enjoyment, hoping that by some miracle Treena will accidentally kill Vera right here, solving all of his problems.

Vera swings the sword incompetently, arousing a sort of deep chuckle in Regan's throat. Treena swipes at Vera with her dagger, this way and that, determined to take some of her flesh. Treena is a vicious fighter and Regan has never witnessed her offer mercy, which is to his liking – mercy isn't the point of the combat calls.

Treena then throws one of the daggers at Vera and it merely skims through her hair and the slight shuffle of Vera's feet to avoid it makes her drop the sword. Treena raises her foot and hoofs Vera in the side, knocking her to the ground. She struggles to pick up the sword, but when she grasps it in her hand Treena comes for her again. Treena holds her dagger right at eye level, pointed down at Vera. All that stands between the blade meeting Vera's eye is a trembling arm that holds a heavy sword. Vera's arm pushes against Treena's in an effort to move the blade further away from her face.

Regan observes as Cole approaches, standing front row to the fight. Regan sits up in his seat – Cole is merely feet away from the fight, so close that if he wants to he could reach Vera and step in. But Cole won't do that, he knows better than to interfere in a combat call. Still, Regan watches with delight and intrigue. It's always suspenseful, watching these things unfold. They are also necessary in order to ensure Tagondo wins in the ceremonies against the Kalians.

Cole sways in his step, crouching forward slightly. He brings his thumb up to his mouth and rests it in between his teeth. Vera manages to push Treena off of her, Cole loosens slightly in his posture. Vera stands and without any notice Treena grabs her from behind and holds the dagger to her stomach. Cole tenses instantly, ready to pounce. Regan notices Cole's eyes shift toward him, he simply gives Cole a smile with a tilt of his head. *Would you really, Cole?* He doesn't think he will. Cole stays frozen, following the rules like a good pawn – one of his favourites, his eyes intently focused on Vera. Rimmy blows the whistle and the fight is over, Regan claps his hands profusely for the show.

# 45

## VERA OF INSIGNIFICANT CANNELLE TAGONDO

Vera sits at the kitchen table in Insignificant Cannelle the next morning with a sore hip from falling in her fight with Treena, but she decides to keep her pain to herself. Pain seems to be an essential part of the Tagondian way, like roots to a tree. In an effort to ignore the particular pain she faces on this day, she scans through the memories she has of Burke, which are few since she never even spoke to the man. But she sees a reflection of Burke within Cole and something about that warms her. She feels for Cole and his pain.

Murdina breaks the silence and with it, Vera's thoughts, "We must leave soon."

"Cole is picking me up tonight."

"Ye best be canny, the lot of ye," Murdina warns.

Vera agrees, "We will."

"How is that poor boy?"

"I'm not sure... As good as one can be." Vera glances to Opi, noting his reserve. He has been quiet since the news of Burke's passing reached him. He leaves the kitchen and walks out the front door in silence.

As soon as Opi is gone, Murdina begins in a whisper: "What is goin' on between you an' Cole?"

"Going on between us? Nothing. Why do you ask?"

"I see more than ye ken. Dinna be messin' about wi' that boy's poor heart."

"I wouldn't mess about," Vera says defensively. And she wouldn't, at least not intentionally.

"Ye best figure it out," Murdina tenses. "I'll see ye tonight at the party," Murdina states as one raised eyebrow lingers on her expressive face. It has a purpose; Vera knows that much.

"See you tonight," she replies.

^

Vera wanders to her room later that afternoon to change into something more appropriate for the celebration of life for Burke of Favoured Pollard. It isn't a fancy party by any means, but she has come to know the expectations for Master Regan's parties. Vera now has a small collection of homemade clothing from Murdina – how Murdina makes the items so quickly, she has no clue. Most of the items are rather eccentric and 'eye-catching;' however, neither of these qualities jive with Vera. But, to her dismay, she can see that her wearing these extravagant items makes Murdina happy and she is beginning to care for Murdina.

Vera pulls out a long, emerald green skirt with flowers stitched across its shining silk fabric – luckily she has a plain black t-shirt to pair with it along with her green scarf. She gets dressed and brushes out her thick waves, leaving her hair down as it so often is now. A knock sounds at the door; it'll be Cole, her heart jolts with a twinge – of what exactly she isn't sure, and so she writes it off as the painful aching of another Almek in mourning.

"Hey," Cole says with the same sullen look that he wore earlier that morning, she purses her lips together.

"Hi."

He breathes in sharply, "That skirt… you look…" his voice trails off. It's a strange reaction to have toward a skirt, but the man just lost his father. Her insides twist.

She clears her throat, "How was your day? Did it go okay?" she cautiously asks as she steps outside. "Bye," she shouts to Murdina and hears a muffled "farewell" while closing the door behind her.

"It was rough. Rimmy came to pick Dad up, took him for burning."

"Do they bury the bones together like the Kals?"

"I don't know what they do. Master Regan has never given an explanation, I'm not sure anyone has ever asked. We're the colony of unanswered questions," he chuckles, though it's half-hearted.

"It's wrong you know. To not tell the people what he does with the bodies."

"Does it really matter? They're gone anyway. He's gone." Cole flops down on the top stair of the front steps, Vera sits down beside him.

"I think it does. Master Oberon taught us that the way someone is buried can reflect their experience in afterlife."

"Do you believe in that shit?" he asks.

"I do, it's better than Master Regan's barbaric neglect and lack of reasoning, *I am Mother Earth*," she mimics, "He's a joke."

"You're a scientist though, don't scientists disbelieve in afterlife?"

"There is a term we use for that, it's called The Almek Passage: a spiritually, scientific way of life. It is the essence of Kala. We are based on scientific belief, but we also practise spiritualism. There's proof you know, that our spirits live on beyond our body's life.

"Where our spirits go depends on the way we live our lives and, of course, our burial. I just don't think it should be a party where people dance and sing and fill themselves with drink. Also, I think the reflection of our lives themselves have more of a determining factor for our spirits."

"That's understandable. What about the spirits, where do they go?" he asks.

"There is no right or wrong answer. Some believe that our spirit stays where we die, others believe we get to choose where our spirit goes."

"Will you choose where yours will go?"

Vera looks up to the tree tops. "Above the trees and into the sky with the birds," she says with a smile.

"You don't think that's weird? A mini Vera floating around up there somewhere? What will the poor birds think?"

She laughs then, "I don't know what's weird anymore. Where would yours go?"

"I'm gonna need some time to think about that. Such a big decision," he snickers.

She can tell he's merely humouring her, she laughs with him.

After a moment of silence he breaks it once again, "What's it like, transferring colonies?"

She needs a minute to think before she finally answers, "It's like I'm a child again, only I'm lost. I keep thinking… if I could just go back to that day… if I had done things differently... Anyways, I guess I'm just trying to keep my head."

He nods as if he somehow understands.

"Well, we should go. Are you ready?" Vera asks as she stands up and begins walking down the wooden steps of Murdina and Opi's home, Cole joins her.

As they walk the footpaths not too many others are on the trails. A memory from their embrace earlier that day burns in her mind, but just as quickly as it emerged she snuffs it out.

"What are you thinking?" Cole asks, interrupting her thoughts, as usual.

"Oh, nothing in particular."

"Well, I was thinking about earlier…" he mentions modestly.

"Oh?" she blushes, now wondering why he can't seem to keep just some of his thoughts to himself.

"It was unexpected, after the other day when you practically ran away from me," he says.

She worries then that maybe she should have run away a second time.

When she responds with silence, he continues: "There's something else. With my Dad passing, it means the merge agreement he had with Master Regan is now revoked… I should note I'm not a Favoured anymore, but an Insignificant, but I don't care about what they call me. If Master Regan wants to set up another merge agreement between Treena and I, he has to get both of our approvals."

"Cole I-"

"Don't worry, I just wanted to mention it. I told you I would be getting out of that agreement somehow. I just didn't have a plan set in motion."

"I don't think right now is the time to discuss this." *Or ever,* she thinks.

"Now is as good a time as any. My dad's passing doesn't stop my life from moving forward. Can't you see that no matter what I don't want to be with Treena?"

"Take a moment and realize the severity of what this means – what it means that your father is gone."

"I lost my mom, Vera, years ago – I know what it means."

"Just soak it in – those feelings of sadness. You can't just up and move on merrily like nothing happened, just like everyone else does. Honour his life. Forget about

Treena and the merging shit, forget about...earlier. Stop worrying about everyone else."

"You want me to forget about kissing you? Vera, I won't. I can't just lie down and roll up into some depressive ball of human flesh and rot in bed for days like you. That's not me."

"That's what you think of me?" she says stunned.

He has no idea what she's been dealing with. *How could he?* Suddenly she can't bear to spend another minute with him, for he doesn't know what demons haunt her. He doesn't know that she is completely unaware of her time in the cave with Cain and that she constantly speculates about what may have unknowingly happened to her. The very thought makes her feel ill.

Cole turns to her, "I don't think that of you, I'm sorry. It's just, we're different with how we cope," he reasons.

"Yes, a little too different I think," she says as she speeds up her pace to reach the stairs of The Master's chamber before Cole.

She hurries up the stairs and enters the building, the musical ones play a joyous beat that opposes how she truly feels while everyone dances. She weaves her body in and out of groups of people, in search of her people - the ones she enjoys being around - which admittedly are only a few sparse beings.

"Where's Cole?" Ezla asks as she catches sight of Vera.

"Not with me."

"I thought you guys were coming together tonight?"

"We were. Hey, you got crutches?" Vera asks changing the subject.

"Yeah, Regan gave the go ahead for the hospital to order the builders to make me a pair... the cane wasn't really working. Getting around is a lot easier now," she chuckles, "What happened between you and Cole?"

"Nothing. I don't want to talk about it."

"Alright. Well, come on, let's get you on the dance floor."

"I don't dance. Especially not at these events."

"Come on V, live a little. Besides, the more fun you have the more pissed Cole will be."

"I don't care if he's pissed. I just want to be away from him."

"V," his hand wraps around her wrist then, cedar and orange scents wisp from the side of her cheek causing movement in her hair. "I know you're mad. Just do me a favour? Don't drink or eat anything here tonight." She ignores his whisper and the tickles that form in her ear.

She knows he's looking out for her well-being, she also knows she doesn't care. She yanks her arm out of his grasp and gives him a cold, indifferent look.

"Let's go get a drink," Ezla shouts over the music, having not heard a word of what Cole said to Vera in that moment.

"Sure," Vera replies as she moves her gaze and feet with Ezla toward the drinks.

Vera forces a large glass of whiskey into her mouth and down her throat - she gags - almost bringing it right back up immediately. She soon has a sudden wave of intoxication wash over her – it's a sensation she discovers that she hates, the lack of control over her own mind and body - it revolts her - enough to make her vomit. Though, she holds the acid in her stomach, she doesn't indulge anymore beyond her first drink. Ezla appears quite familiar with the drink and takes to enjoying several cups – her dancing grows increasingly sloppy as the night progresses, regardless of having to balance on crutches.

"He doesn't take his eyes off of you," Ezla mumbles in a drunken slur to Vera some time later.

"What?" Vera asks.

"Cole. I've known him a long time, I've never seen him like this... so drooly over a woman… Well, I mean there was one… years before Treena… but it would never have worked."

Vera, taken aback, ignores the comment about another woman and forces a chuckle, "Drooly? I'm certain you just made that word up."

"Maybe," Ezla laughs, "He probably would've just settled and merged with Treena, I mean before you came."

"Perhaps he should. She is better suited for him."

"Treena's a huge breach. She isn't well suited for anyone," Ezla laughs some more, "I'm going to go grab a bite to eat, I'll be back," Ezla states as she turns and limps away.

*Funny*, Vera thinks, *I don't think I'm well suited for anyone either.* Vera looks around for any excuse to stop the awkward sway that possesses her hips and legs that night. It's horrid and she hopes everyone is submerged in enough booze to forget her participation on the dance floor, it'll never happen again.

"I know you think you're one of us now… with your hair down and your new shiny weapons. But you're not. You will never be one of us," a voice speaks from behind her.

"Hmm?" Vera turns to face a pale, angry, blue-eyed woman.

"You may have your nails in him Leech, but you and I both know he can do better than you."

"Treena, if it isn't a pleasure to finally meet you," Vera says sarcastically with a sense of shock forming in her lips as she says the words. There's no taking them back now, might as well continue. She'll thank the whiskey for the liquid courage later.

"Listen to me – I'm merging with Cole. There's nothing you do can stop us."

"I don't intend to do anything in particular," Vera chuckles.

"You will do nothing. If you make one stupid move, I'll make sure my daddy sics Rimmy on you. And Rimmy? Well he likes to open up people to play with their insides." Vera shudders at Treena's words, but aims to maintain her nonchalant disposition – for all she knows Treena can see right through her false confidence.

"I doubt that. Besides, Rimmy doesn't instil any sort of fear in me whatsoever," she lies. Rimmy terrifies her – the sight of him alone sends chills of unsettlement through her body.

"Watch it *Leech*. I will bring you all sorts of pain."

"Please, there's no amount of pain you could bring me that I haven't already felt," the realization hits her, of the truth to those words.

"You know that's not true," Treena says, "There will be more combat calls… there will be many more opportunities."

Vera laughs, "Yes, you were good. But I'm not scared of you, or the combat calls."

Treena retorts: "But are you scared of Cain? You know, the guy you met during your time in the cave?" The sinful grin that possesses Treena's lips and the way she presumptuously spits her words suggests that she knows what happened in the cave with Cain. Vera's fingers tighten into fists.

"What do you know about that?" she finds the courage to ask.

"I know that he laid his hands on you. He said you put up a decent fight for a Leech."

"Yes, the burns – I think they suit him just fine."

"He said you were just as he expected though."

"What is that supposed to mean?" Vera asks.

"I'll leave that to your imagination."

Vera stumbles backward as her eyes remain steady on Treena. She backs into a table then turns and runs through the chamber doors – she makes it through right before the vomit spews from her lips.

After retching and unrelenting tears, Vera leans against a tree trunk in deep reflection. It is possibly just as she feared, that Cain might have done more to her. If it is true she is tainted and possibly weaker than she's ever imagined. But what if it isn't true and Treena is bluffing? Through it all a realization comes to Vera: Tagondo is a terrible colony, ruled by a corrupt Master and because of that, it houses troubled people. Master Oberon needs to be made aware. Putting Coakai, One and all of the other nonsensical things Master Oberon does aside – he is the only one with enough power to bring Master Regan down and repair Tagondo.

Vera re-enters the chamber feeling different than the way she left it. A determination soars through her to bring Master Regan down so that all of the troubled Tagondians have a chance at redemption. She walks straight to the table where the servant ones pour drinks and downs a second glass of whiskey. She soon spots Murdina and Opi arrive and she takes her seat with them to eat and drink together.

There's still a sensation in her stomach, only it's more of a burning and less of an ache – the whiskey is to thank. Perhaps she feels some form of hope – hope that Treena is wrong about Cain and that something can be done for the crooked people of Tagondo. Still, Vera tries to convince herself that her conversation with Treena doesn't bother her and yet, she wonders if she should tell Cole about it. Maybe he knows Cain and could put that worry to rest.

She glances over at Cole as he sits looking miserable, still at the front table. She's still irritated with him from their previous conversation, but that doesn't change the fact that he's pleasant to look at. However, not so pleasant a view is spotting Treena's arm glued around his neck as her lips constantly whisper into his ear. All Vera can think is that it'd be nice to separate those two. There must be a reason that Master Regan hasn't switched Cole and Nin's table placement yet as they are technically Insignificant now.

She glances at her water glass to check its hue and realizes then that she has a reason to separate them, at least for a moment – she hasn't told Cole about the black poison and plynth. She meant to tell him earlier, but was caught off guard by the news of Burke's passing.

Vera rises to her feet and rather sloppily jaunts over to Cole, for she still feels the effects of the drink. As she approaches the table his eyes catch sight of her and he grimaces slightly.

"Cole, I need to speak with you," Vera plainly states.

"Are you forgetting about our little talk?" Treena questions her arrogantly.

"Oh no, I haven't forgotten, but I can't promise that I will remember come morning," she lets out a low chuckle, "Cole, can we talk?"

Cole raises an eyebrow, "Yeah," he stands in an instant.

"Come with me," Vera says, a quick look at Treena shows her face in a scowl. Cole follows Vera outside; it's dark for the sun has already set. The air is still chilly for a May evening, Vera wraps her scarf around her shoulders and neck tightly. She feels sensitive to the tension that flows between them - like a current in a river. She shakes her head to clear her thoughts, as what matters right now is that she puts that all aside and focuses on the water. Regardless of their feelings for one another, good or bad, she knows she can trust him.

"What is it V?" his voice sounds impatient, bored even.

"I'll get right to it. I don't want to keep you," she begins. She explains how the herb that Murdina gave her at the Aftermath Party is called plynth and that it counteracts the black poison that was put in her water – even though he knows part of this already. She goes on to explain how plynth is what she tried to give Burke and that she's concerned that Burke was maybe given the black poison as well – which she'd like to test against lethalyn.

Cole pauses, seemingly thinking for a moment, "Hmm. I guess it's possible that they're the same poison."

"It's possible, but I'm not sure how probable it is. I need to test it."

"Why does it matter though?"

"It could've killed me. It killed your father. Don't you want to know more about it?"

"Let's get to the lab then," he says with such indifference, as if the task will be a cinch.

"How?" she asks.

"I'll get you there. We'll go tomorrow night," he confirms.

"Night?" she asks, "But the mammoths?"

"It'll have to be night, I'd rather rumble with a mammoth over the night guard any day. Let's meet tomorrow morning at sunrise at my lookout. We can talk details then."

"Okay, I'll see you there," she agrees.

Cole reaches for the door then and holds it open for her. The solar light suddenly casts across his triceps; shadows accentuate the muscular curves of his arms. The soft, yellow hues meet the black shadows of the night, offering sensuality to the air, at least in her drunken mind. She decides that she likes how his t-shirt rests tightly on his chest all the way down past his ridged stomach.

Possessed by a drunken urge she reaches out her swaying hand and places it on his abdomen. She runs her hand from top to bottom, it feels nice. She notes that her touch seems less heightened than when sober – yet another reason she isn't fond of the drink. She stares, almost absentmindedly, at her hand moving slowly across his stomach.

Cole begins to laugh, "Well, I guess I didn't expect you would listen to me and not drink."

"Nope," she sways, "It feels… really nice," she says, speaking to his muscles.

He chuckles, louder this time, and she notices his hand reach up, he runs his fingers through his hair - his nervous habit, she's sure of that - though he does it so rarely.

It's difficult to pinpoint exactly what makes Cole Pollard nervous. Just then, his eyes glance down to Vera's hand, which sits resting on his abdomen, a wave of embarrassment strikes through her. She quickly pulls her hand away and clears her throat.

"Sorry, I definitely have had too much to drink," she stands beside the door that Cole still holds open for her, swaying ever so slightly. Though the sway is unintentional, she notes that it seems to send a jolt of insecurity through her. Unexpectedly, two Defenders walk around from the side of the building.

"Hey you two, get inside!" one Defender shouts. They do so hurriedly, slipping inside the door.

"I don't mind," he whispers quickly in her ear, quietly enough that she almost doesn't hear him.

Vera soon spots Ezla and Murdina and makes her way back to the table. They have a plan, well the basis for a plan and Vera thinks that will be enough to move forward. However, she doesn't feel ready to share this information with Ezla yet, for a number of reasons, but overall, it's imperative that no one finds out – it cannot get to Master Regan or any of his people. Ezla, being quite heavily influenced by the drink, could do something reckless with such information. She's a blunt person and Vera knows how the drink can alter behaviours, which is primarily how the two of them spend the rest of the night together – intoxicated and highly impressionable.

Ezla lives on the far south side of the colony centre, Vera decides to walk home with her that night after the party comes to an end. Ezla seems to prefer to walk through the forest, as opposed to taking the footpaths, and although Vera doesn't understand her logic seeing as it only makes her hobble with her crutches more difficult – she goes willingly.

Still, she points out: "It's much darker going this way," in a drunken observational slur.

"Yeah. Why? You scared of the dark?" Ezla teases.

"Usually…" Vera admits, but she doesn't feel the typical queasy feeling that burrows itself in her stomach when she's in the dark. She feels the opposite: free, light and as if she could fly. It becomes evident why people get addicted to the drink.

"Shh… look," Ezla says in a whisper as she crouches down.

"What is it?" Vera asks while joining her behind a bush. A line of Defenders march through the forest, carrying large masses wrapped in burlap. They are heading northeast.

"Defenders," Ezla states.

"What are they carrying?"

"Beats me," Ezla admits. Suddenly they hear a voice in the distance coming from behind them. "Someone's out there," Ezla points into the forest.

Vera's first thought is how she hopes it isn't Cain. She isn't ready for his retaliation just yet, she needs more time to ready herself – a few combat calls and some leaves that cause burns aren't going to be enough. They carefully move a few paces closer to the voices as the passing Defenders disappear into the darkness.

"It's Master Regan – looks like he's having a private meeting," Ezla says.

"In the middle of the forest? With who?" Vera lowers herself in an unsteady squat down beside Ezla as she peers through the blurry slits that are her eyes.

"Shh… listen," Ezla says.

"I'm happy it's done. You will be sure to get paid in shares," Master Regan says to his confidante.

"Thank you, your grace," the voice exclaims.

"You left no trails, right? The last thing I need is for that girl to be onto you."

"No trails – she doesn't suspect a thing."

"Excellent. Go now, Murdina may suspect something if you're gone for too long."

“I’ll tell her I stayed late to help with the body.”

“Whatever you need to do,” Master Regan turns then, to presumably head back toward The Master’s chamber. A face reveals to the two friends someone they didn’t expect to see.

“Opi?” Vera questions.

“Oh wow. Of course it’s Opi. How did I not see this!” Ezla says.

“What do you mean, *of course*?” Vera asks, confused.

“He befriended Burke a long time ago, Burke has struggled with his health ever since. Then he up and dies. What else would he be getting paid in private for? Opi killed Burke – 100% it was Opi!”

“Opi? He wouldn’t… This can’t be.”

“Vera, you just saw exactly what I saw. Don’t be stupid. It’s not the first time he’s killed, he killed your dad too, remember?”

“He didn’t though, the origins of his death are kind of… unknown.”

“Of course he did. And Regan’s paying Opi in shares for killing Burke for fuck sakes,” Ezla bellows.

Vera’s head pulsates heavily to the beat in her veins; the sensations of scattered thoughts don’t allow her to focus. No, she definitely doesn’t like this feeling. Her instincts are put on pause and in this moment she doesn’t really care about Opi and Master Regan and their private meeting, nor does she care for Ezla’s accusations. Though she humours Ezla, all she wants is to lie down and have a rest in the bush.

“What are you doing?” Ezla pushes Vera in an attempt sit her friend up.

“Shh… Don’t talk so loud,” Vera complains in a whine.

“You can’t sleep here, Kalian. Move deeper into the bush so Opi doesn’t see us, he’s coming!” Ezla warns.

Just then Opi walks by, but luckily there is plenty of bush separating them from him – he must’ve passed without suspicion. Ezla eventually convinces Vera to resume their hike and helps to steady Vera’s walk, even though Ezla’s own jaunt is clumsy on her crutches. Vera snickers during their journey and behaves with such mannerisms unlike her sober self. She flops her legs about, drags her feet and scuffs the dirt with her shoes among other childlike behaviours.

When they reach House of Insignificant Adder Vera notes that it looks like a shack, perhaps an old garden shed. The front door is slightly crooked with a handle that resembles that of a barn door. Vera hopes that there are beds inside, though she’ll sleep just about anywhere on this night. Upon entry into the house the musky scent of straw wafts into Vera’s nose, its earthiness clings to the hairs in her nostrils. There’s something familiar about the scent, she may have smelled it on Ezla before. Vera notes that the wooden floor is scattered with hay and in the corner of the room is a sad excuse for a kitchen with a couple old shelves that house the few dishes and utensils they have for food and cooking. A bucket full of water sits atop the shelves, it must act as their sink. A few jugs, of what Vera assumes to be safe drinking water line the wall beside the kitchen shelves. There are no chairs, no kitchen table, only an old wooden crate that holds a dirty plate left on it – their table.

A few ragged sheets hang about the room, they seem to act as dividers to distinguish between rooms. Ezla’s room does indeed have a large lump of hay formed into the shape of a bed with blankets in a heaping pile on top. *It’s better than the floor,* Vera thinks. She wonders what sort of condition the bathroom is in as she suddenly has to go – yet another side effect the drink offers. A moan coming from the other side of a grey sheet asks for their attention.

"It's my dad, don't worry about his groans – he's out solid," Ezla explains. "We need to talk."

"Not now, I need to sleep," Vera complains, then flops her body down onto the pile of hay and blankets and immediately falls asleep.

# 46

## Oberon of Favoured Kenoak
## Kala

Master Oberon meets with his Barons early morning as concerns for the colony appear to be on the rise and he wants to ensure he's on top of it.

"With the earth," he greets his Barons.

"May we be cleansed," the three Barons reply, as usual, in unison.

"Where are we at today?" Oberon asks.

Martil starts: "We've been keeping track of the number of people that are asking about the condition of the water, your grace."

"And?"

"Eighty-three," Martil answers, "They want to know what the levels are."

"It's increasing" Oberon notes.

Martil nods, "We must offer them more information than, '*it's going good.'* A more accurate update is needed."

"I know, you've said that before."

"It's hard for me to offer much guidance on the matter, when I myself don't even know the water statistics," she reminds him.

"Yes, I understand, we will have to figure out something else. I'm not ready to divulge the water's ratios just yet. Next," Oberon says with a wave of his hand.

"I have the list of names for merge agreements, your grace," Hogard places a piece of paper in front of Oberon.

"Excellent, this is just what this colony needs," Oberon examines the list of names briefly.

"Lidia of Favoured Peony? So soon?" Quim asks.

"Waiting on a new merge only prolongs the memories of the old," Oberon explains.

"Yes, your grace." Quim agrees.

"We must go over the list and match probable suitors, then meet with the parents of both sides."

Hogard takes the piece of paper back, "Do you want to do that today? It may take some time to gather those names."

"No, we will tend to that list in the coming weeks as you have it ready," Martil suggests, "in the meantime, I have an excellent idea."

"Very well, what is this idea of yours?"

"Well, the Favoured essentially set the tone for the colony, do they not?" she begins.

Oberon acknowledges in agreement, "They do."

"And their jobs are quite exhausting," she pauses.

"Yes. That they are," Oberon agrees still.

"As a means to solve the citizens concerns about the water ratios, and promote a trusting atmosphere, why don't we remove the curfew for the Favoured. That way, it will allow them to work longer hours, more importantly for those who work in the lab, which should bring them closer to the cure. All the people of the colony will feel more trusting," Martil explains.

"Hmm. That involves breaking the curfew law," Oberon hesitates.

"In a round about way it does, but we don't have to break it, per se. We can bend it, for the Favoured. As long as there is progress toward the cure, the Insignificants won't put up a fuss.

"But what of the mammoths?"

"There isn't much we can do about them, aside from making more solar lights to light the pathways to deter them – this will make the people less fearful."

"Very good. Let's do that," Oberon sees no reason to disagree, "As well as increase the Defender count for the night guard."

^

The next morning, Master Oberon has Zev blow the colony whistle three times. Three blows signals a short but urgent meeting in the colon centre. No matter where a Kalian is, no matter what they are in the midst of, they must head there. Thousands of pairs of eyes gather, looking to their Master for meaning. Zev stands at his side, hands clasped.

Oberon stands and addresses his people: "With the earth, my people."

"May we be cleansed," the crowd says back to their Master.

"Thank you for coming to this urgent meeting. It will be brief, I can promise you that. Things in Kala have been improving: There have been no mammoth attacks in eight months time, which is the longest time span we have withstood such troubles. Our water - with thanks to all, but especially to Mother Earth and our scientists - is improving as well.

"It is because things are improving, it is because of all of your hard work, that I have some very exciting news to share with you all. Since we are working so very hard to ensure we reach a cure soon, I have decided to bend the curfew law for the Favoured. With fewer mammoth attacks, I feel more confident in allowing more Almek to roam the paths at night. These Kalians work hard and should have the option to put in more hours; the more they work, the closer we will get to a cure." The Kalians snap their fingers in approval. "That is all, you may return to your posts," Oberon states and the crowd of Kalians leave as quickly as they had come.

Oberon feels a flutter in his chest – he hates messing with the laws. The laws are quite literally carved in stone for a reason, they regulate the people and they keep peace and unity. Though, he needs more time and the only way to get that is by giving more time and therefore extending the curfew – which in turn gives people hope. If a ruler can keep hope at the forefront of his people's minds, that man will forever stay in control.

# 47

# ATTICUS OF FAVOURED NORTH
# KALA

Following Oberon's meeting, Atticus' day continues exactly as planned, much like most days. He spends his morning in class and part of the afternoon foraging to meet his household quota. Later that afternoon, he's nearly back home from foraging when he bumps into a woman hurrying down the footpaths, away from the colony centre. She seems troubled, her face solemn and empty.

"I'm so sorry, are you okay?" he asks her upon their collision while bending down to help her up before collecting his fallen baskets of goods.

"I'm fine, just let me be..." she says in a hurry as she pulls away from him. It's hard not to notice that her cheeks are soaked in tears. When she turns away from him to carry on, he sets his baskets back down.

"What's going on? Is everything okay?" he asks.

"I said I'm fine! Please..." her lips quiver as she speaks. She swiftly moves her body around his and hurries off.

"Wait!" he shouts after her.

"I can't, I have to go. Just... don't follow me," she answers.

The woman runs through the brush not knowing that Atticus has a deeply inquisitive nature – she doesn't know that her saying not to follow is the very thing that indeed makes him follow her, so he begins tiptoeing down the path. He's curious and notes that he doesn't recognize her face, but that doesn't matter as it's not uncommon. He weaves in and out of the forest on either side of the path with a desire to not get caught. The woman rushes along the fields that lead to Lake Cloud, a few loose curls, barely noticeable in the dark, bounce as she hurries. When she slows,

Atticus crouches down and crawls amongst the tall grass. *Where is she going?* The woman stops then, her body facing the lake.

She speaks out loud a prayer to Mother Earth: "Mother Earth, please take me, for I can no longer live this life. Take my body and free my spirit," she says and then steps toward the lake.

*She's going to kill herself.* Atticus stands up and runs then, his arms swinging and his feet pounding into the dirt. The woman holds her foot, hovering over the lake. She releases her frame and her body soars toward the water. His hand grabs her shirt just in time and her body comes to a halt as she tenses over the poisonous waters of Lake Cloud. Atticus quickly pulls her away from its surface.

"No! What are you doing?" she howls in agony as she fights his grasp.

"You can't do this."

"I must. I must go," she continues to fight his hold with small frantic movements of her limbs.

"You mustn't. Stay here, with me," he offers.

"Why, when all I feel is pain? My child is gone; my husband is gone. I need to be gone."

"What's your name?" he asks her as he holds her tightly in his arms. Although he's seemingly much younger, his slender frame towers over hers as he holds her snugly in place.

"Aphria," she manages through sobs.

Suddenly, a connection fires through his brain – he remembers seeing her on the stage with The Masters, and her husband… in The Circle. Her story reminds him so much of Lidia's – the pain, the sorrow.

"Aphria, you mustn't leave because… because there's someone else going through what you are."

"So what?"

"You could talk to her about these feelings, maybe she can help," he offers.

"I don't want to talk. I want to be one with the earth. I want to stop my mind and body from hurting," she agonizes.

"This woman I'm telling you about… what if she needs you too?"

^

Miraculously Atticus was able to convince Aphria to leave the lake and go back to her home of Insignificant Coden on the south side of the colony. An anxious feeling lingers in his stomach – he didn't want to leave her for he worries she'll go back to the lake when he isn't around. Nevertheless, he has to follow through with his promise and talk to Lidia; so, he runs through the colony centre towards the greenhouses where he meets his mother along the way.

"With the earth, Atticus. There you are darling. I need you to run a few tests quickly at the lab: check the lethalyn levels and then the pH of the water please," Ida requests and then saunters off, apparently unaware of the urgency and worry in his expression.

"Okay, mother, I will," he simply calls, then turns his frame and sprints toward the lab. He'll have to find Lidia after he completes the tests for Ida. Atticus pulls out the glass tubes and TXE tester then searches the table for his notebook. Just as he locates his notebook, something else catches his eye: 'Atticus' written in tidy handwriting on a folded piece of paper. Curious, he quickly opens the letter.

Dear Atticus,

'Thank you' doesn't describe well enough the gratitude I have for you. I want you to know that I know you've been following me. I'm unhappy – not blind (I thought that might make you laugh). You're the sweetest man I've known and one day you're going to make a wife very happy – I hope for your sake it ends up being Illandra, I know how you care for her. It has been an absolute pleasure to have known you. Whatever it is that you're looking for I hope you find it. And if you ever get to see Vera again tell her she was my dearest friend, I never got to tell her that.
You'll feel my spirit with you. If you know me well, you already know I'll be with the lilies.
With the earth,

Love Lidia

"What the hell is this?" he says, his voice echoes off the lab walls, "Lidia!" He stands frozen a moment. *Think, where could she be?* "Lilies? Because of Lilith? But why?" he asks. *Where are there lilies in Kala?* It isn't adding up. "There's water lilies," he thinks aloud, dumbfounded. He relives the moment from earlier with Aphria and it hits him, "Oh no – the lake!" Atticus turns and flies out the door, sprinting across the colony centre once again.

The curfew siren wails and the centre is almost empty of people as all the Insignificants flock to their homes, while the odd Favoured still wanders about. However, above The Master's chamber something out of place catches the corner of his eye: red letters. His mind is a scrambled mass of fear, worry and urgency but he stops to read the writing:

"Free us from solitary."

Below the message is a labyrinth symbol. *Solitary?* He glances down at the letter in his hand – it's the same handwriting. He knows where to go, for there's only one place where water lilies grow in Kala: in the lake along the northwest shoulder. His feet glide him down the footpaths toward the lake.

He is fast and used to dodging rocks and tree stumps mid-run, though on a couple instances he fumbles and almost loses his footing. The sun has set and the sky grows black; mammoths howl in the distance, but he won't lose his focus. Soon he sees the waters of Lake Cloud reflecting the slice of tonight's moon, no matter how dim. It is usually beautiful, but on this night the view of the lake sends goosebumps across his flesh.

There she is: her dark figure stands motionless at the water's edge.

"Don't do it!" he forces, out of breath and hopeful that he isn't too late. Her frame turns to see Atticus approaching.

"Oh no… Atticus – what are you doing here?"

"I can't…" he tries to explain in between breaths, "give you… to the lake," he finally gets out.

"It's not your choice," she says with a dull echo in her voice.

"I won't," he reiterates.

"Go home Atticus. The mammoths are out, you're putting yourself in danger for no reason."

"Lidia, I know what you need. It all makes sense now-"

"You can't possibly."

"I saved someone today, just like this. Two women seek to leave Kala by entering the lake on this very day. Don't you see that there's something wrong with that?" he begs as he still huffs.

"Two women?" she seems surprised at the fact that someone else was here, wanting what she so badly wants, "What is her name?" she questions, as if asking for proof.

"Aphria of Insignificant Coden. Do you remember baby Soyer's birthing ceremony? It was a couple of years ago."

"Yes… he had an orange shine to his hair," she reflects.

"His mother is hurting, just as you are," Atticus cautiously steps closer to Lidia who's still at the water's edge.

"Everyone's hurting Atticus, just no one talks about it."

"Let's talk about it. You can talk with Aphria about it," he offers and in that moment he's glad that the darkness shades their faces as he holds back sobs, holding back because he fears he can't afford to waste a single breath, a single second of time.

"If Aphria and I speak of our secrets we'll be forced to face tribulation as Offenders. I'd rather just leave like this, I don't want Oberon and Huron to have the pleasure to see me off," her focus remains on the lake.

"Maybe you don't need her, but she needs you. You know what she's going through, as she knows you. Besides, we can make sure no one finds out about your secrets." Lidia pauses to think for a moment.

"Where is she?" She finally asks.

"At Insignificant Coden, I made sure she got there safely," Atticus' heart races as Lidia's feet shift away from the water's edge.

"I want to see her tonight."

48

# VERA OF INSIGNIFICANT CANNELLE TAGONDO

Her head aches, but only slightly. Her eyes, however, squint in an effort to keep the sunlight out that beams in through the cracks between the boards of wood. The rays would ravage her sight if not for her fingers blocking the yellow laser beams.

"You slept long enough," Ezla says once she notices Vera awake.

"I apologize," Vera moans.

"It's fine."

"No… I apologize for the entire night… my behaviour was less than ideal."

"Don't be sorry. It was pretty hilarious introducing you to the drink."

"Well, I'm certainly glad the introduction is over with – please remind me to never meet with the drink again." Hersh lets out a loud snore.

"He's like the rooster – he wakes me every morning," Ezla laughs.

"Does he drink like that all the time?"

"Yeah, pretty much. Ever since he and Regan had their falling out."

"Falling out?"

"It was bad."

"What happened?"

"We had all just arrived in The Motherland and Master Oberon was speaking to the people about building a better life and learning from our mistakes and so on. Do you remember what happened? A man snuck up behind Regan when he rose to speak up against Oberon, so Regan turned and pulled a dagger on the guy."

"Yes…vaguely… he killed that man," Vera states as the visual runs through her mind.

"Yeah, and why do you think no one did anything about it?" Ezla asks.

"We had just gotten here, everyone was terrified and exhausted..."

"Everyone was terrified of him," Ezla clarifies.

"They probably were."

"Do you know why they were so terrified though?" Ezla inquires.

"Because he killed a man..."

Ezla shakes her head, "It's because that man was his brother."

Vera's stomach sinks, "His brother? How?"

"Hersh, Regan and Taynen: the Adder brothers. They were practically famous back in their small hometown – the best basketball players in all of South Dakota. I mean, ones that didn't play for the state of course."

"What happened to them?"

"All I know is that they didn't have much growing up; their family was poor. Hersh was the best at basketball out of the three and in his teen years his parents wanted to get him a scholarship, but something happened that put all that talk to a stop – he ended up unable to play ball.

"I wasn't alive back then, obviously, but I overheard my mom saying something one time... Something about how Regan got tied up in something and needed out, Hersh got him out... whatever it was. Afterwards Hersh left basketball for good, and took a job in construction for years. Taynen, on the other hand, was an artist and in the midst of building a gallery when the Water Crisis struck."

"And Regan?" Vera asks.

"Apparently he was jealous of all the attention and praise that his two brothers constantly got. Things weren't going well for him, until the Water Crisis. I think he's always been determined to show everyone that he's the best Adder. Even if it meant killing his own brother."

"Oh dear, it's..."

"Fucked up," Ezla chuckles as she finishes Vera's sentence. Suddenly a seriousness washes over Ezla's face. "We need to talk about last night," her expression turns more sterile, "Do you remember what happened with Opi?" she asks. Vera nods, but she hasn't had time to process it all.

"I think Opi killed Burke and Regan is paying him in shares," Ezla spits.

"It's possible. Master Regan has a way of making people do things..." Vera reasons, as she reflects on her conversation about Regan's manipulation tactics with Cole.

"Burke stood up to Master Regan for you and Cole at the Aftermath Party and then he up and dies? *Someone* didn't like it," Ezla suggests.

Vera sits in thought.

Ezla continues: "That conversation we overheard definitely has something to do with Burke. I heard them say something about 'getting rid of a body.' And do you remember the Defenders with the sacks? It could've been his body in pieces."

"Yes... they were marching northeast. There were a lot of Defenders – twelve at least. Have you ever seen them carrying loads like that before?" Vera asks.

"No, never. I've got no clue what they're up to," Ezla admits.

"Maybe that's how Regan disposes of all the bodies though?"

"Huh... I didn't consider that," Ezla ponders, "But it doesn't explain why Opi is accepting payment."

"That's true," Vera reflects for a moment how open and honest Ezla has been with her and decides that she should unload her knowledge of the plant properties and black poison onto Ezla. Furthermore, she reasons that they both have cause to distrust Regan, the face of Tagondo, together.

But first, out of curiousity, Vera needs to ask Ezla a question: "What is D?" and feelings of embarrassment suddenly rush to the surface as she feels her cheeks blush.

Ezla breaks out into laughter.

"What's so funny?" Vera asks, confused.

"It's just that, I was wondering if it was going to be you to ask me that strange question. It took you long enough!" Ezla continues in bellows of gut rumbling laughter. Vera sits in surprise. "Deneen." Ezla finally says once she settles.

"How do you know what D is? I mean… who told you?"

"It was a message I received in a nut shell."

"I'm not looking for expressions, Ezla. I'm looking for answers."

"It literally came to me in a nut shell – a walnut shell!"

"Oh. What did it say then?"

"That at some point I would be asked what D is, and if I wanted change I was to answer Deneen. That's all I know."

"Can I see the letter?"

"I burned it. I didn't want anyone to find it."

"Of course," Vera nods.

With more confidence in trusting Ezla, albeit through her father's strange antics; she goes on to explain what she knows about the plant properties, how she needs to test lethalyn against the black poison, and how it could possibly be the source of Burke's death.

"So that's why they buzz on my skin?" Ezla inquires, intrigued with the plant properties.

"And why I managed to push Issac out of the way during the mammoth attack," Vera explains.

"Shit, it sounds like magic."

"It's not magic. It's science – the evolution of plants."

"This is… insane. How?"

Vera chuckles, "That's all I know. We don't test plants in the lab, all of the focus is on the water, so that evolution theory is my own. But I'm supposed to meet Cole this morning to set up a plan so that I can get to the lab to do some tests. Also, I was thinking that we could possibly look into testing DNA if there is any evidence from the perpetrator left behind at Cole's house. Maybe we can figure out who the murderer is."

"I'm telling you, you're going to discover that it was Opi," Ezla states.

"We'll see. Anyways, what time is it? I need to get going," Vera says then glances at a nearby clock. Realizing the time, she jolts up and runs her fingers through her mane then straightens her shirt and skirt.

"I can help too? You know… I'm not useless with this thing," Ezla offers, as she gestures to her leg.

"I'm sure we'll need you. Thanks Ezla," Vera calls back as she closes the barn door behind her.

^

The sun glows brightly against the east side of the trees, casting shadows along the west. As Vera heads toward The X to meet Cole, each shadow feels cool as she passes through them, sending mild shivers tingling across her skin; the tingles continue until she reaches the sun's rays once again in which she then swoons in all of its glory. Her mother would always tell her that she was made for the sun. Her skin has always been a soft peach, it doesn't change much with sun exposure, only darkens ever so slightly. Her green eyes squint mildly in the light, but it doesn't hinder her sight, unlike her blue-eyed mother, who can't see her own nails upon her fingertips in the right light.

Talks about the Old World with Ezla put Vera's mind in a reflective state, reminiscing on days she spent at the beach swimming in the hot sun, playing in the sand as a child – a desire to swim fills her with yearning. It has been a couple decades since she was able to swim in a body of water. *One day soon*, she thinks, hoping that it can't be too far off. Life always seems to come full circle, and a circle, is ever-moving. That's what she deems to be the best quality of circles, the shape itself allows for constant movement. The only reason a circle stops is when it loses momentum. She can't allow herself to lose momentum – she too, will be ever-moving. *Is that why Cole can't stop after Burke passed away – for fear he'll lose momentum?*

She reaches The X and knows to follow the marked trees to the far end of the row, fifty paces up or so is Cole's lookout. She quickly fluffs her hair and adjusts her scarf over her black t-shirt; she's still wearing the outfit she wore to the party last night.

"Morning," Cole's voice calls, Vera turns to see him approaching her. He rests his hands on her arms in greeting.

"Good morning," she says as she steps out of his grasp with a need to forage her own personal space. "How was your night?"

"It was good," he smiles.

She reflects for a moment on her moment of embarrassment from the night before. He'll probably never let her live it down, how she inappropriately fondled him.

"Where did you go last night? I wanted to walk you home, but you were nowhere to be found. What happened?" he asks.

"That's gentlemanly of you. I went to Ezla's."

"Oh," to her surprise he doesn't push for more. He simply turns and heads for the lookout. Vera follows Cole towards the base of his tree and notes that something is still bothering her: their disagreement over Burke's death and Cole's coping.

"Listen… I'm sorry about our talk the other day, you need to cope with your father's death in the way that you know how," she says.

"She apologizes. Is the world ending? Or just beginning?" he teases.

"Neither, it has merely been put on pause."

"Well, can I hear it one more time?"

"No," she faintly smiles.

They climb the ladder to the lookout and Vera notices that her arm has mostly healed and is of no bother to her anymore, her back too. She notes the ease in the climb without any nagging aches, which is a relief. They soon reach the top of the lookout, the place where there's an endless sea of treetops with their tips creating an illusion of green waves. She stands by the railing with a slight edginess to her posture.

"How are we going to get to the lab?" she asks.

"I've been thinking about that. Actually, I barely slept last night."

"And?" Now she pushes.

"What about the plant, ivani was it? If it offers us a shot of adrenaline, we could get there faster, which means less chance of getting caught."

"Yes, well, it doesn't mean it'll work for you," she notes.

"It'll work for me, why wouldn't it?"

"I sense there are certain things in this world that are not for the simple-minded," she laughs, though she isn't entirely kidding. It's her arrogant Kalian roots that still cling to her feet.

"Oh come on V, let me try it."

"Okay fine, but don't be disappointed when it doesn't work." She searches her bag for the vial, when she finds it she opens the container and holds the ivani twig in her hand. Cole reaches and pulls off a single leaf.

"What do I do?" he asks.

Vera struggles to believe what she's about to say, although she reminds herself that the plant is the reason Issac's life was saved. If it happened once, surely it could happen again. One day she plans to test the plants' true properties in the lab for concrete answers.

She takes a breath, "So if you place the leaf on your wrist, you should feel a slight tingling sensation, that sensation will grow a bit stronger and that's how you know it's working."

"So it's different than just the mild buzzing that happens when the plants brush my skin?"

"It's different. Once your skin has time to absorb the leaf's oils… You'll know what I mean," she explains. "You should expect pupil dilation, accelerated heart rate, a clear mind and…"

"What?"

"Something that feels like superhuman strength and speed… But it's not superhuman, it's just adrenaline," she explains. Cole places the leaf on his wrist and they wait a few seconds.

"I feel so energized. Like… like I could do anything," Cole's voice calls as he rips around the lookout.

Part of Vera hoped that it wouldn't work for Cole – without the lab she feels like she really isn't all that special anymore. Ironically, she's truly Insignificant in Tagondo.

Cole's thumps on the platform drum in her ears as a breeze brushes across her skin. There's a difference though, the breeze that Cole creates is warmer than the current May breeze. His breeze continues to move warmly about the lookout, gently swaying her long brown waves this way and that – cedar and orange are housed within the mild gusts. She closes her eyes, there's no bother to look for she can't focus on him anyways.

"I know you're having fun, but we really need to formulate a plan," Vera finally says to Cole, disrupting him.

"This is our plan," he chuckles.

"Yes, but we need an exact plan."

"What more do we need?" he inquires.

"Why don't we make a list of the essentials? So, firstly, where will we meet?" she rhetorically asks as she pulls a pencil and small piece of yellow paper out of her satchel. She begins writing:

*Escape plan:*
** Meet at lookout upon nightfall*
** Use ivani*
** Cross through The Circle to Kala*
** Go to House of Favoured North to get the key to the lab*
** Get to the lab*
** Test black poison and DNA from crime scene*
** Change*

"I think we have to go through The Circle to avoid the outskirts."

"It's weirdly, the safest bet," Cole agrees.

"There's no chance we could climb the wall that divdes the colonies on the south end of the lake?"

"Not if you want to fall to your death after being sliced by the spikes at the top. Test DNA at crime scene, what's that?" Cole asks.

"Well… I thought if there is something left behind by your father's perpetrator, we could take it to the lab and test it."

"Then we can find out who the murderer is," he breathes. Vera nods and he continues: "There was a glass of water… it has a black tinge in the bottom, I haven't touched it."

"Good, bring that, we can test it. Wrap it in burlap."

"Okay. But I still don't see why we need a list for this?" Cole asks, bewildered.

"Now we know without a shadow of a doubt what we must do. No matter what happens, we stick to the list," she states.

"Seems a little silly to be walking around with our plan for anyone to see," Cole shrugs.

"No one's going to see it, it will be in my satchel at all times. Besides, I know what it's like to set out on a plan and then have something else steal your focus. We must remain diligent. Should we take our weapons with us?"

"Definitely."

"What if we run into the night guard? I doubt anything has changed in Kala – there are no weapons allowed in Kala except for the ones Defenders carry."

"We have ivani, even if we spot Defenders we should be stronger and faster… even if only briefly," Cole reasons.

"True. Also, Ezla wants to help."

"You told Ezla about this?"

"The way I see it, it's us versus whoever murdered your father and tried to poison me, right now. Having Ezla's help can only be valuable."

"How will she be able to help?"

"All I know is that I have to find the murderer and prove that they did it. Only then will we be able to move forward."

"Move forward with what?" he asks.

"With fixing Tagondo."

# 49

## REGAN OF FAVOURED ADDER
## TAGONDO

Later that day, Master Regan sits in The Master's chamber, sipping on his wine. Cole enters upon his request.

"You called for me, your grace," Cole says as he bows.

"Yes. I have important matters to discuss with you," Regan states, Cole nods. "I want to offer you the chance of a lifetime, one that I haven't offered any Tagondian yet. You are the first," he explains.

"I'm honoured."

"Your merge agreement with my daughter has been revoked at the onset of your father's untimely death. I want to reinstate that agreement and offer you the opportunity to take your father's place as Baron. In time, when I am no longer ruler and Treena takes my place, you too, will rule Tagondo at her side."

Cole, taken aback, begins: "I…"

Regan accepts his stunned look as surprise and interjects: "Excellent, it's set then."

"I'm sorry your grace, I'm going to have to turn your offer down."

"Turn it down?" There is no chance he'll accept 'no' as an answer. "You can't turn it down."

"There is no way that I can accept. I'm not Baron material your grace."

"No one is Baron material," he barks.

Cole stands silently for a moment.

Regan fills the silence: "Do you not wish to merge with my Treena?"

"No, your grace."

"Leave, now." Regan bursts in irritation.

He watches Cole immediately bow and leave the chamber – the only man that he's pegged as bearable for his daughter. He's displeased to offer such an opportunity and have it spat back in his face. The anger simmers; he clenches his jaw, and his nostrils flare.

"Rimmy," he shouts as his eyes begin to tighten.

Rimmy appears through the front doorway, "Yes your grace?"

"I want to see Opi of Insignificant Cannelle, immediately."

^

Not too much time passes before Opi comes waddling in with a bow. "You called for me your grace?" Opi says as he awkwardly rises.

"Have you ever wanted something so much that you were practically willing to do just about anything for it?" Regan asks.

After appearing to consider the question, Opi finally speaks: "Yes, your grace."

"And have you ever cheated in order to get that something?"

Opi's cheeks redden slightly as he admits: "Yes."

"Would it be fair to say that you are willing to do anything for me, so that I may get what it is that I so desire?"

"Yes."

"Very good."

"What is it that you desire your grace?"

"I want Cole to merge with Treena. But he refuses, and I know why. It's because of your *daughter*, Vera."

"What does Vera have to do with it?"

"She is a cause for distraction."

"She is?"

"Mhmm. There is to be a celebration tonight at The Circle, all Almek shall be invited – Kalians as well. Be sure to inform everyone. I want Vera and Cole there, but unaware of its purpose."

"As you wish, your grace."

"Also, you will have to miss this celebration. I have another job for you to do."

# 50

# VERA OF INSIGNIFICANT CANNELLE
TAGONDO

Vera leaves her satchel in her bedroom after returning from meeting Cole in The X, and then wanders outside to help Murdina in the garden.

"Princess, would ye help me pick rocks? They come up in the spring, pushed up from the depths below."

"Of course."

"When ye pick the rocks, put them in this pile here," Murdina points to a pile, "Then we'll move on to the holes."

"Okay," Vera immediately begins tending to the rocks and it isn't long before they move on to digging the holes.

Murdina has plants that she foraged from the field, as well as a few from the forest and along the lake. She also has pots with cherry tomatoes and leaf lettuce growing along with some of her favourite herbs.

"You should have been a Kalian," Vera notes, "You have a way with plants – a true botanist at heart."

"Aye, an old hen like me has no business bein' here amongst the pursuers. Twas Opi who chose to reside in Tagondo back durin' the settlement days."

"It's sad, isn't it? Not having the opportunity - the freedom - to choose where one wants to be now."

"Aye, tis. Where would ye choose to be?" Murdina asks.

"What do you mean? Of course I want be back with the Kalians."

"Would ye?"

"Without a doubt."

"Without Cole? He belongs here, doesna he?" Murdina notes.

Vera hesitates then – that's something she's never considered. What if there was the freedom of choice, to choose which colony amongst one could live? What would he choose? *It doesn't matter,* she reminds herself.

"The way I see it… ye were made for both, lass," Murdina states.

"Both?"

"Ye are growing into your inner Tagondian, getting stronger. But still, ye carry the smarts of a Kalian. Tell me, at which one do ye think ye've bin happier?"

Vera thinks about Murdina's question for a moment – about her family, about Lidia and the lab. There's no denying her longing to be back home. Then she thinks of Murdina, Cole and Ezla.

"I don't know the answer to that question."

"Tis not too late to figure it out."

"Murdina, can I ask you a question?"

"Aye."

"How does the Rowan tree offer you good luck?"

"The Rowan tree?" Murdina asks, a clear quizzical look upon her face.

"Yes, when I first came to Tagondo… you said-"

"Oh that's' right. I did say that didna I?" Murdina pauses then, as if she wants to carefully choose her words and then continues: "It helps me reflect on the past an' look to the future wi' hope."

"How does that offer you good luck though?"

"I dinna make the same mistake twice," Murdina reasons.

"Oh." At least it's an answer – something that's trying enough as it is to pull from Murdina.

"That's enough for today Princess," Murdina says as she attempts to straighten her stiff legs. Enough questions or enough gardening? She isn't sure.

Vera walks up the front steps of Insignificant Cannelle and goes in the front door. She decides that it's time to pay closer attention to the contents of her satchel, the plants have been so helpful to her and conversations with Murdina often touch on their finer qualities – it's time she fully accepts them. But, as she walks down the hall Opi comes out of her bedroom.

"Oh Vera, hi – I didn't know you were inside," he chuckles as he pushes his glasses up his nose where he likes them to sit, even though they never seem to stay.

"I just got in… is everything okay?" she inquires. What she really wants to ask is in regards to his reasoning for being in her room, as well as his reasoning for being with Master Regan last night in the forest, but it isn't like her to speak so forwardly.

"Everything is just dandy. I was looking at your door. It's been creaking and I've been meaning to grease the hinges," Opi explains.

"Oh, okay. Well thank you for doing that," she says, glancing down at his empty hands. One would expect that greasing a door would require that person to be in possession of oil though.

"My pleasure."

"Well, I have work to do. I'll talk to you later," she adds as she walks into her room and closes the door behind her. *He is up to something.*

After a quick glance around and not noticing anything out of place, she decides that it was likely innocent snooping on his part and she pulls the contents out of her satchel. It's still an odd realization for her that she carries plants that possess these strange properties, though it has slowly become her new reality and tonight she chooses to entirely embrace it – for if she doesn't, she won't make it to the lab without them.

Still, there has to be an explanation behind the effects of these plants. However, she's getting pulled in a little deeper now, deeper into the properties of the plants and into this life in Tagondo. Atticus would be thrilled at the thought of plants triggering an adrenaline rush. She hopes she'll be able to tell him about it when she slinks to Kala later tonight.

Vera reverts her thoughts back to the plan, maybe there's something more in here that can help them. She pulls out an unexplored vial and reads: "Keenle: put in the tea of a liar, listen with your ears to the truth." Vera likes the sounds of that one. Murdina hasn't come in just yet, she's still cleaning up the gardening tools and Opi just stepped out the front door – so, she takes this opportunity to make tea for the three of them. They often settle in the evenings amongst a cup of tea, which means her making them one won't be deemed odd. However, there will be but a minor change in detail to their evening tea – one they mustn't know about.

"Tea is ready," Vera calls outside a few minutes later.

"We're comin'," Murdina says as she wanders to the shed with her hands full of gardening tools.

It's not long before they both make their way inside and the three sit together at the kitchen table, surrounded as usual by green walls and the whimsical paintings created by Murdina. Vera knows that she needs to stay calm, casual even; the point isn't to formulate an interrogation, but to ask a few simple questions.

"Oh, this smells great," Opi exclaims, and he is right, it does. The earthy and musky tones of the keenle leaf waft about the kitchen.

"Indeed," Murdina agrees, her eyes glancing at Vera's and locking upon them for a brief instant with what seems a glint of intrigue. Perhaps she wants Vera to know that she knows what's in the tea. Still, if Murdina does know, she plays along as though she doesn't.

"It's nice," Vera agrees. They sit quietly at the kitchen table.

"I tell you, that shed back there is good and ready to fall apart," Opi begins filling the silence.

"Aye, we must rebuild it one day, maybe Cole will help us," Murdina suggests.

"I do agree, it is looking worn," Vera adds.

They sip and carry on with small talk – as they always do. It'll be hard to ask the questions that she wants to as she doesn't want to come across as suspicious.

Instead, she chooses to start with something more personal: "I have to admit that I've still been thinking about the probes. I can't seem to get them off my mind. Nor can I shake the feeling of Rimmy and his ill-intentioned ways every time he comes around to do the probes." Does he always do the probes?" Vera asks.

"Aye, he always does. He's an odd man that one," Murdina says, her voice having changed slighty… perhaps more loose sounding. Opi moves his head in agreement.

"Is there a way to have someone else do the probes? He makes me so uncomfortable."

"There isn't anyone else. Rimmy does Master Regan's dirty work – everyone knows that," Opi states.

"Oh, he doesn't have anyone else that does his dirty work?" she asks.

"No," Opi admits. *So that must mean I'm right about Opi and he isn't involved in Burke's death.* Death - she is sure - counts as 'dirty work.' But still, she needs to be certain.

"Does he ever have Rimmy kill people for him?"

"Murder?" Opi gasps, though his speech is slightly slurred, "I think not."

Vera's posture loosens slightly as she realizes the tea must be working, which means Opi is entirely innocent of Burke's death. But who is responsible then?

"Master Regan is a vile man, he is not to be trusted," Murdina warns.

Vera nods, "I really think he's up to something beyond just looking for surplus water with the probes."

"I've heard scarce rumours," Murdina blurts and then looks about the room and towards the windows.

"What kind of rumours?" Vera questions.

"Whispers about an antitoxin. A thing that when taken it allows ye to drink any water. I'm bettin' that's what he's lookin' for," Murdina explains.

"Allows one to drink the water? That must mean it somehow prevents the body from getting sick from the toxins?" Vera asks.

"Aye."

"Are these solely the whispers that are telling you this?" Opi asks Murdina, she nods. Opi waves his hand in a swat-like motion, "The whisperer is nonsense – it's just some bored Tagondian with nothing better to do. I wouldn't listen to them. If there was an antitoxin we'd all be using it by now."

"You're probably right," Vera notes as she thinks about the possibility of something amongst the colonies that offers immunity from the poison that killed billions of people and continues to haunt the world. But, who knows what the antitoxin is, if it's even real or if it even works.

# 51

# IDA OF FAVOURED NORTH KALA

The days fly by in a blur for Ida, mostly because she's trying to keep things straight – who she is and whom she wants the colony to believe she is. She must keep up appearances as she needs everyone to believe she is in a depressive state following Vera's re-birthing. If the people believe it, it will get back to Master Oberon, and what she truly wants is for The Master to underestimate her.

Ida scurries through the colony centre, heading southwest towards a specific cabin. She has business that needs tending to, secret business. The man she is going to see doesn't exactly know that she's coming, but it's better that way – for if he had time to sit on it, to consider her offer, he'd likely turn it down.

She keeps her face pointed down toward the ground and walks quickly. A few people stop and offer her the usual "With the earth," she offers a quick "May we be cleansed," but she keeps moving – she can't afford the distractions on this day. Ida continues through the brush of the forest for ten minutes or so, she then nears the wooden cabin of Favoured Steel. She walks past the house until she catches sight of the shop out back, built specifically for the one who bends steel. She's been here a handful of times over the years, so she knows her way. She travels past the house and to the shop; placing her hand on the metal doorknob, she turns it and lets herself in.

There stands Curshman of Favoured Steel, dressed in his navy coloured carbon armour – a protective thermal suit for burning hot metal. Ida tiptoes in, he glances up at the sound of the door closing.

Curshman lifts his mask, "With the earth," he states, though its not exactly welcoming.

"May we be cleansed," Ida replies.

Curshman puts down his iron tools, “I haven’t seen you over this way in years. To what do I owe this pleasure?”

Ida gets straight to the point: “I have a proposition for you Curshman.”

“Go on.”

“I need you to make me a Favoured North crest.”

“Why on earth would I do that? You know The Master is the one who orders new crests. If I went through with such a request, I could face tribulation.”

“I know that. Which is why I also know that I need to make it worth your while,” Ida pulls a cloth out of her pocket then. She places the cloth inside the palm of her hand and then opens it, exposing its contents. His eyes widen in awe as his head begins nodding eagerly, almost too eagerly. He appears to catch himself and straightens his posture accordingly. She knows he won’t think twice now that he sees what she’s offering him.

“When do you need it by?” he asks.

“A couple days.”

“Done.”

“Thank you,” she says as she wraps the item back into the cloth, she sets it down on a nearby table then turns to take her leave.

“Wait. How can I ensure this doesn’t get out?” Curshman inquires with worry in his voice.

As if she has no empathy for his concern, she simply says: “I have a plan for that. You mustn’t worry Curshman – it won’t be like last time,” then heads back the way she came.

# 52

# VERA OF INSIGNIFICANT CANNELLE TAGONDO

As the sun begins descending and gracing the west with its presence, Vera waits up in the lookout for Cole. She loves a good sunset, to pause and bask in the beauty is simply immeasurable. With no sign of Cole yet, she takes advantage of the view: soaking in the way the palette of the sky melds the soft blues, oranges and pinks into a scheme of elegance. Rare, tiny slits of vibrant pinks and reds appear amongst the crowd of pastels, gleefully and yet calmly debuting its glory for all to see. Each colour, each line of the sky, adds to the treasure. She can't pick a favourite; the appearance of all of it together is that of a masterpiece. It can never be that one hue is more important than the rest – their beauty relies on each other.

"Hey V," Cole calls as he climbs onto the lookout.

"Hi," Vera replies, still mesmerized by the view. Cole joins her, overlooking the trees.

It stays quiet for a few moments before he breaks the silence, "It's really quiet," he ironically announces.

"Yes," her admiration still on the sky.

"Why so quiet?" he asks.

"Do you ever get lost in the sky when you're up here?"

"I want to say no, but I also don't want to piss you off," he jokes.

"I wouldn't be upset, I would feel sorry for you," she simply states.

"That's not a better option."

"No, I suppose it isn't."

"Actually, it might even be worse," he speculates.

She thinks out loud, something she rarely does: "I guess that all depends on your perspective."

"Yeah," he pauses, "You know what?"

"What?"

"You are like talking to a robot when you're looking at the sky," he notes as she is kind of zoned out and a part of her is on autopilot, she laughs then.

"Sorry, lately I find it hard to look away from such a sight." With a calm excitement washing over her she wonders if she merely feels hopeful now that she is finally going back home. Even if it's merely to break into the lab, briefly see her family and then return to Tagondo.

"What if you were being attacked by a pack of mammoths?" Cole asks playfully, breaking her train of thought. She can feel his eyes on her.

"Well, that would be one of the few circumstances in which it would be easy to look away," she says as she brings her eyes to his attention.

"It's like you and me," he says.

"What is?"

"The only instance I could peel my eyes away from you would be if we were under a mammoth attack."

"I don't think so," her cheeks warm.

"It happened once," he reminds her. She remembers when they were under attack, how brave he was, how he protected her... how long ago that already seems.

"I don't know about that," she shakes her head with an internal plea for him to stop gazing at her.

"There's more beauty out there than just what's in the sky, V."

"I haven't seen it."

"One day you will," he states, still watching her.

She hopes he's right.

As the sun takes its leave from their field of vision, Vera wonders if someone else in another part of the world in this moment is being woken up by its golden rays. But, she knows that thought is impossible, the toxic waters have wiped the globe – according to The Masters.

"We should use the ivani now," Cole suggests.

"Okay," Vera says then reaches into her satchel, but she can't find the ivani, "I don't understand, it's not here."

"What do you mean it's not there?"

"It should be right here," she points to the compartment where she keeps the ivani, where Murdina put it for her.

"What's this?" he asks as he points to another plant.

"It's…" she hesitates, she hasn't memorized all of the plants and their labels, she'll need to read it. She eyes the label on the glass tube, "Oh right, it's plynth."

"Which is what?"

"It says: "Rids a body of stein."

Cole laughs, "I always love Murdina's explanation of things. Sometimes it's a riddle, sometimes it's just barely enough to understand."

*Except earlier today,* Vera reflects, for the tea really did work. Then she ponders how she would never need to use the tea on Cole, if anything she needs a tea that offers silence.

"If you could save the world, would you do anything - I mean, absolutely anything - to make it happen?"

"Yeah, I would."

"Even change?"

"Sure, there's nothing wrong with change. Look at the trees – they drastically change every season and they're fine. I think if the trees have the world figured out, we can figure it out too."

"I like that," she says, nodding her head in the darkness, "Even during winter the trees' cells continue to operate. They adapt. We need to be more adaptable," she notes, then reaches for her notebook for their escape plan, "The escape plan list – it's gone too…"

"So? We don't need a list anyways," Cole says dismissively.

"That's not the point. Where did it go? Someone has taken it."

"That and the ivani apparently," Cole notes, "Someone doesn't want us to go through with our plan."

"Master Regan maybe?" she asks.

"That's a pretty sad attempt at stopping us for him – taking a list and a plant. Master Regan would do worse than that to stop us from opposing him."

"Opi…" she says knowingly. He was in fact 'greasing' her door earlier, but who greases a door without grease?

"What good do those things do for Opi?"

"I don't know," it doesn't make sense. She wishes that she noticed the items missing earlier and asked him about it while he was sipping on the keenle tea.

Cole announces: "Oh well, not much we can do about it now. Let's get moving." He climbs down the ladder and suddenly takes off in a steadfast sprint.

"Umm… We have to wait for Ezla, I told her to meet us here at sundown," she shouts while making her way down the ladder.

Cole runs back to the bottom of the ladder and stops abruptly, his hair more dishevelled than normal. For a brief instant she thinks she prefers him this way – with completely unkempt hair. He would never suit the short Kalian hairstyles that the men have over there.

"Woo wee, it's good to be here!" Ezla approaches the base of the lookout, crutches in hand. It has only been a week since the Pursuing Challenge, and although her leg seems to be getting better – it isn't ready for her full weight.

"Shh," Vera instructs.

The three huddle in at the base of the lookout as Vera starts, "There's something I need to tell you guys," Cole and Ezla look to Vera. She hesitates a moment as she doesn't want to spread untruths. Maybe they'll be the ones to help her find out if what she is about to say is a truth.

A moment of silence passes before Ezla says: "Are you going to wait until the mammoths come out to play? Get on with it."

Vera smiles, "There's an antitoxin. I'm not certain, but Murdina told me she heard the whispers."

"The whis-" Cole begins.

Vera interjects: "I know, I'm not entirely convinced that the whispers are legitimate either, but I know that Murdina is. Plus, I gave her a tea that makes one speak the truth – I know she believes it to be true."

"What would this antitoxin be good for?" Cole asks.

"Well, if it's real, it'll allow us to drink the toxic water on the planet and not get sick from it."

"You mean, the water can't kill us like those poor bastards back in the Old World?" Ezla asks.

"Exactly. Which is another reason that we need to get to the lab tonight – no matter what. I need to review my father's notes, and speak to my mother and Atticus, maybe they know something."

"Wow… That means we could leave The Motherland," Cole thinks out loud. Vera nods.

"I'll just about die if it means I can leave this place," Ezla bellows. Vera and Cole exchange humorous glances.

"Avoiding dying is the point here Ezla," Cole quips.

"If I want to die of excitement, leave me to it damnit. It's better than dying at the hand of a Master," Ezla states.

Vera looks to the sky, "We should get going."

The three break into a jog, though Ezla's has a hitch to hers, and quickly begin soaring through the night. Vera struggles to contain the excitement to be back on Kalian soil again, even if only for a short time.

Vera glances at Cole on her left and Ezla on her right then – they are her people though. They don't have books or science, nor fine clothing and tame hair, and yet they help her. It's because of them that she'll make it back home to see her family one last time and to the lab to fulfill the message from Hendrix. She doesn't know what sort of progress the others have made at the lab, but after months of having none she'll be happy with even the smallest amount.

"Every bit counts," she says under her breath as she realizes that it's her friends who have helped her to see it that way.

^

In no time The Circle is in sight. The last time Vera was here was baby Jed's birthing Ceremony. Her pained eyes dart this way and that, anywhere to avoid a glance toward The Circle for she is still deeply marked from its events, *Who isn't?* She recalls Lidia's face then, another scarred by The Circle. She knows that she eventually needs to face The Circle as they need to climb the gates to cross through it into Kala.

As the three renegades get closer, Vera sees the unity symbol carved above The Master's stage. The sphere with two peaks turned inward. *When has that symbol ever represented what they say it does?* They approach the tall fence that surrounds The Circle and quickly realize that they are not alone – there are voices.

When they reach the exterior of The Circle, they see that it is lined with Defenders. It's nightfall, a peculiar time for such a gathering to be in motion. They slow their pace to a walk and enter through the Tagondian gate to find the seats filled with colony people. The Masters and their Barons are all sitting upon the stage; Vera notes that Treena oddly sits amongst the leaders.

"What the hell is going on?" Ezla asks the other two.

"Something odd, there must be an explanation," Vera thinks out loud.

"Regan," Cole states with a husky tone to his accusation, almost as if he knows what's going on. With all eyes on them, they stand to face The Masters.

# 53

# OPI OF INSIGNIFICANT CANNELLE TAGONDO

Opi slinks as quickly as his round body will carry him through the colony centre while everyone else is meeting at The Circle. Vera and Cole will be there, he saw their plan for that night and so he decided to spread the word about Regan's planned ceremony once Vera had left. He did what his Master asked of him, and it was easy. All he had to do was avoid telling her about the ceremony, and take her escape plan. Opi decided it was fair to assume the escape plan involved Cole, which means the two will find themselves at The Circle on this night, completely unaware of the celebration. He also took into consideration Cole's relationship with Ezla, and the fact that she could possibly be involved as well. He knew she would be pursuing all day, and that evening Hersh would be drunk and unaware.

Normally, Opi would also be at the ceremony, seeing as they are mandatory, but he was given an important job to take care of for Master Regan that night, and seeing as Master Regan makes the laws, Opi easily justifies breaking them for his own benefit – which he has on several occasions. No one will pay any mind to Opi being gone, the only one who may possibly notice and speak up about it is Vera, but there is hope that she'll be far too preoccupied with what Regan has planned. He has already given Murdina an excuse – that he was granted sick leave by The Master for a brief return of stomach issues.

The quiet of the colony centre brings a chill to Opi's neck – he has never witnessed such silence. If a mammoth came there would be no one around for miles to hear his screams, he'd be as good as dead. He gives his head a quick shake and reminds himself that it's silly to think about those things, he needs to focus on the job at hand.

Tonight's job is one that links back to weeks prior when Opi actually had stomach troubles and Master Regan, as gracious as he is, admitted Opi entrance to the hospital. It was then Opi formed a friendship with sweet Mae – a necessary friendship in order to complete his task. Mae is lovely and has such soft features. She is much younger than he and far too beautiful, and yet, he can't deny his attraction to her. Regardless, they became friends upon her caring for him and his predicament. She prescribed a ginger root tea and peppermint leaves daily and his stomach has been feeling better in recent days after weeks of following her treatment.

On this night Opi needs to break into the Tagondo hospital and steal as many needles as he can get his hands on. He figures that Mae will likely be the one to notice, as she keeps count of the stock and sterilizes needles for reuse. But, even if Mae does notice, she is such a sweet girl that there is a good chance she may not say a word out of worry for inflicting tribulation upon someone.

Opi creeps toward the hospital building, heading for the room around back that houses the supplies. The window at the back is broken and therefore always unlocked – due to his digestive upset Opi has been in the hospital enough times that he knows most of the quirks of the building. The last time he was here he noted the latch had been busted, he assumes it has been that way for some time. It seems foolish to not maintain the building or for the doctors not to notify a builder to fix the broken window, but he isn't about to make such a suggestion. This foolishness is only benefiting him and he is sure it will again.

As he stalks along the side of the building he runs his hand along the horizontal wood panels. The wood panels are smooth and feel satisfying under his finger tips, offering him some distraction from the quiet. He turns around the edge of the building and stands before the window. It will be a struggle for him to climb it, what with his heavy-set shape. Before sliding the glass across its frame he pushes his glasses up the bridge of his nose as far as they go, a means to secure them in place during his climb. He places his meaty hands on the sill and jumps while simultaneously pulling his weight up, poking his head in through the window. He desperately pulls his body up with his arms while dramatically wiggling his legs in an attempt to shimmy his body forward. When he thinks his tiring arms might give out he presses the toes of his boots against the outside wood panel wall, this additional push seems to be enough to get the core of his body up onto the sill. He slightly shifts and suddenly the top part of his body teeters down and his bottom half goes up, causing him to fall inside, headfirst.

A startling moan escapes his mouth upon impact with the floor. Opi rises to his feet and stiffly moves to the cabinet which houses just exactly what he is looking for; his glasses need adjusting in the mean time. He notices that his heart is thudding, he isn't used to that kind of physical exertion, or any exertion for that matter. He takes a moment to catch his breath then opens the cabinet doors and leans inside with his hands, wrapping his stubby fingers around a box of clean needles. There are two large boxes, he can't take both; instead he empties a box of cloths, one he assumes won't be too missed, and fills it with needles from each of the two needle boxes. *That will do,* he thinks. All he has left to do now is drop the needles off at Favoured Adder and stealthily head home to Insignificant Cannelle before the Tagondians return.

A thought creeps into his head that when his colony members return tonight, they'll likely be returning fewer in numbers – at least that is typically what a gathering at The Circle means. A brief sadness washes over him until he reminds himself of the position Master Regan will promote him to, should he do all that he asks. Baron is all he's ever wanted. His dreams to be Favoured are only getting closer.

# 54

# Vera of Insignificant Cannelle
# Tagondo

"Our guest of honour has finally arrived and is painstakingly late," Master Regan announces, addressing the crowd from the stage.

Vera, Cole and Ezla stand just inside the gates of The Circle, unsure of what Master Regan is speaking of.

"What should we do?" Vera whispers as thousands of faces stare at the three with what looks like disgust - or curiosity - Vera isn't sure what else.

"Vera of Insignificant Cannelle, Ezla of Insignificant Adder – take your seats. Cole of Insignificant Pollard, you belong right here," Master Regan motions to an empty seat on the stage.

"Cole?" Vera urges.

"I don't know what's going on, okay. Just relax: everything will be fine. Go to your seats on the benches," he instructs.

"I'm not leaving your side," Vera chokes with concern as a deep-rooted twinge tells her that something isn't right.

"You have no choice, now go."

"But-"

Cole turns and holds Vera's shoulders, "You've sat in silence for me before – you'll do it again tonight," he says, steadying her.

She turns away from him and immediately her hands begin to tremble. She remembers the first time she attempted to sit in silence for him – he almost lost a finger that night when she didn't fully listen. She knows that she must do as he says – she begins walking toward the bleachers.

Cole suddenly and gently tugs at her wrist and in one quick movement turns her towards him, pulling her in tightly. There they stand, surrounded by solar lights amidst the backdrop of a darkened sky and thousands of eyes, embracing with lips pressed. She doesn't have an opportunity to react as he holds her with a force that she didn't feel upon their previous touch - a touch that both scares her and excites her - for the things that a touch like that could represent. It is that alone which distracts her, forcing her to forget about the crowd who watches them and for her to completely disregard the consequences that she'll face for this act – tribulation is imminent now.

She softens herself into him for the first time, with as much charge as he shows her. She never wants to let him go, at least not tonight. He pulls back then, before she's ready. *How dare he.* He looks at her with a hunger in his eyes and yet at the same time, an unshakable sadness that burrows beneath their heat.

"Making up for lost time?" he smirks.

"You could say that," she offers. He grabs her hands then and looks her in the eyes.

"No matter what happens, it's just a setback. Don't ever give up, because change is still possible," he says it as though he knows what's about to happen, and then he turns and walks to the stage, periodically returning his gaze back to her.

Her heart races for far too many reasons outside of her own control. As she watches him walk the path to the stage, tears begin to grace her cheeks. She moves toward the bleachers and takes a seat beside Ezla, amongst the other Tagondians. Her hands and arms tremble with convulsions and her pulse thumps loudly throughout her head, she leans on Ezla out of pure necessity.

"Are you okay?" Ezla asks.

"No."

"Just hang in there, we'll hear what's going on," Ezla says.

But Vera has nothing left in her to speak in that moment, no words to offer. There is movement on the stage following Cole taking his seat – it's Treena, she whispers to her father.

Master Regan nods his head and steps forward, "I intended for this meeting to be the merging celebration for Cole of Insignificant Pollard and my daughter, Treena of Favoured Adder – but now that is impossible to proceed with," he announces to The Circle.

For an instant an overwhelming sensation of disgust and anger surges through Vera, it makes her stomach twist and her face grow hot. The nerve one must have to force a merge agreement on another – and on stage in front of thousands. She needs to remind herself that Master Regan always sees to it that he gets what he wants and he'll gladly cheat to get it.

"Instead, we will mark this gathering as the re-birthing ceremony of Cole of Insignificant Pollard."

Vera immediately tenses, ready to stand to her feet. She glances to Cole, whose head shakes slightly, the image reminds her vaguely of Hendrix – it is something he would've done. He wears an expression that she can't quite pinpoint. How she wishes in this moment she could speak with him.

Vera darts her eyes about The Circle, she looks across to the Kalians, finding Ida, Atticus and Lidia – sitting together with Lidia's parents. Vera smiles at them, tears tickle her eyes. Atticus waves, normally she would tell him to put his hand down - to sit straight and still - but not this time; this time she waves back. For a brief instance she is occupied with a proud yet faint smile for her little brother and the fact that he has never been one to care about the convictions of others. She misses that about him, she misses him and everyone else. If only she could run over there and hug them. *What a foul world this is; ruled by a foul leader.* But she must remain quiet, nonetheless her hands find fists in her anger.

Master Regan steps forward on the stage, "Who will volunteer to fight?" then he turns and takes his seat, as if to let the thought settle in amongst the people.

Vera leans back into her seat and grasps at Ezla's hand, "A re-birthing ceremony," she mutters under her breath, "How is this just? He has no parents to fight for him."

"Shh… It's gonna be okay," Ezla whispers back as she tucks her arm around Vera. The Masters and their Barons speak amongst one another as The Circle awaits further instruction. Upon their signal, the ceremony is set in motion and as in a typical ceremony at The Circle, Zev takes his place at the podium.

"A welcome to our Masters: Master Oberon of Favoured Kenoak and his Barons of Kala and Master Regan of Favoured Adder and his Barons of Tagondo," the crowd snaps their fingers, "The Masters would like to thank you all for gathering here today, under unprecedented circumstances, for there is no guardian to speak of for this re-birthing.

"Cole of Insignificant Pollard, at twenty-six-years-old, comes from blood of strength. His father was both pursuer and Baron. He is known as the Mammoth Slayer, the only one of his kind and one of the top pursuers of our time. He will make a fine merge for any woman and an equally fine father. Are there any volunteers interested in fighting for the rights to this man?"

Vera stands without a second thought, "I will!" she shouts. The thumping of her heart is a minor distraction, her breathing on the other hand is impossible to regulate.

Master Regan turns to face her once again with a smirk smudged across his face, "So noble and yet in such poor taste. You, my dear Vera, will be facing Tribulation for that disastrous display." She knows he is referring to their kiss.

Suddenly a familiar voice calls out: "I will fight for Cole of Insignificant Pollard." It's Murdina – Vera spots her rising to her feet a few rows back.

"Murdina of Insignificant Cannelle? Isn't this a welcome surprise, I do like surprises I must say. How thrilling," Master Regan taunts.

Vera glances about in search of Opi, he's nowhere to be seen. Instead she catches sight of Zev who stands still, always unemotionally affected by all instances of barbaric nature in The Circle. Though she can't help but question: *What does he stand for?*

Regardless, she won't sit by while someone else - Master or not - tries to decide the fate of Cole Pollard. She's about to walk to the stage when a sturdy hand unexpectedly grabs her arm as she stands alongside the bleachers. Vera turns to see Murdina seeking her attention.

"Murdina," she says in shock, "You can't do this, you can't fight."

"Princess, this day was comin'. Dinna fear for me, for I dinna fear death." More tears begin to fall from Vera's eyes, droplets form on her cheeks. She looks down to the ground and there her gaze stays for a moment.

"Listen, ye best keep yer head up lass," Murdina says as she pushes Vera's chin to face her. "Not another tear. Take this," Murdina says as she pulls a small velvet cloth bag out of her pocket. The bag is a deep burgundy-red and holding it closed is a golden-roped drawstring. Murdina opens the bag and pulls a stone out and places it in the palm of her own wide-set hand.

Vera looks to Murdina quizzically and, as if in response to her confused look, Murdina pulls a tiny piece of paper out of the sack. She places it in Vera's hand and Vera examines its aged and yellowed appearance.

"What is all this?"

Murdina pours the contents of the bag into her hand, "These stones give ye control, unlike anythin' ye've ever seen before," Murdina says as her light blue eyes pierce into Vera's green in a way they haven't before.

"Did you make them? How?" Vera asks.

"Ah pish… these are from yer faither." Murdina's face forms a stern grimace – though when didn't it? It seems like Murdina speaks as if she's insulted on Hendrix's behalf at Vera's assumption.

"My father? How could that be?"

"He made them. He wanted ye to have them."

"Why?"

"They encourage rainfall, that's all I can tell ye," Murdina nods slowly to Vera.

"Rainfall?" Vera echoes, her head spinning with so many questions.

She recalls reviewing studies from the 1900's of attempts to control the weather for warfare – agricultural and other means. At one time she and Hendrix speculated together on what previous scientists had been missing to reap success, though nothing became of those conversations.

"Why?" Vera simply asks again.

"This was his. Now it's yers."

"His project…" Vera wonders if these stones have anything to do with the project he was privately working on.

"Hmm?" Murdina hums.

Vera shakes her head as a means to focus, "He was working on something on his own for years. He never spoke about it and I never asked," Vera proclaims. Murdina simply smiles.

An ache rises in Vera's throat, it tugs at her words as she forces to articulate them: "What about Opi? Does he know about the stones? I think he might be up to something."

"No he doesna ken about the stones. He has darkness… I'd given him keenle tea more times than not, the man never tells the truth without it. No bother, I must go. Fate beckons me, for now, an' listen I must."

"But, what do I do with these?" Vera asks, now holding up the sack of stones.

"Use them of course," Murdina says it in such a way that it should have been obvious – as if one should know what it means to 'use' stones.

Murdina then takes the aged paper, folds it up and places it back inside the sack that sits upon Vera's hand before giving her a squeeze and turning away. After a few steps Murdina turns back, as if her scattered mind forgot something; it's so like her. She holds her index finger up, pointing upward, something she does when she speaks of important matters.

Then says: "Tis all because of the poison in the water – it has altered plant life… it has altered everythin'. Tis the other thin' yer faither said."

A lump forms in Vera's throat threatening to take her voice, still she manages to choke out: "He knew this? He didn't tell me."

"Be wise Princess, use the stones an' plants," Murdina pauses a moment, "Yer a good lass, well-suited for this. Just dinna lose yer head." These are Murdina's last words to Vera before she leaves to fight for Cole.

“Thank you Murdina, for everything,” Vera chokes as Murdina walks to the centre of The Circle. Her rounded shoulders are pulled back and there’s pride in her step that goes unmatched.

Murdina’s gaze stays on The Circle centre – her thick, white curls look brown in the moonlight. There is a humbling essence to her; she needs no praise, no recognition for her good deeds. She is strong too, in every sense of the word, a woman meant to change the world. That night she may very well win the fight and keep Cole where he belongs.

Zev begins: “Thank you Murdina of Insignificant Cannelle for volunteering. We need one more volunteer. If we do not get our volunteer, we will result to the drawing bowls. Are there any families interested in fighting for the rights to Cole of Insignificant Pollard?”

Just then a man walks toward The Circle from Kala, “I volunteer.” Vera instantly recognizes him as the man who had asked her to carry his child right before her own ceremony.

“It appears we have our volunteer: Torant of Insignificant Wells will be fighting for the rights to Cole of Insignificant Pollard,” the crowd snaps, “I would like to remind you all why we gather here at The Circle: we gather to unite as one and we gather to pay respect to Mother Earth. May we be cleansed,” Zev pauses allowing for a brief snapping, and then continues with the typical formality of his ceremonial speech, ending with: “Will the two opponents please step forward?”

Murdina makes her way toward the centre of The Circle, a thud radiates inside of Vera’s ribcage as Murdina’s feet meet with the sand. Meanwhile, Torant’s lanky limbs swing disproportionately long for his torso – his walk is that of a prowl, the servant of death coming to seek his payment. His very appearance sends prickling chills down Vera’s neck and across her arms, her hair follicles react by instantly standing at attention. It’s obvious that this man too houses a sort of evil within his walls and she suspects that it isn’t too far from the surface.

The crowd proceeds the dreadful sound of snapping, a routine to show their approval. *Just what exactly are they approving of? The shedding of blood.* It’s a menacing sound, a steady beat that jabs at one’s core and tests one’s ability to stay calm, at least for Vera it does. She can’t stand listening to it any longer, she needs a plan to get her and Cole out of this mess. *But what?* If only she had her weapons and ivani, she could get to Master Regan faster than anyone could draw a single arrow; faster than Master Regan could put his foot into his own vile mouth. In some form of irony she would secure Master Regan’s sword and run it through his stomach like a stick of butter, and following his slaughter, she and Cole could escape to Kala and fulfill their tasks. But she doesn’t have ivani, or anything for that matter.

“Let us welcome Torant of Insignificant Wells and Murdina of Insignificant Cannelle,” Zev announces to the crowd, interrupting Vera’s reverie. Zev’s voice is once again followed by a choir of snapping fingers filling the air, “Let us begin. Ten, night, eight…” Zev continues, “one!”

Brene sounds the horn then and Murdina and Torant both choose swords and instantly march toward The Circle centre. The fight begins with Murdina and Torant circling one another, each ready for the other to attack; Torant is first to approach, the two swords clang, sounding like thunderbolts of lightening in the moist air. Murdina pulls something out of her pocket, Vera ponders if it’s a stone, like the ones she was given, but she is too far away to pinpoint what exactly it is. Murdina then tosses the object into the air and with a swift swing of her sword she sends it flying up into the sky. It instantly turns into dust, but this dust moves up to the sky, much like a thick, hazy-fog that's difficult to see beyond.

Something is off though, for there is suddenly a shift in the air, Vera senses it. Within seconds the air grows warmer, it's the end of May, but summer isn't quite here – it's something else. Vera looks around her as the sky elusively shifts in such a way that it isn't something one can see vividly, like a raincloud encroaching on a clear summer's day. No, it's subtler than that.

First the stars slowly disappear, one by one, as a grey haze takes over the sky above. As if out of nowhere, golden bolts of lightning sizzle overhead, hurtling their way down to the ground, sparks fly upon contact with the grassy earth. Only now does every single colony member look to the sky for fear of what's upon him or her. However, within The Circle centre the clashing of swords continue as if nothing fazes the two opponents. Amidst the haze comes rain, pouring down on the people – every last citizen instantaneously drenched. The air stays warm, its earthy aroma clings to Vera's nose and with it her memories of the night. The people rise from their seats, their hands outstretched in welcoming.

The raindrops grow larger, crashing down into the dirt of The Circle and sending mounds of its sand up into the air, almost like tiny comets impacting the earth, only without gas explosions or fire. What's odd to Vera is that regardless of the torrential downpour and warm air, nothing else appears to move, not even a slight breeze to sway the raindrops in either direction. Rather, they plummet straight down as if guided through a tunnel toward the earth. Each crashing raindrop sounds a blow and a slight rumble in the ground below Vera's feet.

The lightning bolts continue and sparks fly with each connection they make with the ground. Though terrifying to witness, it's also exhilarating in its own peculiar form: wild and catastrophic. At any moment a bolt can strike and kill instantly upon impact; and yet, it also feels entirely controlled, as though there's a map with markings in which the bolts are meant to target. Vera reminds herself that these thoughts are nonsense and completely illogical; however, so are the last few weeks.

Suddenly, without notice, three lightning bolts hurtle down at one, two, three of Regan's Defenders, clearly killing them in an instant. Their bodies erupt, flying chunks of limbs fall to the ground. Zev approaches the podium, his face as still as a stone statue and his efforts to speak prove useless, his voice cannot be heard. Vera's feet and legs begin to tingle on their own accord, they want to move. She felt a similar sensation the day of her own re-birthing, the sensation to run.

She listens to the urgency in her gut and limbs and leaves her seat in an instant. Her body moves as fast as she possibly can as she runs around the side of The Circle, behind the benches where the Tags sit and towards the stage where Cole remains.

She dodges titan raindrops and bolts of lightning. She's almost there and almost has her arms around him, but something isn't right. Vera turns to glance at Murdina, and without time to warn her, Torant lifts his sword, slashing upward and imprinting a red valley through Murdina's stomach. Murdina falls to the ground as her life force leaves her body. Commotion immediately fills The Circle; desperate, confused chatter erupts amongst the people as to what the strange storm is. Mere moments pass before the storm stops and the haze dissipates.

Zev adjusts the microphone, now able to voice himself: "People of the colonies, please take yours seats. There is no reason to be alarmed as the strange storm has passed. We do have a winner in our midst that we must applaud. A congratulations to Torant of Insignificant Wells!" Snaps sound once again. "But before we give Cole away just yet, I must ask – are there any other volunteers? Anyone else interested in fighting for the rights to Cole Pollard?"

His question sits unacknowledged, which in itself is his answer, and so he continues: "Congratulations Torant of Insignificant Wells, you have won the rights to Cole Pollard." Most go on to snap their fingers while others sit in a daze, still reeling from the trance of the storm. Vera finds herself frozen in shock beside the stage for there Murdina lies, in The Circle centre, her lifeless body in the maroon mud.

Several Defenders make their way toward Murdina's body and encircle her, Zev reaches his arms out in encouragement for all to join, "One with the earth," a singular chant calls as all gaze upon her body. Cole is standing now – his movement catches in Vera's peripheral.

"Torant, come claim your victory!" Master Regan interrupts, desperate to reclaim attention.

As Vera expected, Cole runs, but he runs down the steps of the stage and it looks as though he's making his way toward her. As Cole passes through The Circle to reach her, Torant approaches Cole with his sword in hand, still painted with Murdina's blood. Vera moves her feet, running toward Cole, her feet glide through the mud and she quickly halts in front of him. With Torant in their presence, they freeze.

"What is this nonsense? I said: Torant, claim your win!" Master Regan shouts through clenched teeth. Tortant returns Master Regan's stare with a displeased glare.

"Off with you both," Master Regan then demands of Cole and Torant with a wave of his hand. His Defenders close in to ensure submission. "The tribulation for Vera of Insignificant Cannelle is to be determined," Master Regan shouts as he rises to his feet to rush the ending of the ceremony.

Zev quickly jumps to the podium and begins speaking: "As always, The Masters would like to thank you for coming to The Circle where we gather to unite as one and we gather to pay respect to Mother Earth. May we be cleansed."

"Defenders!" Master Regan shouts as he gestures with a tilt of his head towards Vera.

A group of Defenders close in on her, surrounding her at every step, all the while pushing Cole further away. Two Defenders grasp onto her arms, firmly holding her, and drag her east toward the Tagondo gate. The crowd also surges toward the gates, filling in the empty spaces – the Kalians on the west side, the Tagondians on the east, while Cole and Vera remain restrained, reaching for one another across The Circle. Bodies nudge up against one another in a flood of heat, bridging the gap between them much like Lake Cloud used to – much like it will again after this night. It matters not how hard he fights to get back to her, or her to him. The surge of bodies filter out through the gates without a second glance as there's nothing more to see.

Ida, Atticus and Lidia are out of sight; however, Vera can still see the top of Cole's head in the distance, he's being taken towards Kala. She worries for him and what'll come of him alongside Torant. Where she thinks she'd have tears, she only has anger.

A nameless Defender, one that's at least a little less terrifying than Rimmy, picks her up then - tossing her over his shoulder - and carries her off.

# 55

## Cole of Insignificant Wells
## Kala

Cole follows Torant down the dark Kalian paths to Insignificant Wells, aware that he must go quietly in order stay alive and without tribulation. His heart pulsates in his temples with a deep regret. If only he had known about Regan's plans, he could've avoided The Circle altogether – he could've gotten Vera to the lab as he promised. But as far as he knows, there is no other way to cross into Kala: the fence that divides Kala and Tagondo runs long, and high, no man can possibly climb it. Then there is the matter of the outskirts beyond the fences, no man goes there either, though they knew this. Perhaps their plan was doomed before it even started.

He wonders how Vera is, hoping earnestly that her tribulation is quick, easy. Though he knows Master Regan will ensure her tribulation to be anything but light, after a kiss like the one they shared and in front of the entire Almek. What a stupid decision that kiss was. He should be the one facing tribulation, he did it, not her. But they were on Tagondian soils, and entirely under Master Regan's rule at the time of their kiss. Had Murdina won the fight and kept Cole in Tagondo, he would have owed her his life. Hell, he owes her his life now. He grits his teeth as a painful sadness jabs at his chest. He is going to miss her to no end. If he were kept in Tagondo he would surely be facing something fierce for that kiss. He would face it ten-fold if it meant Vera was exempt of it.

Still he pictures her determination, the way it was quite literally painted on her face – it's also evident in the way her lips force themselves together in a line most days, the way her hands tense and formulate firsts at her sides. She is forever withholding, never sharing what's below the surface. Never sharing anything, really. He decides that's okay, for he too carries a secret with him – one he thought he'd take to his grave. But after that kiss they shared, he knows that to be impossible. He'll have to tell her.

^

The house of Torant Wells is an odd one: a tiny cabin in the woods set back on the outskirts of the Kala colony, surrounded by a wall of stones forming a circle. Animal skulls line the shelves, voodoo dolls hang on tiny strings that are nailed to the wooden walls. It smells of smoke-dried meat and burning wood – a smell Cole is used to from Tagondo.

After spending a few hours last night on the couch, this morning Torant sets up a bed in a tiny room down the hall for Cole, it has no windows, it seems as though it was meant to be a generous closet at one time.

"Your room," Torant says.

"Thanks," Cole replies with a scowl for the man who murdered Murdina – he can't help it. But, he reminds himself it isn't completely Torant's fault – he's a pawn in The Masters' ceremonies.

The two stand in a cool silence, suspiciously gazing at one another. *Man, he is a freak,* Cole contemplates how he'll live with someone so unusual as Torant and a slight chuckle rumbles in Cole's throat.

Torant's jet-black hair has been greased back, his fingernails left long – longer than a male's fingernails ought to be. *How can he hold an axe without the sharp edges of those long nails poking into his palm? How does he chop firewood?* Cole observes Torant's choice in clothing – his pants are tight and oddly short, resting just above his ankle. Cole draws the conclusion that Torant isn't like the other Kalians who care so much about outward presentation. Cole then draws another conclusion: he doesn't fear Torant, it is Torant who should fear him – the Mammoth Slayer.

"So, I need supplies," Cole states.

"Supplies?" Torant questions.

"Rocks, branches, rope."

"You will find rope with the needle-workers in the colony centre, or possibly the builders depending on how much rope you need. The rest in the forest," says Torant.

"I also need a dagger."

"There are no weapons in Kala for daily use, only for strength training."

Cole laughs, "Not that The Master knows about." It's not like him to oppose The Masters so carelessly, but then again it's not like him to be in Kala.

"This Master doesn't miss much," Torant responds coldly. Cole releases a smirk in both humour and annoyance. He knows how The Masters overlook things if it suits them.

"Right… well, I'm going to go make weapons," Cole glances about the gallery of voodoo dolls, "You can get back to making your dolls. But I better not find one of me. Got it?"

"You're going to face tribulation if you make a weapon. But, suit yourself…" Torant replies.

"Don't care, your only concern should be making sure you don't make any Cole Pollard baby dolls. Alright *Tortent*?"

"It's Torant."

"Whatever," Cole says as he walks out the front door and down the footpaths of his new colony.

It looks the same and yet, different. They have the same cabins for houses, the same footpaths – but the difference is in the manicured gardens set throughout Kala. Perfectly groomed bushes and brightly coloured flowers fill these gardens. He thinks that it looks as though this is a cheerful place, but it isn't what he's used to and so it isn't home. The sun rises in the east, a beautiful pink sunrise bids him a good morning.

"With the earth," says a young girl walking in front of Cole, she startles him unintentionally and he jumps slightly from the scare – though he doesn't hold a sting of embarrassment because embarrassment is for the timid-minded he reminds himself.

However, not knowing what to say in return he settles with: "Hi…" she waits a moment, seemingly expecting something more from their interaction, but then saunters off without another word.

Cole continues toward the forest with an urge to construct weapons - he needs them - they are meant for protection from the mammoths and a leader of a colony ought to know that. Cole spots a rope hanging from an old broken down shed on his way down the footpaths. "This will do," he says to himself. On his walk he also procures a few jagged rocks – ones that will file down nicely into a pointed tip, and a few sticks to make daggers out of.

He takes a seat among the brush to grind down the stones into points, pushes the ends into each stick and finishes them off by wrapping the rope around them to secure the sharp stones. It isn't the sort of quality weapons he normally makes, but given the fact that Kala doesn't have the same tools in weaponry making available to citizens - and that his lucky dagger is restrained in Tagondo - this will have to do. Cole assumes that he can likely kill a mammoth with just about anything, but he doesn't want to test that thought too literally.

Once he is satisfied with his handwork, he wanders his way back to the colony centre, beads of sweat glisten on his forehead and a satisfied grin possesses his face.

A tap to his shoulder disrupts his thoughts, "With the earth," a woman says, "Welcome."

"Hi..." Cole replies.

A man walks toward him, "Welcome newcomer," he says to Cole.

"Oh Sedrain, remember we don't like to label the newcomers as such," the woman reminds whom Cole presumes to be Sedrain.

"My deepest apologies, you are so right. Welcome Cole," says Sedrain, correcting himself. The two then wander down the footpath with their groomed hair and tidy clothing.

As the morning progresses and Cole ventures further amongst the Kalian footpaths, it feels as though at least half of the colony has welcomed him. He isn't sure how he feels about that part – a sense that being too friendly to a newcomer is disingenuous. Nobody likes newcomers.

Bright colours from the Kalian gardens engage his visuals at every turn – this he does like. He watches as young children walk single file to school, adult Kalians stopping to engage with one another – which is all kinds of strange for Cole. Then he finally meets Master Oberon: the tall, dark-skinned leader of Kala.

Master Oberon approaches Cole with his uniform walk and expectant eyes. Cole has seen Master Oberon several times over the years; however, up until last night it was always from a distance when he sits atop the stage near Master Regan during the ceremonies. His memory flashes back and the weight of witnessing Murdina fight and die trying in The Circle pushes down on his shoulders and his heart much the same. A clench of his jaw helps ease his thoughts so he can look to Master Oberon in such a way that isn't filled with hate.

Master Oberon's hairless head shines in the yellow morning light and his dark skin blends in amongst his black clothing. Large buttons from his chin down, line the centre of his vest to hold the fabric together; the crisp ends of his sleeves, much unlike Tagondians' ragged attire, rest just off his shoulders. *Kalians must have talented needle workers*. Just below the hem of his shirt, Oberon's muscles grab Cole's attention; solid pieces of brown skin are covered in black ink. He looks like a warrior. Cole bows, but not out of his own agency.

"With the earth, Cole, welcome my friend," Master Oberon says, his voice a deep rumble.

"Master Oberon of Favoured Kenoak," Cole lowers his torso in a bow a second time.

"I trust you are well settled?" Oberon asks.

"Yes, thank you, your grace," Cole replies. However, he reflects that without his weapons it isn't as though he has many possessions in which need settling.

"It would be the greatest of pleasure to show you around," Master Oberon says. "Come, follow me," he instructs, turning to lead Cole through the colony centre.

"I notice you have weapons there," Master Oberon comments, noting Cole's handcrafted spears.

"Oh… these are just for fending off mammoths," Cole explains.

"There are to be no weapons in Kala. They distract us from our purpose here, which is to be with the earth. I'm sure you understand."

"But-"

"Even the Mammoth Slayer isn't entitled to weapons. See that you burn them at The Pit before the day's end," Master Oberon orders.

"Yes, your grace," Cole responds in defeat.

Cole is soon led to the greenhouses, which seem like a sanctuary of some sort. The air smells moist and earthy, yet fresh and floral. Some of the plants sway to the movement of blowing fans while others sit contentedly soaking in the warmth of the space and the rays of the sun. You can't see perfectly outside through the glass, for sweat beads run down the walls of the greenhouse and a fog covers most of the surfaces. A handful of butterflies sail and swoop from plant to plant, seeking nectar, or perhaps just basking in the glory that is the greenhouse. How heart-warming to have all the food one needs and no predators in their wake – though that isn't real life and it hardly seems fair.

Cole stands, mesmerized by its charm. He has never seen anything like this. He wonders if Vera likes this place, how could she not. He closes his eyes then, imagining Vera standing beside him; still feeling the magic of the greenhouse, he doesn't have to see it to feel its presence as it's in the heavy humidity and the thick earthy aroma that clings to his nostrils. Cole notices that Master Oberon has left the greenhouse and appears to be venturing to the next. Cole closes his eyes again to soak in this moment, just then a small hand smacks his arm; though it is gently done, it surprises him.

"Cole," says the voice, as though it knows him.

For a second he thinks it to be Vera for there is no one else who would address him in Kala as though they know him.

He turns and opens his eyes, "Hmm?" The face he sees before him is after all familiar and yet not the face he hoped to see.

"We need to talk," Lidia says.

He sighs, "We do?" he pauses, thinking. Upon seeing Lidia's mouth form a frown in grievance at his oblivion. He confirms, "We do."

"Master Oberon likes to give the tours to the newcomers, come find me here after."

"Okay," he agrees then quickly exits the greenhouse to continue following Master Oberon. Cole casually meets back up with him and they tour through the other three rather large greenhouses with light conversation.

Cole reflects back to a conversation with Vera, he recalls Vera saying that Kala had three greenhouses, not four; perhaps one was built during the spring, after she left to live in Tagondo. Master Oberon and Cole soon saunter down the footpaths, passing several Kalians going about their day and walking lightly on their feet as opposed to the common thumps of running feet pounding into the dirt in Tagondo. No one rushes about here, no one shouts; all but a whisper leaves the mouths of Kalians. Cole wonders how anyone can hear each other, let alone themselves.

"It's so different here," Cole says with his voice booming above the whispers.

"Is it? I haven't had the pleasure of roaming the paths of the Tagondo colony," replies Master Oberon indifferently. "Though I might have guessed."

"Why not? I've never understood why these two separate colonies were created in the first place."

Master Oberon appears as if taken aback: "We speak plenty about our world and how we must care for it, what we can do to improve our imprint, but not typically about Tagondo. We have different views than our Almek-counterparts, we are different people – which is why we are divided amongst two colonies."

"The Tag colony imprints the earth too. Mostly it imprints on the people in it though," Cole replies, taking this opportunity to begin to divulge the magnitude of Master Regan's treatment of the Tagondians. However, Master Oberon appears to ignore Cole's comment as he continues walking with his hands clasped at his lower back.

After a few moments Master Oberon finally speaks: "I don't interfere with Tagondian matters," he explains, "though that doesn't mean I agree with them." He says this in in such a way that signifies the conversation is at its end. Still, Cole wonders how Oberon can wipe his hands clean of the torment that Regan places upon his people.

As they continue their stroll through the colony centre, Oberon leads Cole to the lab. It isn't exactly what one would expect based on its exterior: a large log building with quaint square windows and a small stairway leading to a wooden front door.

"We take pride in our lab, the work being done here is next-generation – especially with the equipment the scientists have built. We will have clean water in no time," Master Oberon beams.

"Can we go in?" Cole asks, hopeful, though aiming for indifferent. He ponders if the antitoxin could be in there, if it's real, surely it would be – where else would it be? He still wants to get it for Vera – for them. His stare lingers at the lab's doorknob.

"No, the work done at the lab is confidential – no one but the scientists go in there." Master Oberon explains. *All the more reason it's in there,* Cole bets. They continue past the lab and walk through the colony centre; all the while Master Oberon stops several times to converse with his fellow Kalians.

A group of colony members greet Master Oberon: "With the earth, Master."

“May we be cleansed,” he announces to them all. Each and every one of them bow upon his arrival and all smile with a wide-eye appreciation, or affection, in the midst of his presence.

As far as Cole can see Master Oberon is a well-respected leader. However, his mind sticks on the fact that the lab is confidential. To Cole there seems to be no real purpose in keeping the progress with the water from the citizens – unless one is hiding something.

“Well that brings our tour to an end, it has been a pleasure my friend. Don’t forget to dispose of your weapons. And Cole? I’m happy you’re here.”

Cole takes his bow of leave, “Thank you, your grace. As I am happy to be here.”

“Now, go ahead and get yourself acquainted with the people. They are all thrilled to meet the one and only Mammoth Slayer,” Master Oberon smiles and saunters off.

Cole is left to his own exploration for the duration of the day – an outsider left to roam the paths of Kala. He knows he’s to meet with Lidia before the day’s end; however, something more pressing calls his attention. He needs to hide his weapons – there’s no way in hell he’s getting rid of them.

# 56

# OBERON OF FAVOURED KENOAK
# KALA

It is disheartening to come to terms with the awareness that his people are not as strong as the Tagondians. They cannot possibly train in strength and combat to the extent the Tagondians do, for the Kalians have much more weight-bearing responsiblilies for The Almek. Still, he's lost many people to The Circle and equally just as many to Regan. However, not this time. This time Kala won and with that comes a certain pride. As a Master one always wants their people to thrive, which is why they created The Circle in the first place. That was the one thing he and Regan agreed upon all those years ago.

Oberon walks the paths in the forest following his meet with Cole, admiring the colony he built with his own two hands. It's a joyous walk because there are grey rain clouds gathering in the sky, but not only that, things are looking up for Kala. After Vera and Hendrix left Kala, he noticed a shift in the community. The people were more sluggish, the whispers increased. He wasn't sure why their departure triggered such negative responses, but he hopes that Cole, the Mammoth Slayer, will bring great blessings to the colony. Maybe his presence will give the people hope. After all, who doesn't feel protected while living amongst the Mammoth Slayer himself?

*"Liar,"* the whispers begin and he glances around nervously, the whispers are the only reason he doesn't enjoy his walks through the forest. He speeds his pace to make it back to The Master's chamber – it's far easier to ignore them than to give them a second thought.

When he reaches the chamber he hurries in a means to escape the accusatory whispers. He has it in his agenda to draw up some plans for making the merge celebrations livelier, but he's surprised by the unexpected presence of his Barons. They sit upon their seats as if patiently awaiting his arrival.

"With the earth," he greets his Barons.

"May we be cleansed," they respond together.

"I wasn't aware we had planned to meet today, and this late in the day?" Oberon begins.

"It wasn't on our schedule. However, we must speak with you, your grace," Martil says.

"What is it?" Oberon takes his seat at the table.

"There is much talk amongst the people, we are growing concerned for their questions," Quim notes with eyebrows angled upward, showing his nerves.

Martil carries on, clearly wanting to get right to the point: "Since Murdina of Insignificant Cannelle made rain at Cole of Insignificant Wells' re-birthing ceremony, the colony members have been doubting your sole ability to communicate with Mother Earth in regards to encouraging her to make rain for us." The room remains silent for a moment.

"They think anyone can do it," Hogard adds.

"Oh dear, this is quite the predicament. I do not know how Murdina pulled off what she did. However, she is one with the earth now, so there's no need to worry about that any longer," Oberon says - trying to deter their worries - but his chest begins to pain with anxiety. He knew her death wouldn't be the end of their questions, he'll need to do something to remedy it. If only he knew just how she went about inculcating rain from Mother Earth... that would make it easier for him to fix the problem. *Was her way anything like mine?* Surely not, only he can pull off what he does, with Educator Ferris' help of course.

"Another Coakai isn't going to be enough to prove to them that you are the vessel, it's not out of the ordinary anymore," Martil interrupts Oberon's thoughts.

"We would be able to help you more strategically if you told us how you encourage the rain from Mother Earth," Hogard explains.

"Absolutely not, Mother Earth won't allow it," he states.

His Barons are right though: another typical Coakai ceremony won't do the trick. He'll need to go bigger, step outside of his comfort zone a little.

"I have it. I will report to them the toxin levels in the water. This is something I've never done and will both surprise and appease them."

"That won't likely be sufficient enough to keep their faith in you," Quim disagrees.

"What are the levels?" Martil shifts in her seat as her wide eyes take in all of Oberon, anticipating his response. Oberon exhales then, long and slow. In all the eighteen years of The Almek, progress in the lab has never been disclosed.

"0.3 mL of toxins in the water. Still, the best it's been to date. Eighteen years ago when we settled it was 1.2 mL."

"Excellent," Martil beams, "But as Quim suggests, it's not enough."

"How do you think she did it?" Hogard asks. Master Oberon releases a sigh, he has no clue, but a Master must always have the answer.

"I believe that Murdina of Insignificant Cannelle was secretly experimenting with chemicals. I think she made some kind of toxic and volatile instrument, which forced Mother Earth to rain unnaturally," Master Oberon explains. The Barons gasps of shock fill the room.

"That is terrible," Martil begins.

Hogard adds, “Absolutely horrid.”

“How could she? How could an Almek?” Quim bursts.

Master Oberon exhales, “I know, I know. It is unnerving, and with all of the hard work we have done to help Mother Earth heal…”

“We must tell the people this,” Martil urges.

“Very well.” Master Oberon agrees, “You may be excused,” He states and the Barons stand and prepare to take their exit.

“Yes, your grace. With the earth,” the three speak in unison.

“May we be cleansed,” he says before the Barons close the door upon their leave.

57

# VERA OF INSIGNIFICANT CANNELLE
# TAGONDO

Vera sits tied to the column outside The Master's chamber awaiting her tribulation for having kissed Cole. It's considered a crime, such treachery, and in front of the entire Almek no less. The Tagondians close in, awaiting The Master's word. Master Regan is really thinking on this one, with his fingers grazing back and forth across his chin. The thoughts one must have as they contemplate the creative ways in which they will make another bleed. That alone is something Vera can't fathom, not even in reference to an animal, let alone a human being.

She contemplates more on Ezla's story about Master Regan and how he had gotten into trouble in his younger years – the speculating helps ease her mind, and her anger, as it distracts her. She wonders what kind of trouble it was, and what exactly Hersh had to do to get him out of it.

Master Regan rises to his feet and begins pacing the landing. The Tagondians perk slightly at the movement, like tiny rodents tend to do. But are they really prey? They stand behind their Master; his actions and his beliefs herd them. Maybe they're a bit bigger than a rodent, maybe they're sheep. Vera's not sure which alternative is better. After several hushed words into Rimmy's ear, Rimmy steps off the platform and disappears through the crowd.

Regan speaks, "Thank you all, for joining us on this night… I know this evening's events did not go as planned." Vera glances to Treena who stands at the lead of the crowd, never at the rear, with a scowl resting upon her face. "And what do I say when things don't go as planned?" *You find someone to torture?* The crowd stays silent. "I say: 'It's good to keep things interesting.'"

The Tags break out in their ceremonious chant, "He, he, he."

Just then Rimmy appears, walking up the steps of The Master's chamber with a chain in his hands. Vera's stomach drops.

"This is what I like to call, keeping things interesting," Regan announces.

Rimmy knows exactly what to do without further instruction from Regan; he's good at this – hurting people. He takes two ropes, tying them up high upon each pillar. After cutting Vera loose, he reties her wrists, only this time, one to each rope. Her wrists are now restrained up above her head. As she faces the crowd of Tags, they watch with tentative stares. Vera can see that there is fear in their stares though.

Vera's feet rest on the wooden platform and the rope burns against her wrists as she watches Rimmy, his face is expressionless as usual, expressionless like the way you'd expect one to look when folding laundry or tending to weeds in the garden.

"You just keep fucking up," he whispers to her as he stands in front of her. His whispers almost sound humoured at the fact.

Although she'd really like to spit in his face, because that's about all she could do in this moment, she doesn't. He's not wrong.

"I don't mind this," he says.

*Tell me something I don't know*, Vera thinks.

He continues, "I like the way you look," And his paws reach up, instantly tearing her shirt and undergarments off. She winces.

Master Regan speaks next, "When you offend in Tagondo, you are only hurting yourself." His eyes wander to Vera with purpose, and then back to the crowd.

Though she stays tight-lipped in an attempt to hide her own fear, her stomach aches with a pit the size of a crater. *Keep your head.*

"In light of this particular offence, I'd like Rimmy to use the chain. Rimmy," Regan says with a nod and takes to his seat.

"You're awfully quiet," Rimmy notes as he tugs on the rope by her wrists to ensure it's sound. "I wonder why." His eyes wander to her chest – he takes in the view of her. Vera's hands roll into fists.

The chain Rimmy holds is six feet long of braided steel – Vera rationalizes that without teeth on the end of it, it's not nearly as defying as the ceremonial chain.

"I just want to get this over with," she says between her teeth, while tensing her body in preparation for what is to come.

"You're the grin and bear it kind, not many are like that," he circles behind her, hammering the steel chain into the wooden boards as he walks.

She closes her eyes expectant for what is to come, though not truly knowing the extent. The chain shuffles, its reaction time is much slower than the leather whip, which makes the second before it thumps into her back even more unbearable. Another shuffle, and a second later the chain hammers into her again. The clatter of the chain, the moan of Rimmy exerting his strength and Vera's grunts of disdain are all that is heard.

She squeezes her fists tighter – surely it's possibly to cut the circulation off of one's fingers by doing such an act. Three and then four lashings slam into her body – it's as if she can feel it thumping through her muscles and into her bones and organs. Her legs threaten to give out; she struggles to stay standing. She opens her eyes, barely able to see past the water they're now filled with, and notices a Defender off to the side watching her intently with his light hair highlighted by the solar lights. The fifth blow assaults her back and just when she thinks she can't bear anymore, Regan stands.

"Let it be known. This is what happens when one's promiscuity gets the better of them." The crowd stops their feet in agreement.

Rimmy instantly begins untying Vera's wrists. She caresses her wrists as soon as they're free, noting the raw wounds from rubbing against the rope - they are minor - her back on the other hand, is damaged. Though to what extent she doesn't know. All she knows is this feeling. She imagines it's comparable to having run into a brick wall. Her knees buckle beneath her and she settles onto the floor. A part of her is uncertain if she'll be able to walk. The Tagondians begin to clear out, and the Defender who had been watching form the side approaches her.

"I'm going to pick you up," he says. She nods slowly in response, with her arms tightly embraced across her chest.

He scoops below her bottom and across her back, she winces – but she knows there is no way to limit the pain.

He walks down the steps of The Master's chamber and says, "I'm going to take you to my place." *Leave me be*, she thinks. But she is too weak to protest or inquire further.

The unknown Defender walks with her in the dark of the night and through the quiet paths she can only hear his breathing. A part of her imagines that it's Cole carrying her again, only this time she wants to cooperate, to enjoy it.

Almost as if the Defender read her mind he asks: "Was it worth it?"

She doesn't know this man, she only knows him as the Defender who follows Rimmy around during the probes. Still, somehow she knows what he's asking – he's asking if kissing Cole was worth the tribulation. Though she doesn't think she can bring herself to speak, for the pain of talking is too great, she pushes herself to.

"Yes."

^

Vera awakes the next morning on a bed, still shirtless from the tribulation. She's lying on her stomach, with a cool object pressing against her bare back. She attempts to move, but it isn't just the pain that holds her down, an object on her back holds her in place. She glances behind her as best she can, only to find that she's tied down. A surge of panic runs through her.

"Whoa, whoa. It's okay," the Defender from last night says as he walks in the room wearing track pants and a t-shirt. It's strange to see a Defender out of uniform.

"What is this?" she asks, her mouth dry.

"It's just something I rigged up to stop you from turning over. You were moving a lot in your sleep and I needed to keep that ice pack on your back."

"Oh. Thanks. Can you untie me now?

"I can, just be careful getting up. Take it slow."

"Okay."

He fiddles with ropes at her side and pulls the compress off of her back. Reaching out his hand, he helps to slowly pull her into a seated position. It isn't easy – moans of pain escape her mouth without warning.

"You're tough, Kalian."

"Am I?" she asks, truly unsure of her answer.

"I've seen others break from something like that."

"I feel broken. Does that count?"

"No. It's different." He retrieves a glass of water off the bedside table and sits down upon the edge of the bed. Vera offers a hesitant glance and takes the glass from his hand.

"It's safe water," he says as he moves over to the light switch and turns on a lamp, which allows her to see the shade of the water more clearly. She inspects the contents. It's not tainted with yellow or black hues and it smells normal, so she takes a drink.

"You helped me. Why?" she asks, not knowing the possible repercussions that he could face for doing such a thing should Master Regan find out.

"You needed it and I was able to," his observant eyes watch her as she drinks. He glances down and notices her hands clenching the bedsheet across her chest. "Shit, sorry." He grabs a shirt out of the dresser drawer and hands it to her.

She passes him the glass of water and slowly struggles to get the shirt on. "But is it allowed?" she asks. He shakes his head. "So you risked yourself, your safety, why?" She gulps back the water thirstily.

"Because I had a feeling."

"A feeling?" She scoffs slightly.

"It was a calculated risk."

"I don't know what you mean."

"I've been watching you, for a while."

"And what did you come up with?" she asks.

"Why did you look so closely at that water just now?"

"I wanted to make sure it wasn't tinged yellow – to make sure it wasn't Lake Cloud water."

"So you weren't worried about it being black? From the black poison?"

Her breath hitches slightly. He knows about the black poison. Which presumably means he knows about the plant's properties.

"So what if I was?" her fingers toy with the glass in her hand.

"It would mean you know more than you let on," his eyes gaze at her attentively.

"What is D?" she suddenly asks him.

"What is D? I have no clue, what is it?"

"Nothing, never mind." She realizes in that moment that she never asked Cole her father's question, and yet she trusts him more than any Tagondian. "So, say I know more, what does that mean to you?"

"It means that you can help. I've heard whispers about an antitoxin… and those whispers didn't start until you came to Tagondo."

"I have nothing to do with the whisperer, or the antitoxin. I don't know even know if it's real."

"But you're a scientist, you must know."

She scoffs, "I don't even know you're name."

"It's Finn."

"Well, Finn, I hate to break it to you but that's all I know about the antitoxin – that it may or may not even exist. But, I'm looking for it. Actually, I think Master Regan is too – I think he's looking for the antitoxin when he conducts the probes…"

"Huh, maybe."

"What do you know about the black poison?" she asks.

"I know that he stores it in a hut on the east side beyond the border. I've never been, I've only heard talks of it."

"What does he need it for?"

"I wish I knew."

“Take me there,” she insists.

“You need a couple day’s rest.”

“Tomorrow night,” she says. He nods.

“In the meantime, I’d like to try and help you. I’ll try to find out more about the probes. It might be hard, Master Regan has his select group of ‘elite’ Defenders –they seem to be the only ones fully accordant with his dealings on the probes.”

“I have yet to see a Defender who isn’t accordant.”

“I’ll see what I can do.”

“You might have to get elite, Finn.”

# 58

# ATTICUS OF FAVOURED NORTH
# KALA

Atticus sits in botany class deep in thought. He pays no attention to the lesson that day, how can he? Educator Wade Peony, Lidia's father, rambles on about the temperature of a greenhouse – Atticus already knows all of that. So, instead, his mind is focused on the newcomer. *I can't believe he's here. I'll kill him.* Cole Pollard has made an Offender out of his sister. He knows that she would never have spoken to a Tag, let alone kissed one in public on her own accord – Cole must have forced her into it. Atticus could tell from fifty yards away that she didn't look herself, with her hair down and wild. Cole must have brainwashed her. He's a coward and a cheat, just like the Kalians say about all of the Tagondians. If Cole is the reason that Vera is in Tagondo, then the only meaningful thing in Atticus' life that he can possibly do right now is to avenge his sister.

Suddenly, Atticus wishes then that his uncle Merek were still alive. Atticus doesn't even recall meeting Uncle Merek, for he was exiled not long after their settlement days when Atticus was merely an infant, but from the stories that his parents used to share it sure seemed like he was a resourceful guy – although he apparently had a temper.

Even though Vera claimed to never like him, Atticus likes the idea of him from the stories he has heard. He bets that his Uncle Merek would know what to do and even be able to save Vera from Tagondo, but that's not an option. Atticus will have to find someone else to help him, but he knows that if he speaks about this to anyone there's a greater chance that he'll get caught and his plan will be ruined – except he doesn't have a plan per se, he's more spontaneous and slightly hotheaded at times, especially with his teenage male hormones fluctuating and adding to his inconsistencies.

*Make Cole Pollard suffer*, he decides is essentially his plan. How he'll go about it will have to be an in-the-moment type decision. He likes those kinds of decisions; they make him feel empowered. He has made some of his best decisions in the moment – some even purely based on curiosity. Atticus reflects upon the fact that he's seen enough of what goes on in The Circle to understand how to kill a man. He's observed that there are tons of tools and tons of approaches in which to utilize those tools. Sure, Cole is bigger and way more muscular than he, but that hasn't stopped several smaller men from winning in The Circle. He'll start practising and convince his friend, his best friend, to train with him. That's about as far as his planning will go – he will practise the combat that he's seen other men perform countless times before.

Class lets out and Atticus searches for his friend, Ulyd, a skinny boy similar in stature to himself only slightly shorter in height and much darker in skin tone. They have been an interesting duo: two tall and lean teenage boys that struggle slightly with pimples due to their changing hormones and greasy faces. They both fashion somewhat untidy hair, at least for Kalian standards, and long, filthy fingernails were usually of no concern – though this is all changing as they get older. Atticus and Ulyd are entirely different, which is why their friendship formed in the first place many years ago. Ulyd is quite intelligent and his education is focused on specializing in the laws of the colonies, he has hopes that one day he'll be an Educator.

Ulyd admires all the great Educators, including his mother, Rumi - the Eldest Educator - as well as Educator Ferris who teaches science, to name a few. However, he is particularly drawn to Educator Barlow. Ulyd greatly appreciates his knowledge and passion for the laws, Atticus doesn't – his hate for Barlow goes beyond the workings of the classroom, it covers Kala like a storm cloud floating omnisciently, growing in plain sight.

Atticus now stands at the doorway of Educator Barlow's law class, he sees Ulyd speaking with Barlow and they are the only two in the classroom. Ulyd is such a teacher's pet, a *snub* Atticus calls it, and likely scouting for further opportunities to improve his class grade.

"Ulyd," Atticus calls into the classroom.

"Oh, Atticus. It's only you," Educator Barlow says as he looks up, abashed.

*Only me?* Atticus questions sarcastically to himself, while also noting that his sarcasm has been ramping up as of late – both internally and externally. *Who is Barlow expecting, or avoiding?*

"Is Ulyd done?" Atticus asks with a glimmer of impatience to his tone.

"Oh yes, we were just finishing up," Educator Barlow says in an agreeable manner, which Atticus notes as not typical.

"Thanks James," Ulyd says then turns toward Atticus, who is still standing at the classroom door. Even Atticus doesn't call Educator Barlow by his first name, and they've spent countless meals together.

"Anytime Ulyd, anytime," says Barlow. The two boys walk down the hallway towards the exit together.

"Why are you spending more time around that creep? And you're calling him *James* now?" Atticus asks.

"He's giving me extra assignments, you know, to increase my grades," Ulyd explains.

“Don’t be such a snub. You’re already at the top of all your classes. What more could you do?”

“I know, he’s helpful though. He actually cares about my future and me. He wants me to become the next Law Educator – when I’m old enough.”

“Just be careful with that guy.”

“You don’t know him like I do.”

“Whatever man,” Atticus says with a huff. The two walk outside and venture along the footpaths.

“So listen, I need your help practising something,” Atticus says, breaking the silence.

“Practising what? I know you’re definitely not talking about practising school work,” Ulyd thinks aloud, though his words are hopeful.

“No, definitely not. Okay, I’m going to let you in on a secret – you have to promise never to tell anyone. Okay?”

“Okay, I promise,” Ulyd agrees.

Just then two Kalians walk by, one whispers to the other: “Finally another win!” Atticus rolls his eyes, it’s all people have been talking about since the Kala win at The Circle during Cole’s re-birthing.

He moves in closer to Ulyd as a means to be careful that no one overhears him, “So, Cole of Favoured Pollard is here now, living amongst the Kalians…”

“So what?”

“Between you and me – he brainwashed her.”

“How do you know?”

“You just… you don’t know her like I do, she would never kiss a Tagondian, let alone volunteer to fight to keep one in Tagondo with her. Anyway, I know he’s the reason she is gone.”

Ulyd shrugs, “Well, what do you plan to do about it?”

“I need you to practise in combat with me. Like with swords.”

“Where the heck are we going to get our hands on swords?” Ulyd asks.

“I know where the weapons are stored for the ceremonies – we can break in and get them.”

“I don’t like the sounds of that Atticus.”

“Come on, don’t be such a waste,” Atticus teases, it’s his favourite term for when Ulyd is being apprehensive, as he so often is.

“I’m not… I just-”

“Waste. Waste. Waste,” Atticus chants.

“Alright, fine,” Ulyd sighs in defeat. “But why train in combat?”

“I’m going to seek revenge on him Ulyd, and I’ve made up my mind so don’t try to convince me otherwise.”

Ulyd opens his mouth as though he wants to say something, but he doesn’t. They continue through the footpaths and drop their bags off at their respective homes. Atticus ensures he’s quick and quiet about it since Ida appears to be fast asleep on the couch in her nightly-wears. Atticus reflects upon how it’s a matter of pure luck that Master Oberon or Huron hasn’t caught on to her mildly depressive behaviour just yet. Nonetheless, Atticus slips in and out of the house without notice and the boys meet at the main footpath that leads to The Circle as agreed.

They saunter down the path, passing the broken-down hut that sits off to the side in the bush along the way. Atticus wonders why no one ever fixes that hut, it could be used for something – maybe people are hesitant for fear it will topple over on them. There is something about that hut though, something that sparks his curiosity.

"So, where are the weapons?" asks Ulyd, pulling Atticus' curiosity away from the hut and back onto his mission.

"At the back of The Circle there's a stage door. The ceremonial weapons are locked in there."

Ulyd speaks, bewildered: "How do you know that?"

"I'm an observant guy. Don't you know that?" Atticus quips.

Ulyd snorts, "No."

"Well, I am. At Cole's re-birthing ceremony I watched Huron slip around the back of the stage and he reappeared with the ceremonial weapons."

"Oh."

"Yeah, I think they usually try to get them set up before the ceremonies, but that ceremony didn't go quite as planned," Atticus beams, "Anyway, after I left I climbed to the top of the gates and saw the door, which I assume is where Huron got the weapons."

"How do we get them out?" Ulyd asks, seeming mildly more confident as they approach the fence that encompasses The Circle.

Without replying Atticus begins climbing the fence, it isn't easy though Atticus manages to climb to the top and there he sits awaiting Ulyd. Ulyd gives in and begins his ascent, but he slips and the edge of the wooden fence scrapes his arm.

"Ow!" Ulyd shouts.

"Shh, you're going to get us caught," Atticus warns.

"My arm," he wails.

"It's not that bad, barely any blood," Atticus observes from his perch.

"Easy for you to say."

"Pull your sleeve down, it will soak the blood and keep it hidden."

"It stings. Ouch."

"Digger does worse damage to my face on a daily basis," Atticus teases.

"Yeah well, I'm thankful I'm not you," Ulyd says as he pulls his sleeve down over his dark skin and with much less enthusiasm climbs the fence once more. He reaches the top and follows Atticus, jumping to the sands of death in The Circle. "This is eerie being in here."

"It's not that bad, just don't look to the centre."

"What if it's haunted by the ghosts of all the people who have died here…" Ulyd reflects.

"It's not haunted. Besides, all those spirits have been cleansed. They are long gone – enjoying their afterlife."

"I still don't like it."

"It's daylight – the sun is shining. Don't be a waste. You're lucky we didn't do this when the moon's out," Atticus teases innocently.

Ulyd doesn't reply and so Atticus wonders if he is too focused on the usual thudding in his chest to humour further conversation – he knows his friend fairly well. The two walk behind the stage and just as Atticus said – there's a door. It's a wooden pallet door built of cedar and a lock hangs over the latch, fully intact.

"We need to find something big and heavy – like this rock…" Atticus says as he picks up a rock and tosses it back and forth between his two hands as if debating its girth, "…and we'll smash it off."

“I don’t-” but before Ulyd can finish his sentence Atticus hits the rock against the steel clasp, the rock drops and rolls to the grass. He hits it again and again, until his face begins to grow warm.

“It’s no use, Atticus. Let’s go,” Ulyd says, it’s obvious he has an urgency to flee.

“It’s going to work,” Atticus states determinedly and he picks up the rock once again and with all of his strength, which doesn’t seem like much, he hits the lock once more and this time the lock breaks in half as the rock smashes to the ground.

“I can’t believe it worked,” Ulyd says, though his voice is anything but excited.

“I can,” says Atticus with a grin stretching as wide as his cheeks allow.

59

# VERA OF INSIGNIFICANT CANNELLE
# TAGONDO

Finn returns home to Favoured Malek at sun down after his shift. Vera spent the day there in rest and sadness, after both agreed that Opi would be too distracted with Murdina's death to ask any questions about her whereabouts. She had let loose enough tears during the day that upon Finn's entrance her eyes were still red and puffy.

"How's your back?" he asks as he enters the room in uniform.

"Better." However, in actuality, her body is still very bruised feeling, and walking is extremely uncomfortable, but the ice helps. Still, she doesn't want to complain, nor does she want him to suggest putting off their plan.

"So, you were right."

She perks, "About what?"

"Rimmy announced to the Defenders that protocols for the probes have increased. Searches have now extended to any and all buildings on a Tagondian's property and we are to report any plant-matter, suspicious substances and weapons to him immediately."

"I knew it… Well it isn't quite proof that the antitoxin is real, but it does mean that Master Regan is an even bigger cheat than we thought," she says.

"If Master Regan is looking for suspicious substances and plant-matter, I would be willing to bet that it's real," Finn states. She's not quite ready to have that much faith in Master Regan though.

"Well, I should get going – Get back to Insignificant Cannelle before Opi let's something slip."

"I'll walk you."

"Won't that be suspicious?"

"Defenders walk with civilians all the time, especially upon nightfall," he reasons. She nods.

The two walk down the pathways lit with solar lights – it's quiet out, with the exception of howls of laughter in the distance caused by a few teenaged Tagondians seeking mischief no doubt. On their route they'll soon pass Insignificant Pollard – she doesn't think that when they pass she'll be able to look, but she does and it isn't without effort. She pushes onward and soon they reach House of Insignificant Cannelle.

"I'll be back here to get you tomorrow night."

"I'll meet you at the rowan tree… I don't want Opi to see you."

"Okay," Finn agrees then simply turns and makes his way back down the path, disappearing into the black forest.

Vera walks up the steps of Insignificant Canelle and enters through the front door. Opi sits at the kitchen table.

"Where have you been?" he asks.

"I should ask the same of you."

"I can't say."

"Neither can I."

He pushes his glasses up his nose, "Is that how it's gonna be?"

"I guess so." She replies then turns down the hall to her room – the house feels different without Murdina here, colder. She knows it's not just the dark that makes it so. Vera carefully flops on the bed and quickly finds sleep for the night.

^

"Wakey, wakey!" Ezla's cackle pulls Vera from her sleep.

For a split second it feels as though she's back at the cave during the Pursuing Challenge, with Cole about to walk in with their bounty.

"Hi," Vera moans sleepily, wanting to stay in bed, to be left alone.

"We're going. Come on, get up."

"Going where?"

"I was doing some digging, after your water was poisoned that night, and I noticed that Master Regan's water always has a single leaf in the bottom of his glass. Treena's too. I have eaten lunch there several times recently. At first I thought they were just adding flavour from a mint leaf, but then when I got a closer look I saw it wasn't a mint leaf. The edges were pointed and tiny streams of faded black releases into the water."

"What kind of leaf do you think it was?"

"I don't know. But I wondered if there was a connection with what was put in your water."

"The black poison? It doesn't make sense… they wouldn't poison themselves."

"Duh. I wish they would though. What if a small amount of this leaf's oil is safe, but too much is dangerous?" Ezla says.

"I guess it would depend on the leaf. I might be able to get some black poison tonight."

"Huh, how?"

"I might have a friend in high places…" Vera smirks but doesn't say any more.

"Be careful. Not everyone that says they want to help you, actually wants to help you."

Finn helping her recover right under Master Regan's nose surely proves his word is worthy. "I will."

"Ezla nods, "We should get going then. If we're going to be on time, you need to get dressed now."

"But where are we going?"

"I've been asked to show Treena how to make her own arrows. It's pretty pathetic that she's just learning now at her age…"

"I haven't learnt that yet."

"Yeah but, you're just a scientist."

"*Just* a scientist?"

Ezla laughs, "You know what I mean. Anyway, I thought if I brought you with me, while she's distracted, you could somehow get a leaf from her."

"Me? Go into Treena's house? Are you nuts?"

A wide grin spreads across Ezla's face, "Yes." Vera rolls her eyes. "Oh, I almost forgot, I got this for you." Ezla holds out Vera's handcrafted dagger that Cole made for her then, and something else below it.

Vera grasps the items and then nudges her dagger to the side to see what rests below, "Cole's lucky dagger… how did you get these?"

Ezla shrugs, "It was nothin'. Master Regan keeps a pile of confiscated weapons in a shed behind Favoured Adder. He asked me to go back there to find a couple arrows for Treena to reference. She's good at aim, but she stinks at the making part. Anyways, I saw them at the top of one of the piles… he won't miss them."

"Thanks Ezla."

Vera gets dressed as quickly as she can manage then the two wander the footpaths toward Favoured Adder. Treena's is the last place in the colony that Vera wants to be, but she believes there must be some significance behind Ezla's instincts. They reach Favoured Adder and Ezla knocks on the door.

Treena opens the door and lays her eyes upon Vera, "What is *she* doing here?"

Ezla waltzes in, "Leeches, am I right?" Vera scoffs to herself at Ezla's comment. "This Leech needs a lesson, if not as much as you do, more than you do."

"I would say she needs it considerably more," Treena spits.

"And that's why she's here. Let's get started." Ezla empties her burlap sack of sharpened stones, sticks and rope.

"How do the rocks get like this?" Vera asks, playing dumb.

"I use a rock like this, and just rub them against one another. After a time, the friction causes the edges of the rock to flatten and sharpen. This isn't quick work."

Treena and Vera pick up the rocks and tend to the friction that Ezla speaks of. It is some time before a sharp edge with a tip is formed.

Vera decides to stand and walks toward Treena's side of the table, to presumably grab a couple more rocks, when truly her goal is to get closer to Treena's glass that sits on the edge of the table. The glass is made of metal, but a quick glance inside and Vera can indeed see a leaf situated at the bottom. She decides that now is the time to act and slinks her hand very quickly toward the pile of rocks, while intently allowing her arm to bump Treena's cup, sending it to the floor in a crash. Water covers the table and floor.

"What have you done?" Treena shouts, apparently the water didn't only cover the table. A quick glance to her lap proves that Vera soaked Treena as well.

“I… I’m so sorry,” Vera crouches down, eyeing the leaf that sits sprightly in her peripheral. With one hand she very obviously reaches for Treena’s glass, with the other she inconspicuously collects the leaf and sticks it into her pocket.

“You Leeches, you’re all worthless,” Treena stands and runs out, presumably to her room to change.

“Treena, I’m so sorry. If it makes you feel any better, I got soaked too,” Vera calls after her, while offering a wink to Ezla. “In fact, I better go and get changed too.”

“Vera, you dumb shit. How could you!” Ezla calls for the effect while Vera slinks out of Favoured Adder with the mysterious leaf placed in her pocket.

# 60

## ATTICUS OF FAVOURED NORTH
## KALA

The swords are neat; they are heavy, shiny and absolute death instruments. Atticus thinks that he can definitely master the use of one of these things. All he has to do is mimic the men in The Circle. Easy. *A lot of things are easy*, he reflects. *You just have to try your hand at it*. However, when it comes to things that are hard, Atticus doesn't like to invest a whole lot of effort into them. Though he supposes 'hard' and 'easy' are subjective anyways. Avenging his sister, in his confident young mind, that will be easy. He just needs all but a few minutes to pull that off. Atticus and Ulyd leave The Circle and flock towards the brush surrounding it.

"Let's go over here in the forest, so no one sees us," suggests Atticus.

"Okay," Ulyd says with uncertainty.

"All you have to do is practise swinging. Try to stop my sword with your sword," Atticus instructs his friend.

Ulyd does as he asks and all that can be heard for miles is the sound of swords clinging and the grunting of two teenage boys that have no idea what they are doing. It is amazing they don't get caught.

"These are so heavy," Ulyd whines.

"They're not that bad. Besides, they're only going to give us muscle."

"I don't need big muscles to be an Educator."

"You don't need to have big muscles but you should want them," Atticus argues. "You could have to volunteer in The Circle one day."

Despite Ulyd's efforts, Atticus convinces Ulyd to continue practising for a little while longer. Unlike Atticus, Ulyd doesn't have the same kind of motivation to keep at it though. Before long Ulyd grows tired of the games and holding the sword itself.

"I want to go now, I'm hungry and my mother will be wondering where I am," Ulyd huffs.

"Fine." Atticus isn't mad, only slightly irritated that Ulyd doesn't see the value in all this. But Ulyd doesn't know Vera as Atticus does; of course he doubts his theory. Why wouldn't he?

Atticus needs to prove it to Ulyd. *But how can I prove it without proof myself?* He'll confront Cole of Insignificant Wells first, he decides.

"Can we meet back here tomorrow morning? I don't have class until the afternoon," Atticus asks.

"Sure," Ulyd agrees.

Ulyd has a way about him to make plans and then not pull through though. Atticus hopes he'll pull through on this one because tomorrow they will confront Cole together with their weapons. Just then, they hear movement amongst nearby brush.

"Shh, get down," Atticus says to his friend who jumps down in a hurry – if he can count on Ulyd for one thing it's that he listens well when he's fearful.

"Defenders," Atticus whispers. He knows that they can't get caught, even though Master Oberon is on his day of rest – they would still face the same tribulation when he returns.

"Apparently it's in pill form," says one Defender to another.

"What exactly is it?" asks the other.

"They're calling it an antitoxin. It allows for consumption of the toxic water."

"But how? Who has it?"

"I've only heard the whispers. I don't know who has it, but whoever does have it could control the colony." The two Defenders carry on their march, their voices turning into faint mumbles as they walk into the distance.

"An antitoxin!" Atticus says with a clear understanding of the significance of such a word.

"How can that be?" Ulyd asks in bewilderment.

"If it's true it means we are about to see change."

"What kind of change do you think?"

"I don't know Ulyd, could be good – could be bad," Atticus states. The sun is starting its descent and Atticus is motivated to get home before it sets, "We better get going."

Atticus tucks the two swords under a thick bush beside a pine tree and notes its short trunk. He places them just below the lowest branches that almost rest upon the ground. The two boys then stand and head back towards the colony centre, where they then go their separate ways.

# 61

## COLE OF INSIGNIFICANT WELLS
## KALA

Cole hides his weapons at the base of the rock wall that surrounds Insignificant Wells. In his brief time in Kala he notes that no one ventures as far south as here, as it's near the edge of the colony. He ponders why, while not minding the peace and quiet it produces. Still, he grabs his weapons on his way to the forest to forage. *There's a first time for everything*, he thinks. Although he isn't one to instinctively oppose the laws of The Masters, there's no chance that he'll wander the forests without weapons. Master Oberon is mad for allowing his people to be so vulnerable. Although mammoths rarely roam the forests in the daylight, Cole knows it's not unthinkable. They are animals, and animals are always unpredictable. He walks the footpaths with intentions to head toward Lake Cloud, to stand upon the Kalian side of the lake. Part of him wishes that he was on this side when Vera had been, though he doesn't know how their friendship would fare being in her colony, on her terms.

*"Have faith,"* the Whisperer sings. *So they are in Kala too*, he notes. Just then Kalian's Lead Defender Huron approaches him.

"Insignificant Wells. I have been looking for you," Huron states, "I also see you still have yet to dispose of your weapons."

*Shit.* Day one with his weapons and he's already caught. Maybe he's not as stealthy as he thinks, or perhaps Huron is a better, more attentive Defender than Rimmy.

"I was getting rid of them, as Master Oberon has asked of me," Cole lies.

"If that is true, you would be on your way to The Pit. All Tagondian transfers are instructed to burn their weapons at The Pit," Huron notes.

It's amazing to Cole that there have been Tagondian transfers to Kala at all, due to their lack of strength in comparison to the Tags. Still, he recalls the few fights over the years where a Kalian has won. He also remembers how Master Regan worked them harder following those defeats – he doubled the amount of combat training to ensure that Tagondo would win the next time, to ensure they'd never lose again. And they haven't lost – not in six years. Not until Torant. Cole wonders what kind of shit Regan will be giving his people. Regardless, in Kala there has been no sign of a fellow Tagondian; they must already be brainwashed and altered to look and act as one of them. He notes that he will never transform, never cave in to the Kalian way. He likes his long hair and ragged clothing – there is nothing wrong with them.

"I'll go right now," Cole says.

"Too late. Besides, I have a charge against you," and without notice Huron forces the weight of his paw on Cole's shoulder. Huron's girth and size are considerable, though he isn't quite as large as Rimmy.

"Where are we going? What is this charge?" Cole asks as he allows Huron to push him down the footpaths.

"To see The Master."

It would be considered a torturous walk down the paths and across the colony centre if he weren't Cole - once Favoured - Pollard. All citizens who pass them eye Cole with a suspicious and accusatory glare, though it doesn't bother him. Besides, how can he blame them – he's an Offender, in more ways than just one. But these people don't need to know that, even if they look at him as though they do – they aren't wrong. As they cross the colony centre he hears Kalian whispers that perk his intrigue, whispers about The Master.

"He's not the only one who can encourage rain fall," he overhears.

"That Tagondian woman did it, but how?"

"If she can do it, any one of us could."

Cole lifts an eyebrow in surprise of their whispers, but his thoughts are quickly redirected as Huron guides him into The Master's chamber. Once through the entryway Cole sees Master Oberon with his three Barons at a long rectangular table located towards the back of the room. Cole bows immediately.

"Cole of Insignificant Wells," Master Oberon welcomes.

Cole rises and greets his new Master: "Good day, Master," but Huron immediately smacks Cole on the back of his shoulder, "With the earth," Cole forcefully corrects himself.

"May we be cleansed," and after a slight pause Master Oberon continues, "I won't beat around the bush with you Cole. News of your Offending has reached the chamber today and likely all of Kala. We must initiate a form of tribulation."

"Tribulation? For carrying around a couple makeshift weapons?"

"Not only have you continued to utilize your weapons on Kala's land, you have broken into the weaponry and stolen the ceremonial swords."

"I am not a thief, your grace."

"Those words are difficult to believe Cole."

"Where is your proof?" Cole asks.

"The very items that rest in Huron's hands," Master Oberon says. Huron holds in his giant-sized palm the sum of Cole's averagely crafted weapons.

"My weapons? Those are not the ceremonial swords!" Cole replies, "Where is your proof that I am the one that stole the ceremonial swords?"

Oberon nods, “The weapons are missing, the lock to the weaponry is broken and the single thing that has changed in recent days is your presence – not to mention your interest in possessing weapons. That I say is sufficient enough evidence to order tribulation. Cole of Insignificant Wells I sentence you to jail. The timing and details of your tribulation will be discussed upon and you will be informed in a few days time.”

“Jail? Wait!” Cole calls is disbelief.

Huron reaches for Cole then, his single palm wraps around the back of Cole’s neck – there is no fighting such a grip, not from Huron. They leave the Master’s chamber and head directly to the next building.

Just then a whistle blows signalling for the colony to meet upon The Master’s request. Cole is aware that he will miss the meeting, but hopes that he can listen in. Huron leads him in through the jail’s wooden door and swiftly throws Cole into a cell, locking it behind him.

# 62

## ATTICUS OF FAVOURED NORTH
## KALA

The following day after foraging, Atticus walks into House of Favoured North and sees that Ida is in the kitchen making dinner.

"With the earth, Mother," he says.

In a groggy inflection Ida responds: "Hi dear. May we be cleansed."

There's been a permanent dullness that resides in Ida of Favoured north since Vera's ceremony. So many things have drastically changed and are forever gone. It pains Atticus, and yet through the pain he holds onto the fact that he can still make his mother laugh.

"Care for a shot of corn-whiskey? It'll make your belly hot and your head twitch," he says with a smirk on his face. Ida laughs as he predicted she so would.

"Sure, honey. Thanks," is all she says.

Ida drinks more frequently after everything changed. She hasn't gotten out of control, if anything, with the corn-fermented booze she expresses feeling more 'in control' – perhaps that's the problem though. Either way, it seems to get her through the long nights without Hendrix and - on a rare occasion - she'll even let Atticus have a two-finger glass, which he much enjoys. He just turned eighteen and if anything the booze makes him feel like more of a man. Perhaps it isn't so much the act of drinking the booze, which makes his taste buds scream and his belly burn, as it is simply holding the glass of golden liquid. *Is there power in that?*

He's noticed his body beginning to slowly change over the months since Vera's leaving – though he doesn't believe the booze is to thank for that. His muscles are thickening, and in many ways he's the man of the house now. He is responsible for fixing things, such as: the front door that rotted and fell off from years of water exposure; the step in the house that always creaked – he even built up Ida's garden so she could plant flowers confidently and without worry that the rabbits will eat her hard work. He likes to keep busy, it helps him, especially when he's missing Vera and Hendrix. It is true, without them it's more difficult for he and Ida to make their shares each week, but they manage by cutting back and making their meal portions a bit smaller to last them a couple extra days. They make it work and are fortunate to be Favoured. Atticus is now accustomed to the science of portion controlling food – knowing where to cut back and what they can go without. Ida works full time at the lab and when she isn't working she often tends to her garden, or lies on the couch.

Atticus and Ida sit down to eat a simple and small meal – tonight's dinner is potato soup. Ida has made enough for two more meals each.

"Did you hear that Cole of Insignificant Wells was put in the jail?" Ida asks.

"What? No, I didn't."

"Apparently he broke into the weapons department at The Circle," she says.

Atticus freezes. *Shit. That was quick.* He realizes then that he left the two swords lying in a bush just outside of The Circle – he assumed they would be safe there. Who would go looking in the forest for weapons? No one - especially not in Kala - he thought. However, he realizes in this moment that he lacked to consider that someone might find the lock to the weapons department broken…

He wonders why they've jumped to the conclusion that it was Cole who broke in though; he supposes all Kalians are secretly suspicious of any newcomers. At least Cole is trapped right where he wants him. It'll be even easier now, vengeance is not far off. The best part about this is that no one will care what becomes of him because Cole is now a thief. Atticus can take care of business and no one will have the slightest inclination or care. Cole will be dead, Atticus will relocate the swords to a better location for a Defender to find them and all will be settled. *But*, he reminds himself, *I'm not going to over-plan it. I'm going to wing it.*

"Atticus? Did you hear me?" Ida interrupts his thoughts.

"Oh, sorry mother, long day. That's unbelievable."

"It's saddening when transfers don't work out like that."

"Yeah it is. What a dumbass, getting himself locked up," Atticus chuckles.

"Atticus. It's not a laughing matter – this is someone's life we're talking about. Who knows what Master Oberon will do with him. Hopefully nothing too gruelling," Ida explains. *If only you knew what my plans are for him*, he thinks.

"You know he got Vera transferred right? Made her an Offender." he notes.

Ida shakes her head, "No. I don't believe that."

"I overheard… someone, speaking about it," he says, aware that he can't expose Lidia and the fact that she was at Favoured Wells.

"It can't be true. Our Vera isn't an Offender," Ida dismisses.

Vera didn't become an Offender on her own accord though – she was forced into it. Ida isn't thinking straight, if she were she would understand that. She would be furious. But, he also hates seeing his mother upset, Atticus is pretty sure that Cole dying will ultimately neither hinder nor hearten her feelings though.

^

The next morning Atticus hurries back to the bush where he left the swords and still finds them hidden there. As he gathers them he concludes that he needs a better temporary hiding place - one not too close to The Circle - seeing as he isn't quite finished with them.

*"Hurry,"* the Whisperer speaks.

Atticus scurries back through the forest and finds himself back on the footpaths, still unsure of where to hide his contraband. Suddenly he hears nearby voices – someone is coming his way.

*"The hut,"* the whispers call into the breeze.

Atticus looks around and notices the broken-down hut and decides that it isn't a bad idea. In an instant of panic he tosses the swords into the hut.

"With the earth," a man and a woman say as they appear through the trees and pass by.

"May we be cleansed," Atticus nods in relief that these two are not Defenders, and then continues to scurry down the footpaths.

He decides to head to the jail next, that is until he crashes right into Digger. Atticus falls to the ground and Digger remains standing, almost as if untouched. It's no secret that Digger has a way with torment.

"Ow," Atticus says as he hits the ground.

"Watch it *goon*," Digger says.

"You were standing in the middle of the path, you could've moved," Atticus stands up; however, Digger only pushes him back down to the ground.

"Stay down, where you belong."

"I'm kind of in a hurry, so I'll need you to move," Atticus replies.

This sort of thing happens often enough and he is growing sick of Digger's persistence. All Atticus wants is to be left alone. Why does Digger not understand that?

"I don't give a shit, you little stump."

Atticus stands up again, "Get out of my way," he warns, though it is a sad excuse for a warning.

"I'll tell you what, you stay away from Illandra and I'll let you go," Digger threatens.

Atticus has liked Illandra of Favoured Steel for quite some time, though he has only recently found the courage to act upon his feelings and befriend her.

"Is she your new catch of the week?" Atticus sarcastically backfires; he's fully and unfortunately aware that Illandra and Digger have been in merge agreement for some time, not that it stops Digger from messing around. If the laws can't stop him then not even Illandra can.

Atticus has a mind to report Digger, but he has always been taught to keep the peace – to be quiet at all costs. Only now he realizes that 'keeping the peace' is code for allowing his own face to be bashed in countless times for the rest of his life, and above all else, shutting up about it.

Just then Digger winds up his arm and comes at Atticus' face with his right fist. His punch lands on Atticus' cheekbone, the force of the blow knocks him to his ass – a boulder to a melon. Atticus stays on the ground for a moment. He places his hand on his cheek as he begins to feel a wetness that wasn't there before. His hand is now covered in blood, the warm liquid oozes down the side of his face.

"Great, that's just great," Atticus shouts to Digger as he walks away. So much for moving under the radar.

"There's more where that came from. And Atticus? Watch your back," Digger warns.

"This dating game of yours will end pretty quickly once Master Oberon finds out," Atticus retorts back.

Digger jolts his body then, as if signalling that he's coming back for Atticus, and naturally Atticus jumps and begins running away. No, Atticus isn't boisterous, or strong, or overly intelligent, though he certainly isn't stupid. Luckily, he's tall and a fast runner, so he does have that on his side.

After a few minutes of running, Atticus slows his pace. His face throbs to a steady beat, much like the drums of Coakai. He is sure to get a black eye. *Mother will be pissed*, he thinks. How he dreads the conversation he'll have to have with her about it. She'll be worried and he'll have to convince her not to be – she won't act on her worried feelings anyway. He hates Digger. However, even though Digger beats him to a pulp time after time, he still doesn't hate him as much as he hates Cole of Insignificant Wells, which surprises him slightly – it turns out the anger he has for someone harming his sister can overtake a lifetime of someone harming him.

Atticus makes it to the jail, and seeing as he has no particular time frame mapped out, he's right on time. He waits a few moments for the guard to carry on with his rounds. Seeing as there is rarely a prisoner in Kala, there is never a full time guard positioned at the jail. The guard does his last check inside the jail and turns to leave. Before the door closes and locks behind him, Atticus quickly slips his fingers around the edge of the door. Following one last glance around him to ensure no one is watching, he turns and slinks into the darkness. Only having been in the jail a time or two before over the years, he can't remember exactly where the cells are located inside and so, as he enters, he enters on high alert.

"Who the hell are you?" A voice from within says.

Atticus stands there, silent and with his eyes fixed on Cole who gazes back at him in confusion. Over the last two days this moment has been all Atticus has thought about. And yet, it feels like a lifetime since he dreamed up this meet with Cole. He envisions his sword fitting in-between the cell bars and slicing Cole from head to toe – something he will fulfill tomorrow with Ulyd. Today, he has merely come to speak with the man who took his sister away from him.

"I'm Atticus of Favoured North," he states, a smirk displayed on his lips.

"Atticus? Vera's little brother, Atticus?" Cole asks as he sits up on the bed.

"Yes."

"I'm Cole," he says and the two remain still in silence for a moment. "So… why are you here?" Cole asks.

"Vengeance."

"Me too. I am most definitely in the market for some vengeance – in a round about way. Who's the unlucky bugger on your list?" Cole asks.

"You."

"Me? I… see," Cole says then pauses. "You're spirited like your sister," he notes.

"Unlike my sister I don't put up with people's shit though."

"Is that what that is?" Cole asks, gesturing to Atticus' bleeding cheek. "You not putting up with people's shit?"

"I do what I have to do sometimes," Atticus wipes at the blood that is still seeping out of his wound, as if to erase its presence altogether.

"We all do, don't we?" Cole states, "So, what have I done to deserve such a visit?"

"Vera's in Tagondo," Atticus' voice is cold in a matter-of-fact tone.

"Yeah."

"How'd that happen?" Atticus asks.

"Listen buddy, I'm not about to give you the rundown on The Master's ceremonies. Where's your mom? Ida right?" Cole asks as he rises to his feet and moves toward the bars.

Cole leans casually, clearly wanting to get a closer look at Atticus. He doesn't wait for Atticus to respond.

"You do look like your sister. But not as much as I would have thought," Cole adds.

Atticus swiftly reaches through the bars and grabs Cole's shirt, slamming him up against the bars.

"How did it happen, Cole?"

"The fuck do you mean?" Cole asks, irritated.

"You brainwashed her. Admit it," Atticus screams.

"Shhh. Keep your voice down calf. I did not. Are you a lunatic?"

"You forced her to talk with you one day at The Circle – you lured her over. Lidia was there. I know, so don't try to deny it."

"Fine, yeah, we met. I didn't tie her hands down and hold her hostage or anything. It was her choice."

"Did you or did you not plan to lure her to Tagondo?" Atticus asks.

"I didn't!"

"Why should I believe you?" Atticus asks.

"I don't care if you believe me. I cared for her, and I still do. We were friends damnit!"

Atticus loosens his grip on Cole's shirt and eventually lets go.

*"He speaks truth,"* the Whisperer says.

"Thank you," Cole says in reply as he fidgets with his shirt to straighten it once again.

"You hear the whispers?" Atticus questions, though he's not entirely sure why he's surprised. He thought the whispers were only meant for the Kalians, as if the ears of a newcomer couldn't hear them.

"Yeah, probably better than you. What is your deal?" Cole asks.

Atticus takes a deep breath – sometimes when things don't go as planned it's a huge disappointment, other times it's an unexpected surprise and Atticus likes surprises.

"When I found out Vera had met with some Tagondians and Lidia said it was you, I knew she had to have been forced... lured. She'd never agree to speaking to the likes of a Tagondian – nor develop a relationship with one. Something still feels off though… why do you think Vera went to Tagondo?"

"Her name was drawn at random, just like everyone else? I didn't know that she hated Tagondians that much," Cole ponders.

"Well, it's true," Atticus states.

"Now that you mention it, it did come up a couple times," Cole beams.

"What was she like over there, on Tagondian soil?"

"She was stubborn."

"Sounds like her."

"But she was learning how to throw axes and use a bow. She organized an escape plan… we were to leave Tagondo and travel here to Kala together, but that didn't work out the way we planned it."

"She wanted to escape Tagondo?" Atticus asks while wrinkles of humour form on his face.

Cole nods his head in confirmation, "Just to get to the lab to do some tests."

"I wish she made it, I would've gotten to see her one last time."

"You miss her."

"I do."

"Me too."

"I'm glad I came to talk with you first… you know… before I planned to mark you with a sword."

"No kidding," Cole chuckles.

"So, I hear they think you stole the ceremonial weapons," Atticus notes.

"Yeah. My guess is that was you?" Cole asks.

"Yes… But I'm going to put them back."

"Since you successfully, and anonymously, broke into the weaponry, do you think you can break me out of here?" Cole asks with a smirk.

"Maybe, why?"

"I'm in here for the wrong reasons, and I'd really like to bring Vera back to Kala so we can finish what we started."

"She trusted you," Atticus firms. "I think I can figure out a way to help you," he finally decides.

"What is the meaning of this?" a Defender shouts as he suddenly barges into the jail through the front door – they've been caught. Atticus hopes that no one overheard the beginnings of their potential alliance.

"I-I…" Atticus stumbles over his words.

"He came to ask me where I put the swords," Cole states to the Defender.

Atticus looks at Cole whose eyebrows are slightly raised as the glimmer of a smile levels across his lips.

# 63

# VERA OF INSIGNIFICANT CANNELLE TAGONDO

Vera slips out the front door at four in the morning, when she assumes Opi is asleep. Finn waits on the far side of the Rowan tree – she can see a slight curve of his shoulder in the dark protruding from the silhouette of the tree trunk, but only because she's looking for it. She stands by his side without a word – he begins walking east to lead the way to the hut.

"By the way, I got this for you," Finn holds out Vera's satchel, she must've dropped it during her tribulation.

"Oh, I wasn't sure if I was going to see my satchel again. Thank you." The two walk in silence until they reach the Tagondian border.

"It's not far past the Tag border," Finn whispers. She nods. They walk another half hour or so past the border until they come upon a thick grouping of tall bushes.

"This is it," he says. Vera gazes at him with a quizzical look. "It's hidden. Camouflaged," he explains.

Finn walks into the bushes and Vera follows. There sits a black hut beyond the wall of thick greenery. He pulls a light out of his pack then presses his fingers upon the doorknob giving it a twist, Vera's heart thuds slightly with excitement and fear. If she gets caught at least she's with a Defender – they could make up a story.

Just then a series of footsteps sound nearby and mumbles of a conversation fill the space between the trees. Finn instantly presses the door closed and releases his hold on the knob.

"Quick, behind the hut," Finn warns.

Vera runs behind the hut and freezes in place with Finn coming a close second after her. Both stand with their backs pressed slick up against the hut with their chests huffing.

"Yeah, I did it," a voice says.

"That's Rimmy," Finn whispers. "The most brutal Defender of us all."

"Did Master Regan ask you to?" another voice speaks.

Finn continues with the commentary, "That's Creek… he's a close second."

"Are they both a part of Master Regan's elite Defenders?" Vera asks.

"Yes."

The door to the hut opens and the men walk inside.

"I'm the Lead, I don't need permission."

"So how'd you do it, how'd you kill Burke?" Vera's eyes shoot to Finn's in terror. He raises his finger to his lips, a warning for her to keep quiet.

"With this, the black poison. Too much of this stuff and it shuts the organs down in the body… for humans at least."

"What about the scientist?"

"Yeah, I tried to take care of her too, but some pieces of shit got in the way. They're gone now though."

Finn must see her posture tense, and her hands find fists because he whispers, "It's okay."

A third voice sounds from much further away.

Whoever it is, they must be calling for Creek and Rimmy because Creek hears it too, "Shit, we gotta go." A moment later the door closes and the scuffing of the Defenders' boots in the grass soon fades away.

Once it's quiet, Finn speaks, "Let's go."

The two round the hut and enter the building – it smells of a thick piney scent. Finn pulls out his light once again, which highlights potted plants that fill the hut.

"Stein," Vera says, "And its been here all along."

"We better hurry."

"I'm taking some."

"Here," Finn offers Vera a pair of tiny hand crafted scissors to cut a stem off.

She quickly pulls the leaf from Treena's water out of her pocket and holds the stem of the black poison plant up in her hand to compare the leaves, "Shine your light over here."

As Finn aims a spotlight upon the leaves, it is evident that they are the same – both with the dark green hue that almost looks black and points all along the edges of the leaves.

"What's that?" he asks referring to the single leaf in her hand.

"Finn, I think Regan and Treena are drinking the black poison. But it doesn't make sense… if Rimmy used it to commit murder…" Vera shoves the stem and the single leaf into her satchel.

"I don't know. We better get going though." Vera nods, and the two leave the hut closing the door behind them.

"It just doesn't make sense, why hoard this much of it? Why keep it hidden?" Vera asks as they leave the bushed enclosure.

Just then several thuds radiate into the ground.

"Run Vera!" Finn calls as he tugs on her arm.

"What is it?"

The silhouette of an enormous creature appears in front of them and a growl so loud that it seems to shake the soil she stands upon leaves its mouth. Vera freezes, she can't move. If she moves it will chase her, catch her, and tear her apart. As her mind races within the millisecond before acting, she decides if they could climb a tree fast enough, they might survive. Finn begins running.

She doesn't know what else to do, other than to follow him. She breaks out into a sprint – following closely behind Finn. The mammoth immediately pursues them, close on their heels – if only she could press the ivani onto her wrist for some sort of adrenaline rush, but she can't, there's no time. She pushes her legs as fast as they will go, but the mammoth creeps up on her now. It's so close she wonders if she can feel its breath on her neck, or if she's imagining it. Finn moves much faster than her, he now runs several paces ahead of her. His zigzags are difficult to follow, impossible to predict.

"I'm going to lead him south – you go north," Finn huffs, and the two seperate.

After running full speed for several minutes, she slows her pace and eventually pauses to scan her surroundings. All she can see is endless forest, a forest that she is unfamiliar with. The sun begins to rise, offering her some form of hope. She reminds herself that she has an internal compass of sorts – a force that tells her which way is north, she can lean into that pull and let it guide her.

Speaking of guidance, Vera pulls the tiny velvet sack that Murdina gave her out of her satchel. She holds the pouch up and pours the rocks out into the palm of her hand; their edges soft and round and their surfaces as smooth as her own skin, just like the day Murdina gave them to her. There's a delicacy about them, which seems odd for rocks, rocks aren't delicate items, and they shouldn't need to be stored in a velvet bag – they are insignificant objects that move up from the Earth's crust, travelling amongst layers of dirt. *What makes these rocks different?* She pulls out a piece of paper from the velvet bag, hoping that it will give her information on the stones. It reads:

miss ,
your KindnEss aNd patience will undOubtedly serve you.
it's your stubbornness thAt you must overcome. don't
fear the setbacKs… sometimes they are your friend.
keep seeing north, except when you must look elsewhere first.
Always ,

> HN

The first thing Vera notes about this message is the fact that Hendrix wrote it with such poor form – the reason is entirely beyond her. He must have written this note in a hurry, though his writing is usually unkempt. The second thing she notices is the fact that the letter is entirely unimportant. There is no valuable information, no genius line that explains anything – not the antitoxin, not the plants, not even the stones themselves – all things that she needs explanations for right now.

But she misses her father, and reading his words only remind her of that. A single tear falls from her eye and meets with the yellowed paper. A growl sounds in the distance – the sound startles Vera and the stones fall to the ground. She can only hope that Finn got away safely…

As she bends down to collect the stones her hands begin to tremble. The stones sit, spread across her hand, a white collection of fractions. Tiny, singular pieces that appear to be their own entities and yet, in some way, she feels as though they are a single unit.

She begins walking with part of her concentration on the forest's depth in front of her and the other on the stones. She also has a fragment of her conscious on the mammoth sounds that come from somewhere behind her. That unknown force instinctively inside her tells her where north is, she can't explain it, but as a result she can easily decipher the other cardinal directions; she heads northwest. She puts the stones and the letter back in the velvet bag and places it in her pocket.

*"Kala,"* the wind whispers.

"Yes," she says out loud in response, appreciating the reminder. She does need to get to Kala - to fulfil step number three - but also to tell Cole who murdered his father.

# 64

# COLE OF INSIGNIFICANT WELLS
# KALA

There's a way out of this for Cole; that much he knows, he just can't see what it is yet. Besides, the Whisperer did tell him to have faith. Hopefully something will work out with Atticus, either way, he isn't the first man in the history of humankind to be wrongfully imprisoned and escape, he'll figure out a way with or without Atticus' help.

Despite being imprisoned, Cole has been fine for four days. The Lead Defender, Huron, brings him food and water routinely and he drinks the water without hesitation. There's a reason they are keeping him in jail alive and have yet to exile or force tribulation upon him for stealing. Stealing is an offence that Cole has not yet been fully convicted of – they'll need to locate the ceremonial swords as evidence first. Still, he knows that right now, in every Kalian's eyes, he's an Offender. *Great start to being a Kal*, Cole thinks, though he feels confident that he'll be able to change their outlook on him, and if he can't it won't bother him all that much.

The thing he struggles with most while being in jail is the lack of stimulation – not being able to see outside of the jail walls, with the exception of a tiny window which sits abnormally high. His days in Tagondo were spent amongst nature; being one with the forest, at least he can overhear the odd conversation of passersby. He also enjoyed the thrashing of a thunderstorm the night before – a pleasant surprise for all in the colonies. But none of it is as satisfying as seeing it.

So, he spends his time doodling on the walls of the cell. He dips his finger in a glass of water and draws stick figures because that's about as far as his artistic ability goes. He draws until his index finger becomes slightly raw from friction against the wooden walls, upon which he switches fingers. It doesn't take long until his drawings dry, absorbing into the porous fibres of the wooden wall. The moment it all finally fades and he has nothing more to look at, he begins drawing again. Eventually, when he gets bored of sitting in the same spot, he'll move to a different location within the cell to create his works of art.

Huron will eventually come in with food and Cole will then stand to stretch his legs out. He always forces physical exertion before eating: push-ups, sit-ups and jumping jacks. Then he'll sit and enjoy his meal with his water. Cole is aware that each time he drinks a glass of water, there's a chance it could be tainted with the black poison. Still, it doesn't stop him, he looks for a black or yellow tint and down the hatch it goes. After he eats he moves back to the corner to continue on with his doodles.

"Did Master Oberon address the antitoxin whispers?" Cole overhears a voice outside the jail window speaking to another.

"Not yet, when it came about yesterday he was away on his day of rest."

"Every week on the same day. We should take a day of rest too when he leaves from now on."

"We couldn't possibly – he'd find out," the man responds, seemingly concerned.

Cole glances up to the window and from his angle he can see the trim on the window sticking out. The voices fade into the distance, but his focus remains on the trim now. He contemplates that it looks slightly out of place. The crooked, outward angle of it makes it appear as though it has been taken off at one time. He stands up, but the window is still an arm's length above his head. He should forget it, it's likely just a piece of trim not put on straight upon its build. Still, he stands and stares at the window – that window could be his only chance for escape.

Through his moments of ogling over the window and contemplation whether or not his frame could fit through it, he notes that there are marks of some sort by the edge of the trim – it looks like scratches. Maybe someone else has already attempted an escape. Curious, he decides after all that he wants a closer look.

Standing on the tip of his toes allows him to just barely touch the bottom piece of wooden trim. He stretches up, grips the trim with his hands and tugs at it, but the nail doesn't quite release itself from the indentation it makes in the wall. His plate will help – it's a thin piece of wood made from maple; it should be firm enough to provide some tension. Cole slips the plate up in the crack between the wall and trim and uses it as leverage to pry the trim off. The wood cracks slightly before it rips the piece of trim away from the wall. Now the scratches are fully exposed, which upon further survey he thinks the scratches to be writing. Cole leans the trim against the wall so that it's standing upright and parallel to the wall. He places his foot on the edge, and pulls himself up while gripping the ledge of the window. Now he can see directly out the window, he can see the lab and the greenhouses. He looks back to the edge of the window and can clearly see the writing – artfully scribed into the wood:

He who seeks honour. – Creaosis

*"Honour,"* the wind wisps.

"Honour?" Cole thinks out loud. "Who writes about honour on a jail wall?" Cole finds the irony amusing, "I guess Creaosis does," he answers his own question with a rumble of laughter. *But who is Creaosis?*

Then his thoughts shift back to how he plans to get out of the jail and what he is going to do when he gets out. The window is likely too small for him to fit through and when it appears that there is no other way out, he decides that breaking out isn't the best idea. If he could just speak with Master Oberon, but how and for what reason could he offer? Huron would not likely agree to take Cole to The Master's chamber for any reason.

Before he gets caught for destruction of the jail cell, Cole lines the trim back in place and uses his plate to hit the nails back where they belong. He begins to hum then, because that's another thing Cole enjoys doing in his free time, and these days he has a lot of free time.

"What's all the noise?" Huron asks as he enters the jail.

"Huron, just the man I wanted to see."

"You're not a quiet prisoner," Huron says disappointedly.

"Unfortunately for you, I don't generally do quiet."

"You're free to go," Huron says as he slips the key into the lock.

"Huh?" Cole responds, baffled.

"Torant of Insignificant Wells, the Weapon's Keeper, came forward with a claim. He says that he lost his keys for the weaponry and had to break in to clean the swords from the last ceremony."

"No kidding," Cole says agreeably. "Well, Torant being the Weapon's Keeper is news to me."

"The man does a fine job. He keeps those weapons clean and sharpened for the ceremonies."

"I'll bet he does," beams Cole as he reflects on the attentive detail that Torant puts into his voodoo dolls.

"Master Oberon requests your presence," Huron states.

"You got it."

"He's in The Master's chamber. Follow me," Huron explains as he turns to exit the building.

Cole, entirely surprised by the turn of events, follows Huron to the chamber and they quickly make their way inside. Cole immediately bows to Master Oberon and his three Barons: Quim, Hogard and Martil. Martil is the only female Baron to ever grace the colonies with her presence. It's Cole's understanding that she's a fierce lady, she has deep, red hair that reminds him of the colour of blood, the way blood darkens as it dries. She also lets her S's linger a little too long when she speaks, reminding him of a snake.

"You have come. With the earth," Master Oberon says to Cole.

"May we be cleansed. I had a choice?" Cole asks.

Hogard cuts in upon a nod from Master Oberon: "No, this is a mandatory meeting."

"We would like to discuss our indiscretion," says Martil.

"Ah, you mean putting me in jail for no reason," Cole replies.

"Without good reason," Martil corrects, lacking any emotion.

Quim gestures with his hands, using them as he speaks: "This has been a first on our part and we do apologize."

"Apology accepted," says Cole, though he doubts its legitimacy.

"Now, you did hold your homemade weapons illegally in Kala, however, we are willing to forget this indiscretion of yours. We would like to make amends for our own, if you will, and in doing so we would like to open the floor for suggestions on how we may do that," Martil announces.

Cole thinks for a moment – it sounds as though The Master owes him a debt. His heart races, only slightly, at the realization that he can ask for anything.

"Vera North," Cole spits the words out in such a hurried fashion that he barely articulates them clearly.

"Pardon?" Quim asks.

"Vera North," Cole repeats.

"Vera of Insignificant Cannelle… what of her?" Hogard asks.

"She shouldn't be in Tagondo."

"No," Master Oberon says, "I've warned you once already about mingling with Tagondian affairs."

"It is not within our power to manipulate the Tagondo colony. All things are untouchable beyond our side of The Circle," Hogard explains.

Cole is entranced with how the four of them speak rhythmically together, almost in sync. Their sentences carry on from each other as though he is speaking to only one person. Though, he assumes, people working in such close quarters for eighteen years together would likely do this.

"But she's one of the Favoured," Cole pleads.

"Not now that she is a Pursuer," Hogard reminds him.

"Grant me permission to go to the Tagondo colony," Cole asks for if he can just get over there he could find Vera and free her himself.

"No," Master Oberon says.

"The laws are clear, Law #29: None shall leave their respective colony unless exiled by The Masters or upon becoming one with the earth," Martil states.

Cole exhales, "So, I can ask for anything that resides on this side of The Circle?"

"Yes, within reason," Master Oberon answers.

"Who is Creaosis?" Cole asks. The four look at each other, speechless and wide-eyed. Shock slowly fades from their faces and morphs into anger.

"Why have you asked us this?" Hogard inquires.

"How have you come to know such a name?" Martil interrupts.

"That name is not to be spoken," Master Oberon's voice booms to end the discussion.

"I was just curious," Cole shrugs. Each spoke as if they are somehow insulted or betrayed, Cole is unsure which is true.

Their eyes still fixate on Cole with an anger that he can't seem to understand. They are the rulers of their colony – he supposes with that in mind comes a certain level of intensity.

"If we didn't owe you a service for our shortcomings, I would have a mind to take your life," Martil booms.

"No, no, no… no need to do that," Cole chimes with his hands up in submission as he knows it can be done with the flick of her wrist if she so desires. And so, with that in mind, he opts to keep the whispering winds and the message on the jail wall to himself.

"What is your amendment suggestion?" Hogard asks, as if desiring to put the meeting to an end.

Cole can't help but think about Vera in Tagondo and how he can ask for nothing to help her while she's on the other side of the lake. He considers her desires then, reflecting back to her talks of cleansing the water, the plants' properties, the antitoxin, the lab – everything. He decides the best thing he can ask for is a sought-after position in the colony where he can continue implementing Vera's plan and learn as much as he can in order to find the cure... or the antitoxin.

"I would like to request a position in the lab," he finally says. Gasps and stares of disbelief fill the room.

"That is not possible," Master Oberon rules. *Damnit.* Though he won't stop there – he'll try the next best thing.

"Fine then. I want to work with the plants in the greenhouses," Cole states.

"That is a sizeable request," Hogard says, his response seeming more agreeable than the previous responses he's received.

"No one has been appointed such a position before," Quim replies.

"Being born into our higher-ranking positions has always been how we do things," Martil notes.

Quim adds, "Higher ranking positions mean less share requirements."

"He is a Pursuer," Hogard argues.

"He is here now, no longer a Pursuer," Quim reasons.

"This would make House of Insignificant Wells turn to Favoured," Hogard states.

All the while Master Oberon sits quietly as the three appear to debate amongst themselves. He listens patiently, clasping his hands up into a fist and resting his chin on them.

"We do need more botanists," Quim notes, "After Vera left and Hendrix's... passing, Ida and Atticus of Favoured North have had to focus most of their efforts in the lab."

"That doesn't mean we promote Insignificants to Favoured on a whim," Martil says.

Cole decides to add to the debate: "Yes, I am a pursuer, but I can assure you that I am the best damned pursuer the Tags have ever seen. It's not just because I am good at pursuing, I work best amongst nature and I work hard to get good at whatever I'm up against. Or in this case, what I'm working with. Give me this opportunity. Besides, if you guys go over and above to make amends it only shows the colony how fair you are to its members." Silence follows Cole's speech for a few long moments.

"He's right," Quim finally says.

"Cole Wells," Master Oberon states, "consider yourself and your home one of the Favoured."

# 65

# ATTICUS OF FAVOURED NORTH
# KALA

Atticus leaves class for the morning and sits on the grass outside of the school eating his lunch and analyzing his recent encounter with Cole. Regardless of how he first felt about Cole, after meeting him Atticus decides that he likes him – the feeling was almost instant. Atticus has always been instinctual in deciding how he feels about a person, and often quick to trust – Vera always thought that was his downfall. For years he believed her, agreed with her; however, now he thinks maybe she's wrong about all that. One day he will tell her why, for if she is wrong about this, she could be wrong about so many other things.

Atticus has always, always been agreeable with Vera. She's smarter, braver and more capable – she's everything he isn't. It wasn't until she left that he began growing slowly into the young man he wants to be. Now he feels smarter than ever, braver and more capable. And yet, he still finds himself seeking, unknowingly searching for someone to look up to. He is, after all, only eighteen and still has a lifetime of learning ahead of him. Perhaps, he decides, that's why he likes Cole so much. Though he doesn't want to admit that he needs someone to help guide him. Atticus reminds himself that he is a Favoured and so his unlimited learning is at his fingertips. He can go back to school for more botanist or science training if he wants to in the future.

*"Find the antitoxin,"* he hears a soft whisper.

"Hmm?" he says in response, looking around him.

*"The antitoxin,"* it says again.

"What is the antitoxin?" he asks to no one in particular it seems.

The wind begins to blow and the Whisperer speaks louder, *"Go."*

“How do I get it?” Atticus waits for a response, but one does not come. He wonders where such a thing - an antitoxin - would be kept. Then he remembers the Defender he overheard mentioning an antitoxin and that it’s in pill form. *Maybe it’s in the lab.*

Atticus despises being in the lab and frankly he misses the greenhouses. Between work at the lab, school, foraging and home maintenance on Favoured North, he hasn’t had much opportunity to spend time in the greenhouses with Lidia – and the last thing he wants to do is spend more time at the lab, and yet, Atticus can’t ignore the whispers. The antitoxin could very well be in the lab. He’ll check there first.

He gathers his things and walks through the colony centre in the direction of the lab. He isn’t exactly clear as to what he’s supposed to do or look for and so when he gets there he simply wanders around. He looks in cupboards, inside binders and underneath tabletops in case something is fastened to the underside in secret. His search comes up empty. Alternatively, he could search the paperwork, but he has already read over all of Vera and Hendrix’s notes from the last eighteen years – he’s a fast reader, even when struggling to read Hendrix’s mammoth scratches. Alas, he is sure that there is no note on the antitoxin in all of his readings over the past few months.

Although he falls short on finding the antitoxin, he praises himself on the fact that the water is the closest it has ever been to pure. After three months of Atticus sampling different minerals within test tubes he has lowered the toxin ratios by 0.3, which is huge in the grand scheme. Still, it isn’t cured and it isn’t the antitoxin. He reflects then on how Ida hasn’t been much help – she struggles to remember how to use the instruments and tools. Mostly she’ll just answer his questions about minerals and keep the lab tidy when she’s there; though, organizing isn’t her strong suit either. She wants desperately to stick to what she knows, she’s the best botanist to date. Lidia, her mentee, has become a close second – or so Atticus thinks. She will become the best – so long as she stays away from the lake.

Atticus glances at the spring water, it’s lowering in quantity and although Master Oberon tried to tell Atticus it’s because the pipes need work, he figures otherwise. He’s come to understand the way an underground spring houses its water source and it isn’t an unlimited source by any means. He knows the Almek are going to run out of safe drinking water one day and from his calculations it isn’t too far away.

As a result he desperately needs to find the cure or possibly just the antitoxin - whatever that is - at this point either will do. He wonders more about taking things out of the water as opposed to putting things into it. It always seems to be the manmade solution to add as a means to change something – rarely does man subtract.

Atticus begins drawing: he isn’t very good, but he isn’t horrible either. He draws up plans for a suction pipe that attaches to a giant vacuum and divider of sorts that will filter out the toxins and separate the water from the debris. One pipe carrying the toxins will lead to a large vat of boiling water – using the system of a boiler it will boil the toxins into steam. Once they are converted into steam, they will no longer be considered a toxin – they morph into oxygen. He draws this pipe leading to the greenhouse, which will help the plants grow. Meanwhile, the other pipe, which moves the garbage and debris out, will lead to a large cremation bin. Once the ashes mix with a particular combination of plants and dirt, within the year they will eventually turn into compost. The smoke from the cremation bin is his only problem. *How can I filter the smoke or prevent it from harming the atmosphere?* He finishes his diagram, adding a large question mark beside the smoke pipe.

*"Keep looking,"* the whispers call as they wisp in through the cracks of the lab windows.

"I know," he replies, "I know there's a solution."

"What's that darling?" Ida inquires as she enters the lab.

"Oh, nothing just talking to myself."

"What are you drawing there?"

"Just a silly diagram… an idea I have for pulling toxins out of the water."

"Let me see," she says.

He hesitates, as he isn't sure if it's an outrageous idea – one that's far-fetched and illogical. Though in his head it makes absolute sense – mostly. He moves his sketchbook over so she can see it more clearly.

Ida scans the page meticulously, "You've actually got a pretty good idea here," she says, surprise in her tone.

"Thanks. I'm just not sure what to do with the smoke."

"That's a tough one. It contaminates everything: water, soil, air."

"I know."

"Keep looking," she simply says. He glances at her, *Is she the voice in the breeze?* She acts so oblivious to his gaze though, no sign of a wink in her eye.

"I will," he responds as he stares at her for an instant longer, his right eyebrow rising in suspicion.

"I'm going to be out foraging this afternoon. We are cutting it close for shares this week," Ida tells Atticus.

"Sorry, I know. I've been busy with… well just falling behind I guess," he responds.

He doesn't want to mention his run-in with Cole to her or the fact that he stole ceremonial swords in which to kill Cole with – which, now, all seems far too juvenile a thing to do. He'll have to apologize to Ulyd for putting him through that and risking both of their places as Favoured. Ulyd will forgive him, he always does. Atticus isn't unfamiliar with making mistakes, but one thing he's sure not to do is make the same mistake twice.

He spends the rest of the afternoon theorizing on his vacuum idea, or as he begins calling it: The Distillation Project. When he grows tired of staring at the page, Atticus decides to go for a walk. The footpaths are busy this time of day in the late afternoon. Most colony members end their day of work or school at about this time and go on to do their last-minute errands before the sun sets and the mammoths come out.

"Hey," a voice calls from behind him. Atticus turns to see Cole standing there – a free man.

"Cole? What are you doing out of jail?"

"They let me out."

"Oh no, are they onto me?" A sudden worry fills Atticus' chest.

"No, no, you don't have to worry about that. Turns out Torant didn't actually want me in jail and covered for me."

"He did? What did he say?" Atticus is surprised to hear that Torant helped Cole, which means there is one less thing on his list to worry about now. An interesting turn of events this is though, especially from Torant of Insignificant Wells.

"I've been promoted to a Favoured too," Cole adds.

"No way. They do that now?" Atticus asks.

"Not really, they owed me some form of payment for their misjudgement, turns out they don't often misjudge – never, actually. I guess that's because none of you Kals stir shit up. Anyways, I'm working in the greenhouses now."

"Good for you. Geez, you're here only a few days and already you've been arrested, held prisoner in jail, almost murdered, released from jail and made a Favoured. You're something else Cole of Insignificant Wells," Atticus laughs.

"You mean Favoured Wells," Cole retorts with a smirk.

"Right."

"It's been… not quite a pleasure, but something maybe close," Cole chuckles.

"Well, I'm glad things are looking up for you – Vera would be happy to know that," Atticus notes. The smile from Cole's face fades, his brows lower.

"I wanted to get her out of Tagondo, but they can't touch anything beyond The Circle they said," Cole explains.

"I know," Atticus says.

"One day - soon - I will get her out of there though," Cole assures him.

"I believe you want to," Atticus says, fully aware that wanting to and being able to do something are two different things. Then again, Atticus realizes that he too wants things that seem unreachable.

^

Atticus is aware that he owes a debt to Torant for covering for Cole because in turn Torant's act of loyalty covered him. Perhaps it wasn't loyalty that motivated Torant; regardless, his actions helped them all.

It's just before nightfall when Atticus arrives at the broken-down hut – he needs to bring the swords directly to Torant without getting caught. However, Atticus quickly learns that removing the swords is going to be more of a challenge than getting them in for when he goes to open the dilapidated door the top half falls while the bottom hinges still hold onto the frame of the building. Eventually he moves the door and gets in. The hut is tiny, a 10x10 space at best. It appears as though it was once used for some form of storage, holding shares of some kind.

As he looks around more closely, he sees that there are all kinds of foraging tools inside. There are tiny axes, funny looking knives that are bent, small handheld rakes and several pairs of handmade scissors. *Why would someone need so many tools?* he wonders. The Kalians have always foraged just fine without tools, mostly with their hands – it's rare to take a tool foraging.

As Atticus continues looking around, it's obvious that the hooks and shelves that hang on the walls of the hut were put there many years ago as they are barely still hanging. Like rocks on the edge of a cliff, the slightest movement may send them tumbling down the landscape. He tries to keep his movements slow and steady for the wood of the hut has mostly rotted from time and abuse from the elements.

The history of this place intrigues Atticus though: *Who last used this hut? Why did they stop using it?* Aside from its broken appearance, there are oddly no cobwebs or signs of being abandoned on the interior, as one would expect. He moves his feet and below him an unsteady square cuts into the floor, teeter-tottering slightly. *Perhaps it was an old ice fishing hut at one time.* On the ceiling there's a tiny door, it appears to be an attic entrance as a small, circular handle sits on the surface of the four-sided piece of wood.

He places his two fingers around the handle and pulls. The attic entrance swings down, dust and debris sprinkle overtop him and onto the floor beneath his feet. It's a small opening, smaller than a window – he won't be able to go up and will be less likely to even fit through the door, but he can't deny the intrigue of what might rest up there. So, he finds an old wooden crate and props himself atop it, sticking his head up through the door. It is indeed dusty and hot up here and a suffocating sensation engulfs him – it's the kind of space where one must hold their breath and so he does for worry of inhaling the filthy particles.

There is straw and string and some random pieces of torn cloth. It's obvious that some kind of animal - likely birds - made a nest up here at some point or another, there is no telling how long ago that has been as no carcasses are in sight. He reflects that this is the condition in which he expected the entire hut to be in. Something catches his attention then: a glimpse of a word from underneath a piece of torn cloth. He moves the nest materials so that he can clearly investigate what caught his sights. It's an inscription that reads:

He who pursues knowledge. – Creaosis

Atticus wonders who Creaosis is, for all he knows Creaosis is someone who resided in this very hut before the Water Crisis. He doesn't know anyone in Kala that goes by such a name. Maybe he'll ask Ida, though after further thought, he decides that she likely won't have an inclination.

*"Knowledge,"* the whispers sough and with that Atticus climbs out of the attic and carefully places the door back where it was prior to his entrance.

He collects the two swords and wraps them in a blanket so none will be the wiser as to what he has in his possession. He then exits the hut, carefully replacing the decrepit front door back where it was as well pausing to consider the best path to Torant's – if he cuts through the forest instead of the footpaths he'll be able to come out the other side closer to Torant's house as opposed to going all the way through the colony and risking his prestigious role as a Favoured. He can't have anyone finding out about his indiscretion, of which he is dreadfully embarrassed about now.

Then, as if the whispers mean to only add to his unsettling feelings, it speaks: *"The Cobra."*

"Who is The Cobra? What is it?" he asks in return. He really doesn't know what to think of it and ponders why the whispers have warned him about this. But he doesn't get a response so he continues on, marching along the outskirts of the forest.

"Atticus of Favoured North – where are you off to?" a deep voice that somehow sounds like angry clouds crashing off in the distance calls, it's Huron. He's a fool to think that he could go unnoticed – he should have known better, he should have known that someone is always watching. Huron startles Atticus, making him jump, even though his eyes saw him before he spoke.

"Oh, with the earth Defender Huron. Just running errands before going in for the night."

It doesn't matter Atticus' position, the fact is that he is illegally in possession of the ceremonial weapons could be the end for him. Huron has a way about him and it's certainly an uncomfortable way. Something about his eyes and the way he so tentatively focuses on him, or perhaps it's the way his jaw clenches and cracks as though he's chewing on bone. Either way, Huron's brown beams stare at him -

unwavering, unblinking - as if looking right through him. Atticus is sure that Huron has scared the few freshly growing hairs off of his maturing chin.

"May we be cleansed," Huron nods once. "What's that you got there?" he asks.

Atticus reflects that even though Huron is the Lead of the Defenders and therefore the keeper of peace, he causes the most harm out of anyone. Ironically, he seems to be responsible for most acts of violence, mischief and so on. Atticus' heart races and underneath the blanket his hands begin to sweat profusely.

"Just something I am taking care of for a friend," Atticus responds.

"Then you won't mind if I take a look?" Huron asks.

Though Atticus is nearing 6' tall, it feels as though Huron towers over him with muscles that bulge out from the fabric of his shirt. *He's a house*, Atticus thinks. There's no possible or reasonable explanation to ever say no to Huron.

"Sure," Atticus says nervously.

His heart thumps in his chest and drips of sweat suddenly begin pouring down the sides of his face. There is no doubt that he looks entirely suspicious, he is sure of that. Huron eyes him up and down. *This is it – I'm an Offender. I'm going to face tribulation – the second Favoured to ever face tribulation.* He's ashamed. *What will Mother think?* His family has worked hard to build a good, respectable name for themselves and in a rash decision he's ruined it all like the reckless, thoughtless teenager he is.

Huron reaches for the swords as Atticus still carries their weight. Huron begins lifting the blanket off and the blades of two filthy swords are exposed. Dark red blood, dried and crisped to the edges of both swords becomes apparent – they look almost as if they have rusted, which could never be as they are handcrafted with the finest of steel made by Curshman of Favoured Steel himself.

The golden handles carved with elaborate designs reveal themselves, Atticus has never taken the opportunity to admire their decorum until now, and he never will again. His hands begin to shake and the swords clatter against one another. *Death*, he thinks. *Death will surely be the form of tribulation that I will face.*

# 66

# VERA OF INSIGNIFICANT CANNELLE
# TAGONDO

After walking for some time, Vera notes the hungry ache that she felt earlier, now fading away – it's funny how some aches will stop, if you ignore them long enough. It's early morning and the beginning of summer, the re-introduction to true warmth. Vera realizes then that June means she has survived three whole months in Tagondo. A lot has happened in that time, she glances down at the scar on the side of her arm. It was not all that long ago that she would cringe simply at the sight of that scar. *There's no going backward, only forward*, she thinks.

She travels northwest for a while, until the voices of fellow Almek murmur beyond the forest, which means she's close to the colony – though she can't afford to be spotted, not if she's going to get to Kala. She must go around Tagondo so that she can get to The Circle and pass through it.

She slumps down in front of a tree for a break and presses her back against the trunk of the birch tree – it is tall with rounded pieces of its white bark sticking out in random tags. She used to pull at the pieces of bark on birch trees that jutted out when she was a child – back in the Old World – she wouldn't dare to anymore. Her eyes examine the tree's outer layer: how a tree works is in essence science, though at a glimpse she can see how it appears almost magical to the average person. Though she knows that not to be true, still she respects the greatness that resides within a tree, reincarnating every change of the season and yet staying at its core the very same. Her mind flips like a switch back to scientific analysis of nature and the sad fact that over the past few decades the trees have come to release more aerosol emissions – also known as VOCs. Humans are to blame: they created more air pollution and in turn higher emissions. Trees' VOCs then meld with manmade chemicals and create

SOAs. These elements all affect climate and precipitation which lead to the reality she, and all Almek, live in. Vera reflects upon how she learned about this state of the world in science class with Educator Ferris. Though this sort of research isn't the focus in the lab: the water is.

Her eyes catch a glimpse of what looks like a carving in the tree trunk and her thoughts instantly fade. She moves closer to inspect the writing:

She who seeks courage. - Creaosis

"Creaosis?" she says out loud. *Who is that?*

*"Courage,"* the wind soughs with whispers. *Courage?* she thinks, but the thought quickly passes. Instead, she finds herself more intrigued at the unusual name that's engraved before her eyes. The name is familiar. She knows that she's heard it once before and yet she can't recall where or from whom. She realizes that the name itself makes her hair stand on end and her arms tingle with electricity, the way a storm sends prickles down one's limbs before it shows its face. She has an unexplainably bad feeling. *Or is it a good feeling?*

"Well, well, well...who do we have here?" a man appears through the trees, sifting grass with each step. "Just the woman I was looking for. Mind you, you're not exactly where I expected you to be."

Vera jolts to her feet in an instant and takes a couple steps back, passing the birch tree with the inscription. She's confused at first until she gauges who her visitor is and in that moment she stumbles in her step. It's *him*: the man from the cave – Cain.

Her insides shake with fear for she is still hazy about what took place in the cave that day. But, she is certain that if this man wants her dead, he'll be successful.

"I guess we should pick up where we left off, no?" he says, still inching closer. She's at his mercy once again, this time out here alone in the forest.

"Please..." she manages, still letting her steps guide her backwards a few more paces as her mind fights to find focus.

"I believe I had your hair, tangled in my hands. Your neck at the tips of my nails," he says as he holds his hand up, his fingers spreading open to symbolize his clutching claw of a hand once wrapped around her.

"I don't want any trouble," she pleads, terror causing her voice to crack. She has always hated the way her voice sounds when it shakes – no one has made it sound so shaky, not like how this man does.

"Trouble," he repeats. "You said that last time. And yet, you keep causing trouble." Cain turns his face, showing proof of the trouble she's caused him – revealing raised and unnaturally pigmented scars from the thone leaf. "If I'm honest, and I may as well be, after all we've been through... I have always found a sweet side to trouble. And once again Cole isn't here to save you."

"I..." Vera stammers as he continues to walk toward her.

"You see, Master Regan promised me a hefty reward for killing you – he even ordered me to break into Insignificant Cannelle," he explains as he dangles a pair of keys in his hand. "Of course, he can't kill you himself. He needs it to look like he's had nothing to do with it."

She shudders, "Please..."

"Come on, you must've known that he can't let you display such promiscuity – what would the rest of The Almek think?" he questions rhetorically.

Vera shakes her dizzying head.

Cain continues: "But me, well, Master Regan said he will pretend as though the case of Vera of Insignificant Cannelle's murder is inconclusive. Hell, he may even decide to state that it's a suicide for being separated from your Offender-lover," he pauses to chuckle, "And then, in secret, he will reward me for a job well done." Vera tries to process what Cain is saying, though her thoughts are mangled.

"I faced tribulation for that kiss," she says. "Regan and I are even."

"Even? With The Master?" Cain chuckles, "The tribulation was just a show. He wants you gone." His smile stretches wide, bearing his teeth and gums.

She continues to move slowly, her legs trembling as she edges backwards as far away from her attacker as she possibly can get, but with each step he moves forward, closing in on the space between them.

"If you kill me… what makes you think he will spare you tribulation… or death?" she finally asks in an attempt to sway Cain's loyalty.

"Master Regan has helped my family and promised me a high-ranking position – but either way, it's worth the gamble," Cain spits.

There is no use, he'll have his way with her and end her – he'll stop the rhythm in her heart by day's end. She begins to cower, slowing her step until she freezes. This man has a power over her, one she can't seem to break free of.

*"Survive,"* the whispers whistle.

Her ears perk and her hands form fists at the word. *Survive*, she thinks. *Oh yeah, survive*. She likes the word, it has a sort of invigorating appeal. It makes her suddenly feel hopeful. She pushes her hand into her satchel.

"What do you have there?" Cain asks suspiciously, "Better not be more of that plant," he warns.

A flock of birds suddenly fly from the trees, creating a welcomed commotion in their wake. While Cain is distracted for a brief instant, she runs her fingers along the fuzz-covered surface of the velvet bag. *The stones*. She inconspicuously reaches into the bag and takes a stone out. *Survive*. She has no clue what to do with the stone, but then she remembers how Murdina threw hers up into the air at Cole's re-birthing then rain followed, but not just any rain. Without another thought, Vera throws the stone up into the air.

Cain darts his eyes from the birds and toward her, "What are you up to?" his voice scratches and he reaches for her. But, as soon as the stone is above the treetops it bursts into particles. The stone's dust seems to reach the heights of the sky, she has no idea what to do next and so she waits, something is coming though, she can feel it. Clouds appear through the sun-filled sky and rain begins gushing in large deposits and the earth erupts in tiny, brief explosions upon each impact.

"What the fuck?" Cain exclaims. She is just as shocked as he. "You're gonna die today. I'll tell Cole you said goodbye," he smirks then smacks Vera across the face, she falls backwards onto the ground.

She quickly rises to her feet, but her attacker charges at her again. His fist collides with her face and she falls once more with her back slamming into a tree. A rasping sound escapes her throat – for a moment she can't breathe.

*"Survive,"* the whispers speak as she struggles for air. She crawls on her hands and knees and sees that the velvet bag has fallen from her pocket. Vera fumbles to collect the bag with her trembling hands while the rain begins to pour down, thick and harsh, creating a wall between her and Cain.

She wonders if the stones have an expiry, a time when the rain comes to an end. But she realizes even with an expiry, the stones *will* help her survive; she rises to her feet once again and glances into the bag of stones. White, smooth, dense and yet they turn into a dust-like substance upon impact. *But what do the stones come into contact with up there to cause them to burst and make rain?* she thinks, *Exposure at a high altitude of oxygen... aerosols?* It's the only thing that can possibly explain the rain: aerosols made from particles released by trees and altered in the atmosphere. *Are aerosols the missing link to weather control?* People in the Old World dropped gunpowder and ionizers to create rainstorms at one time. *Cloud seeding*, she thinks, referring to when researchers sprayed silver iodide into the clouds to increase precipitation. The trees weren't so volatile back then, their emissions of aerosols were not so concerning for the atmosphere – for the earth. That was then.

Vera grabs another stone and throws it up into the air above the trees – an attempt to thicken the wall of rainfall between her and Cain. A white dust forms like a cloudy umbrella over the treetops. It's ironic, the ionic stones encasing the treetops, absorbing the aerosols and forming a negative charge of ions to create SOAs… It's exactly what The Almek need to create more rain. She wonders then if it's too much like playing God – the thought irks her and yet it enthralls her. This outcome, she decides, is good for The Almek – they need more rain. A surge of courage streams through her, she stands taller for she holds the power of rain in the palm of her hand. But not only that, The Almek can drink rain water. A squeal erupts from her throat at this realization. The rain plummets down, all she has to do is get out of the ionic cloud.

"There is a way out of this," she shouts to Cain through the storm as he clearly attempts to fight against its force.

"The only way this ends, is with you dying," he yells, "I can't go back empty handed. Not again. But to be honest, killing you will be thrilling. You've made me suffer Vera… and I don't like suffering."

"I'm sorry about the burns. I'm sorry I lied," but she is anything but sorry. He's the one who should be sorry, sorry for threatening her and Cole.

"You will be sorry."

"We need to create change in this world," she shouts as water pours down over her face.

"This is all we have. Insignificants and Favoured. Oh, and poisonous waters that turn our bodies to mush. I'm only ensuring my future as Baron. Besides, you fucked me over. You had this coming," he shouts back.

There is no need to disagree, he's right, she did fuck him over and he has the burn scars on his face to prove it – his assault is visible and known. There was likely backlash from Master Regan when he showed up with a plant that burns instead of a plant that cleans the water, he likely added to Cain's scars.

"You could be right. But we have to try," she says. He stands silent for a moment below the easing raincloud, the rain slowly tapers off and he's not but a few feet from her.

"You want to change things here?" he asks, "All the more reason you need to die," and within an instant he swipes his fist at her, she ducks and sprints to the backside of a nearby tree.

"We have to work together," she continues, "We need to stop listening to Regan."

"Master Regan has led me for half of my life. You have been nothing but a pain in his ass since the day you arrived." Cain's face contorts into fury and hunger; it isn't the first time she's seen his face like that.

She readies herself with fists up and out front. As he approaches she jabs her knuckles into his right temple, thankful for her brief combat call training. He grabs her arms and throws her. Her body flies as if it were a sack and lands in the mud, only her arm lands in such a way that it bends where there is no joint. She bellows out a scream of pain as she attempts to pull herself up to a seated position. She holds her injured arm tightly to her side. "Even if you did get away and you come back to Tagondo – Master Regan will find a way to kill you," Cain calls as he approaches her.

Vera glances about in desperation; relief washes across her face at the realization of what sits in front of her. *Ivani.* Growing out of the ground in a round plentiful bush, staring right at her as if attentive and grown just for her – it's a promising escape.

"I guess this is it… I just thought that perhaps, you came in search of me for something else…" she says, a means to stall him as she slowly moves toward the ivani.

"You fucking slut," he bellows. *Not what I meant.*

She shimmies her body just a little closer, still on her bottom. Every move, no matter how subtle, causes a burning throb to shoot down her injured arm – her sore back now far out-shined by the pain in her arm. She bites her lip to keep herself quiet.

"That's what I can't stand about you goddamn Insignificants. You're pathetic. Little puppy dogs begging for some attention. Just like Jeanne," Cain continues.

"I'm not Jeanne," she states.

"Yeah well, it was her fault. She couldn't just have casual sex."

Vera grits her teeth, "There must be something about you that she couldn't live without," she says needing to get just a little closer to the plant.

He grins a hungry grin, "Seems to me you are of similar interests."

"Am I?" she asks as she now sits beside the ivani bush, "How does one know?" His eyes glance up toward the trees – he obviously thinks he can afford the distraction.

"How did you do it?" he asks quizzically. Then, almost as if they are two friends having a casual conversation, "How did you make the rain?"

"I'll tell you, I just need reassurance that you won't kill me." Just then she rips an ivani leaf off of the bush, her heart is sure to bound out of its ribcage and through her flesh.

"Huh, not this again. You want to make another deal," he states.

"Something like that," she says as she places the ivani upon her wrist.

A moment passes with Cain in thought. Her fingertips begin to buzz, her vision tunnels in, adrenaline begins coursing through her veins – she knows she can move faster now. Before she rises to her feet to flee, she takes a moment to glance at Cain's face. She notes a bruise forming on the side of his temple from her blow earlier. She guesses that her arms will soon be red with the markings of his grasp on her skin, like a trade: pain for pain – that is what they seem to do. At least he will go back to Master Regan empty handed again and this will cause them both great anger, but she will be long gone and out of their reach by that time. All she needs is to get to Kala, and if she gets her hands on the antitoxin, she'll be leaving Tagondo for good. It's a hopeful thought that she has then – that this is the last time she'll ever see Cain of Favoured Fenwick. She stands and breaks out into a sprint, allowing the adrenaline to sore through her veins.

# 67

# Lidia of Favoured Peony
# Kala

Weeks have passed since Lidia's attempt at meeting with the lake. Initially she was frustrated with Atticus for having found her, but it made her realize that she does have a right to be here. A right to work through her own personal struggles, even if it must be in secret. The private discussion she had that night with Aphria helped her to see that there are those who want to listen and support, they are merely fearful of tribulation. It also showed her that there are those who need it just as badly as she, and although the discussion helped her, it wasn't enough.

As Lidia waters and prunes the plants while deep in thought that morning she feels a new found appreciation in caring for the plants. the first watering of the day seems to awaken them as they stand a little taller, open their buds a little wider. *It's like magic*, she thinks. She has always felt a closeness to them, a connectedness that goes unexplained. Knowing what they need so passionately and being able to fulfill those needs without much conscious thought has been her calling, like a mother hen. She wonders if Lilith will have a connection with the plants like she does.

"Lidia, can I ask you what you are doing?" Master Oberon asks as he enters the greenhouse unannounced.

"Oh, my apologies Master Oberon," she says, startled. "I was in deep thought. With the earth, your grace."

"May we be cleansed. In deep thought regarding?"

"Just how to get these tomato plants to avoid the rot," she lies, she was thinking about Lilith. The suspicious look on his face suggests that he doesn't believe her lie – perhaps he wants her to know that.

"Very well," he says, "I need you to train Cole. He must become a true botanist and that is where your focus belongs," there's a warning within his tone.

"Yes, Master," she says with a bow and watches him leave as suddenly as he appeared.

Train Cole? It is strange enough that Cole is in Kala, never mind that he'll now be working in the greenhouses alongside her – and that she's the one responsible for his training. *How did Cole come into possession of a Favoured botanist position in the colony?* The thought doesn't sit right with her.

Lidia can't help but call upon in her memory the day that she and Vera met Cole and Lincoln at Lake Cloud. As far as she can tell, meeting Cole seemed to be the start of all of Vera's troubles. At the last ceremony, Cole's ceremony, it didn't appear as though things were looking up for her still – she is sure to have faced tribulation for that kiss. However, through these thoughts, Lidia knows that she'll eventually have to speak to Cole if she is to remain an abiding citizen of Kala. Furthermore, she wants to understand how her friend had been doing all those months in Tagondo.

Thoughts of Tagondo thrusts her mind to engage in the memory of Lilith once again and although she didn't know Lilith for all that long, she can't ignore the maternal bond that tugs at her insides. She knows she cannot tell The Master this. She knows she is to carry on as if it never even happened.

Still, in Lidia's fair mind, Master Oberon has a point. She should not let her focus on the plants dwindle for something that she cannot change. She owes it to The Almek, and to Mother Earth, to keep the plants flourishing.

She thinks back to her conversation with Atticus and how there has to be room somewhere to acknowledge her suffering. *What do other women who lose their babies and husbands in the ceremonies do?* Surely they struggle, as Lidia does. She can attest to how holding the memory of carrying an infant and losing it has scarred her. She knows that Aphria can too, and surely many others. Lidia decides she needs more beyond a one off conversation, but not just for herself, for the others too. She looks down then and notices an inscription carved into the wood that encases the tomato plants:

She who seeks compassion. -Creaosis

"Hmm… I haven't noticed that before," she notes to herself out loud.

*"Compassion,"* the wind whips in through the doorway and she hears the whispers.

*Compassion is important*, she agrees with the whispers. But it isn't exactly present among The Almek. *Who are The Masters to decide what the people can and cannot feel, think or speak of?* It's practically emotional abuse, unethical in every form. All the women out there – mothers who have had their children kidnapped from them are suffering in silence. Men too. Lidia decides then that she doesn't want to be quiet any longer. She will reach out to those affected by the ceremonies. Seeing as she has already connected with Aphria and understands her pain, that is where she'll start. It will mark the beginning of compassion amongst The Almek. The first secret communion created by the people, for the people.

# 68

## COLE OF INSIGNIFICANT WELLS
## KALA

It's an exciting day for Cole: he is to receive his Favoured crest. Although it isn't so much the repossession of the Favoured name that excites him as it is becoming a botanist – he hopes that he will gain more understanding of the plants' true properties in this job. As he walks through the colony centre with Torant, he notes how the Kalians veer as far as they can from them, creating a wide lane with moving bodies on either side for Torant and Cole to walk through.

Cole glances at Torant curiously, "Wow, they're terrified of you."

"And it pains me that you're not."

"Why though? Why are they so scared of you?"

"I don't care to speculate."

"You must have some idea."

"I have one."

"So? Let's hear it."

"It'd do you better if you didn't know," Torant says.

Cole shakes his head; Torant is the most tight-lipped bugger he's ever met. They approach The Master's chamber and greet Huron who stands beside the wide doorway.

"With the earth," Cole says.

"May we be cleansed," Huron speaks with a slight nod and opens the door for them to enter, eyeing Torant as they walk by.

The instant Cole's eyes see The Master he bows, "With the earth, your grace." Torant bows beside him, but says nothing.

"May we be cleansed," Oberon says in welcoming them.

"Today marks your Favoured ceremony, you must be thrilled to be among the top of our people," Quim smiles.

"I am – we are," Cole says. Torant subtly nods his head in agreement.

"Well then, should we get on with it?" Martil asks.

"Yes, indeed," Oberon rises from his seat and descends to the front of the platform.

Cole takes in the ceremonial scene around him: it's a quaint ceremony compared to others, only Master Oberon and the Barons are present among Torant and Cole. However, Cole notes the musical ones sitting off to the side, the light hum of drums begin and a quiet, intermittent shaking of a tambourine takes place. Candles fill the edges of the stairs. Huron slips in then through the door and walks to the other side of the room where he stands across from the musical ones.

"My Lead," Oberon acknowledges Huron with a nod, "Huron will be our witness." Cole nods. "Come forward," Oberon instructs his Barons.

Quim, Hogard and Martil make their way around the table and descend the stairs to stand beside Master Oberon. Cole notes the mild grimace on Martil's face.

Master Oberon continues, "It is with great pleasure that I welcome you, Cole and Torant of Insignificant Wells into the Favoured of Kala. We have much respect and expectations for our Favoured. You must make an oath to swear to uphold the laws of our Motherland and of Mother Earth herself.

"You must swear to act in alignment with our visions of Kala, do what is requested of you and set a good example for our Insignificants. If you make this promise, you are promising to me, the Barons and you are promising to Mother Earth. If you agree with this statement say 'aye',"

"Aye," Cole states.

Torant shuffles in his step before speaking: "Aye."

Oberon's focus shifts directly to Cole, "Furthermore, Cole, you have no botanist training. You will need to begin apprenticing immediately at the greenhouses. Lidia will get you up to speed and tutor you as well in some of the course curriculum for botanists. Her father is Educator Peony, so she has a wealth of knowledge. If you are prepared to partake in a steep learning curve, both mentally and physically, and commit to caring for our plants wholly say 'aye'."

"Aye," Cole states again.

Oberon nods in contentment, "Then it is my honour to bestow upon you, your Favoured crests," Master Oberon announces then attaches Cole's silver crest to his shirt. Cole and Master Oberon bow at one another simultaneously. Master Oberon then attaches Torant's crest and he and Torant repeat the gesture of bowing to one another in acceptance. "It is done."

"That's it?" Cole asks, surprsised.

"It is a simple ceremony, though it represents a great deal."

"Yes, I understand," Cole notes.

"You may get on with your day my Favoured," Oberon says with his arms spread wide and a smile brimming across his face.

"Thank you, your grace," Cole says as he bows once again before taking his leave. Torant mimics Cole's bow and they exit the chamber. For the first time, Cole walks across the Kala colony centre as a Favoured.

# 69

## ATTICUS OF FAVOURED NORTH
## KALA

The end of Atticus of Favoured North is coming. As Huron still stands before him, he closes his eyes and holds them tightly shut. He doesn't want to see Huron's face morph into anger, nor witness Huron's hands wrap around his thin body as if he is a mere strand of grass in which one can manipulate. Atticus reflects how Huron could quite easily tear him in half, though he thinks Huron to be far too proper and respectable to kill a man with his bare hands. Even in his most fearsome moments Huron isn't an animal, Atticus is pretty sure of this.

"The ceremony swords?" Huron questions. Atticus raises his shoulders and shrinks his neck down into them, unable to muster a reply. Huron continues: "That's right. I bumped into Torant earlier today – he did say you would be bringing him the swords."

"He did?" Atticus asks.

"Yes, he mentioned that he requested you to help carry them to Favoured Wells."

"Ohh, yes. He is getting weak in his old age," Atticus nods enthusiastically – arguably too enthusiastically. Of course Torant isn't all that old, maybe fifty, if Atticus has to guess.

"Old age? Right. Well, you best get those back to him for cleaning right away. They're filthy," Huron says as he turns and walks back down the footpath.

Atticus inhales slowly as his breathing stabilizes from the scare. *That was a close one – the closest one yet*, he reflects. He looks at the swords once more then and notes that they are indeed filthy, one more so than the other – covered in the dried blood of Murdina of Insignificant Cannelle. He needs to get these swords out of his possession – his legs immediately move into a light jog.

He approaches Torant's house, which is always an eerie place to walk by – it's as if the ravens caw a little louder and the trees move their branches like flailing arms here. Torant's a strange man with his slick black hair and long fingernails; he isn't what one would expect a Weapons Keeper to look like, though Atticus isn't usually one to put labels on things. Aside from Torant's peculiar nature and eerie house, he keeps to himself and as far as Atticus can tell he is an abiding citizen of The Almek. Atticus approaches the front door and knocks, Torant opens the door moments later.

"Come in," Torant greets Atticus, though it doesn't sound heartfelt, it sounds more like boredom. Atticus walks in and for the first time absorbs the inside of now Torant of Favoured Wells' home. Animal skulls are one thing, not overly strange, but voodoo dolls are an entirely different thing.

"With the earth" Atticus says to Torant.

"Sit," Torant replies sternly gesturing to the kitchen table. Atticus places the swords on the kitchen table; Cole walks in the room as Atticus takes his seat.

"Cole, I'm glad you're here," Atticus says, relieved. Following a glance at Cole's new crest he continues, "I see you guys are officially Favoured now."

"Yeah, I'm looking forward to doing my part."

"Well, if you ever need help, don't hesitate to ask."

"Thanks calf. Hey did you thank the weird man for saving your ass?" Cole asks.

"Uh, no. Thank you Torant. I had made an ill-mannered decision… it won't happen again. I do appreciate you putting yourself in an unruly position to help us," Atticus says sincerely.

"My involvement does come at a fee," Torant states. Atticus glances down at his hands, they're already worn and aged looking for an eighteen-year-old, the bulk of the effects happened in most recent months.

"What kind of fee?" Atticus inquires.

"It's a difficult thing, to know what *the man who sees all* needs. But there is something," Torant notes.

"Sees all?" Cole asks with a confused, unbelieving look to his face.

"The Shadow," Atticus says knowingly.

It explains why Lidia visited Torant – he must have given her information. Atticus wonders what form of payment she gave him. Torant smirks at Atticus' comment.

"I remember hearing stories of you when I was a child. But I thought they weren't true," Atticus continues.

"Parents will tell their children just about anything to get them to go to sleep at night – that's one thing that hasn't changed from the Old World to this one," Torant grins slightly as if conjuring a specific memory in his mind.

Cole sits dumbfounded, he clears his throat, "What are we talking about here?"

"A tale about a man who lives amongst the people. He knows all that goes on in the colonies. He neither fears the mammoths nor The Masters. You can't do anything without The Shadow knowing," Atticus replies.

"That's not creepy at all," Cole says sarcastically.

"It's both a compliment and a burden, I assure you," Torant notes.

"Is that supposed to explain the dolls? Cause I still don't get that," Cole asks.

"Yes… and no…" Torant says.

"Do you give any straightforward answers?" Cole asks.

"It's not in my nature," Torant simply states. Atticus and Cole remain sitting while Torant paces about the kitchen.

"His nature is to know, not to tell," Atticus explains. "So what is the fee?"

Torant sits down, "Master Oberon refuses to place me in a merge agreement, for years he has refused."

"What exactly do you want from us?" Atticus asks skeptically.

"We don't like men, man. I mean, I don't," Cole states.

Torant shakes his head, "There is one, whom I would do unthinkable things for."

"For or to?" Cole teases.

"Who?" Atticus asks.

"Your payment is in keeping my secret and helping me in return, in time," Torant urges.

"That is not a very clear request of payment," Cole argues.

"Shh," Atticus hushes him.

"Two of your lives I have saved, not just one," Torant notes.

"Spit it out *Tortent*, what do we do about this love interest of yours?" Cole asks, "Anyway, I don't see how much help I can be when I can't even stay on the same side of the lake as mine."

Torant pauses, then, "Ida of Favoured North."

"My mother?" Atticus asks, baffled. Torant nods. "You love my mother?" Torant nods again.

"Surely, you realize, there is nothing we can do about your affection for her," Atticus says in sympathy.

"Oh, but there is," Torant notes with a hopeful look in his eyes.

"What?"

"In time. For now you will keep my secret. Hold it as if it is your own and utter its existence to no one," Torant states.

"Why'd you tell him then? Isn't it obvious the guy has a big mouth?" Atticus asks gesturing to Cole.

"Hey! I can keep a secret, wise guy," Cole spits back.

"You must keep my secret. If you die, my secret dies with you," Torant says.

"Seems like a drastic thing to say, but okay." Cole agrees.

"Agreed," Atticus says.

There is no denying the human nature behind secrets, Atticus reflects. Part of him thinks that's some of what being a human means – we keep secrets and only divulge them to those we trust. Even then, we don't always share them. Atticus told Vera everything, he would've even told her about the swords and she would've told him he was being reckless and probably would have convinced him to not follow through with it. But if she were still in Kala then he wouldn't be in this mess.

Upon deciding that he has no reason not to trust Cole and Torant, and in an attempt to gain their trust, Atticus decides to share one of his own secrets: "I'm trying to create a machine that can suction the toxins and garbage out of the water."

"Yes," Torant replies knowingly.

"You're smart for a calf," Cole teases, but in a complimenting sort of way. "When are we building it?"

"I don't know… the plans are still rough."

"Keep at it, the sooner we can find the cure the better," says Cole. *Or the antitoxin*, Atticus thinks.

"I just need time to sit and focus is all," Atticus explains as he notes that Torant hasn't given his opinion on the matter.

There's a strange sense of relief for Atticus in knowing that the story of The Shadow is real though. Don't all kids want their childhood stories to come to life? He never dreamed that some of his came from true facts.

A short time later, Cole sees Atticus off at the doorstep. Following his leave from Favoured Wells, Atticus wanders to the lab to check on Ida. When he arrives she is filing through papers at the desk. She offers a hurried glance up at him, above the stack of papers in her hands, as he approaches from beyond the entrance. Her eyes quickly dart back down to the papers upon identifying him.

"With the earth, Mother," he greets her.

"May we be cleansed," though her voice sounds tiresome and her eyes look light with a sort of restlessness to them.

"How was your day?" he asks.

"Good, good, I'm a bit busy right now dear. Can we catch up later at home?"

"Sure. Do you need help with anything here?"

She replies reassuringly: "No, everything's fine."

He doesn't believe her, but the way her hands flip desperately, keenly even, through the papers tells him she is truly occupied with something – and as far as he can tell, that something is better than nothing. It's weird how she has these on and off moments, but he ponders how differently each individual must feel internally upon even the very same circumstances. It's like when two people eat the very same meal, he wagers their taste buds don't ignite in exactly the same way.

"Okay, I'll see you at home then," he states.

"Yes dear," she responds with her eyes still glued to the papers.

After leaving the lab, Atticus wanders the field as a means to forage before heading home. Though he collects a small sum of goods, he is more so spending this time in thought. He thinks about Torant and how he possibly could know *everything*, and even more absurd, how Torant could be in love with Ida. He thinks about his plans with The Distillation Project and how he is not a true scientist, nor an inventor – though he doesn't come up with a solution to that ordeal. He thinks about the antitoxin, and how he can learn more about it. After some time, his thoughts form an idea and he eventually heads home.

When Atticus sits down on his bed that night, his face still throbs from his recent encounter with Digger, but it doesn't matter, he has bigger things to focus on. Atticus notes that between Torant's all-knowing abilities, the watchful Defenders and the whispers, he has never truly been alone. Even out in the thick foliage of the forest, someone is always watching – every Almek knows this fact though. He knows that he has heard things about Torant through the whispers and about a person referred to as 'The Shadow' – although those whispers don't connect Torant to The Shadow outright. He has heard of an antitoxin through the whispers, among many other things. He is also fairly certain that all The Almek have heard these whispers. All of these things, he decides, must have a story, an explanation of sorts. Torant knowing all must have an explanation, so too the rumours of an antitoxin. If there is one thing that is never spoken of, one thing that even the whispers don't comment on, are the whispers themselves.

# 70

## Cole of Favoured Wells
## Kala

It's his first day on the job and Cole finds himself to be quite thrilled. It isn't everyday that one wakes to the notion that they are now one of the Favoured, but not just a Favoured – a botanist too. That doesn't happen to anyone, for any reason. He infers in his mind why Master Oberon gave in to such a request. But, he's pretty certain it's because he and his Barons have never wrongfully accused someone before. Still, it was a bold move, requesting to become one of the Favoured. Now he just needs to figure out his next move. Strategies aside, he'll fall into his new role with great attention.

"With the earth, Lidia," he greets as he enters the greenhouse.

"May we be *cleansed*," she says with an edgy look to her.

"Everything… okay?" he asks hesitantly.

"Everything's fine. What's with the hair?" she asks.

"What?" he asks dumbfounded.

"If you're going to play the part you should probably look the part," she adds in a hushed warning.

"If you think I'm going to-"

"At least comb it," she offers.

"My hair is fine."

"Very well. So, if you look over here," she gestures toward the entrance where a table sits covered in strange utensils that Cole hasn't seen before, "these are all of the tools we need for this greenhouse." As she speaks, she speaks in a sombre tone and a flat expression possesses her face.

“What are all these weird squirt bottles filled with?” Cole asks as he picks up a bottle that’s filled with a puke-coloured green substance inside it, his mouth forms a frown as he examines it.

“Mixtures of things that are good for the plants – all of which are plant based blends.”

“Oh good. Cause I was going to ask if someone heaved and then…”

“Gross, Cole,” she says seeming mildly sickened, he chuckles.

“So… what else do I need to know?” he asks.

“Umm… I always start the day by turning the fans on, some of the plants depend on a constant breeze to prevent too much moisture from collecting on their leaves.” Her response a series of weary mumbles.

Cole can’t ignore the mumbling, the knowing that this isn’t Lidia, “What’s going on? Everything is not fine,” he finally announces. Lidia shakes her head in objection, and he assumes she simply doesn’t want to talk about it. But if they are going to be stuck working together in this place, they are going to talk about it, no matter what it is.

She sighs, “Fine. I’m just, struggling okay? And seeing you here isn’t helping,” she says as her eyes focus loosely on the ground.

“Okay… Well what is it? If it has to do with me becoming a botanist, I can promise you that wasn’t my original plan.”

“No, it’s not that.”

“Spit it out already,” he says gently.

“Remember the first day Vera and I met you and Lincoln at Lake Cloud?” she asks.

“Yeah.”

“That’s when things started to change. Horrible things followed V after that day. It might even be why she is in Tagondo. Anyway, since she left, they’ve followed me too.”

“I didn’t know.”

“Now you do,” she says.

“It’s not just you and her though.”

“You just became a Favoured botanist… on the spot. The first ever to be appointed in Kala. Doesn’t seem as though your list of problems is all that long.”

Taken aback by her assumption, he carries on in explanation: “My life was a breeze until Vera came into it. I knew what The Masters demanded of me, I put my head down and did it. Then she came and suddenly I was too busy worrying about her to give a shit what The Masters wanted of me. You think I want to be here? I’d rather be over there, stuck facing tribulation next to her. Instead, I can’t be with her and I’m stuck living with the colony creep. All the while, for a period of time her little brother wanted me dead. If you want to hear anymore about my shit list of problems… it’s racking up pretty high these days.”

Her eyes soften slightly upon the completion of his words, “I didn’t know.”

“Now you do,” he says mimicking her earlier comment.

“I’m just,” Lidia takes a deep breath, “I’m worried about her. I’m worried about me too… Maybe I’m just trying to find someone to blame.”

“Blame The Masters,” he shoots back.

“You’re right. I’m sorry,” she says sheepishly.

“It’s okay, I get it,” he says calmly and nudges at her shoulder gently with his fist. “Now, teach me how to make plants happy, would ya?”

A timid smile overcomes her lips and he catches a glimpse of the Lidia he remembers meeting that day at the lake, "Okay, let's start at the beginning. First, some plants can either thrive or dive if they're planted next to the right or wrong neighbours."

"What about this one?"

"Those are cucumbers, no melons or potatoes can be planted near cucumbers. This here is oregano, when planted beside the cucumbers it works as insect deterrent."

"You're worried about insects in a greenhouse?" he asks quizzically.

"You can never be too careful," she says with a faint smile.

The day progresses as Cole and Lidia care for the plants. Cole learns that it is a routine-based job, but there are so many plants to tend to that it creates some diversity. All in all, he's just happy that he's out of jail and can work towards finding the antitoxin and getting Vera back to Kala. He decides that first he needs to figure out how he can possibly sneak into the lab.

After a full day of 'intro to botany,' Cole says goodbye to Lidia and makes his way back to Torant's house. As Cole wanders the colony centre he notes how quiet it is as the day's light slowly fades. He walks near the school and the bushes that surround it when he notes a rustling sound coming from behind the school. Curious, he wanders around the building to the back. The rustling fades and a cry of sorts fills the air.

At first he thinks it might be an animal, the high pitch moan reminds him of a rodent. However, when he rounds the corner he sees her: a young woman surrounded by bushes upon the ground. She sits, leaning against a tree, her legs spread open as her dress dangles over her knees. He's about to speak, naturally to say something sarcastic about her strange behaviour in the bushes, but then he notices her stomach. It protrudes outward and it becomes very obvious that this woman is pregnant.

A realization overcomes him then and he speaks it out loud: "Holy shit. Are you… are you having a baby?" he asks, astounded.

The woman looks up at Cole, "Help me, please," she manages through gritted teeth.

"I haven't ever…"

"It's okay," she takes several quick deep breaths, "Just put your hands down here and be ready."

"Ready for what?" he asks, but he doesn't truly want to know.

"To catch the baby, help guide him out," she explains.

"How do you know it's a boy?" he asks, obviously panic-stricken.

She raises her voice: "Catch him!"

Cole urgently shoots his hands where the woman has asked him too – he looks up at her, her face is dewy with beads of sweat, moistened hair sticks to her pink face. A look to her eyes shows both terror and excitement – he's sure of that. Then he thinks staring at her in this moment might make her uncomfortable, so he looks down. His heart races at the thought of what he's about to do. He's hunted deer, outrun Cain - the fastest Tagondian - and has even slayed mammoths; still, this makes him quiver.

"Do you always stare at ladies' goods like that, newcomer?" she asks through quick breaths. His eyes dart away, unsure of where to settle his stare.

"I'm sorry, I don't know where else to…" he moves his gaze upward then, focusing on the brush that sits beside them, it seems to shield them from the sights of others.

"It's okay, you're not the first man I've ordered between my legs," she releases a giggle and though cute, it sounds anything but innocent – it's borderline crazed. Surely cute and crazed can't be one in the same, or two things at which to describe the same thing. Still, he's stuck with those words in his mind. Cole of Favoured Wells is speechless. He says nothing in response. Instead, he'll keep his eyes fixated on the brush. The details on the green leaves, the ridges and lines… He's not removing his eyes from those leaves.

She chuckles again, "Don't worry newcomer, most men that are ordered between my legs desperately seek to return," she speaks with assurance.

"My name's Cole, Cole P… I mean Wells."

"I know who you are, Mammoth Slayer," she says.

"Can I help you to the hospital?" he offers.

"I can't go there," she says impatiently.

They sit in silence for some time, the woman's moans and exhales of discomfort are the only sounds made. When the curfew siren rings it startles them both and causes Cole to jump slightly. He can't recall a time when he's been so on edge.

"Easily scared, are we newcomer?" she speculates as she stares at him.

She must've seen the hairs on his neck stand, for he is most definitely nervous. Though scared, he'd argue, he isn't quite there just yet. However, he reminds himself that he has nothing to prove, not to anyone and especially not to this woman that's about to give birth.

"Sure," he says with a smirk. She laughs a light giggle. "Is there any way to speed this up? We're definitely missing curfew tonight."

"Oh Cole, are you worried about being out late?" she asks in a taunting tone.

"I'm worried about us getting caught. I don't generally seek to break the laws."

"Well The Master removed the curfew for Favoured… so that means one of us is in luck. And sadly, there is no way to speed this sort of thing up. Well, there is one way," she quips.

"There is? What is it? We should do it," he suggests. Defenders will be roaming the paths, there's a good chance they'll get caught, especially if her moans grow any louder.

"If you say so…" She tugs at the buckle on his pants.

"Whoa. What are you doing?"

"You asked if there was any way to speed it up. This is the only way that I know of," she smiles, her eyes devious.

"What are you, crazy?"

"Some say," she replies as she runs her fingers through the ends of her hair, twisting the strands together.

Cole shakes his head in shock and decides to say nothing more to her; she seems drastically unpredictable. Maybe it's the traumatic experience leading up to birth – he's sure it must be terrifying and confusing all at the same time.

"This is it," she utters.

After a series of grunts and pushes, which may or may not end up traumatizing Cole - he's undecided on that fact - the baby comes down the birth canal and lands in Cole's hands. He wraps the baby in his sweatshirt, noting there is in fact a penis – she was right.

"Is he okay?" the lady asks.

“I think so,” he then places the baby on the woman’s chest and she moans in relief, allowing herself a second to take in her blood-soaked son. “Wow, that seemed way easier than I expected…” Cole notes.

“Easy?” she barks.

“Sorry… Not easy. Quicker?”

She rolls her eyes then looks directly at Cole, “You will tell no one of this.”

“This isn’t exactly the highlight of my day either lady,” he says.

There is no way in hell he’s telling anyone, or ever reliving the past 30-minutes of his life again. Perhaps that night he’ll take to the bottle to erase the memory of her swelling and enlarging vagina – not to mention the mucus and blood that covers his hands. For a moment he wonders if he may vomit, but through that concern, he can’t deny that it’s incredible what women’s bodies can do.

“If anyone finds out, I will face tribulation as an Offender and he will have a birthing ceremony,” she says looking at her newborn baby boy.

“I’m not going to tell anyone. But can’t his father fight for him? I can’t see you hiding the birth of a child from The Masters forever.”

“His Father, Reed, disappeared. Hunted by a mammoth last month. He saved me – the mammoth was coming for me.”

“Coming for you?”

“It wanted me.”

“Well, I’m sorry,” Cole says, knowing mammoths aren’t intelligent enough to have targets – they are animals that simply follow their instincts. Unfortunately for the colonies, these animals instinctively hunt people.

“I plan to leave this place once I’m well enough,” she says.

“This place? You mean The Motherland?”

“There is nothing left for me here,” she says sorrowfully.

A woman fleeing The Motherland with a newborn baby is ludicrous. He redirects the conversation: “Where do you live? I’ll help you get there.”

“I can’t go home to my parents, they will have no choice but to turn me in or they too will be tried as Offenders. Besides, the Defenders are looking for me and they’ll check there without a doubt. My parents must act as though they don’t know.”

“How have you been surviving? Obtaining food?” Cole asks.

“I’ve been sleeping in the hut behind the school since Reed died. There are a couple school kids who drop off berries and nuts – I’m making due,” she explains.

“I’ll help you,” Cole states, “Come with me to my house.”

“And live with Torant of now Favoured Wells? No fucking way.”

“What does everyone have against the guy? He’s only a little weird,” Cole notes humorously.

“I just can’t, I need another option.”

“You don’t have to live with us. Let’s just go talk to him, maybe he has an idea.”

“Other than to cook my body into a soup? Not likely.”

“He’s not like that…At least I don’t think he is. Besides, how else will you keep your baby hidden?”

“I have no one,” she admits, “My parents have disowned me after they found out I was pregnant with Reed’s child.”

“Okay,” he thinks for a moment. Cole knows no one else in the colony, aside from Atticus and Lidia, and there’s no way he’ll put this on either of them. The only person who knows what’s coming and is able to deal with this is Torant: The Shadow, he’ll know what to do. “Our only option is that you come with me-” Cole begins.

"I won't-" the woman interjects.

"I understand you have your own ideas on Torant and that's all fine and dandy. But lady, if you want to live, Torant is your only option as far as I can see. At least for the meantime we can hide you both there. No one - not even the Defenders - go as far as Torant's. Take it or leave it," he concludes.

Her face contorts in odd ways as she appears to contemplate her choices and possibly what living with Torant will mean. Her brow rises then furrows; her mouth purses then loosens. *She is rather dramatic*, he thinks, though reasons that the poor girl just had a baby, hormones will be skyrocketing and hurtling back down to earth with little to no warning.

Finally, she kisses her baby's forehead and looks up at Cole: "Okay, fine," she says, "For him."

"Do you think you have enough strength to get there?" he asks.

"I don't think I can even stand up."

"I'll carry you then," he says without hesitation.

Cole scoops her and the baby up in his arms as though it's nothing. The woman confidently tells Cole which way will be the safest route to get to Torant's house and they are lucky, for no one sees them on their travels.

As they enter House of Favoured Wells, Torant sits at the kitchen table awaiting their arrival – it turns out one person did see them.

"You took longer than expected," Torant says.

"Yeah well, I'd like to see you help birth a human being and get back in decent time," Cole jokes, still holding the woman and baby in his arms.

"It's not the least noble thing you've done in your life," Torant notes. Cole ignores him, he can't let banter get in the way of helping this woman right now.

"Can we let her stay here? At least for a little while?" Cole asks.

"Not a chance. It is a terrible idea," Torant says.

"What is a good idea? Letting her die in the forest?"

"That wouldn't be so bad," Torant says thoughtfully.

"I told you," the woman says as she wiggles out of Cole's arms.

"Shhh, relax. He doesn't want you to die in the forest," Cole reasons.

"It makes no difference to me in the end," Torant says, his voice cold.

"Would you shut up?" he warns Torant.

Cole then wraps his arm around the woman and helps her to the kitchen table. Torant and the woman sit, stares of hatred upon their faces.

"So… do you two know each other?" Cole asks. Neither respond, only lingering stares of disdain sit upon their faces.

"This is gonna be wonderful: us all living together," Cole says with a forced smile.

"Three days," Torant says.

"Three months," Cole counters.

Torant looks at Cole, "I can't hide an Offender for three months."

Cole ponders over the petty time that he has known Torant and reflects that he has seen him mildly outraged a handful of times. In this moment Torant appears to be just that, which Cole deems to be a good sign as extreme outrage would be a definite 'no.'

"You can, you will find a way. She needs the time to recover – the baby too," Cole explains.

A silence washes over the room for some time. Torant stands to his feet and paces about the kitchen. Cole understands the risks involved in accepting the woman and her child into their home. He also knows that they don't have a choice. To ignore her would be to kill her; the blood would practically be strewn across their hands. No one in the colonies would know; but they would.

Finally Torant speaks: "You are responsible for whatever harm she causes – both outside and inside of this house."

"I-," the woman begins.

Cole interjects, "Done," then he looks to the woman, "You and the baby can have my room. Do you need a bath… to clean up?" he asks.

"Yes," the woman says.

"Okay. Be good *Tortoise*," Cole demands as he leaves for the bathroom to draw her a bath. When Cole returns, Torant is gone. "Where's Torant-the-terrible?" he asks the woman, still sitting at the kitchen table.

"Out to run his nightly errands. Why he is not terrified of the mammoths baffles me," she says.

"He is a peculiar one," Cole agrees, "How are you feeling?"

"I'm fine. Thank you for doing all this," she says.

"You're welcome. I just realized though that I don't even know your name."

"Isn't that something? You know what I look like down there," she points to the space between her legs with a smirk on her face, "and yet my name has never crossed your lips." She laughs. "I should add, I don't always look quite like this…"

He clears his throat, "So, are you going to tell me your name?"

"Almay."

"Almay, that's nice. Well the bath is ready, I'll watch the baby."

Cole rinses his arms and hands in the sink, while Almay takes to her bath. He then sits and takes the baby in his arms. Not much stirs the nerves inside of Cole, but holding a newborn baby does. He barely moves, he barely breathes as he holds the sleeping infant. Surely he'll scare him or hurt him in some way if he moves. In fact, when he tries to adjust his arm the baby wakes and begins to cry, Cole establishes that no one is supposed to move when holding a baby.

Almay comes back into the room with her golden brown hair now darkened with dampness, she's dressed in clean clothing.

"Where'd you find the clothes?" he asks.

"In Torant's room… there is a drawer filled with ladies' clothing."

"That's not odd," Cole says sarcastically as he wonders if there's a legitimate reason why The Masters won't offer him another merge agreement.

"How is he doing?" Almay asks.

"He's good… I think. Still very breakable."

She giggles, "I'm ready to bathe him… You can come if you want."

The two take to the bathroom and Almay bathes her son while Cole watches nervously, offering help when she needs it. It's a stressful thing, bathing a baby, he thinks. It's out of his realm of understanding; he'll never be good with babies.

"Look at his toes," Almay says.

"They're tiny." A laugh erupts from Cole's chest, Almay laughs too.

"It's beautiful, isn't it? The whole thing," she says.

"Should I answer that truthfully or…?"

She laughs, "Of course, you should answer truthfully. Just don't answer stupidly."

"Oh, well in that case. My answer is: yes and no," he laughs again.

"I see what you did there," she notes with a smirk.

"Difficult to get into trouble with an answer like that."

"Yes, and you don't want to piss me off," Almay says in a matter-of-fact way.

Torant stands in the doorway of the bathroom then, "What is this?" he asks.

"Bathing a baby. What does it look like?" Cole says, unmoved.

"The guy who just convinced the greats of the colony to make him one of the Favoured is wasting his time bathing a baby?" Torant scoffs while his face shifts. His eyes widen right before he turns and walks away.

"Hey, lay off. Almay needed some help," Cole calls after him.

Torant turns back, his voice grows louder: "There are forces Cole, forces at work. Which means you need to be working too," he threatens. The baby begins to cry.

"Excuse us," Cole says to Almay then leaves the bathroom and guides Torant down the hall. "What is your deal doll man? I'm struggling with your lack of understanding for what she's been through. Do you know her lover died a month ago and now she's forced to raise this baby alone?"

"I know all of that," Torant barks.

"Okay, listen, I understand Almay coming here isn't ideal. But without us, her and that boy will die – she wants to escape, but I know they won't make it. I just haven't thought of another plan for them yet," Cole says.

"It is a grave mistake bringing a stranger into this house," Torant says.

"But you brought me here," Cole retorts.

"That's different."

"Help me figure out a way to convince her to stay. And to hide the baby from The Masters."

"She can't stay forever. If you are going to take us down this path you must hide it from the people too," Torant pauses, "You don't know what they are willing to do with an unaccounted for child. For it is written that: no child shall be exempt from the birthing ceremonies."

"I know. But where do we start?" Cole asks, desperate for help.

"She must stay indoors at all times. Keep the child quiet."

"No one ventures out this far anyway-"

"Keep the child quiet," Torant shouts.

"Okay, I'll tell her," Cole agrees then turns back down the hallway to talk with Almay.

As if out of nowhere, a previous thought returns to his mind, something he wants to mention to Torant so he turns back again and makes his way to the kitchen.

"What is the antitoxin? Don't try to pretend like you don't know," Cole demands in a whisper. A smirk spreads across Torant's face as though he's pleased that Cole should ask him such a question.

"You're late, Cole. But better late than never."

# 71

## Vera of Insignificant Cannelle Tagondo

Vera slinks quickly through the forest while still feeling the adrenaline effects from the oil of the ivani leaf that sits on her wrist. Her arm, the one Cain injured, fiercely aches and so she holds it across her stomach. It's not a kind of nag she's experienced before – it doesn't rest upon the surface of her skin: it's deeper, more invasive. Though she tries to ignore the pain, it's a constant throb that tells her that she needs to get medical help.

She has heard the voices of Tagondians for quite some time, though she somehow hasn't come across anyone. In no time she arrives at the edge of the forest where the clearing leads to The Circle. She has her satchel, the two leaves to compare and test for black poison in the lab, as well as the knowledge of who killed Burke – all of which propel her forward with her mind set to get to Kala undetected.

Nevertheless, she is nervous about continuing her plan on her own, she doesn't necessarily feel good about it, but she doesn't feel horrible either - it's something in the middle - like snowstorms in May, pretty to look at, but unsettling to truly acknowledge. It's the underlying reason that's cause for concern – snow storms in May are a sign that the Earth is upset, out of balance, which is how Vera feels about executing her plan without Cole. She is well aware that sneaking into Kala could mean death, but it could also mean reuniting briefly with her loved ones and finding the antitoxin. It could also mean, getting through to Master Oberon – the only one with enough power to overtake Regan.

Nightfall is just upon her as she stands along the tree-line in Tagondo. She stares into the beyond, into the field that leads to The Circle. The ivani plant begins to burn on her wrist – a sign, she thinks, that it's expiring and all of its oils absorbed. She removes it and wanders past the threshold of the tree-line. As she begins her trek across the field, Vera contemplates that she should have retrieved another ivani leaf. She wonders then just how much oil one's body can safely take of the plant.

A sudden noise sounds in the darkness: a creak amidst the bushes. Unexpectedly something collides with her head, and with the thud everything goes dark.

# 72

# OPI OF INSIGNIFICANT CANNELLE TAGONDO

"Tell me everything – every conversation you've had with her," Master Regan demands as he sits upon his textured chair in The Master's chamber, his hand squeezes around his whiskey glass.

"Well, a number of weeks ago she asked about the probes… Murdina told her about the antitoxin."

"Damnit. What did you say? Were you under the influence of the kneele tea?" Regan asks.

"No, your grace. She tried, but Murdina used kneele tea on me often enough that I eventually caught on. From then on I took breenga leaf everyday to counteract the kneele tea. I was in complete control of my words. I told them the antitoxin isn't real, that the whispers are nonsense."

"And?"

"They believed me, without a doubt."

"It's Vera I'm concerned about, Murdina is but a spike of grass amongst the fields by now."

Opi's chest twinges in sadness, but he brushes it off for his Master, "You're right, I believe Vera fell for it. She looked to every word that Murdina ever said and Murdina seemed to agree with me."

"Good. That's the last thing I need, Vera out gallivanting and getting her hands on my antitoxin."

"We will find her, your grace."

"Yes and when we do, we must see to it that she dies."

"Master, she couldn't have escaped Tagondon on her own," Opi reasons, suggesting that the possible helper should be the one held accountable. Though he doesn't want to see Vera dead, he won't disobey his Master.

"I don't care how she escaped," Master Regan spits the words. "She has already subjected me to enough headache, let alone this act of defiance. Treena is in the middle of a meltdown – she had just seen Vera right before her disappearance with Ezla. I've got Defenders questioning my ability to keep my colony on lockdown. Soon the people are going to be asking questions."

"I understand. But with all due respect your grace, Vera couldn't have gotten away without help. Someone must have helped her. If we find them, we find her," Opi reasons.

"What are you suggesting? And make it quick."

"Is there someone in the colony that is close with her? Someone who also despises you?" Opi asks.

Master Regan sits with one leg crossed over the other, one hand grazing at his jawline deep in thought. Opi's glasses begin to slide down his face, he uses his index finger to push them back up into place; the sweat that pours from his forehead causes his glasses to slide more than usual. If he's honest with himself, he's frightfully nervous as Master Regan is mere minutes away from ordering a death by stoning tribulation for Vera in the colony centre. He's about to send out the search party for her and Opi is trying desperately to convince him otherwise.

"There is someone…" Regan finally says, thoughtfully.

"Who your grace? We should interrogate them."

"My niece…"

"Oh…" Opi has no intentions of messing with The Master's niece.

"Follow her, would you?" Regan sternly demands.

Opi nods his head and offers his Master a bow before frantically making his way out of the chamber. As he leaves, he stumbles down the chamber stairs and falls to his knees. A clumsy nature has been the way of life for Opi, though he never lets that bother him. But as of late, his clumsiness has seemed to ramp up – maybe it's in relation to his nerves.

He rises to his feet once again and scurries down the paths to Insignificant Cannelle. He has a feeling suddenly that someone is following him – it's a terrible feeling, but it isn't the first time. He hears then the quiet scuffing of feet against grass. It also isn't the first time that he turns his round body, as quickly as it is capable of, to find no one on the path behind him. He exhales and continues on.

The sudden sound of stomping feet approaching him from behind just about knocks him on his bottom. He turns once again, sure someone is set to attack him, but it is only a couple of children running in a zig-zag motion across the path, now releasing squeals of pleasure. This time his nerves are satisfied, it was likely the children all along.

Opi enters Insignificant Cannelle aware of the grave difference that vaguely haunts him without Murdina here, but only if he pays mind to it. If he just keeps his mind distracted, if he doesn't think about her, it's easier. Besides, it's all a part of his Master's plan.

His legs carry him through the living room and over to a cabinet, he pulls up a chair and brings the weight of his short, wide body to stand upon it. Reaching for the top cabinet door, he opens it and moves a pile of books to the side. He pulls out a bundle of the black poison then to the kitchen table he goes, spilling the bunch across its surface.

"What are you good for, huh? Why does The Master want you?" Opi says aloud to the plant, with a knowing that it doesn't cleanse the water.

If only this bundle were the antitoxin – how useless plants seem in comparison. Sure, Murdina always suggested there is great value in their properties and maybe in some respect she's right, maybe there is value. But the antitoxin is life - even though he tried to convince Murdina and Vera it isn't real - he believes it's very real and he'll be the one to find it for his Master. More than anything Opi wants a respectable position in the colony – Baron will suit him just fine. If Opi of Insignificant Cannelle finds the antitoxin, why, Master Regan might just appoint him as Baron right on the spot.

# 73

# ATTICUS OF FAVOURED NORTH KALA

It's a rare occurrence for Atticus to be sitting in the office of Rumi of Favoured Epillow, Ulyd's mother; however, if he had to choose an educator to be meeting after class with she is by far his preferred. Her office is a small and resided space, because she is also Eldest Educator. Or Principal, as they used to call it in the Old World. Atticus notes her unique disposition, a level of unconscious sophistication that he hasn't noticed in any other Kalian – he admires that about her. Truth be told, Atticus asked to meet with Rumi, but not in search of ways to be uppity with his marks; no, today he comes to her in seeking answers.

"What can you tell me about The Shadow?" Atticus gets directly to the point as he takes his seat.

Rumi chuckles, "With the earth. Surely there is nothing more important than our greeting?" She says, but he can't tell if it's with sarcasm or not.

Still, he quickly responds with the accepted greeting, "May we be cleansed."

Rumi continues: "My dear boy, where are you hearing such profound nonsense about this *Shadow*?"

"The whispers…" He doesn't want to admit that he's met Torant and never mind been to his house. The whispers from the Whisperer on the other hand, he assumes, are public knowledge.

"The whispers. Hmm," Rumi pauses.

"Can't you tell me anything?"

"My dear Atticus, you are such an inquisitive young man, but… we should not be discussing such things." Though she offers no explanation as to why.

"What about the antitoxin then?" Atticus asks as he anxiously taps on the top of Rumi's desk with his fingertips.

A sigh escapes her brown lips, a nervous whisper follows, "Our world is so sensitive, so fragile in this day. It saddens me," she musters.

He waits in silence, a means of implying patience, which with Atticus' patience, it must be made apparent.

After a moment she continues: "I have heard the whispers of an antitoxin, though in a place such as this, it is difficult to decipher their truth."

"Well what have you heard about it?"

"That it shall rid our bodies of the toxins in the water, pulling them through and out of us like a magnet."

"Do you believe it?"

"I don't believe in much without proof... Now listen, you should be getting on with your day."

"Do you ever talk with Ulyd about this stuff?" Atticus asks, desperate to continue the conversation.

"My son has less interest in fixing the Broken World than a bird has to the likes of a snake," she says, "But no, he doesn't ask such questions and so I do not bring it about. Truly – the less he knows the better. Same goes for you."

"I guess. He's determined to learn the laws, to follow in Educator Barlow's footsteps anyway," Atticus notes.

"I suppose that you are right," she replies.

Rumi has always appeared reserved and quiet, Atticus shouldn't be surprised by her lack of answers for him. But in a place like this everyone is tight-lipped. Still he is grateful for her leadership and that she and Ulyd are a part of The Almek, even if they have an air about them that says they are far too humbled to speak out of line – humbled or scared.

Rumi is from Nigeria, but moved to Wisconsin with her husband when she became pregnant with Ulyd and was offered a position as a Principal at one of the high schools there. They hadn't spent much time in Wisconsin before the Water Crisis unfolded and at that time Ulyd's father died from drinking the toxic water, which meant Rumi came to The Motherland as a single mother with an infant.

Her eyes are as dark as the night, they haven't changed or faded over the years as some do. Atticus imagines that they are wells, wells of information and knowledge because being Eldest Educator means that she's well read in books and people. Rumi's particular profession multitasks in the realm of people: understanding people, listening to people and reading between the lines with people. Surely it includes sourcing out illegal commodities.

"Do you think we could get our hands on the antitoxin?" he persists.

"It's inconceivable."

"Why though? If there's talks of it – it must be out there somewhere."

"You shouldn't waste your time listening to the whispers."

"But what if they're true?"

"Regardless, The Masters don't like us speaking of the Whisperer nor the whispers themselves – you are going to get yourself into trouble young man."

"I can't help but wonder about their legitimacy. I can't ignore the whispers anymore," he admits.

She smiles as her watery brown orbs glance toward Atticus, “You, my boy, are unusual. Though I suspect that you are so because you’re meant for changing the world – and I trust that one day you will.

# 74

# LIDIA OF FAVOURED PEONY
# KALA

"With the earth. Master Oberon requests your presence," Huron reverberates into the greenhouse.

Lidia startles, practically jumping out of her boots, or is it her skin? She can't see him, but she can picture his stance in her mind – a certain level of confidence that is abnormal among The Almek for most walk amongst eggshells, at least she feels she does. Perhaps it is normal for The Master's Lead to house such arrogance within his build.

She walks around the fig bushes to place him in her sight, an uncomfortable twinge moves across her spine – Huron always imposes this reaction within her. She fears him like the mammoths at night, surely everyone does though.

"May we be cleansed. Okay, thank you," she manages indifferently then places her gardening tools on a nearby table before following him out of the greenhouse.

The stares of the people are skeptical in her mind, which abash her petty self-confidence so she looks to the ground. Perhaps they are merely curious and she couldn't see that if she tried. Private meetings with The Master are never for law abiding Insignificants and rarely for the Favoured – more often they are for the troubled. *Am I troubled?* Maybe it doesn't matter. Most people don't actually like true facts – they only like the speculating surfaces of what makes up a person, like shiny white veneers.

Huron leads Lidia up the front stairs of The Master's chamber and she enters with a bow to The Master and his barons.

"With the earth," Master Oberon greets Lidia.

"May we be cleansed," she responds.

"Lidia of Favoured Peony, we thank you for answering our call for your presence," Quim says.

"Does the girl know why she is here?" Martil asks no one in particular.

"She must have an idea," Hogard states.

"I apologize, I don't want to assume that I know The Master's ways," Lidia says.

Hogard leans forward, "You have been lazy and moping about. You're falling behind on your duties as Favoured in the greenhouses." A stab to her ribcage suddenly pains her side.

"Have I? It hasn't been that bad," she thinks out loud.

"Some of the shares that have been coming from the greenhouses are rotten: an issue that magnifies a lack of care," Master Oberon states.

"I didn't know that people were receiving rotten shares, no one told me," she says, baffled.

"Let this be a warning. Forget your troubles of the past and fulfill your duty," Martil notes, "or you will have no place here at all."

*No place here at all?* Lidia questions herself, shocked, for she has been working herself to exhaustion day in and day out.

"Yes, your grace," she simply replies as she fights back the sudden tremors that threaten her knees to bend and cause her legs to snap beneath her.

"Should this meeting not prove useful and you ignore this warning, tribulation will come for you," Master Oberon states.

"Yes, your grace," she says.

"Off with you – clean those greenhouses up," Master Oberon orders.

Lidia bows before leaving the building, her steps soft tiptoes.

As Lidia mopes through the colony centre, mostly successful in ignoring the countless accusatory stares, she makes her way back to the greenhouse. Like a sad, pathetic mouse of a human her eyes attempt to timidly steady themselves with their gaze forced upon the ground.

*I'm a dud. Why did Atticus have to stop my meeting with the lake?* No, this is not his fault. However, is she truly inadequate? The idea of rotten vegetables is shocking and upsetting. It must be a lie, as far as she's concerned, all produce leaves her greenhouses in deliciously crisp conditions. For all she knows she's being set up. *How or why?* She can't be certain.

"Damnit," she says out loud, "I've done everything here. Everything! And with zero help. How can they say this place is failing?"

"*Keep going,*" the whispers howl in through the doorway, "*The shed.*"

"The shed? The garden shed!" she exclaims with a sudden shift in her disposition. It reminds her that she has yet to arrange the gathering that she had wanted to with those who need it, mainly for the simple fact that she hadn't a clue on a safe location for them to gather. The garden shed will be perfect though, it's the exact space that she needs right now to solve one of her two problems. But first, she'll finish up with the greenhouse and then she'll contact the women who seem to be suffering by passing the message in whispers from one to the next.

# 75

# ATTICUS OF FAVOURED NORTH KALA

A few days following their last conversation about the Broken World, Atticus receives a meeting request from Rumi – a message passed on by Ulyd with a suspicious eye. Ignoring the wary gaze, Atticus nods in response and saunters down the hall without a word to his friend. He returns to Rumi's office for the scheduled time of the meeting, uncertain as to what the details of their exchange will reflect – though he is hopeful it has something to do with the antitoxin. Regardless, he's looking forward to it; Rumi is a wealth of information.

Upon Atticus' arrival she informs him that she has been thinking a great deal about their discussion and that she wants to help him. Apparently, she's rather impressed with his initiative and obvious passion for the circumstances surrounding the colony. Rumi suggests that in order to show Atticus how she can help him, they must take their meeting outside.

As the two stand in the colony centre midday, the sun shines so brightly that it beautifully illuminates the entire centre and all of those that walk across it.

"You must listen to their whispers," Rumi says.

"But I thought you said any whispers were-" Atticus begins.

"Forget what I said, and do as I say," though she interrupts him, her voice stays calm, steady, like the treetops on a windless day.

So, there they stand in the colony centre. Atticus takes in the scene: the school sits adjacent to the lab, which is beside the greenhouses, and from there the jail is situated between the school and The Master's chamber. This is the busiest place in the colony, especially at the beginning and end of the day, it's a central path in which the people travel to get to the forests for foraging, to run their errands and travel back and forth from their work to home. Atticus stands in the centre, amongst the moving bodies, all the while Rumi stands not inches behind him. He watches the people without blinking and they continue on with their day, seemingly entirely unaware of his presence.

"I heard about an antitoxin," one says.

"What is that?" another asks.

"It attracts the mammoths," one speaks again.

"No, it brings the rain," a third voice states.

Atticus turns to look at Rumi with one eyebrow raised in amusement. Rumi continues to stand tall and proud, her hands clasped together behind her back and the faintest of smiles curves her lips upward. Maybe the knowledge here is that the citizens rarely speak the truth.

"This sounds like nonsense," he says to Rumi as he twists his upper body to glance at her again.

"Just listen," she urges.

He contemplates why Rumi is suddenly on board for listening to the Kalian whispers – he contemplates truths. Maybe the words that these people utter are *their* truths, things they believe to be true. *But what if they know their words to be untrue?*

"But some of these whispers are absolute garbage," he reiterates.

"With experience comes clarity," she simply replies.

"So I have to experience the lies to know the truths? How do I tell them a part?" he asks.

Just then Doctor Theodus and his wife Surni of Favoured Harrow walk by with their fingers linked in a loose knot. Surni's blonde locks are tied back as the rest of The Almek women and her part pushed over to one side. The odd tiny strand lingers, hanging loose as it blows in the wake of her steps – she's a beautiful woman, though Atticus tries not to stare. She is much older, in her early forties, but this point does not stop his heart from racing in her presence.

Her merger, Doctor Theodus, is a well-respected man amongst the colony. He runs the Kalian hospital and graciously accepts his duty as humbly as any man can. Surni works as a nurse under his lead and the two appear to be the embodiment of happiness, 'a merge agreement gone right,' as Ida would say.

"With the earth," Doctor Harrow says to Atticus and Rumi.

"May we be cleansed," Rumi responds. Atticus locks eyes with Surni and a teasing smile rests upon the lips of the doctor's wife.

^

Several weeks pass and Atticus still has not obtained what he is in search of – the antitoxin. The whispers send him in no more clear direction than the mysterious spoken words of Torant of Favoured Wells. He has been awake more hours than he sleeps, showers less often than he cares to admit and hasn't fuelled his body with food and drink as much as he should, but still, he sits through his botany class with as much enthusiasm and concentration as he possibly can. Though he usually enjoys botany class, he wants to focus more of his efforts on his Distillation Project as well as his more recent undertaking with Rumi as his mentor.

Atticus reminds himself that he is running out of time, for this December - the end of his final year of school - he must choose his profession: botanist or scientist. However, there is a possibility that a request will be submitted for him to join the scientists seeing as Kala has lost two. Atticus can only assume that Master Oberon will request him to become a scientist and research assistant to Educator Ferris, who was recently promoted to laboratory head. He doesn't mind Educator Ferris though.

Atticus gathers his belongings and leaves the botany classroom on his way to meet Ulyd, who should be out of his law class by now. The past week hasn't offered much time for him to spend with Ulyd – he's hoping that this afternoon can prove promising, though he hasn't confirmed with Ulyd about this yet.

Atticus ambles toward Educator Barlow's classroom only to find it empty, but a door at the back of the classroom behind the bookshelves catches his attention. Atticus has never paid mind to it before, but in this moment beyond its wooden frame, a clatter of noise sounds and it pulls his focus. He begins approaching the door and just as it's within his reach a thumping begins on the other side.

A muffled voice speaks sternly: "You're going to do exactly what I tell you and if you don't – consider this punishment to be a treat."

It's difficult to make out, but it sounds as though the muffled speech is in the British accent of Educator Barlow.

"Yes, sir," says the whimper of another voice.

Atticus doesn't have a clue what's going on behind the door, but he swings it open without a second thought and there is Ulyd – bent over with his pants down around his ankles and James Barlow whipping his ass with a belt. Barlow's face appears concerned and terrified by the intrusion. Time seems to stand still for Atticus. Redness emulates heat off of his skin as his face flushes in confusion, but also anger. He knows then, that he wants to rip Barlow's head clean off. He also knows that he can't.

He remains frozen, unable to react in the moment almost as if his feet are planted, glued even, to the floor below him; as a result of his hesitation this gives Barlow the opportunity to snag Atticus in his grasp. Barlow wraps his hands around Atticus' neck and violently pulls him into the closet then instantly begins beating Atticus with the belt that's still clutched in his hand. In between cracks of the belt James fights at pulling Atticus' pants down – Atticus can't focus, nor fight back, his head reels with panic.

"The lot of you are going to pay for this intrusion," James yells.

Atticus questions internally what he has done wrong, for he was simply curious. *What has his poor friend Ulyd done wrong?*

"In experience, comes clarity," Atticus whispers, though he doesn't know why the words leave his swelling lips.

"What?" Barlow shouts.

Atticus raises his voice and says it louder this time, ignoring the thought that he should just be quiet, "In experience, comes clarity."

"You're going to experience my foot up your ass if you don't shut it," Barlow shouts then violently kicks Atticus' face with his boot.

Barlow finally ceases his thumping upon Atticus and moves toward the door. Atticus spits to relieve the taste of iron filling his mouth. *In experience comes clarity*, he chants in his mind.

James stands in the doorway and stares down upon the injured teenagers, "I'll take care of you both like I took care of Elle," Barlow barks, the anger on his face fades into something else… uncertainty perhaps.

Atticus watches Barlow for a moment – he looks like an ordinary man, but the blood - Ulyd's or Atticus' blood - is smeared across Barlow's forehead. Atticus decides then that any man who wears the blood of another is not ordinary. He also decides something else: James Barlow is a murderer.

# 76

# Lidia of Favoured Peony
# Kala

The Tarnished: it has a nice ring to it and Lidia prides herself in creating it. She has created a gathering of women and it is hers to lead. It isn't that she has a particularly deep desire to lead, although she is an organized woman and nurturing others does come naturally to her. She deems that it's an organic formulation of her strengths... and possibly even her weaknesses. Sometimes everyone needs nurturing, for what a dismal place this world would be without those of an empathetic nature – no one would feel understood or appreciated. And what exactly happens when people don't feel understood? When they don't feel appreciated? Chaos. Evil doings.

As if the Whisperser reads her mind they call: *"Be watchful of The Cobra,"* though Lidia still isn't exactly sure who or what The Cobra is.

Brushing the whispers aside, Lidia reflects upon her, albeit mild, evil doings for she has been sneaking out at night and wandering the colony. There is a purpose though: she is tracking the night guard's watchful route upon nightfall. She knows that there's only ever one Defender on shift during the late hours, so she's been following him without a peep. No matter who's working they seem to take the same route every night, which works in her favour – she has been able to tell the women which routes to take and at what time.

Now that she has a meeting location - the shed behind the greenhouses - and safe routes for her members to take, she is ready for The Tarnished to meet. They gather that night for the first time.

"Lidia, I'm concerned we'll get caught," Aphria whispers.

"Nonsense. There's really no need to worry. Ida North has assured me that no one uses the garden shed on a regular basis, which means we should have no surprises," Lidia says assuredly.

"So long as you're sure," Aphria says.

"I'm certain. Ida was so gracious to offer us the keys."

Lidia didn't tell Ida why she needed the garden shed; she felt that information impossible to share with anyone outside of The Tarnished. She has permission and the keys – that's what is important.

The shed that the two women are currently gathering in consists of wooden walls that house the extra gardening tools among other items for the greenhouses. It's pretty rare that Lidia herself needs entrance to the building since most necessary items to run the greenhouses are in their rightful building. Aside from gardening items there really isn't much else in the shed; however, Lidia took it upon herself to bring a couple blankets to lie out on the floor in the centre of the shed to add some comfort.

As far as she knows, there are two more women who plan to come to this first meeting. Just then Ursai walks into the shed, hesitant at first, but there's fierceness within her fair complexion.

"Hello Ursai of Insignificant Tullum, it's a pleasure to meet you. Thank you so much for coming," Lidia welcomes Ursai, while intentionally avoiding the accepted Almek greeting.

"Likewise," Ursai says. Behind Ursai in steps Emille.

"Emille of Insignificant Quilian, I'm so happy you've come," Lidia welcomes as well.

"Thanks," Emille says as her eyes dart about the shed.

Emille's ebony hair blends in with the shadows of the night and the darkness surrounds her. It reminds Lidia how she met Emille once before and by accident – it was a warm afternoon a few years ago, they were both delivering shares to division and Emille had dropped hers, Lidia helped to pick them up – Emille's hair was midnight black, daylight didn't change that.

It has been a couple weeks since Lidia last saw Aphria and passed onto her the message that would help organize their first meet. Beyond giving her the secret message, Lidia has seen Aphria in brief passing, intentionally locking eyes in recognition of one another, but unable to communicate much beyond their heartfelt stares. It seems as though Aphria is doing better – she gives hope, and sometimes a small amount of hope is enough to help someone out of a rock and a hard place.

After brief introductions the four women sit in a circle upon the floor of the shed, silence fills the air. The crickets creak – their music loud enough to be heard through the thin wooden walls. The night sky is speckled in stars that are visible through the windows at the front of the shed; however, awkward glances and flat smiles are highlighted by the candlelight. Lidia grows worried that her vision isn't going to turn out the way she planned. Of course they will be hesitant, fearful of getting caught. She needs to make it worthwhile for them to continue showing up. She must share her story first.

"Thank you all for coming, for this our first meeting – let us begin. I would like to start off by saying that I, myself, have suffered a great deal these past few months. The birth of my daughter Lilith followed by Kobe's death means that I never really got to be her mother." Sighs fill the circle. Lidia continues: "Sadness grew into a darker sadness. Until I felt like I was living a lie, living someone else's life because it couldn't possibly be my own. With no one to talk to I… almost left Kala. Upon this rude awakening by a dear friend I began to wonder: what do other women in the colony do with their grief? And so, here we are."

"Did you try to talk with anyone about it?" Aphria probes for the sake of the other two women as she already knows Lidia's story from that night they both had minds to leave Kala.

"I had… briefly. You may remember Vera of Favoured North? She was my closest friend. She listened to my grieving in the early stages, but after she left for Tagondo I've had no one to listen to my songs of sorrow. Master Oberon and Huron both gave me lectures that I should move on and not think of them… actually… Master Oberon has threatened me with tribulation as of late."

"How can he?" Emille questions.

"It's wrong," Ursai joins.

Lidia continues: "You're right Emille – how can he? Well he's The Master of a colony, that's how. There seems to be no room for empathy, let alone freedom in ruling some four thousand people. But why not?" Lidia proposes.

The four women sit, each nodding their heads or releasing sighs of agreement. It's obvious they begin slowly warming up, Lidia notes it in the way they let their postures slink ever so slightly and the way they eventually unclasp their hands.

So, Lidia goes on: "Aspects of my life have been taken right from under my nose like a carpet being pulled away as I stand upon it, though leaving everything else in its rightful place. However, without that carpet my feet are cold," Lidia says, rubbing her hand across her eyes.

"Me too," Aphria says. The others share hums of agreement in unison, pained expressions upon their faces.

"You all have suffered similar anguish. Please share with us your stories."

"I'll go next," Aphria volunteers.

"Please do," Lidia encourages.

"It was two years ago now that my husband, Cyprus, was murdered and my beautiful son Soyer was taken to Tagondo. It has been the most depressing time in my life. It's torture living day in and day out in the memories – it almost led me to greet the lake. How I wish I could hold my baby in my arms. I think what hurts the most is the knowing, knowing that Soyer has no idea who I am. If he were to see me, he'd think of me as a stranger," Aphria explains with a rattle to her voice.

Lidia reaches for Aphria's hand and offers it a gentle squeeze, "Oh Aphria, I'm sorry for your loss and all that you have gone through. You'd be a truly wonderful mother."

"I question myself if I could ever have another pregnancy, but I don't think I can go through that again," Aphria pauses, "especially knowing the experience of the potential outcome."

"But we have no choice in the matter," Emille notes in worry, tears soaking her cheeks.

"I am nearing the age of change and without a merge agreement in the works, I may get through unnoticed," Aphria explains.

"Master Oberon notices everything. If you think you're under the radar, you're probably next in line on his list of projects," Emille states.

"Why do you say that Emille?" Lidia asks.

"My husband died in The Circle and my baby went with a Tagondian family some four years ago. My lover and I have been secretly planning to escape this place… but we suspect that Master Oberon is on to us…"

“A lover?” Aphria asks unbelieving, Emille nods bashfully. “Where will you guys escape to?”

“We planned to go to beyond the border, to the Iron River.”

“The Iron River? But all the water on the planet is littered with toxins. It’ll be suicide,” Ursai says.

“We want to see what else is out there… to get away from this place. In our desperate minds trying our luck outside the Motherland seems better than staying here. But I recently found out that I’m pregnant – with my lover’s baby.”

“Has this news changed your mind?” Lidia asks.

“No. It’s the news from Master Oberon that has me worried. He has recently requested a merge agreement between myself and Gaffus of Insignificant Dire,” Emille states.

“Have your parents agreed to it?” Ursai wonders.

Emille shrugs, “I haven’t heard just yet. But I can’t stay here with this child growing inside of me.”

Suddenly a woman barges into the shed: “You can too!” she states.

“Hi, can we help you?” Lidia asks, worried about who this intruder is.

“I’m here for the gathering, I heard the whispers,” the woman announces, “You can stay here and hide your pregnancy – I should know, I did it for nine months.”

“What whispers? Is this true? What is your name?” Lidia asks, perplexed, as she quickly stands and closes the shed door.

“Almay Vennesh,” she states.

“How did you hide your pregnancy from The Master?” Aphria asks.

Almay walks onto the blanket, without taking her shoes off as the others had, and sits down. Lidia ignores this and returns to her spot, cautiously intrigued about the newest Tarnished guest.

“I made my own clothing – made them larger. And when I began to show and could hide it no longer, my mother and father found out and kicked me out. I understand the risks involved in hiding someone… I’ve been sleeping behind the school ever since.”

“Why have you come?” Lidia asks.

“Because I too have suffered a great loss,” Almay says.

Lidia hesitates, but ultimately decides to ask: “Why don’t you tell us about it?”

The words begin pouring out of Almay, unfiltered: “The mammoths got my lover and now I’m stuck living with Torant the Terrible,” she blurts out.

Ursai asks: “Not Torant of Insignificant Wells?”

“He’s Favoured now,” Almay notes in a gossip-like tongue.

“How did this take form?” Aphria asks.

“Cole-” Almay begins.

“Cole what?” Lidia interjects.

Almay clears her throat, as if miffed by the interruption, and states: “Cole Of Favoured Wells. He birthed my son, whom I have decided to name Elan. Cole took me to his home to help care for me and the baby and he happens to be staying with Torant for an unfortunate and undetermined amount of time,” Almay explains.

“He birthed your child?” Lidia questions, wrinkling her nose.

“Mhmm. He was practically meant for the job. Listen, I was wondering – do you guys know how one can request a new merge agreement?” Almay inquires.

“Cole is spoken for,” Lidia says, harsher than she intended.

“What, you?” Almay asks, appalled.

“No, Vera North,” Lidia retorts.

“Vera North? You’re joking. That woman has caused more trouble for me than I can stand,” Almay says.

Lidia looks Almay in the eye: “I’m not.”

“That’s ridiculous – Cole can’t be spoken for by a Tagondian. That merge agreement will never happen.”

“That doesn’t matter right now. Anyways, how exactly did you find out about us and this meeting?” Lidia asks, shaking her head as if to rid the unpleasant words Almay pressed upon Cole and Vera.

“I told you – the Whisperer,” Almay states. “I was on the footpaths and heard a wisp in the breeze… I don’t usually pay any mind to them – I actually find it annoying how this voice tends to travel between the trees. But I heard it say something about a group forming to seek justice. I was intrigued and so, here I am.”

So the whispers in the wind led Almay here, maybe that means that Almay should rightfully be here. However, Lidia struggles to ignore the irritation that Almay’s presence seems to bring to The Tarnished.

“Okay. But it’s strange that there are whispers about us as I invited these women by way of secret spoken messages,” Lidia says thoughtfully.

“Maybe someone is on to us,” Aphria suggests.

“Oh no, already?” Emille whines with the palms of her hands covering her cheeks in an instant panic.

“No, a Defender would be here arresting us and taking us to jail if that were true.” Though as Lidia says these words she instantly regrets them – these women don’t need a visual of their possible demise, especially not when all they’ve come for is some clarity in this mixed up world. “I mean… trust me – if someone is on to us, we would know,” Lidia firms.

“You’re probably right. They wouldn’t let us get away with it – not even this one meeting,” Ursai agrees. This fact seems to settle Emille and Aphria.

“If you left letters Lidia, you were likely not careful enough,” Almay taunts.

“I told you, we passed verbal messages – they were the most discreet thing I could arrange for,” Lidia defends herself.

“You’re definitely risking our lives right now,” Almay states.

“If you think lives are on the line then why are you here?” Lidia questions Almay while knowing right well all of their lives are on the line.

However, she also knows that point isn’t fair and she longs to change that fact. Almay stares at Lidia with a troubled smirk upon her face, Lidia decides then that she doesn’t like it one bit.

“I think you should go,” Lidia firms, while simultaneously and internally deciding that The Tarnished need a different way to communicate.

“Fine. I hope you guys don’t get caught,” Almay sings the words as she rises to her feet, “Also, tell your friend Vera that Cole is taken,” she adds with a wink and the release of a kiss blown off her hand.

Almay slowly exits, but slams the door on her way out and the energy of the gathering shifts, the women look to Lidia as if for guidance. Their wide-eye stares and tightly clenched mouths tell her that they are not impressed, she herself is on edge too. *Now I’m going to have to lecture Cole*, she thinks. *Why does he seem to continually make stupid decision after stupid decision?*

"That was odd. I do apologize for the intrusion. I don't know Almay and would've gladly welcomed her into our gathering if it hadn't been for those things she was saying about my friends and our gathering," Lidia notes.

"Vera's gone though, why does it matter?" Aphria asks.

"It is a solid point and a very fair question. Why does it matter?" Lidia muses, "It matters because if Almay is so willing to betray or harm one of us, she cannot be one of us. I must also admit that I am still rooting for Vera and Cole…"

"It has to be over between them, they are forbidden to speak or see one another," Emille says as her brow rises in a worried wrinkle. Lidia reflects how that law didn't stop them that day at the lake.

"Yes, there is a law stating that Kalians are not to socialize or engage with Tagondians. But why? It's a pitiful law," Lidia pauses, "Anyways, I'm fully aware that things for Cole and Vera are beyond complicated."

"I don't believe Almay was able to hide her pregnancy all that time," Ursai speculates, changing the topic slightly.

"It seems risky, but I have heard whispers of others doing the same," Aphria adds.

Emille thoughtfully glances toward the window, "I guess she left the baby with Cole while she came here."

Lidia attempts to bring the women back to the focus of their meeting: "I understand that we all have faced difficult times, it's in our difficult times that we witness the worst in ourselves – right before we get to see the best," Lidia decides that she needs to tell the women just exactly what Master Oberon said to her during their most recent meeting. Perhaps that will refocus their sense of betrayal to their Master, "While my friend Vera was here, it was as if it was easier for me to cope with Kobe and Lilith being gone. However, after Vera left I dove into a deep depression. I could barely work and I barely managed to fulfill my shares. I was spiralling downward into a darkness I've never known before.

"I thought I was just coming out of it, then Master Oberon called me in for a private meeting. He told me to cry in isolation - or to not cry at all - and that it wasn't doing any good for the colony members to see me in such disarray. He threatened tribulation on me if I couldn't keep myself in line." A tear escapes out the side of her eye at the memory and she lets it continue to travel down the side of her cheek – here, with these women, she doesn't have to hide.

They sit with faces that show that they feel her pain, faces that tell her that they are here for her.

"I think there's a valuable lesson we can all take away from this," Lidia adds, "There are so many things in this world of ours that are out of our control, but the one true thing we can control is how we persevere," she notes, almost as if she's speaking to herself, she needs these words as much as the next woman.

There is an empowering, calming shift upon this realization. Yes, it is true – so many laws and lack of freedom are stacked against them, but for now these women need her and she needs them. They need this safe space that will allow them to feel what one wants to feel - what one needs to feel - and in doing so she will gladly salute a splendid *fuck you* to The Masters.

# 77

## Cole of Favoured Wells
## Kala

Almay storms in through the front door, startling Cole as he holds baby Elan – the baby begins to cry from the unsettling noise and Cole's sudden movement.

"Shhh, Almay. What's your deal? Where have you been?" he asks, irritated. "It's okay baby Elan," he whispers.

Seemingly ignoring his mention of Elan, she speaks heatedly and short of breath: "I went to this stupid gathering. A gathering where they told me I was wrong for having Elan and wrong for being with you."

"Where'd you go?" he asks again.

"To a group of women that call themselves The Tarnished. Turns out, they are exclusive."

"What are you doing out past curfew? You're an Insignificant, if they find you they'll take you home to your parents. It wouldn't be all that hard for the Defenders to find out you've had a baby."

"I heard whispers of a rebellion – I had to look into it," Almay replies, "Turns out they were just a couple of depressed widows."

"Maybe you should contact your parents, they might be helpful through this. Your mom – she's birthed a child," Cole suggests.

"I want to stay here with you," she pleads as she sits down beside Cole and Elan on the couch. Her voice has a slight whine to it, one that Cole finds difficult to decipher.

"That's fine, I'm just saying – I haven't birthed a baby before. So, I don't know exactly what you're going through," he adds as he puts Elan down in his basket on the floor, "and I haven't been through losing my lover to a possible mammoth."

Almay slithers her way onto his lap, his pants tighten almost instantly at the gesture against his intentions.

"I said I was looking for a rebellion, not a support group. But I can see you want me to stay here too," she says looking down.

Distracted he says under his breath, "I don't, I don't mind if you stay."

She must take his protrusion as an invitation for she reaches down then, her hand grasps at him, while she forces his gaze to meet hers.

Cole pulls away, "Whoa! You just had a baby."

"I heal quickly. Besides, it's already been a few weeks," she leans in once again.

"You're still healing," he firms.

"I can't wait to have you. I am literally ready to go," she says desperately as she tugs at her clothing and pulls her shirt up over her head.

"Almay…" he says as he removes her hand from behind his neck then picks her up off of his lap and sets her down on the couch beside him. "I hope I didn't give you the wrong impression with helping you and Elan… but I can't do this."

"Of course, you can, it's been awhile for you… I can tell," she says while still breathing heavily. "It shows in the way that your heart pounds against your chest… among other things," she winks.

He swallows, "Yeah, it's been a while. That doesn't mean I'm going to jump at the opportunity," he notes, though he's undecided if he feels offended by her grand assumption.

"I thought it's what you wanted," she says, looking up at him.

"I do want it, but with someone else."

"It's Vera, isn't it?" she ridicules.

"How'd you know?"

"Everyone knows," she scoffs and turns away from him.

Cole can't help it, but his eyes unintentionally linger on her chest – plump and enlarged, ready to fall out of her undergarments. Upon noting his unconscious stare, he quickly diverts his gaze. Almay gets up and walks to her bedroom where several loud noises follow: a knocking on the wall, a slamming of the closet door. Cole gets up and goes into the room.

"Listen, it's not that I wouldn't want to. You're beautiful, graceful… even determined. It's not easy. But I met Vera before I met you and I'm hanging off this hope that I'll be with her again one day."

She pauses her outburst, "You think I'm beautiful?"

"Gorgeous. Far too pretty for the likes of me," he says with a smile.

"That's sweet," she says as she walks over to him and leans her head against his shoulder. "You're the sweetest man I never got to bed."

"You say that like you've taken a lot of men?" he questions, although indifferently.

"Oh… no. Not nearly enough," she smiles a smile that means to look innocent.

He likes her smile, the way her thick lips move and part as they curve upward. She can even gracefully move her body in such a way that would drive any man out of his pants. She's right, it is hard to turn her offer down – what other man in his right mind would? Surely none. Unless of course they are already in a merge agreement or those that follow The Master's laws religiously – most seem to.

Even though his heart pounds against his chest cavity and the pulsating at his pants has yet to subside, he knows it's the right thing to do. He also reasons that she should be focusing on caring for her son, not taking men to bed.

"Besides, you should be seeking a merge agreement with someone closer to your age," he suggests, even though following one's twentieth birthday age isn't a factor in this world – he simply says it as a means to take her focus off of him.

"I've had younger, and in my experience a well-aged man knows how to please a woman," she says and she stands without her shirt on still. She begins to step toward him as if her determination to have him has not been laid to rest yet.

"Okay, well, I'm going to go for a walk," he says in a hurry as he turns and practically runs out of the house. His breathing quickens and once he gets far enough away from Torant's house he takes a slower pace to stabilize it. There is no way that he can live everyday like this, on edge and uncertain of when she may try to pounce once again, like a lioness in heat. But he isn't going to be her lion, he is going to be a giraffe – calm and with the kick of a thousand men, as a giraffe can fend off a lioness any day, he reasons.

*"Be watchful of The Cobra,"* the whispers warn through the trees.

He tries to ignore the whispers though – there is no reason for him to fear anything, especially the likes of some person named after a reptile.

Cole walks the footpaths until he reaches the colony centre. The buildings look different at night, when everything is still and lit by solar lights. Can he not just leave right now? Run to Vera and rescue her from Tagondo. If he sees Vera this very night he could tell her his secret, the one that has been pecking away at his chest since the day they met. He also debates in his mind if she will ever know, or tell him for that matter, what may have happened between her and Cain while she was stuck in the cave with him.

A noise interrupts his thoughts, a thumping sound as he stands in the middle of the colony centre. Quietly and patiently he waits for the noise to sound again, one thing that serves him from all of his years in pursuing is that his ears are well trained. When he hears the noise a third time he can tell that it's coming from the school.

He walks over to the front door of the building and of course they keep it locked after school hours so he needs to find a way to get in. He creeps to the side of the building where the windows are low enough to be within reach – it's stuck but not locked. Cole pushes his fingertips onto the glass, gripping hard as his hands shake – eventually with enough force he slides the window open.

He climbs into a classroom – which one, he can't be sure. It's dark and he doesn't know his way around the school so he pauses to listen again. The thumping continues and so he follows his ears, cautious not to trip or bump into anything – a careful intention to not notify anyone of his presence. He holds his arms out in front of his body, allowing his hands to sense objects before he may collide with them. Years of wandering the Tagondian forest at night must've allowed his vision in the dark to become more trained for he can make out the objects around him in the darkness.

The thumping grows louder then, until he enters a classroom and can now hear the rattling of a doorknob coming from the back of the classroom. He grabs an item off of a desk and tosses it on the floor in a crash as a means to observe the following reaction of the thumping behind the door. The thumping stops for a moment and then begins to pound harder than before. Muffled screams call from the other side of the door and Cole instantly runs toward the back of the classroom. His hands guide him to the door's handle and he opens it.

"Hello? Who's there?" Cole calls into what seems to be a storage closet.

"Cole? Is that you?" a familiar voice questions in the darkness.

"Atticus?" Cole asks.

"Yes, it's me," Atticus replies. "Go to the Educator's desk, I know Educator Barlow keeps a flashlight in there."

"Ok," Cole says as he turns and walks to the desk. "What are you doing in here?" he calls back to Atticus.

"I'm not in here by choice. James Barlow locked me in here. Ulyd too."

"Who's Ulyd?" Cole asks.

"My best friend."

"Are you both okay?"

"Yes," Ulyd whispers.

Cole returns to the closet once again and shines the light at the two boys whose faces are swollen and red with blood.

"Oh shit, what did he do to you?" Cole asks as he bends down to help untie the restraints that are tied around the boys' wrists.

"He beat us," Atticus says.

"Who beats two teenagers and locks them in a closet?" Cole inquires.

Atticus adjusts his position. "A bad man," he huffs as Cole helps him to his feet.

"He isn't really all that bad," Ulyd says in defence.

"He has you brainwashed – he's evil," Atticus coughs.

"What does Educator Barlow teach?" Cole asks.

"The colony laws," Atticus says with a raised eyebrow all the while acknowledging the irony.

"More like human mutilation. This guy must be messed up, he's breaking laws left, right and centre," Cole says in amazement as he too helps Ulyd stand.

"We need to go before he comes back. He will probably be back soon to check on us," Atticus notes.

"How long have you been in here?" Cole asks.

"I found Ulyd last night after school let out for the weekend."

"What was he going to do with you guys when school starts back up Monday morning?" Cole questions.

"I doubt he thought that far ahead," Atticus states.

Cole shakes his head, "Come on, come with me. You'll be safe at Torant's house."

They quietly make their way back outside - exiting through the same window on their way out - Cole closes it behind them. Light footed in their jaunt, Cole guides the boys in a hurried fashion.

"Who do we have here?" a Defender says as he approaches the three on their walk to Favoured Wells. The man grips tightly at the club in his hands.

"With the earth, sir," Cole nods.

"May we be cleansed," the Defender replies.

Cole grasps his crest and faces it toward the night guard to show his Favoured identity then subtly smacks Atticus' arm to do the same. As Atticus holds his crest out for the Defender to inspect, Ulyd catches on and follows suit – the shine of their silver reflects the guard's solar light.

"All Favoured here, sir," Cole notes.

"So I see. What's all this?" the Defender asks, gesturing to the blood smears across the teenagers' faces.

"I-" Ulyd begins to speak.

Cole interrupts him: "I was working in the greenhouses when I heard some commotion going on outside. That's when I found these too slugger-heads beating on one another," Cole says.

"That is strictly prohibited," The Defender responds, his brow creases.

"That's what I said. They were trying to help guard the colony from mammoths. But I told the-"

"That he's the Mammoth Slayer!" Atticus interjects.

"The Mammoth Slayer? *You're* the Mammoth Slayer?" the Defender asks, with a brief flicker to his eyes as he inspects them once again.

The Defender shines his flashlight across their faces and extremities looking for something more that seems off, anything will do. It only has to be a minor suspicion that can get them arrested, reported and placed in the jail – especially as they are out past curfew, even though it's allowed for Favoured it's still monitored strictly.

"Yes, I am," Cole sighs, never wanting to use his mammoth-slaying ability to get out of anything. "But we're just on our way home now," he adds.

They stand in silence a moment, perspiration beads across Cole's forehead. He feels responsible for the safety and care of these two boys – he doesn't want anything more terrible to happen to them, especially nothing that could go against their family records.

The Defenders have a way about them that always makes you feel as though you've done something wrong with just a single glance. One thing is for certain though, Cole knows it's best for these two that this Defender doesn't find out the real reason behind their blood-smudged faces.

"Very well then," the Defender finally says, though Cole argues in his mind that he thinks there's the slightest disappointment in his voice at the lack of rebellion.

The man gestures with his flashlight for them to continue on their way. Cole releases a quick sigh of relief and nods to the guard as they continue.

However, Cole can't help but feel irked by Atticus' careless addition to the conversation with the Defender, he walks in silence the rest of the way. For all he knows they could wake up to Defenders on their doorstep the following morning, claiming that the Mammoth Slayer thinks he's above the law.

When Cole and the two sore teenagers make it back to Torant's house, Torant is there looking quite displeased, which isn't out of the ordinary. The house is dark except for a glimmering candle on the kitchen table, which is where Torant sits, the rest of the house is quiet, Almay and baby Elan appear to be in bed.

"Why have you brought more trouble into my house?"

"Look at them Torant, they've been beaten."

"Beaten for their own stupidity. All people should be beaten for poor choices. Why should I have to be inconvenienced by it?"

"I didn't know what else to do with them. Have a heart."

"It's difficult to have a heart Cole, when all one has is a fluttering mind," Torant sneers.

"Well, try to understand then. We need to keep them here at least for the night. I'll take them to their rightful houses tomorrow."

"I can see I have no say in the matter," Torant says as he raises his slender body to his feet.

Cole notices that Torant's stature is deceiving for he is not very tall, average height one would say, but it's in his thinly framed limbs that makes him appear tall despite his muscles being arguably concave. His jet-black hair is also thin and as always slicked back on his head emphasizing his pale blue eyes that pierce in whichever direction they look. To most he's an eerie presence in the colony, but to Cole he's simply odd – a geek of sorts that plays with dolls and says abstract things.

Nothing too specific comes out the mouth of Torant of Favoured Wells. This aspect reminds him of Murdina.

"Who was their captor?" Torant asks, though he asks the question in such a presumptuous way. He must already know the answer. Still, Cole humours him.

"Educator Barlow, do you know him?"

"Yes, I know him, though not personally," Torant says.

Cole notices Atticus and Ulyd awkwardly standing still by the door, like a couple of terror-stricken deer. He walks over and guides the two boys to the couch.

"You'll rest here for the night," Cole informs them, then turns to address Torant in the kitchen once again, "What can we do about this? There's got to be some way we can bring this to Master Oberon's attention and have Educator Barlow held accountable?"

"There is one thing we can do," Torant says with a sigh.

"What is it?" Cole asks.

"You're not going to like it."

"Spit it out."

"Kill James Barlow," Torant indifferently suggests.

Cole steps back, "I'm not going to kill a man."

"Not yet anyway."

"Any other *brilliant* ideas?"

"None aside from that. So, what will it be Cole? Kill James Barlow or have him come back to seek revenge?" Torant says with piercing eyes.

"You know, you can really talk some bullshit when you want to."

"Be that as it may, you must decide which course of action you will take, will you choose life or death? And whose?"

^

It's an unimaginable thought that in choosing life for himself means choosing death for someone else, but not just anyone else – James of Favoured Barlow. A man whom Cole hasn't even had the pleasure - or displeasure, depending on one's perspective - of meeting. Yes, he is an Educator, one of the Favoured, but does that mean he's allowed to abuse a couple of teenage boys? He needs to pay for his crimes, but at the very least and for the time being, he needs to be confronted.

So the next morning, before everyone wakes, Cole ventures to Favoured Barlow. Atticus explained the previous night that Barlow recently moved to an empty cabin that sits deep in the woods on the north side – a place where he can live away from the suicidal home that plagued the colony since Master Oberon set fire to his old house some weeks earlier.

As Cole approaches the property he notes that this new house, although it's anything but new, is quite tiny and placed amongst the trees. The roof is covered in moss, which makes the cabin greener rather than brown – the trees above create plenty of shade allowing the moss enough moisture to flourish. The mossy roof is also scattered with fallen fragments of the different trees that hang above it, clearly Barlow doesn't care about curb appeal as his home looks quite unkempt. Trees have a way of doing that though, dropping particles and fragments at even the prospect of a breeze.

Cole marches up the wooden stairs, which have begun the breaking-down process with loose nails protruding out past the stair boards. Years of exposure to water and no sunlight to dry them have left the deck boards feeling soft upon his step. The place looks practically ready to fall over, but anyone would avoid living in the confines of a suicidal home in comparison. He reaches out and knocks on the front door while nervously fiddling with the dagger in his hand – a makeshift one that indeed could find him trouble, it's the sole weapon he has kept without anyone's knowledge.

As Cole awaits Barlow's answer, he reflects on how he fought off and killed a mammoth, a couple actually, with all but his lucky dagger and one with his bow and arrow. Sadly, he doesn't have his lucky dagger anymore – still he is pretty sure he can handle James Barlow if it comes down to it. Cole knows that people like James Barlow, evil people, do unpredictable things. It is in their pleasure to catch others off guard. It is in their pleasure to not play fair.

A man of average build opens the door and to Cole's surprise he looks just like everyone else in Kala. He wears clean, well-made clothes and his brown hair is short on top of his head, nicely combed and his face is clean-shaven.

"To what do I owe this visit?" he asks in an accent that sounds proper, elegant even, as it rolls off of his tongue. *Like Issac*, he thinks, though Issac is rightfully the opposite of elegant.

"James Barlow?" Cole asks.

"Yes. Educator Barlow," he replies with a skeptical glare.

"I don't want any trouble, but I've come to let you know that I found Atticus and Ulyd," Cole states, making sure to keep a steady eye on Barlow while simultaneously studying his surroundings in his peripherals.

It's just the two of them out here and the sun has yet to rise in the east, which means it's dark – dark enough that the mammoths could still be roaming.

Something changes in James' face then, it contorts and his mouth opens in a grimace. He closes his eyes and his brow wrinkles. He brings his fingers up to his temples and holds them there for a moment.

"You best leave newcomer," James snarls, "If you know what's good for you."

Cole takes a step back, "I'm not here to threaten you." *At least for now*. "I'm just here to make sure this doesn't happen again."

"If I hear whispers that you've spoken to anyone, I'll have your head," James says through gritted teeth then slams the door shut.

Cole backs down the stairs, intently keeping his gaze on the front door. He doesn't turn his body away from the house until he's about twenty yards away, at which point he turns and runs – he has it in his mind that his turned back is his weakness. Even though he can hear an animal approaching from 30 yards away, he hasn't dealt with this kind of animal before. Then he thinks of Cain of Favoured Fenwick and realizes that perhaps he has.

It's important that Cole makes it back to Torant's house before everyone leaves for the day, so he runs quickly through the footpaths leading back to House of Favoured Wells. When he walks in the door the four are sitting at the kitchen table having breakfast.

"Cole," Atticus calls, "I had the weirdest dream last night. You were a mammoth."

Torant drops his fork and it slams against his plate of eggs then falls to the floor. Torant awkwardly collects it without uttering a word. When the commotion passes Cole finally responds to Atticus.

"Did I hunt any humans in it?" he laughs half-heartedly.

"Yes. And James Barlow tried to kill you."

"Well, I'm pretty sure James has the guts of a squirrel – he could never take on a mammoth. But, did he kill me?"

"No. You killed him. I woke up covered in sweat."

"Ah," Cole squints his eyes and swats at the air nonchalantly, "That explains it, take a shower. You'll learn that no woman appreciates it when you don't."

"You know what women appreciate, Cole?" Almay asks far too playfully for his liking, he laughs a nervous laugh while the other three look at each other quizzically.

"I went to see James Barlow this morning, I told him that I found you two boys," Cole states.

"You did? What did he say?" Ulyd asks seemingly mortified.

"He threatened me not to tell anyone or he'll have my head."

"You better listen to him Cole, he sticks to his word," Ulyd says.

"He is a troubled man, troubled people do inexcusable things," Atticus adds.

Cole rests his hands on Atticus and Ulyd's shoulders, "Well, you guys shouldn't have any more trouble from him. If you do, let me know. In the meantime, keep your distance."

"We can't not go to school," Ulyd replies.

"Okay, so only go into the class when other students are in the classroom too – and no staying late, even if he asks you to," Cole instructs, the two nod in understanding.

After breakfast Cole walks the boys to their respective homes. Atticus insists they tell their parents that they had a run-in with a mammoth and that Cole saved them, but there is no way in hell that Cole is going to take part in spreading a story like that, he deems they will stick to the story they told the Defender – that Atticus and Ulyd were caught up in a brawl. Though it goes against his greater judgement, he understands that it's best they continue the same lie, especially while the boys are still in school with Barlow – he doesn't want Barlow to come after them a second time.

After dropping Ulyd off and making sure he gets inside safely, they soon arrive at House of Favoured North and Atticus invites Cole in.

"Cole, oh my goodness," Ida says as she embraces him in a hug.

"Hello," he pauses. He isn't sure what he's to call her, or is he sure if he should say the whole 'with the earth' thing that everyone seems to say to one another. He decides he'll just follow Ida's cues.

"Ida. Call me Ida..." she beams, "So, this is the famous Mammoth Slayer. I wondered when you were going to come by. Gosh, you are so rugged and masculine. But, you've killed a mammoth so one would expect you to be nothing shy of burly."

Cole merely smiles, unsure of how to respond.

"So, tell me about Vera," Ida eagerly asks. Cole assumes, much like Atticus, Ida is probably wondering what life has been like for Vera in Tagondo. He doesn't want to tell them the nitty-gritty of it all though, it will only make them worry more and there is nothing they can do, at least not until he rescues her.

"She... well-" Cole begins.

Atticus cuts him short though: "Mom, I already told you everything he said about how Vera is."

"I know honey, I just... I like talking about her," Ida explains.

"Her favourite thing was watching the sunsets from my lookout," Cole interjects.

"She does love sunsets," Ida sighs.

"More than I think she lets on," Cole chuckles.

They laugh together as they reminisce and share stories of the woman who means different things to each of them.

"Oh Cole, I want to give you something," Ida says then wanders out of the kitchen.

She reappears with a silver object resting in her hand, "Here," she says holding out her hand.

He opens his hand, unsure of what is soon to be his, but ready to accept whatever it is.

She delicately places the object in his palm, "I know that Vera's not here… and well, you two haven't merged just yet… But I know that one day…" Ida's speech veers off. "I want you to have this. It was hers." Ida holds out a Favoured North crest.

"But Ida-" Cole begins to say.

Atticus interrupts: "You think Master Oberon will let them merge one day, Mother?" he looks at Ida with a confused expression.

"Ida, I don't think I can accept this," Cole says slowly, for accepting this makes them all Offenders: Ida for gifting it, Cole for accepting it and Atticus for witnessing it and not reporting it – he's also uncertain how Vera would feel about this.

Cole stares down at the North family crest in his hand: a shiny, grey steel instrument crafted by one who bends steel. In shape it is entirely unlike his old Favoured Pollard crest nor is it like his crest of Favoured Wells. This one is in the shape of a compass, there is one larger point than the rest and at the tip of it sits an "N" signalling both the family name and cardinal direction of north. Although, it doesn't act as a regular compass – it's meant for displaying upon one's shirt just like all the other family crests in The Motherland. However, to Cole it holds such significance beyond just it's tinted charm, it represents Vera of Favoured North.

"Cole, I want you to have it. She *will* understand."

"I'm, I'm not sure what to say."

"Say you'll wear our crest."

"I would," he says as he watches her smile fade to disappointment. "I mean, I will. I'm honoured," he states, regretting the words the instant they leave his mouth.

How can he wear the North crest and not be an Offender in the colony? But how can he let Ida down – the mother of the woman he cares for? He can wear it under his jacket, while still keeping his Favoured Wells crest displayed at the very front of it. At least in some ways then he's able to keep his end of the agreement.

He reaches down and lifts his jacket, attaching the North crest on the fabric of his t-shirt. It has been several weeks since he said goodbye to his father's crest - the eastern phoebe - but he did it because he had to. He isn't a Tagondian any longer, he reminds himself of that. Cole looks to Ida and Atticus with appreciation, noting how his crest now matches theirs. His part-time crest, he'll think of it as – at least for now. Ida's mouth forms a smile that stretches from ear to ear in contentment. He exhales.

"Mother, I don't understand… you allowed that dreadful ceremony to take place all those months ago and didn't step in to break the laws then – why now?" Atticus asks with a perplexed look.

"I'm just trying to make Cole feel welcome, darling," and with a squeeze of Atticus' cheek Ida turns and heads for the kitchen.

78

# IDA OF FAVOURED NORTH
# KALA

Ida watches as her Favoured North family crest reflects the low light that a candle sitting upon a wooden crate offers. It is cool and damp in the cellar, and though she has been coming down here for almost two decades, the dampness isn't the bother – The Masters are. The way they designed the colonies was out of their own selfishness, their own desires. She needs help if she is to make a difference – they all do.

And so, that's why Ida has chosen Cole. If he has interest in her daughter and her daughter in him then there must be something of value in him. But she isn't one to trust without reason - much like Vera she needs proof - cue giving Cole the Favoured North family crest. She knew Cole would of course be honoured in being gifted such an item and that he'd be stupid enough to wear it – and although it seems drastic, she knows a tribulation will be the result.

The laws of The Motherland ensure The Master's control over crest distribution and the moment Cole is seen in possession of the North crest, tribulation will be ordered. But it mustn't be just any act of rebellion to get him there, it has to be a choice, one he makes on his own. However unfair, it is necessary. Ida figures it will be a fair tribulation for wearing a wrongfully assigned crest – nothing too barbaric, a whipping perhaps. Though she sees it as a necessary sacrifice, his pain for her trust – he can handle it. She may have to lie once he gets caught, but truth be told, she's been lying for years – at least since they came to The Motherland and especially these past few months.

Everyone in Kala thinks they know her: a distraught widow, and although she is both distraught and a widow, she keeps her head. Besides, no one truly knows her, not from a hole in the ground and for now she'd like to keep it that way. At any rate, eventually she'll need to offer Cole an explanation for all of this - including a reason for breaching his privacy - and in time she will and in turn he will offer her forgiveness. It is all quite clever, she thinks, planting a microphone on the crest she gave him. Over the years Hendrix taught Ida many tricks, one of them being how to rewire old electronics and bury a microphone into melted steel.

Ida has been able to listen in on Cole during several occasions now. Almay seems to be of some concern – Ida will need to find a way to get her out of Favoured Wells. Distractions will do Cole no good.

As if by pure luck, as she sits in the damp cellar, a conversation begins between Cole and Torant: Cole admits that Atticus has made him aware of the dire water situation and that the water is running out. This is a piece of information that Ida has already calculated herself, though she has told no one. A sense of pride for being the mother to the son that figured this out on his own beams through her as she listens to Cole reiterate it all to Torant. Atticus has apparently laid it all out for Cole – six months to live.

Cole finishes his speech and Torant responds: "We need to focus on the antitoxin, now more than ever. We will tend to Vera once that is sound."

"Hell no, I'm working on a plan. I'm going to go get Vera and bring her back here. I need her help with the lab," Cole retorts.

Ida notes that Cole's response - above all else - is to help Vera. Even though this confession isn't enough to earn her trust just yet – the upcoming meet will be a true testament. It's easy to spout words of any form, but actions are the true indication of who a person is – and she knows exactly the kind of person that she needs. He will put Vera before his own life, yes, but will he put his own life on the line so that the water may be cleansed? That is the kind of ally she is looking for – to Ida that is as good as gold.

# 79

## Vera of Insignificant Cannelle
## Unknown

Vera wakes from nothingness, it doesn't feel as though she had been sleeping and yet her eyes squint and open in mere slits of haze and fog. She tries to glance at her surroundings, but there is a weight to her body that is unexplainable. She can't move, though still she tries. Through her minuscule efforts her arm nags – the one she speculates that she broke from her altercation with Cain. *Cain,* she thinks. How long has it been since she saw him in the forest? It feels like days, weeks. She doesn't know. She notes that she now feels nothing upon thinking of him. Not a stir of fear or anger. It could be the fog that encompasses her conscious thoughts though.

There's movement, it's coming from beyond her. She can hear something in the distance, though it's muffled. Her left hand searches and barely feels the soft granules of something below her. It trickles through her fingers, cool and damp. Dirt. Someone appears in her sight then, a figure crouches down over her body – they're wearing a black mask.

"Ple…" she tries to speak, but there is an instantaneous heavy feeling that prevents her from being able to articulate anything more.

The person, her captor or whoever it is, adjusts something that's attached to her arm and her eyes close again, she returns into the nothingness.

# 80

# ATTICUS OF FAVOURED NORTH KALA

There is something to be said about time viewed in its linear form, infinite and yet constricting. For Atticus, there seems to simply be not enough, which is where the constricting part comes in. Maybe it appears that way to everyone – not having enough time, he doesn't know. How can one have an infinite supply of something and yet, feel it thinning as evident as the trees in the fall. Still, the way the weeks soar by in a hurried blur fuel him with a fire to move faster, and yet he feels that if he stops then motion sickness will encompass him, as though perhaps moving constantly with time is the thing to do. So, he works intently, learning alongside Rumi. He is still waiting for her to explain why she suddenly began listening to the whispers.

Through the intangible essence of time Atticus attends classes, works in the lab and during his sparse instances of calm, he forages. However, those instances have been brief, so much so that when he has the opportunity to forage he runs, only now he runs not because it feels freeing or because Vera is there for the chase, but because time is constricting him.

Atticus walks toward the school as his thoughts fall upon James Barlow and the notion that he is a murderer. He tells himself that Barlow likely confessed this to him and Ulyd as a means to scare them – to keep them from talking. But what should one do with such information? Then there is the knowing that the colonies will eventually be out of fresh drinking water. Which knowledge is more important? James Barlow could take lives, just as the water can. Atticus argues that the water will take more in comparison.

If Educator Ferris knows about the water, it seems likely that Master Oberon does – surely he knows everything that goes on in the lab. Although, Atticus can neither be sure nor can he conclude if he should approach Master Oberon on the subject matter – on either subject matter. But he can't go to The Master armed with just his words. All the more reason he needs to figure out what the antitoxin is and who is in possession of it. He just has no idea how. He needs to figure it out sooner rather than later because in a few months, they will all be dead. There is no definite timeline, but the end is coming.

Atticus decides that regardless of the past abuse that he suffered alongside Ulyd, he won't let it wear on him – he does not have enough time to worry about the past. He has chosen to move forward though, still, at a safe distance from James Barlow. He will not allow fears to dictate his behaviour, instead he will focus on his goal: to gain knowledge of the antitoxin. As he believes, like his Father: in knowledge, there is power. Some knowledge is meant to be kept to one's self, whereas other knowledge is meant to be passed on – he isn't sure yet which is which.

"*Knowledge,*" the whispers sough.

He hears it, the whispers have repeatedly wisped the word in his ear on and off for weeks. He nods his head in acknowledgement. *Yes, you're there, whoever you are*, he says to himself.

There's a part of him that wonders if it has been Torant, The Shadow, all along. Who else knows all there is to know about the colony and its people? He assumes that the whispers know all, as they always seem to know just precisely where he is at any given moment – or someone follows him down the footpaths, which is more likely. One would think that would cause a scare, or at least some form of unsettlement but it doesn't in Atticus, for he has already come to terms with the knowing that he is never alone. In actuality, it offers him comfort – so long as it isn't Digger.

^

Atticus enters the school with thoughts still wandering when a hand gently grasps his elbow.

"Have you had any more visits from Educator Barlow?" Ulyd asks as he falls into step with Atticus.

"No. I just do my work and get the hell out. What about you?" Atticus responds, still slightly unfocussed.

"Yes, he's been asking me to meet him after school," Ulyd admits.

"And you agreed?" Atticus asks in disbelief, Ulyd nods his head in defeat. "I don't understand, what is this power he holds over you?"

"I don't want to talk about it."

"Come on Ulyd, I already know it's something weird and offending," Atticus widens his eyes in all seriousness. Ulyd releases a sigh that seems to cause his chest to concave dramatically.

"Fine… but you can't tell anyone. I mean it, not anyone," Ulyd says as he looks hesitantly around for listening ears. Atticus waits a moment, but just a moment for he can't stand to wait any longer.

"Well?" Atticus pushes.

Ulyd's eyes find the ground, "James Barlow… wants to merge with my mother."

"He what?"

"Yeah."

“So what does that have to do with us? Cole risked his life for you when he went to talk to Barlow. And the one thing he asked us not to do was to meet with him.”

“I know, I’m sorry. It’s just, I caught him in relations with my mother a couple months ago… before Vera left, and since then he finds any reason to lock me in his closet and beat my ass red.”

“I don’t understand…”

“He doesn’t want me to tell The Master. Don’t you see? If I were to tell Master Oberon that he is courting my mother, Barlow would be an Offender and face tribulation.”

“Still doesn’t make sense why he beats you.”

“To stop me from talking. And I won’t talk. Every time he takes me in there I can’t sit for a week afterwards.”

“Does Rumi know?”

“Of course not.”

“You have to tell her Ulyd. You have to tell Master Oberon. What if James Barlow gets a merge agreement with your mother… do you really think the beatings are going to stop?”

“He promises that they’ll stop once they get an agreement.”

“They’ll never stop!” Atticus shouts at his friend louder than he intends, for he should know, he’s thought the same of Digger. *They never stop.*

^

That evening chaos ensues. Atticus and Ida are home before the curfew siren rings when a woman’s shrill scream sounds through the footpaths and filters in through the cracks of their windows.

“A dead body!” a voice yells. Atticus looks out the front window as two people run by his field of vision, their hands smeared in red.

“Mother, what’s going on?” he asks.

Ida appears by Atticus’ side and glances out the window, “I don’t know,” she says then hurries out the front door to scan the area, Atticus follows her. Several colony people roam the footpaths, a sense of panic painted on their frames.

Atticus stands with his hands resting on the wooden railing, “What should we do?” A shift in Ida’s step shows her nerves.

“We should go inside, lock the doors,” she instructs.

“Mother, why would we hide when we don’t even know what’s happened? Let’s go to Torant’s, he’ll know something.”

“No. Absolutely not,” Ida states.

“Why not? Maybe Torant will be able to give us some insight.”

Atticus can’t understand why Ida holds so much animosity toward Torant – he’s never even seen them speak to one another. Atticus looks at his mother, she is such a pretty woman. Her hair has begun its transition as light grey strands replace their brown counterparts, though it doesn’t make her look any older, only more beautiful. In many ways, change in one’s body signifies time and experience on this earth. The wrinkles that form on her glowing, freckled skin are predominant around her eyes and mouth, and when she laughs their lines are accentuated, like a fish creating ripples in a lake with its fins. However, she’s not laughing on this day or on many days as of recent. Instead, her brows raise in worry, her eyes widen with concern.

Ida appears to disregard Atticus' suggestion and paces the front deck as if she's waiting for something. *What are you waiting for?* he thinks, for there's something about sitting idle in such a precarious time that seems senseless. He loves and trusts his mother dearly; however, he is itching to take action – any form of action will do at this point.

Atticus speaks more sternly this time, impatience tickling the edge of his voice, "Mother."

Ida expresses inaudible mumbles of concern – a steady hum from the other side of the deck. The hum resembles the bees, they could be building another nest at the side of the deck for all he knows. After all it is mid summer, nearing the end of July – the warmth is at its peak and so too are the bees. Her eyes flutter from side to side, though her face remains parallel to the deck.

"Mother," he speaks louder this time. A sudden jerk of her head and her eyes dart toward Atticus.

"What-what?" she stammers.

"I'm going to go to Torant's." He attempts to look her in the eyes, though they continue to flicker back and forth. A wonder of how she isn't getting motion sickness crosses his mind. At least she stops pacing. He continues: "Everything is going to be okay. You go inside, lock the door. Don't come out until I knock three times."

Her eyes come to a halt and she glances up at him, "Okay," she whispers in both surprise and defeat.

Atticus, though surprised by her sudden mood shift, guides Ida in through the front door and closes it behind her. It will take him no less than ten minutes to sprint to Torant's – he's fast. Once he hears the door lock he begins his jog down the deck stairs and heads for the footpaths.

Screams continue to echo off the trees, he ignores them. It's all too theatrical in his mind, besides, he can't afford the distraction. As he approaches the colony centre he sees that there is a mob of people forming a circle, their heads are turned toward the ground. Atticus pushes his way through the crowd – he needs to see what everyone is gaping at.

When he makes it to the centre the marks of blood catch his eyes first, but someone other than the corpse has painted it. Theres a body lying on the ground face up, with lines of red spread around a ten-foot radius. It soon becomes evident to Atticus that the body is that of a man, his clothes are torn to shreds and his stomach has been sliced open. His neck has also been strangled, because of the bruises that have been left there. As Atticus scans over the face, which is pale and swollen, he knows it to be none other than Theodus of Favoured Harrow.

"It must've been a mammoth attack," one comments. *Or James Barlow.*

"Oh, we must all get indoors. Right away," another says. Kalians aren't unfamiliar with the sight of blood, for they see it fairly regularly at the ceremonies – in that context it has become routine, expected even, like eating breakfast. However, finding a corpse in the middle of the colony is certainly not an ordinary occurrence here. At least not up to this point.

Atticus speaks to the crowd: "Everyone should get inside. It's not safe out here right now," and without further pause he leaves the mob and continues in the direction of Torant's house.

He jogs down the footpaths on the south side of the colony centre, as it's generally quieter on that side. Soon nature is all that surrounds him – he is out of the colony centre's sight, and so he slows to catch his breath. In the stillness he hears a noise, a grunting of sorts. It sparks his curiosity and naturally he follows the sound.

As he moves closer toward the grunts, he is fairly certain that they belong to a person. Atticus peers around the base of a wide oak tree and his suspicions are proven right. He notes the white flesh of a man's ass, some fifteen feet away, moving back and forth – pinning a woman up onto the tree behind her. It is then that the grunts make complete sense to Atticus. *But what an odd time to be partaking in such activities... When a man has just been found dead,* he thinks. *Suspect number three: Digby of Favoured Espen.*

The last eighteen years of knowing Digger and being subject to his abuse is reason enough for Atticus to consider him a suspect. Now, combine that with Digger's current state of affairs amidst an uproar in the colony – it's pretty suspicious. *However, there is a chance that Digger and his lover don't know about the body in the colony centre,* he argues internally. But they are close enough to the colony centre to at the very least overhear the commotion. Even if they don't know what has happened, anyone can tell by the screams that something troubling is taking place. Would one not go to inspect or seek to help? Apparently not these two lustful creatures as they continue to ignore the shrill sounds and instead celebrate their bodies.

Atticus decides that it's highly disrespectful to fornicate in the forest – a child could walk by at the change of a minute. His eyes focus on the woman whose face is knotted in pleasure. He knows that face – it's Surni, the wife of Kala's now deceased doctor, Theodus of Favoured Harrow.

The hairs on Atticus' arms stand. It seems far too coincidental that these two should be here right now. Then he remembers the flirtatious look Surni gave him some weeks ago. *Would she seek pleasure in me if I were the one to come across her in the forest alone? Or did Digger pursue her?* It's hard not to wonder how two entirely different people come together under such odd circumstances.

The woman's sighs of contentment continue as the two bodies collaborate effortlessly. Her face is so pretty, especially when all dishevelled. Atticus' pants begin to tighten and he can't stop it – so the experience goes for teenage boys and their fluctuating hormones. He panics and places his hands down over his pants to hide the protruding mass at his front, forgetting that it's more pertinent that he himself not be seen. The change in his focus causes him to lose his footing and he trips over a stump.

"Digby!" Surni whispers to her lover in concern.

"What?" He continues to pump her body against the tree trunk. Would he stop if she asked him too? It seems debatable.

"Someone's there," she says.

"Huh?" Digger turns his head and his eyes instantly lock with Atticus'. Atticus jumps to his feet in a hurry.

"It's okay, I didn't see anything," Atticus calls.

"Goon!" yells Digger furiously while pulling his pants back up around his waist.

"I have to go, excuse me," Atticus says as he turns with the intent to flee.

However, Digger is quick, always a step ahead of Atticus. He approaches Atticus from behind, wraps his giant paws around either side of his arms and swiftly throws Atticus into a large pine tree. If Digger doesn't one day become a Defender, Atticus would be surprised because his size for a teenager his age goes unmatched. And though Atticus is tall, Digger is tall with thick, dense muscles that compliment his height.

Expecting another blow to the head, which is Digger's speciality, Atticus cradles his skull with his hands and arms. Instead, Atticus watches, from the corner of his eye, Digger sticking his hand down into his own pants pocket and suddenly holding something up in his fist. Curiosity seems to outweigh Atticus's fear briefly, for he removes his shielding hands from his head and looks up at Digger with inquisitive eyes.

Digger looks down at Atticus, an evil glare to his soulless eyes, "If this doesn't kill you, you'll be half the pitiful person you are now," he says then opens his hand and lets fall a powdered substance that Atticus can only assume is intended to take his life.

Atticus reacts, moving his hands to cover his face, though he doesn't move fast enough. Particles of some sort fly at his face. It happens so quickly and he can't make out if the particles are a dark green or black. A coating covers his eyes, like the way pollen collects on the surface of the lake. No amount of rubbing or blinking removes the powder and it stings fiercely, as if his eyes are being held to fire – a moth to a flame.

There is a sort of panic that urges him to scratch his eyes. He rubs his fingertips and nails across his skin furiously. If he wasn't in his right mind he would claw them right out of their sockets. He's willing to bet that's the idea.

*"Be still,"* the Whisperer says.

Atticus hears the whisper, it reminds him that he's not alone, a sudden sense of stillness encases him then and he breathes through the pain. He rubs his shoes together in a restless motion, a helpless motion. He hears nothing but the pulsating in his own ears of his blood pressure skyrocketing, and yet the rest of his body lies still. He falls back on an internal chant, merely out of habit: *In experience comes clarity,* he thinks. The chant seems to help calm him.

Slowly the burning sensation that nags at his eyes fades into a sharp ache. Though 'a sharp ache' isn't nearly enough to describe this kind of pain – perhaps a rusted-metal dagger to the cornea would be more accurate. *Or to the testicles*, he thinks. Through it all he can feel his eyelids swelling. Atticus breathes intentionally large intakes of air and his exhales release wheezes of pain. Eventually the ache subsides altogether and he is present once again. He can smell the earthy scent of the moist ground that he lies upon; he can feel the dampness that lingers on the grass; he can hear that Digger and Surni have reconvened about their business. The sounds of sex fill his ears, and if he listens closely he can still hear, faintly in the distance, commotion at the colony centre.

Through all the scents, feelings and sounds that he is experiencing, it's hard to ignore what he is missing: his sight. He can't seem to tell if his eyes are open, though he is pretty certain they are. He moves his eyelids, closing and opening them as if the next time he opens them will be the time that he'll look up and see the trees standing proud above him. Hoping to witness the umbrella of branches enveloping the mossy ground below and the cracks of sunlight surging their way in between leaves like laser beams, only pleasant ones. But to his dismay that doesn't happen. Digger and Surni put their clothes back on, he knows this because he can hear the rustling of fabric brushing across skin – a bra strap smacking against a back, a zipper moving on pants. The faint sounds of footsteps veer off in separate directions and eventually fade into the forest. They have left him for dead.

# 81

# IDA OF FAVOURED NORTH
# KALA

Immediately after Atticus leaves, Ida leans her back against the front door of Favoured North. She didn't know that Atticus has been spending time with Torant of Favoured Wells and truth be told, she hates the idea of it. But one thing she does know is the likely name of the person who has been found dead, she is pretty certain. She heard whispers a few days ago about him: Doctor Theodus Harrow – she knows him fairly well, as well as one Almek knows another, which isn't all that well now that she thinks of it. Still, she knows that he's a man of nobility and he has been helpful to The Almek in many ways. How she hopes that it isn't him… though she feels it in her chest, the guilt setting in. She heard the whispers; she should've acted upon them.

Once she's certain Atticus is long gone, she double checks the lock on the front door and hurries toward the basement. A hutch sits blocking the basement entrance, Ida pushes it across the floor with enough space to be able to open the door – thankfully Hendrix ensured it was made on wheels. She swiftly closes the wooden door behind her and rushes down the stairs.

It isn't a spacious area by any means, it's really more of a cellar – a place where one might normally house their wine on racks and store jarred food. Instead it is a place of secrecy, a place Vera and Atticus have never been nor do they know of its existence. The floor is dirt and the walls are rock – no one would suspect it to be occupied. Most cabins in the colony don't have basements, but she and Hendrix picked this cabin when they moved to The Motherland for that reason and that reason alone.

She figures she has at least 30 minutes before Atticus returns, maybe more if she's lucky. Ida rummages through files that Hendrix made on all The Almek citizens. He merely instructed her to keep track of those who die. Hendrix made notes on their previous lives before the Water Crisis, as much as he could gather, without looking suspicious. She scans through the H's. Harrow, Theodus: A man born and raised in Kentucky, Tennessee. *Southern as the day is young*, Ida reflects. He was married in the Old World, no children to speak of and a doctor by profession as well back then – surgical. Ida wonders what lead to Theodus getting himself killed. Or perhaps it's an unmarked murder; perhaps it really was a mammoth.

She stares at his photo for some time – barely letting her eyelids form a blink. Then she turns on the old receiver that she and Hendrix smuggled in from the Old World to listen in on Cole:

"It's not my problem, nor is it yours," Torant's voice cracks over the speaker.

"What does it mean for the colony though? If a mammoth has rampaged the colony, these people could be in danger – unarmed and no combat training. What if more mammoths return?"

"The mammoths are not my concern," Torant says.

"What is your concern then?" Cole asks, though his tone is condescending.

"Theodus Harrow."

"Who is that?"

"The one whose blood has been spilled in the centre."

Ida flips the switch off and wipes the sudden sniffles forming at her nose. She grabs a marker and scribes "DECEASED" across the front of Theodus' file.

The planted microphone has been an asset to her and yet, there is one she has not brought herself to listen in on. Months ago, as soon as she found out about Vera's re-birthing ceremony, she took an old steel spoon and melted it over the fire and placed a microphone inside the circle of the Cannelle family crest – she has Hendrix to thank for temporarily obtaining possession of the newly made Cannelle crest. Though, she hasn't had the courage to turn it on and hear her daughter's voice. She's heard rumours that Master Regan of Tagondo is even more fierce in his ruling than Master Oberon, which means that death could be the possible form of tribulation that Vera faced following her kiss with Cole. Ida decides that she desperately needs to know if Vera is still alive.

She takes a deep breath and turns the receiver on once again, adjusting it to tune into Vera's microphone, all that fills the speaker are waves of static. Best-case scenario: it isn't working. Worst-case scenario: Vera has been killed. Ida punches the desk and then throws the receiver across the cellar.

"Fuck!" she shouts.

# 82

# ATTICUS OF FAVOURED NORTH KALA

*"Move,"* the whispers howl.

Atticus has lost count how many times he's heard the whistling words of the Whisperer since Digger and Surni left. He knows that he needs to get up, to move. However, it's not easy as his body trembles, likely from shock, and his head aches as if Digger bestowed upon him the usual poundings that he so graciously gives. There's a foggy sensation that encases him, a disorientating sort of awareness, as though he should be somewhere else, doing something else. To top it all off his head holds a certain pressure, like a bubble rising in the lake, and when he tries to stand the pressure begins to reach the surface – he's worried it will pop just the same. Maybe the pressure in his head popping is possible, or maybe he himself will pop, explode into a million tiny fleshy pieces. He doesn't know what digger has done to him, so anything is possible at this point. He does know that he needs to move.

It speaks again, *"Move."*

Atticus coughs out a response, though he doesn't know to whom it is for, "I know. I know I need to move." The truth is that he's dreading to.

He props himself up on one foot, his hand rests on the ground for support. He pats his other hand across the ground and up the base of the tree that his body was slammed into. By leaning into and gripping the tree he is able to pull himself up to his feet, the pressure he felt moments ago lingers, unchanged. At least his head didn't explode. If Atticus doesn't know what it's like to walk on jellied legs, he will after this day.

He straightens his posture, as much as he can manage, but his head pulsates now, allowing the pressure to come in waves. *Just go*, he tells himself. Atticus steps forward then, a jagged, rough step. His hands stretch out in front of him, as if to feel his way through the forest, but he walks, albeit disoriented and seeing only blackness. Within a few steps he staggers into a bush that sits lower than the reach of his hands, he feels like a child learning to walk again, maybe in some ways he is.

Suddenly noises of people moving about inform him that he is nearing the footpaths. Footsteps seem to be approaching him, though he doesn't falter.

"Atticus?" a voice huffs.

"Illandra?" he asks, though he is quite certain that it's her as her soft speech flows smooth like syrup.

"Yes. Are you alright?" she questions.

A sting of embarrassment taunts him – of all the people, of all the weird and wonderful people that could cross paths with him in this moment, it has to be Illandra. The simple girl, the caring girl – the one he has masturbated to countless times over the course of his teenage years. If he's honest with himself, he cares for her deeply in a number of ways though.

"I'm fine," his voice cracks. "but, I could use your help."

"Sure, of course," she pauses, "Um Atticus, what's wrong with your eyes?"

"I don't know, but I can't see right now. Can you help me get to Favoured Wells?"

"Why can't you see? What happened?" she questions.

"I don't know just yet. It's going to be okay though," but as he says the words he's not entirely sure if it will.

Her voice lowers, "Okay." After a moment's pause she continues, "But Torant Wells? What do you need to go there for?" He should've expected hesitation. Who wouldn't be concerned by such a request?

"Cole's there. I think together they may be able to help me," he replies.

She doesn't seem to think a second more for her shoulder slips in under his arm and in an awkward movement she pulls his arm up and around her while she wraps her other arm around his waist. She is much shorter than he and to guide a wobbly nearly six-foot-tall guy to a house through the forest won't be easy.

"Are you okay?" he asks.

She replies, "Of course." Atticus attempts to offer a smile, though the discomfort in his head doesn't allow for it.

"Thanks," he musters then pauses a moment, he should talk to her. He can't very well accept her help and not at least attempt a conversation with her, regardless of how unwell he is. It is after all, Illandra. He clears his throat, "So, what are you doing out right now anyway?"

"Well, what do you mean?"

"With the commotion happening at the colony centre…"

"Oh? I didn't hear about a commotion. I just got back from foraging by the lake," she explains so innocently.

It's just like her, innocent and naïve of the horrors in human nature. Most who are also naïve think it was a mammoth that killed Theodus of Favoured Harrow – Atticus is skeptical of that though, but he's even more skeptical of James Barlow. *Digger,* he reminds himself. *Don't forget about Digger: the one who tried to kill you a second time.*

"I hate to be the one to tell you, but you should know – so you can protect yourself. A man was found dead in the colony centre." Atticus feels Illandra jump ever so slightly, his chest pains at the thought of scaring her.

"Oh no! What should we do?" she asks with sudden fear in her voice. He reminds himself to speak lightly, so not to scare her more.

"Right now, the best thing we can do is get inside," he instructs.

Illandra doesn't say anything, she's nodding her head as he thinks he feels a subtle movement against his arm, but upon reflection he actually feels slightly numb as pins and needles radiate throughout his body. In fact, he realizes that he can barely feel anything. *Shock, it must be shock*, he tells himself.

To his surprise she asks: "Any idea about what happened to the man in the colony centre?"

"No, the body was still there when I left. Master Oberon and Huron were nowhere in sight."

"Hmm, could it have been a mammoth?" she inquires.

"I'm hopeful that's what it was."

She pauses a moment, "Hopeful, but not convinced?"

"Definitely not convinced," he says and although he's serious, he fights back a chuckle that's rising in his throat. They've spent enough time together in school over the years for Atticus to know that Illandra doesn't often ask the obvious questions, but rather asks about what's missing. Atticus likes that about her.

"Almost there," she notes.

"Good. Thanks Illandra."

"Of course."

A thought crosses Atticus' mind, "How do you know where Torant Wells lives anyhow?" he wonders as most colony members only know that he lives on the outskirts of Kala.

"I saw a lot of him as a kid, my parents were friends with him."

"Were? So your mother isn't friends with him anymore?"

"I don't think so. He stopped coming around the time my father died and mother was sent into a new merge agreement."

"Your mother merged with Curshman Steel, right? The one who bends steel?"

"Yes – a much older man."

"I wonder what Torant has against Curshman…"

"Your guess is as good as mine. Torant was really close with my father, I figured that he was just hurt that he died. And seeing my mother with another man… that's been hard for a lot of us."

"Torant is an odd man, I struggle to see him being close to anyone. I struggle to see anything right now though," he jokes, surprising himself that he has it in him.

She laughs, but it's only a fraction of the song he'd like it to be. "Tell me what happened to your sight," she urges once again.

"To tell you would be to risk your life. I'm not about to do that."

"You're always so humorous Atticus," she adds – her voice a light tease, but there is a soberness that overtakes it.

In reality he's merely aiming to be logical. But he won't tell her that – he doesn't have the heart to take away her pleasure for he only dreams to add to it. The backside of his left hand grazes a rock wall, the only rock wall that he knows encases Favoured Wells.

"Here we are," Illandra says as she pushes Atticus' arm off her shoulder and envelops the back of his arm in her hands to help him up the stairs.

Illandra guides him up the steps leading to the doorway of Favoured Wells. Atticus treads carefully, bringing two feet onto each stair before moving to the next, the way a young child would, or perhaps an elderly man. Each step brings him closer to Torant and Cole, and to their aide in fixing him – so he hopes. Atticus hears Illandra opening the door without knocking, for a moment he wonders why she didn't knock. Then he decides it's likely her nerves.

"Can you help us?" Illandra speaks urgently as they enter the kitchen.

"You made it, calf," Cole calls. "Are you totally blind?" he asks, as if he's been contemplating the answer all day.

"You know?" Atticus questions then hears movement, though he doesn't know what to make of it as he is unaware of who is where and what they are doing.

Torant answers Atticus' inquiry: "Yes. But there's no time for that now. Come, lay on the table."

Atticus can hear Torant's voice clearly and it's obvious that he is fairly close to him – at least his ears are working. The sensation of Illandra's touch wraps around his elbow and she guides him to a table – it's the one in the living room with shorter legs and a longer top than the kitchen table and from what Atticus recollects, it will be suitable to hold his size and weight.

Atticus hears more movement about, though all he sees is black. Cole and Illandra - he can tell by their touch - help him lay down on the table. The surface he lies on is unexpectedly soft and fuzz-covered, it's not the cool, hard finish he was expecting against his skin – someone must have put a blanket on it for him. As Atticus settles in, a clinking sound comes from the kitchen. Mumbles are heard, which makes Atticus believe that Torant is in the kitchen and is likely the one responsible for the clinking.

Still, Atticus asks: "What's that?"

"Torant is mixing some things together," Illandra whispers.

"I have something that may help you," Torant's voice grows close again. "You will likely feel a bubbling sensation on your eyes. It's going to hurt a little," Torant explains.

"Go ahead," Atticus says while clenching his teeth in preparation for the peculiar potion.

Someone marches away and within seconds their steps return.

"Bite down on this," Cole instructs as he gently places a cloth in Atticus' mouth.

"You're going to want to close your eyes, but you must fight it. Keep them open, above all else," Torant states then he begins to pour the mixture into Atticus' eyes.

Deep groans of disdain escape from Atticus' throat, the cloth muffles them. His body stays unmoving, all but his clenching jaw, and he holds his eyes open though it isn't without an unyielding urgency to close them. Continuous groans are unleashed – they are hardly controllable. He hears Illandra move her body to settle on the floor next to him and he can ever so slightly smell her sweet scent. A soft hand slips into his and he squeezes it gently.

She whispers in his ear then, "You're going to be okay."

No amount of pain can numb him of her presence, or the fact that her lips brush his ear, whisking his hair with them – he wants it to be his lips being brushed by hers. But even he knows this is neither the time… nor the place.

When Torant finally instructs Atticus to blink, a bubbling sensation tingles at his eyes, like soap bubbles brushing up against skin - just as Torant said - though it's much more painful than Torant noted it would be.

"How do you feel?" Torant asks.

"I feel... okay, I guess," he musters. Someone dabs around Atticus' eyes with a towel.

"What can you see?" Torant asks.

Atticus was hopeful that Torant could help – that the pain would be worth it, but as he moves his eyes across the room he reasons otherwise. Blackness. All he can see is a never-ending sea of black.

"I can't see anything," Atticus states. Illandra's hand leaves his and he feels a breeze move across him, she has left his side. "Illandra?" he asks.

"Yes, I'm here."

"Try this," Torant says as he pours a spoonful of a mixture into Atticus' mouth.

Atticus twitches, it's worse than the burning of whiskey – it sears his tongue and he wants to spit it out.

"Swallow," urges Torant.

Atticus swallows as the woodsy-tasting oil coats his throat; it takes a minute or so before the burning sensation halts.

"Look more closely now, look at us," Torant instructs.

Atticus does as Torant asks: he focuses on the three people that he knows in his right mind stand before him. He can picture them in his mind, bent at the waists and leaning overtop him; he imagines an umbrella of people as opposed to tree branches. Instead he sees nothing.

"What was that stuff?" Atticus asks.

"The poison that Digby forced upon you?" Torant questions.

"Wait… Digger did this?" Illandra asks, her voice now deep.

Atticus can hear her breath falter and then quicken, the combo of the two are not a good sign – she must be frightened for her reaction is followed by the soft paddle of her footsteps distancing themselves from the group.

"Illandra, wait!" Atticus calls. The door shuts. "Torant, why did you-"

"She needed to know," Torant interjects, "For her own protection. If you don't know that boy, then you're a fool."

"I wasn't ready to tell her, it's not safe yet," Atticus explains as he pushes his body upright. "She really shouldn't be opposing Digger right now. You've seen what he does to people that object to him."

"On the contrary, was it not you who said: *In knowledge there is power*?" Torant retorts.

Atticus knows that he said that for of course there's power in knowledge. If one knows then one mustn't be fearful. Atticus thinks back… he didn't say those words to Torant though. *What exactly does Torant know and how does he come to know it?* If there is clarity in anything right now, it's in the knowledge that The Shadow's intentions are never truly known.

# 83

## LIDIA OF FAVOURED PEONY
## KALA

Lidia spends weeks coaching Cole in the greenhouses. All the while she decides against speaking with him about Almay's presence at her Tarnished gathering – maybe Almay had been dishonest about Cole or, maybe, Lidia is about to learn more about who Cole of Favoured Wells is. So, she has decided to be patient.

Regardless, she's impressed with how quickly he's picking up on his greenhouse knowledge. Earlier that day he churned the soil in two greenhouses and clipped the lower leaves on all of the tomato plants – both of which are time-consuming jobs. If she's honest, she is thoroughly enjoying the productivity he provides. If anything, it makes up for her skeptical thoughts about him and what he's been up to since coming to Kala – at least until the tomato plants need trimming and the soils churned once again.

Upon completing her work for the day, she heads home to Favoured Peony. When she gets home she arrives just on time for dinner and the three family members sit in a kind of continual silence that carries from one day to the next, like the way most houses only sound in the wee hours of the morning. Either way, it suits Lidia just fine.

Lidia's Mother, Bethin, drops her fork and it crashes against her steel plate. The sound startles Lidia, pulling her from her reverie.

"Oh, Lidia, I've startled you," her mother apologizes.

"It's okay."

"You've been distracted lately," Bethin notes.

Lidia's aware that many things have been claiming her attention lately – her parents seem to only be aware of one: Lilith. Lidia simply nods her head.

Bethin's eyes gently and intently focus on Lidia's, "I know how hard this all is. To just move on after…"

"But you don't know Mother. You never gave birth to a child and had it taken away from you," she says through a sudden surge of emotion.

"Now, Lidia," Wade, her father, begins, "this is not exactly an acceptable conversation to be having."

Lidia rises from her seat, "I know. Because we're Almek."

^

Later that evening Lidia makes her way to the shed for a meeting with The Tarnished; the sun is setting and the sky takes on the dark blues and blacks of the night. When she arrives she can faintly see that the three women are waiting beside the shed – they are hiding, tucked between the building itself and a large bush. Lidia keeping tabs on the night guards' routes proves successful as the women know which paths to avoid and when, and in turn they have yet to be caught. They will never be caught as far as Lidia is concerned.

Aphria comes out from the hiding spot upon seeing Lidia. Lidia unlocks the door and they enter the shed, locking the door behind them – after Almay's intrusion Lidia installed a lock on the inside of the door as well.

"Hi everyone, before we get started I want to outline how we will communicate going forward. We must be creative and we must improvise. We must not use anything that can be tied back to an individual, nothing that can hold us accountable or blatantly give any information about our intentions.

"Letters can be found, they can be traced. Words can be heard, at least outside of this shed they can be. However, objects, like rope or string, can be left in certain places without much suspicion, so this will be the basis of our signals and communication. Of course, the object will need to be placed in just the right location…"

Lidia continues on, explaining to the women that they must use objects that will be accessible all year-round throughout the different seasons. She decides that a tiny rock placed at the foot of their doorstep means there will be a meeting that night at the shed. A twig placed beside the door means the meeting for that night is cancelled. A strand of thread placed upon the front window sill means possible danger: someone is onto them and all communications must stop for a period of time, until there is another signal. A pebble tossed at one's window is a call for an emergency meeting asap at the shed.

She explains that these chosen objects are neutral in colour and appearance, meant to blend in. The return of the rock at the doorstep some time following the danger signal means the danger has lifted and there will be a meet that evening. If the women need to communicate something to Lidia, they are to place a rock upon her doorstep, for a one-on-one meet that night at the shed. A meet is always no earlier and no later than midnight.

"Does everyone agree?" Lidia asks following her instructions. The women all nod agreeably. "Perfect. Now, let's get started. How was everyone's week?" Lidia asks.

"It was another sad excuse for being an Insignificant," Aphria says. "Having to reach more shares just because I'm an Insignificant is hard. I live alone and my roof began leaking a few days ago."

“I can imagine it’s not easy living alone and having to take care of all that a house requires – let alone what the colony requires. Did you get your roof fixed?” Lidia asks in concern as she knows that colony members who are without family must continue to live in their marital homes.

Even though Lidia is struggling being back at Favoured Peony, she’d rather be there than living in that other house alone – her home that Lilith once lived in with her, even if it was only for a short time.

Aphria shrugs in disappointment, “No, I tried nailing a couple more pieces of wood on top. It didn’t work, and I can’t afford to pay shares to a builder.”

“I’ll come help you tomorrow. I’ll ask my father what to do,” Lidia offers.

“Thank you, Lidia. I can pay you, somehow,” Aphria offers.

“Nonsense, I won’t accept payment. It’s my pleasure,” she says while offering a gentle hand squeeze to Aphria. Aphria mouths the words ‘thank you’ and Lidia continues, “Emille, let’s hear from you, how was your week?”

“I haven’t been feeling well from the pregnancy, but still I have to fulfill my shares. So, my lover has been helping me,” Emille replies.

“I’m so glad he is caring and helpful,” Lidia says.

Ursai sits quietly with her head tilted toward the floor. A glance in her direction tells Lidia that Ursai needs some time before being called upon.

Unexpectedly, Ursai opens up: “I was abused in the woods.”

Lidia’s voice rises in shock, “Oh Ursai… What happened?”

“I don’t think I can…” Ursai’s thoughts trail off.

“It’s okay, you don’t have to say anything that you don’t want to. We’re here for you,” Lidia assures her.

“What did he look like?” Aphria curiously asks.

“I didn’t get a close look, he was medium build, light hair I think. I’ve never noticed him before. Usually all the faces in the colony are at least familiar,” Ursai explains slowly.

Emille stirs in her seat, clearly wanting to speak but feeling timid – she seems to be more on the quiet side, and cautious, like a mouse.

Finally, Emille speaks: “I have come across many unfamiliar faces. And… I was abused once too. I know who my abuser is though.”

“Who was it?” Aphria asks, as though she doesn’t even consider the fact that Emille may not want to talk about the specifics.

“Curshman Steel,” Emille states in a whisper.

“The guy who bends steel?” Lidia asks in surprise, for he’s a reputable Favoured in Kala. Emille simply nods her head.

Aphria’s face turns vengeful, “I want justice. He should be killed,” she suddenly spits, “as should my abuser. If only I knew who he is…” Lidia’s head jolts back slightly in shock, she sits speechless for a moment. All the women look to her with expectant eyes.

She swallows, “Justice… is a… tough word.”

“Why?” Aphria asks rather curtly.

Lidia chooses her words with care, “Justice… is up to The Masters.”

“They don’t seek justice,” Aphria retorts, “They seek satisfaction in torture… in placing fear upon the people. Yes, they say they inflict tribulation on those who are Offenders, but what about my Offender? What about Emille’s?”

In seeing tears take form in Aphria’s eyes Lidia knows - without sharing the direct experience of what Aphria speaks of - she knows how the decisions of The Masters can hurt. She also knows that those tears of Aphria's are likely not just tears of sadness, but anger-fuelled tears.

How The Masters will The Almek to do what they so desire, forcing people into troubling circumstances, Lidia will never understand. The Masters have created a community in which their people fear even just the thought of speaking about their concerns. Lidia can't remember ever hearing her parents speak of going to The Master for anything, it simply isn't done. So how on earth could someone like Emille approach Master Oberon with the story of an abuser – and to accuse Curshman of Favoured Steel nonetheless. It's laughable. And Aphria, how can she seek justice when she can't even call forth who her abuser is? *Who will seek justice for these women? Who will enforce tribulation on their Offenders if not The Masters?*

Aphria pulls Lidia's attention back to the meeting, "Why don't we just kill Curshman?" she laughs following a brief pause.

"Kill?" Lidia repeats the word, the word feels weighted on her tongue as she says it; heavy, like thick oil in her mouth.

*Murder? Who are we to decide when someone's life should be over?* It seems like such a drastic decision to make, one she wants no part of, besides, is killing actually justice? She doesn't know the answer to that.

"Aphria, that's not what we're here for. We're not here to develop organized crime," Lidia notes.

Aphria appears to contemplate Lidia's point, "Okay, maybe *killing* him is a little drastic. But what if we don't kill him, what if we just scare him a little bit?"

"What would you have us do?" Lidia asks with sincerity.

"Let's fight for justice on our own terms," Aphria's hand forms a fist, she thumps it into her other hand.

"We are fighting for justice right here, right now. Every time we gather we lessen the hold they have on our minds – on our healing. Isn't that something?" Lidia asks, though she knows it's certainly something. What she doesn't know is if it's enough.

"Maybe, but I want those responsible for my loss to feel loss as well," Aphria argues, "What's that saying? An eye…"

"Yeah," Emille agrees.

"I do too," Ursai adds.

"An eye for an eye…" Lidia says in response to Aphria's question, her voice low, almost as though she's dreading the outcome.

"That's the one!" Aphria muses.

Suddenly the whispers call: "*Justice.*"

"Did anyone hear that?" Lidia asks the group.

"Hear what?" Aphria pauses. "The silent sounds of bloodlust rising in our midst?" Aphria looks at the others with a very different look across her face – one that Lidia has not seen before.

"I heard something," Emille reasons.

Ursai nods her head and whispers: "Justice."

They all glance at one another, anger clearly rising in their chests and pouring out onto their faces. They want revenge, but this group isn't about revenge – at least that's what Lidia didn't originally intend. Their world is full of hatred, killing and trivial laws, and yet horrible things continue to happen – things that are against the laws of The Masters. It may not be just the women who feel misunderstood – maybe the men do too. But, maybe, understanding and appreciating people isn't enough.

Lidia glances down at her family crest: a circle with a flower. The shape of the petals represent her last name, Peony, and the circle represents the ties and responsibilities that her family holds to The Circle, The Masters and The Almek. She glances at the others' crests, the steel that they are made from glints in the candlelight. She reflects how Curshman of Favoured Steel made all of their crests and how that must be a constant nagging reminder for Emille.

A thought crosses her mind, like a spark igniting a flame: these women need more than just sitting in circles and holding hands in secret – they hunger for the blood of their Offenders. Lidia must figure out how to feed and contain that hunger.

# 84

# ATTICUS OF FAVOURED NORTH KALA

It's a depressing realization for Atticus to come to terms with the fact that his eyesight is gone - taken - and for what? So Digger could have his daily fill of orgasm? He'll take Digger's hands if it means he can't hurt more people. It would be hard to do that though, seeing as he can barely function on his own – even when he had his sight that was a stretch.

He has missed the last few weeks of school, but he can't very well read the textbooks. Work is challenging, after he trips his way around the lab he eventually finds his seat, but then he struggles his way through knocking objects off the desk and trying to catch them – never mind being productive. He can't even hold a test tube in his hand to save his own life now, there is no way he'll be able to reference Hendrix and Vera's notes anymore either. It suffices to say, his chances of being appointed a scientist position come December have lessened drastically. In addition to his uselessness in the lab, he is also useless at home. Ida continues to fuss over him: she helps him get dressed and cooks all the meals, there is no other way to be, he is helpless.

"It's going to be okay," she says to him one August morning.

"It's been weeks, nothing's getting better. Nothing's okay."

"It seems that way right now, I know," she reassures him.

He sighs and fumbles up the stairs to his room. It's hard being around her – she doesn't just let him feel down as he so wants to. He stays in his room for days.

^

"Oh, Cole," Ida answers the front door. "With the earth," she says. Atticus can hear them from his bedroom.

"May we be cleansed. Can I see Atticus?" Cole asks. Atticus doesn't know why, but every time he hears Cole say 'may we be cleansed' it sounds like an award winning joke and he half expects Cole to burst into howling laughter.

"You may. If he feels up to coming down," she says. Atticus hears footsteps moving toward the stairs and then Ida calls up: "Atticus, you have a visitor."

Though he doesn't feel much like talking, he has known Cole to be helpful in the past, so he will go down. Atticus hobbles down the stairs.

"Calf, you hangin' in there?" Cole asks.

"Hardly."

"You need to get outside and get moving. Listen, Torant made you something. He said it will help you walk."

"What is it?"

"Here," Cole says as he places a tall, thin object in Atticus' hand. Atticus moves his hands up and down, assessing the object.

"A stick?" he says, bewildered.

"A cane," Cole corrects.

"What am I going to do with this?"

"He says you'll be able to walk better with it."

"Like the gimp that I am."

Ida interjects: "You're not a gimp, you're just…"

"Different," Atticus finishes her sentence. "Tell Torant I said thanks." He turns then and fumbles up the stairs with his cane. Ida releases a sigh.

"He's not doing so well, is he?" Cole asks her.

"Not at all. I don't know what to do to help him."

"I know what to do," Cole states.

Atticus can hear footsteps moving up the stairs and toward his bedroom. They come in without knocking – it must be Cole.

"You're coming with me," he demands.

"No, just leave me alone," Atticus retorts. Cole scoops him up then, throwing Atticus over his shoulder – Atticus still holds his cane in his hand as Cole travels down the stairs.

"Cole, put me down. This isn't a joke."

"It's not a joke, you're right about that. But I'm not putting you down. You're coming with me."

"Where are you going?" Ida asks.

"To see Torant and then to train," Cole states, as if everyone should understand what it means 'to train.' Cole puts Atticus down and then says, "Hop on my back."

"I'd rather not."

"Just do it," Cole adds with a huff.

Atticus releases a sigh, and with guidance, hops onto Cole's back. Cole walks out the front door and down the footpaths, carrying a lanky and angry Atticus on his back.

"I'd rather you not carry me through the colony centre," Atticus notes.

"You want to stumble your way there?" Cole asks.

"No, but…"

"Well those are your two choices."

"Fine," Atticus gives in.

Atticus can soon hear the hustle and bustle of the colony centre – the odd body brushes up against his feet that dangle out from Cole's sides.

"Can you go any faster?" he begs. The last thing Atticus wants is to run into Illandra looking like this. He hasn't brushed his hair in days and with Cole carrying him like a damsel, he'll just about lose his lunch if Illandra sees him.

"I'm going as fast as I can while carrying a teenaged baby."

"Hey, uncalled for," Atticus whines.

Cole chuckles, then his voice turns serious, "Did you hear who the man was that they found dead?"

"Yes, I saw him."

"Doctor Theodus of Favoured Harrow… You knew him?"

"Not well," Atticus admits.

As though someone had been reading his mind, "With the earth," a woman says. She's nearby and has a sombre tone to her voice – he thinks it to belong to Surni.

Atticus can't see her, but he knows the voice and it brings him back to that moment when he found Digger balls deep in Surni while her husband lay dead upon the colony centre, though he keeps those thoughts to himself. He remembers how he felt before Digger knocked him down, how naïve he had been. Digger isn't just a roughhousing bully - he's an attempted murderer - maybe worse. Atticus feels a twinge of pain shoot through his eye sockets.

They stand in silence a moment. "Let's go, Cole," Atticus says.

"Wait. Atticus…" Surni begins.

"I don't want to hear it," Atticus states.

Cole doesn't say a word, he merely continues walking. They eventually reach Favoured Wells and upon entrance it's easy to notice that Torant is vibrating with urgency.

"I've got it," Torant exclaims as soon as they enter the cabin.

"Got what?" Cole asks as he helps Atticus down and to a seat at the kitchen table.

"This," Torant says. Atticus feels oblivious.

After a moment of silence Cole asks, "What is that?"

"It's why I requested you to bring Atticus," Torant pauses, no one says anything. "He must eat it."

"What's it gonna do to him?" Cole asks.

"I can't be certain, but my hope is that it will help."

"I don't think he wants to take some mysterious pill."

"I do," Atticus interjects with desperation.

Cole opposes: "You do? Atticus – you don't know what could happen."

"I want to take the pill." Atticus places his hand out, palm upward, expectantly.

"Just know that I don't know how the rowan flowers will interact with your blood… but from my knowledge of the rowan tree it should help in some way," Torant explains as he places the pill on Atticus' palm.

"What are the risks?" Cole asks.

"I have no experience with the plant that I think Digby put in Atticus' eyes, so there's really no telling," Torant says.

Cole scoffs and throws a series of questions at Torant: "You don't know the possible risks? Could his life be in danger if he takes it? What plant do you think it was?"

"Stein. Some call it the black poison."

Atticus interjects again, "Do I just swallow it?"

"Wait. Atticus, what if it has terrible side effects?" Cole asks.

"I am willing to take that chance."

"You're sure? What's it called?" Cole inquires further.

"Kinsmet. Don't forget – my help comes at a fee. And if my records are correct – I am still owed a debt for helping the day your sight was taken in addition to the day I stepped in with the ceremonial swords," Torant reminds him.

"I'll do whatever you want," Atticus says as he pops the pill in his mouth and swallows.

A knock sounds at Torant's door. Atticus hears a familiar sigh – it's Illandra. He is sure that he can hear Illandra's heart beat quicken as her footsteps move closer to him. *Weird*, he thinks.

"What can you see?" Torant inquires, ignoring Illandra's entrance.

"What's going on?" Illandra speaks into the quiet anticipation of the room.

"With the earth," Cole says in a humorous tone, but maybe only Atticus hears it that way.

Then Atticus says: "I can see something."

A force of some sort flows through his veins making him feel more capable, allowing him to see something other than just black. He sees an outline of their frames, like lines drawn on a map to signify a body of water. Their outlines are smoky grey, which stands out from the rest of their bodies. The space that fills them is that of a soft grey. He can see their shapes, which reminds him of shadows – this excites him.

"You can see what exactly?" Cole asks, surprised.

Though he struggles to put it into words, Atticus finally says: "I can see shapes."

"Stars, hearts, flowers – what kind of shapes, calf?" Cole questions.

"I can see your frame, Cole, like a shadow of you. And Illandra, your…figure," he gulps, "and Torant; you, I can see you too," Atticus says.

"The rowan tree is of good luck to you, Atticus of Favoured North. You should thank Mother Earth," Torant states.

"Why? How?" Illandra asks.

"His blood has accepted the rowan tree… it isn't for all," Torant explains.

"This is…" Cole begins.

"Like magic?" Illandra interjects, seemingly fascinated. "He's gone from being entirely blind to… to seeing shadows."

"It's the exact opposite of magic – it's science. In essence, it's the Earth. The plants have not failed us yet," Torant states.

# 85

# COLE OF FAVOURED WELLS KALA

Cole sits in the greenhouses at work with Lidia, he tries earnestly to focus solely on the plants, but there is a building sense of guilt creeping over him. He has been struggling for weeks in trying to juggle his new demands as a Favoured Kalian. Between the work in the greenhouses and foraging for shares, he has had little time to offer Atticus with his new training. There is also the important task of finding out more about the antitoxin and rescuing Vera – two things that can't be rushed, they must be executed at just the right time. And making any drastic moves directly following his appointed position as Favoured botanist is not the right time.

Since Atticus has been able to see shadows it has given him a sort of unrelenting determination, which is a good thing. However, it also makes reasoning with him and trying to squeeze in the training sessions whenever Cole can next to impossible. They train in the field by Lake Cloud – their own personal combat call. Atticus is allowed to use his cane, but that is it, and Cole uses nothing for he is already at an advantage. Cole made it clear though that he makes the calls, from the combat stance to what moves Atticus should use and when. He needs to know the basics first, before he's ready to move off of instinct.

When Cole is able to take a break from the greenhouses the odd afternoon, him and Atticus practise, only for him to return that evening to finish his shift. He knows that Atticus also works with Rumi and Torant – *the kid is going to burn out*. Cole thinks that he should take a break and slowly ease into his new way of life. After all, seeing shadows doesn't mean he is back to normal.

However, Atticus clearly expressed his need to stay busy so that he doesn't fall into the abyss that his visuals live in every day. In some ways Cole understands that as he too is keeping busy by means of taking on the search for the antitoxin and developing a flawless plan to get Vera back into the lab. Not to mention he is continually distracted by Almay and must try to at least keep an eye on Torant's suspicious late night conversations with some unidentified Almek.

It wasn't until recently that Cole noticed Torant sneaking out like a rebellious teenager. The mysterious meetings are always in the middle of the night and always outside, but inside the rock wall that surrounds Favoured Wells.

Last night he watched as Torant went through the front door and around the back of the house. Torant must have thought everyone in the house was asleep, but Cole watched as the dark figure met Torant. The visitor looked to be a man, slightly taller than Torant and possessed a soft, genuine voice. It wasn't a voice he could recall hearing before, and so he couldn't identify the person. Still, he tried. Cole snuck out of the window and managed to overhear the conversation between the two men:

"Torant, do you recall when I told you there would be a bump in the road?"

"Yes, you never mentioned why though?"

"There's a group forming… their intentions are unclear."

"What more must I know?"

"You know just as well as I that certain things may not be accounted for before they must," the man reasons.

"Yes."

"However, it will come to involve the antitoxin."

"I will keep my eye on it," Torant assures the man.

"I must go now, before we're caught. Until next time," the man states, though it wasn't clear to Cole where the figure slinked off to.

"Cole, can you cut the lettuce? The first rounds are ready." Lidia's voice startles him, though it's silly – he knows that she is here, he merely forgot while deep in reflection.

"Sure," he says as he retrieves the large strainer and scissors and begins cutting the leaves at their base.

He starts with the outside leaves and cuts his way inward. He has several plants to prune, which will likely take him the better part of the day. He remembers the hysteria that ensues when the Tags get fresh lettuce shipped in from across Lake Cloud. The stigma that they only eat meat is laughable, seeing as the lettuce rations don't last long. Now he radiates with a sense of pride in knowing how these plants are procured.

"So, what did you do last night?" Lidia asks.

This is one of her many interrogative questions that she asks him daily. Although he argues in his own mind that it's strange that he deems them to be interrogating.

"Not much, I helped Atticus with his training," Cole replies.

It's a lie and how he hates lying. In reality, he was scheming Vera's escape, though he can't tell her. He knows how excited Lidia would be, he wishes he could share his plans with her, but it's safer to keep her in the dark.

"How nice," she says flatly. She has no clue that he's lying, he is sure of that.

"What about you? What did you get up to?" he asks.

Her eyes shift toward the plants, "I was just at home with my mother and father, nothing exciting," she says as she moves her foot across the dirt floor.

There's a falseness in the air, Cole hates the taste and it isn't coming from just him. Though he can't blame Lidia, lies are the norm for The Almek – and keeping one's thoughts to themselves is standard for the people of Kala. Except, not behind closed doors. How else do people hear the secret whispers in the colony?

"That's boring," he says with a chuckle.

"Yeah, that's my life. Boring," she says.

He wishes he could say the same, but his life is anything but boring – especially since meeting Vera. *Damnit*, he worries about her often. He worries what sort of tribulation she faced; he worries what sort of things Rimmy will try to pull – but mostly he worries about her vulnerability to Cain. He swears that if he ever gets within an arm's reach of Cain he'll incapacitate him – he'll have the pleasure of offering Cain his own sort of tribulation for all of his wrongdoings, there have been far too many. The dangerous part is that Cain doesn't just act under the regard of his Master – he acts under his own twisted rules.

Honing his thoughts back to his work, Cole reflects that although there have been brief instances in which he has been overwhelmed, he tries to tackle his responsibilities with grace and accuracy. Lidia has even expressed her sincere appreciation for his determination.

Lidia is a thorough teacher, patient and guiding in her ways. He regrets that he can't confide in her of his escape plan for Vera – it has nothing to do with a lack of trust in her, but everything to do with not trusting anyone else, especially since he worries that his thoughts could easily become the whispers of the colony and flutter in the wind amongst the soughs of other secrets.

^

That night, following work in the greenhouses and a brief training session with Atticus, Cole resumes plans for Vera's escape. He lays on the couch, pencil and paper in hand, sketching the layout of the colonies. He knows the Tag forest like the back of his hand and he is not too worried about coming across any mammoths. The only thing that could stand in his way in Tagondo will be Regan's Defenders, and he can't forget about Cain.

Regardless of the obstacles, Vera has to be the one to foster change – to cleanse the water. Murdina believed it and so he does too. It seems as though he was bred with the instinct to protect, to save her. Even with Murdina gone, now one with the earth - with or without the agreement - he will save Vera. In order to complete his plan, he takes an unsolicited piece of advice from Vera and he begins to make his own list. Only, this time, it will be in the form of a map showing his route to Insignificant Cannelle – he hopes that's where he will find Vera.

Previously, he planned to cross the border at the The Circle; however, he recently overheard a conversation about more Defenders being placed there after the scare of the ceremonial weapons being taken. Conversely, on the south side of the lake there is a wall, built many years prior, meant to separate the colonies. He can't attempt to climb that wall, it's a sure death sentence. Not to mention, he isn't entirely sure if Regan has Defenders placed there too. His only other option is to swim through the poisonous waters of Lake Cloud, as Master Oberon has increased the Defender count at The Circle, and going along the mountains is far too dangerous – many think the mammoths live in the mountains too. But no one has survived such a swim across the lake before. He will though – he has too. Which means he needs the antitoxin more than ever, luckily now he knows that Torant understands exactly what the antitoxin is. Next, it's convincing Torant to give it to him.

# 86

# Opi of Insignificant Cannelle
# Tagondo

In recent days Tagondo has been pulled apart in a mass search lead by Rimmy to find Vera. Master Regan has become enraged with an obsession to locate her. The things Master Regan says he'll do to her causes Opi to shudder in fear. He is a powerful man and he does what he has to and all pursuing has even been put entirely to a halt while Defenders and colony members search the woods.

Opi admires Master Regan and only wants to please him, so when Master Regan asks Opi to tend to more private business for him, Opi gladly agrees. It has been requested that Opi conduct a probe of sorts on Insignificant Pollard. Nin is the only living member in Tagondo of the Pollard family and she's neither considered a threat nor one who would put up a stink against The Master about the house being torn up. So, that afternoon, as Tagondians fill the forests, Opi enters Insignificant Pollard.

It's eerie being here and a cool feeling sweeps across Opi's skin. He wonders if spirits live where they've died – if so, Burke could be watching his every move. Opi tries to ignore his racing heart and shortened breaths for he must pretend as though it doesn't bother him as he walks past the kitchen where Burke's body laid when life left him. *Focus,* he tells himself, he has to focus and complete his job for Master Regan before Nin returns.

He continues on to Burke's bedroom and as he rummages through his old friend's things, Opi tries earnestly to be mindful of what he is moving and to put the items back in their rightful places. A part of him doubts that Burke even has the item of desire, for if he did he likely wouldn't be dead. But still, Opi has to try for his Master.

After some time of searching through old clothing, books and blankets, something catches Opi's attention. It shines a metallic yellow in the poor light and it fits just right in the palm of his hand. Its weight is sufficient to provide exactly what is needed. Yes, he has found what he came for. *Master will be pleased.* Opi quickly places the item in his pocket and flees House of Insignificant Pollard.

^

Later that day Opi takes the item of desire to The Master's chamber and upon his entrance he sees Ezla, standing in front of The Master.

"Opi, what ideal timing," Master Regan welcomes.

"Sorry, your grace," Opi turns to leave.

"No, no. Please stay. I'd like you to be here for this."

Master Regan's two barons sit in their sits rather quietly.

Opi nods and walks a few paces forward to stand in-line with Ezla, though slightly off to the side.

"Ezla, you have come upon my request," Regan reconvenes.

"Have you brought me here for tea? Oh please, dear uncle, let's do tea," her voice rasps as her sarcasm causes Regan's nostrils to flare.

"Enough."

"No tea then?"

Regan continues, "You saw Vera of Insignifcant Cannelle the day before she disappeared." Ezla nods. "What was your path with her on this day?"

"I took her to your lovely daughter's house. Both needed training on how to make arrows. Then she left, I haven't seen her since then."

"I didn't request for you to train Vera in such a task, I requested that you train Treena."

"You didn't mention the training to be exclusive," she shrugs.

"Are you forgetting one important fact?" his eyes pierce into hers, making Opi feel uncomfortable. "My daughter is Tagondian royalty."

"You're right. How could I forget? I'll be happy to give her exclusive training," Ezla exclaims with a humourous tone, "training in the colony's abstinence laws that is."

"What is the meaning of your statement?" Master Regan demands.

"Your daughter might be royalty, but she is also the colony whore."

Sweat beads instantly appear on Opi's head, this wasn't the conversation he thought he'd be having with his Master on this day.

87

# ATTICUS OF FAVOURED NORTH
# KALA

Atticus has been training with Cole in combat calls for the last few weeks and they are going as well as they can, given the circumstances. He continues to reel off the excitement of being able to see shadows, it makes it possible for him to walk without running into everything. He sees things around him in greys and black, which for most is a rather depressive thought, not seeing in colour; however, at least it's something. He can make out the shapes of the buildings, the swaying grass, bodies of people walking past him in the colony – all he has to do is take a pill every day to make it happen. However, he notices that once he creeps toward the 24-hour mark since last taking a pill, the crispness of the shapes begin to blur. The various shades of greys slowly meld into the black shapes and before long it all becomes a desolate black hole in front of him, the way it was when he first became blind. He will never stop taking the kinsmet pills – they are everything to him.

Upon walking through the colony centre one morning, with his cane in hand and shadows at his orbs, Rumi approaches him:

"With the earth, young man. How are you feeling?" she asks.

"May we be cleansed. I feel good, actually, really good."

"I'm happy to hear that. Have you reported your injury to The Master yet?"

Rumi's question is a stark reminder of his avoidance on the matter – Atticus gazes upward, taking a moment to view grey clouds amidst a black sky. Truth be told, he hasn't told Master Oberon yet because he's hoping kinsmet has something more to offer him, that his vision will fully return.

Atticus finally responds, "No, I haven't…"

"Atticus of Favoured North, I have withheld reporting your lack of attendance in class to The Master as a favour to allow you time to adjust and come to terms with your new reality, but that time is up. You will tell him today. If you do not, I will."

He knows that he's in the wrong, Rumi should have reported his lack of attendance to Master Oberon the first day he missed class. He will need to lie to cover for Rumi, he can say that he thought he had meningitis and experienced days of fever followed by vision blurring and eventually vision loss… he will be ordered to the hospital and will be poked and prodded, but that is better than anyone facing tribulation. He will say he asked her to grant him a couple sick days once the fever began. All of that should, at the very least, cover for her lack of reporting him.

"You're right. I will go right now," he states.

Rumi smiles at Atticus, he knows because he can hear the quiet chuckle under her breath, even over the hum of the colony centre, which is odd.

Atticus walks toward The Master's chamber with his legs trembling. He's discovered that the cane does help in guiding his jaunt, which now he is happy to have the extra help in balance. Still, he hates carrying the stupid thing around, some days he has half a mind to toss it in the lake – but only on the harder days and only when Cole isn't looking. He isn't allowed to go down to the lake alone anymore, in case the vision he does have fails him and he falls in. It's horrendous: the lack of freedom he now faces. Although he knows that if Vera were here, he would be wound on a much tighter rope. *I wouldn't even be allowed to walk the footpaths alone*, he chuckles under his breath at the thought.

"*The truth,*" the whispers tell him through the trees.

He says out loud in response, "Shall set you free."

He doesn't know where the words come from, or if he has heard them before, but they ignite a series of thoughts: *What if Digger retaliates since he didn't successfully kill me as he presumably planned? What if Digger tries to harm Illandra, to seek revenge?* Or his final thought: *What if Digger truly is responsible for killing Theodus of Favoured Harrow?* Atticus wouldn't be able to bear it if Digger were to cause more suffering amongst The Almek, or towards Illandra. If he is to attempt to avoid that, he will need to tell Master Oberon the truth, even if it means possibly facing backlash from Master Oberon, or even from Digger, should word get out of Atticus' reporting of him. *Perhaps, protecting the safety of another is far more worthy a cause than protecting one's self,* he reasons.

As Atticus approaches The Master's chamber, Huron stands outside the front doors with his arms crossed and for once Atticus is thankful that he can't see faces. As usual, Huron stands quiet, resolute.

"Huron?" Atticus asks, if only just to ensure it is whom he assumes it to be.

"Yes," Huron's low voice fills Atticus' ears – crisper, clearer than normal if that's possible.

"With the earth," Atticus says.

"May we be cleansed," Huron pauses a moment before continuing, "Atticus of Favoured North, what brings you to The Master's chamber?"

"I would like to request a private meet with The Master, if you please." Although Atticus' voice is calm, his insides are anything but that, for what he is about to do is so drastic, so permanent. And sometimes the truth isn't good for everyone.

"Excuse me a moment," Huron states then turns and enters the building through the front doors and closes them behind him. It's customary for the Defender on watch to enter without permission for discussion with The Master.

When Huron finally returns, he announces that Master Oberon is able to meet with him. Atticus ignores his racing heart and tells himself that the truth is necessary and rarely pretty – a pep talk of sorts. But as he follows Huron in through the doors - his cane and ears guiding his jaunt - he overhears the quiet murmurs of the Barons. He imagines their statuesque appearances and freezes. He can imagine their harsh eyes, burning across his skin with their fiery stares. It is a familiar sensation, while also being completely foreign to him.

Atticus has been in The Master's chamber a handful of times with others, but never for a private meet. This is the first. *What does that mean?* Maybe it's not a good idea to overthink though, *But is my plan still a good idea? What was it that I said about the truth?* All he knows in this moment is that he is uncomfortable, fearful, and he fixates on the sudden weighted, constricting hold that his shirt now imposes upon his neck. He reaches his hand up, hooking his index finger just over the edge of his collar and gently tugs at the fabric to loosen its arrest.

Sadly, the speech that he gathered in his head before entering the chamber is now gone, locked away for a time and inaccessible by way of jittering nerves.

Huron pauses, it's obvious because the sound of his steps come to a halt. Then, within a millisecond following his pause a gust of wind, if one could even call it that, of the most insignificant breeze brushes by Atticus, and Huron is at his side, reaching his hand around Atticus' arm. Huron now guides Atticus forward – there is no backing out now, he will have to face whatever Master Oberon is to rule in favour of.

"With the earth, your grace," Atticus says as he bows, holding his cane steady.

"May we be cleansed. Atticus of Favoured North, what can I do for you?" Master Oberon asks.

Atticus assumes that the fact that he is blind must be seen across his entire build, sticking out like a sore thumb. If the cane doesn't give it away, his posture will, or his expression. For he speculates that the way he once held his face must be very much unlike the way he holds it now. It matters not, however, because in a moment's time the truth will be out in the open, like Dr. Harrow's remains in the colony centre.

Regardless, Atticus knows he must tread lightly, as he still needs to find a way to cover for Rumi, "I have come to report that I have missed several days of class because I…I can't…"

"Well, get on with it child," Martil urges with impatience. Although Atticus can't see her, he knows it's her because she is the only female Baron.

"I can't see," he finally states.

On the far right side of the room, Quim shifts in his seat with a sigh; Atticus knows that Quim is the most soft-spoken Baron – the least intimidating, the one who always sits at the far right on the end.

"What do you mean to tell us boy?" Martil asks.

"I'm blind," Atticus responds.

"Blind?" Master Oberon repeats, as if allowing the words to register. In all of The Motherland, Atticus is the first.

"Yes, your grace."

"How can this be?" Master Oberon asks.

"A substance of some sort was put into my eyes and…" he cuts himself off, mainly for fear of how ridiculous it all sounds now that he speaks these words out loud.

"What substance? And by whom?" Hogard orders.

Atticus wraps his fingers around the handle of his cane firmly; he squeezes it so tightly that he can feel the skin stretching overtop his knuckles.

Following a sharp intake of air, he speaks: "I don't know what the substance was."

"Who did this?" Master Oberon sternly repeats.

Atticus reminds himself of the whispers and how they ignited his plan to share the entire truth, no matter the consequences.

He inhales a choppy breath, "Digby of Favoured Espen." Gasps of surprise fill the room and the tone of the chamber shifts.

"Digby? Are you certain?" Master Oberon asks.

"I saw him with my own two eyes. I mean, right before he blinded me with the substance."

"Why did he do such a thing?" Quim asks.

"I saw him… doing an illegal act. He wanted to punish me for seeing him, to prevent me from talking. But… I'm here to speak the truth." Now, more than ever, Atticus needs The Master's protection from Digger.

Master Oberon continues the inquiry: "What illegal act?"

"Sexual relations with a woman in a merge agreement, your grace," Atticus says quickly, the words leave a sour taste, a worry of regret surges through him, though he's not quite sure just yet if he should regret this.

Gasps escape the Barons' mouths once again. It is sad, if he's honest, how clueless they all really are. He prays to Mother Earth that they won't *shoot the messenger*, but he must unload the whole truth, if he's to ensure safety for The Almek from Digger.

"Sexual relations with Surni of Favoured Harrow on the night her husband, Theodus, was found dead in the colony centre," he pauses, "Digger has been bullying me, beating me up for years. I can't walk the paths without getting bruised and bloodied. Something needs to happen. I cannot defend myself anymore."

"We should have been informed of this sooner," Martil quips with a snap.

"I apologize, I was fearful to come to you with any of this." Though his hand still grips his cane as if it is his life force, he wonders if it's actually easier to be in the room with them now that he can't see their faces.

"Does anyone else know of these happenings?" Master Oberon asks.

There is no way Atticus is mentioning the names of those who know; furthermore, he sees this question as an opportunity to help those who need it: "Well, I do need to admit that I've lied recently, to avoid the truth. Not only did I lie to my mother, I lied to Educator Epillow. I told them that I had meningitis and experienced days of fever which affected my vision at the time. Neither questioned me due to my symptoms."

"Very well, Atticus. We will do some investigating into Digby and this behaviour you speak of. I will also need to have a private meet with your mother, Rumi and the sexual Offenders," Master Oberon explains.

Atticus swallows, "Yes, your grace."

"However, sadly, given your circumstances, I believe that you are no longer fit to fulfill your Favoured duties. We must immediately demote you to Forager. You will no longer be able to work in our labs or greenhouses, but your North name will stay Favoured because of your mother's role. Now go, and keep your distance from Digby as we resolve this issue."

"Thank you, your grace," Atticus bows and leaves the chamber.

He stops briefly beyond the exterior of the door, his limbs quiver like the surface of the lake on a breeze-filled day. He hastily makes his way to the nearest footpath and just as soon as he is covered by bush, he collapses to his knees into the dirt. His tension-riddled hand finally releases his cane in a stiff withdrawal and he stills. He takes a series of deep, desperate breaths and then he calms. *That was close.* He lost his Favoured position, but he didn't lose an arm, or worse. He did the right thing. He prays once again in his thoughts to Mother Earth that Digger will be locked up in jail. Surni too.

^

Atticus was supposed to meet up with Cole this afternoon for a training session – he's enjoying training in Cole's combat calls and learning sightless fighting techniques, he's learning to rely solely on his hearing and his strength. But Cole cancelled on him today, so instead he decides to go for a walk down the footpaths. He can hear another set of footsteps coming from a mile away; they are soft and delicate, the steps of a person who walks on their tiptoes. They are slow and hesitant, not the kind you would expect from a Defender. The footsteps approach him.

"Illandra?" he asks.

"Hey Atticus, with the earth," Illandra replies, "I hope I didn't scare you."

"May we be cleansed… No, not at all."

"You heard me coming?" she asks.

"Yes."

"How did you know it was me?"

"A feeling," he says with a smile.

"Do you want to go for a walk with me?"

"Sure, but I stick out like a rotten tomato."

"No, you don't."

"Have you seen me lately? I can't exactly blend in anymore," he says.

"You never blended in. Besides, I don't want you to blend in anyway, I want you to stand out, or not – I don't care," she says.

"You don't care?" he asks.

"No, I don't."

"You want to spend the entire afternoon looking into these lifeless orbs?" He doesn't know if he is looking to rid her presence, which isn't like him, or if he is fishing for compliments – a reassurance of sorts. It is likely the latter.

"Atticus, they're not lifeless. They're still a part of you."

"They don't scare you?"

"No. Sure, your eyes are different now, but it was never your eyes that I always liked anyway, it's your smile," she notes.

"Okay," he says, feeling slightly embarrassed, while also relieved. "But what about Digger?"

"I'm not speaking to him right now after what he did to you."

"But you're in a merge agreement with him, you can't just ignore him."

Illandra doesn't respond, so they walk in silence. He soon hears rustling on his left side, so when her hand slips into his he's half expecting it and they walk this way for some time. He keeps his ears peeled, to listen for other Almek walking the paths, or Defenders. The only one he can't detect is The Whisperer, as they make no sounds other than their quiet messages. He stays alert because the second he hears anything they must unclasp hands.

"Want to go to the lake?" she finally speaks.

"Yes."

Atticus has only been to the lake with Cole since becoming blind and so it will be a nice change to go with Illandra. If he has to be babysat, he prefers it be her anyways.

They saunter through the trees and along the lakeside where they release their hold, knowing that the clearing at the lake isn't a place to be embracing. He can tell how far they are from the lake based on the insignificant waves that the breeze creates. Closing his eyes and without looking at the lake's shadow, he guesses it's about ten feet or so from where they stand. He opens his eyes and looks down at the ground to look for the shadow of a rock. He spots one and picks it up, closes his eyes once again, and tosses it toward the lake. The water splashes upon impact from the rock; he has always liked the sound of rippling water. Eyes still shut, he turns and walks with his cane in front of him in a straight line toward the water's edge. It feels daring to walk in complete blackness when he could open his eyes to see at least the surrounding shapes if he so wants to. But with one foot in front of the other, as if he is walking across a log, he counts the steps to the edge of the lake. Suddenly his cane breaks through the water's surface, he opens his eyes.

"Be careful! You better move away from the edge," Illandra says.

"Ten!" he calls. "Ten feet!" Atticus celebrates as he notes the strength in his other senses – even if his eyes fail him, the rest of him is strong. He looks down and can see tiny slits of shadows moving through the water: fish.

# 88

## LIDIA OF FAVOURED PEONY
## KALA

"With the earth," Lidia says as she bows to The Master and his Barons.

"May we be cleansed," Master Oberon states as he gestures to the centre of the room where all that address The Master stand.

Martil begins: "Lidia, we have summoned you here today to discuss with you new opportunities."

"What kind of opportunities?" asks Lidia.

"The kind concerning merging," Master Oberon clarifies.

Lidia reflects how it has only been five months since Lilith's birthing ceremony – she still needs time.

"Yes, your grace," she says though.

"We think it is time we make arrangements for you," states Hogard.

"We have reason to believe this merge will do you good," Master Oberon notes.

A memory flashes through Lidia's mind – back to two years prior. She stood in this very room and was told those very words – back when Master Oberon formulated an agreement between her and Kobe.

"I..." she begins. She wants to say that she isn't ready, that they can't force her, but she knows they can and resisting will only make it worse. "I am honoured."

The chamber doors open then, Burelle of Insignificant Oaklyn walks in. Lidia, surprised to see Burelle, assumes he is likely the one that she is to merge with. She hasn't spoken to him in years, not since they were in school together in foraging class.

An odd, fairly recent, memory flashes through her mind of Burelle walking hand in hand with a woman through the colony – their hazel eyes appear to match one another's. *Isn't he in a merge agreement?* It's the only thing that could explain their hand holding – the only thing that would make it legal. Who was she though?

"With the earth," his silvery voice greets The Master and Barons upon a bow.

"May we be cleansed. Burelle, please," Master Oberon says as he gestures for Burelle to come stand beside Lidia.

"What is this?" Lidia mumbles beneath her breath to Burelle as he joins her, a question of course that cannot be posed to The Master. Burelle simply eyes her curiously.

"Lidia, Burelle Oaklyn comes from blood of hardworking foragers – having never faltered on their shares. Burelle has proven himself worthy of merging with one of the Favoured. Burelle, Lidia Peony has blood of brains with her family being botanists. She is of child-bearing age and as a result of her previous agreement, appears to be quite fertile." Master Oberon pauses for a moment; Lidia shuffles her feet in a sudden self-consciousness.

"With that being said, we consider this a promising decision – we would like to put in place a merge agreement. Having already met with your parents, the decision is final," Master Oberon states.

Lidia looks at Burelle, with his fair skin and slim muscles that flow across his chest and arms under his shirt. He is fit, but not overly muscular as the Tagondians are. She finds her thoughts wandering back to the woman that walked with Burelle in that memory of hers. What happened to their merge agreement? As always, The Masters only share with the public what benefits them though.

"It will be my honour," Burelle says as he bows and turns to rest his lips on the back of Lidia's hand. He glances up, his hazel eyes look contentedly into hers.

"As it is mine," she says, with the sensation of pink forming on her cheeks, though she doesn't know if it's from anger or embarrassment – she decides it's likely both.

Still, an alarming urge overcomes her, she needs to know about the other woman, if not for the sole reason that The Masters have only revoked a handful of merge agreements in the history of The Almek.

"Wait," she suddenly says. "Isn't Burelle already in a merge agreement?" she asks, desperation in her voice.

She knows she could very well face tribulation for asking such a question, as past merge agreements are not to be spoken of, but where did this woman go? Lidia realizes that she has never seen that woman since. It was maybe a month ago when she saw the two walking hand in hand. The Barons look to Master Oberon, then shift their stare to burn upon Lidia, her organs rattle.

"Your grace?" Hogard asks in alarm.

Master Oberon steadies his eyes on Lidia, "I'll allow the question."

Lidia's heart sinks in relief, and though she feels the warmth of Burelle's eyes on her too, she chooses not to look.

Master Oberon goes on to explain: "Burelle's previous planned merger disappeared. Her whereabouts are unknown. However, since a merge didn't actually take place, thereby, we are moving on."

"Moving on? What if she returns?" Lidia asks.

"We did a search for her and it came up empty – no one returns from the outskirts, it is considered a guarantee that the mammoths got her."

Interestingly, Lidia doesn't recall a search being done, or one ever being announced for that matter. Maybe they did it discreetly.

Oberon continues: "Now then, where were we? Oh yes – it's settled then. We will speak with your parents about setting a date for the merge to commence. In the meantime, Lidia, you will keep house for Insignificant Oaklyn up to and beyond the move-in date."

"Thank you, your grace," Burelle says, bowing as he still holds Lidia's hand warmly in his own.

Lidia matches his bow, but only because she knows she has to – and just like that the course of her life has changed again. They walk out of The Master's chamber hand in hand: a woman forced to have more children than she cares to and a man who will eventually be forced to risk his life in The Circle to keep those children. That's what the merge agreements come down to.

Once they are outside Burelle turns to Lidia and professes: "I hadn't a clue that was going to be happening."

"Me either," Lidia says while still in shock herself.

"Is this weird?"

"I'm not sure how I feel right now."

"I mean, we were friends before you and Kobe…" his words trail off.

"Friends?" she inquires.

"In school… so quite some time before you and Kobe," he reasons.

"Sure."

"It's weird, having not spoken in years," he notes.

"It is… I suppose," she pauses, "I'm sorry, I have to go, excuse me."

"Okay," he calls after her as she hurries away.

Lidia runs through the colony centre, her heart races in a way it hasn't before – she needs to speak with Atticus. She flies past the lab and down the footpaths that lead to Favoured North. She bangs on the wooden door several times.

"Atticus," she shouts, "You in there?" There is no movement inside, no sounds of a presence. *Cole.* He'll do for now.

She heads for Favoured Wells next, and if she's honest Cole is probably the better choice – at least for now. She feels terrible at the thought of bothering Atticus with her troubles, he has his own to deal with right now. When she reaches Favoured Wells she doesn't bother knocking - she has grown tired of unopened doors - so she swiftly opens the door and walks in. The scent of herbs and meat fill her lungs.

"Cole?" she shouts.

"Hey," Cole says as he appears from down the hall.

"I need to talk with you," she says out of breath.

"What's up?" he asks casually.

She catches her breath and continues, "I've just been placed in a merge agreement with Burelle of Insignificant Oaklyn."

"Congratulations!" he says as her face forms a frown. "Or… I mean… my condolences?"

She sighs, "I don't know what to do – he was placed in a merge agreement with someone else, but Master Oberon revoked that agreement."

"Okay, calm down. Maybe he has a good reason for revoking the agreement for him."

"But they rarely do it. They did it for Vera because she was transferred," she notes.

"Why don't you talk with Burelle – he should know," Cole suggests.

"The woman disappeared, Cole!" she panics.

"Oh… You're not thinking… that he did it?"

"Well now I am," she admits.

"What are you thinking exactly? That he made her disappear?" Cole asks, bemused.

Lidia's chest heaves up and down as she still attempts to catch her breath, "Killed her maybe? I don't know. You just put the idea in my head." Her voice rises into a whine, "What woman up and leaves The Motherland by herself and without word – especially knowing that survival in the outskirts is a guaranteed 0% chance?"

Cole places his hands on her arms, "Calm down. When is the merge scheduled for?"

"I don't know, in the near future."

"Okay, well, you've got some time to get to know him before it's official at least."

"What makes you think I want to get to know him? They have no idea where she is and are just *moving on*… him too… it's suspicious."

"Why are you so worked up about this? What other choice does he have but to move on and not question The Master? Are you just worried because they are forcing *you* to move on?" he asks sincerely.

"It's weird, Cole. Don't you think it's weird?"

"Not really. Look at me – they appointed me a Favoured position, that's something they've never done in all the history of The Motherland," Cole points out. Just then Almay walks down the hall with baby Elan in hand.

"Almay, I wasn't expecting to see you," Lidia says disappointedly.

"You two know each other?" Cole asks.

"Sort of," Lidia replies.

"Well, here I am. Waiting for a man to take us away from this place," Almay's eyes dart to Cole. He looks at Lidia and raises his eyebrows in innocence, or discomfort.

"I can see that some of us are in a less ideal spot than others…" Lidia says referring to Cole's position of being stuck with Almay. "I better go."

"Hey, let me know how things go. Be safe," Cole states.

"I will."

"Oh Lid, question for you: have you heard of The Tarnished?" Cole inquires.

"No… Why?" Lidia answers quietly, noting that thankfully Almay is now out of earshot.

Conversations with The Tarnished and what has been taking place under The Master's nose are precisely why she's so skeptical of the sudden urgency in ending Burelle's merge agreement and invoking one for her.

"There's been whispers in the colony about a group of people... not sure on their intentions. I was just curious."

"Oh, haven't heard of it."

"Be careful, keep your eyes peeled," Cole says with concern.

"Thanks," Lidia says as she turns and walks down Torant's front steps. The door closes behind her. A rough hand suddenly squeezes her arm; it's Almay.

"I'll have you know, I have been hearing the stirring in the colony. I also know that your little group can't hold up to the reputation it's bellowing. But try, I dare you. If you don't, I will spread your name through these paths like wildfire," Almay states sternly.

"You're a miserable woman. I truly wish that you find peace," Lidia simply says as she pulls her arm out of Almay's grasp and walks away.

"Wildfire!" Almay shouts.

Lidia needs to meet with The Tarnished that night and make sure the women aren't spreading whispers and causing mischief. It has to be one of them, or Almay, for no one else in the colony knows about their alliance. She hurriedly navigates through the colony and places a rock at the doorstep for each Tarnished woman.

^

Upon their meet that night, Lidia quickly begins: "There's whispers in the colony, I think they're talking about us."

"I've heard them too," Ursai says while the other two women nod in agreement.

"Where have these whispers come from?" Lidia asks the women.

"Don't know," Aphria replies.

"We can't have it continue, it's dangerous. Almay has already threatened to identify us to the public," Lidia states.

"Then we kill her," Aphria says.

"No, we're not killing anyone," Lidia raises her voice. She has grown sick of the talks of killing people.

"It's easy for you to say, you've never been abused or mistreated," Emille says.

"I've been mistreated, I've been forced into circumstances that I don't want to be in. It doesn't mean those people should die," Lidia states.

"Says the girl in the new merge agreement with one of the most desirable Insignificants in all of Kala," Aphria says.

"You heard?" Lidia asks, shocked that word has spread so quickly.

"We all did," Emille notes.

"I was going to tell you. I just don't think I've really had a chance to let it sink in. I feel that I'm still trying to cope with losing Lilith and Kobe."

"Coping is important, but so is justice," Aphria taunts.

Lidia thinks for a moment as the shed sits in silence. Lilith, her baby, was taken from her – her one true love in this world. She glances at the women who sit in the circle facing her. They all have red cheeks from the lack of air circulation in the shed, sweat beads down her forehead.

"You're right, Aphria. Look at us, in this moment. Hiding our thoughts and feelings in a shed like a flock of sheep. Why do we have to be the sheep? Why can't we be the wolves?" Lidia questions as she is sick of The Masters making her life's decisions for her.

"I want to be a wolf," Emille sings.

Lidia thinks for a moment before she speaks, "I've decided… I want justice." The women rejoice quietly at her words, "But we mustn't be brutes, or barbaric in nature, but wolves that are fair and seek justice. We must be compassionate to our enemies and loyal to our friends."

Lidia pauses before listing her utmost expectations of the women before her, "If we are to seek justice, we must follow a set of rules – The Tarnished Rule. There are three: no murdering, we must keep our identities secret and we must stay loyal to our pack. That's it."

Lidia takes a moment to gaze upon her wolves – they are awestruck.

She continues: "We know what it's like to be disrespected and kept in a cage, and we will know what it's like to break free of that cage…"

# 89

## Cole of Favoured Wells
## Kala

Swimming through Lake Cloud sounds as though it would be easy enough – so long as he gets his hands on the antitoxin. He hasn't gone swimming since he was a young boy, but his body has been well exerted on a regular basis and he knows that if he can source out ivani he can make it through the clearing that surrounds the lake faster – meaning less chance of being spotted by mammoths or Defenders. Once he's on the other side of the colony he'll track his way through the Tagondo forest and locate Vera. The only flaw in his plan is swimming the lake if he doesn't get the antitoxin.

Cole has just finished work for the day and is on his way home to Favoured Wells before the curfew, though it doesn't really matter anymore if he's out past it.

"What are you doing out here at this hour?" Cole asks as he approaches a tired-looking Atticus who sits upon the rock wall that encases Favoured Wells.

"Took you long enough," Atticus says with a slight whine to his tone.

"Long enough? I work every day until this time… unless you bug me to train."

"We need to talk. I've got to get some things off my chest," Atticus states.

Cole sits down beside Atticus with a sigh, "Shoot."

"First off, I told Master Oberon all about Digger."

"You told him everything?"

"Everything."

"Even about how you're *not taking his shit*?" Cole chuckles, though he means to be heartfelt as he references the first conversation Cole and Atticus had back in the Kalian jail.

Atticus releases a smirk, "Even that part."

"So what now then?"

"I'm waiting to hear The Master's decision – what kind of tribulation he will place on Digger."

"You mean if he even acts on it."

"Of course he will, he has to. I'm blind because of him."

"We'll see. I hope he does, for your sake." Cole notices Atticus' mouth form into a slight frown then, "But hey, regardless, I'll have your back."

"Thanks."

"Speaking of that. I have something I want to tell you," Cole begins.

"But… I'm not done yet."

"It'll only take a minute to explain," Cole goes on to unload his plan on Atticus about how he plans to get to Tagondo, get Vera and bring her back to Kala.

Atticus sits in thought for a moment before responding, "Cole, I want her back here as badly as you do, but my first thought is what if this antitoxin doesn't actually work? What if it's not even real? What if she gets caught in the lab? A tribulation of death would be certain."

"It will work. I've even heard the whispers about the antitoxin, have you not?" Cole asks. "Besides, even if it fails us – Vera will know what to do."

"Okay, if you're sure. Have you thought about the risks?"

Cole looks out into the trees; lines of trunks sit sturdy and still. What if he can't get the antitoxin or the ivani? Atticus is right – he won't make it without those things.

"I worry… if you do this, you might wind up getting yourself killed," Atticus adds.

"There are risks everywhere; mammoths, The Tarnished, and I've heard whispers about something called The Cobra – it seems as though any of these factors could strike at any moment. Not to mention Digger, James Barlow…"

"That's true, though their attacks seem to be more targeted," Atticus suggests.

"Especially Digger's," Cole teases with a light press of his knuckles on Atticus' arm. "The way I see it, I'm as good a target as any," Cole pauses, "I'm the only appointed Favoured in Kala and a Tagondian at that – come on, Atticus, I've thought it through.

"Worst case scenario: I can get her back to Tagondo before sunrise and no one will know she was even here. Best case scenario: we get our hands on the antitoxin and she doesn't have to go back, we all just leave this place."

"I'd like that." Atticus pauses in thought, "I appreciate you doing this Cole. Especially since I can't… I really hope your plan works.

"It will."

"Just be careful. Let me know when you're going to go," Atticus pauses before divulging more important information. "So, the other thing I need to tell you is that our water is going… and fast. My calculations say we will be out by February."

"Running out of water?" Cole questions.

"It's top secret, of course; however, The Master must know… at least I would assume."

"Shit," Cole sits in thought a moment. "But six months is enough to cleanse the water."

"Cole, they've had eighteen years to cleanse the water."

"Another reason why we need Vera back then."

"Listen, there's something else… something is odd about my calculations. We're going through the spring faster than we should be with the number of people we have utilizing it between Kala and Tagondo. Although it's been a while since Master

Oberon has provided the lab with an accurate population count of Tagondo, there must be around six thousand Almek…" Atticus' words trail off in thought.

"How much time?"

"I told you – six months, at best," Atticus says.

"How accurate is that? How do you know?"

"Pretty accurate. Before I… before this," Atticus gestures to his face, "I was consistently measuring our consumption: each person uses seven hundred and fifty gallons per month – which is substantially less than people consumed in the Old World, but even still we go through approximately three million gallons every month."

"And?"

Atticus sighs, "The release amount is lessening, which means the volumetric water content is lowering. Our numbers should be less than three million gallons every month with all the lives we have lost at The Circle, exile and general deaths. At the release amount rate, I calculated the amount of water being stored in the aquifer to be at eighteen million gallons, which gives us about six months."

"Shit."

"Yeah, shit is right," Atticus says. "If we don't cleanse this water in less than six months – we're all dead."

# 90

# VERA OF INSIGNIFICANT CANNELLE
## UNKNOWN

A nag at her arm brings her to wakefulness, only it isn't the kind of alert wakefulness that it should be. She opens her eyes, this time she can move her head and so she glances around to groggily gauge her surroundings. Dirt. Dirt encases her, all around her. Only it isn't as though she's been buried, it's as though she's in a room, built underground. The ceilings are fairly high, seven feet at least. She glances to the other side of the room, revealing the room to be about eight feet wide, and sees a makeshift table. The table is made from a large rock and has a flat surface on top; it holds a plate with what looks to be a series of medical-type equipment.

She slowly lifts her head and inspects her body, but can only manage minimal movement, as her limbs feel heavy - weak - as if someone has sucked the energy right out of her and she's more or less a vegetable. There is a blanket overtop her, knit from some kind of scratchy yarn. Her slight movement causes pressure, a tugging at her arm – the one that she's certain is broken. *A sling?* Someone has taken it upon themselves to wrap her arm in a sling. Her arm is bent at the elbow and lies across her stomach, she can't move it. Her other arm, the left one, has a needle pricked into it which is attached to some kind of tube and beyond that a bag. She wonders what her captor has seeping into her veins? She wants to rip it out – to run and escape, but she can't, she is far too weak.

Her captor appears then from a tunnel beyond this room. They are still wearing the same black mask, only showing their eyes. Vera attempts to gaze into them, if she could only see more of their face she could possibly identify who it is that has kidnapped her. The black mask, her captor, holds in their hand a needle – they seem to intend to put more of an unidentified substance into Vera's veins. She wants to scream, to kick and punch – there is no use though, her body isn't quite connected to her mind the way it once was. The black mask presses a needle into the port that already resides in her vein. Instantly, the sleepy haze overtakes what little amount of consciousness she still had and it carries her away with it.

# 91

## COLE OF FAVOURED WELLS
## KALA

Unlike Atticus, Cole occupies the figurative space that is the fine line between a thinker and a doer. He knows that he can't just sit around and do nothing while also patiently awaiting the most ideal time to strike. He isn't extremely spontaneous, but in some respect and with appropriate timing, he can be.

He walks through the colony centre at sundown, following the curfew siren. The door of the lab calls to him, beckoning his attention. How he needs to get in there… At least a quick peek to ensure there is nothing suspicious happening inside its walls, to confirm if there is in fact an antitoxin, and then he'll leave.

Cole pulls out a piece of thin metal wire that he carries up his sleeve - something that Torant uses to make his dolls - it will allow him to rig the lock to the lab. With no Defenders in sight, he flies up the steps in a hurried fashion. Pushing the metal wire inside the lock on the doorknob, he gives it a spin and a jiggle. He then places his hand on the knob and it turns, opening the door. He slinks inside.

Finally, after all this time, he has made it inside the infamous and top-secret Kalian lab. He can't be too careful though, and he knows that. The air inside smells of plastic, it isn't pleasant, although it isn't terrible. The solar lights from the colony centre shine in through the windows, lighting the place decently.

Cole looks around and immediately notices three large cylinders that house water. Upon a quick inspection he sees that there is a large filter in each machine, which appears to suck the water from the bottom and pull it up to the top creating the steady sound of a running tap. It seems to grow louder as each minute passes; he wonders how anyone can work in such a space with such noise. Granted, he isn't used to noise caused by machines.

He notes that one tank has yellow-tinged water and easily identifies it as water from Lake Cloud. He isn't entirely sure what the other two have within them though, he assumes one must be the safe drinking water from the spring – it's only partially full.

Cole walks through the lab, there are all kinds of odd-looking tools strewn across the desks and papers with written notes on them. Items are scattered all over that he believes in some form or another must hold significance. In the back room there are hooks with several lab coats hanging. If it weren't for a double glance Cole wouldn't have noticed one particular lab coat with the words: "It's in the setbacks," needled in cursive on the left breast pocket – nor would he have noticed the protruding bump that appears behind the blue-letters. He recalls a conversation that he and Vera had at one time when he referenced something merely being a setback. The face she made when he said it told him that phrase held some form of significance to her. He said it again, before he left her side at his re-birthing ceremony – she made the same face then too with wide eyes and a straight-lined mouth that told him he tugged at a soft spot, though he didn't know why then nor does he now.

Cole checks the pocket out of curiosity and finds a piece of paper in which he stuffs into his own pants pocket. He glances down then and sees a pencil with "V" engraved on it, even after all this time there are still pieces of her here. He lets his fingers graze the sides of the pencil, he imagines her soft hand on it and he wonders when she had carved the "V" there. Was it on the day they first met when he had gifted her the nickname? She's a secretive woman though, especially when she doesn't want the world to know how she feels. But, when she can't possibly admit her own feelings to even herself, they tend to slip out. At first that drove him nuts about her, but he has grown to miss that after all this time away from her.

He continues to rummage about, trying earnestly not to make a suspicious mess of things – he doesn't want it to look like someone broke in. Cole pushes through the papers that are dispersed across the desk - antitoxin - that is what he is looking for, any sign of it and he will be satisfied that he's on the right track. His eyes catch a glimpse of a paper that belongs to Educator Ferris, entitled "Prospect." Cole scans the page.

"What in the?" A diagram, hand drawn, references some kind of weird wind in the forest. Cole releases a chuckle of sorts. "These scientists…" he shakes his head. Still, he thinks that maybe Torant will have some insight on this, so he folds the paper and puts it in his pocket.

His ears perk when he hears a jiggling at the front door – the only door. *Shit. Someone is coming.* His heart pounds suddenly, but he needs to keep his senses sharp.

"The door was left unlocked?" he hears a worried voice articulate.

As one trained to be aware of his surroundings from growing up within a forest littered with mammoths, he knows there is a window in the back. Cole slides into the back room and tugs on the window desperately to escape. Footsteps enter the lab. He will face tribulation, but not lashings, worse – there is no way Master Oberon will let him live after this. His fingers grip at the smooth surface of the window, pushing it with tense limbs, but his fingers slip. He realizes then that there is a lock on the window and he hasn't unlocked it. *For fuck's sake.*

His thumb and index finger swiftly unlock the window, he pushes it open and bounds forward through the frame to the outside world. Miscalculating the height of his fall, he lands on his knees and a wince of pain escapes his mouth. He stands to his feet immediately and runs. As his chest huffs, his legs carry him through the woodland forest beyond the greenhouses.

Cole quickly returns to Favoured Wells without being spotted. He forgot to lock the door behind him after entering the lab, for that he's pissed – there is no room, no allowance, to be so careless. He takes a moment to catch his breath before entering the house. Torant is nowhere to be seen and Almay seems to be finishing a feeding. He greets her and Elan quietly and then sits down at the kitchen table. After a few minutes Almay is ready to put baby Elan to bed and so the moment he is left alone he retrieves the folded pieces of paper out of his pocket.

The note that came from the lab coat is a list of some sort. There is a good chance that Atticus will know what it is for, so he places the piece of paper in his leather bag for safekeeping. Next, he examines the paper that belongs to Educator Ferris – he hopes it won't be missed. He studies the drawing: its lines indicate some kind of movement on earth, but there's also a series of letters scrawled randomly on the page, like words, only they don't form coherent sentences.

A noise from outside startles Cole out of his intrigue in the paper – he quickly tucks it in his leather bag and hurries to peek through the front window of the tiny cabin. There, just beyond the front stairs, but still inside the rock wall, is Torant. But it isn't just Torant himself, he is speaking to the mysterious Kalian again, the one that only lurks outside their home in the wee hours of the night when the mammoths roam and the Defenders are sparse. Cole discreetly cracks the window open in an attempt to listen in.

"There is interest spiking in the antitoxin… You must prepare."

"When?" Torant asks.

"Soon."

"You know I need more than that."

"In due time," the unknown Kalian says. "Here."

There's an exchange of sorts, only Cole can't tell just what it is. Cole tightens the window back to its frame as a means to not get caught for eavesdropping. Though, in retrospect, Torant likely already knows what Cole is up to.

When Torant enters the house some time later Cole holds out the drawing with the name "Educator Ferris" etched on top of it.

"What's this?" Torant asks, though Cole assumes he's bluffing and knows just exactly what it is.

"I was hoping you could tell me."

Torant pulls the paper out of Cole's grasp. "Prospect," he inhales heavily and as a croak escapes his throat he begins coughing.

"What does it mean?" Cole probes.

"It means we're in trouble."

# 92

# LIDIA OF FAVOURED PEONY
# KALA

Life, she thinks, is infinite – death isn't the end. How could it be the end? It's like a second chance. But when she walks by the woman's body that lies by the greenhouses with deep red slashes in lines across her stomach and bruises around her neck, she questions those beliefs – right after she releases a scream of terror.

It's early morning, the sun graces the sky with its glory and a beam of light shines through the cracks between the trees from the forest, resting upon none other than the lifeless face of Alva of Insignificant Retner. It's as if the sun highlights her emptiness – a spotlight for the broken. Or the light is a good thing and intends to take her soul, envelop it in its warmth before guiding it towards afterlife. At any rate, it's eerie and distressing the way her lifeless eyes stare back at Lidia – dark pits that look as though they are meant for haunting.

"Help!" Lidia asks the empty centre.

Her eyes look about to see no one in sight. She seems to be the first out upon the sunrise on this day. What can she possibly do for this poor woman? Her hand shakes as she bends down and closes the woman's eyelids.

"One with the earth," she chokes as tears pour from her eyes.

"What's going on?" a woman approaches Lidia, her voice very clearly naïve to what is happening.

Lidia's words scratch at her throat as she glances up at the woman, "It's Alva of Insignificant Retner."

Her saddened gaze shifts back down to Alva as the colony member comes to the realization that the woman lying upon the ground is no longer living. Lidia, with the observation that Alva's body is a shade of grey with no sign of the pink pigment that once occupied its cells, contemplates to herself who might have murdered this woman. The bruises and clean-cut lacerations definitely don't appear to be the markings of a ruthless mammoth. Come to think of it, the blood seems settled in precise lines, dried even – it would be unusual for a mammoth to leave behind such a tidy-looking corpse.

"How did this happen?" the woman gasps, terror-stricken.

"I don't know. A mammoth…" she says to humour the woman, knowing that is what she wants to hear, but she struggles with the absurdity of anyone thinking this is the result of a mammoth attack and continues, "Or..."

"Or what?"

"… Or a murderer," Lidia stammers.

The woman crouches down beside her, fear painted on her delicate-looking face. Lidia knows that the woman did not want to hear the word *murderer*. She wasn't prepared. It's as if the word itself has been wiped from their vocabulary to make room for the ceremonies at The Circle – to make them disassociate "murder" with what goes on there – in The Circle it's not murder, it's called winning.

"Murderer?" the woman questions in disbelief, the word sounds foreign dropping off of her tongue.

"Well, does it look like a mammoth has done this?"

"Yes," she says at first without thought, though she clearly thinks for a moment longer and then glances back at Lidia's watchful eyes. "I suppose not. I'm not sure."

"The Cobra…" Lidia speculates.

"The what?" the woman asks.

"Never mind."

"Master Oberon… when he finds out about this – he will make everything fine again."

"Sure," Lidia doubts that though. "I better go find Huron so he can tend to this."

First thing in the morning Huron can usually be found walking the footpaths in the forest just behind The Master's chamber so Lidia heads in that direction. It's never all that difficult to find Huron, a man with the girth of a giant surely stands out amongst a crowd, even if the crowd is a crowd of trees.

"With the earth," Lidia calls to Huron timidly.

"May we be cleansed. What brings you out this early?" he asks, his voice a low boom.

"I've been… making up for lost time."

"Good, as you should be," he turns to continue his route.

"There's something you should know… There's a body in the colony centre, by the greenhouses," Lidia explains.

He turns, "A body?"

She nods her head, "She's…dead." Lidia shudders at the word, "Has Master Oberon risen yet?"

"He is gone for the day – it's his rest day. I will tend to it," Huron says without flinching.

How convenient, she thinks, a body turns up in the colony centre and The Master has disappeared for the day.

"Get back to work," he instructs her as his steps thump toward Alva.

Strange, he didn't ask Lidia to lead him to where the body is. Nevertheless, Lidia hurries to the greenhouses and it isn't long before she hears the screams of Kalians fill the colony centre – the terror digs into her skin as she worries what another murder in the colony could mean.

^

At the end of the day Lidia heads directly home to Favoured Peony, dread washes over her when she remembers that her mother has invited Burelle over for dinner. It's the last thing she wants to do especially after the day she's had. For all she knows Burelle could have murdered his first merger and now Alva. Maybe Master Oberon knows all this and hired him to take her and The Tarnished out for their vigilante attempts at justice. Maybe it all has something to do with the rotten produce... That is a silly thought she attempts to convince herself. She waltzes in the front door to see Burelle sitting at the kitchen table with her parents.

"With the earth," Wade greets Lidia.

"May we be cleansed," she nods. "Mother."

"How was your day?" Bethin asks as she stands up from the table to get Lidia a tea.

"It was… strange," Lidia notes.

"Did you hear about the body?" Burelle asks.

"I found the body."

Bethin gasps, her hand finds its place across her chest, "Oh my."

"Mammoth or murdered," Lidia debates out loud. Her father, Wade, isn't the chatty type; rather his words are always meaningful and made to count.

"Mammoth," Wade states.

"Wade!" Bethin gasps before composing herself. "We will hear tomorrow, following The Master's rest day."

Lidia is tempted to say that they likely won't hear the truth but the version he wants them to hear – instead she purses her lips and the table sits in silence for a time.

Burelle interjects the silence after a while: "I saw you cleaned the kitchen yesterday Lidia… at Insignificant Oaklyn. I wanted to say thanks," he smiles.

She clears her throat, "You're welcome."

"Do you want to have dinner with me there, tomorrow night?" Burelle asks. Her eyes dart between Wade and Bethin, back and forth, assessing their reactions.

When Bethin offers Lidia a reassuring and excitable nod, Lidia agrees, "Sure."

If she ends up dead in the colony centre like Alva, it will be her mother's fault as far as Lidia's concerned.

# 93

# OPI OF INSIGNIFICANT CANNELLE TAGONDO

Opi walks into The Master's chamber, just as Treena is in the midst of another fit with her father, he stands off to the side. There's a brief exchange of words where she expresses that he's not challenging her enough, not giving her enough responsibility. Though Opi has heard similar conversations in the past between the two of them, tensions seem to be amping up as of late. Suddenly Treena turns and marches out of the chamber, anger seethes from the movement of her limbs.

"I am at a loss with her. I can't have the people seeing the way she behaves." Master Regan throws his hand up towards the doorway where Treena has exited.

"She is fiery, your grace. You should be proud," Opi offers.

"I knew it from the day she was born, and yet I had no idea her flames would be used against me – her own father."

"Things will get better, she will start behaving… she can't misbehave forever," Opi suggests, trying desperately to aide the unease that seems to reside in his Master.

"That's just it, how to get her to behave?" Regan appears in thought as he grasps at his chin, "That's it! You, Opi."

"Me? What about me?"

"You will keep an eye on her – encourage her to behave. That will settle things down."

"What would you have me do, your grace?"

"Whatever it is you think will encourage a change in her. I'm counting on you." Opi nods nervously. "In the meantime, I was thinking that you should take a visit to your friend Mae, see if she knows Vera's possible whereabouts," Master Regan adds.

^

The Tagondo hospital is small, Master Regan hasn't placed much significance on having a large one, nor does he place effort on how it's run – except for implementing the law whereby Tagondians must seek his approval for entrance into the hospital for treatment. It doesn't matter what form of treatment, the patient could be holding their own leg in their hand and hobbling upon the other one – approval is needed.

The Doctor who is in charge of the hospital, Doctor Yani, is well trained. Apparently she was a Nurse Practitioner in the Old World and trained to gain her Doctorate of Medicine thereafter. Though, Doctor Yani is not working on this day, Opi knows that it's Mae's day to run the hospital. Mae is sweet and kind, and in her own naivety always sees the good in others – even when there isn't any good to see.

"Mae," Opi greets as he waltzes into the hospital with a bouquet of wildflowers from the field.

"Oh Opi, how are you doing today?"

"Fine, just fine. Here, these are for you – wildflowers for a wildflower," he says to her and with a smile he hands her the flowers.

She giggles at the compliment. What she doesn't know is that some compliments said off the tip of such a tongue are actually a shield for deception.

"Oh, they smell marvellous, thank you," she offers him a quick peck on his check.

"I had a couple questions for you, flower."

"Mhmm?" she says as she busies herself with placing the flowers in a metal vase with water.

"Did you know Vera of Insignificant Canelle?"

"Not really."

"What about Cole?" he questions. Opi is aware of the soft spot that Mae holds for Cole, though he doesn't know why she holds it.

"Yes, I knew Cole quite well." She glances down to the floor and a brief pained expression passes over her face. "What does that have to do with Vera?"

"It's just that Master Regan is growing tired of searching for her. I wondered if you know of any special places the two might have gone?"

"No, Opi, I truly don't. Cole and I… didn't really talk all that much after Vera showed up."

"Did either of them say anything to you about an antitoxin?"

"No, I've never heard of such a thing. What is it?"

"Oh, nothing of importance," he taps his knuckles upon the flat surface of the table at his side. "Well, that's all for now I think. Enjoy those flowers," and he kisses her forehead before leaving.

If the antitoxin is in the hospital – Mae would know. At least Opi can scratch that off his list.

# 94

## Atticus of Favoured North
## Kala

As each day passes Atticus betters his combat stance and general straight-forward movements, but not only that, his mobility while running is improving. Since their last venture at the lake together, Illandra seems to make many appearances, which does wonders for his spirit. She makes him happy, even though his eyesight has stayed much the same – seeing only shadows, so long as he takes kinsmet daily.

Due to his and Lidia's increase in work production, Cole has some time off from the greenhouses during the weekends now, so he trains with Atticus in the clearing by the lake. Atticus wants to learn how to manoeuvre, but not just that – he wants to learn to fight, something he's never had the possibility of learning before. And to think at one time he wanted to take Cole's life – that would have been a big mistake.

They train through the heat of August, when they feel the sun-like flames on their shirtless backs. Atticus teaches Cole to cover himself in the sap of an aloe plant, which helps protect their skin from the rays of the sun. Cole teaches Atticus lessons in combat stance, balance and quick reflexes. Atticus is aware that it is also important to rely on his hearing more, considering as he now sees less than before his altercation with Digger. Even though he at least can see shapes, his ears can very well save his life, just as Cole's have for him in the past.

Cole comes at Atticus with his sword, Atticus hears the movement in front of him and holds up his cane to block the strike. It works this time.

"Again," Cole demands.

Cole comes at Atticus from behind this time – Atticus hears the rustling in the grass and ducks right before Cole can thump the stick into his back. Illandra snaps her fingers in delight as she watches from the shade of the trees.

"Again," Cole repeats.

Cole tiptoes toward Atticus and throws his body into Atticus' side and he falls to the ground. It wasn't the first time and it certainly won't be the last that Atticus misses a cue.

Cole holds his hand up to Atticus' throat. "You're dead," Cole says. "Again."

They continue, relentlessly, on Cole's days off, and only when they are certain there are no Defenders around. Atticus is tired, but the desire that twitches at his fingertips is stronger. He wants to know how to protect himself – he wants to know how to protect Illandra, his mother, Vera, Lidia and many others. The kinsmet is what gives him the sight of shadows, and therefore it's what gives him hope. It makes it so that he doesn't slump into a depressive bag of bones. He can never go back to pure darkness, he won't. However, if he is going to take out people like Digger and James Barlow, he'll need more than just intuition and kinsmet pills.

^

Master Oberon announced earlier in the day that there is to be a One celebration following dinner this evening, and so, Atticus ventures to the colony centre to meet Illandra for a walk before they head to The Pit. He reflects upon how they have been walking down the paths a lot together over the last few weeks.

He can see her shadow just passing by the front of the hospital. Her dress is tight at the waist and bows out into a tiny bell that rests just below her knees while her hair sits back in a bun with a couple loose curls dangling.

"You look beautiful," he says, but he whispers this to ensure no one else hears.

"You couldn't possibly know," she laughs.

"But I do."

"You're a peculiar boy, Atticus North," she says.

He can hear her smile, the joyful, subtle sound that lips make when they spread wide in pleasure. Since taking kinsmet, he recalls hearing noises that he's never noticed before taking it. Maybe he was just numb to hearing such subtle sounds, back in the days when he was more reliant upon his eyesight. He ponders if that is the norm for everyone, if the use of sight hinders the other senses, or if taking kinsmet has done something to enhance his hearing.

"Man," he clears his throat, "A peculiar *man*," he corrects her comment, a smile forms on his face.

She giggles, "Technically."

"Are you holding my lack of proper eyesight against me?"

"I would never," though playful sarcasm tickles her voice.

He gasps playfully at her comment as they walk.

"Eyesight or no eyesight, I will still call you boy," she teases.

"So long as I'm your boy," he abruptly says in a moment of pure innocence. Illandra makes him happy, but it's a rash assumption, to suggest that he makes her just as happy. An awkward silence follows.

"Someone's coming," Illandra whispers, but Atticus heard their footsteps long before her warning.

"With the earth," the man says to them as he passes.

Atticus and Illandra speak in unintentional unison, "May we be cleansed," and a chuckle arouses from their throats.

Following a stroll by the lake and the sun's descent, the two eventually head back toward the opening of the colony centre. The sky grows dark above them as it does later in the evenings during the summer months. Atticus can see the fire gleaming through the trees down at The Pit, the celebration is beginning. They walk down the solar-lit path of trees that lead directly from the colony centre to The Pit, the familiar smell of burning flesh and bones cling to the air.

Kalians take to their seats upon the wooden benches around the fire, Master Oberon sits in silence at the head of the circle – zoning out to the steady reverberations of the drums. The Defenders stand in rows behind Master Oberon, lining their backs along the edge of the forest. The light of the fire touches various angles of their faces, creating shadows in other parts.

Atticus views the beginnings of the ceremony in greys and blacks, but he knows exactly what it is he is missing, he doesn't need to see their features to know the fire is casting shadows upon them. The musical ones continue their gentle low pats to the drums and many colony members hold drinks in their hands. Atticus assumes that they've likely already missed the dancing at the beginning, but that is okay as others are still arriving. There will be more dancing to come, following The Passing.

"Want to sit here?" Illandra asks him, among the designated Favoured seats.

"Wherever, you lead the way."

Illandra sits down and Atticus follows suit.

"Hi, darling," Ida's voice says, she takes the seat beside him and it's obvious that she's been drinking – her breath reeks of whiskey.

"Hi, Mother. I guess we better walk home together tonight, we're both sort of compromised right now," he chuckles.

Ida holds her head back and laughs joyfully, "Yes."

She never laughs like that anymore, it is sad to think that it takes the drink to make that laugh return. Though he can still make her laugh sometimes, it's never quite as it used to be, when Hendrix was alive.

Master Oberon stands, which means Alva of Favoured Retners' bones have all been retrieved and cooled. The colony members take their seats and the drums stop.

He begins addressing the crowd: "It is time, my friends. The time has come for The Passing. We pass Alva around the fire with love and in unity. With a vision that if we work together, one day our water will be cleansed and we can expand beyond The Motherland."

"One," the crowd hums.

"Now we must pray," a slight pause in Master Oberon's speech. "Oh Mother Earth, we pray for you to carry this woman's spirit to her afterlife and to bless us with abundance on this Earth for the rest of our days," Master Oberon says as he faces his people.

Alva's bones rest in a heap at Master Oberon's side, already cooled. Atticus reflects upon how it is said that the fire cleanses her from her life as an Almek as well as her wrong doings, her mistakes. He wonders what mistakes and wrong doings of his own will need to be cleansed one day. Atticus watches as he sees Master Oberon's shadows pick up one of her bones and one after another he begins passing them to his right after giving, what looks likes, each piece a careful caress.

Atticus caresses the bones differently than he had before – this time he does it knowing that one of these times this could be him… depending on what Master Oberon decides with Digger. He hopes that in the event of his own celebration of life, others will do the same for him. The Passing is a lengthy ceremony as there are, after all, over 200 bones in the human body – All the while the fire crackles and that is the only sound, it's oddly peaceful and easy to get caught up in – the entire ceremony is.

Ida leans into Atticus and whispers, "Vera hated these ceremonies," as they continue passing the bones.

"She *hates* a lot of things," he responds.

"With fair reason… mostly," Ida smiles, though Atticus can't see it, he feels it.

"Right. There is always a reason," Atticus agrees.

Once all of the bones are passed around the fire, as a good luck omen Master Oberon readies himself for the final prayer.

"One with the earth," the single chant is spoken by all.

The Defenders then place Alva's bones, respectfully, in a wheelbarrow and roll them off toward the bone hut, which is some four hundred yards from The Pit, and tucked in behind The Master's chamber – it is essentially their cemetery.

The drums pick up once again and those who wish to can stay for more drink and dance.

"I think I'm going to go home," Illandra yawns, Atticus can hear it over the steady beats of the drums.

"I'll walk you home. I'll come back for you Mother," he says as Ida turns and waves them a good-bye.

"I should be walking you home."

"Don't say that," he hates the idea of being useless when he longs to protect her.

The colony centre is empty – all Kalians are either home or at the celebration. Still, the sounds of The Pit fill the centre of the colony, so too the shadows and flickers of light from the fire, though Atticus sees it all very differently than Illandra does. The greys and blacks sway and flicker and he imagines it all in colour in his mind. Over beside the hospital Atticus comprehends a commotion of some sort happening between shadows.

"Get down," he urgently instructs Illandra in an effort to avoid the confrontation.

They crouch down behind some nearby bushes that sit in front of The Master's chamber, just beyond its fence. They watch as one shadow swiftly wrangles an opposing shadow, though Atticus has no clue who is who and what they are doing. There are screams and grunts of exertion and suddenly more shadows appear. One of the shadows begins moving, rather fast, heading deeper into the forest.

"What is going on?" Atticus whispers to Illandra.

"There are five shadows," she responds.

"Wait, you see them in shadows too?"

"Four of them are wearing dark cloaks… They blend in with the night."

"What are they doing?"

"They're restraining someone… a man… I can't tell who it is."

"Who are you?" the man whines as the four figures drag his body toward The Master's chamber.

A shadowed figure speaks in a deep, husky voice, "The Tarnished," it states.

"Crouch down lower and stay quiet, they're coming this way," Illandra instructs.

The night is quiet, with the exception of drumming from The Pit and the grunting of the five shadows. Now that he thinks about it, the drums are kind of eerie as they build suspense for what is going to happen amidst this strange altercation.

"What are they doing?" he asks Illandra.

"Oh Atticus, it's horrible…" her voice fades with a flinch.

Atticus can hear the straining of bodies, the clash of metal brushing metal, and then the sudden ear-piercing wail that echos off the trees as it sounds followed by a final snap.

"What's happening?" he asks more urgently.

Another shrill scream echoes off the buildings in the centre.

"Shears…"

"Shears?" he repeats, not understanding the significance of such a word at a time like this.

"They just cut off his… with shears… I think I'm going to be sick," Illandra's body jolts to distance herself a few feet from Atticus.

"Hey, hey, it's okay," he soothes, though he doesn't actually know if that fact is true.

"They are tying him to the pillars out front now," she manages to describe, though she sounds unwell.

The smacking of a fleshy limb hits a surface near them.

"One of the cloaks threw his… *member*… on the stairs of The Master's chamber."

"Whoa," he chokes. "It's… it's okay," attempting to keep her calm as a means to stay unnoticed. He can't imagine the pain, the finality of it all. "But why?" He nudges his body beside her once again.

"To expose him… it seems," she says. "But I don't know why."

Suddenly the man shouts in a crippling voice: "Let me fucking go, right now!" Atticus swallows, the gulp tugs at his throat because after hearing the man's voice now a second time, he knows exactly who it is.

"I think he has been doing unspeakable things," Atticus says in a hushed tone.

Illandra shudders at his words, he feels it against his arm. All of a sudden it seems as though a breeze sweeps across the centre and everything feels cooler. Maybe it's the knowing that the man before them is Digger.

"One of them is painting words on The Master's chamber," and she continues as each word becomes visible to her: "Tribulation… for… sexual… Offenders," she reads. "Who is that man I wonder?"

"It's Digger," Atticus states.

"Digger? Are you certain?"

"Quite certain. I can tell by his voice."

"Has Digger been a sexual Offender?" she asks.

"I think so," he replies. However, he knows so.

"I can't believe The Master has arranged for me to merge with him. How could he?" she questions, bewildered.

"There's flaws in the system, Illandra. Deep flaws," Atticus replies. Though he wonders how this altercation will affect Digger and his possible upcoming meeting with Master Oberon.

"I can't go through with it," she states.

Atticus looks to Illandra, "I'll never let that happen." And they watch as the four cloaked shadows run off into the night.

^

"My eyes aren't changing, they're not getting better," Atticus explains to Torant the next morning.

"They will stay as they are, always seeing in the form of shadows," Torant states.

"I wish there was another way."

"There isn't."

"Tell me, how did you know it was Digger?" Atticus asks.

"Hmm?" Torant questions back.

"How did you know it was Digger that did this to me?"

"You said so."

Atticus sighs; he's growing impatient with Torant's constant avoidance of the truth. "I didn't. I said nothing before you began telling Illandra," he argues.

"Oh, is that right?" Torant says as he slowly moves about his kitchen.

"Tell me," Atticus demands.

"Boy, you cannot talk people into confessions. Haven't you learned the way of The Masters yet?" Torant asks.

"What is the way of The Masters?" Atticus retorts.

"Manipulation, threats, abuse…"

"I haven't seen Master Oberon do such things," Atticus notes.

"I don't suppose you have," Torant says.

"Are you not going to tell me?" Atticus provokes him once again.

"I do not tell people things that they do not need to know."

"Fine."

"There is one thing, however, that you do need to know," Torant says.

"What is it?" Atticus asks.

Torant freezes then and his words are but a faint whisper: "Change is coming, and we must prepare."

# 95

# LIDIA OF FAVOURED PEONY
## KALA

Wolves, Lidia has always admired them – their sophistication, bloodlust and loyalty. She has never associated herself with the mark of such a proud animal, for she always thought of herself more as a rabbit – timid, scared, although fast and instinctual. A sheep, she scoffs at the comparison, there is no way she and her group of Tarnished are sheep, not anymore. They are fierce, thought-provoking women who need more – they need a voice, they need action. Aphria is right, and Lidia is glad she finally sees it.

Weeks following Alva's One, The Tarnished head for the colony centre in the middle of the night. With a mixture of water and pureéd beets, the four women paint their words like forbidden art across the colony: "Eliminate the ceremonies" and "Freedom to Feel" are written on the paths in the dirt and upon the buildings in the centre. On The Master's chamber Lidia writes: "May the fires in our bellies stoke that of our voices – The Tarnished." The Defender on duty is pacing the southern paths at this hour.

Emille turns to the group, "This is so dangerous."

"That's why I like it," Aphria replies.

"It's more painful to live in silence," Lidia reminds them.

"You don't think we'll get caught?" Ursai asks.

Lidia stands with a smirk, "To hell with them!"

The heat of the summer night and their daring mission brings the women back to a time in their lives before the Water Crisis: a time when they biked the streets aimlessly with their friends and caused mischief as children do; a time when they didn't have to fight for their rights or fear for their lives; a time when no one feared the poisonous waters; a time when one could marry whomever they so wished. The air smells fresh, like dirt and lilacs, to Lidia it smells like opportunity. Change is in the air and she can feel it – it's as evident as the stars in the sky and as bold as the moon's glow. She proudly glances at her allies, whose faces are sternly focused with the thrill of the freeing sensations of the night.

^

The aches of physical exhaustion possess her limbs the following day, but it's not like the emotional life-sucking exhaustion that she once felt. This is an empowering exhaustion, one that makes her feel as though she finally knows what it means to live. Still, she works through the day at the greenhouses, relatively unchanging in physical workload.

Following her shift, Lidia has plans to spend the evening at Favoured Oaklyn. Plans were made during dinner with her parents and Burelle a few weeks earlier - he asked her to join him for dinner the following evening - but being partially busy and partially leery, she cancelled his invitation numerous times. Tonight's dinner is in place of her previous cancellations as she has run out of excuses for avoiding his offer.

She arrives at her soon-to-be home and hesitantly knocks on the door, even though she isn't required to since they are to merge.

"With the earth," Burelle says in greeting.

"May we be cleansed," she forces. Burelle motions for her to come in.

"So… I hope I haven't made you feel put on the spot by asking you to join me for dinner here," he says.

"No, no, you didn't. I'm sorry I cancelled, it's been a strange couple of weeks for me," she says.

"It's not a problem," he replies as he directs her to the kitchen.

Lidia looks about, in the living room sits an old chessboard upon a small coffee table, a stack of books rest beyond it; his items are all aged and obviously date back to the Old World. The couch looks rather comfortable though, as far as couches in the colony go. The kitchen is a part of the living room, with the kitchen table in the very middle, which seats two. Burelle motions to the table and they sit.

"So what do you want for dinner?" Burelle asks.

"I can make it," Lidia says, instantly pushing her chair away from the table readying herself to stand.

"No, no, I invited you. I want to do it."

"Ok," she sits back down. "I'm not really sure what to have."

At this point, Lidia doesn't actually care. She's exhausted from The Tarnished's late night and a long day with the plants. The only mental focus she has enough energy left for is her suspicions toward Burelle and his previous merge, but even that is lacking today.

"I know what I'll do," he says as he gets up and begins gathering various items to prepare a meal. He chops vegetables and adds them to a pan on the stovetop, he tilts his body in her direction, "So how do you like working with the plants in the greenhouses?"

"I love it. There would be no other suitable profession for me."

"That's really nice… to be placed somewhere you want to be," his voice veers off.

"Why? Are you happy? Where would you want to be?"

Although she is skeptical of him, she knows just as well as the next Kalian how to humour a conversation – exhausted or not. Besides, if he should try something, her Tarnished will take care of him like they took care of Digger.

"Happy… I'm happy to be alive, to be one of the survivors from the Old World. But am I doing what I enjoy? No."

"I think about that all the time – the fact that I survived."

"Out of the 9 billion people on the planet… Why us?" he adds then stops chopping the vegetables and looks up at her, she meets his gaze for a moment and realizes that there is a sense of ease that washes over her in looking at him, though she looks away just as quickly.

"Yes, those 9 billion people who dropped dead."

"Oregon seemed to be the last to get hit. I don't know why."

"Maybe the earth was just over populated and that was her way to cut back – survival of the fittest, or most observant at least."

It was a thought she'd never considered, but the idea gives her shivers, "Maybe… maybe the ones that died from drinking the toxic water didn't heed the warnings, therefore didn't have reserves before meeting up with Hendrix."

"Anyways, we aren't supposed to talk about the Old World," he says in a whisper and Lidia simply nods her head in agreement.

It isn't long before he brings over two steaming plates filled with zucchini noodles and fried vegetables – it's simple, it's Almek. For the most part they eat in silence and following dinner Lidia clears away the dishes and washes them. Burelle thanks her for spending the evening with him and she leaves Insignificant Oaklyn feeling surprisingly light.

# 96

# IDA OF FAVOURED NORTH KALA

She's keen to watch Cole's plan unfold in trying to rescue Vera – even if she doesn't know if Vera is alive. Still, Cole needs to be the one to go find out, he's the only one who can truly survive the journey. She knows that there is something she can do to help his plan along: cause an interference, but not just any interference – she'll have to put Almay's life on the line.

That night Ida scurries to the broken-down hut that sits to the side of the footpaths near the lake and carefully opens the dilapidated door. Underneath the falling-down structure there is a brown object that protrudes out of the dirt and she slips a note inside.

"Sorry Almay," she whispers. It isn't long on her walk back through the paths that the whispers sound, they only ever seem to speak when one is alone.

*"Have faith,"* the whispers say.

She chuckles then, only it isn't a genuine, joyful chuckle, "Have faith. Ha!"

Having faith seems like a difficult thing to do due to recent events, never mind the fact that her son is now blind and suddenly spending an undesirable amount of time over at Favoured Wells. It's true that she is pained by Atticus' blinding; however, she will ensure that justice is met. Aside from taking care of Almay, there is something else Ida needs to tend to on this day, so while she knows Atticus is out she heads back home and flies in the door, locking it behind her.

She walks directly to the hutch that blocks the cellar door, pushes it to the side and heads downstairs. Sitting on a wooden crate she pulls out Hendrix's files. "Alva Retner," she whispers to herself as she scans the rows of papers.

A few moments later she pulls the R files out and locates Alva's. Inside are whatever details Hendrix was able to gather on Alva and her family from the Old World – she had two sons and a wife – there is no indication as to where they ended up. Alva was from Denver, Colorado and worked as a detective in a local crime unit. She must've been in Oregon for a different reason that day. Ida wonders how Alva wound up getting herself killed… After a moment of thought, Ida reaches for her black marker and writes "DECEASED" across the front of her file then places it amongst the stack of other files that belong to the dead. She is struck by a gnawing awareness that her pile is only getting bigger. It is time.

# 97

# COLE OF FAVOURED WELLS
# KALA

Cole doesn't know Digger nor does he know what he has done to deserve such a tribulation, though whispers spread throughout the colony like dandelion seeds willed by the wind. He's still unsure who the whispers belong to, but he hears them just the same. Maybe Creaosis, the woman's name, so he assumes, that is carved on the jail wall, has something to do with the whispers.

He is unsure if what The Tarnished did to Digger the night of the One ceremony is just – perhaps they don't seek justice, perhaps they are in search of something else. As a result of The Tarnished's display, The Master has called a meeting with only the Favoured colony members. This is a rare occurrence and seems to be rather poorly planned – to cram a couple hundred people into The Master's chamber is a trying feat, although not nearly impossible. They stand in rows like soldiers, only much less intimidating, facing The Master at the front of the room. They take their bow in unison.

"With the earth," the group says then remain standing in silence.

"May we be cleansed. My dear Favoured, we have but a dire situation. There have been several scandalous acts, offending acts, happening here in our very colony. Should any of you know whom is responsible, please step forward." The room sits still. "I will no longer allow such acts to continue. It is against our laws. Our laws – the very values that hold us together like glue, without them… The Almek will fall to ruin. It is a delicate balance, as I'm sure you know, keeping thousands of people in sync and in turn our civilization a float. Therefore, if any one person is caught partaking in an Offending act, they will face immediate tribulation and there will be no waiting period. Depending on the severity of the crime and that of the law that has been broken… immediate exile or death will be the verdict."

Even though Cole is a new member of Kala, he knows that Master Oberon has never taken to enforcing immediate action – he always investigates offending acts and finds a fair tribulation. That is all beginning to change. The Favoured share concerning glances, though they aren't glances that suggest any of them are specifically Offenders – it's merely the finality of Master Oberon's words that send an unsettling into their minds. Kala is changing.

"I know this comes as a scare – and I do trust that my Favoured are all respectable, law-abiding citizens. I suspect that these acts are being done by the Insignificants," Oberon explains, as if the Insignificants are suddenly less than, possibly the scum of The Motherland. Though, somehow, it still sounds respectful and justified coming from his lips. Several Favoured nod their heads in agreement.

Master Oberon continues: "Which is why I have asked you all here today. The first person to come forth with knowledge on those identifying as The Cobra or The Tarnished will be repaid a handsome reward."

"What's The Cobra?" whispers spread amongst the people.

"Silence," Master Oberon demands. A hush falls over the crowd once more. "A handsome reward, such as no share requirements for the remainder of the year, will be available." Whispers fill the room yet again – questions in wanting, everyone wants to know who The Cobra is. Who are The Tarnished? The Kalian whispers come up empty in identifying them though.

"We don't know, your grace," one man speaks out.

"Haven't a clue in the slightest," a lady offers.

"I have a question: what are you going to do to ensure the public's safety?" Cole shouts.

Master Oberon's eyes meet Cole's. "Cole of Favoured Wells," Master Oberon begins, "Your mouth seems to find trouble for you often."

"Master Oberon, it has and I'm sure it will again. But more often than not it has aided me. Now I'll ask you again – what do you plan to do to keep the public safe?" Cole asks.

"The people of Kala are perfectly safe. If we stick to our laws, respect one another and the Earth – we will be safe."

"What about the deaths?" Cole probes.

"Do not fear, my people, we will ensure there are Defenders out on watch as always. The Cobra will be caught, so too will The Tarnished."

Master Oberon squints in the light that beams in through the windows, his gaze soon rests notably upon Cole's jacket. Cole doesn't realize that his jacket is open, and inside it, resting on his shirt underneath his Favoured Wells crest is the Favoured North crest. A sliver of the unauthorized crest sticks out from underneath his jacket; the dual glint catches Master Oberon's attention.

"What is it that you carry behind your Favoured Wells crest?" he asks Cole.

"Hmm?" Cole questions as he innocently glances down and notes the edge of the North crest sticking out, visible to all. He quickly pulls the sides of his jacket closed together.

"Huron, retrieve that object," Master Oberon orders.

Huron approaches Cole within a millisecond and instantly one large hand wraps around Cole's neck, practically encasing it in its entirety. Huron grips tightly, so tightly that Cole can't move even if he wanted to for his grip will surely choke him.

With his other hand, Huron reaches behind Cole's jacket and rips the North crest off of his shirt.

"It's a Favoured North crest, your grace," Huron's voice booms as it always does, only today it feels louder as it echoes off the hundreds of bodies in the room.

"Where did you get that Favoured North crest?" Master Oberon inquires. *Uh Oh.*

"Umm, I was-" Cole begins, unsure of what to say.

"Stolen. He was at Favoured North a month ago, maybe a bit longer, your grace. He must have stolen it when I wasn't looking," Ida interjects.

Cole looks to Ida, a sense of betrayal washes over him. *She set me up.*

"Is this some sick joke?" he questions Ida.

"Have you no control over your own household, Ida North?" Master Oberon asks.

"I… I do. Yes."

"But you had a family crest taken from you, the very thing that represents your family – our circle," he says accusingly.

"I suppose I lost control briefly, but just for a moment," Ida explains, her frame trembling.

"I thought better of you. I expect better of you," Master Oberon shakes his head in clear disappointment.

"Master Oberon, it was taken from me without my knowledge," she pleads.

*She wants me dead. How could I let her set me up like this?* Maybe she also blames Cole, as Atticus once had, for Vera's transfer to Tagondo.

"That is inexcusable and quite frankly disrespectful. Huron, take these Offenders to the colony centre – I order twenty lashings for Ida of Favoured North for insubordination. Ten lashings for Cole of Favoured Wells for being in possession of an unauthorized family crest."

And just like that, Master Oberon follows through with his threat of immediate action on Offenders. As it turns out Cole isn't the only one in shock over this change as commotion arises across the room. The crowd retreats to form a pathway for Huron to reach Ida.

Several thoughts swarm through Cole's mind, thoughts surrounding Master Oberon's intentions with Ida and his own place in the unraveling of all of this.

"You've made a mess again," Torant whispers to Cole as he appears at his side.

"Yeah well, I clean up my messes – Ida has sure made a mess for me."

"Is that so?"

"What do you want Torant?"

"I came when I heard."

"Heard what? About my lashings?"

"Never mind your few measly lashings – Ida of Favoured North is about to die."

"Did you not hear the verdict? Clean out your ears old man – he said lashings for Ida, not death."

"The lashings will be the end of her."

"What can I do?" Cole asks.

"Keep quiet. An unfiltered voice only causes damage. You better learn that sooner than later."

"Anything other than that?" Cole asks, "Staying quiet is really not my strong suit."

"Take this to Ida – she'll know what to do with it. And tell her to meet me at Favoured Wells," Torant passes Cole a familiar leaf, a leaf from an ivani plant. "And go accept your ten lashings," Torant states, then instantly disappears.

Cole wonders why Torant didn't just give Ida the ivani himself. Regardless, he needs to move quickly and so he walks through The Master's chamber and hastily makes his way to Ida, he notices that she is wearing a backpack, but for what?

Nevertheless he must move quickly as Huron already has Ida in his grasp, her hands tied behind her back in a thick, brown rope. Cole runs at Huron and with all his might he forces his shoulder into Huron's side – Huron falls to the ground with a growl, as Cole grabs Ida's wrist and instantly presses the leaf on it.

Her pupils begin expanding and it's evident the oils of the plant are beginning to seep into her bloodstream. Cole wonders then why Torant didn't give him two ivani leaves, then he considers that it's probably to ensure he graciously receives his ten lashings; after all, Torant isn't all that fond of him. He wonders if he should indeed continue and follow through with Torant's orders. Torant, a man who isn't a friend of Cole's – hell, he wants to let Cole suffer ten lashings. Maybe it is all about helping Ida, the woman who set Cole up and made him out to look like an Offender. Torant is in love with Ida, of course he wants to help her first. Then he thinks of Vera, Ida is her mother and she'll be heartbroken if she dies – he decides then, he'll do it for V.

"I can't believe I'm actually going to do this after what you just did… but you must go and meet Torant at Favoured Wells," he quickly whispers in Ida's ear. Huron rises to his feet and restrains Cole by forcing his wrists behind his back.

"You won't regret this…" she says as she runs, her voice but a mere wisp in the breeze followed by the chamber doors swinging open then closing with a forceful gust.

"What is going on?" Master Oberon shouts as the doors cause a stir.

"A ghost," shouts one.

"A witch," shouts another.

"If I may, I think that is all nonsense. And there are serious, horrific, Offenders at play here," reasons another.

Master Oberon raises his hands, "My people, calm yourselves. Where is Ida of Favoured North? Show her to me." The crowd freezes, eyes search the room. "Huron, find Ida North at once. In the meantime, Defenders, take Cole of Favoured Wells to the colony centre and ready him for his tribulation."

Two large hands place a rope around Cole's wrists behind his back. Another set of hands push him forward, toward the doors. A brief thought crosses his mind, he wonders whose hands will be at the other end of the whip.

# 98

## VERA OF INSIGNIFICANT CANNELLE
## UNKNOWN

Vera lies awake upon the dirt floor of the room her captor holds her in. She is growing more and more wakeful by the day, although she still feels as though her head is encased in an unrelenting fog. She can keep her eyes open for a few minutes at a time now before falling back into the abyss. The IV needle is still attached to her, so too is the sling on her injured arm.

When she wiggles her toes, tears tempt the corners of her eyes at the fact that she can finally feel her feet again – though she can't move them to the extent that she needs in order to escape. It's in these little things that she finds hope. She needs to look to these little signs of assurance otherwise she'll fall into a depressive state upon her few wakeful moments. If she can feel her body more and more by the day, one day maybe she'll feel it enough and will walk again. One day, she'll leave this place – wherever it is.

She still has no visual of who her captor is, though they appear to come in daily and now bring food and water. She is alert enough that she can lift her neck and bring her hand to her mouth to put food in and hold a cup to her dry lips. It appears as though they are nursing her, but she can't understand in her right mind how someone can consider this good help. She doesn't know how long she's been kept here for, or when it's day or night.

The black mask arrives once again, down the tunnel from beyond. A dark, slinking figure from the shadows appears.

"Hello?" Vera calls, she can speak more coherently now. "Who are you? Can you please tell me how long I've been in here for?"

The black mask doesn't respond, they merely add more substance to her port and away she goes, back into the darkness that she's been living in for far too long.

# 99

# COLE OF FAVOURED WELLS
# KALA

He is tied to a post, his arms wrapped around it in front of him, for the remainder of the day – put on display for all to see just how tormenting it is to be an Offender. No water, no food and baking in the hot summer sun for hours on end awaiting his official tribulation.

Two Defenders sit watch for no one is to speak to the Offender and the Offender is to speak to no one; though, for the first time in a long time, Cole doesn't want to speak. His mouth grows drier by the minute, parched from dehydration. He doesn't move, granted he can't for the way his arms are tied. He doesn't shuffle his feet nor rotate his head, instead he saves his energy for what is to come.

Since he can't move, or talk, all there is to do is think. He thinks about Vera, about the water, about Ida and her gimmick. He has been wronged by others before - it's never stopped him - and it won't stop him this time. He thinks about Torant and his ability to remove Ida and keep her safe. Torant always seems to have a way to make it out of disaster – if he so chooses. It seems intentional that Cole is exposed as an Offender and readied for tribulation, but he reminds himself that part is Ida's doing. Still, Torant played his part. He decides then that if he is going to keep this secret about Ida's escape then Torant owes him knowledge of the antitoxin. Fair is fair. Besides, most men would kill Ida for what she did to Cole.

It's just before sundown when the Defenders encircle him in the colony centre. The Master and his Barons appear, standing in the shadows with their hands clasped neatly at their fronts. Cole closes his eyes as the drums sound an eerie hum that is much unlike the celebration of life drums. They beat faster; they force one's heart to race. The drums are a signal for tribulation – an invitation of sorts. The people eagerly accept and join the gathering – Cole can hear the swarm of Kalians gathering around him. He opens his eyes to glance around at his spectators. His head pounds from dehydration – such an unpleasant feeling. *The lashings will be worse*, he warns himself.

Huron approaches, whip in hand – so those are the hands that will wield the whip. He figured it to be so. Huron is always the first in line to do The Master's bidding. *Just like Rimmy*. He supposes that all Masters need someone that's willing to mark another's life.

"The time has come," Master Oberon speaks to the crowd.

Cole feels the weight of two large hands - the hands of a giant - manipulate his body by forcing him to stand. Huron grabs Cole's shirt in two fistfuls and tears it away from his body, exposing his back, exposing his old scars.

"Let's get this show on the road, shall we?" Cole taunts. He isn't scared – he's had lashings before. He knows that the lashings will come and then they will be over.

"Anxious to get started, are we?" Huron asks.

"It's nothing I haven't done before."

"You've never had a lashing done by my hand," and with that Huron swings the leather whip and Cole hears in a nanosecond the whip thrashing away, distancing from him and then anchoring back toward his body. The *swoosh* in his ears comes immediately before the blow.

"Ah!" he moans and the sting spreads goosebumps across his back.

The whip returns, again and again – each strike more painful than the last. He counts them: the fourth one splits his back open, he knows by the way the whip burns deeper into his flesh – the way it burns beyond his outer skin. Fluid streams down his back in small rivers.

"You're right, Huron," Cole pants, "No one whips quite like you."

The fifth whip comes and relentlessly bounds his torso into the post. He gets back to his feet and readies himself for the sixth. As Huron forces blow upon blow to Cole's back, speckles of blood splash across the post from the movement of the whip. Trying to distract his attention, Cole wonders who will have the job of cleaning this post – The Masters never like bloodshed being left expelled like this.

"Still want more?" Huron mocks.

"May we be cleansed," Cole says then tenses through his gritted teeth as the whip collides with his back once more, slashing his flesh and exposed muscles – he has no idea how much this tribulation has mutilated his back.

His back begins to slightly numb and the pain that he does feel is where his flesh is split open, where his insides are vulnerable to the breeze.

The tenth thrash comes swiftly and knocks him to his knees. His vision blurs, but only slightly. He looks to the ground below him as he feels warmth immediately encasing his knees – stewing in a puddle of his own blood.

# 100

# Atticus of Favoured North Kala

Atticus sits on the rocks outside Torant of Favoured Wells' house moping and awaiting news. He ponders Torant's words, "Change is coming." He didn't imagine that change would include Ida leaving him, just like the others have. It sure feels as though everyone close to him leaves. Vera, Hendrix and now Ida - even Lidia attempted to - at least she didn't. However, he hasn't seen much of Lidia over the past few months, so in some ways she's left him too.

Atticus' thoughts wander back to a question that nags at him: why did Ida lie about the crest? He contemplates what her motivations could possibly be for lying about Cole stealing their family crest. Cole didn't steal it, she gave it to him and Atticus was right there, he heard the entire transaction. He wonders what Ida is up to.

Maybe he's being melodramatic. Surely Ida has a good reason for what she did... His caring, smart and reasonable mother. He just hopes she's safe and that he will one day see her again – he will ask her then. He realizes that he can't confidently say the same for Vera though. However, he has to trust that Torant got Ida away safely. Trust doesn't come all that hard to Atticus, especially since he knows that Torant is in love with Ida – he will ensure her safety.

As he sits outside of Torant's house, he notes that there is someone else missing – it seems as though Almay is not home and in fact he realizes that he hasn't seen her since before the Favoured meeting. A wonder of where she's snuck off to crosses his mind. Still, he wishes there is more he can do to help during this mess, instead of sitting stagnant – instead of hearing Cole face his lashings, that was painful yesterday, for Atticus to stand by the colony centre and listen to the sounds of disdain and torment. To see the shadows move in such unpleasant ways that displayed the lashings to his mind's eye in black and shades of grey, which made the whole experience even more teeth clenching. It doesn't matter though, he had to be there, he had to witness – the drums are a mandatory attendance, not an invitation.

Atticus reflects upon how in the wake of two Favoured offending, Master Oberon appears to grow in anger. He notices that significantly more Defenders roam the footpaths by the week's end and now a Defender stands at every footpath, increasing pressure among the law-abiding citizens – which can only mean that more Defenders results in less foragers and in turn raising the share obligations of families in the colony. Now that Ida is gone he will soon be an Insignificant household and will be able to go unnoticed throughout the colony as most Insignificants do. He assumes that he will be getting an Insignificant North crest in the coming days.

The Tarnished haven't left their mark in a while, he knows this because there haven't been any messages from them upon the colony centre. However, two men were recently found dead in the forest – both strangled with sliced stomachs. Atticus comes to think that the strangled necks are a symbol - a symbol of power - Alva and Theodus had this symbol placed upon them too. But there is no knowing who the murderer is, Atticus has his own list of suspects though.

The victims were probably approached from behind, as Cole taught him to do in their combat calls. *But who would do such a thing? Really kill someone... and for what reason?* He supposes someone who wants desperately to prove a point. *Could James Barlow or Digger be capable of such things? Could either one be The Cobra or The Tarnished?* He struggles to understand how people can treat each other so barbarically. Some acts seem to be intended to end a life, and seem to be randomly executed. While others seem more targeted but are merely warnings – like Digger's altercation. Atticus ponders the purpose in their differences and who is responsible for which act.

Atticus sits feeling defeated and bored on the rock wall surrounding Favoured Wells when suddenly footsteps patter quickly towards him.

"Atticus, you must come quick!"

"Illandra, what is it?" he asks her.

"The exile – it's going to start any minute," she speaks through trying breaths.

Atticus is dumbfounded, "What exile?"

"Digby's."

"I don't understand, what happened?"

"I told my mother everything. Master Oberon apparently spoke with your mother too before… well, before the ordeal yesterday, because of what you reported to him. He revoked our merge agreement and has ordered Digby be exiled."

Though there's excitement dancing on her voice, it seems to hold sadness that he can't quite place. She should be relieved.

"You don't sound too happy about that."

"I mean, he's being exiled, I feel terrible – no one survives out there, in the outskirts. But, I'm glad that I don't have to merge with him."

"When is it happening?"

"Now – we must go. Can you run?" she reaches for his hand.

"Hell yes, I can!"

Atticus feels the warmth of Illandra's tender hand slip into his as she tugs him forward and he is right, he can run. He still needs to have the cane in his other hand, just in case, but all of the training with Cole has helped immensely in his recovery.

Atticus can confidently fly through the forest, only not nearly as fast as he once used to.

Illandra and Atticus make it to the colony centre where a mob of Kalians gather. The siren rings once to signal there is an exile to take place. There stands Digger, at the front of the mob, his head hangs sorrowfully at his shoulders. Following the siren, Master Oberon signals for Digger to begin walking – every Kalian knows the place that they send off the exiled. Master Oberon follows Digger, his Barons walk closely behind him and the rest of Kala comes after. The Defenders encircle everyone as they walk.

Digger leads the colony through the forest, beyond Favoured Barlow's moss-covered cabin and towards the border where Kala meets the outskirts, the unknown. There is a field at the border, as far as the eye can see beyond the tree-line in Kala. Everyone halts in silence as eyes focus on Digger. Master Oberon stands with his head held high, his gaze looking just beyond Digger, out into the grassy field. Atticus thinks that they release the exiled at the field so that all can watch for some time as the exiled walk away and if they should try to come back, the Defenders would see.

Master Oberon steps toward Digger, "Digby Espen, you have brought great shame to the Kalian name. Your actions have spoken, they have said things that I do not want shared within our borders. It is time to let Mother Earth have her way with you. Be gone and never return."

Following his speech Master Oberon simply waits. He says no more words in these moments, for there are no more words to be said. Digger has done horrible things, things that his victims will have to live with for the rest of their lives. Atticus feels no remorse for him – in fact, as Digger takes his first step out into the field, a smile the size of his jawline stretches across his face.

# 101

## Lidia of Favoured Peony
## Kala

Lidia has been spending an increased amount of time at Insignificant Oaklyn as of late, mainly to prepare it for her upcoming move. On this day, Lidia cleans the bedrooms and prepares the one at the far end of the house for herself. It's customary for the woman to move into the man's house, and lately that doesn't bother her all that much because it means she can get some space away from her mother. Bethin is the main reason for Lidia's newfound agreeable nature in regards to moving into Insignificant Oaklyn. If he turns out to be involved in his previous merger's disappearance, she will find out and The Tarnished will take care of it. However, the more time she spends with Burelle, that thought becomes increasingly outlandish. Burelle is gentle, soft even – at least he is whenever she is around him.

As she makes her soon-to-be bed she reflects upon recent events. She knows Ida has disappeared and Cole is in rough shape at Favoured Wells, she hopes they are both safe. As natural as the pigment of green is on grass, Lidia worries for them. She worries about the terrible things that could happen to Ida. Ida is a smart woman, but all she knows is plants – she's no warrior. To fend for herself in the wild, to face the unknown with mammoths… death will be sure to find her.

And what of Cole? He's a warrior, apt in every physical regard and yet his body lashed to the point of being bed-ridden. He will need weeks of recovery before he can move about as normal. Her teeth graze back and forth on the right side of her bottom lip, the pace quickens in her most worrisome moments. Also, to her dismay, she has grown so accustomed to Cole's presence. She prays to Mother Earth for some form of guidance. The Mother always has plans of her own – perhaps this is all a part of her plan.

"With the earth," Burelle says as he enters the bedroom.

"Oh, you startled me," she holds her hand up to her chest. "May we be cleansed." He smiles.

"I apologize, I didn't mean too, I…" he begins.

"It's okay, really."

"How are you making out here? Do you need a hand?"

"No, you're supposed to be relaxing after a long, hard day foraging while I clean," she reminds him.

"Yeah, so The Master says. I like cooking, so maybe I'll go make dinner then."

"Again?" she asks in shock. It isn't the male merger's duty to cook, and yet he has done it all week.

"Sure, why not?"

"It's just that…" she hesitates.

"It's not typical?" he asks.

It isn't the word she's looking for, and yet she nods her head. It's something along those lines… She reflects how she practically waited on Kobe hand and foot and with no thanks.

"Can you make that stew with the mushrooms?" she finally asks, feeling only a slight sense of guilt for her request.

A smile of satisfaction spreads across Burelle's freshly shaven face, "Of course."

^

Despite the increase in patrol and danger, The Tarnished continue to meet almost nightly. Seeing as Lidia isn't quite living with Burelle just yet, she doesn't have to explain a thing to him in regards to her late-night whereabouts, at least not yet.

Lidia still spends countless nights watching the guards from the shadows, understanding their nightly patrol – especially after Master Oberon increased Defenders. The increase does make things more challenging, but not impossible. Lidia discusses with the members about taking a strategic break. She voices that it's possible to prove their point while keeping their heads about them and that it would be foolish to attempt a drastic move while Master Oberon is so outraged and unpredictable.

"What of Ida North?" Aphria asks.

"I don't know her whereabouts, but it doesn't mean she's dead," Lidia says. In some ways she says this in an attempt to convince herself.

"Let's pray," says Ursai.

"Yes, let us pray to Mother Earth. She will guide her," Lidia states. The women sit, holding hands in prayer. Lidia speaks: "Mother, please keep Ida North safe. Please guide her in her journey. Bring her back to us, when the time is right." The group sits in silence for a moment.

"Ida's such a sweet woman, I don't know her well but we would often cross paths at Division and exchange pleasantries," Emille reminisces.

"She is the most pleasant woman, so kind and caring. She was my mentor through the years in the greenhouses. If there is anything I can do to bring her back, or keep her safe, I will," Lidia explains.

Aphria changes the subject: "When will we run the paths again?" seemingly anxious to make another mark.

“When Master Oberon calms down. I don’t want any of us to be found,” Lidia states.

“But people are out there, women are suffering – men too,” Emille adds.

“You’re right. But we won’t be able to help them if we can’t help ourselves,” Lidia pauses, “I’m sure things will settle in a few days.”

“What’s next on our list then? For when it’s time,” Ursai asks.

“I’ve heard The Whisperer comment on a peculiar merged couple that live on the northwest side…”

# 102

## COLE OF FAVOURED WELLS
## KALA

Forced to lie on one's stomach for weeks on end is surprisingly not the worst part of Cole's recovery – being taken care of by Torant Wells is.

"We must redo the bandages," Torant notes.

"Leave them be, they're fine." He's had enough of the poking and prodding, not to mention the oil that Torant pours over his wounds smells of stale, moist leaves, the way they soak into the ground at the onset of fall. Cole neither likes the smell nor the tingling feeling that it offers his back.

Each time Torant walks by, he creates a tiny breeze that brushes across Cole's body – the slight pressure of the draft shoots painful stings across his back. "Would you just sit still?" Cole begs.

"It's not easy to sit still when there is work to do."

"But you're not doing anything. You're just pacing."

"I'm waiting."

"For what?"

"For your back to heal. It is agonizing," Torant says with a knowing smile – as though he knows exactly when Cole's back will be healed. Cole wonders why on earth it's so frustrating for Torant to wait for *his* back to heal. Doesn't Torant see that it's far worse being in Cole's shoes?

"Must be so hard being an all-knowing expert with insight of the future in his hands," Cole barks.

"It is harder than you think. The urge to step in and…" Torant's hands shoot up into a grasping motion, as if gesturing to squeeze the very thing he wants to change… whatever that is.

"To step in and what? Change it?" Cole asks, his interest spikes as do his accusations.

"That's not what I was going to say."

"Then what were you going to say?" Cole retorts. Torant doesn't respond. "Where is Ida North, *Tortund*?"

"I have told you – she is safe."

"Where? Did she leave the colony? She will die out there you know."

"She is perfectly fine."

"You're acting pretty nonchalant about this whole thing. As though you're not worried about her – were you ever truly worried about her?"

"You're smarter than you're given credit for," Torant proclaims.

"I'm just sick of people using me for their own selfish reasons. Ida tricked me – are you a part of her ploy too?"

"She had to."

"Where is she? And where has Almay gone? I haven't seen her and baby Elan since before the Favoured meeting."

"It is for your own safety that you do not know where Ida is. Almay left with baby Elan, of course."

Cole thinks about Torant's words for a moment. How is anything either of them have done for him for his own safety? He is sick of the bullshit. On the other hand, Almay leaving The Motherland with Elan makes total sense, as it was something she was planning to do. Though, why she wouldn't have said goodbye surprises him.

Cole turns his head to look Torant directly in the eyes, "You know what, that's enough of the fucking riddles old man. Tell me right now – where can I get my hands on ivani and the antitoxin. I need them both to rescue Vera."

"I…."

"If you don't tell me where I can get them – I'm going to announce to the entire colony that you're hiding Ida North," Cole threatens.

Torant drops down into a chair at the kitchen table without a word. He presses his fingertips on the bridge of his nose. Cole sits up right, though it is slow and with immense pain, and he watches Torant in bewilderment.

"The fuck are you doing?" he asks, growing impatient. "Fine, I'm going right now. I'll hobble my ass down to the colony centre if I have to. So long as everyone finds out what you've done." Cole stands to his feet, groans of pain and discomfort grumble in his throat.

Torant stands and walks over to Cole. "Sit down. You're not to move about just yet," he guides Cole back to the couch. Cole is in no position to fight back, still he pushes Torant's hands away.

"Then tell me," he manages in painful exhales.

"You could get us both killed," Torant hesitates.

"You will end up dead either way, my friend."

Torant sighs, he knows Cole to be right. "I keep ivani here, I have plenty of it. The antitoxin is… " he clearly fights to say the words, potentially because he knows of the trouble it will bring – Cole doesn't care though.

"Spit it out old-timer."

"It's here…" Torant confesses.

"You make it?" Cole asks.

"Not exactly." Torant sits down across from Cole.

"If you don't make it, where does it come from?" Cole questions.

"The rowan tree… among other ingredients.

"The rowan tree… but isn't that what…" Cole begins connecting thoughts.

"Kinsmet is made of?" Torant interjects, "Yes, they are one and the same."

"You have been giving Atticus the antitoxin?" Cole asks unbelieving.

"He needs it for his eyesight – he doesn't know what all it can really do though."

"You've put his life at stake! What if someone finds out? There are whispers about the antitoxin through the footpaths, everywhere."

"I know," Torant admits, "that's unexpected."

"So the rowan tree offers us immunity from the toxins in the water? And it helps the blind see?"

"Basically, yes... among other things."

"What?"

"It causes a shift in the cerebellum in the brain."

"We don't all speak voodoo doll – English please."

"It heightens one's senses when consumed. The longer one takes it, the better."

"So what does that mean?"

"I take it back," Torant says with a judgemental glare.

"Take what back?" Cole asks.

"What I said about you being smart," Torant states.

Cole huffs, "The antitoxin, the rowan tree, makes our senses stronger? But how does it allow us to drink the toxic water?"

"Does water not move oxygen through our bodies? And are our bodies not made up of sixty percent water?"

"I guess so?" Cole wonders.

"That is your answer."

"Need more, Tortoise."

Torant sighs and continues, "The toxins prevent the water from moving oxygen throughout the body, it enters the blood stream and does the same. Thereby within minutes, a human being dies from lack of oxygen to the brain. The antitoxin allows the passage of oxygen to continue."

"Was that so hard?" Cole asks sarcastically. "Then why can't we touch the water?"

"It is absorbed by the skin and enters the blood stream."

"Hm. So it essentially suffocates us no matter if we touch it or consume it?"

"Just like our pollution has done to Mother Earth, yes."

"Is the antitoxin always taken in pill form?"

"Yes."

"Can I have some?"

"If I give you some, you are at risk. At least Atticus is unaware of what he has in his possession. Sometimes the less you know – the better," Torant tries to reason. Once again, Cole doesn't care though.

"I don't give a shit. I need it to rescue Vera," Cole says growing impatient. "Listen," he speaks more calmly now, "I've been sketching out a plan for weeks: I'm going to use the antitoxin to swim across Lake Cloud and then ivani to get through the Tag forest and to Insignificant Cannelle."

"How do you know she's not already dead?" Torant poses the idea.

"Do you know? I don't have any logical reason other than a feeling," he admits, "but it's enough to make a go."

Torant ignores his question, "And you don't think there is anything else that you should be doing?"

"I'm doing this."

"Very well," Torant stands to his feet and wanders to the cabinet that sits above the sink. He reaches inside a tin can and pulls out a small burlap sack. Torant turns to Cole, "Don't tell a soul."

"I won't. I just need it to help Vera."

"I am giving you this because you've proven yourself worthy. But take heed, Cole, if you try to travel right now with those wounds – they will likely get infected. The probability of you dying is far greater than you succeeding."

"I'm not going to go just yet," Cole puts his hand out and Torant places the bag in his palm. Cole peers inside the small sack, there has to be at least 100 red pills sitting inside the tiny bag.

"Keep your head about you Cole," Torant warns.

"So, I take one pill once a day, like Atticus does?" Cole asks, glazing over Torant's warning.

"Yes, for each day you will be consuming or in contact with the poisonous waters."

"Can you get more?"

"Yes."

Cole stuffs the sack in his pants pocket and reflects that Torant must have a secret ally, someone who produces the antitoxin, then he thinks of the mysterious figure that lurks by Favoured Wells at night. No, the antitoxin won't cleanse the water, but it can save The Almek from meeting their deaths when the spring runs dry.

"Good, 'cause we're gonna need *a lot*."

# 103

## OPI OF INSIGNIFICANT CANNELLE TAGONDO

As instructed, Opi has been following Treena closely throughout Tagondo as the search for Vera continues. This is the longest a search has ever run, but Opi knows it is imperative for Master to find Vera before she compromises his search for the antitoxin. Master Regan has Rimmy organizing the search in shifts, they have ensured that Opi and Treena share the same schedule so that Opi is able to keep an eye on her and so far she's none the wiser.

Opi walks with Treena this sunny afternoon as they and twenty other Tags scour the woods. Each day the searches go as far as the Tag border, but no further. He often wonders if Vera's dead and they just haven't found her body yet, after all a soft Kalian like her wouldn't survive a run-in with a mammoth.

As others glance up in the trees Opi studies the bushes. One of these days he's sure he'll find body parts. Though, as they explore the forest, he can see eagerness in the others that he struggles with locating within himself. Finding Vera alive means she will be killed. What if he is the one to find her? He will have no choice but to turn her in. And so, although he is a seeker, he simply hopes that he is not the finder.

A Defender approaches Opi, "Any sign of Vera?" his voice sounds indifferent, though bordering on hopeful. It's both terrifying and awe-inspiring how Master Regan has his Defenders fully accordant to his wishes.

"No, Defender Malek, I haven't seen anything."

"Call me Finn."

Opi whispers, "Well, Finn, between you and me I'm betting she's already one with the earth."

"Vera? I find that hard to believe. You have yourself a good day, Opi."

Opi strolls to catch up to Treena, huffing and out of breath he begins his attempt at swaying Treena's poor behaviour, "You know, your father is such a good man – he is trying his best to find Vera." Opi doesn't mention her father's reason for continuing the search, as he doesn't know if Treena is aware of the antitoxin. But he does know the good that the antitoxin will bring for The Almek.

"I won't be satisfied until I find her body lifeless and in pieces."

"You think a mammoth has gotten her?"

"I'm counting on it," Treena beams. "It's only a matter of time until we find her." Opi nods knowingly. "And, my father can be as useless as an Insignificant," she spits. "So I'm betting I'll need to tend to it and find Vera on my own accord."

"You don't mean that. You need to go easier on him. He only wants what's best for you," Opi offers as they continue walking along the brush, eyes constantly scanning.

"He only wants what's best for *him*."

Opi attempts to reason through his panting: "Surely what's best for him, is in turn, good for you as well."

"That's not entirely true. But we'll see. All will be known on my twenty-fifth birthday."

"What's supposed to happen on your twenty-fifth birthday?"

"When we first came here he made a promise to me – he promised that he will give me a portion of the colony to rule upon my twenty-fifth birthday."

"Oh. When is that?" Opi inquires.

"December fifth."

"That's only a few months away."

Treena looks at him with a sly smile, "Yes, the clock is ticking."

^

Opi walks through the paths later that evening, after he and Treena go their separate ways from their day of search for Vera. Luckily his new task of watching Treena isn't a twenty-four-hour round-the-clock venture. So, at this time, he's headed to Favoured Adder to report to Master Regan.

As he travels, he admires how the solar lights illuminate the footpaths as well as the edge of the green pines and wild spruce trees. He reaches the colony centre and turns down a walkway alongside The Master's chamber and walks to the back of the building, his focus remains on the trees, but suddenly his side vision catches sight of two people – their bodies repeatedly plunge into one another.

Opi quickly backtracks to hide behind the other side of the building – he needs to leave right away – *Trouble* - that's all these two people represent. *But who are the two people?* People who choose to hide their fornication and yet are unable to wait for a more opportune place for such an act. Their impatience leads one to believe they hold a certain passion for one another. His curiosity outweighs his urge to flee – hopefully he won't get spotted if he just peeks around the edge of the building quickly.

The moans that filter through the air are deep and low; the breeze blows, rustling the branches in the trees as if attempting to cover their groans of pleasure. He sees the lovers then with their pants-less asses exposed, one thrusting into the bare flesh of another. The grunts are those of two men.

Squinting his eyes in the darkness as if willing them to focus, even with his glasses on, Opi eventually catches a glimpse of the men's faces in the warm yellow solar lights – a croak escapes his mouth in sudden shock. As their moans grow louder it amazes Opi that no one else can hear their pleas for climax.

They finish and it is Lincoln who playfully speaks first: "Did that meet your expectations, your grace?"

"Turn around," Master Regan replies. "Tonight, you're mine."

"I was yours last night and the night before that too," Lincoln chuckles.

"And you'll be mine again."

# 104

## Atticus of Favoured North
## Kala

Toward the end of August, Atticus waits for Huron to come take his Favoured crest. Though his crest won't be confiscated until after he leads a search for Ida. Cole is still recovering and so Torant takes to training Atticus; however, his training is unconventional. There are no textbooks in which to study, no duals to train his reflexes and ears, but instead they train the use of his hands.

It was decided between Cole and Torant that Torant is to show Atticus how to read with his hands. No one conferred with Atticus on this, but seeing as he spends much more time at Favoured Wells in recent days than his own house, it makes sense. During his lessons, Torant notes that the pressure of any pencil upon a piece of wood or paper leaves an indent and he'll need to silence his mind and focus his efforts on his fingertips - his sense of touch - to decipher this. Atticus soon admits that his sense of touch seems different after exploring this new skill, and so he does as Torant instructs, grazing his fingertips along paper after paper. He soon notices that the grooves from one piece of paper to the next feel different, which makes it difficult to make out the words. Upon feeling the slightest indent, Atticus excites himself thinking that he's gotten it, only to lose his focus and with it the spark of sensitivity at his fingertips.

"Is this an H?" Atticus asks Torant.

"That's incorrect."

"What's this? An M?"

"No," Torant simply says.

It's unclear how Torant expects him to get anything right when he doesn't offer the slightest clue or assistance. Though Atticus isn't one to get frustrated easily, he may in due time. Even so, he persists, and when he needs a break from reading, or when they have some spare time, Torant teaches Atticus how to improve his fine-motor skills without the use of his eyes.

Torant has chosen to do this by means of introducing Atticus to one of his hobbies: making dolls. Atticus faintly watches as Torant's hands move about as he cuts the fabric and wraps twine around a piece of wood to make the shape of the body. He then places twine atop the heads and carves each a face in wood with a tiny piece of wire, among other utensils.

"Is this how you made my cane?" Atticus asks.

"Yes, I have been carving and whittling wood since I was a boy."

"How can I do it? I mean, without cutting myself…" Atticus asks.

"Feel the wood, feel the tool. Once you have the body shape, the face comes naturally."

Atticus watches with what sight he has, as Torant's grey hands move this way and that, elegantly conducting the movement of his fingers; seemingly as if he's playing a harp or some other delicate musical instrument.

"You see all, right Torant?" Atticus decides that now is as good a time as any to push for some information.

"More or less. Less or more."

"Do you know where my mother is?"

"Young man, your mother is safe and sound," Torant states.

"Will I ever see her again?"

"That, I cannot say."

"Did she know about the kinsmet pills? I never told her I was taking them."

"Well, if it isn't time that we have something in common."

Atticus sighs, "You didn't tell her either then?"

"It would not have sat well with her."

"Probably not. Do you know anything about the antitoxin?" he finally asks.

"Quit asking questions and focus," Torant instructs.

Atticus knows that Torant is withholding the truth, for he walked up the steps of Favoured Wells just the other day and overheard a very interesting conversation between he and Cole. Atticus now knows that he's been in possession of the antitoxin all along – it's the kinsmet. He also knows that, supposedly, his senses are heightened – the thought is strange though. He also now knows about ivani, where it is and what it can do for him.

Seeing as Cole has already told Atticus the plan to get Vera, and Cole can't go, maybe he will. He can run now and use his cane as protection, even if it'll be haphazardly. Thanks to training with Cole and his heightened senses – he's doing better. It is, after all, time he takes action.

## 105

## TREENA OF FAVOURED ADDER TAGONDO

"It's not enough that she's missing, I need to see her for myself," Treena spits to Cain the next morning. She's growing sick of the on-going search and has convinced herself that Vera is simply playing games.

"There's no way she's alive, I'm telling you I broke her arm that day I saw her in the forest. There is no chance in hell she's survived living out there, let alone with a broken arm," Cain argues.

Treena sits upon the stairs outside of The Master's chamber, with not so much as an attempt to hide how she truly feels.

"That's not enough though," she whines then lies back, shifting her weight to her arms that now stretch out behind her, settling her hands on the floorboards of the stairs. Cain sits beside her. She pushes her chest out, her crest out. Cain ogles, as he always does. She counts in her mind: *One, two, three,* he licks his lips.

"Find her, Cain, and let me see her. I know you're the only one who can bring her to me," she says coyly.

"I am. I'll do it," he replies.

She sits up then, leans over to him and brushes her lips overtop his forehead, "You're so good to me."

"I will always be good to you," he whispers.

She doesn't fully believe him, but his words are enough for now. If he finds Vera, that will be worthy of her faith in him as, truth be told, Cain isn't all that bright. All she has to do is flaunt her crest and breasts in front of his face and he's willing to do just about anything. But she knows that she needs men like Cain, she practically thrives off them. She holds his balls in the tiny palm of her dainty hand and she loves nothing more than giving them a squeeze, not enough to cause pain per se, just enough to keep him impressing her. Hunger and desire, she thinks, are the best ways to motivate a person, because everybody wants something.

# 106

## LIDIA OF FAVOURED PEONY
## KALA

August is nearing its end and Lidia reflects how she will miss the warm temperatures that come hand in hand with the summer months. Although, there is something that spikes her interest for the months ahead: Master Oberon has set the merge date for her and Burelle in one month's time, the first of October.

She stands at the kitchen sink of Insignificant Oaklyn washing dishes as she hears the front door quietly open and then close. It's Burelle, for there would be no one else walking in uninvited. Her eyes stay focused on the soapy water in the sink as an arm reveals a bouquet of some unknown plant in front of her face. She closes her eyes and reopens them to focus.

"It's sorbis," Burelle exclaims.

"Oh, how nice."

"They're for you."

A warm sensation tingles her cheeks as she rinses the soap off of her hands; she dries them and then reaches up to accept the bouquet. The pea-green leaves tingle against her skin, and she immediately notices that this plant buzzes more powerfully than any others she has felt. She wonders more for a moment about the tingling, how the plants came to evolve into buzzing against one's skin like the wings on a bee.

"I've never heard of sorbis before. The leaves are beautiful," she says as she inspects the light green leaves that encase veins intersecting in circles, not just lines. The leaves' shapes are round and plump with pointed tips on the very ends.

"Smell it," Burelle encourages.

Lidia lets the edge of her nose move in close to the plant while she eyes Burelle curiously, not knowing what sort of smell to expect. In her experience, she either loves or hates a plant's smell – there is no in between. As she inhales a sort of warm floral scent brushes at her nostrils, she smiles, though she isn't surprised by its soft, warming scent, considering how intricate and beautiful its leaves are.

"Thank you, it smells and looks so beautiful. What do I do with them? Do you cook with them or are they simply for aesthetics?"

"You can cook with them or you can put them in a jug full of water. I'll let you figure out the rest," he smirks.

Suddenly an unexplainable urge soars through her arms as she springs forward and wraps them around Burelle's neck, pulling him into an embrace.

^

When the moon glistens off Lake Cloud, everyone is still for the night and the mammoths roam the colony, so too do The Tarnished. They have someone in their sights, someone who needs to be held accountable for their actions – and it can't wait any longer.

The peculiar man, Thode Musk, has a wife whose skin is tainted with the scars and colours of abuse. However, this is still an assumption - The Tarnished only act upon truth - they need to be certain, without a shadow of doubt, they need proof. So, proof is what The Tarnished seek.

One can obtain proof in many ways, such as watching, waiting. If one watches long enough, people are bound to show their true colours, it's in their nature because nobody can be someone they're not, not forever. It's in these vulnerable moments that The Tarnished get what they need. And so, off they go, dancing in the forest amongst the fireflies as if the pathways are lit just for them. They creep to the window of Insignificant Musk, light-footed and vigilant.

"Shut up, Agnes, you're worthless!" he shouts, his voice seeping outside through the cracks of the windows.

"I'm sorry, I-I," Agnes' soft voice fumbles over her words.

He stands then, flat on his feet, and winds his arm up. When the backside of his hand collides with her face she instantly falls to the floor. *Proof.* Lidia immediately engages their plan and throws a rock at the front door: something to stir a sense of curiosity in Thode. Two of her wolves, Emille and Ursai, stand back a bit farther on watch. Lidia throws another stone, he opens the door then and peers out, his maddening stare shoots out into the dark, but nothing can be seen for the wolves are out of sight – waiting and ready to pounce. Emille cracks a tree branch, a signal of a welcome invitation. He will come. They always do.

"Come if you dare," Lidia whispers as she scales back into the trees with a giggle, though knowing he can't hear her, it's purely for her own enjoyment.

He soon descends down the stairs and stomps along the short footpath into the abyss of the forest where no one is truly safe.

"Where are you? You bastard!" he shouts. When silence answers he calls, "Show your face you sack of shit!" Emille cracks another branch for good luck, or for no reason at all. "Fight like a man," he says with his fists up, because it certainly couldn't be a woman out taunting him at this hour of the night.

Then, without notice Aphria whispers in his ear, "You mean a woman," then smashes a large branch against his head, knocking him down unconscious. Ursai diligently ties his hands behind his back as Agnes comes out of the house, presumably to see what the ruckus is all about, she simply stares at her still husband lying on the ground. Though she's a fair distance away as he is amongst the trees, she can see enough to know the body is his.

"You're safe now," Lidia says to Agnes.

"Who are you?" Agnes asks through the darkness, through tears and blood-soaked lips.

"We're The Tarnished," Lidia states from the shadows of the trees.

"Are you… helping me?" Agnes asks, dumbfounded.

"Yes, that's what we do. We protect those who cannot protect themselves."

Agnes nods then, as if she understands, then says: "Where are you taking him? What if he comes back?"

"The mammoths will deal with him now," Lidia explains.

It isn't technically murder, for they will not be the ones to stop his heart, and so the four wolves then slink through the paths while they carry with them the weight of a brute.

They leave Insignificant Musk and stop to tie Thode to a tree in the forest – they know they can no longer use The Master's chamber as their stage, at least not to tie a man to as the Defenders are constantly on guard there now. Besides, here in the forest, the chances of a mammoth coming for him are greater.

The women then slink through the shadows and stop just before where the solar lights by The Master's chamber touch the trees. They watch as a Defender walks across the centre and past the hospital. As soon as he reaches the forest beyond the hospital they run to the chamber for they'll always find time to make their mark in the colony.

Aphria hastily paints: "Men that use their hands against women should have no hands at all – The Tarnished" across the chamber wall.

"I tied his hands significantly tight. If he still has them come morning they'll be black and blue," Ursai says.

"Good. Thode is no more, but the rest of The Almek – they must understand," Lidia states.

As soon as Aphria completes their notice, The Tarnished turn and run through the footpaths with the moon on their backs and a bramble-filled forest ahead of them. In the distance the mammoths howl their unearthly songs; there was a time when these songs used to give Lidia a fright, the kind of fright that makes one's flesh ripple with goosebumps, but she doesn't get that anymore. *In some ways, we're a lot alike*, she thinks regarding the mammoths. *Tarnished, broken, hungry – seekers of the night.*

# 107

## VERA OF INSIGNIFICANT CANNELLE
## UNKNOWN

When Vera wakes she wakes to a light, almost airy, feeling. She notices that she can move her right arm today – the sling has been removed and it no longer aches the same way. Still, her body feels weighted, but it's not quite as heavy a feeling as usual. The IV is still lodged into her vein, she is pretty sure it's the culprit of her drowsiness. Vera reaches her right arm over and gives the tubing a tug – only her muscles are weak, as they haven't been used in an undetermined amount of time, which means she doesn't have the strength to pull the IV out.

She glances down at her body: her clothes have been changed. That realization sends a disturbing sting through her stomach for someone has seen her naked, the details of which are entirely unaccounted for in her memory. As her awareness grows, so too does her fear of who has been keeping her hostage. She decides to explore her surroundings the best she can while she has the energy. Her eyes spot a plate that sits just off to the side of her waist in the dirt – bread, some vegetables and a glass of water are within her reach, her mouth begins to water at the sight.

She struggles to prop herself up on her left elbow, it sinks into the dirt below her as she shakily reaches for a piece of bread. She doesn't think twice about the food or the water's origins before letting them touch her lips. As she drinks back the water, as though she's been without it her whole life, she decides that if it kills her, it'll be worth it. She doesn't eat all of the food though – she doesn't have the energy for a healthy appetite.

After some time her captor comes again, only this time instead of talking she decides to rest her head and close her eyes. She pretends to sleep, as that's what they seem to want her to do. She can hear the black mask walk about the room, checking the IV bag and collecting her used dishes. She tries not to budge, not even the slightest of muscles, for if she does they will give her more of that strange substance. She catches herself holding her breath and realizes that isn't a normal thing for a sleeping person to do, so she focuses on releasing regular, steady breaths. When she's sure the black mask has finally left, walking into the beyond, she opens her eyes.

# 108

## Atticus of Insignificant North
## Kala

Atticus leaves his meet with Master Oberon where he officially surrendered his Favoured North crest and in turn was provided an Insignificant North crest. As it turns out, there is no special ceremony for such a thing. He doesn't want to cling to losing his Favoured crest, it is simply not what's important – time is what's important and right now it's slipping away. September is here already and he knows that he needs to move. He's decided that if the colonies are going to survive, the lab needs Vera – The Almek need Vera. He is now of the Insignificants, and can no longer tend to the water in the lab. Therefore, Atticus has secured his plan to leave – tonight he's going to Tagondo to bring her back.

He walks with one hand tucked in his pocket and the other grasping his cane, and with a glance up to The Master's chamber he sees the remnants of The Tarnished's words still smudged across the exterior wall. It has only been a few days since the most recent rebellious act took place. It's a bold move - to vandalize Master Oberon's building - what's more, to tie a man and leave him for dead in the forest. It was otherworldly, and not in a good sort of way. Who knows what Thode had done, maybe he was just another Digger, or maybe he was entirely innocent – no one will ever know now that he is dead.

^

That evening Atticus wanders to Favoured Wells, but not for his typical reasons, tonight he is in search of something – actually two things. He comes to find that Cole is asleep on the couch and Torant is nowhere to be seen, so Atticus takes this opportunity and acts quickly.

He rummages through the kitchen cupboards in search of ivani leaves and more antitoxin. He is damn determined to get Vera and the best part is that he is capable, now knowing what kinsmet truly is – anything seems achievable. He finds a tin pushed to the back of a cupboard and reaches his hand into it. There he finds another sack, presumably more antitoxin – he guesses that Torant got more after giving a bunch to Cole, but there's something else. He feels a piece of paper, creased with folds. He places the sack in his pocket and pulls the paper out and unfolds it in his hands. He gently places his fingers along the curved and pointed indents the letters create on the piece of paper. But, he can't make out what it says. It must hold some significance though.

Just then Torant barges into the house from outside, startling Atticus and almost making him drop the paper.

"Atticus, you must leave Kala at once," Torant exclaims as he flies into the kitchen.

"Why?"

"It is pertinent to your safety..." Torant glances down at the folded paper in Atticus' hands, "What is that? Where did you get that?"

"I found it." Atticus sees the shadow of Torant's hand reach up to grab the paper from his grasp and quickly pulls it away from his reach.

"You shouldn't have that. Give it here," Torant demands.

"What is it?"

"It's... not important."

"Then it won't matter if I keep it," Atticus smiles then shoves the paper into his pocket.

Torant releases a rumble of displeasure in his throat, "I knew you would be trouble," he says under his breath. "Listen, you must leave Kala, I-"

"You what?"

Torant sighs, "I promised your mother that I would keep you safe, and I can't do that here... not tonight."

"Ohh, me leaving is doing you a favour?"

"You shouldn't see it that way. It's doing *you* a favour – giving you a chance at survival."

"Okay, I'll leave for you, Torant, so that you can keep your promise to my mother. But on one condition," Atticus barters, knowing right well that he plans to leave Kala on this night regardless.

Torant stands with his hands resting upon his hips, "Well? What is this condition of yours?"

"Just tell me one truth: are you certain that the antitoxin protects people from the toxins in the water?"

"Young man, out of all of this – that is the one thing I am certain of."

"Good, I was hoping you would say that."

"Now listen, don't stray too far from the borders of Kala, you must be able to find your way back and you need only be gone for the duration of the night. If you are to see a mammoth..." Torant begins to warn.

Atticus cuts him off, "I'm not running from anything."

"You're a brave, but stupid boy."

"Why does everyone keep calling me *boy*?" Atticus throws his hands into the air.

"You must leave now, you must get out of Kala before..." Torant hesitates then swiftly grabs the paper out of Atticus' pocket.

Torant then turns, slams the piece of paper onto the table and draws the lake, the Kalian borders and a circle at the bottom left side of it, "If something happens that it doesn't appear safe to return to Kala, go here."

"Why?" Atticus asks as Torant passes the paper back to him. Atticus runs his fingers briefly along the heavy indent that Torant's writing imposed upon the paper.

"For now, just do as I say. Don't let anyone see that paper."

"Okay…" Atticus says cautiously then puts his backpack on and walks to the front door.

"Atticus?" Torant calls, "Don't speak with anyone – especially if they welcome you. Find a place to hide."

Atticus turns without a word and travels into the night: a blind young man with the antitoxin and ivani in his possession hell-bent on bringing his sister home.

# 109

## LIDIA OF FAVOURED PEONY
## KALA

A persistent knocking on the front door wakes Lidia in the middle of the night. Thinking it's one of her wolves and not wanting her parents to wake, she flies to the door in a hurried spring, only she opens it to find Torant of Favoured Wells panting upon her doorstep.

"Torant? What are you doing here?"

"I do apologize for the intrusion at this hour, but I need to tell you: Atticus is gone – he took ivani with him and has fled to Tagondo to try to save Vera."

"You let him go, you-"

"There was no stopping him… not technically," Torant cuts her off.

"Well, where's Cole?" she asks.

"He's in bed, I haven't told him – he's in no condition to be out gallivanting."

"I'll go find Atticus and bring him back," Lidia states.

"Yes, but there's something I need you and your wolves to do first," Torant warns.

Lidia falters at the sudden realization that Torant knows of her wolves. She reminds herself that Torant of Favoured Wells knows all – supposedly. She also reminds herself that he likely won't share her secret for he's known for his tight-lipped reputation – not to mention he has helped her before. She is still in his debt.

"What do you need us to do then? I'm worried for him," she says.

"Cause a distraction in Kala. Bring the citizens out of their homes. It's time their eyes are open."

"Okay, I'm on it."

"There's more…" Torant notes.

"What?"

"You need to know there's an antitoxin and Atticus has it, which means he's in trouble now. If word gets out that it's in his possession, it won't be good for him. It's why I told him to leave."

Lidia raises her voice instinctively, "You told him to leave?"

"He planned to leave anyway, and him being here on this night will be dangerous."

"Wait, what does this antitoxin do?"

"It's been made to let us drink the toxic water without repercussions."

"Holy shit," she exclaims. "That's better than gold!"

"Here's the hard part. I want Atticus to get here," Torant shows Lidia a copy of a map, and points to the location that he drew out for Atticus. "I need your help. It is time you pay back your debt. After you cause a distraction in the colony, I need you and your wolves to catch up to Atticus and get him to this spot."

"What's there?"

"You'll find out when you get there. It's time Lidia – to stir up the colony. Do what you and your wolves do best – leave a mark," he states then turns and leaves.

Lidia flies into her bedroom and picks up her clothing off of the floor, she pulls them over her body and hurries out into the night. She runs and though her legs are tired from the previous night's vigilantism they carry her swiftly without fail.

Lidia reaches the colony centre and creeps through it quietly. There is something she needs to take care of before rounding her wolves, something that will otherwise stand in their way tonight. As she peeks around the corner of the school, her eyes catch sight of Huron standing outside of The Master's chamber entrance on watch – his arms are crossed, his face stern. She calms her breathing and walks into his sightline.

"What are you doing out past curfew Lidia of Favoured Peony?" Her core shakes, nothing in her wants to be alone with Huron in the darkness like this.

"I was just doing some work with the plants, I'm heading in for the night now though," she lies.

"Very well then, I will walk you home," he orders as he moves toward her.

His hands reach out to her, to claim her, to guide her home as if she's a child, but she isn't a child. Without a moment's notice she spins a knife out from her boot and pulls a cloth soaked in herth from her bra, the tip of the knife already rests on Huron's thick neck.

"You're going to let me go and you're going to stay quiet about it," she whispers in his ear.

"Okay," he agrees as he is clearly stunned.

"On your knees," she demands.

"Okay," Huron's hands rise in submission as he lowers onto his knees. However, when she least expects it his hands soar back up, he grabs a hold of her wrists and instantly rises back up to his feet.

"What do you think you're doing, mouse?" he demands.

"I don't need strength to take you," she spits in response to his power over her.

His fingers tighten around her wrists, likely leaving lines of pink. *Bruises,* she thinks. She hates men that bruise women. The herth cloth falls to the ground then and in one quick motion she reacts, stabbing the tiny dagger that she still grasps into the fleshy part of Huron's hand. He fumbles and let go of her, holding his now blood-soaked hand. Lidia reaches into her pocket - she always carries a backup - and grabs the second cloth then presses it against his face – instantly his eyes begin to roll back into their sockets.

She quickly pulls her scarf up over her airways as he stumbles down to his knees, fighting the sleepy weight that pulls him, beckoning him to rest. Lidia promptly anchors her left leg and swings her other boot up, slamming it into his head and knocks him to the ground unconscious.

^

A small pebble pings off of the window, enough to wake her fellow Tarnished wolf, but not enough to break it. Lidia travels fleetingly through the colony to gather her band and they soon meet at the shed where she tells them of Torant's message. They are to make a stirring, cause a distraction and then catch up to Atticus. Perhaps there is more reason for the stirring, she speculates, regardless, without doubt or fear The Tarnished race into the night with cloaks on and hoods up – no one can be identified, for the price is too costly.

They approach The Master's chamber – Huron's body still lies asleep where Lidia left him, just to the side of The Master's chamber. She begins to paint and just like every other night she proudly paints the words that the people need to hear. The other three wolves stand guard, watchful and patient. Nothing is more important to them than their cause.

The message is displayed in large letters across the chamber: "There is an antitoxin to save us from the toxins in the water. What are you going to do about it? – The Tarnished." The question is not only posed for The Master, but for the people as well. The Tarnished then set fire to the tips of their wooden stakes and run through the footpaths, howling at the moon, at the people – or at nothing at all. The Tarnished run past the houses in dark flashes, their cries bring the citizens out of their sleep – they call to the people, beckoning them from their homes.

"There is an antitoxin! We can drink the toxic water on the planet, question The Masters. Come, question your Master. Question your Master," the wolves chant.

People see the cloaked figures, hear their cries for answers and hear their shouts of hope. It's enough to pull them from their doorways. It's enough to make them question. Their words cause a surge of Kalians to wander outside, toward the colony centre. Their job is done. The Tarnished dig their stakes into the dirt at the centre and swiftly meld into the shadows once more to watch as it all unfolds.

"Hey, did you read that?" a man inquires.

"An antitoxin. It's like they said," another answers upon reading The Tarnished's message.

"What is it though?" The voices of the people now fill the night air – concern, fear and excitement within their words.

The citizens soon crowd the footpaths and travel to Favoured Kenoak. There they send blow after blow to the door until he appears. Master Oberon walks, with two Defenders at his side, out into the view of the people amongst the forest.

"What is the meaning of this?" Master Oberon demands.

"Come to the colony centre, Master. Come see for yourself," someone shouts.

"We seek answers," another calls.

The Defenders take immediately to a combat stance, readying themselves to fight off the Kalian mob that appears before The Master by raising their clubs. However, Master Oberon waves his hand – an asking for them to lower their weapons. He walks down the wooden steps of Favoured Kenoak, still in his nightly wears. The mob opens, allowing a path for him to walk through, and as he walks towards the colony centre they follow closely behind. Lidia continues to guide her wolves through the cool darkness, to sit and watch beneath the moon.

# 110

## COLE OF FAVOURED WELLS
## KALA

Cole wakes to the whispers coming in through an open window.

*"Fuel the fire,"* the Whisperer says.

He hears it, but in his groggy wakefulness he doesn't pay much mind to it. He rises off the couch to his feet, it feels good to stand and stretch. He's been walking a lot more the last couple days, movement is something he's missed. He wanders the tiny cabin in search of Torant, but there's no sign of him. Cole gets dressed, though it isn't without pain for his back is still a scabbing wound, slowly healing, but allowing him to begin feeling slightly more like his old self in recent days. A bitter realization hits him that the oil Torant offers daily is after all working.

He walks outside, each step sending painful aches down his back, but a noise pulls him out. Beneath the chaos he hears whispers nearby – he peeks his head around the side of the cabin and there stands Torant at the back corner of the property talking to the mysterious Kalian. Cole staggers along the wall of the house to get closer to the conversation.

"Yes, Almay and Elan left Kala," Torant confirms.

"Good. What of Atticus?"

"He left – went to Tagondo to get Vera, but I'm trying to intercept."

"Very well," the voice whispers.

*He went to get Vera?* Cole turns and walks slowly down the footpaths, baffled at the turn of events, he ponders if Lidia knows anything about it. *How in the hell did the calf get enough guts to go?*

Cole has been working so diligently on a plan, every detail, every move is thought out – just as Vera would want. He has been bedridden for weeks with so much free time to ponder on the ways of the forest and the ways of the colonies. That's supposed to be his victory. But he couldn't survive a trip to Tagondo in his condition. He's weak right now, even being the almighty Mammoth Slayer doesn't prevent this kind of weakness. Actually, in recent days it feels as though he's grown entirely soft. He doesn't much like the feeling.

Human voices, muffled and scattered, sift through the trees calling his attention. A light glows off in the distance and as he approaches the colony centre he sees two, three – four lights. As he gets closer he sees the mob of people, their shouts more audible. Now, in clear view, the glowing stakes and the marking done by The Tarnished on The Master's chamber pulls his attention.

"Damnit," he says out loud. *Now everyone knows about the antitoxin – now no one is safe.*

He pushes his way through the crowd, breaths of pain escaping his mouth as he searches for Lidia. Defenders line up in front of The Master's chamber, their voices speaking in attempts to calm the citizens of Kala. Cole can barely hear his own thoughts as the crowd's calls abuse his ears all around him. On this night, for the first time, they are not listening to the Defenders. They don't bow to their Master nor offer silence when requested. That fact alone is worrisome. Maybe it's a good thing Atticus isn't here.

"Lidia?" he calls, but he can't see her in the colony centre.

He decides that if she isn't here he'll go to Favoured Peony next, he begins heading into the forest towards her home. Suddenly two dark figures move across his eyes, and they begin moving in on him. Suddenly two more appear flanking their sides.

"What the hell?" he says.

"Shh," one of the shadows replies and moves to stand in front of him. He pulls its cloak back ever so slightly, just enough so the moonlight touches their face and he can see who it is.

"Lidia, what is going on?" he asks in surprise.

She places her hand over his mouth, "Shh, I said. Keep your voice down."

Cole glances at the other black figures that now surround him. He looks to Lidia with a concerned expression resting on his face.

She laughs, "It's okay – they're fine."

"Does 'they're fine' mean your cloaked, faceless friends aren't going to try to kill me?" He taunts in a whisper, though he means the question in all seriousness, as he knows that he's not in a place to easily fend off any unwanted assailants.

"They won't hurt you… unless… unless I tell them to," Lidia teases, though still glancing at their surroundings to ensure no one approaches. Her wolves appear to be watching too.

"I'm not sure that makes me feel any better," Cole states.

She laughs once more, "Listen, Atticus left for Tagondo – he's gone to get Vera."

"I know, the guy has more guts than I thought."

"He is brave… Braver than you think."

"I'm not saying he's not. All I'm saying is – the calf surprised me."

"He is good at surprises," Lidia smiles, as if calling upon a memory. "We're going to go find him though, and guide him away from Tagondo once he gets Vera."

Cole nods. "Why are you dressed like that? What are you, *the rebellion* or something?" he teases, though he does wonder who started the chaos in the colony centre.

“The Tarnished, to be specific. Are you surprised?” she smirks with raised eyebrows.

When Cole realizes that she is serious, he’s about to shout in shock, or excitement, or both – but Emille interrupts his train of thought.

“Someone’s in the forest,” whispers Emille with urgency.

“It’s time to go,” Lidia says.

“Should we look to see who it is?” Aphria asks.

Lidia pauses, “If we do, we must be quick.”

The group follows Lidia away from the footpaths and into the thick brush; they know to be strategic in their approach, which means never approaching a target head on – Cole knows this too. He follows them, though his pace doesn’t match that of The Tarnished. Through the brush and around the wide-set tree trunks they follow the noise, like curious beasts of the night.

The instant they catch sight of the target an unknowing ambush surrounds Cole and the four women from all angles and without warning. There must be ten, maybe twelve, figures – Cole can’t count them all, but they all stand now frozen in place.

“We mean you no harm, we will go in peace,” Lidia speaks.

The figures do not reply, instead they stand still – dark statues that blend in with the trees. The ambush begins moving, closing in on them. The moments following are a blur because the instant a cloth is placed over Cole’s face he passes out.

# 111

## VERA OF INSIGNIFICANT CANNELLE
## UNKNOWN

Vera paces the dirt room, unaware of how long she's been anxiously travelling back and forth. Although her legs feel stiff they move her from either side of the space, offering her something to do. She's growing bored and longs to escape, only she has no clue where she is or how she got here. For all she knows her captor could be sitting at the other side of the tunnel, awaiting her getaway attempt. Maybe they are even counting on it. *Then what?*

After countless minutes pass she finally builds up the courage to peer into the beyond – the tunnel that houses a world of uncertainty. However, it's as black as the lake in the night, only nothing reflects off the tunnel.

She hears whistling then – the black mask is coming. She quickly moves over to the place where she sleeps, lies down and closes her eyes. She hears the black mask sets a plate of food and a jug of water on the floor beside her, then turns and leaves.

*Now is the time – move or what? Become one with the earth in this place?* She can follow him. *Him,* she assumes. Though she decides that thought is possibly presumptuous and even sexist. It could very well be a *her*.

She rises to her feet. Her captor walks down the tunnel with a light in their hand – if they need a light, she most certainly will, so she scoops her solar light up off the ground, just in case, then steps into the tunnel of blackness.

Up ahead the captor walks, whistling a familiar tune – one that her memory can't pinpoint. It's muffled and doesn't echo off the walls as one might think it would, the dirt offers a sort of sound barrier as it swallows the tune.

As Vera walks, she drags a single finger in a line along the dirt wall marking her trail – something she learned from Cole. The reminder of him and his guidance casts a closed-lipped smile on her face with a sombre wonder if she'll ever see him again. Her shoes press into the cool dirt and she hopes that her captor will lead her out of this place.

Her captor's jaunt speeds up as she follows, some thirty feet behind him, trotting down the aimless pathways. He takes a sudden turn and his solar light begins to fade until she can see a dull line of light on the wall of the tunnel across from the path he ventured down. But that petty light begins to fade more drastically as other voices begin speaking.

In almost complete darkness now, she sees a tiny beam of new light up ahead – just beyond the entrance that her captor turned down and some forty feet beyond where she stands. She needs to find out where that light is coming from. She moves her feet in a hobble thanks to her trying muscles that are still adjusting to movement from possible weeks of lying stagnant.

She stands underneath what looks to be a skylight and realizes two things: one, it is daylight, and two, her lungs have missed the clean air from above. She hears voices grow louder, which tells her that her captor is returning. Without a definite clue as to where the exit is, and for fear of what they may do to her if they know she has escaped, Vera runs back the way she came.

Moving her legs as quickly as they can carry her, passing the tunnel her captor is in and continuing onward, in no time at all she makes it back to her room and immediately lies down, slamming her body into the dirt. Her chest heaves up and down at an impossible rate. The whistling sound down the tunnel creeps closer – that same tune. Her thoughts don't drift to ponder on its name again, this time she is far too distracted. Forcing deep, long breaths she finally lowers her heart rate and breathing.

Her captor walks in. He is wearing no mask and in that brief instant, peering through her eyelashes, she sees his face. *Those eyes–.*

# 112

## Atticus of Insignificant North Tagondo

If he were one to sit back and let fate happen as it should, he wouldn't be Atticus North – nor would he be a brother who could call himself loyal. He knows there will be consequences, as to what they may be, he can't be sure. However, he believes that nothing in comparison can be as terrible as never seeing his sister again. The sooner he gets to her, the sooner he can ensure she gets to the lab to try to cleanse the water.

Atticus slinks that night to Lake Cloud with the antitoxin, ivani in his bag and his cane in hand – he bets on his and Vera's lives that these items are enough. The sun has set some hours ago, which means the sky wears its deep blue specs of light like a blanket. In some ways Atticus prefers the night, it's in his knowing of how others' eyesight then lacks when his neither falters nor improves – the shades merely grow darker or lighter with the colour of the sky. It will always be this way, so long as he has kinsmet pills. He finds comfort in this – he supposes that it's easy to find comfort where there is hope.

As Atticus moves through the forest and approaches the lake he can hear the chaos, the noise coming from the colony centre. Normally he'd be inclined to investigate, though he knows he cannot be a part of that noise – not on this night. From his view among the brush, Atticus can see the shadows of Defenders scattered around the exterior fence of The Circle – the night guard has greatly increased in numbers with Master Oberon's stricter rulings. Dark grey mounds of living, breathing, moving objects patrol the colony.

He reaches into his pack to grab the ivani – now is the time to use it. His fingers grapple at the place in his bag where he knows he's placed it, only it isn't there. He searches desperately, contorting his fingers this way and that across the bottom of his bag. The ivani is gone. *Shit.* He can't go back – not at the risk of someone seeing him.

It's an in-the-moment decision that he decides to continue onward. He moves to the lake and soon stands at what he knows to be its yellow, toxic waters. There is no other way to cross into Tagondo, The Circle is bombarded with Defenders and the fence on the opposite side of the lake, which is more like a wall, is some twenty feet high – there is no climbing it. That massive fence extends so far as to reach just beyond the Tagondian and Kalian borders and touches the forest where it's considered 'the outskirts.' No one survives the outskirts – that's guaranteed mammoth territory and there is no way in hell he's going there. He'll have better luck with the water.

There, in the still night, Atticus enters Lake Cloud. The cool water hugs his skin, and his limbs feel light and airy in a way they haven't before. His clothing sticks to his body, similar to the way the rain makes it cling, only not as profound as when fully submerged. As he slowly walks deeper into the waters, he thinks back to Vera's recollections and stories of swimming in the Old World. He doesn't know how to swim – for he's never swum a day in his life, but that isn't something that's going to get in his way.

As his toes pull away from the depths of the lake he leans back and releases his body to the water, just as Vera once described to him, knowing it will keep his face out of the water and be the easiest position in which to float, or so he thinks. The water instantly swallows him, marking an enclosing circle of fluid around his face; it trickles into his ears.

He moves his feet slowly in and out in an instinctive paddle. In this slight panic he finds ease in the realization that if he were going to die by touching the poisonous water, it would've already happened. So his confidence grows in Torant, which he can't quite put into words.

It's both relaxing and eerie gliding across the surface of the lake as no man or woman has touched these poisonous waters and lived. He remembers the day Digger had almost pushed him into the lake all those years ago, then how Lidia and Aphria almost met with the lake with intentions of leaving Kala – none of those fears, the things of the past, will affect his present, not for the worse. He steadies his breathing and continues to slowly travel across the lake.

"Hey you!"

Atticus' body jolts in the water at the sound of a man's voice. The call came from somewhere amidst the darkness. He looks around, but can see no shadows. He moves his feet faster.

"What are you doing in the water?" the voice speaks again.

This time Atticus can tell it's coming from the Kalian shoreline. He keeps moving. A whistle blows – the man is alarming the other Defenders. Atticus moves quicker as he hears several voices forming by the lakeside in Kala.

"That boy must have the antitoxin, he's in the water and unharmed," one shouts.

"And he's headed for Tagondo," another warns, but there's nothing they can do.

Atticus finally reaches the Tagondian shoreline – he stands to his feet, dripping wet, and his steps make a sloshing sound when he walks, but he doesn't care, he has to keep moving. Luckily, if any Tagondian Defenders hear the whistles of Kala, they won't know what they mean.

Atticus carries on, moving towards the south side of the Tagondo forest, and although he doesn't know his way around Tagondo and can't fully be guided by his sight, he has something of an internal compass and always knows which way north is. It isn't something one needs sight for, it is something one feels. A steadfast and unwavering sense of determination gets him hastily to the edge of the Tagondo forest. He ventures south along the tree-line. He notices that it is quiet and calm on this side of the lake for the winds are at rest. He continues to walk, his breath a huff. But then there's a disruption amongst the quiet.

"Freeze!" states a voice from somewhere in the trees.

He freezes, for until he can at least identify where the voice is coming from he needs to cooperate. A firm grip remains on his cane that he holds in his right palm as he raises his left hand in surrender. His clothes still drip the poisonous waters of the lake.

"I come in peace," he says.

"A Kalian," the voice states, intrigue brushing against their words.

"Yes, that I am." He knows that there is no sense in trying to lie.

"What have you come to Tagondo for? It's illegal, you know."

"It isn't safe in Kala right now. But more importantly, I am in search of someone," Atticus replies.

"Who and why?" they question. It's a female's voice, stern in its tonality.

"I need to speak to Vera North."

"Do you mean Vera Cannelle? I'm looking for her right now too. What do you want with Vera anyhow?"

"I am her brother, Atticus North. Why are you looking for her?"

"Brother? I didn't know she has a brother. How'd you get past the night guard, Atticus North?"

"I swam."

"Makes sense, you are dripping wet after all. Which also tells me that you must have the antitoxin," she beams playfully.

"I had just enough to get me across," he lies.

"I'm sure. You mentioned trouble in Kala?"

"I was warned to get out, that's all I know."

"Come with me," the woman says as she turns to lead Atticus northeast.

"Where are we going?" he asks.

"Oooh you're not scared, are you?"

"No, but I can't see. I just need to know where you're taking me. Are you taking me to Vera?"

"Sadly, no. But there's someone else who will be thrilled to see you."

"What's your name?" he asks the woman.

"Treena."

# 113

## VERA OF INSIGNIFICANT CANNELLE
## UNKNOWN

"Torant Wells!" she says louder than she intends into the empty room.

Of all the people, of course it's him. She has dwelled on this for what she assumes to be several days now, with making only small moves toward escaping. Today is the day she makes her big move – though she'd really like to find a large rock, to possibly do to Torant what she's seen Defenders do to Offenders in tribulation, but there's no time.

Regardless, she wonders why he captured her, and how he's in Tagondo to do so. One good thing to come from being under his watch is that it appears as though he's healed her arm. Her IV is long gone, perhaps that means he wants her to be more wakeful now – she also finds herself stronger in recent days.

After making it her mission to explore the tunnels and find the exit, she continues to move through them with her light, marking her way with her finger many times now. With a mixture of dirt and spit she paints her growing path on her arm with a series of cardinal directions and checkpoints, and makes sure to slide down her sleeve to cover her escape plan. Still, even in this place, wherever she is, she feels that pull that tells her where north is. Each time she ventures out she's gone farther, and today she'll go all the way. After retrieving her light and observing that her captor, Torant Wells, is nowhere to be seen, she ventures into the darkness.

With her sleeve pushed up once again, she follows her directions that are brushed on her arm while praying to Mother Earth that no one sees her. There is no telling what he, or the others might do. She moves her limbs as quickly as possible, urgency flows through her to get above ground while suspense grows in wondering how long she's been under for. She makes it past her first few checkpoints and peers every which way to ensure there is no light or sound coming in her direction, she continues on. She has determined that the first three she can sprint back to the room that she's been kept in less than five minutes. There's eight checkpoints, the eighth took her twelve minutes to navigate to – beyond that last checkpoint is unknown.

Upon checkpoint four, there's many voices coming from a large room – there usually is at number four. She scurries past the entrance, while keeping her light off as a means to not call attention to herself. *It's a cult!* It has to be – especially now knowing that Torant is the one who brought her here. The man is more than off-putting, he reeks of evil doings. After all, he is the one who killed Murdina.

Laughter sounds from behind her, from checkpoint four – she breaks out into a sprint. It's something she doesn't like to do, rushing through her checkpoints is not ideal as she could pass one, she could slip up. She turns southeast around a corner and comes to a complete stop to glance back the way she came and sees two dark figures walking her way, one holds a light that barely casts yellow upon their chins. She turns and runs toward checkpoint number five. Her lungs pull oxygen in hungrily, but with each inhale she's left feeling an unappeased appetite for air. She feels slightly claustrophobic down here, or maybe it's the attempted escape making her feel this way. She must turn her light off and walk in complete darkness if she doesn't want to be seen.

The lights from the two people walking behind her creeps up on her, they're quickly approaching. As they advance, now some fifteen feet behind her, the two speak in a heated conversation:

"They say it's going to happen tonight," one man says.

The other man retorts: "I don't know if they are ready."

"Are you kidding me? Eighteen years. Eighteen years!"

"Time isn't always a determining factor."

Vera melds her body into the dirt, willing her spine to stiffen into its contours as she holds her breath. Surely the movement of her heart slamming into her chest will be enough to alert them. *Keep your head,* she reminds herself – she's almost at checkpoint eight.

The two approach the entrance to Vera's sixth checkpoint and continue on, presumably entirely unaware of her presence. A dramatic release of air exits her lungs and mouth. She decides to follow the two, hoping they will continue in her planned direction and possibly go a step further – leading her to the exit.

Vera stays a fair distance back, possibly thirty feet. Checkpoint eight approaches and her leaders continue on by it with her on their trail. At this point it would take her twelve minutes to walk, or nine minutes to sprint back to her room – assuming she doesn't miss any turns. She moves along now uncertain about what lies ahead.

After a series of turns that she is unable to record, she sees a light up ahead – bigger and brighter than any she's seen before. The two men turn and she continues on to approach the light, now able to see that there is a set of stone steps leading upward. She wanders toward the stairs and places her right foot upon the first step. *This is it. There is no going back.* Something dangling beside the staircase grabs her attention, it's her satchel.

"Hey, there she is!" a voice calls from behind her.

There's no time to think – she grabs the satchel and sprints up the stairs, her lungs gasp for air while her eyes yearn for darkness. It's brighter, greener up here – it's almost as if she'd forgotten. As she reaches the surface her eyes adjust and she soon notices that the brightness is timid as the sun sets, still it is harsh compared to the darkness she has lived in. Her feet move upon the grass, this surface below her is less pliable than in previous days, weeks, months – however long it has been since she was encased in dirt.

She glances down behind her, into the black pit of tunnels, and although they called out in acknowledgement, no one comes for her. *Strange.* They're probably alerting the others. The urge to move fast – to get as far away from this place as possible fills her.

She frantically begins pushing her way through the large gathering of bushes that hide the entrance to the hole. Vera moves, and finds another set of bushes to sit behind, not nearly as far as she'd like, but the desire to sift through her satchel calls for her. She sits upon the ground, still shielded by bush, and her hands immediately rub against the soft, limber strands below her – they prickle her skin from their tips and a scent wafts by, it's like forest trees in the heat of a summer night. Though what month it is, she's unsure. If she is to guess, it's probably the end of August, early September.

She sits and glances upward to see trees enveloping her, their branches gazing down upon her like quiet giants. The ceiling, walls and floor of dirt are gone – for that she is grateful. They have been replaced by fresh air and greenery for miles - as far as the eye can see - and a dusk sky. She begins sorting through her satchel – everything that Murdina gave her is still here, even Burke's glass and a tiny test tube labeled: "Black Poison." The black poison leaves, and Treena's single leaf from her water glass still resides in her satchel as well, as she hoped.

The slender frame of an object within her bag catches her eye – she pulls it out. The silver tip of a blade reflects the diminishing light of the sky. She turns the blade on its side to see the familiar engraving on it: "V," and a sudden rattle of emotion reverberates through her chest. She breathes the evening air in again, its aroma earthy and moist, and yet drier than the scents she smelled in days past while she was below, she exhales slowly. *I survived.* A wonder why Torant took her still tugs at her thoughts. As she settles her knife inside the satchel a second shine glimmers from within, she pulls it out. It's Cole's lucky dagger. She is pleasantly surprised to see these items again after her kidnapping. She swallows heavily, pushing the rock in her throat back down, all the while thankful to Ezla for having retrieved the daggers for her in the first place.

A familiar velvet sack catches her attention then. She pulls it out of the satchel, this small bag holds the rainmaking stones and the letter from Hendrix. She opens the sack to confirm that those contents are still present. Satisfied, she unfolds the letter and examines the distorted writing with odd spaces between the words – she thinks more on how it isn't like her father to blather, as he so seems to in this letter. The lack of significance in his words still irks her.

miss ,
your KindnEss aNd patience will undOubtedly serve you.
it's your stubbornness thAt you must overcome. don't
fear the setbacKs... sometimes they are your friend.
keep seeing north, except when you must look elsewhere first.
Always ,

> HN

*"It's a map,"* the Whisperer says.

She doesn't question the whispers – she simply and curiously places her finger upon the ground and draws an arrow pointing north into the dirt. She turns to sit facing north as she hypothetically compares the note to a compass. Imagining that the top is north and the bottom south, she runs her finger along the spaces in between the words. *West, northwest, west, northwest.* But where is it leading her? She glances at her surroundings, and notices that behind her sits the wall that separates Kala and Tagondo and along her side the trees are marked with K's representing Kala's border. A sense of relief washes over her, she's so close to the Kalian lab. But before she can go to the lab, she must follow Hendrix's map and figure out what he's trying to tell her. She turns the paper then, so that "Miss" is sitting where east would sit, she traces her finger once more.

"West, southwest, west, southwest." she quietly notes to herself then rises to her feet and stares westerly. It appears as though the letter is a message after all, just not in the way she initially expected. It's guiding her through Kala's outskirts. *I knew it. It wasn't just some nonsensical letter.* A smile graces her face at that thought.

The map directs her west so she gathers her things and decides to follow it. When she reaches where it leads her, she will find a way to get to Kala's lab – she must fulfill step number three and she must also find Cole and tell him who is responsible for killing his father. With the plants and stones on her side, it should be a breeze to get there.

She moves, darting through the footpaths and continually scanning over her plan in her mind, which she soon realizes isn't genius or overly calculated by any means. She can't afford the time to sit and think it through though – she will need to trust her father's map. A thought crosses her mind then: she is free and no one knows this, besides the people in the tunnels... They have probably told Torant by now. It would be easy for her to just leave The Almek and never return – to take a chance with the wild with the mammoths, to take a chance on the water… Vera knows that she would rather die by drinking the water than live another day in Tagondo – or be held prisoner in another jail like the one she's just come from. But she can't leave Atticus, Ida and Lidia… and she can't leave Cole.

With her back to the east, where the moon rests, and her satchel across her shoulder, she carries onward. She opens her satchel to glance at the array of plants that are once again at her fingertips. The things she'll be able to do with it all excites her – the things she realizes now that she's missed doing.

She looks down at the map noting that the path zigzags as opposed to moving in a straight line, but still, it'll lead her to the destination on the map – the place Hendrix wants her to go. She thinks of the tunnels then and how they too move in a zigzag motion, but ultimately lead her to the exit. *The setbacks. They all happen for a reason.*

## 114

## Cole of Favoured Wells
## Kala

A breath of air escapes Cole's lungs as he opens his eyes to see it's still nighttime. He lies in the forest, occupying the same space where the ambush occurred and can still smell the substance that was forced upon him – its minuscule fibres stick to his nose, something about it smells like the cooling fermentation of potato vodka and makes his head twitch. He isn't fond of the smell or the taste of vodka, which makes the lingering effects of it cause him some displeasure beyond just a foggy head. An intention to pull himself up proves to be more trying than he hoped. His body still feels slightly drowsy from the substance, which is clearly used to put people to sleep.

A glance around tells him that he's alone – Lidia and her Tarnished are gone. He wonders where the attackers have taken them. With noise still commanding the colony centre and having no clue how many hours has passed, he opts to return to Favoured Wells. Though, due to his concern for The Tarnished, he reasons to at least wander through the forest and toward the edge of the Kalian border in search of them on his way back.

The night air slowly descends in its temperature, September is here and it is only a matter of time before the snow comes now. This realization reminds him that this also means the end of their fresh drinking water is getting closer. Cole walks with his hands out as a means to steady his swaying steps and every few paces he stops to listen for signs of movement. He walks southbound for some time and when he makes it to Favoured Wells he decides to walk a bit farther – past the Kalian tree-line marked with K's carved some eighteen years earlier. He's never been out quite this far before, but he can't help but feel that the attackers took The Tarnished outside of the colony – it would make sense as there is nowhere inside the colony that an attacker can hold four people hostage without someone finding out. Cole notes how Atticus and Ulyd's kidnapping proves case and point.

The forest is even thicker beyond the Kalian line. At some points one can't look up and see the light of the moon at all, for the trees and brush are plentiful in this uncharted territory. A tree branch cracks and he freezes for a moment, then slowly moves his body up against a grandfather oak tree. He glances around the tree, his heart begins to race but he holds his gasps steady with long, slow breaths. Possible causes of movement include mammoths or other forest creatures; however, it's more likely the latter as the smaller ones always seem to be the louder of the two – or it could be the attackers.

Defenders never walk beyond their colony line – the tree-line in which The Masters put in place to keep people safe, though it is more or less a pointless boundary of trees marked with either a 'K' or 'T' depending on one's colony. The line itself keeps nothing out and no one in. It's The Masters themselves who keep the people in with their laws, brutality and fear mongering.

Cole stays still, mimicking the straight frame of the tree, blending in with its shadow. The cracking grows louder, closer – his heart rate accelerates and his arms buzz with anticipation. As the sound approaches from behind him, he hastily dances his feet around the wide trunk now leaning on the north side. The shadow of a person passes by the tree he hides behind – he isn't scared, but this person, he deems, should be scared of him.

Cole isn't one to pick a fight for the sake of fighting, so he watches as the figure moves slowly through the forest – a dark figure with a scarf wrapped covering their face. He sees a white piece of paper in their hand as they walk; perhaps they are following directions of some sort, though he can hardly guess what for. He decides that it isn't any of his business what this person is up to and that person is proof that searching the outskirts is likely only to find him trouble.

So, as soon as the figure is out of sight he turns around and heads back to Kala as there are no signs of broken branches or scuffed up ground from the remains of kidnappers pulling victims to an isolated place. It isn't long before Cole approaches the rock wall at Favoured Wells once again, and just as he arrives Torant comes slithering from the shadows behind the house.

"Cole," Torant calls.

"Tortoise."

"There's no time for games," Torant barks, "Things are getting worse at the colony centre – people are standing up to the Defenders. You must retrieve your makeshift weapons and go, now."

"I'm hardly in fighting shape at the moment," Cole regretfully admits, "What am I supposed to do?" Torant holds out in the palm of his hand a tiny green pill.

"Take this," Torant states.

Cole scoffs at the sight of what sits in front of him, "You've got to be kidding me. Another one of your mysterious pills. What is this one? The cure to being Almek?"

"This isn't just any pill. You'll be happy you took it."

"Wow, you must've worked on that for a while," Cole ridicules.

"If you are to fight with the people and protect them, you must take it."

"Risk assessment – come on old man, we've been over this before. What are the risks? What does it do? What is it made of? And, go."

Torant sighs, still holding his hand out flat in offering, "As far as I know there are no risks. But I can't guarantee it. What I can guarantee is that it will relieve the pain from your wound. The ingredients are a combination of plants, that's all I know."

"No. I'm not taking that voodoo shit," Cole shakes his head wildly in disagreement and walks inside the rock wall to retrieve his weapons, "But I'll go back to the colony centre and try to help the others."

"As you wish. I would advise against going in your current state though."

"I get it, I'm slower right now and some movements aren't possible. But taking a pill that causes a wound like this to feel no pain… that's unnatural," Cole reasons.

"I don't intend to argue with you, but I'm curious, at which point would you be willing to take it?" Torant asks.

"If I was desperate," Cole says, huffing with a chuckle.

Cole makes his way to the rock wall and stuffs his dagger into his boot, places his bow and arrows over his shoulder and holds his spear tight in his grasp. They aren't his steel weapons from Tagondo, but they will have to do. He leaves Favoured Wells and heads for the colony centre.

# 115

## Vera of Insignificant Cannelle Outskirts

After a few hours of rest up in a tree, Vera climbs down. She retrieves her dagger from her satchel, on edge in the dark night, she begins following the map. Initially she walks along the outskirts of the Kalian border, but now she walks with no landmarks to recognize exactly where she is, she can merely assume that she is somewhere deep among the outskirts in the forest. Fresh, unexplored forest envelops her, until she approaches a clearing.

She walks just beyond the tree-line and spots a small cabin that's a mere ten feet or so away from the edge of the forest. A metal fence encases the entire cabin, covering a radius of about eighty feet. The steel fence is massive, reaching up fifteen feet, and atop it spikes poke upward preventing anyone from climbing in - or possibly - to prevent whoever resides within its walls from getting out.

She approaches the enclosure, peers through the metal bars and sees that the tiny well maintained hut has layers of solar panels on its roof. She squeezes her eyes shut and rubs them, thinking that perhaps she's seeing things, following the past few months, she'd think just about anything possible though. Perhaps Torant drugged her and she's hallucinating. She opens her eyes and cautiously reaches her trembling hand out to touch the bars. *Please be real.* She doesn't want to be crazy, *But then again a crazy person never truly knows they're crazy...* So maybe it doesn't matter when her hand grazes the cool grey surface of the post. Still, she exhales.

Looking past the fence the scene appears quaint, peaceful even. It is early morning and the sun is just rising and casts a warm light across the tiny land of grass inside the fence while bearing shadows in other places. Vera notices that there are a couple toys scattered on the front lawn, a doll and some books. A couple trees sit clustered in a corner inside the fence blocking her view from the rest of the yard inside.

She looks around and scales the fence with her eyes and spots a rounded edge of a steel handle. Why not give it a try? She's gotten this far, not to mention Hendrix's map has led her here for some reason – she needs to find out why. She walks over to the gate, places her fingers on the handle, presses down with her thumb and pushes – and to her surprise it swings open.

Without a hint of naivety she grasps at the wooden handle of her dagger and walks inside, her steps long and slow. The few trees that are inside the fence still stand before her, blocking what is beyond them. A pivot of her heels in the dirt allows her to glance around them. A sudden noise grabs her attention. *Laughter?* She peers through the trees that still block her vision. There she sees a little girl, who has to be about ten-years-old, playing in the grass with a black dog. Her giggles tickle the trees in the forest.

"Now, now Luna, don't tease that dog of yours," a woman says.

"But Mom, I'm not!"

"Come, let us read," the woman says.

Vera sees the woman sitting upon a blanket in the grass. The girl runs toward her, the dog follows, and they land on the blanket in a crash. *Why has my father led me here? Who are these people?* Vera moves forward deciding that she needs to find out. Besides, she figures that she's likely the more dangerous one.

She slowly walks around the trees and faces the woman and child. The woman looks up then, her eyes wide with terror that Vera knows she's responsible for.

"Mommy, who is that?" the child asks. Her mother pulls the girl to her feet.

"It's okay sweetie – go inside. Remember? Just like we talked about." The girl runs inside.

"I'm not here to hurt you," Vera speaks. The woman's eyes flicker upon the dagger in Vera's trembling hand. Vera quickly tucks it in her pocket.

"What do you want?" the woman asks.

"I just want to know who you are. Why you're here," Vera inquires. "Truly, I mean no harm."

"You need to leave," the woman states cautiously.

"Please. I have to know. I have a map from my father, you see," Vera pulls out the piece of paper and holds it up. "It led me here and I don't know why."

"If I tell you, it'll put your life at risk. But more importantly, it puts hers at risk," the woman gestures to the house.

"Mine is already at risk. I wouldn't be here if it wasn't."

The woman stands in silence, she must be contemplating her next move.

Vera continues: "Look, I'm not leaving without the information that I need. The sooner you tell me, the sooner I leave." The woman's eyes dart toward the front door of the hut, the one where Luna entered and now resides within.

"Okay. What do you want to know?" Her spooked eyes now rest on Vera.

"Who are you?"

"My name is Minx. The girl is Luna." Vera pauses, waiting for a last name – as if that matters out here. "Kenoak," Minx says with a nod of her head and a steady stare. "That's what you want to know right? Who her father is? It explains why we're out here."

"Kenoak?" Vera questions, confused. She glances down at the letter from Hendrix, and focuses in on the erratic capital letters. To put those letters together in order they spell Kenoak, a clue of sorts should she have questioned the map or struggled to figure it out.

"The girl in there, she is the most beautiful and wonderful thing to ever happen to me. Don't hurt her."

"I said I'm not here to hurt you guys – just help me understand. How are you Kenoaks?"

"I lived in Tagondo once, eleven or so, years ago. But then I got pregnant with my dear Luna and we have lived out here ever since."

"Tagondo? What is her father's first name?" Vera asks, though she is certain she already knows the answer and that it's not a coincidence.

"Oberon."

It hits her then – Master Oberon has an unaccounted-for child, and with a Tagondian no less. A child who should have had a re-birthing ceremony, a child he should have fought for in The Circle. Suddenly she realizes how stupid they all are – The Masters have been playing them. Cowardly men who seek only the greed of power so that they can continue their own selfish biddings. She always thought Master Oberon as a sincere man, a good man. She scoffs at imagining what Master Regan's secrets are.

A quote dances in the back of her mind then. It's something she vaguely remembers from the early settlement days. It was taught to the children by one of the eldest settlers at the time - a woman, Arless - who has long since passed. She was an ancient woman and said things that were mostly scattered, but she was sweet and often sung songs and played games with the younger children. Vera hasn't thought about her in a long time.

"Hello?" Minx attempts to get Vera's attention. "You said your father gave you that map? Who is *your* father?" Minx continues.

But Vera turns and walks at a much slower pace than she ought to, beyond the steel fence and back into the forest. She heads for Kala, there is not much more she can do besides getting to the lab to take care of her to-do list and reuniting with her family, it is time to tell them everything she knows.

As she walks, she continues to think about Arless and the words she taught Vera comes to her. Words she hasn't thought about in a long time, words that she hears Arless' crackling voice speak in her mind.

*The greed of man shall be his downfall.*

Maybe Arless wasn't just old and senile – maybe she was actually trying to teach them something.

She ponders The Master's ways, his rest days in particular, and how it is a secret from all of The Almek. How his greed to keep his family safe from the ceremonies has led him to break the laws of The Motherland and thereby betray his people. Her stomach twists at the realization that she, Vera North, holds Master Oberon's greatest secret.

# 116

## COLE OF FAVOURED WELLS
## KALA

Cole walks purposefully to the colony centre, the commotion going on there is louder than before. As he approaches through the trees his visuals are pulled not towards the mob of crazed citizens, but to a certain part of the school building. It's on fire – the flames are raging and begin dancing and tickling the branches of the trees above it.

"Oh shit," he calls.

Kalians are spread across the entirety of the colony centre in battle with the Defenders. There are numerous bodies strewn across the ground covered in blood, many appear lifeless at his feet – men and women alike. The sun begins gracing them in the east, casting light upon the bloody scene. He reaches for his makeshift dagger to protect himself should someone attempt battle.

An entire line of Defenders stand guard across the front of The Master's chamber, thrusting their clubs upon any Kalian that approaches them, protecting The Master and his Barons as Cole assumes they will be tucked safely inside. His eyes shift to The Tarnished's words, still painted across the chamber's wall. Now knowing who The Tarnished are, he hopes that their words make a difference. He also hopes their words aren't responsible for this bloodshed.

Suddenly someone charges at him, a man one he's never met before. The man runs at Cole with his bloodshot-crazed eyes, his hand seemingly ready to wrap snugly around Cole's neck. Cole is shocked, this brutality is so unlike Kalians, so he freezes – knowing right well that if he needs to he can kill this man. The man reaches for Cole and firmly plants his hands on Cole's shoulders.

"Do you have the antitoxin?"

Cole shakes his head stunned, "No."

The man shoves him and runs off. Cole falls backwards, landing on his ass, a shot of pain soars across his back. One of the seemingly lifeless bodies lying on the ground beside him begins to move. The blood-soaked man reaches for Cole's ankle and tugs on it. Raising his head, he stares at Cole in desperation and fear.

The man croaks: "Please, help me."

Cole can see this man is on his last breaths, "I'm sorry."

"Do you have the antitoxin?" he asks.

"No, I wish I did," Cole lies, as the bag is right in his pocket, but it wouldn't be safe to disclose this information in this moment – otherwise he'll end up like the bodies in the dirt. "Where is your family?" he asks the man.

"Dead. They're all dead."

"How? Why?"

"The Defenders…" The man's words become inarticulate, more choked and inaudible, until finally his head flops face down into the ground and his hand releases its hold on Cole.

Cole rises to his feet and holds his dagger snug in his fist. He doesn't want to use it, but if he has to he will. Now what? Everyone he cares enough about are somewhere else – Lidia is gone, so too is Ida, though he's not entirely convinced he should care about Ida. Atticus is off in Tagondo - which is actually a good thing now that Cole sees the state Kala is in - and Vera… she is in Tagondo.

He watches as Kalians run every which way across the colony centre, holding kitchen knives as defence against the Defenders – though Cole can see the Defenders are simply protecting their Master and themselves, they aren't out to kill everyone for the fun of it. The citizens, on the other hand, are all shouting and seeking the same thing: the antitoxin. More fires flare about the colony and the sounds of crackling fill the early morning air.

"Give me the antitoxin," a man shouts as he runs at Cole with a knife in his grasp.

Now that Cole fully understands the mayhem taking place here, he reacts quickly. He turns his body and in one abrupt movement grabs the knife out of the man's hand and twists the man's body around so that his back rests against Cole's chest. Cole now holds the kitchen knife to the man's throat. The stranger freezes.

"I don't want to hurt you, but if you don't stop what you're doing I'm going to have to," Cole warns.

Just then, out of the corner of his eye, Cole sees Huron appear atop the chamber steps with what can only be assumed to be one of the ceremonial swords.

"If you do not go back to your homes, you shall pay the price," Huron's voice booms across the colony as he holds the sword high above his head, looking quite unlike himself, for his face and shirt are lined with the markings of Kalian blood. He looks crazed. He must be because when the commotion carries on he walks forward and begins slaying everyone in his path – he is no longer just protecting his Master or himself.

Huron's powerful arms swing aggressively, slashing torsos and throats as he walks by. Blood sprays across the dirt, it's almost impossible to take a step and not fill your sole with it. Kalians begin screaming, not just for the antitoxin now, but also for their lives. Cole grits his teeth. All they have to do is go inside; they are losing their heads - their sanity - like a bunch of helpless sheep. The only way to make this end is to get everyone to evacuate the colony centre.

Cole pushes the man from his hold and runs across the colony centre, "Get inside," he shouts. "Go home!"

Many can't hear him for the shouts of others and the few that do hear his warning don't listen – it isn't working, he'll have to get rid of Huron. He tightens his grip on the dagger in his hand and stalks toward Huron. Cole glances all around him in an effort to ensure he moves unnoticed, but as he approaches the brute, a figure appears through the trees from the southwest side of the forest and his peripheral view catches sight of something familiar: a green blur. *No, it can't be.*

He looks back quickly and his eyes settle upon a woman who from this distance resembles Vera. The green blur, now crisp, no longer in his peripheral, sits in the exact focal point of his stare. A scarf rests across the bottom half of the woman's face, concealing her identity. He must be seeing things. He shakes his head desperately, opens his eyes and looks back at the place where he saw the woman – she is still there. Creeping out from behind the trees she locks eyes with him. Emerald green eyes.

Forgetting entirely about Huron, his feet begin moving quickly towards her, he doesn't know if his eyes are deceiving him, still he moves. She stands frozen. Her wide emerald orbs stare into the chaos of Defenders killing civilians and then look back at him. Upon his close proximity he doesn't need the scarf withdrawn, he knows it's her, his body meets hers in an embrace – it's really her.

Cole wraps his arms around her, and hers around him, as he lifts her feet a few inches off the ground. He then puts her down, grabs her hand and runs with her into the forest. He stops about twenty feet in from the colony centre and tucks them both inside a thick gathering of trees to shield them from the sights of others. Cole stares down at her, sure that his heart has stopped beating, or perhaps it's simply beating at an unthinkable speed – he can't tell which it is. He pulls down her scarf, exposing the rest of her face.

"V," he whispers, out of breath, "how did you get here?"

"It's a long story," her voice rasps, "it's good to see you."

"Now is not the time to be tight-lipped," he warns her with a smile, adjusting his hold on her so he can view this face that he has missed.

"I couldn't even tell you all of it if I wanted to."

"Well… I guess we both made it to Kala after all," he says with a reflective pause. "How did you get out of Tagondo? Tell me that, at least."

"I was kidnapped. But I escaped."

Cole gasps, "Because I wasn't there to protect you."

"It's over with now. I'm here."

"You look different," he finally decides.

She nods knowingly, "I feel different," and after a pause she adds: "So do you though. You brushed your hair." He can't tell if she's being sarcastic, but she smiles when she says it.

"You noticed."

"It's kind of hard not to."

His fingers run through the strands of hair on his head again then his arms reach out and envelop her. He pulls her in and as she looks up at him, he presses his lips to hers. He has missed her, more than he even knew. How she ended up here, he may never know, but one thing he decides in this moment is that he'll never let her go again – he'll never stop protecting her. Their lips part and they remain still together for just a moment longer.

"We don't have a lot of time," she says delicately. "We need to talk."

He agrees, "There's things I need to tell you too."

"Make it quick." She gently urges.

"A lot has happened here in the last few months… But it's not just that. There's something about me that you should know…"

"I know that you're a Kalian now, but we don't have time for pleasantries," she says in a playful tone.

"I did something, back in Tagondo…"

"It doesn't matter to me. We've all done things," she looks to the ground. He wonders what it is that she has done, but it doesn't matter – she could stab him with his lucky dagger and he'd still forgive her. "Where is everyone? My family? Lidia?"

"They're all gone. I don't know where, except for Atticus – he went to Tagondo to save you."

"Oh no. You're not serious?" she exclaims as she looks off into the bushes, appearing to collect her thoughts.

"I wish I wasn't."

She suddenly moves, urgently stepping off to the side and out from the shield of the trees, "We need to go, I need to get to the lab. Now. And then I need to go get him."

Cole reaches for her wrist then, "Wait. You said you had something to tell me."

She moves in closer to him and in a hushed tone speaks, "It's Master Oberon, he has a secret in the outskirts. A family."

"Like a wife?"

Nodding her head, "And a child."

"Living out there?"

"For years," she confirms.

"Holy shit!"

"There's something else…" Cole interrupts her words briefly by wrapping his hand around Vera's wrist, willing her back into the trees with him. "I know who killed your father."

His step falters slightly, "What?"

"Rimmy. He used the black poison and he tried to kill me too."

"What, that night at the celebration?" She nods. "How do you know it was him?"

"I overheard him telling one of the Defenders. I'm really sorry."

He blinks the tears out of his eyes, "He'll get what's coming to him."

"Don't do anything reckless. You're still stuck in Kala, remember?"

"You don't have to worry about me," he says with a sad smile. "I have something for you." Cole pulls a small burlap bag out of his pocket and a piece of paper, "I don't know what this is, but maybe you will be able to figure it out," he says as he hands her the paper. "Also, here's the antitoxin," he says as he gives her the bag. "Don't let anyone know you have it, or that I was the one who gave it to you. That's why the colony is in chaos."

"So it is real!" For the first time Vera's expression appears lighter.

"It's real alright. And our spring is running low… now that you're out of Tagondo, you should get out of here, go hide somewhere outside of the colonies. I'll get more and I'll track down the others, we'll come to you. First I need to help those Kalians at the colony centre though."

"The spring is low? Everyone needs to know."

"You will face tribulation if you say anything. You need to go now."

"I can't leave. I have to get to the lab… if these pills are truly the antitoxin I need to dissect them, figure out what the ingredients are," Vera explains as she glances down at the paper.

"Where did you say you found this?" she asks, referencing the paper.

"In the lab in one of the coats. It had some words embroidered on it."

"It's in the setbacks?" she asks and he nods. "It was my father's. It was…" her voice lowers as though a realization has come over her: "Step number three." He looks at her curiously, but doesn't say anything. "You have no idea how much this means to me." She tucks the antitoxin and piece of paper into the inside pocket of her jacket.

"I have something for you too," she adds clearing her throat, as she reaches into her bag and retrieves a shiny object, one that only Cole would know its true history, it's true significance.

"My lucky dagger! How did you? What did you?" He accepts it with pure excitement.

"Ezla."

"Of course," he beams.

"We better get moving," Vera says as she steps out of the tiny cocoon of trees, Cole follows a few paces behind her. She is standing out on the path for only a moment before a body instantly appears in front of her, Cole freezes, he's still tucked in behind the trees and out of sight from the unwelcome guest.

"Vera, what an odd thing it is to see you here," Huron says.

"With the earth, Huron," she speaks with sarcasm.

"I should've known you'd have something to do with all this… This despicable display of rebellion."

"You're mistaken."

"We'll let The Master be the judge of that. You're coming with me." Huron encases his fingers, which are more like long confining snakes, upon her arms.

"Unhand her Huron, she's not going anywhere with you," Cole calls, appearing from behind the trees.

"If it isn't the Mammoth Slayer. Didn't I teach you a lesson already?" Cole knows he's referring to his lashings, and no, no he didn't teach him a lesson of any sort.

"No, doesn't ring a bell," Cole smirks.

Just then Huron raises his arm to wipe the sweat from his brow – the telltale sign of a nervous bruiser. That's his cue. Cole moves instantly then, breaking out into a sprint. With his lucky dagger in hand he jumps and bounds his foot into a nearby tree, pushing off of the tree and turning his body one hundred and eighty degrees he lands on Huron's back. Huron's hand releases Vera in response while his other hand drops the sword – he fights to contain Cole. Cole knows what a big guy like Huron is capable of, he also knows what sort of combat movements he'll likely attempt. A guy like Huron always relies on his strength, which in Cole's opinion is foolish. If one is to win in combat, one needs more than just strength, one needs intelligence, strategy and speed.

In one sudden movement Cole pierces his lucky dagger into Huron's neck then pulls the blade out of his thick flesh while pouncing off and landing swiftly on his feet – all the while a stabbing of pain radiates down his still injured back. Huron's hands move to his neck to caress the wound that now pours his very life force out from his body, he falls to the ground on his knees in moans of agony.

Cole runs to Vera then, placing his hands on either side of her face. "You have to go, now," he says as he steadies his brown eyes upon her emerald orbs.

"I can't leave you… I can't leave without getting to the lab," she says.

However, one thing they've done - that they shouldn't have - is assume that Huron is out of commission, for he rises to his feet then, grabs the sword that rests upon the ground and wraps his wanting hand around Vera once again. He pulls her body into his and away from Cole.

"Well that was rude, we were in the middle of a conversation," Cole quips.

"Keep talkin' Mammoth Slayer," Huron says as he places the sword against Vera's neck.

"Okay, Okay. I'll shut up. I'll do whatever you want. Just don't hurt her."

"Back up twenty paces," Huron demands.

"Okay." Cole backs up, his palms up in submission, his eyes on Huron.

"Now, I want you to stay there. But I don't trust you'll stay there. Put your hands behind your head."

Cole presses the palms of his hands to the back of his head, while gritting his teeth. He knows he must do as Huron says for a sword rests across Vera's throat.

There is a rustling behind him then and Vera begins screaming, "You! Get away from him!" she threatens. Cole squints in confusion at Vera's remarks.

"Torant of Favoured Wells, am I glad to see you," Huron says while holding Vera steady. "Do me a favour and pick up that dagger," Huron instructs.

Cole turns to see Torant who offers him an uneasy stare, but he does as he is told – he must if they are to keep Vera alive. Cole rises to his feet as Torant picks up Cole's lucky dagger off the ground.

"Now I have someone who can make you stay put," Huron says to Cole. "Torant, take that dagger and pin his hand to that tree. Make him bleed."

"But-" Torant begins.

"Don't do as I say and I'll see to it The Master knows about that girl you've been hiding."

Vera screams in anger, her words are mostly inaudible. Cole glances back at Torant and offers a subtle nod, no one else would have noted it but Torant. Torant raises the dagger, as Cole leans his left hand against the closest tree, and stares straight ahead, his gaze locked upon Vera and Huron while he bites down on the collar of his sweater. Cole feels the blade of his lucky dagger slide into his flesh, he releases a moan of pain through the fabric that fills his mouth. His eyes begin to water and so he closes them. His knees buckle below him – folding like a broken tree branch as his knees meet with the ground, stretching his pinned arm out straight. The movement causes tension on his new wound, and sounds of pain release from his throat. More cries erupt from Vera, inaudible howls – helpless and scared. Cole wishes that Lidia and her wolves were here.

"Mammoth Slayer? It's not even true is it? Your blood doesn't run strong… you have blood of the weak," Huron spits, and then looks to Torant. "Keep him there and she doesn't die," Huron states and then begins backing up toward the colony centre, still pressing the sword against Vera's throat.

Torant places his boot upon Cole's shoulder to restrain him and the pressure only worsens the agonizing pain of his wounds. The instant Huron is far enough away, Torant removes the blade from Cole's hand and he slumps down to the ground. While he is on the ground, he realizes that for a few moments he was entirely distracted and deaf to the commotion in the colony centre. But it still continues, possibly louder now than before. Cole watches Vera disappear as the forest lights up with the fires spreading.

After a moment of lying still, his head pressing into the dirt and Torant finally speaks, “Are we desperate yet?”

“That’s a yes, Tortund – I’m gonna need that green pill now.”

# 117

## VERA OF INSIGNIFICANT CANNELLE
## KALA

Huron carries Vera through the smoke and flames of the colony centre. A few Kalians stop at the sight of her – it is her screams that grab a hold of their attention, they rage louder than the troubling fires and the shouts of panic.

"Vera of Insignificant Cannelle of Tagondo!" Huron shouts to the other Defenders and instantly they move, taking shape into a large circle around the two of them. Consecutively, word must've gotten to Master Oberon quite quickly, as he appears in the doorway of The Master's chamber and walks in through the circle of Defenders.

"Vera? Why have you dared to trespress upon Kalian soils?" Master Oberon questions.

Huron pushes her forward so that she has to face her Master, but he keeps a single hand wrapped around the back of her neck – it's a warning, like a rope around an animal, meant to ensure she doesn't even question the possibility of escape, it's meant to make her accept her leash.

Just then Oberon nods his head to Zev, a motion to blow the whistle once for an immediate gathering. Zev does as he's asked, inviting all of Kala to gather in for a tribulation. This could be it – this could be her end. Of course her trespassing would result in tribulation. She must think quickly.

Though what she is going to say, she has no clue until the words come out of her mouth. "I have come to help all of you," Vera shouts in desperation to stay alive. The Kalians quiet even more so and begin gathering behind the Defenders to sneak a view.

A scornful smirk passes over Oberon's mouth, "You have come to help us? Please, elaborate."

She glances at his Barons who stand by the doorway to The Master's chamber, observing the commotion. Movement highlights in her peripheral – it's Cole. His torn shirt barely clings to his upper body, blood covers him – his own and Huron's. She wonders how he's able to stand at all following the pain that Torant imposed upon him. His eyes move to hers and they stare at each other in terror.

"I have come to help," she repeats as she collects her thoughts.

Huron's fingers squeeze tighter around her neck, her lead shrinking, she must act quickly.

"Get on with it," Oberon warns.

She clears her throat, "Secrets. Have you ever had one?"

Cole slowly shakes his head knowingly. His eyes tense at her, his body bends at the waist – he's ready, but to do what, she's unsure. The rest of The Almek offer blank stares.

"Alright, enough. Huron – the stones," Oberon says as he moves toward the edge of the circle of Defenders.

As if wheelbarrows stay filled and ready for such an event, a Defender appears with one packed with stones then dumps them in the centre. Flames tickle the trees as the breeze taunts their blaze. This is where she must decide if she is to tell Oberon's secret. A secret that will better the lives of The Almek, but will also save her own life from this stoning.

The Defenders stand ready with rocks filling the girth of their palms.

"Wait!" she shouts with her hands up in plea. "You have all heard rumours that there is an antitoxin. I'm here to tell you that those rumours are true. There *is* an antitoxin."

Cole looks as though he's about to be sick. His brown eyes that stare so intently upon her fill with tears. He shakes his head once again, this time less heated, more sorrowful.

"How do you know?" someone asks.

"Have you seen it?" another questions.

"Yes, it exists!" She responds, as hushed mumbles follow across the colony centre. "I'm here to tell you something else. Another secret that will change your lives forever."

"What is it?" someone shouts.

"Get on with it," another muffled voice says.

Just then faces appear beyond the colony centre through the trees. The Defenders turn and stand guard, suspicious of the newcomers.

"Tagondians!" someone shouts.

The Tagondians stand silent, watchful, while Master Regan stalks through the brush.

Vera stands tall, ready to say the words that would most likely have Master Oberon guided to the centre of this circle set for his own stoning. He would be gone, as all of The Motherland would know of his terrible crime. If she goes through with this, what will become of Minx and Luna? Will The Almek welcome them as their own? Surely, it's not their fault that Oberon has kept them divdied and exempt from the ceremonies. But what if The Almek want their blood too?

A sudden impulse overtakes her – a change of heart, for she can't bear to be responsible for the death of Minx and Luna. This secret is as much theirs as it is Master Oberon's. Evidently, she does need Oberon on her side – she remembers that he is the only one with enough power to take Regan down.

She stops then – she sees Cain walking up the wooden stairs of the lab and inside without hesitation. She wonders what he's up to - it can't be good - but she must act quickly.

She nods to Cole, her head pointing in the direction of the lab. She can only assume Cain is about to raid the lab. Cole's eyebrow rises in curiosity, then, in understanding. Though he hesitates to leave her, he turns and begins walking toward the lab to do as she has asked.

Vera pulls her attention back to The Almek and addresses the crowd: "The spring is running out, we don't have much time until it is dry," her voice is steady, strong as she speaks – it surprises her. This information - she justifies – the people deserve to know.

To her astonishment Huron releases her in shock then, gasps by all The Almek outweigh the crackling flames. No one knew that the water is dwindling.

Treena enters the circle of Defenders, approaching Vera and speaking so that only she can hear her, "I have to admit I'm surprised to see you alive. And, once again, you're wrong. But, you're wrong about a lot of things, Leech."

"You know nothing of the water," Vera spits.

"I know more than you think I do. For starters, I know that your Re-birthing wasn't by chance – Master Oberon meant for your father to die and ship you off to Tagondo."

A breath escapes her but she pushes forward, "You couldn't possibly know that."

"Believe me, don't believe me. It isn't going to change the outcome for you," Treena smirks. Treena turns then to the people. "Our fresh drinking water is no more," she bellows for all to hear. "It is time for all Almek to get their hands on the antitoxin." Sighs release from the crowd in shock and uncertainty.

"What are you talking about? What have you done to the water?" Vera whispers to her. The people's sighs quickly turn to shouts.

"I might have asked for Cain's help with something, you know, to keep things interesting," she smiles.

"How could you?"

Treena raises her voice to the people once again, "Now, she claims there is an antitoxin. Well where is it Vera? And why are you keeping it from us?"

"Here!" Vera shouts as she pulls the tiny bag out that Cole gave her, "Here is your antitoxin!" She raises the bag above her head. Treena swiftly reaches up and snatches the bag from Vera. Obviously she didn't think that through very well.

"Did you make it?" someone asks.

She shakes her head, "I don't know anything about it and that's why I have returned to Kala – I need to figure out the formulation and dosage requirements to produce more for The Almek, right now there isn't enough for everyone."

"You don't know anything about it?" Treena shouts, "You heard her – she has no antitoxin knowledge to offer us, and now, she doesn't even hold the antitoxin. Vera of Insignificant Cannelle has no reason for being here, and yet she walks upon Kalian soil illegally. Death to the Offender!" Treena announces. Vera notes the irony though – Treena, nor any of the Tagondians shouldn't technically be here either. But they will condemn her just the same.

Regan approaches The Master's chamber and as he walks he asks the people: "Do you want to survive? Do you want the antitoxin?" Howls of desire erupt in response. "Then prove that you're a survivor. Come and get it."

Regan takes the bag of antitoxin from Treena, and the citizens of The Motherland - both Tagondian and Kalian a like - begin battling one another in an attempt to get as close to Master Regan as possible and claim their survival, all the while knowing there isn't enough for everyone.

"Defenders," Master Oberon nods and they immediately charge at Vera while the rest of The Almek continues to riot.

What follows is a loud, ear-piercing event that carries on beyond the treetops – Vera knows this because she glances up in a moment of internal peacefulness, right before the Defenders take hold of her, and catches sight of the birds fluttering erratically, almost as though they're looking for somewhere safe to land. *Not here,* she thinks. *Don't land here.*

The Defenders grab her with their titan strength, she doesn't fend them off – there is no use. Her focus returns to the colony people carrying on with their screams, vociferous, gut-wrenching sounds. She feels partially responsible for the chaos, but also realizes that this has never happened before in the history of The Almek – she realizes this is the sound of change. *Finally – change.* Maybe Vera understands The Almek saying now, after all these years – it means change. If that is the case then, *May we be cleansed.*

Acknowledgements

There are a few people whom this book would not be possible without. Firstly: my husband, Alex, and our children, Averi and Owen. Your support and unwavering belief in me has been both essential and a blessing – an essential blessing. No one has believed in and supported my writing dreams like you three. I am forever grateful that you are *my people*. Seeing you three read this book will bring me more joy than you know (Sorry children, you have to wait until you're eighteen).

My developmental editor: Jessica Beck-Ciurko, who I can't thank enough. Jess and I were introduced sometime in 2017 when I reached out to her knowing I needed an editor, someone to highlight my countless grammatical (and beyond) writing flaws. And so, in the winter of 2017, she began editing my short stories and sometime after that the first draft of my novel. After more than two and a half years of sending this novel back and forth we landed on the final draft. While I did expect an editor to fix my grammatical errors and content inconsistencies, I didn't expect the support, dedication and guidance that she offered. In so many ways Jess was like a writing coach and at points a motivator. The ways in which she has helped me and this book is innumerable.

My final copy editor, Vicki Cloutier. Vicki and I met at a Christmas party in the winter of 2019 and connected through our love of books. I'm so thankful for our connection and want to say a huge thank-you shout out to her for all of her wisdom and expertise. Not only did she read this book once as a beta reader, she read it a second time as its final edit. Each time, her suggestions on sentence flow and her ability to catch flaws always amaze me.

Lauren Kyte, my life-long friend and the designer and illustrator of the cover and map for this book. The patience that my dear friend has shown me over the past year, with all of the changes and fixes for both cover and map, has been so appreciated. It was quite a process nailing them down, especially since it was a learning curve for the both of us. But we got through it, and she made (in my mind) a cover and map that depicts the essence of the story beautifully. Without her touch and talent this book would not be what it is. I thank her for all of her love, time and efforts.

Thank you to my family and friends who have believed in me and shown me support in the many ways that you have. I hold onto your kind words - the uplifting and the critiquing - they have propelled me forward.

My beta readers: Ryan Murphy, Nikki Murphy, Kate Williams, Laura Jull, Lena Robins (Author of The Viralist Series), Vicki Cloutier, and my husband, Alex Jaffray. Thank you all, for taking the time to read this novel and offer your valuable and much appreciated - and needed - feedback.

To a few of my fellow indie author friends: Lynelle Barette (Author of Kiss & Consume), Shamika Lindsay (Author of Popularity Rules), William John, Joseph Hood (Author of My Friend Nick), Elias J. Hurst (Author of Europa & Planning a Prison Break) and Melissa Frey (Author of The Secret of The Codex) for offering your support with the ways of self-publishing, book synopsis issues and general indie author book chats. It has been so much appreciated.

To my other fellow indie authors and writers in the online (specifically Instagram) community, thank you for your continued support. It means the world to have connected with such an inspiring community of creatives.

I would also like to thank my readers. Whether you're lounging in your PJ's, sprawled out on the grass or cooped up in a waiting room somewhere, I hope this story has moved you – thank you so much for supporting an indie author.

**PLEASE POST A REVIEW**

Reviews largely impact the success and number of sales of my books, among other indie authors like myself. So if you enjoyed reading Age of The Almek, please leave a review on amazon.ca and goodreads.com.
Your input is much appreciated.

**KEEP AN EYE OUT FOR BOOK 2 OF THE ALMEK SERIES**

To stay up-to-date on Tara's work visit:
www.taraalake.com

For regular posts you can find Tara on Instagram and Facebook:
@tara.a.lake

Visit Amazon to purchase Tara's work

About the author

Tara A. Lake lives in Southern Ontario, Canada, with her husband, two children and dog, Kali. When Tara isn't writing, she enjoys kayaking adventures and board game nights with her family, nature photography and painting.

Manufactured by Amazon.ca
Bolton, ON

15315243R00296